RANCHO CUCAMONGA
PUBLIC LIBRARY

D0049234

# MAXIMUM VIGILANCE

# MAXIMUM VIGILANCE

## STEVE PIECZENIK

**WARNER BOOKS**

A Time Warner Company

Copyright © 1992 by Steve R. Pieczenik
All rights reserved.

Warner Books, Inc., 1271 Avenue of the Americas, New York, NY 10020

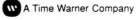 A Time Warner Company

Printed in the United States of America
First printing: July 1992
10  9  8  7  6  5  4  3  2  1

**Library of Congress Cataloging-in-Publication Data**

Pieczenik, Steve R.
    Maximum vigilance / Steve Pieczenik.
        p.    cm.
    ISBN 0-446-51556-6
    I. Title.
PS3566.I3813M38    1992
813'.54—dc20                                          91-50401
                                                          CIP

*Book design by Giorgetta Bell McRee*

To Secretaries of State Henry Kissinger, Cyrus Vance, George Shultz, and James Baker for their continuing support in allowing me to play a serious role in foreign policy and crisis management.

To Sharon and Stephanie, my daughters, who accepted the moments of crisis as a challenge to be conquered without remorse or regret.

And most of all, to Birdie, my wife, who navigated through the storms of change with aplomb, grace, intelligence, and perseverance. As always with my deepest admiration and love.

# ACKNOWLEDGMENTS

I would like to thank the following people:

Mel Parker, my editor, who never lost sight of the big picture and who through gentle persuasion, encouragement, and an uncanny intuition helped me attain that vision. Many thanks.

Nanscy Neiman, my publisher, who helped burnish my writing with her infectious enthusiasm, uncompromising high standards, and provocative wit.

To Larry Kirshbaum and William Sarnoff, President and Chairman of Warner Books, who made me feel part of the Warner family.

To Robert Gottlieb of the William Morris Agency, my long-standing supporter and friend.

And to the courageous and spirited people of the Commonwealth of Independent States who broke the yoke of oppression at a most inopportune time—forcing me to rewrite major parts of this novel.

Last, but not least, to Birdie, my wife, the front-line editor who corrected this manuscript with unswerving devotion, energy, and intelligence.

The faults, failures, and contrivances are clearly all mine.

And, hopefully, the enjoyment of reading this book will be all yours.

# FOREWORD

Steve Pieczenik is one of the smartest people I know. There aren't many people who make the rank of Captain, United States Navy, at 34; who zoom through medical school without breaking a sweat; or who find medical residency so boring that along the way they pick up a Ph.D. from the Massachusetts Institute of Technology just to keep their time occupied. Steve did all these things.

The MIT sheepskin is in International Relations, and married to his medical degree and experience as a psychiatrist, it expands Steve's intellectual horizons well beyond the mundane practice of medicine.

Steve is one of the world's leading experts on crisis management. He's worked for our government, and he's been essentially subcontracted out by the Department of State to places that needed his expertise. He's a professional bubble-burster. Steve calls 'em as he sees 'em, and since he will never be the sort to suffer fools gladly, he has a valuable talent for cutting through all the nonsense and finding real solutions. A secondary result of this is that he is not the most popular person in the community which he serves. The fact that they keep calling him back is a statement on Steve and that community. I wish I knew all the things that he does. There might be one hell of a book in it, but he's too honorable to reveal things that others routinely leak for their own benefit.

Of this I am certain: Steve knows what he's talking about. Diplomacy and crisis management remain a human experience. Steve's observations and analyses have served our country well in some of the most unlikely places. He specializes in identifying human factors that find their way into the most institutional of activities. What distinguishes him from others who write about these matters is that he's really done and seen the things he writes about, and that's more than anyone can say about me. Steve Pieczenik is one of the people to whom I go for advice.

—TOM CLANCY

# MAXIMUM VIGILANCE

# PROLOGUE

Major Roger Gross, Troop Commander, 5th Squadron, 11th U.S. Armored Cavalry Regiment, struggled with his problem.

It wasn't going to be as easy as Washington thought to start World War III.

Perched on the turret of his M1A1 Abrams tank, astride the M109 self-propelled howitzers, he peered over the verdant rolling hills of Wildeck, Germany. All he could discern through his binoculars were the scorched barrels of the Russian T-72 battle tanks, peeking through overgrown bushes, shrouded with pink-petaled flowers. It all appeared so halcyon, just like the glossy pictures in an expensive guide book pointing the way to Johann Sebastian Bach's ancestral home only a few hundred yards away.

He directed his "Tonka Toys," three M60A3 tanks with hydraulically operated dozer blades, toward his right flank. Their assignment, along with the M9 armored combat earth mover, was to build a ten-by-twelve dirt furrow across the autobahn that would serve as a barrier to the advancing Russian forces.

It was all supposed to be so simple.

According to Field Manual 100-5, the new AirLandBattle Plan stressed initiative, depth, agility, and synchronization. As far as he could tell, he was certainly demonstrating initiative. His Tonka Toys, moving into a forward position, could easily be construed by the Russian troops in what was once the Democratic Republic of Germany as unnecessarily provocative. He had taken advantage of an unforeseen opportunity that could block a potential Russian advance.

Directing his howitzers toward the ravine, Gross covered his left flank, ordering his forward-based Sheridan tanks, with their Shillelagh missiles, back toward the rear. They were too valuable to be exposed so early on.

True, he could lob a 155 millimeter shell into the jagged cluster of those flowering bushes and blow away a few T-72s. The ensuing exchange of fire would last only a few minutes. But the T-72s would only respond with a few 125 millimeter shells of their own. And that would be about it.

Perhaps he could create a situation where the Russians would trip-wire a Special Atomic Demolition Munition, a man-portable nuclear land mine designed to wreck an autobahn junction. That certainly would start things rolling. But on second thought, this approach seemed too passive. The Russians might confuse the explosion as an engineering attempt to clear away the wooded lands surrounding the autobahn.

Suddenly, one of nature's vagaries inspired him. A cloud of dust raced toward him at thirty miles an hour. Peering through his binoculars, Gross saw six eight-wheeled Russian-made BTR-60 armored personnel carriers concealed within the approaching dust cloud, approximately eight miles away. And he discovered the solution to his problem.

"Black Horse two five . . . Black Horse two five . . . this is Tonka Toy One . . . over," Gross shouted into the Combat Net Radio.

"This is Black Horse two five, over . . . I read you loud and clear." The frightened voice added, "Six Belly Tango Roger Six Zeros raining down on us like hailstorm. What do we do, sir?"

"Hold fire until otherwise instructed. Do you read me, over?" Gross could hardly contain his enthusiasm.

"Sir, Belly Tango Rogers are almost upon us. Permission to fire." The crackling voice started to break up.

"Hold fire! This is Tonka Toy One! Hold fire! I repeat! Do you read me?"

"Belly Tango Roger within range," the voice replied.

Closing his eyes, Gross prayed.

# CHAPTER
## 1

"The first rule of crisis management is that there are no rules." Dr. Desaix Clark, the forty-eight-year-old Deputy Assistant Secretary of State for East Asian and Pacific Affairs walked across the stage of the small, overcrowded auditorium at the Japanese Foreign Ministry in total command of his audience. His swarthy good looks and dark, penetrating eyes were like a magnet to the diplomats seated in front of him, but there was also something about him that looked dissipated, even unsavory. He spent a good part of his adult life trying to dispel that licentious look, bred into him during his boyhood in the French Quarter of New Orleans.

His friend, Yutaka Imai, Japan's fifty-four-year-old Deputy Foreign Minister for Political Affairs, fidgeted nervously in the back of the auditorium, concerned that Desaix might be disappointed by the formality of his listeners. He had had a hard time arranging for this brief overview of the "Principles of Crisis Management" with the world's preeminent expert. It was a great honor that, on the day before their treaty negotiations were to begin, Desaix was willing to donate several hours of his time. Desaix had placed friendship before exhaustion after his fourteen-hour nonstop flight from Washington, D.C.

Desaix laughed to himself, even as his audience maintained its deafening silence. His now blunted angular features screwed into a mask of playfulness. "You make it up as you go along!" He paused purely for effect. "That's it! The lecture is over! Thank you for coming!" Then he watched his bewildered audience as they tried to decide whether that meant they now had to leave.

Imai broke into a cold sweat. Like his colleagues, he was taken completely off-guard. The lecture and discussion was supposed to last an hour. Mischief was certainly one of his friend's endearing qualities, but it was not appropriate during such a serious occasion.

Before the murmurs of confusion grew too loud, Desaix raised his right index finger in the air and waited for his audience to regain their composure. "The first, second, and third rules of crisis management are control, control, control. You must be able to control the different elements of a crisis—time, information, media, image, and the decision-making process."

The audience's bewilderment was swiftly replaced by laughter. Desaix's prankish technique had worked. It was clear to them that the famous Dr. Clark, whose first name, Desaix, rhymed with betray, had just made his point with the subtlety the Japanese prided themselves on. He had thrown them off-balance and just as quickly regained control.

"For those of you who may have drunk one glass of sake too many last night, I want you to remember a mnemonic, a word that will help you remember what I am saying." He picked up a felt pen from the flip chart on the stage and slowly wrote in large red letters: "TIMID." "In a crisis don't be afraid to be TIMID!"

The audience laughed again. Imai was relieved that his colleagues could appreciate Desaix's unusual sense of humor. This was the Desaix he treasured.

"T stands for time. Make certain you control the time element in a crisis. Otherwise, you will feel psychologically pressured that you have only a few options. Time allows you to find and create options that might not have been obvious from the start." He paused to make certain that everyone understood him. "I is for information. Collect all relevant intelligence—but share it sparingly."

"Dr. Clark, how can one collect information from everyone but only give it to a few?" a sprightly middle-aged Japanese asked in a clipped English accent.

"That's a good question. The answer is to remember that crisis management is a delicate balance between collegial cooperation and self-interest."

"You mean take what you can from others, but share very little?"

"That's right!"

"You mean we should just be ourselves?" the Japanese replied with a hint of sarcasm in his voice.

"What do you mean?"

"It's very Japanese to take from others and give back very little. So it will be easy for us to be good crisis managers."

The audience nodded in unison. Desaix was pleased by the unexpected spontaneity.

"You will become great crisis managers as long as you remember that you are now a major economic and political superpower. And you must not be afraid to act that part. You can decide how much to take and how much to give. You can no longer isolate yourself from the problems of the world. Either you will control them or they will control you."

The audience stood up and applauded. Imai was proud of his friend.

Desaix smiled, loving the anticipated response he received, realizing that here was both his weakness and his strength. He loved the spotlight, especially when he connected like this to his audience. And he loved being in the center of a crisis for the same reasons: the intellectual challenge and the opportunity to show off his talents. But it was *wanting* the opportunity so much that often left him vulnerable to manipulation.

"Please . . . please . . ." Desaix motioned for them to sit down so that he could continue. He felt like a TV evangelist intoxicated with his own ability to manipulate the holy trinity of hope, expectation, and adulation. But he was mindful of his responsibility to allow them to regain their composure before they became embarrassed by their sudden emotional outburst.

By temperament and disposition, Desaix was indeed in his element. He relished the fact that his profession put him on the stage of history. Measuring his self-worth not by the mortal standards of wealth, health, or daily successes, but through action. Physical action. Sexual action. Moral action. Mental action. Dramatic action. But by training and profession, he prided himself on being an outsider, able to walk away from the action when it was necessary. A deadly combination in the international game of crisis management. As a psychiatrist with a doctorate in international affairs, both from fine Ivy League universities, in his mind he still remained a professional in search of a profession.

For Desaix, a fourth-generation Huguenot from New Orleans, the son of a martinet general medical practitioner and a frustrated music teacher, he pursued life as if it were an extension of the natural rhythms of zydeco, searching for the raw, vital spirit of that strange soulful mixture of the bouncy, fiddle-topped Cajun music and the bluesy accordian. But the only meaningful actions he courted avidly were associated with historical imperatives, especially those that might footnote his participation. He referred to this compulsion as his "histrionic" destiny.

"The letter M in TIMID stands for media," Desaix continued. "If you do not manage the media, it will determine the outcome of the crisis. The optimum situation is a complete news blackout like the one we had during the Iraq War against Saddam Hussein. Failing that, you must be able to co-opt the newsmakers as much as possible with your own TV footage and information. Otherwise, the crisis becomes *their* story."

"But we are democracies. We cannot simply shut the press out. They have a right to know," an elderly Japanese diplomat interjected.

"That's correct. But it's all a question of timing. Holding back the news a few minutes or hours can make all the difference between life or death in a crisis. But it won't change the outcome of the reporting."

The old man shrugged his shoulders in resignation as he sat down.

"The second I in TIMID stands for image, or perception. In a crisis, it is important to know yourself, the situation, and your adversary. And it is equally important for you to project an image to the world that you are in full control of the situation. That, at all times, you know exactly what you are doing."

"But we Japanese are always portrayed as secret and sneaky," a brash young foreign service officer yelled out.

"Well, are you?" Desaix challenged.

"Quite frankly, yes."

"Then either change your behavior or your image," Desaix replied emphatically, standing squarely, hands on hips, almost daring the audience to contradict him.

"How would you recommend that we do that, Dr. Clark?" The young man asked defiantly, reinforced by the supporting murmurs in the crowd.

"How many of you have seen the movie *Snow White and the Seven Dwarfs?*" Desaix asked, barely containing his enthusiasm as he watched the bewildered audience raise their hands hesitantly. Early on, he had learned the lessons of spiritual conversion from his Cajun evangelist cousins: Shock them into believing in you. Keep them entertained. And leave them with plenty of hope. Then you got yourself a bona fide God-fearing soul.

"There were seven dwarfs," Desaix continued, "each of whom had a completely different personality—Sleepy, Dopey, Sneezy—"

"Are you saying that we must act stupid or make believe we have a cold?" the foreign service officer asked sarcastically.

"No. What I am trying to say is that Japan must stop presenting itself as a nation of inscrutable samurai warriors intent on dominating the world through economic means. Let the world see you as you are—a composite of different individuals—"

"Acting sleepily, stupidly, or sickly . . ." the young officer interjected.

"Why not? If that's what it takes to convince the world you are a nation of individuals."

"So you recommend that we should first see *Snow White and the Seven Dwarfs* in order to learn how to project multiple images during a crisis?"

"As a matter of fact, that's not a bad idea," Desaix replied half seriously, realizing he had inadvertently stumbled on a potentially effective teaching technique—the American movie.

"What other movies would you recommend that we Japanese diplomats watch in order to learn your lessons of crisis management?" the young officer asked.

"My dear young colleague, I think that's an extremely interesting question." Desaix paused, trying to recall some of his favorite films. As a movie and theater addict, he knew he had ample material from which to draw. "There are many films I could mention. But of course the one that comes to mind most readily is . . ." Desaix paused as the majority of the audience cocked their heads in eager anticipation. He was always impressed by the universality of interest in movies and their ability to overcome differences of language and culture. He strutted across the stage, leaned out toward his audience, and whispered sotto voce: "*The Wizard of Oz.*"

Following his lead, the audience became silent, something that Desaix had not anticipated. So he raised his hands in the air, as if conducting an imaginary orchestra, and began to sing the well-known theme song from the movie. "We're off to see the wizard . . . the wonderful wizard of Oz . . ." Encouraging the audience to sing along with him, he soon had almost everyone either humming or singing.

Even the stern Imai participated. He suspected that his clever friend was using this familiar song to break down the formidable psychological barriers that normally existed between an Occidental lecturer and an Oriental audience. But he knew that within the apparent innocence, if not silliness, of Desaix's approach, the *tatemae* was a very serious message, the *honne*.

"We're off to see the wizard . . . the wonderful wizard of Oz . . ."

Suddenly Desaix stopped singing. By this time, the audience was not surprised by his abrupt change. They were beginning to get used to his theatrics.

"If you want to manage a crisis successfully, you must imagine it as an enjoyable movie with a beginning, middle, and end." Desaix spoke seriously as he grabbed the felt pen and hurriedly wrote the word "STRUCTURE" on the flip chart underneath the word "TIMID."

"*The Wizard of Oz* works because above all else it has a well-constructed screenplay. Within the first few minutes, we know who the main character is, what she wants, and what obstacles she must overcome to achieve her goal. There is a very definite beginning, middle, and end." Pointing to the cocky young officer, Desaix asked, "What does Dorothy want?"

"She wants to get to . . . the Emerald City, to meet with the wizard so that he can send her back to her home in Kansas."

"Good! Now tell me, what were the obstacles along the way?"

"The Wicked Witch of the West . . ." He hesitated, "or was it the Wicked Witch of the East?"

"Don't worry! It was some kind of wicked witch who flew on a broomstick. Then what happened?"

"Along her . . . journey . . . on the brick road . . . the yellow-brick road, she met a straw man . . . that . . . scares . . . away birds. He wanted a memory. Then . . . she . . . finds . . . a man made of . . . I think . . . it's tin . . . who needed a heart. And, of course, there was . . . a lion who wanted . . . to be . . . brave. All three together fought . . . flying monkeys. But at the end of the movie, they reached the city . . . They discovered that the Wizard was . . . how do you say a . . . fake."

"That's right, they discover that the Wizard of Oz was an impostor, or fake." Desaix paused. "I see that you know your movies."

"I spent two years in graduate school at UCLA."

The audience chuckled.

"In reality, it turns out the author had written *The Wizard of Oz* as a parable of the domestic political crisis in the early part of the twentieth century, involving William Jennings Bryan, the problems of adopting the gold standard, and the farm crisis in the Midwest. What is important for you to remember is that a political crisis and a movie have the following points in common: a protagonist with whom the viewing public can identify, and an objective which must be obtained by overcoming a series of adversities and obstacles. And the element of time enables the drama to play itself out in the final scene of the crisis, which more often than not involves some type of action. So both the screenwriter and the crisis manager must be in control of his material and process at all times."

"Are you saying that we must become writers . . . of . . . screenplays . . . before we become crisis managers?" the young man asked.

"It wouldn't be a bad idea. But I don't think it's necessary. A good crisis manager must have creativity, imagination, and discipline. He must be able to impose his view of the crisis over the limiting demands of reality. And at all times he must be in control of his characters, strategy, and tactics.

"Which leads me to the final point about the letter D in TIMID. D stands for decision maker. And one must never forget that the first one in and the last one out with the ultimate decision maker, in our case the President of the United States, is the one who has the final word." Desaix checked his watch. "Well, my time is up, and I want to thank you for the opportunity to talk to you. I hope you enjoyed it as much as I did." He bowed, exhilarated by the standing ovation he received.

"Oh, one more point," Desaix shouted above the applause. "Don't forget to game out your management of a crisis with someone who can play the role of your principal adversary. In a real crisis, you must always know beforehand how your adversary thinks and responds."

"What if you don't have an adversary?" an elderly man yelled out.

"Then create one!" On that command, Desaix left the stage, shaking hands as he walked through the audience toward the exit.

"Thank you so much for your witty and insightful talk." Imai had remained until the auditorium was empty. "Just as you requested, the police helicopter is on the roof, waiting to take you to your next appointment."

"It was my pleasure and honor. I'll see you tomorrow," Desaix replied.

The two men shook hands and then bowed to each other.

Ironic, Desaix thought as he walked toward the waiting helicopter, how facile he had sounded about the need to control a crisis. Only an hour ago he had learned that a major crisis was brewing in Western Europe between the U.S. and the Russians. And here he was in Japan, not part of the action loop. But business would have to wait. Right now, he could only worry about the evening he would be spending with his good friend Sasha, the ultimate gamesman. Time was of the essence. The crisis would have to go on without his intervention.

\* \* \*

From the air, Desaix saw Tokyo as a sprawling metropolis expanding with amoeboid elegance from the congested harbors of Tokyo Bay on the southeast to the bucolic suburbs of Chichibu to the west. And in the distance, the snowcapped mountain peaks of Mount Fuji beckoned him forward.

In a few minutes they landed in front of a fifth-century Shinto shrine, and Desaix rushed up the flight of faded stone steps toward a physically trim man in his late sixties, standing half naked in front of an oversized bronze Buddha beneath a vaulted wooden ceiling.

"Sasha!" Desaix hugged his inebriated friend, a sybaritic ex-director of the Funzi Military Academy and currently a senior officer in the Russian Army.

"You son of a bitch! Where the hell have you been?" Pointing to his Rolex, Sasha scolded unconvincingly in his thick Russian accent, "You Americans are supposed to be punctual! And it is we Russians who are supposed to always be late!"

"General, I see that you have already started without me." Desaix started to unbutton his shirt.

"Look! They are all assembled, all ready to start! A few seconds more of waiting, and I would have had a riot on my hands. All because of you!" Like the Pontiff blessing the masses at the Vatican, Sasha stretched his arms as if he were inviting the religious ceremony to begin.

As far as the eye could see, Japanese men and women filled the square, with a group in the middle carrying a large wooden phallus over their shoulders. The crowd began to walk slowly toward the two men.

The police helicopter that had brought Desaix hovered above the milling crowd. At the same time, baldheaded priests swathed in orange tunics, locked arm in arm in a human chain, were applauded by onlookers at a respectable distance.

In the center of this religious procession of several thousand people was a group of sexually enticing women, dressed in flamboyantly decorated kimonos, throwing chrysanthemum petals at the oversized wooden penis carried on the shoulders of the young novitiates marching somberly in front of them.

"Tell me, Desaix!" Sasha spoke in a heavy slur, made almost unintelligible after two bottles of sake. "What are two dissipated, decadent characters like us doing in this godforsaken country? Haven't you heard that your country and mine are having some problems. We should be back in our own countries, preparing to kill each other."

"My dear friend. Have you learned nothing about peace and war?" Desaix was having a hard time propping Sasha up as several men and women slowly mounted the stone steps toward them. "In peace, we crisis managers are an extravagance that neither side can afford. And in war, we are simply unwanted nuisances."

"In Russia we have a saying that crisis managers are like Siberian mushrooms. Keep them in the dark and feed them horse manure!" Sasha grabbed Desaix by the shoulder and looked him straight in the face. Tears streaked down his face. "Please, Desaix! Of the two of us, you are the more clever. Do an old friend a favor. Figure out how we both can get into this situation before it's too late. Otherwise, it will be a catastrophe! We both may miss the most important crisis of our lives!"

"Patience, my friend. Patience." As Desaix replied he noticed a lithe young woman approach him with outstretched arms, her long jet black hair glistening in the afternoon light.

"Patience? You, an American, who cooks his prepackaged cardboard dinner in a one-minute microwave and devours it in half that time, consoles me, a Russian, to be patient? Hah! That's a joke!"

Desaix recalled the countless days and nights they had spent in group sex encounters over the past several years in Japan, celebrating the Great Phallus Game. Last year they had been placed on opposing teams, each one composed of Buddhist monks and specially selected women.

As usual, the women were instructed to sexually excite any member of the opposing side in any way they could, with the objective of finding out which team player could sustain an erection for the longest period of time. The male whose engorged penis subsided last, despite relentless distractions from the opposing team, was declared the winner of the game. Both the *harigata*, the artificial penis, and the *higozuiki*, the ring hastening erection, were actively used, either in consort with another person or all alone.

What both men enjoyed about the Great Phallus Game was that anything and everything was permissible. If nothing else, these two friends were gamesmen who loved a challenge to their sense of masculine identity: aggressiveness, competition, power, and control.

For the moment, Desaix thought, his friend was headed for defeat, given the amount of sake he had drunk. It would take nothing less than a combination of an esoteric aphrodisiac, like rhinoceros tusk, and the sexual guile of a Japanese courtesan, to make Sasha potent again.

"As a disciple of Amaterasu, the Goddess of the Sun, I would like to pass through the Royal Door with you!" The young Japanese maiden spoke to Desaix in English, and began to gently stroke his chest.

"My friend is in a hurry! In a few hours, he must leave for his country. Perhaps you could help me to help him." Desaix redirected her amorous attentions.

"You are a good friend! A very good friend!" Sasha shivered as he felt dainty fingers caress his crotch. "But I must return soon to Mother Russia! They will call me into action! You will see! So make a plan for us, my dear Desaix." He tore open the woman's diaphanous kimono as he yelled, "We must conspire together! Otherwise we will both be finished! We will be nothing more than fornicators!"

"First enjoy yourself, my friend! Then we'll worry about making ourselves indispensable to our governments."

Desaix took hold of a mature woman standing before him and began to fondle her with all the enthusiasm of a diplomat who must attend yet another cocktail reception. He tried to forget the admonition of his supervising psychiatrist in New Orleans—"Every crisis offers you extra desired power. And each extra power forces you to seek out another crisis, in an endless cycle of continuous dissatisfaction."

As the procession of the Great Phallus ascended the stairs to the Shinto shrine, Desaix penetrated the Royal Doors.

# CHAPTER

## 2

***M****uzukashii.* It is difficult. After two grueling days, negotiations were not going well.

Desaix felt extremely frustrated. While yearning for the captivating commotion of the mounting crisis in Western Europe, the senior State Department official felt trapped, enveloped by smooth-skinned Orientals in an elegantly decorated conference room on the sixth floor of the Japanese Foreign Ministry.

Ignoring the unruly behavior among the six members of his negotiating team, Desaix stared through the green-tinted windows overlooking the National Government Offices on Sakurada-Dori. He felt a strong identification with the Imperial Palace, located a few blocks away, surrounded by useless gawking tourists strolling lazily around the Sakurada Moat, filled with different types of symbolically important goldfish.

He picked up the highly classified position paper from the conference table in front of him and scanned it.

### TOP SECRET/EXTREMELY SENSITIVE/NO FORN/NO CON
#### Differences in U.S.-Japanese Negotiating Styles

| JAPAN | U.S. |
|---|---|
| 1) Closed internal process of consensus | Open public process of consensus |

| | |
|---|---|
| 2) Understated, vague opening position | Overstated opening position |
| 3) Leak position before formal presentation | No leaks, all positions are formal |
| 4) Work with domestic press, isolate foreign press | Adversarial press relationships |
| 5) Reveal details of ongoing negotiations | Maintain complete secrecy |
| 6) Case-by-case practical solutions | First establish principle, then find solution |
| 7) Compromise difficult, offer meaningless concessions | Compromise too soon |
| 8) Stress areas of agreement | Stress winning argument |
| 9) Avoid confrontation | Adversarial |
| 10) Negotiate to avoid failure | Negotiate to win |
| 11) Probe, push, panic strategy | Ad hoc strategy |
| 12) Negotiations are continuous | Negotiations lead to final solution |

Desaix was disturbed by Imai's ability to reverse the so-called typical Japanese negotiating style. If he didn't know better, Desaix would have sworn that Imai had a copy of this highly classified document. His only remaining hope was to try to co-opt the Japanese negotiating strategy described in point eleven. But he wasn't optimistic. He now saw himself as a misplaced ornament, enticing to examine, but of no real practical consequence to anyone. After ten years in the system, four at the National Security Council and six at the State Department, he tried to fight the feeling of being the misbegotten outsider. He knew that his need to highlight his differences often arose when things weren't going according to plans. But his disconcerting mood swings had become an annoyance both to himself and to those who cared about him.

Neither of his four previous wives nor his two past mistresses interpreted this personal pathology as anything more than a crumbling rationalization for the ordinary fear of being mortal and mundane. They accepted his behavior as insufferably wearing but exciting, and each tolerated his moodiness and infidelity up to a point because he was a caring and patient lover.

After having acquired and practiced three completely different vocations—physician, psychiatrist, and diplomat—Desaix knew that he now stood the risk of being considered a professional dilettante by those few professionals in the crisis management business whose opinion he respected. And for him, that was intolerable, if not inexcusable.

Under normal conditions, he would have taken pride in what he was currently doing, negotiating long-term agreements for the National Security Agency's Signal Intelligence network in Japan. But these were not normal times. A series of unusual events had been escalating in Western Europe that resulted in a heightened state of worldwide tension according to this morning's National Intelligence Directorate, the daily bible for some two hundred senior-level bureaucrats at State, DOD, CIA, and the White House. As of 0800, U.S. forces the world over were placed on DEFCON TWO— one notch below the maximum state of alert. Maximum Vigilance.

Desaix was certain that the crisis management mechanisms at both the White House and the State Department were already set in motion. And no one had called him. At least not yet. Had he been once again an orphan of bureaucratic preoccupation? Or, perhaps, worse, purposefully kept out of the information and action loop. Instead, here he was, assigned the task of conducting negotiations with the Japanese because the Sec State, so he had said, needed someone out there who wasn't a member of the Chrysanthemum Club, a derogatory term assigned to those Foreign Service officers in the department who were completely enamored with Japan or anything to do with Japan. Nippon lovers.

Desaix returned his gaze to the room and rested it on Imai. He was both disturbed and impressed by Imai's charm, wit, and negotiating skill. A diminutive man with a piercing sensitivity to Americans and the way they thought and did business, Imai was typical of the new breed of Japanese diplomat who retained only the faintest trace of bitterness toward the Americans for Hiroshima and Nagasaki. Instead, like many others in the Japanese Foreign Ministry, he felt grateful for the compassionate way the Americans had treated Japan during the postwar years. But as Desaix knew, this overriding sense of gratitude didn't necessarily translate into a negotiation strategy of accommodation for renewing the U.S. intelligence network in Japan. And to make matters worse, while Desaix was considered one of the U.S. government's finest negotiators and crisis managers, his negotiating team was definitely out of control.

Desaix was having difficulty implementing his own variation of point eleven, what he termed the Japanese three Ps of negotiating: Probe. Push. Panic. Probe the opponent's point of weakness. Push it open large enough so that the opponent is convinced of his own vulnerability. Then intimidate him into a state of panic where he believes that there is no alternative other than the one presented.

But Desaix was expending all his energy trying to make some sense of the bickering among his team members.

Lieutenant General Richard White, a taut, ashen-faced, highly decorated electronic engineer with large, rough hands was Director of the Office of Signal Intelligence Operations at the National Security Agency, responsible for both Communications Intelligence and Electronic Intelligence. He was contradicting James Ball, a ruddy-faced former CIA station chief who looked and acted like a compassionate Peace Corps worker, informal in both dress and manner. He headed up the Office of Scientific Intelligence, which was responsible for a wide range of scientific data collection, including encoded telemetry, secret signals transmitted from spy satellites. Ball was also Director of Desaix's favorite CIA section, the Center for Leadership Analysis, where they developed the psychological profiles of well-known world leaders, affectionately known as the Office of Sluts and Nuts.

Theirs was more than the usual bureaucratic turf disagreements. Desaix was certain they were engaged in some form of personal vendetta that had found its way into their professional life. Each had consistently torpedoed the other's proposals.

And he, Desaix, was too distracted by visions of his impending involvement in the crisis in Europe to focus seriously on their bickering. If he could only wire himself into the loop, he thought. Damn White and Ball! They were simply prolonging the unnecessary agony of this negotiation.

In total contrast to the basic precept of his lecture, Desaix realized he was not in control of this negotiation and it was quickly unraveling for reasons he didn't understand. In the past, he would have stopped the proceedings and walked out without any explanations. But this time he was unable to walk away. The fact that he didn't understand what was happening fascinated him and kept him glued to his seat.

"Let us examine the facts behind your installation at the Ashiya Air Force Base on the island of Kyushu." Imai cocked his head backward.

"Excuse me, sir," White interrupted.

"Let him speak!" Ball interjected.

Desaix shook his head in disapproval, indicating to both White and Ball that he wanted them to cease and desist.

Without saying a word, Imai moved his head ever so slightly from side to side. *Haragei.* Belly laughter. Nonverbal communication. The use of vagueness, silence, and subtlety to convey Imai's desire to be cordial. Like all Japanese, Imai had been taught since childhood to avoid any and all forms of social conflict.

"With all due respect to you and your colleagues, Dr. Clark, I must reiterate my disapproval of your previous proposal to allow the 9132 Mobile Radio Unit on the island of Kyushu."

"Again, Mr. Imai, may I interrupt you for a moment?" White did not wait for permission to continue. "The 9132 Mobile Radio Unit cannot, under any conditions, be considered for possible termination."

"Wait a minute, Richard," Ball jumped in. "Everything is up for grabs. That's why we're here—to negotiate our differences. Not to dictate terms." His face reddened.

For the first time in their five-year collegial relationship, Imai glared at Desaix. The *haragei* was obvious—get your team in order.

Uncharacteristically, Desaix squirmed in his chair, feeling trapped by Imai's deftly designed strategy. By encouraging the discussion of proposals that he, Imai, knew would be divisive, he had been able to split Desaix's team right down the middle. Consensus through unanimity, a primary U.S. negotiating goal, was being effectively undermined.

In contrast, Imai was expected by his country to use whatever inherent differences might exist on his team of fifteen bureaucrats to find a solution that was satisfactory to everyone. His young bureaucrats were expected to be like fierce samurai, while the older, more mature governmental officials, like himself, were expected to keep their bureaucrats under tight control. And Imai's team sat silent and watchful as the American team continued sparring with one another.

"Only those Signal Intelligence sites not considered critical to our collection capability should be discussed."

Desaix bent slightly forward to get a good look at the speaker, Daniel Fitzpatrick, a longtime friend about whom he was concerned.

Fitzpatrick was a wily, seemingly distracted, red-bearded ex-professor from the University of California, Berkeley, who was, as far as Desaix was concerned, the finest NSC senior staffer on the Commonwealth of Independent States that had ever been appointed to that position. Fitzpatrick was responsible for coordinating all intelligence from the CIA, DIA, DOD, NSA, and State Department Intelligence and Research that was in any way related to the different republics that once comprised the Soviet Union. He also arbitrated differences among these agencies with respect to any intelligence report they might present to the President. Fitzpatrick reported directly to the President through General Thomas Mapplethorpe, the National Security Advisor.

Staring at Fitzpatrick, Desaix wondered what the hell his good friend was doing here. His presence in Japan didn't make any more sense than his own. Even before the mounting crisis between the U.S. and the Commonwealth of Independent States, General Mapplethorpe had insisted that Desaix take Fitzpatrick with him to monitor and arbitrate differences among the various agencies represented on the negotiating team. Since that was Desaix's ostensible job, and not Fitzpatrick's, Desaix had protested. But Mapplethorpe had insisted.

"By critical you mean Modern Magic or Yellow Cloud?" White questioned Fitzpatrick as if he were demanding a staff briefing.

"No," Ball interrupted again. "By critical we mean the ground stations at Edzell, Scotland, as well as the ocean surveillance facilities in Argentina and Newfoundland." He spoke with an air of defiance, waiting to see how White would respond.

Desaix was incredulous. In less than two minutes, both White and Ball had revealed more classified information about the highly secret U.S. Signal Intelligence system than the team had ever intended.

Leafing through all the classified documents in his folder, Desaix grimaced as he stared at the bold lettering marked across both the top and bottom of each sheath of paper: TOP SECRET/NO FORN/NO CON. It couldn't be more clear. Signal Intelligence should not be discussed with any foreigners (FORN) or contract employees (CON). What the hell was wrong with these guys?

Imai spoke. "Am I to assume that we are agreed on removing the 9132 Mobile Radio Unit from Ashiya Air Force Base in Kyushu?" He waited for a response.

"I think we've explored this issue as deeply as we're going to," Desaix interrupted, trying to minimize whatever damage had already been done. True, Japan was an ally and the U.S. shared common intelligence concerns with her, but Imai had no need to know about any of the electronic assets specifically targeted against Russia and the other independent republics. Even if Imai was only probing to see how far the U.S. was willing to defend its national security interests vis-à-vis Japan.

"Perhaps you gentlemen are correct. We should not examine any particular Signal Intelligence installation, but instead discuss the pros and cons of basing them in Japan. Or as you Americans like to say, let us examine the big picture."

Desaix scrutinized the reaction of his team members and was surprised at their complete indifference. Maybe they didn't understand that Imai was trying to expose further the U.S. team's vulnerability.

"Mr. Imai, are you really asking us to review the need for a Signal Intelligence capability on Japanese soil?" Desaix knew that the question would serve no purpose other than to antagonize Imai and provide some fodder for his own team's gossip mill. But as a willing student of bureaucratic behavior, he had formulated a rule: the State Department bureaucracy could function with zest and efficiency only if there were seventh-floor principals, including the Secretary of State and the three different Under Secretaries of State, present at a negotiation. This way, the bureaucracy could vent its spleen by leaking damaging news stories about a certain faux pas, forcing Congress to initiate hearings and produce an overwhelming flow of irrelevant reports.

The corollary to the rule stated that in the absence of a clear national goal or ideology, bureaucratic behavior and imperatives dictate the course of national action. And these two principles could not have been operating more clearly than in this room.

But why now? What was their reason for revealing Signal Intelligence? He knew that any attempt on his part to impede their behavior would be met with disdain, derision, or back-channel chatter. The last thing Desaix needed was cable traffic back to the department through Roger Channel in which the worst elements of the negotiation, real or imagined, would be described in lurid detail. It was important that his reply curtail all further discussion.

"We are not authorized to discuss anything other than the leases on specific Signal Intelligence installations. In order to do what you have just suggested we would have to return to the States, hold an interagency Principals' Coordinating Committee, from which we would receive a report that would go to the White House. Fitzpatrick would then convene a Deputies' Coordinating Committee, after which the President might . . . I add might . . . issue an executive directive authorizing us to negotiate the Signal Intelligence installations in Japan. Now, I don't think you, or we, want to engage in such a protracted process that really has nothing to do with the problem at hand."

Imai nodded his head in silent approval. His friend Desaix had just outwitted him using the time-honored tradition of *tatemae* and *honne*. What Desaix had said was very clear: the U.S. bureaucracy works very slowly. That was the manifest content of the statement—*tatemae*. But what was far more important for Imai was *honne*—what Desaix thought. The general message was understood. Japan would have to remain in a third-party status in joint U.S. intelligence gatherings, along with South Korea.

"In time, many things will change." Imai made certain that Desaix realized that his *honne* had been understood.

"Many things must change in time. But time has a way of preparing us for the inevitable." Desaix was now practicing *awase*, a negotiating style that emphasized the importance of proper form and process over substance. Like any good Japanese negotiator, Desaix was trying to achieve maximum tactical flexibility by avoiding a direct confrontation with Imai, while at the same time informing him through *honne* that the future status of U.S.-Japanese intelligence cooperation would depend very much on the outcome of the present lease arrangements. Particularly the 9132 Radio Mobile Unit on Kyushu.

Both Imai and Clark understood that there was more involved in this discussion than simply a renewal of Signal Intelligence leases. What was really being determined was nothing less than a new social order of power and international alliances. Each man knew, all too well, that the hierarchy of intelligence alliances determined almost a full half century ago was seriously outdated. What had been missing was any notion that Japan would become a formidable economic and political force fifty years later. Imai merely wanted current reality reflected in the new alliance agreements. And Desaix understood this.

For the moment, there was nothing else Desaix could do but contain the damage on his side. And this might mean to return to Washington as soon as possible. He started to assemble his papers.

"*Muzukashii.*" It is difficult. Imai bowed his head in contrite acceptance of the inevitable. He had failed to resolve the impasse in this negotiation. Perhaps he had pushed too hard.

"*Sho-ga-nai.*" It can't be helped. Desaix motioned to White, Ball, and Fitzpatrick, but they remained seated. A test of bureaucratic wills.

Imai and his team of fifteen waited to see what Desaix would do with this apparent insubordination.

Desaix stood up, tucked his folder of classified material beneath his right arm and signaled his team to do the same.

"*Cojones*," Fitzpatrick hissed the Spanish word for "balls" beneath his breath. It was Desaix who always defended him whenever the seventh-floor policymakers at State wanted to get rid of him. Often at great personal risk to himself.

"Let us continue to discuss the leases on the other Signal Intelligence sites in Japan," Ball continued as if nothing had transpired.

"Let's take them one at a time, starting with our unfinished discussions on the 9132 Mobile Radio Unit," White replied with the guarded impatience of a man who realizes that he has acquired a new lease on life.

In an unexpected move, Desaix sat down again and opened up a folder consisting of classified material. He had instantly assessed the situation and decided that he had only one option left—accepting as gracefully as possible his own rule of bureaucratic survival. Never go against the will of the system. No bureaucrat would invite a charge of insubordination from a Deputy Assistant Secretary of State unless he was being protected by someone from above. Way above!

Desaix was certainly not going to martyr himself to the system. At least not before he had a chance to be involved in the crisis developing in Germany. His contest of wills was over—but only for the moment.

Imai tried desperately to restrain the emerging smile on his face. His friend Desaix was certainly no samurai. He had lost his Bushido code of honor as well as his pride. Just another typical American eager to make a deal. But he felt sorry for his friend. How he wished to tell him what was really on his mind—his *honne*. But that would not be possible. Not now. Not in front of his American colleagues. He owed this gesture of friendship to Desaix. It was his *on*. His obligation.

"Besides the 9132 Mobile Radio Unit on Kyushu," Desaix continued as if nothing embarrassing had transpired, "we will discuss the installations that are primarily targeted toward collecting Signal Intelligence against Russia and other republics in the Commonwealth of Independent States."

He was bothered by the fact that so many U.S. intelligence assets were directed against Russia at a time when the country was still in continuous turmoil. The Commonwealth of Independent States had become less and less of a military threat to the U.S. That's why the deployment of both U.S. and Russian troops didn't make much sense. But if he wanted to be part of the action, he knew he had to first resolve this Japanese mess.

"We want to maintain the overflight and basing privileges for the rotational EP-3B aircraft from the installation on Guam. The Tori station on Makiminato as well as the location on Hokkaido are all essential parts of our Signal Intelligence system in Japan. Isn't that right, Mr. Fitzpatrick?" Desaix was eager to bring Fitzpatrick into the negotiations before he tuned out completely.

"That's correct, Desaix," Fitzpatrick replied appreciatively.

"We might add that there are fifteen other major Signal Intelligence installations that we would also like to negotiate," Ball added, perplexed by Desaix's sudden change. And suspicious.

"We will also have to lease more land around the Tori station in order to maintain its effectiveness," White added, not wanting to be left out.

"Let us examine the merits of the present lease for the 9132 Mobile Radio Unit," Imai said, refocusing the discussion, hoping it would help his friend. "Let us see where our differences lie. Perhaps there are not as many as one would imagine . . ." He paused, and added with deliberate emphasis, "Or fear." He continued nonchalantly, "From there, if we are lucky, we may proceed onto our next case and see where there are points of convergence. We should always try to avoid, if possible, any major points of contention. Let us try to settle them in a harmonious fashion."

*"Zensho itashimasu."* I will do my best. Desaix nodded his head in agreement.

*Haragei.* Imai would understand the need for Desaix's sudden acquiescence. He could no longer fight both Imai and the members of his own team.

He would now submit to the accepted rituals of the negotiation. First, there would be discussions concerning practical problems and solutions. A case-by-case method would be established. In each different situation the practical solution would always precede the principle that would eventually determine the outcome of the next case. If compromise were difficult, one or the other side would offer a meaningless concession in order to allow the other side to save face. But if that were not possible, a fictional principle would be created by which both sides would agree to abide until some later point in the negotiation when, again if both sides agreed, the principle would be dropped and another, more convenient one would be created. In this ritualized manner of negotiation both sides could avoid any points of conflict or contention. But it would be clearly understood that the real negotiation would occur in the informal discussions between Desaix and Imai. That would be where the most important issues, like the practical problems of implementation, would eventually be ironed out.

Desaix was now ready to play his part in the Kabuki of a proper Japanese negotiation.

Closing his eyes, Desaix sensed that familiar surge of sexual discomfort that always arose when he encountered an episode of frustration or personal disappointment. At some point between his first and second wife, or was it his first and second mistress, he had vowed to give up any pretense of self-understanding. Whatever value self-awareness held for him lay primarily in the province of seduction.

"Gentlemen, it has been a long and difficult beginning. I propose that we adjourn for the day. And in the spirit of friendship I would like to invite you all for some drinks and an evening's relaxation." Imai smiled. *Haragei.* He knew his friend Desaix well. In the past they had shared many moments of joy and disappointment together. He knew how frustrated his friend must be now.

Desaix blew a mock kiss across the room and relieved the tension that existed in the room. Everyone broke into laughter.

"Terrific suggestion," White said. "For a moment there, I was worried that we would be up all night negotiating. I love my country, but not that much." He gave Desaix a hearty slap on the back.

Not to be outdone, Ball went up to Imai and shook his hand vigorously. Only Fitzpatrick seemed visibly disturbed by the news of impending merriment.

"What's the matter, Danny? Doesn't the White House also have a right to a night's indiscretion?" Desaix was puzzled by Fitzpatrick's palpably angry silence. "Don't worry. I promise you'll get all those leases signed, sealed, and delivered no later than close of business *mañana*. You have my word. Trust me." Walking over to Fitzpatrick, Desaix placed his arm in a comforting gesture around his shoulder. But Fitzpatrick still seemed preoccupied and sullen.

"Why not?" Fitzpatrick gathered his classified papers, shielding them from Desaix.

"What's wrong, Danny?" Desaix asked, concerned. "Is there anything that I can do?"

"No, thanks. I just have a few odds and ends to collect here. Nothing too serious." Fitzpatrick spoke in a nonconvincing, self-mocking tone. The more he tried to dismiss his tense behavior, the more inviting he became to Clark's innate suspiciousness.

Desaix recalled another favorite maxim, this one derived from his delinquent youth in New Orleans: *Qui s'excuse, s'accuse.* He who excuses himself, accuses himself.

"Come on, Desaix, it's getting late!" Ball led him out the door toward the bank of elevators located in the middle of the glistening pink-marble corridor. They descended to the ground floor, where several black Cadillac limousines were waiting.

"A little touch of home." Imai gently steered Desaix by the elbow, inviting him to sit with him in the back seat.

Fitzpatrick, White, and Ball entered the second limousine.

The limousines sped off into the traffic of swirling headlights toward the Ginza. The night was illuminated with a festival of twisted, multicolored neon signs. Every conceivable brand name was prominently displayed atop or astride buildings.

"I'm sorry about the negotiations. But I want to thank you again for your lecture. Everyone has been telling me how much they enjoyed it."

"Imai, remind me next time to follow my own advice about control, or better yet, to keep my mouth shut." Desaix laughed. He appreciated Imai's attempt to make him feel good. As a matter of fact, after his escapade with

Sasha two nights ago, Desaix had no desire to go to the geisha house. But he knew that Imai would be deeply offended if he didn't accept his offer.

"Don't worry, my friend. Ours has been a long-standing relationship with many ups and downs."

Watching the people and the traffic, Desaix felt he had entered a new house of worship: the twenty-first century, in an orchestrated cacophony of sound and bright lights. There was no place for man and his sense of self. Only the modern vestige of man's spirit remained—his need to be continuously in motion.

Yet Desaix felt comfortable in this urban sanctuary. The Ginza, the Forty-second Street of Tokyo, was the most honest distillation of man's prurient intentions that Desaix had ever seen anywhere in the world. Only Bangkok provided him with a clearer sense of man's genius to delude himself with regard to his immortality. There, the fluorescent pantheon of the night was Patpang—a downtrodden area of iniquity catering to the proposition that man was indeed destined to enter the inferno of eternal sin.

When they arrived at their destination, Imai directed Desaix toward the entrance of a fairly large wooden inn built in the traditional Japanese style, with a sloped roof made from dark red ceramic tiles.

Accompanied by Ball, White, and the reluctant Fitzpatrick, Desaix entered a foyer formed of paper-thin sliding walls. Each man was greeted by a hostess dressed in a colorful diaphanous kimono. When a fifth hostess approached Imai, he quietly demurred and, turning to Desaix, bid them all a good night, saying he had to go home. It was his daughter's birthday.

Desaix was completely surprised. This was the first time Imai had not participated in an evening's frivolity with him. He was trying to decide what this might mean as his hostess guided him gently but insistently to a private room, the *tataki*, where he removed his shoes before entering. The hostess, an attractive Oriental woman in her mid-twenties, offered him sake. After a few pleasantries, Desaix undressed, and still preoccupied, lowered himself into a wooden hot tub sunk into one corner of the room.

Removing her kimono, the now naked hostess followed his lead. With a bar of soap, she began to lather his body. He felt tense, and it was her job to relax him. After massaging his entire body for a considerable period of time, she was taken aback when Desaix started to knead the muscles of her shoulders. No *gaijin* had ever done that before. But Desaix wanted to make her feel a little bit special. And this was a good way, he knew, for him to relieve his own tension.

He ran his fingers over her incredibly smooth skin. She felt good—full and inviting. He pulled her toward him and gently placed his lips on her breasts. She stroked his loins, and with the subtlest of motions reached behind Desaix to lift a prophylactic from a wooden shelf.

With equal grace, she placed it over his erect penis and quietly mounted him. Slowly, the head of his penis entered her vagina, guided by the gently swaying movements of her pelvis. He ran his tongue over her large brown nipples as she moved ever so rhythmically on top of him. After several minutes, he could feel himself dissolve into her self-assured movements.

The hostess smiled at the moment of his release.

A second later, Fitzpatrick's naked body came crashing through the paper thin walls.

He had been shot through the right eye.

# CHAPTER

3

For all practical purposes, Colonel Alexander Lvovich Pushkin did not exist.

He was as much a contrivance as was his Abyssinian ancestor, Alexander Pushkin, the renowned Russian poet. Like his ancestor, the colonel had the disturbing habit of rubbing his callused, powerful hands together with nervous intensity. But he was a man who long ago had forgotten the emotional imperative to appear appropriately distraught.

He had come to terms with himself as much as any wistful Russian could. At the promising age of thirty-five, Colonel Pushkin had achieved a certain measure of success as commander of the Russian 107th Guards Airborne Division, a Spetsnaz diversionary brigade that was conveniently misplaced on most, if not all, the military organizational charts.

But to the Uzbeki lieutenant who had saluted the colonel as he walked briskly down the ornately decorated hallways of the Kremlin, with its stalactite icicles of glittering chandeliers, the colonel represented the realization of a young man's dream. To this underpaid, overfed lieutenant, the Spetsnaz colonel was the remaining embodiment of an ethos and fantasy that provided spiritual sustenance to all armies: a warrior of the state. A man who would still die bravely and honorably in the service of his country. The body-fitting green tunic jacket, bracketed by the red and gold epaulettes, broadcast the claim of his being a man of integrity and valor.

Had she been alive, Colonel Pushkin's mother would have been appropriately proud. As Colonel Pushkin was wont to admit, it was precisely because of his mother's disappointments and entitlements that he owed his presence in the Kremlin. First and foremost, she had bequeathed him his strikingly good looks. His dark, palpably sensuous presence unnerved women and made immediate friends of husbands who felt both uneasy and vulnerable.

She had convinced him, throughout childhood and into manhood, that he was special—a point she chiseled into the granite of his life-template by naming him Alexander Pushkin, despite the fact that he was four generations and five cousins removed. She had reinforced this fiction by frequently having him recite Pushkin aloud, which not surprisingly reaffirmed her fears for the imminent invasion, if not destruction, of Russia:

> *"Know, O people of Russia*
> *What no one does not know:*
> *I have ordered new uniforms*
> *From Prussia and from Austria.*
> *I am fat, well fed, in very good health."*

As Colonel Pushkin walked through the double set of oak doors into the red-carpeted antechamber of the inner sanctum sanctorum reciting the verses of his ancestor's poem, he finally encountered the bureaucratic intrusion to which he had long ago inured himself.

"Identification!" the ruddy-faced captain of the Palace Guards demanded. As an afterthought, he added, "Please."

Colonel Pushkin inserted his right hand into his tunic and removed the plastic identification card that afforded him access to any part of the Kremlin.

Pushkin watched carefully as the captain pushed a sequence of buttons on the electrical console next to him and waved him through the double doors. He proceeded briskly down a dimly lit corridor where once had hung the poorly painted portraits of all the previous General Secretaries of the Communist Party. Now the dull walls were decorated only with photographs of the Presidents of the independent republics, which comprised the Commonwealth of Independent States. Above them was the portrait of the pragmatic Igor Ivanovich Zotov, President of the Russian Federation, the most important and powerful leader of all the republics. More than any other person, Zotov held the destiny of Russia's fate in one of his "new free market initiatives." The bureaucratic plan had varying significance, depending on one's assessment of whether Zotov could survive within the tightly knit, truncated State Council, the highest government body, consisting of the leaders of all the republics.

Zotov had become widely popular as a witty man always ready with a bon mot. He had become best known for paraphrasing Marshal Suvorov, the military genius who had defeated both Frederick the Great and Napoleon, and who, when confronted with the need to suppress some internal incidents, replied, *"Pust khuzhe, da nashe."* Let it be worse, but let it be ours.

Pushkin liked this type of strong nationalist sentiment. *Kvasnoi patriotizm.* It was the basic, earthy nationalism of the *mujeek*, peasant, with which in an admittedly patronizing way he could identify. My country right or wrong.

Checking his watch, Pushkin realized he had exactly thirty minutes. After that, the young lieutenant would be making his rounds according to standard operating procedures. So it was important that he be on time for his appointment.

The door to Gospadin Nikolai Pavlovich Kurasov's office was open and unattended. Years before when there were more people than jobs, Pushkin would have had to pass through a phalanx of secretaries before he could have entered this office. But times were different now. Unless, of course, one wanted someone from Tashkent. But no one in the Kremlin was that desperate.

"Please come in, Colonel Pushkin. You are precisely on time, and timeliness is a virtue I have long come to admire." Kurasov, Executive Secretary to the President of the Russian Federation, spoke with the authority of a man who knew that no matter what he said, or how he said it, he had a captive audience by virtue of his office.

Kurasov was considerably larger than Pushkin had expected, about two inches taller than Pushkin, and thirty pounds heavier. That, in itself, might present a problem, Pushkin thought, but not an insurmountable one. Kurasov moved restlessly about the room, which resembled a richly decorated brothel covered with red wallpaper and bright multicolored Bokhara rugs. Worst of all was the overpowering scent of lilacs, which stood in a vase sitting precariously on the edge of a mahogany table. On the shelf was a large bottle of Stolichnaya vodka.

Pushkin felt himself gag.

"Are you all right?"

"Fine. Just fine."

"Good! Then let us get down to business. As you know, President Zotov received very disturbing news this morning. Several divisions of the U.S. Army 5th Corps have initiated highly provocative maneuvers around the central sector of Germany, at Wildeck."

Pushkin wasn't surprised. Kurasov's news was significantly less disconcerting than his nauseating lilacs.

Pushkin spread his arms over the back of the leather couch and made himself more comfortable. He knew he had to do something that would distract his attention from that smell and help him to focus on his agenda. He checked his watch and realized he had precisely twenty-five minutes left.

"Excuse me, but what exactly do you mean by 'provocative maneuvers'?"

Kurasov walked to his desk and sat down.

"The Americans are moving a group of their Abrams M1A1 tanks toward the Eisenach border without having informed us beforehand. I would say that's provocative." Pausing to assess Pushkin's indifferent reaction, he continued, "When we pulled the majority of our forces out of Germany between 1991 and 1994, we left behind several divisions, most of them comprised of Spetsnaz soldiers. We left them there as an insurance policy against any potential problems that might arise from the newly unified German state.

This was part of the agreement that was made between President Gorbachev and Prime Minister Kohl. We repatriated 365,000 Russian troops, in return for the Germans paying us fourteen billion deutsche marks for what was called military housing."

Kurasov was impatient. Did he have the right Colonel Pushkin?

For his part, Pushkin could not believe that this bear-like man with the small feet, who was beginning to sweat profusely, could be the same infamous colonel-general, code name Papa Rimski, once Chief of the Second Directorate of the Komitet Gosudarstvennoy Bezopasnosti, or the KGB as it had once been known. For a man who was so highly regarded by so many different General Secretaries, Soviet Presidents, and Republic Presidents as an effective Executive Secretary, Kurasov seemed unduly agitated by such a minor provocation.

Could it be that Kurasov senses that something is wrong, wondered Pushkin.

Pushkin could not ignore that Kurasov was the legendary creator of Service A—Sluzhba Aktivnykh Meropriyatiyi, Active Measures Service. He had created the infamous organization out of the old dysfunctional Disinformation Department. Taking a group of burned-out novelists and poets, he had placed them in legitimate front organizations like the Novosti Press Agency and the Academy of Sciences. There, those intellectual misfits were assigned the task of fabricating, distorting, and disseminating whatever false information was required to undermine the *Glavni Vrag*, the main enemy, which, even after perestroika and glasnost, was still the United States of America.

From there, Kurasov had gone on to head the Twelfth Directorate and then the Second Chief Directorate under President Boris Yeltsin, before becoming the Executive Assistant to his successor, President Zotov. Pushkin had to admit Kurasov was impressive. No, Pushkin corrected himself, Kurasov had been impressive. That was then. Times had changed!

Pushkin massaged his large, thick fingers as if he were warming them up for a virtuoso piano recital. He glanced at his watch, and at a lamp cord hanging loosely from a recently purchased Tiffany lamp still bearing the price tag.

The lamp cord had a serpentine quality to it.

"We need your special services." Nothing further had to be said by Kurasov.

In return for their loyalty to President Boris Yeltsin during the failed August 1991 coup attempt, the Spetsnaz soldiers were now respected as an elite, versatile combat unit under the direct command of the President of the Russian Federation. When traveling around the Commonwealth of Independent States, they were allowed to wear the khaki uniform of the airborne troops. Overseas, particularly in Poland, Germany, and Czechoslovakia, they were forced to disguise themselves as members of the less impressive Signal Corps. As Kurasov knew all too well, the Spetsnaz detachments were used as multipurpose instruments of the operational component of any naval, airborne, or army combat unit to inflict direct or indirect damage to the enemy.

But Spetsnaz soldiers always served dual masters—intelligence and terrorism.

"I want you and your men to parachute exactly fourteen kilometers behind the 11th Armored Cavalry Regiment and destroy their communications lines and logistical support capability."

"Is that all you need?" Pushkin stood up and walked toward the mahogany table.

"What do you mean?"

"Intelligence?" Pushkin tried to memorize the layout of the room as he spoke.

"We could use some," replied Kurasov defensively.

"Some?" Pushkin fingered some dead lilac leaves. They smelled putrid from decay.

"Yes, some!"

"Am I to presume then that you already have as much intelligence as you need?"

"No, you are not to assume that! Collect whatever intelligence you feel is needed. The tank commander will give you all the help you need. What we really need is far more important."

"What could be more important than intelligence?" Pushkin wanted to hear from Kurasov's own lips the words he seemed to be having a hard time saying. He rubbed his fingers clean with total disregard for Kurasov's obvious anxiety.

"Make certain you get a copy of the AirLandBattle Plan! I want to know how the U.S. intends to win a war with us, if there is to be one." Pausing, he added, "Why there should be a war in the first place is still not clear to me."

"Is that all?" Pushkin came up alongside Kurasov.

Without a moment's hesitation, he placed his right thumb over Kurasov's eye orbit, just at the point where the facial nerve exited the eye socket, and pressed as hard as he could.

Kurasov raised his head and threw it back like a bucking bronco trying to dislodge his rider.

He raised his arms straight upward and grabbed Pushkin's throat. Pushkin's face turned blue. His thumb pressure over Kurasov's eye started to weaken. At the same time, he could feel his legs begin to buckle. With barely any strength left in his body, Pushkin grabbed the loose coil of lamp wire, reached up, and wrapped it tightly around Kurasov's neck. He loosened his grip around Pushkin's throat.

Taking the thick callused heel of his right hand, Pushkin rammed it up against Kurasov's nose, driving it into the base of his brain.

The sounds of pain stopped as Kurasov's head fell limply onto his chest. Pushkin felt the drops of Kurasov's cerebral spinal fluid drip into his hands.

It was a complete mess. There could be no point of pride for Pushkin.

He dragged the body over to the couch, poured some vodka from the bottle on the shelf into Kurasov's gaping mouth, drank some himself, and then folded Kurasov's arms over his face as if he were taking a late afternoon nap.

The door swung open. The young lieutenant walked respectfully into the room, saluted, made note of the fact that both men looked disheveled, and concluded from their appearance as well as the loud noises he had heard that both men had been carousing together.

Colonel Pushkin indicated with the barest of hand gestures that Kurasov had drunk too much and was taking a nap. Standing up, Pushkin motioned to the lieutenant that they should both leave.

As they closed the door, Pushkin placed his arm around the young lieutenant's shoulder and in a reinvigorated voice finished the last lines of the poem:

> "Here comes the furtive assassin,
> Decked out in garter and star,
> Drunk with rage and wine."

# CHAPTER
4

The smell of sex permeated the darkened room.

Beneath the four-poster brass bed, above the quilted comforter, hand-sewn by those candy-striped handmaidens of charity frequently found wandering aimlessly about hospital corridors, lay a man and a woman, totally disrobed, gently stroking each other with the care and delight of those who have known love.

They heightened the intensity of the moment by probing each other for the telltale signs that only long-term lovers can readily identify.

Choirboy, her nickname for him, ran the tip of his tongue along the alabaster folds of the nape of her elongated neck, bequeathed to her by patrician parents.

Milkshake, his nickname for her, had learned early in life that not even sex was for free. A cynical, perhaps even cruel lesson, which, despite all its misanthropic overtones, was nevertheless a helpful guide for her survival. But at this moment of passion, Milkshake could only concern herself with the consequences of not anticipating her lover's movements—silent and gentle as they might be.

Choirboy's fingers brushed along Milkshake's pendulous breasts with the synchronous precision of a high school drum major leading a halftime band.

Milkshake bit her lower lip, hoping that Choirboy would not notice that she was ticklish. But, as if anticipating a deviation from some self-contrived norm, Choirboy burst into laughter.

"What is wrong with you?" Milkshake asked with all the self-righteous indignation to which she knew she was not due.

"What's wrong? You're what's wrong."

"Me?" She pummeled him with small, playful fists.

"Yes, you!" Choirboy pinned both her arms against the mattress.

"Ouch! You're hurting me!" She mock-complained, although her self-righteousness was a sham. Milkshake enjoyed the range of emotions Choirboy could elicit within her. God only knew how accommodating Choirboy could be. Perhaps too accommodating.

"You broke the moment of silence," Choirboy responded with the false pain that only the very entitled know how to evince, overtaken by his need to appear innocent. It had earned him the sobriquet of Choirboy. He had, in fact, been a choirboy at an exclusive gentleman's prep school in which a cathedral dominated the campus. It was there that he learned the essential ingredients of hypocrisy—ask for divine forgiveness after screwing your best friend's girl.

Milkshake didn't respond. She simply wanted to inhale his presence. She strained her head upward to lick the beads of sweat sliding down his cheeks. It tasted and smelled like that other part of his anatomy that had a thick, musky aroma. And it excited her. It was her continuous need for oral gratification that had earned her the nickname Milkshake. She tried to loosen her arms, but he wouldn't let her go. The more persistently she tried, the more forcibly he restrained her. Invariably she became more excited. She knew that he knew this. That knowledge excited her even more.

Choirboy released the hold on her arms and straightened his back. His six-foot frame didn't lend itself easily to this game that genteel lovers play. By temperament and physique he was suited to the more comfortable patterns of traditional sex. Only a man of his fifty plus years could understand the need for the missionary position. It was a God-sent respite for the tired and weary. All one had to do was make the barest of hip movements.

Milkshake lowered her body under his in order to have unimpeded access to his lower torso. With the aplomb of an accomplished lover, she stroked the insides of his loins with the tip of her long pointed tongue, ever so gently fashioning a path of excitation to which he would eventually succumb. As they both anticipated, he rolled over on his back and closed his eyes.

He could feel the rush of warmth spread over his body, ready to paralyze him into blissful helplessness. He gently massaged her scalp in a rhythmic pattern that mirrored the subtle sway of her body over his. Reflexively, he raised his hip and thrust his penis into the disciplined rotating movement of Milkshake's tongue. His fingers dug more deeply into her scalp as her tongue movements became more circular and invasive.

There was a point at which he could no longer assume any control over himself. At this very moment, she possessed him. He welcomed the all-embracing caress with her mouth as if it were the ultimate sanction of their union.

What transpired next was from Choirboy's point of view strictly a matter of conjecture. All he could recall was a momentary flash of pain somewhere between his groin and belly button, as if someone had pierced his abdomen with a stiletto. With a sudden thrust of both his hands he threw Milkshake off of him.

"A polite no would suffice," she complained gently.

There was no response.

Choirboy was quiet. Lying stiffly, eyes shut, he wasn't protesting his innocence. Something was definitely wrong. Milkshake wanted to scream, but he had warned her that under no condition, short of death, should she shout for the help that was on the other side of the door.

"Come on, Choirboy! This is no time for games." Milkshake grabbed his large head, and ran her fingers over his deep-set eyes and long, fleshy nose. They felt cold. "Come on, Choirboy! You don't want me to call in the Goons!" My God, she thought, he's having a heart attack. Raising her right fist into the air with all the force she could muster, she brought it down on his chest and watched him closely.

A shroud of white began to envelop his body.

"Oh no! Oh my God, no!" In the two and a half years they had been together, she had never been confronted with an emergency in which she had to call in the Goons. But if she waited any longer, Choirboy might die. She hesitated once more, hoping that by some divine providence he would revive.

"Scare you?" Choirboy opened his eyes and raised himself slightly on his elbows.

Milkshake couldn't decide whether to smother him with kisses or choke him.

"What the hell happened?" She took his head between her hands. Some of his color had returned. She licked away beads of sweat crowning his forehead.

"Don't, please!" He wasn't in the mood any longer.

"Sure, baby. Whatever you say."

"Hey, don't treat me as if I just passed away. Did I scare you?" he asked again, smiling at her.

She smacked him playfully. "No! I was just waiting for the resurrection," she replied sarcastically.

"What about necrophilia?"

"You bastard! Why didn't you tell me about your Houdini act?"

"Because I don't know anything about it."

Milkshake looked into his glazed eyes and knew he was lying. He couldn't look directly back into hers. Clearly, this episode had occurred at least once before. But she wasn't going to press the point. She took his long fingers and began to massage them, kneading the blood back in. They had a certain elasticity she had not noticed before. She had always admired his agility and nimbleness. But this was literally the first time she noticed that she could take his index finger and extend it backward.

"I'm glad that you didn't call the Goons."

"Why? What the hell was I supposed to do?" She could feel herself getting angrier. "You're a goddamn sadist, you know?"

"I think it's time for us to call it an evening." Choirboy started to sway as he stood up. He grabbed her shoulder for support.

"I can't let you go! You're in no shape to go."

He clutched his stomach with both hands, as if he could blunt the pain.

"Tell me what's bothering you."

"Nothing, Milkshake, nothing."

"You're lying!"

"It's an old ulcer. Occasionally it flares up." He paused and looked at her. "Especially if I get too excited."

"Don't bullshit a bullshitter!"

"Honestly!" He crossed himself as he began to dress.

She stared at him. If only he understood how much she loved him, he wouldn't be so flippant with her.

Choirboy adjusted his clothing as they walked toward the door. With a reassuring wink, he opened the door and walked quickly down the darkened hallway, accompanied by two men in dark suits.

The three men walked down the back staircase of the four-story apartment building in the gentrified section of Adams Morgan in northwest Washington, D.C.

A petite woman dressed in a two-piece suit opened the back door of the black nondescript Ford station wagon for the men and returned to the driver's seat.

Before the men could enter, a disheveled black man in his late thirties staggered over, pint bottle in hand. It was an unusual entourage of people congregating at four in the morning. He reached over and grabbed Choirboy.

Reflexively, Choirboy turned around and punched the man in the face, landing him flat-out on the ground, and entered the station wagon without looking back.

The bodyguards rushed over with .38 Smith & Wessons fully cocked, ready to fire.

The drunk looked up at the gun barrels as the station wagon screeched away.

# CHAPTER
## 5

President Donald Westview, the youngest president elected to the office since John F. Kennedy, paced nervously around the Oval Office. For the first time in a very long time he felt claustrophobic. The room was by any contemporary standards of comfort extremely small, certainly for a man of his unusual size.

The desk, constructed from the oak wood planks of HMS *Resolute*, a salvaged British frigate, was one of those Victorian gifts of gratitude that reminded him of his favorite ribald tales of Frank Harris. It consumed almost one quarter of the room. Laden with all sorts of National Intelligence Directives, National Security Directives, and Presidential Directives, the oak desk had acquired a certain Proustian charm, continuously reminding him of the never-ending demands of the office.

Behind the antique desk stood a concession to modern times, a brown leather-bound swivel chair lined with sheets of Kevlar, a protective fiber that was both lighter and more durable than steel. The chair was designed to protect Westview from an assassin who might sneak up behind him, point a .348 Magnum, and fire at point-blank range. As far as Westview was concerned, it would have been a lot cheaper, and probably more effective, had the General Accounting Office moved the goddamn desk away from the window to the other side of the room.

Throughout the room was an assortment of reminders that Westview was, indeed, the President.

On the small table alongside his desk was a vanilla-colored STU-3 telephone console that allowed him to access all government agencies on both an unsecured and secured basis. The rectangular screen on the top of the console would inform him of the name of the person to whom he was talking, his or her telephone number, and whether they were or were not on a secure channel. It would tell him the level of security of the conversation; whether it was CONFIDENTIAL, SECRET, or TOP SECRET. The STU-3 was the neuronal extension of the President. But like all privileged functions it worked best when it didn't work at all. The STU-3 was completely unreliable the day after it was installed. But Westview was used to such disappointments.

He had grown up in a household where self-reliance and ambition were both nurtured and simultaneously crushed by the overriding accomplishments of his patrician father, a man who was as comfortable directing an investment banking house as he was cutting a deal in the coatroom of the Senate.

Westview grew up with all the necessary edicts and prerequisites to be a good son, brother, father, husband, and public servant. However, destiny, a euphemism for emotional dyslexia, prevented him from becoming fully accomplished in any one of those areas. At best, he was a good son, a reliable brother, an adequate father and husband, and a talented but professionally stunted politician. His beliefs, such as they were, had no central core. Much like his political mentor. If he believed in anything, it was in the importance of maintaining the status quo. Change was anathema because, by its very nature, it disparaged the past and heightened the prospects of uncertainty. If nothing else, the patrons of wealth had always taught their progeny to avoid change—it conveyed the dangerous connotation of the need to restructure the social order. Today's haves could be tomorrow's have-nots. If change must occur, then one had an obligation to make certain that those unfettered forces could never do injury to one's own person or interests.

If his father had taught him nothing else, President Westview had learned to co-opt everything and everyone. In turn, he became extremely cunning and wily in a pleasing, acceptable way. Those around him wanted to work for him because he knew how to instill in them a sense of belonging to a cause worthy of their efforts. He was able to impart a feeling of genuine gratitude and appreciation, making them feel special and needed. Invariably, anyone who remained loyal to him knew that in time they would be amply rewarded.

As a student at a privileged boy's academy, he learned the value of becoming a team player. Participation in a group was a way of making certain he never had to have an original idea or had to attempt anything on his own initiative. Instead, one could always borrow from teammates. And always with grace and charm. A smile and a thank-you would become his shibboleths for success. It would allow him to neutralize his opposition with the minimum of personal effort and discomfort.

Once he organized a car-rental service that provided his college classmates with the ability to attend their Harvard classes in style. He was so taken with the fun of setting up the business venture that he had forgotten that people went into business to make money. So he tried to enlist the help of his friends. The collaboration never materialized because his friends realized that there was no business to be had. But Westview had learned two important lessons from that experience: never venture out on your own and always cover your ass. As he became increasingly more dependent on his social skills and personal contacts, politics became one viable profession in which he could employ the skills of co-opting people and covering his ass. Most importantly, with politics as his métier he would never have to be accountable for his actions again—at least not to his father.

On the other hand, he had discovered early on in his professional career that he had a knack for appearing nonthreatening, all the while ruthlessly pursuing his political ambitions through guile. He appointed a cabinet that everyone felt was significantly smarter than he was. Yet not one of them had been able to implement any new programs without his direct intervention, either with the Hill or with the bureaucracy. Despite the rhetoric of an open government, he had compartmentalized his Presidential Directives so that only he would know all the elements of the order.

Above all else, he was a hard worker who understood his own shortcomings and tried to compensate for them through self-improvement and willful change. He had assiduously studied the master political strategists throughout history—Sun-tzu, Machiavelli, Clausewitz—and applied their respective precepts to his everyday exercise of power.

But it was from his friend Desaix Clark and his writings on crisis management and diplomacy that he learned the important lessons of integrating politics and psychology into a systematic approach to governance, devoid of ideology and dogma. He accepted Desaix's basic edict that a leader must impose his own subjective reality on the political process in order to control it. Otherwise he becomes hostage to timeworn preconceptions and behavior patterns.

Walking about the Oval Office, he riffled through the day's NID. Filled with one-page narrative summaries of the day's most important events, the NID, with its glossy paper and colored photographs, was often compared to *Time* or *Newsweek*. Often these national magazines covered the same news events as the NID, but they did it more accurately and without all of the problems associated with classifying secrets. Westview wondered what would happen if the government had to rely only on the news provided by the major newspapers and magazines? He was certain that it could save hundreds of millions of dollars and probably get as accurate a picture of what was happening in the world.

Westview didn't like what he was reading. Events were getting out of hand. How could he not be nervous today, with dangerous tensions between the Americans and Russians looming over the horizon?

He had already convened a meeting of the Crisis Management Group of the National Security Council—principals only. That meant there would be an incredible amount of bureaucratic jockeying to attend the meeting.

He could expect each of his cabinet secretaries to implore him to be able to bring only one indispensable staffer.

He could have predicted that the biggest pain would be the Chairman of the Joint Chiefs of Staff, General Ronald McCormick, who would refuse to come unless he could bring an entire coterie of light and full colonels, all of whom would be equally as indispensable as the next one. Fat Ronald, as the general was affectionately called by his peers, was, in fact, mean, lean, and trim. But at Harvard, where Westview and he had first met, Ronald was portly. That was before he transferred to West Point.

"Excuse me, sir, may I come in?" Randy Newmann, Westview's appointments secretary, stood in the doorway.

"Of course." This thirty-three-year-old, well-proportioned blonde with an infectious smile had been a staff assistant on his presidential campaign and was considered by everyone who worked with her sufficiently competent and attractive to have performed a wide range of campaign-related chores in a nonthreatening way. And since Westview picked people around him who posed no real threat to him, Randy was perfect. Even Margaret Westview, the twice-married First Lady, who could smell a sexual overture a quarter of a mile away, found Randy "sufficiently pleasant." When translated into the jargon of power politics this meant that if Randy kept herself inconspicuously concealed behind a facade of Midwestern charm and competence, she would go far. In terms of realpolitik, however, Randy was the second most important person in the White House.

"Come on in, Randy," the President said.

"Sir, they are all waiting for you in the Situation Room downstairs."

"Everyone?"

"Yes, sir."

"Randy, how long have you been working for me?"

"Is there something wrong, sir?" She adjusted her brown Harris tweed jacket nervously.

"Yes, there is something wrong." He placed his large hand on her tense shoulder. "Please stop calling me sir."

"Yes, sir."

"Why don't you try Mr. President."

"Yes, sir."

"Or, better yet, Your Excellency." Westview chuckled at his own joke.

"Yes, sir, Mr. President."

"All right, I give up." He laughed mischievously. "Come on! We can't keep the garden party waiting."

Strolling down the narrow carpeted hallways, Westview nodded his head to the different Secret Service agents stationed along the route.

"Zorro is on his way down! Hold the elevators and block the entrances!" Special Agent Maureen "Mary" Dougherty, Section Chief of the Presidential Detail, talked into a plastic microphone coiled along the inside sleeve of her blue blazer.

Mary was the first woman to become head of the Secret Service detail that protected the President of the United States. Not a bad accomplishment for a first-generation American whose parents had fled from the ceaseless violence of Northern Ireland. But making a living in Boston was harder than her bricklayer father had imagined. When Mary was three years old, he fled his paternal responsibilities and became the very thing his wife had always accused him of being, a bum. Mary, in turn, vowed that she would atone for whatever deficiencies her father might have had. And, at the same time, she would try to make her mother proud.

She was never certain which of these two goals presented her with the greater psychological burden—her father's negligence or her mother's unrealistic expectations. But at this point in her life she made certain that she would keep herself so occupied that she wouldn't have to worry about it.

The only person she really had to worry about now was the man codenamed Zorro. Where he went. What he did. Who saw him. Whom he saw. She was his for twenty-four hours a day, seven days a week. And no one, but no one, could see him, no matter what time of the day, without her clearing that person first. There were only two things she had to know about that person—a Social Security number and a birthdate. Once she received that information she fed it into the computers at the Treasury Department and within seconds would find out whether that person was a potential threat to the President.

She had assigned Westview the code name Zorro because, like the legendary masked man who was always being chased by the Spanish authorities, the President also had his bête noire: the Secret Service. Wherever he went, they followed. Whatever his sins, they forgave, or more importantly, forgot. All they saw and heard remained within the sanctity of silence and discretion. There were no paper trails to leave any incriminating evidence against the President of the United States, only the professional deaf and dumb witnesses of the Secret Service. They carried a responsibility that exceeded that of a physician or a priest. Confidentiality was literally a matter of life and death. But protecting Zorro was becoming increasingly more difficult. And no one could ever know.

The principals of the Crisis Management Group were already seated around the rectangular conference table in the White House Sit Room when Westview entered.

The room, like the Executive Dining Room and other White House additions, was surprisingly small. It was twenty by thirty feet long, with dark square walnut-paneled walls, annoying fluorescent lighting, and a rectangular teak conference table that could seat half a dozen people. One could easily mistake it for any executive conference room except for one small fact— one needed a specially coded badge in order to enter.

On the far wall was a multicolored flattened map of the world inscribed on a pane of glass. A stream of moving light showed the time of day in any part of the world. Concealed beneath this Hong Kong–manufactured clock, tucked in behind the square walnut panels, were the latest state-of-the-art paraphernalia of American crisis management: two Japanese-made video monitors; a Taiwanese-assembled four-color printer; two German-made high-resolution projectors; five STU-3 telephones subcontracted to a European electronics consortium; and a Filipino-assembled intercom.

Westview realized that crisis management, like horseback riding, required a subtle combination of discipline and courage. Too much daring and the horse becomes uncontrolled. Too much control and the horse offers no challenge. But the ultimate challenge of crisis management was to realize that it was primarily a game of interpretation, manipulation, deception, and execution.

"Well, gentlemen . . ." Westview waited until Mary cleared the room of all unnecessary personnel, including herself. "I see everyone is here except, of course, my National Security Advisor." He made a mental image of the group. Seated to his immediate right was his good friend and trusted advisor, Secretary of State Chester "Chet" Manning, a shrewd, heavyset ex-congressman in his early fifties with a rugged, weatherbeaten face, who, when properly prepared and directed, could be extremely effective. Their relationship was based completely on mutual respect and trust. Neither one owed the other any more than their friendship. And, when the political game would be all over for both of them, they had vowed to remain friends.

A few years older than Manning, Westview felt and acted like an older brother. And Manning was smart enough to nurture whatever pretense was created in the heat of their friendship. For Manning knew that like all other asymmetric relationships, this one would would either realign itself or fade. He believed that all people and events had a natural dynamic.

As a professional politician, Manning was mistrustful of the bureaucratic technicians in the room today. Like Sam Rayburn, the most powerful man in Congress four decades before, during the Johnson administration, Manning would have been far more comfortable and impressed if any one of the other presidential advisors had been elected even sheriff of a small town. At least then some could understand and appreciate the realities and constraints of the real political world. For now, he could only give these honorable gentlemen the benefit of the doubt. At least for now.

Seated across from Manning was Larry Jenkins, a small, thin, well-coiffed man with delicate, almost effeminate facial features, who prided himself on his elegant handmade Italian suits. As Director of the Central Intelligence Agency, he had climbed his way up the "greasy pole" of the intelligence community through the "other side" of the house, eventually becoming the Deputy Director of Operations. He sat comfortably back in his chair. In his more daring days, he was credited with having cleverly engineered the entrapment and capture of some very prominent terrorists. That's how he earned the moniker Master of the Sting. Some ten years before, he was

Ambassador Westview's station chief in Warsaw where Westview was biding his political time between the two presidential elections.

"Mr. President, we're running fifteen minutes behind schedule," said Secretary of Defense Randolph Merck, a physically imposing, self-assured man whose warm, penetrating hazel eyes bespoke a quick, inviting intelligence. At forty-eight years old, he had been the CEO of a Fortune 500 company, Bowes, Merck and Associates, a major military contractor, initially built with the help of a minority grant from the Small Business Administration. He was the first black Sec Def, and the man to whom the President would often turn to shepherd his more important social legislation through Congress. By temperament, he was least cowed by protocol or convention. He had built his business empire through unorthodox means. And like all men of unusual talent, he was impatient with himself and others. The President's lateness had now put him behind schedule.

"Randolph, I know you are a busy man, but if you don't mind indulging your President for just a few more minutes, I know he would appreciate it." Westview liked Randolph's impertinence. He liked a self-made man who owed nothing to anyone.

Westview had high hopes for Merck. There were rumors spreading throughout the Republican Party that depending upon his performance as Sec Def, Merck stood a good chance of becoming the first black Vice President of the United States.

Merck smiled broadly and pointed to General Ronald McCormick, the tall, taut, silver-haired man with cold blue eyes and unruly eyebrows, sitting on his left.

"In all truth, this is the man who is driving my schedule."

"Good try! You're becoming quite the bureaucrat." Manning laughed. He knew that Merck was far from becoming anything other than what he was: a street-smart hustler. If he really wanted to learn how to be an aggressive bureaucratic in-fighter, three-star Air Force General Ronald McCormick, the Chairman of the Joint Chiefs of Staff, could always teach him.

"You bet, Chet! By the time I finish with him, this here Sec Def will be able to cover his ass on almost any issue without ever taking his hand off the throttle."

General Ronald McCormick, like several of his predecessors, was a fast-tracker. He only knew one method of operating—do whatever is necessary to accomplish the task. Then find out if what you did was correct. Questions and doubts should always follow implementation. He had begun his career as an ROTC ex-Vietnam fighter pilot who flew F-4 Phantoms over North Vietnam, logging in one hundred and fifteen sorties and officially credited with three kills.

As Chief of the Air Force, McCormick was proud of maintaining a significant modernization program under one of the tightest budgetary restrictions ever. He had been instrumental in converting the fighter squadrons deployed in Iceland and Germany, as well as the Air Force Reserve, from F-4Es to F-15Cs. But for the moment he was doodling.

"Sorry, I'm late," a diminutive, harried-looking man with drawn, pale features said as he walked into the Sit Room. It was General Thomas Mapplethorpe, who at sixty-eight had a chest filled with all types of military awards despite the fact that he had seen little combat in his life.

"At last, my National Security Advisor decided to show up," the President said. "How kind of you."

Mapplethorpe was the chief villain. He was cautious beyond the point of being reasonable. McCormick never understood what two former Presidents had seen in this guy, other than that he looked and acted like the cautious West Point professor of modern strategy he had once been.

Mapplethorpe was good at one thing, thought McCormick. He knew how to manage the information flow coming into and out of the White House. And with all due respect, he knew how to manipulate one agency against another, especially DOD and CIA. Mapplethorpe would never try to pull that shit against State, he thought. Manning would eat him alive.

"As some of you may not know," Mapplethorpe said, "Dr. Daniel Fitzpatrick, my senior staffer for the Commonwealth of Independent States, was murdered late last night in Tokyo. He was my rep on Desaix's negotiation team for renewing the leases on our Signal Intelligence installations in Japan."

"Are you certain?" Westview asked, visibly disturbed.

"Yes, sir." Mapplethorpe pulled out the Night Action cable, which described in detail the circumstances of the death. He handed it to Westview, who read it carefully and then passed it around the table.

"Has this been picked up by the press yet?" Manning asked. "We'd better get some press guidance out there as quickly as possible."

"What in God's name is Desaix up to this time?" Merck asked incredulously.

"Don't be too harsh on Clark," Jenkins interjected sarcastically. "I'm sure he was simply providing some R and R for our exhausted negotiators." Jenkins wondered what it would take for Manning to get rid of Desaix once and for all. Instead of firing the SOB, he promotes him to a Deputy Assistant Secretary of State position. As long as Desaix was up to his usual shenanigans, everyone would assume that the Agency was behind him. He gave the Agency a bad name and, worse yet, he didn't even belong. Moreover, he could never belong to a world of continual compartmentalized paranoia.

"Larry, did your people know anything about this?" Westview asked, sounding irritated.

"Well no . . . not really . . ." Jenkins replied.

"What the hell do you mean?" McCormick shot back.

Mapplethorpe gave McCormick a stern glance, as if he were completely out of line.

"I wasn't aware the Agency was within your purview," Jenkins said, as he turned sideways and shook his head with disapproval. "One of our men was with Desaix and Danny—"

"You mean in that whorehouse?" McCormick asked, smelling blood and like a hammerhead shark pursuing the scent.

"Let go, Ronny! Larry's man could have been a target just as well," Mapplethorpe said, retaliating against McCormick's hostility. He picked up on the sense of the group that they had had enough of McCormick's sarcastic comments.

Westview didn't say a word. He wanted the underlying tension within the group to build up sufficiently so that he could intervene at the proper point. He believed in Desaix's concept of managing through constructive tension. It kept his cabinet members continuously on edge.

Jenkins directed his response toward Manning. "James Ball, our Director of the Office of Scientific Intelligence, was in the room next door. But he claims he didn't see or hear anything. The gun must have had a silencer."

"Any make on the pistol?" Manning asked nonchalantly, as if he already knew the answer.

"Any motives?" Merck asked, scribbling several words on a piece of paper: Federal Security Agency, the old KGB, other hostile intelligence, and personal reasons. He circled FSA.

Jenkins replied, "None that we can ascertain at this moment." He felt uncomfortable having to answer questions to which he had no answers. He was in the business of spying, not investigating crimes. If any nationality should be thorough in their investigation of a murder, it would certainly be the Japanese.

"I'm glad you asked that question, Randolph." Westview said, eager to get to the matter at hand: what to do with the intensifying crisis in Germany. "Gentlemen, we'll investigate the murder of Fitzpatrick until we find a culprit. But now we must proceed to the next matter . . ."

Did you mean *the* culprit instead of *a* culprit? McCormick thought to himself. There was something disconcertingly cavalier in the President's approach.

"At this moment in time, we have a far more serious problem," Westview continued. "If we don't resolve our situation in Germany right away we may well end up at the threshold of disaster." He paused, then looked around the room. "First of all, we need an intel briefing. What exactly is the status of our forces at Wildeck?"

No one responded.

Mapplethorpe asked, "Ronny, what does the Defense Intelligence Agency have?" He was not surprised by the absence of any response. This embarrassment should shut up big-mouth McCormick, he thought. The Joint Chiefs of Staff were always good at criticizing others, but notoriously poor on delivery of their own products. He was eager to hear Ronny's excuse. It should be a whopper.

McCormick simply shrugged his shoulders.

"What does that mean?" Mapplethorpe said, showing he could smell a bureaucratic bleeder. It would only be a short time before Ronny would be out of the Joint Chiefs position without any good prospects for a future job.

McCormick replied defensively, "It means simply what I just said. Or in this case, what I didn't say. I ain't got none!"

"How is that possible?" Westview asked.

Manning interceded. "Hell, Ronny could have just bullshitted us and no one would have known the difference. We should be grateful for his frankness." He knew he was playing in dangerous waters. One wrong slip—a little too enthusiastic an endorsement—could have brought a reproach from the President. This way, Merck and McCormick owed him one each. Not bad. He just got himself a twofer.

"Randolph, do you have anything to say?" Westview expected to hear something more. Merck shook his head in the negative.

"Are you sure?" Mapplethorpe asked him, wanting to give Merck every opportunity to share exactly what he knew.

Merck replied, "No, I stick by my Chief. If he says we have nothing, then, by God, we have nothing. I am sorry, Mr. President, I wish it were otherwise."

Westview nodded his head in reluctant approval. No fool is this Sec Def. He understands the importance of loyalty.

Loyalty to superiors. Loyalty to subordinates. Loyalty to an institutional position. Even if loyalty meant you had to profess ignorance when, in fact, that wasn't the case. Westview knew from his own independent sources that Merck knew the troop deployment on both sides. Because of the way information flowed, his Chief may not have known. Merck was just applying the rules of the game. And one of the principal rules of crisis management, at least in this administration, was always to remain loyal to the President and the team. No grandstanding. No backbiting. Ignorance could be forgiven. Poor preparation would be tolerated. Even incompetence could be carried along for some period of time. But a loose cannon, a man who decided to go it alone, a man like Desaix, well, that could be tolerated only under special circumstances.

Looking around the table, Westview wondered what it would be like if Desaix were sitting there. He concluded that it would be a living nightmare. Although he personally liked and even admired Desaix, he was still anathema to Westview. Unlike the others here in the Sit Room, Desaix was the type of man who prided himself on his independence at the expense of being an effective team player. He recalled how Desaix had walked away from a crisis when he felt he was not being given the chance to manage it his way. Similarly, if there were a lacuna of information, Desaix would find it incumbent upon himself to expose it. If there were an iota of incompetence, he would have to deride it.

Manning, Desaix's self-appointed protector, had assured Westview that

Desaix was beginning to learn how to be a team player. But what made Desaix and men like him particularly dangerous was the fact that they were dedicated to accomplishment rather than to the mere acquisition of power. Men like Desaix, although often indispensable to the successful resolution of a crisis, were also totally mistrusted because they, in turn, mistrusted the bureaucracy and its processes. For the most part, everyone knew that these processes entailed attending an endless series of meetings and the preparation of position papers, frequently intended to do nothing more than avoid implementing a course of action. But Desaix just couldn't go along with life as it was in the bureaucracy. For Desaix, a bureaucracy, by definition, meant a collective group of individuals who were well intentioned but poorly directed. They represented the complete antithesis of his core belief that "trust is good, but control is better." His model, Secretary of State James Baker III, ran an effective foreign policy in the early 1990s because he personally managed the entire process with no more than a handful of extremely talented young people, located in the Secretary's Policy Planning Staff, to the complete exclusion of nine thousand members of the professional Foreign Service.

Like Desaix, Westview believed that the ultimate decision in any international crisis was made by one or two people. And despite Desaix's mercurial temperament and his unwillingness to play the game as a team player, Westview knew that in the final crunch Desaix always came through with a creative insight or strategy. The President also enjoyed Desaix's Louisianian weltanschauung, inspired by an eccentric mother from the genteel precincts near Audubon Park, which viewed life as a series of Mardi Gras fantasies filled with flamboyance, high drama, and all sorts of personal and political craziness. So everything and anything was allowed as long as the job got done.

As he surveyed the room once more, Westview took comfort that these men, including the abrasive General McCormick, were team players. He didn't have to worry about any surprises from them. They were manageable, to one degree or another. Except, perhaps, for his best friend, Chet Manning, who typically always had a hidden agenda.

Mapplethorpe stood up and pulled down a map of Central Europe. "As far as we can tell, and please correct me if I am wrong, Larry, this is the present situation, to the best of our knowledge."

Using his favorite metal pointer, Mapplethorpe began a briefing that Manning suspected had been rehearsed. "First and foremost, one can say with a definite degree of confidence that there are no Warsaw Pact countries or NATO forces on the battlefield." Mapplethorpe smiled as everyone in the room broke out into laughter. For the past seven years there had been no more NATO and Warsaw Pact forces poised against each other. Ever since the dissolution of the Soviet Union, all defense requirements in Europe had been fulfilled by the U.S. and the Russian Federation.

Mapplethorpe turned toward Merck. "Along the central portion, over here, we have the 5th Squadron of the 11th Armored Cavalry Regiment, as well as on these forward positions. Is that right, Randy?"

Merck looked at McCormick for approval. By having Merck turn to McCormick for the corroboration of the information, Mapplethorpe in effect had released Merck from his self-imposed loyalty. McCormick nodded his head in approval, releasing Merck from his vows.

Merck replied. "Yes. We have approximately a half dozen M60 tanks on the right flank located around hill 401. Another four M109 self-propelled howitzers are positioned about two hundred yards away."

"Thank you, Randolph." Mapplethorpe added, "About four hundred yards away, toward this heavy black line here, are a group of Sheridan tanks with their Shillelagh missiles."

Mapplethorpe paused to make certain he hadn't lost anyone. Only Westview's eyes had started to glaze over. He knew that the President was a "big-picture man" and hated these map briefings because everything looked alike to him on these topos. He confused the brown hills with the green valleys and the black roads. These three-dimensional repesentations of battlefields were merely a testimony to the imagination of the cartographer and to the pervasive influence of Crayola crayons. Nothing made sense on these maps, unless you literally memorized the color codes, which, of course, were too numerous. The importance of these topos lay with the air of authenticity and legitimacy they provided.

"The 5th Squadron in Wildeck is opposed by a half dozen Soviet T-72 battle tanks," Jenkins interjected, "and a dozen BTR-60 armored personnel carriers, all remnants of the old Soviet Army that were allowed to remain in the eastern portion of Germany after the Two Plus Four Accords, agreed to in 1990." He added, "According to Signal Intelligence, the armored personnel carriers moved toward the autobahn and are simply prepositioned there. Waiting."

Jenkins felt it was safe to share this valuable piece of intelligence. Normally, he would have held on to it until he was able to see the President by himself, adding an even greater sense of importance and urgency to the matter than normally existed. This was a classic Agency ploy. Hold off until the last moment. Don't share unless you feel it absolutely imperative. If you have to share, be discreet. One-on-one with the President, if possible. Failing that, see the National Security Advisor.

"One simple question, Larry," Westview asked ingenuously. "Why are they fighting?"

"The cover story that the Agency has contrived . . ." Jenkins paused to choose his words carefully, "for public consumption is that renegade Spetsnaz units refuse to go back to Russia. Instead they want to precipitate a war with the U.S. in order to drag their fellow countrymen into one last hurrah."

"What's the real story?" Westview riveted his eyes on Jenkins. He was waiting to hear how much the DCI would deviate from what everyone in the room knew was the truth.

"Reliable HUMINT informs us that Zotov wants to precipitate a confrontation with the U.S. as a pretext for him to mobilize the entire Russian Army. He then intends to conquer the other independent republics, unifying them under one ruler—himself."

"A new Russian expansionist version of the old Soviet Union," Merck added.

"Something like that," Jenkins continued, "but for the moment, Zotov is providing the Russian people with the excuse that the 'bad American capitalists' are taking unfair economic advantage of the 'poor downtrodden Russians.' So he must fight the Americans, if need be, in order to defend their honor and redress their grievances."

"Have the Russians broken out toward Wildeck yet?" Westview asked. He had an uncanny sense of what the key issue would be in a battle like this.

McCormick finally felt comfortable enough to participate in the discussion. "If the Russian armored personnel carriers break out of that furrow of earth that we have been able to contain them in, then we will have a very serious problem. We can't bring in enough reinforcements to contain the breakout if one were to occur soon." McCormick's past ignorance only cost him a few minutes of nonparticipation. Sustained arrogance or abrasiveness could have cost him complete ostracism.

Westview asked as if he already knew the answer, "So how would you summarize the military situation, Randolph?"

"I think it would be fair to say that barring any unforeseen events, it looks quite stable. What do think, Tom?" Merck didn't want to commit himself to any assessment that might come back to haunt him later on.

"I'm pretty much in accord with you." Mapplethorpe paused. "Except for this caveat: this crisis could get out of hand pretty quickly. And then we will have an incident of major proportions. It would be wise for the Department of Defense to develop contingency plans, including the use of Special Operations Forces. I will prepare an executive order directing the United States Special Operations Command to implement its April 16, 1986, authorization to unify all Special Operations Forces under one commander." Mapplethorpe wanted to make certain that everyone in the room understood who would be in charge of this DOD operation.

Westview was becoming noticeably impatient. "We will officially designate this crisis as Low Intensity Conflict, and we will treat it accordingly." He was distracted. His eyes were bothering him. As in the past, images were becoming increasingly blurred. He never liked discussions concerning details. They bored him. And, at best, they were irrelevant. He prided himself on being a strategic thinker.

Mapplethorpe directed his concern toward McCormick. "We'll need contingency plans for airlifting our troops."

McCormick felt good. "I've already placed a thousand cargo planes on notice for a possible airlift to Ramstein Air Force Base in Wiesbaden." He could sense that he had just salvaged his reputation as a hard charger with a minimum amount of damage.

Westview was pleased. "Good. Good. Now what about the political ramifications, Chet?" His good friend would do whatever had to be done. But in a Crisis Management Group meeting, Westview didn't want to evince any preference. He wanted to hold that in reserve.

Manning looked disturbed. "Well, Mr. President, the situation isn't as upbeat on the diplomatic front."

Mapplethorpe smirked. It was a typical Chet technique of lowballing expectations, developed during Westview's presidential campaigns. Mapplethorpe knew it by heart: bad-mouth yourself up front so that if the worse occurs, it simply fulfills the poor expectations you had originally created for yourself anyway.

Manning continued. "As you might imagine, we have tried to contact President Zotov both through our ambassador in Moscow and our back-channel sources. But nothing seems to work. He is conveniently away or absent every time we send our ambassador to the Kremlin. Some very strange things are happening over there."

"What do you mean?" Westview asked, feeling revived despite the fact that he was still having trouble focusing his vision.

"I think Chet is right," Jenkins said. "Something is going on besides the usual disturbances in the independent republics. Our station chief in Moscow has been reporting strange rumors, including one that . . . there may be an attempted coup against Zotov." Jenkins said the last words slowly.

He knew he had a little gem in this piece of information. Rumors always elicited more interest than fact. There was very little that could be done about a fact, particularly a fact that had already occurred. By its very nature, a rumor had a salacious connotation, promising the possibility and opportunity of hope. A rumor implied an event that had not yet been acted upon and, therefore, was susceptible to change. Like the readers of the national scandal magazines, senior government officials loved good gossip and juicy rumors.

"What else is new, Larry?" Merck asked matter-of-factly. In his undergraduate days at Amherst, Merck had majored in Russian studies and still maintained an active interest in the area. "The Russians are always in the process of having an impending coup."

"You're right, Randolph," Jenkins interjected. "Except for one minor point. Zotov's Executive Secretary, his closest political ally and friend . . ." He paused for a moment and thought of adding the comparison to Manning, but dismissed the idea as too risky, "Nikolai Pavlovich Kurasov, was rumored to have been murdered in his office in the Kremlin literally only twenty feet away from the Russian President's suite of offices."

Manning shook his head in disbelief. "That's playing guts ball. It explains why we've been having such a hard time reaching Zotov. Kurasov was our man in the Kremlin who would set up appointments. Why didn't I hear anything about this?" Manning was annoyed with Jenkins and his bureaucratic games.

Jenkins responded defensively, "As I said, it was reported as a rumor. The Russians have been reluctant to admit that anything is wrong." He disliked the fact that Chet was trying to intimidate him. But there was no way that Jenkins would have deprived himself of the opportunity to report this jewel. Had he placed the rumor in the morning National Intelligence Directorate, it would have been stale news by now. And fresh news, like fresh eggs in the bare Moscow markets, had a real value in terms of garnering favor and, therefore, power. But in a meeting such as this, in the world of the righteous and the mighty, a rumor could accrue a disproportionate value. And he wasn't about to give up that prerogative—either to Manning or to the President.

Jenkins continued, "Unfortunately, that isn't the worst part of the rumor." Without waiting for a response, he added what he knew would be the pièce de résistance. "Well-informed sources in the Kremlin believe that the United States was behind the assassination."

"What? Why?" Westview asked, incredulous.

"Since 1991," Mapplethorpe added, "all conspiracies in the Commonwealth of Independent States, particularly the Russian Federation, eventually lead back to us or the FSA." He was becoming nervous now that they were spending so much time discussing a mere rumor.

Westview was concerned. "Was Russian President Igor Zotov injured?" He recalled how the FSA had orders to kill either Gorbachev or Yeltsin.

Jenkins replied, "We were informed that Zotov was on a tour of Moscow's newly renovated automobile factories."

McCormick was intrigued by the notion of a conspiracy. "Any relationship between Fitzpatrick's murder and Kurasov's murder?" He was beginning to envision a worldwide conspiracy—but against what and for whom? It didn't make much sense. But neither did the murders.

Jenkins demonstrated with his hands. "The victim's nasal bone was fractured by a direct blow and then rammed into the base of his skull. People in the Kremlin believe that only the CIA could have committed such a heinous crime." Jenkins was on a roll. He could feel the excitement mount in the room. He suddenly realized that what he needed over the coming year were some ghoulish murder stories. They would rebuild the prestige and power that the Agency had lost during Judge Webster's staid stewardship.

"Why not the FSA or some elite military unit?" Merck added. He remembered that the Russian coup of 1991 had been attempted by elite units of the then KGB and the Black Berets.

"Not according to our reliable sources, who inform us that since the Russian Federation had taken over control of the FSA and the Russian Army there have been absolutely no problems," Jenkins replied. "No dissensions. And no attempted coups. They feel that this is strictly an outside job."

Westview laughed. "Listen, did you Agency guys do it?"

Jenkins sounded indignant. "Mr. President, I think you know the answer to that question." He was fully aware of President Ford's Executive Order prohibiting the CIA from engaging in the direct assassination of anyone, particularly a head of state or any of his associates. And given the present emasculated condition of the Agency, it would be close to impossible to find anyone who would even be technically qualified as an assassin. Those days were pretty much over.

Mapplethorpe stood up. "Well, gentlemen, what we need now is a well-integrated Scope Paper that explores all the relevant issues, problems, and options relating to the effective resolution of this crisis. I expect it here by close of business tomorrow." After delivering those words, he began to put away the topo map. It was a signal to the rest of the group that it was time to leave.

Westview stood up to shake each person's hand as they left the room. "Thank you for your constructive participation. Keep pushing your staff to produce some creative solutions to this sticky problem. And don't forget to play hands-on ball. Remember, our primary goal is to resolve this crisis as quickly as possible."

After everyone left, only he and Mapplethorpe remained in the room.

"How bad is it really?" Westview asked anxiously.

"Honestly?"

"Yeah."

"We could use Desaix," Mapplethorpe said, grateful he didn't live in those times when the ruler executed the bearer of bad tidings.

"That bad?"

"Maybe. Maybe worse. Events are getting out of hand."

"What's the worst that can happen?"

"Mr. President, without either side wanting to, we could literally obliterate each other."

"But what about—" Westview stopped short.

# CHAPTER

# 6

Pushkin sensed that he was a marked man.

Walking briskly past Moscow's Rizhsky Market, he knew he was being followed. He decided to be a few minutes late for his first *Shicht* (Shield) meeting.

As he strolled up to the attractive round-faced woman behind the vegetable stand, he picked up a green tomato and examined it.

"Tell me, my beauty, what is this poor excuse for a tomato that you are selling? Aren't you ashamed of yourself?" He held the green tomato high in the air and looked surreptitiously around him. For a moment, he thought he had caught a glimpse of someone following him.

"Listen, Colonel, if you don't like what you see, don't buy!"

"Don't get me wrong. Why did I choose you amidst all these other attractive fruit and vegetable stands?" Raising the tomato, Pushkin saw someone dressed in a black coat turn away, trying to avoid eye contact.

"Give me back that tomato and find yourself a better-looking one, somewhere else."

Running his fingers slowly over the smooth skin of the tomato, Pushkin took her hand and placed it under his. "Feel that my little one! Tell me that doesn't feel good."

"Leave me alone, you pest! You have no right to come up to me—and waste my time!"

"You fool, let the soldier have a little fun with your tomatoes. What harm can it do you? Stop acting like some old maiden."

An old lady hawking apples shouted, "Colonel, come over here! I'll let you play with my fruits." She coughed as she laughed.

Raising the green tomato in a gesture of appreciation, Pushkin recited one of his ancestor's poems in a booming voice:

> *"Why do you sit there, old woman,*
> *Mute by the corner of the window?*
> *Is it the long sobs of the wind*
> *That weary you, my friend,*
> *Or have you drowsed off*
> *To the murmur of your wheel?*
> *Let us drink, steadfast companion*
> *Of my poor young years!*
> *No more sorrows! Where's the jug?*
> *Let our hearts be gay!"*

"Very beautiful, my dear fellow." The old lady's smile revealed a missing front tooth that reminded Pushkin of those silly American Halloween pumpkins.

"Thank you for your vote of confidence." He bowed dramatically as several passersby applauded.

The toothless lady threw him a stale apple. Catching it, Pushkin took a big bite and tossed her a kopeck.

She threw it right back.

"Save it for your young lady friends. I'm too old to do anything worthwhile with a gentleman's money," she cackled. "Take out the tomato lady friend of yours!"

"Listen, I don't need any of your nosy interference into my private life." The tomato lady pushed Pushkin out of the vegetable stall.

Tamara Ivanovich Popov watched Pushkin's show as she leaned lazily against the wooden frame of the broccoli and cauliflower stand. If she had the time, she would have bought some white cauliflower for her special new Chinese dish. But right now, more important matters occupied her thoughts. She couldn't keep her eyes off the strikingly handsome Spetsnaz colonel who could recite Pushkin as if he were the poet himself.

Major Tamara Ivanovich Popov, or Tamara as she was called, was on assignment from the GRU, Glavnoye Razvedyvatelnoye Upravleniye or the Chief Intelligence Directorate, a division of the Russian General Staff. She reported directly to the First Deputy Chief of the GRU, which carried out military intelligence work for the Russian Army in the Moscow area. Using the covers of the Russian Foreign Ministry, the Ministry of External Trade, Aeroflot, and the Academy of Sciences, Tamara had a distinguished career as a military intelligence officer.

After only two years on the job, she had recruited six different intelligence assets, including foreign military attachés, members of military delegations, and American businessmen. She was most proud of the fact that she didn't have to use sex in order to recruit them. Once she had recruited a grateful diplomat from Zimbabwe who shook uncontrollably every time he was around her. Her boss, a boorish man, had suspected that the African had fallen in love with Tamara, so he gave her extra money to allow her to encourage the relationship. She had taken the money and bought the Zimbabwean antimalaria medication, which stopped the shakes and "cured" his lovesickness. He was so grateful for the badly needed medicine that he ended up spying for her.

So what, she wondered, was she doing standing next to the broccoli, watching this attractive Spetsnaz officer making a fool of himself in front of a group of farmers' wives?

By anyone's standards, she was extremely attractive. Not quite thirty-four, she was tall, blonde, and well proportioned. She had warm blue eyes that, combined with her hesitant smile, clearly conveyed an impression of feminine vulnerability and unspoken sexuality. Ironically, she was too attractive to be a truly effective agent. She had learned to downplay her physical beauty, so that men would not be too intimidated to approach her. By nature, she was a timid individual who preferred the company of animals to that of people. Needless to say she owned several pets: two cats, one midget rabbit, and a one-eyed hamster that continuously ran around in circles. But she invested most of her free time and almost all of her energy into her job. At a time when most of her colleagues and childhood friends were leaving the security of government work to start their own restaurant cooperatives or day-care centers, Tamara had decided to dedicate herself to working for the welfare of the Russian people as an intelligence officer. Her mother, a worldly woman, thought that she had had a mental breakdown.

But Tamara had her own reasons for joining the GRU. She was infatuated with its ignominious history. Throughout her whole life, she had always supported the underdog. And in the annals of the old Soviet intelligence, the GRU was considered to be the least important, least effective of all the organizations. She also wanted to have a chance to resurrect her besmirched family name—Popov.

At an age when most children are enchanted with Tolstoy's fables, Tamara read stories about Mother Russia and the GRU. And now, at a time when Russia was disintegrating in front of her eyes, she felt she would be needed, more than ever, to defend her beloved country.

From its very inception in the spring of 1920, the GRU was an illegitimate afterthought of the then succesful NKVD. After the Polish Army invaded Russia in the spring of 1920, driving deep into the heart of Ukraine, Lenin ordered the former Polish Count Dzerzhinsky, father of the KGB, to create an independent Directorate of Intelligence under the jurisdiction of the General Staff to collect military intelligence relevant to a forthcoming Russian invasion of Poland.

Failing to predict the formidable resistance of the Polish people to the subsequent Russian onslaught, the GRU was almost disbanded as quickly as it was formed. And in 1939, the GRU once again failed to predict the impressive resistance of the Finns to Stalin's invasion. But it was not until World War II that the GRU gained any semblance of respectability. As a result of the daring exploits of Richard Sorge, who was stationed in Tokyo, the GRU was able to provide extremely valuable intelligence that had a major impact on the favorable outcome of the war.

Following a short-lived success, the GRU encountered its first major postwar defeat—the discovery that one of its most successful operatives, Lieutenant Colonel Yuri Popov, was a CIA agent. Popov was Tamara's grandfather. Two generations later, she felt it incumbent to rectify the family name. And the GRU was willing to give her that chance. In their eyes, she could become an effective agent, if only she didn't become distracted by other matters.

"May I help you?" Pushkin's mellifluous voice took her completely by surprise. How had she missed his approach?

"Well no! Of course not!"

"All right, as you wish."

"Who are you?"

"Listen, beautiful blue eyes, I've been watching you watching me for the past half hour. And you still claim that you don't know who I am?"

She couldn't find the right words to respond to his question and started fidgeting with her nails.

"What are you doing? Your nails are as beautiful as you are." He took her hands. "Beauty is not something with which you can tamper so lightly."

She pulled back her hands. She was taken aback by his boldness and didn't know what to do. No one had prepared her for this type of encounter. She was always the one who hunted the other person down.

"For whom do you work?"

"I am a housewife. I do not work for anyone."

"Okay, have it your way." He grabbed her arm brusquely and started to pull her away from the broccoli stall, past the cucumbers and leeks, standing her firmly in front of the rotten cantaloupes and melons from Tbilisi, Georgia.

"What do you think you're doing?" She tried to pull her arm away from him. But as much as she hated to admit it to herself, she felt an incredible sense of excitement when he grabbed her so firmly. One part of her just wanted to be carried away without any questions asked or answered. But the other part of her was incredulous. How could she feel this way? She was a professional. She rarely met anyone so forward, so forceful. The men around her were either afraid to approach her or too deferential.

"I don't know. You tell me."

She tried desperately to regain her composure.

"What vegetables did you buy?"

"What business is it of yours?"

"You said you were a housewife. And since this is a vegetable market, I think it's only reasonable to ask you what type of vegetables you bought? Zucchini?"

"It is not the season."

"Potatoes?" He asked with a broad smile.

"Too healthy." She replied.

"Too healthy? You don't buy foods that are good for you?"

"It depends. When I feel in my American mood, I buy only fruits and vegetables to lower my cholesterol."

Pushkin liked her mischievous banter. For the most part, he found her quite attractive, but as far as he was concerned, women were to be admired, possessed, and betrayed. In her case, she was already betraying herself. She must be GRU.

"What type of mood are you in right now?"

"Why?"

"If you are not in your American mood, there is a possibility you might be in some other kind of mood, which we might be able to satisfy together. One never knows, of course."

"This is crazy. I don't even know you and already—" She stopped suddenly.

"And already . . . what?" He was amused by the crimson flush of her neck. He wondered if his own organization would have sent someone to follow him who was so shy.

"Nothing." She started to pull away from him before she was too attracted. "I must be going."

"Where are you going?" Pushkin held her arm fast so that she couldn't walk away.

"None of your business!" She pulled against his firm grip. Was he as ruthless as people said? Was the poet Pushkin truly his relative? Did he write poetry? What type of women did he like?

"Come with me!" he ordered. He grabbed her by the arm and led her toward Timiryazyev Park, where old women, bundled up in tattered overcoats, hovered over steaming pushcarts selling baked potatoes. Behind them stood empty wooden tool sheds. Children were running about as if on a holiday.

Pushkin walked up to one woman wrapped in a tight brown babushka and bought two potatoes. He handed one to Tamara.

"Be careful, it's hot."

They blew on their potatoes.

"Why are you doing this?" She was uncomfortable with this turn of events. None of this was supposed to happen. He was on his way to a meeting. She had been instructed to follow him. Instead, she was standing in the middle of a park blowing on a baked potato with the very man she was supposed to catch.

The hunter had become the hunted.

"What exactly am I doing that seems to disturb you?" His dark eyes were relentless. They kept boring in on her. She felt completely vulnerable.

"You know."

"No, I don't."

"You are teasing me now." She felt like a schoolgirl uttering those words.

"All right. I'll tell you exactly what I am doing. I am trying to co-opt my adversary by relaxing her. If a three-kopeck baked potato and a little bit of kindness can loosen your tongue and entice you to reveal the big, bad secrets about your hush-hush mission then the three kopecks will have been well spent. Don't you think?"

"You really are sure of yourself." She enjoyed his playfulness.

"Nothing like what they told you that I might be?"

"Not exactly. You must admit that your reputation isn't exactly . . ." She was having a problem finding the right word. She didn't want to be either insulting or hurting. Yet there was nothing about him that revealed any sense of fragility.

"My reputation among whom?"

Tamara wanted him to stop talking. She placed her index finger on her lips, indicating silence.

"Don't become silent now," he said.

"Why?"

"Because I like the way you speak."

He pulled her toward him and gently caressed her face, her hair, and the nape of her neck. As cold as it was in the park, she felt increasingly warm.

The old ladies huddled around their pushcarts and nodded their heads in approval. So this is what happens when you buy one of their baked potatoes.

Pushkin steered her into one of the maintenance sheds and kicked the door closed. For a split second, Tamara wasn't certain whether he would make love to her or strangle her. Her instincts told her not to pull back from his wandering hands. She decided to take control and thrust her body into his. They stood locked together, against the wooden wall.

She could feel excitement pulsate through his body. Whatever he had been and whatever atrocious acts he had committed were suddenly dissolved into a moment of anticipatory euphoria. She thought only of his hands finding their way inside her coat, then underneath her dress. His callused hands felt surprisingly soothing, self-assured. For the first time, using sex to keep her quarry in sight didn't seem like a bad idea.

She moved her body in a circular, inviting motion.

Her hands probed his body in an insistent, caressing fashion, urging him to continue this ritual of love.

Suddenly she stopped and pulled away.

"What's the matter?"

"I can't!" She adjusted her dress.

"Aren't you supposed to entrap me?" Pushkin said with a slight smirk.

"No!" she replied angrily. "I was supposed to . . . never mind."

"I'm sorry! I didn't mean that," Pushkin said, trying to comfort her. "I was carried away by the passion of the moment."

"If you were the only one with that particular feeling, then we wouldn't be having this problem, would we?" She looked at him with fearful anticipation.

"What exactly is this problem?" He wanted to touch her, but he was afraid she might bolt out of the shed like a frightened kitten.

"It's just not right! You catch me following you, then the next minute we're making love. You don't even know my name."

"Well, in that particular case you have the distinct advantage. So just to make it official, I will begin by intoducing myself," he said, bowing from the waist. "My name is Alexander Lvovich Pushkin."

"More precisely, you are Colonel Alexander Lvovich Pushkin, who at thirty-five is the one of the youngest commanders in the history of the 107th Guards Airborne Division, a Spetsnaz diversionary brigade."

"It's clear that you have learned a lot about me. I hope I do not disappoint you."

"No! On the contrary! You are far more charming and handsome than I had ever imagined."

"Then what is the problem, my sweet blue eyes?" he said, trying to reach out to her. But she pulled back. Something was wrong, he thought. She seemed too skittish to be a GRU agent. Maybe this coquettish resistance was all part of her professional routine to trap the quarry. So be it. The least he could do was enjoy it.

"You should know! In our business we should never allow our emotions to cloud our professional judgment." She began to fidget with her hands. She wanted to leave, but she couldn't. His sensuous hazel eyes beckoned her forward.

"Business . . . business . . . !" Pushkin spat out. "You sound like an American. Has the GRU also lost its soul in this madness we call democracy?"

"Please, don't be angry with me!" She reached out toward him.

"You know, I don't even know your name." Pushkin took her arms and placed them around his waist.

"My name is Major Tamara Popov of the First Directorate of the GRU."

"You work for the General Staff?" He ran his hands over her body. She began to tremble.

"Business . . . business . . ." she whispered in his ears as she felt his hands caress her loins.

"Are you related to Lieutenant Colonel Yuri Popov?" He felt her body start to move in a circular, inviting motion.

Her hands probed his body in an insistent fashion, urging him to continue.

Suddenly, he lifted her up from the ground, his strong arms supporting her buttocks.

She wrapped both her legs around his waist. And in the moment of a passionate embrace, he entered her with the gentleness of a lover whose only concern was to make her happy.

They moved rhythmically together. She whispered, ever so softly, "He was my grandfather."

In one way or another, we are all traitors, he thought to himself. His mind wandered to the meeting of the *Shicht*.

The coup would have to wait, yet another day.

# CHAPTER

## 7

All morgues look and smell alike.

The fact that this one was located in the basement of the Japanese Police Prefectory in the Chuo-Ku area, a few blocks from the heart of the Ginza, was of little or no significance to a completely distracted Desaix.

Desaix's mind was somewhere over the Pacific. Fundamental rules of crisis management ran through the fog of formaldehyde that permeated his senses: First, find out who is making out the invitations to the crisis. Second, get yourself invited. Third, don't grandstand, unless you have a sure thing. Addendum, there is no such thing as a sure thing.

For Desaix, the hardest part of managing any international crisis usually was being invited to participate. And there was no doubt in his mind that he was purposefully being excluded from this one. Apart from one short conversation with Mapplethorpe about Fitzpatrick's murder, no one in the States was returning his phone calls from Japan. Almost anyone who might be involved was either "out of town" or "in meetings for the better part of the day." Finding out who might be involved in the crisis was becoming a small feat of its own. An intelligent observer might assume that a crisis involving the Russian Federation and the United States would involve the Russian desk at State, the Russian Division at the International Security Agency, a part of the Department of Defense, often called the mini–State Department, the Russian National Intelligence Officer at the Central Intelligence Agency, or the Deputy Director of Operations at the Agency.

But more often than not, Desaix knew that logic was not a compelling force behind the management of a crisis. It was conceivable that none of those agencies would have any significant role. But that was no consolation.

Somehow he had to find a way to get in. It seemed as if the gods were against him. Yesterday he was on his way to finishing up a negotiation that would have allowed him to proceed stateside. Now, ordered by Mapplethorpe, he had to remain in Japan until he cleared up the mystery of Fitzpatrick's death.

Desaix had wanted to vomit when he saw the stiff naked body of Daniel Fitzpatrick splayed out on a glistening steel table. The truth was that twenty years after medical school he still wasn't used to seeing cadavers.

"We took out some small fragments of metal that we think may be part of a 9 millimeter bullet. But quite frankly we are not certain." Dr. Oda Nobunaga, Chief Forensic Pathologist for the Prefecture Chuo-Ku, trained at San Francisco General Hospital, waved the pieces around in the air.

What interested Desaix more were the small clusters of yellow blisters on the palms of both of Nobunaga's hands. It reminded him of a time when he had acquired a similar array of blisters. About ten years ago when a chemical tanker-trailer had flipped over on the highway.

"Where did you find those pieces?" Desaix examined the fragments. They didn't look like the fragments of any bullet that he could recognize. Lifting them up to his nose, he discovered they had a strange aroma. But not gunpowder. Just not too dissimilar from the smell of that chemical tanker-trailer.

"These pieces came from the posterior part of his right occipital lobe."

Nobunaga walked around the body with the bravado of a hunter who had just bagged his first elephant.

Even Imai, who felt some responsibility for the murder, winced at the false sense of pride. The good doctor had just eviscerated a body. The large and small bowels were coiled up alongside the cadaver as if they were a boa constrictor ready to strike.

Nobunaga was about to weigh the organs to determine whether in the process of death they had gained or lost weight. What relevance this procedure had to solving the crime was certainly not clear to Desaix. But even in death, Desaix realized, standard operating procedures had a place of prominence.

"How far away was the assailant when he fired the gun?"

Desaix tried to look at the body with a newly constituted dispassion. But he was clearly having trouble. He tried hard to remind himself that this was not the body of his good friend. This was not the body responsible for preparing the all-important annual National Intelligence Estimate 11-3/8 on Soviet strategic capabilities and objectives. This was not the body that had predicted the disintegration of the communist empire five years ahead of his time. This was not the body that had recommended the disavowal of first-strike capability.

Although they had always had their differences, Fitzpatrick would often accuse Desaix of practicing "diaperology"—using psychosexual constructs to explain world events.

In turn, Desaix would accuse Fitzpatrick of distorting historical facts in order to justify his policy decisions. But those were simply the arguments of close friends, bureaucratic colleagues, and longtime friendly competitors.

Staring at the rigid planks of tissue, muscle, and fiber torn apart at the abdomen, Desaix felt a visceral sense of resentment and anger at Fitzpatrick. Why had Fitzpatrick listened to him? It was clear to everyone in the room yesterday that Fitzpatrick really didn't want to go for R and R.

As a matter of fact, something had been bothering Danny. Could Fitzpatrick have known that something might happen to him if he went out that evening? Perhaps he would be alive today if only he hadn't listened to Desaix.

But guilt was a luxury that a fourth-generation Huguenot had long ago learned to displace in the run-down brothels of the Latin Quarter in New Orleans. Desaix had replaced it with the sense of the Big Easy—an attitude of taking life at its face value. Not more. Not less.

But now, a sense of remorse overwhelmed Desaix and he allowed himself the indulgence of recognizing pain and loss. In part, he attributed this feeling to Fitzpatrick's death. In greater part, he related his sadness and guilt to his not being back at the department. In fact, the more he thought about Fitzpatrick's death, the more angry he became at the seventh-floor principals at State. Had Secretary of State Chester Manning not sent him out on this mission to negotiate the Signal Intelligence agreements, this never would have happened. Furthermore, had he been requested to fly back immediately and attend to the more important matters of managing the ongoing crisis, this death would never have happened.

But externalizing responsibility for Fitzpatrick's death was not operating very well for Desaix today. The blame was his. His alone.

Imai carefully watched his friend Desaix walk slowly around the body, meticulously examining it.

"From the impressive size of the entrance wound and the large amount of burn marks around the wound, I would say that whoever did it was at very close range," Desaix said nonchalantly.

"How close, doc?" White's manner was impatient and aggressive.

"Take it easy, White! All we're talking about now is a postmortem. There is nothing we can do to bring him back," Ball warned.

"Maybe no more than five feet, at most." Nobunaga enjoyed the brusque questions. They were so refreshingly American. It reminded him of medical Grand Rounds at San Francisco General.

Strolling over from the far end of the table, Ball examined Fitzpatrick's chest. Although he wasn't a medical doctor, he had extensive experience with medical problems. He was in charge of the CIA's Center for Leadership Analysis, which collected human intelligence about different world leaders, including everything from what they excreted in their urine to their sexual preferences, and used that information to develop psychological profiles for State Department policymakers like Desaix.

Ball recalled with some pride a recent psychological profile of a well-known Palestinian leader. It was Ball who had figured out that the PLO leader was both a homosexual and a pedophile, spending much of his time in Palestinian refugee camps recruiting young boys for his terrorist organization—and for himself. But what that information would mean in terms of developing or implementing foreign policy was never very clear to him. He had always assumed that senior policymakers at State, like Desaix, could integrate all his disparate psychological and medical information into one coherent political strategy.

Examining Fitzpatrick's chest carefully, Ball noticed a series of scratch marks. Long furrows of dried blood stretched all the way from one nipple to another, almost as if he had been attacked with some small, sharp, pointed instrument.

"Dr. Nobunaga, please, take a look at this! What do you make of it?" Desaix asked.

Ball watched Desaix probe the gaping necrotic wound in the right eye with a pencil. "Find anything interesting, Desaix?"

"What about those scratches?" Desaix replied without even looking up.

"Those scratches could have been made by a human hand." Nobunaga was mindful of Desaix's tone of disrespect.

"Like a woman's long nails?" White asked. He watched Desaix probe the eye wound. He had never seen him so totally absorbed.

"Are you certain this was done with a gun?"

"We're pretty certain, Dr. Clark."

Imai was concerned that Nobunaga seemed so unsure of himself. "What are you getting at, my friend?" Imai boldly asked. He wanted to do whatever was necessary to solve this crime. More than anyone else, he felt responsible for Fitzpatrick's death.

"Smell it!" Motioning Nobunaga forward, Desaix pointed to the hole.

"What?" Nobunaga was startled by Desaix's peremptory tone.

"Smell it, please!" Desaix was impatient. Nobunaga was acting like the typical county medical examiner who was too busy to make the proper diagnosis. A gaping necrotic hole was automatically considered a gunshot wound because it was a hell of a lot easier to make that diagnosis than to find out what it might really be.

"I don't know what you are getting at." Nobunaga looked frightened.

"Does that or does that not smell like gunpowder?"

"Hey, Desaix, take it easy on the doc. He's on our side, remember?"

Desaix responded to White's comment with a look that said he should mind his own business. "I don't think you will find gunpowder in there. Furthermore, I doubt if the fragments that you found in the posterior occipital lobe were in any way, shape, or form any part of a bullet, particularly a 9 millimeter bullet." Short of calling Nobunaga a liar, Desaix had thoroughly insulted him. But intercultural sensitivity was the least of his current concerns.

Without asking for permission, Desaix pulled down the electrical bone saw that hung from a metal pole over each examining table in a morgue. He flicked on the switch and made a straight incision, starting from the top of the sternum extending all the way down to the xiphoid. Then he separated both sides of the chest and exposed the pulmonary cavity.

"Clear the table! Take a few steps back!" Desaix shouted and then started to cough as a vapor of gas escaped from the body cavity. When Desaix pushed on the outer linings he could feel that both lungs were congested with water.

"Oh, shit!" Desaix quickly withdrew his right hand. He rushed over to the sink and flushed his hand with cold running water.

"Get me a syringe with 10 percent calcium gluconate and 4 percent novocaine. I'll also need a magnesium oxide–water soluble paste with a 20 percent glycerin base. And, if one of you big bruisers could bring me a chair, a scalpel, and rolls of gauze and bandages, I would be eternally grateful."

Ball rushed over with a chair as Nobunaga barked some orders in Japanese to a group of attendants who had appeared suddenly from nowhere. They disappeared, and then reappeared with all the requested equipment.

Imai walked over to steady his friend. Desaix's face was turning white. His cough was more pronounced.

"What the hell is going on here?" White asked as he began to probe Fitzpatrick's cavity with a pencil.

"Leave that frigging body alone," Desaix shouted across the room.

"Who the fuck are you talking to? I'm not one of your slant—" White didn't finish his sentence. He didn't have to. Everyone in the room could have completed it for him. "Sorry," White apologized.

"I think we are all a little bit upset," Imai said. "So much has happened in such a short period of time." Despite his conciliatory tone of voice, Imai would never forget what General White really felt. His *honne* was like that of so many other Americans—the Japanese were still the slanty-eyed bastards. There would be time for retribution.

"So what does he have?" Ball asked, having felt he had initiated Desaix's line of inquiry by asking about the scratch marks.

"Dr. Nobunaga," Desaix said, totally absorbed in the procedure, "take the syringe and mix a half-and-half cocktail of 10 percent calcium gluconate and 4 percent novocaine and inject it at the base of the second and third fingers of my right hand."

"You want a nerve block?" Nobunaga asked.

"I'll take whatever you can give me. But please, make it gentle and, above all else, swift." The pain in Desaix's hand was becoming unbearable. Large blisters filled with yellow fluid were beginning to swell his second and third fingers.

"Desaix," Ball said, annoyed, "will you please tell us what the hell you found." Ball held Desaix's right hand down on the metal counter. He turned his head away as Nobunaga inserted the tip of the two-inch needle into an imaginary point one centimeter below the juncture between the second and the third fingers.

"Oh, my God!" Desaix groaned, then bit his lower lip as he watched the syringe needle burrow deeply into his palm. For a moment, he felt as if the bones of his hand were being crushed by a nutcracker and the nerves and arteries were being sadistically torn apart.

"Desaix, tell me all about those wonderful Creole dishes your mother used to make," Imai said, trying to distract his friend.

"Chicken gumbo . . . I love . . . Oh, my God, it's killing me! But chicken gumbo, I love it. Big juicy pieces of chicken immersed in . . . ahhh . . . Jesus!"

Nobunaga inserted the entire two inches of the needle into Desaix's hand. He moved the needle around in order to make certain that all the novocaine anesthetic permeated the necessary areas. How ironic, Nobunaga thought, that in order for him to prevent pain he had to create even greater pain. So this was the way of modern medicine.

"Shrimp gumbo . . . and . . . oh, my God, when is this going to be over?"

"Soon, Doctor . . . soon. I just have a few more milliliters of fluid left in the syringe."

"Desaix, what the fuck did you find?" White interjected. He started to feel queasy. He wanted to leave Japan as quickly as possible to report to his superiors.

"Catfish prepared in Cajun style, a lot of black pepper, now that's a delicacy," Desaix added.

"Come on, Desaix, what gives?" White asked, as he placed his hands around Desaix's throat in a mock gesture of choking him.

"That's what happened, General. Someone grabbed Danny from the back, muffled his screams by placing their hands over his mouth—"

"That's why no one heard anything, right?" Ball was excited. This was far more interesting than any psychological analysis of some depraved world leader.

"No one heard him scream . . . Oh, Christ! It's killing me!"

"Sorry, I was just pulling out the syringe." Nobunaga looked up to see White turn ashen gray. "Are you all right?"

"Yeah, I'm fine! I just need a little fresh air." White sat down on a chair Imai provided.

Nobunaga unpacked the surgical kit that had been brought to him. Withdrawing the fine-edged scalpel, he placed Desaix's two anesthetized fingers on the metal counter and draped the surrounding area with surgical towels.

"I want you to cut both nails off," Desaix said. "Follow the cuticle line on top and come down on the sides. Then lift them off their nail beds. Put some magnesium oxide on them, and wrap them up in gauze." Desaix was surprised by his memory. It had been almost ten years since he had practiced any medicine. But like riding a bicycle, he would never forget what he had once learned. At one point in his medical career he had become an expert in burns, and the key to success was to act quickly and prevent the burned tissue from corroding, either into a blister or into necrotic tissue. Prophylaxis was the most effective antidote to chemical burns.

Nobunaga painted Desaix's nails with a brown antiseptic. He made a careful incision along the side of the nail of the second digit. Desaix didn't feel anything. As Nobunaga made the incision along the eponychium, the flap of skin above the cuticle, Desaix screamed.

"Oh, I'm so sorry!" Nobunaga apologized in a questionable tone of contriteness.

"You're cutting too far up. The anesthetic block doesn't work there."

"Apparently not." Nobunaga wiped the blood away from the surgical field and cut along the borders of the cuticle.

"Desaix, your friends are waiting," Imai said, impatient to clear up this mess and save face. Plus, it would distract Desaix from Nobunaga's work.

"Hydrogen fluoride." Desaix breathed with a sigh of relief as Nobunaga started to bandage his two fingers.

"What the hell are you talking about?" White asked. "Isn't that the fluoride that is put into toothpaste to prevent tooth decay?"

"Yes. Whoever killed Fitzpatrick did it with a highly concentrated dose of hydrogen fluoride or hydrofluoric acid. At least two people were involved. One stood behind him while the other poured acid down his throat, causing him to die almost immediately from pulmonary edema, or water in the lungs. And just to be certain they hadn't missed, they rammed a hollow metal tube into his right eye and poured the hydrofluoric acid down it."

Desaix stood up, thanked Nobunaga, and walked over to the cadaver. "Don't touch it! As you can see from my hand, this body still contains a lot of active acid."

"How did you suspect the diagnosis?" Nobunaga asked with a certain tone of bewilderment, but pleased with the minor operation he had just performed on Desaix.

"By carefully examining the first piece of evidence."

Desaix took both of Nobunaga's hands. "You see, Doctor, I take nothing for granted, not even the blisters on your hands. Smell them! They smell just like the metal fragments you showed me. If you carefully examine the so-called bullet wound, you will see a small cluster of these blisters scattered throughout the wound site." He felt a little apologetic. The only thing he hadn't done was call Dr. Nobunaga incompetent.

"What does this all mean?" Ball asked, fascinated by Desaix's process of deduction.

"If it's true, that is." White wanted everyone in the room to know that he didn't buy Desaix's explanation. He still liked the smoking gun thesis. It was a hell of a lot easier to understand.

"I don't know what this means, Jim. All I know is that someone went out of his way to have Fitzpatrick executed. The key question is why?" Desaix said.

"Why go through all of this just to kill him?" White liked his explanations simple. "Why didn't they simply put a silencer on a 9 millimeter Beretta? It would have accomplished the same thing."

"Dick's got a point there, Desaix." Ball was trying to recall a similar type of death using a corrosive chemical. But nothing came to mind.

Desaix didn't respond. The answer to the question would have to be found at the scene of the crime, as well as with the woman Fitzpatrick had spent the evening with at the inn. The longer he stayed at the morgue, the more time he was wasting.

"I'm sorry, gentlemen, but you'll have to excuse me. I need some time to recover. I'll see you both back at the hotel." Desaix bade farewell to Nobunaga as well and motioned Imai to accompany him. Both men left the police station. He asked Imai to take him back to the inn.

They sat silently together in the back of the limousine as the chauffeur drove slowly past the American Embassy in the Roppongi district, toward the shopping and entertainment district of Shibuya.

Passing the Hachiko bronze statue of a dog, Imai noticed that they were taking a roundabout way toward the inn. Without wanting to alarm Desaix, Imai asked the chauffeur in Japanese what he was doing. The chauffeur muttered that he thought he was being followed by a car that had pulled out of the driveway of the American Embassy when they drove by.

"Desaix, our driver thinks we are being followed by one of your embassy cars. Does that make any sense to you?"

"Just tell him to keep driving slowly so that he doesn't lose the car behind him. And when we get out of the car, don't look around."

When they arrived at the inn, Desaix couldn't resist turning around. But he didn't see any car. Maybe the chauffeur was overanxious.

Once inside the inn, Desaix tried to find the hostess who had been with Fitzpatrick before his death. He was told that she wasn't there, and hadn't come to work that day. The manager of the inn gave them her home address, but he added that she wouldn't be there either.

Walking slowly down the long, narrow corridor, they retraced their steps from the previous night toward the room in which Fitzpatrick was murdered. The room had been sealed off by red tape. Desaix had been prepared to see a room that looked as if it had been devastated by a typhoon. Instead he found two tatami mats neatly rolled up alongside a small wooden table that held a half bottle of sake and a cracked blue porcelain lamp. Other than a lamp cord that had been torn from its base, it looked as if the room had been cleaned up right after the murder.

"Has anyone been here since yesterday?" Desaix asked.

"Not according to the innkeeper." Imai felt uncomfortable playing the role of criminal investigator.

There was a wooden hot tub at the far end of the room, similar to the one in which Desaix had made love. They walked slowly around it, carefully checking the wooden slats of the barrel for any unusual marks or stains. Imai was uncertain of what he was looking for, but he trusted his friend. Despite the unfortunate circumstances under which they were cooperating, Imai was grateful to share a few intimate hours with Desaix. It had been such a long time since they had collaborated. Even if a death had to be the reason, Imai preferred this cooperative approach to an adversarial relationship. While it might be selfish of him to have such thoughts, they merely expressed his yearning for a friendship that he feared may have been displaced somewhere, sometime ago.

"Come over here, Yutaka."

On the other side of the hot tub, Desaix moved a sharp-edged metal spigot around on its ball joint. Water splurted upward in a steady, full stream.

"Fitzpatrick must have been interrogated and tortured right over here." Desaix peeled away a thin layer of crusted blood from the mouth of the rusted spigot. "They must have rammed his right eye socket into this sharp pipe. Look at the diameter of the pipe, it's almost the same width as his eyesocket."

"But why? Why go to such extremes to torture a man?" Imai felt nauseated, envisioning Fitzpatrick having his head rammed into a pipe. "Who would do this?"

"I don't know, but clearly it was someone who was extremely comfortable with terror and violence."

"Could he have simply slipped on it and injured his head?"

Ignoring Imai's question, Desaix continued to look around the room. Something was bothering him. Despite a few broken pieces of furniture, nothing in the room looked sufficiently disrupted to indicate that there had been a serious confrontation. True, the paper-thin wall adjoining his room was completely shredded. But that resulted from Fitzpatrick's having crashed through.

The more Desaix thought about it, the more he was disturbed by one simple fact. He had not heard any noises coming from this room. If there was any interrogation or torture conducted last night, Desaix should have heard some screams or shouts. At least, some incriminating noises. But there were none.

Something happened in this room last night that contributed to Fitzpatrick's death. But what was it? And where did the hydrogen fluoride come from?

Desaix walked slowly around the room, examining every corner, knocking on walls to test for any hollow sounds that might reveal the location of pipes containing a chemical.

"Desaix, look!" Imai pointed up to the ceiling.

"Don't touch it!"

The two men watched as small droplets of fluid traveled slowly across the wooden beam spanning the small room.

When a drop achieved a certain critical mass, it fell slowly into the hot tub. Just like molasses. It reminded Desaix of that time in Vermont when he and his first wife went to ski at Killington, but found themselves spending most of their postcoital time watching farmers collect maple sap from the trees.

Desaix paused. For a moment, he thought that he had heard some footsteps coming from straight above him.

"Something wrong?"

"I don't know, maybe. What's up there?"

"I think there is nothing up there. They told me downstairs that it is simply a storage room."

"Come on, let's see!"

Imai followed Desaix out of the room.

They rushed up the poorly lit wooden staircase. Striking a match, Desaix saw that they were in a storage room filled with rusted canisters and large metal beer kegs. As far as he could tell, there was no one else in the room.

Desaix lit another match and located the point above the hot tub. Both men pushed aside several rusted kegs and looked through the broad spaces between the wooden slats of the floor. Desaix could see the room below.

"This is it!" Desaix gingerly picked up a black-oxidized canister with prominent Japanese lettering in red. A clear fluid leaked out from the bottom of it onto the floor through freshly cut jagged edges.

"What does it say?" Desaix asked.

"This canister is used to fumigate houses for insects and rodents. It's made from methyl sulfonyl fluoride. There's a warning here that states that this liquid is dangerous. It says that if you accidentally swallow the chemical or get it in your eyes, you must wash it out well with water. Then see a doctor." Imai looked upset.

"Ninety percent of all accidents and nonphysically related deaths occur within one mile of one's own house. I would have hoped that the same mathematical principle operates when one is in a whorehouse." Desaix discovered a strange sense of relief. Perhaps Fitzpatrick's death was a freak accident. No grand sinister plot. No paranoid collusions. No betrayals. Just a fucking series of accidents.

But, more importantly, he felt a strong need to believe in something other than his own delusion of omnipotence. He was tired of having to construct paradigms of behavior that seemed to explain everything, but in fact revealed very little. He didn't want the responsibility of having to uncover the Veritable Truth. It was just a lot easier to believe in accidents and random chance.

A creaking board startled him. He gestured for Imai to remain still, and walked slowly around the room. What would he do if he encountered another person in the room?

"Stand back, Dr. Clark!" A muffled voice reverberated through the dark.

"Who is there?" Desaix motioned Imai to leave the room. He refused. Instead, Imai started to circle in the opposite direction.

"Please, Mr. Imai, don't mirror your friend's foolish actions. Just stand there quietly and no harm will befall either of you."

As best as Desaix could ascertain, the voice was coming from behind a wall, twenty feet away.

"If you don't want to hurt either one of us, then why are you hiding?" Desaix kept advancing toward the wall.

"I'm a nocturnal creature. I like to hang out in cold, dark, clammy places. This hiding place is as good as any other. Furthermore, it gives me a distinct tactical advantage over you."

"You sound like a bat."

"Doctor, I didn't realize you were a comedian."

"Why don't you just take it easy and tell me who you are and what you're doing here."

"Dr. Clark, I wasn't aware that you were allowed to practice psychiatry anywhere near Tokyo." The voice sounded impatient.

"What do you want?" Desaix advanced another five feet.

A burst of rapid gunfire erupted. Desaix and Imai fell to the ground.

"Greetings from the International Arms Import Corporation. This is their welcome wagon—a Sig Sauer Model P226, the finest combat pistol in the world. It's a double-action 16 round capacity, 9 millimeter Parabellum. It has a white-accented combat sight for rapid target acquisition in low light conditions. Just like this situation."

"Can we get up now?" Desaix crawled a little closer toward the panels.

"Please don't play any games, Dr. Clark. Mind your Ps and Qs. A little politeness goes a long way with me."

"Who are you?" Imai stood up slowly.

"I am, Mr. Minister, simply a functionary, just like yourself."

"You're too modest, Mr. Functionary." Desaix was trying to identify some characteristic speech patterns that might allow him to remember the man at some later point.

"Please, Doctor, don't try to accord yourself the same privileges that I now possess. Sarcasm doesn't become you. At least not at this very moment."

"What do you want?" Desaix was frustrated, but tried to conceal it. "By the way, how should I address you? You seem to know our names. Should we call you the Man Behind the Wall?"

"I would suggest that you say as little as possible." He paused, then added, "My reason for being here is quite simple. I'm here to find out who killed Fitzpatrick."

"What? You must be kidding. You think we killed Fitzpatrick?" Desaix replied.

"Who killed him?" the man asked, sounding annoyed. He fired a shot into the air.

"Please take it easy," Imai said. "On my honor as a Deputy Foreign Minister in the Japanese Foreign Ministry I can swear to you that we know nothing about the reason for his death or the identity of the perpetrator. Quite frankly, I assumed that it might be you."

"How do I know that you are telling the truth?" the man asked.

"For the same reason we are not certain that you didn't kill him. Why would a U.S. government official want to kill another U.S. government official? It doesn't make sense," Desaix added.

"Doesn't make sense, huh? Did you ever hear of Baltimore?" the voice replied.

"Yes, the capital of the state of Maryland."

"Nice try, Doctor! Annapolis is the capital of Maryland, not Baltimore."

"You must have been quite an inspired schoolteacher in your earlier life," Desaix replied.

"Doctor, I suggest that you control your sarcasm. Now then, did Fitzpatrick ever talk to you about Baltimore?"

"No! He did seem to be quite upset and distracted toward the end of our negotiations, but he never mentioned anything about Baltimore." Reflecting for a moment, Desaix added, "By the way, what is Baltimore, if it's not a city?"

The man didn't respond for what seemed like nearly a minute.

"Why don't you come out?" Imai asked, feeling more comfortable.

"The less you know about me, the better off you will be. Trust me."

"So what is Baltimore?" Desaix repeated before he was knocked to the ground as the gunman ran past them. It was too dark for Desaix to see the gunman's face.

Lying bruised on the ground, Desaix thought to himself, Thank you, Fitzpatrick. Your death has not been in vain. He realized that somehow Fitzpatrick's death in Japan, the mounting tensions with the Russians, and "Baltimore" were all related. In his business, there was no such thing as an accident. From experience, he knew that usually two or more seemingly unrelated events involving a political murder and an international crisis were usually connected by threads of deception, duplicity, or conspiracy. And there was nothing more tantalizing for him than the opportunity to unravel these knots of political connivance. It afforded him the chance to utilize his skills in order to uncover and manipulate the conflicting motivations, the insatiable ambitions, and the outright malice behind the mystery of these seemingly unrelated events.

# CHAPTER

## 8

No one, but no one, wanted to go to Room E-406, the Baltimore Room.

For most people working in the White House, there was no need. But for those who were involved with the most intimate secrets of the United States government, Baltimore, like its namesake fifty miles to the north of Washington, was a safe haven of national security secrets and highly classified intelligence.

Lieutenant Colonel Sonny Shaw walked briskly across Executive Lane, the limousine-lined street connecting the West Wing of the White House, where the President and his National Security Advisor had their offices, to the Old Executive Office Building.

A hard-bitten ex-wrestler, he was having a difficult time catching up with Air Force Lieutenant General Thomas Mapplethorpe. Unlike his boss, Shaw was not an intellectual. More importantly, he didn't have any pretense to being erudite. Like a domesticated, submissive housewife, he was content to bask in the intellectual penumbra of the spouse; or in this case, the General, as he affectionately called Mapplethorpe. He particularly enjoyed the fact that anyone who met both men wondered what it was that each saw in the other.

Colonel Shaw received, like most men in the military, a clear sense of self through the prescribed relationships of the social order. And in the military, the pecking order was very clear. It was based on the notion of the authoritarian personality, which, by definition, required immediate and complete obedience to the person or position above while, at the same time, requiring the complete submission of the person immediately below.

Had Erich Fromm, the renowned social psychologist been alive, he would have found the relationship between Mapplethorpe and Shaw a perfect case study in the Authoritarian Personality. Without mention of word or effort of motion, Shaw knew almost instinctively what Mapplethorpe wanted. Theirs was the communication of intent.

Yet no two soldiers could have been more different. Mapplethorpe was a pale, bookish man in his mid-sixties, who had spent considerably more time in the library than he had on the battlefield. In fact, he had spent very little time in battle. But it certainly wasn't for lack of courage, because in danger-ous situations Mapplethorpe was known as a man who could be enticed to appear, if not act, courageously.

Although not a man of robust valor, Mapplethorpe had a quiet persevering manner in the face of insurmountable odds, a trait that made him the master of both the intelligence and national security bureaucracies. Still, behind his back, he was often called "the old woman" because of his prim manners and his thin, reedy voice.

In contrast, Shaw, a forty-five-year-old burly man of coarse features, wearing the short-cropped haircut from his drill instructor days at Fort Dix, New Jersey, lived only for combat and action. A career Army man who left the ski slopes of Breckenridge, Colorado, immediately after graduating high school, he joined the Special Operations Forces at Fort Bragg, North Caro-lina, where he rotated through one Ranger regiment, two Psychological Operations battalions, and one aviation company, flying modified MH-47E and MH-60K assault helicopters. He fought alongside the contras in Honduras and Nicaragua in his official capacity as an "observer," and had the unique distinction of having been one of the few American advisors to the noncommunist resistance groups, ANS and KPLNF, fighting in Cambodia against the Soviet-backed Vietnamese-supported PRK.

As expected, Shaw comported himself with honor and distinction. He had been awarded several purple clusters as well as numerous other meritorious commendations. But like all men in systems that discard their personnel after having served their initial purpose, Shaw remained in the backwaters of career advancement. Despite excellent recommendations from his superiors, Shaw would never be destined for promotion until he renounced his Special Operations Forces career track.

Since World War II, from the OSS days of Wild Bill Donovan to the John F. Kennedy era of the Green Berets, the mainstream Army had always had a basic mistrust and dislike of elite combat units. By definition, these units were not under the normal line of command, so anything they did or requested was the subject of suspicion. In any other Army unit, Shaw would have been a full-fledged colonel by now.

Mapplethorpe had met Shaw when he was intimately involved in the implementation of the Special Operations Forces Command and Control system legislated by Congress in 1986. Shaw had helped develop the United

States Special Operations Command at MacDill Air Force Base in Florida. USSOCOM had been created prior to the Iraq War as the central area of management and oversight for all Special Operations Forces resources. It had maintained the highest standards of training, interoperability, and readiness as evidenced by the overwhelming military success in the Gulf War. In principle, USSOCOM could bypass all the regional Commander-in-Chiefs' capability to employ Special Operations Forces in their respective regional theaters.

Walking through the side door of the Old Executive Office Building, Mapplethorpe turned toward Shaw.

"MEECN?"

"Secured," Shaw responded reflexively. Their communication had been boiled down to monosyllables. MEECN stood for Minimum Essential Emergency Communication Network: a two-way hardened teletype link between Strategic Air Command headquarters and the Minuteman silos.

"GWEN?" This was one of the few times that Mapplethorpe smiled. It sounded as if they were talking about some promiscuous woman.

"She's on board." GWEN was the Ground Wave Emergency Network consisting of seventy-five relay stations, each containing a three-hundred-foot transmission tower. This was the backup communications system that would theoretically survive a nuclear attack.

"Fleet Satellite Communications of the Navy is fully operational." Using this network, Mapplethorpe could still communicate directly with the Trident and Polaris nuclear submarines after a Soviet first-strike nuclear attack.

"MILSTAR?"

"All systems are go on that one." This was the Pentagon's latest toy, thought Shaw. It was the Military Strategic Tactical and Relay System, which provided some of the most sophisticated hardware in the spy/navigation business. As best as he could remember, it contained three polar and four geostationary orbit satellites that would provide navigational and communications backup during a nuclear attack.

After entering the building, the two men rode in the small walnut-paneled elevator up to the fourth floor and proceeded down shining marble corridors under high-arched ceilings.

Glancing quickly at the titles on the large oak doors, Shaw was impressed by the titles. There was an Assistant Deputy Counselor to the President for Minority Affairs. Next to that one was the Office of Public Communication as well as the Office of the Special Assistant to the President for Community and Religious Affairs. The only office that was missing, thought Shaw, was DOBS, the Director of the Office of Bull Shit.

"Here we are," Mapplethorpe said as he punched out a secret code on the black buttons affixed to the door, marked Room E-406, Office of the National Security Advisor. But the door wouldn't open. "Sonny, what's wrong here?"

Whenever Mapplethorpe was upset, he would call him Sonny. Otherwise, he addressed him as Colonel Shaw.

"Sir, I think today was the day that we changed the code combination."

"How the hell am I supposed to have confidence that MILSTAR or GWEN works when I can't even have my office door opened?" Mapplethorpe paced up and down in front of the door as Shaw tried out different code combinations. None worked. "I don't believe this! What the hell am I supposed to tell the President? I'm sorry, sir! I wanted to help you out, but I couldn't get into my office."

"I'm very sorry, sir." Shaw banged on the door.

"Hey, General, do you think the President is trying to send you a not-too-subtle message?" the Vice President's staff assistant said, smirking as he walked by. He was happy because the VP along with the Speaker of the House and the President of the Senate pro tem were all on a two-week fact-finding trip to the Far East.

"Wipe that shit-eating grin off your face or I'll do it for you," Shaw answered, but then was angry with himself.

"There is no reason to be abusive to one of our colleagues, is there?" Mapplethorpe interceded. "Please apologize to the young man, Colonel."

"Yes, sir." Shaw snapped to attention. "On behalf of General Mapplethorpe and myself, I would like to express our deepest apologies for any insult or injury that you may have experienced as a result of my inappropriate comment."

"Thank you, Colonel. I appreciate that." The staffer responded with an off-handed salute and continued sauntering down the hallway.

Finally, someone opened the door to the Baltimore Room from the inside. It was quite impressive. In contrast to the cloistered, ascetic tenor of the White House Sit Room, this room was large and well appointed. The high ceilings were crowned by hand-carved baroque molding, a vestige of President Harding's corrupt administration. The impressively long windows were framed by heavy silk-brocade drapes. In the center of the room stood a large rectangular mahogany table with antique brass inkwells placed before each of twelve seats. The sides of the room were decorated with different types of communications equipment, from the simple telephone, to the STU-3 secured telephone, to the TAC SAT, a portable secured communications system.

Hanging from the ceiling at each corner of the room were colored television sets tuned to each major TV network. By far, the most important for the management of an international crisis was Cable News Network, which had become the alternative intelligence venue to the CIA, the State Department's Office of Intelligence and Research, and even the Defense Intelligence Agency. Mapplethorpe himself had even begun to rely very heavily on CNN. It provided him with the most up-to-the-minute live coverage of ongoing events. At one point during a previous crisis, when Mapplethorpe was trying to overthrow a Latin-American dictator, each of the two principals had communicated with the other through public pronouncements on CNN, rather than using an unreliable CIA back channel.

On the far end of the room were rear projection screens that gave Mapplethorpe the ability to monitor any and all parts of his national security apparatus as well as his military force structure. At any given moment, he could determine the latest deployment of troops anywhere around the world.

The room had been developed by a National Security Advisor several administrations back. At that time, it was intended to be a communications relay depot through which all secured and nonsecured traffic from both State and CIA would pass. However, it was perceived by various senior officials as a way of monitoring their agencies. As a result, many agencies refused to have their communications lines pass through Baltimore. No cabinet officers were willing to attend meetings in the room, claiming it was too far out of their way. In short, no one wanted to visit Baltimore if they didn't have to.

But Baltimore was the center of Mapplethorpe's power base. He had successfully accomplished what no other National Security Advisor had been able to do. He had mandated, through the President, that all departments, agencies, and offices involved in any way with national security, military, or intelligence matters had to route their communications traffic through this room. There were to be no exceptions, bar one: the National Reconnaissance Office, the most secret and sensitive of all the agencies. It was responsible for managing satellite reconnaissance programs for the entire U.S. intelligence community.

At the moment, he needed to get a status report on the deteriorating situation in Wildeck, Germany. He flicked out the lights and the twenty people working in the room stopped what they were doing. The rear projection screen started to descend slowly.

Mapplethorpe looked carefully at the first slide marked TOP SECRET/ NO FORN/NO CON/CODE WORD: CLOSE LOOK.

The photograph showed a formation of six Russian T-72 battle tanks and one dozen BTR-60s surrounding a half dozen American M1A1 Abrams tanks. The tanks appeared to be moving toward a howitzer 109.

"Colonel Shaw, what can you tell me about this situation?"

"Sir, a Major Roger Gross, Troop Commander, 5th Squadron, 11th U.S. Armored Cavalry Regiment, is completely surrounded by the Russians."

"Have they started firing yet?"

"No, but they're a hair trigger away from an all-out war."

"Shaw, get me Major Gross directly!" Mapplethorpe sounded angry. Events were out of control.

"Do you want me to go through the National Military Communications Center?"

"What did I say?"

"Directly, sir."

"Yes, directly!" Mapplethorpe repeated.

Shaw sat down in front of the portable TAC SAT equipment and began to transmit. The transmission signal was completely distorted by interference from the downtown office buldings. TAC SAT could only work if there were unimpeded transmission of its K-band microwave to a passing WWMCCS satellite, which would then be bounced back to an InterSat transponder in a geostationary orbit. From there, it would downlink to an antennae farm in Wiesbaden, Germany, to Gross's M1A1 Abrams tank.

"Sir, I'm sorry, but I can't seem to reach him."

"Are you certain?" Mapplethorpe was impatient with Shaw. First, there was the matter with the door. Now, a serious problem with the transmitter.

"All right, forget it!" Mapplethorpe pressed the clicker. "Let's see what we have available if the situation gets out of hand. At the rate the crisis is escalating, we may have to begin to think about using one of our more unthinkable options."

"Sir, I've got Gross on the line." Shaw was excited to have overcome the man-made urban obstacles of concrete and steel.

"Gen . . . e . . . r . . . a . . . Map . . . p . . . l . . . e . . . t . . . h . . . , we' . . . re . . . unde . . . r . . . h . . . e . . . a . . . v . . . y . . ."

"I'm having a hard time understanding you." Mapplethorpe pressed the telephone receiver tightly to his ear.

"T . . . 72 . . . s . . . B . . . M . . . Rs . . . in . . . f . . . a . . . n . . . t . . . r . . . y . . . Mi-. . . 24 . . ."

"Mi-24?" Mapplethorpe deplored his own lack of knowledge about sophisticated weapons. Because he had little battlefield experience, he had to rely on a visual memory of a written description of most of the new weapons. He occasionally went over to the Aberdeen Proving Ground in Maryland to see some new weapon being tested. And Russian weapons, especially, were less clearly ingrained in his mind.

"Mi-24 Hind is a low-speed rotary wing ground attack aircraft." Shaw embellished the description slightly so that Mapplethorpe's ignorance would not appear as serious.

"It's a goddamn high-speed Russian helicopter, is that it, Shaw?"

"Yes, sir."

"Need . . . p . . . e . . . r . . . m . . . i . . . s . . . s . . . i . . . on . . . to detonate the S . . . A . . . D . . . M."

"Permission denied." Mapplethorpe knew only too well that SADM was the acronym for the Special Atomic Demolition Munition, a man-portable nuclear land mine designed to wreck an autobahn junction or block a valley. It was no bigger than a picnic basket and no heavier than a home set of barbells. Detonating the SADM would certainly precipitate a nightmare. Gross had his orders. And they didn't include precipitating a nuclear attack.

"E . . . n . . . c . . . o . . u . . n . . . t . . . e . . . r . . . i . . . n . . . g
massive amounts of . . . Category I D . . . i . . . v . . i . . . s . . . i . . .
o . . . n . . . s . . . C . . . a . . . n . . . n . . . o . . . t . . . r . . . e . . . s
. . . i . . . s . . . t . . . f . . . o . . . r . . . l . . . o . . . n . . . g . . . if . . .
t . . . h . . . e . . . y . . . f . . . i . . . g . . . h . . . t . . . ."

"Permission denied! Do you read me? Under no condition will you detonate the Special Atomic Demolition Munition. Is that understood?" Mapplethorpe didn't hear any response.

The situation was obviously worse than Mapplethorpe had anticipated,
but he was determined not to be drawn into a worst-case scenario. President
Westview would have to be notified quickly of the sudden turn in events.
Now Mapplethorpe understood why McCormick, during the morning's Crisis
Management Group meeting, had claimed that the Defense Intelligence
Agency didn't have any recent intelligence. That was unmitigated bullshit.
There was no way that McCormick, an Air Force general, didn't have
access to his own KH-8 Close Look or KH-9 Big Bird satellites. They were
controlled by the Air Force and their final processed photographs were passed
on to the NRO and then to him at the NSC. The son of a bitch had just
wanted Mapplethorpe to be the one to present the bad news to the President.
Did he really think that DOD would be insulated from any responsibility for
the impending mess?

"Sir, is there anything wrong?"

"Get me General McCormick, STAT!"

"What about Major Gross?" Shaw couldn't hold the connection on TAC
SAT too much longer. The communications link was breaking up.

"Keep him on the line as long as possible." Mapplethorpe had to know
exactly what was going on and who knew what, before he could execute any
further orders. "Where the hell is McCormick?"

"His secretary told me that he is in a meeting and cannot be disturbed."

Shaw looked around the room, trying to elicit support from the others.
But they were too smart to have any direct dealings with a boss they collectively judged to be mercurial and excessively demanding. Each professional
in the room had been secured from one of the military or intelligence
services, so their basic allegiance to Mapplethorpe would always be suspect.

"Tell his secretary that the President wants him on the phone right away.
Tell her to interrupt his goddamn meeting."

"Yes, sir." Shaw listened as the frightened secretary again explained that
it was impossible to interrupt her boss. She could get fired.

Mapplethorpe grabbed the phone. "Damnit, madam! I must talk to General McCormick now! Is that understood?" There was dead silence on the
other end of the phone. Mapplethorpe was certain she had gone to get
McCormick. What a joke, he thought. Sixty percent of crisis management
was convincing some scared GS-15 that her boss had to answer his telephone.

"What's so urgent, Tommy?" McCormick's smooth voice was a welcome sound to Mapplethorpe.

"Why didn't you tell me that there are Category I motor rifle divisions surrounding Major Gross and his troops?"

"Is this what you got me out of the meeting for? You couldn't wait another thirty minutes?"

"I may not have another thirty minutes. I've got Major Gross of the 11th U.S. Armored Cavalry Regiment on the other line and he's ready to use the SADM in order to stop the advancing Russian troops."

"What the hell can I do about that now?"

"I need to get an accurate reading of what our men are confronting before I send in reinforcements."

"What makes you think I have any better access to intelligence than you do?"

"Ronny, don't make my life more complicated than it already is."

"Tommy, don't you think you might want to leave these problems just where they belong, with the Commander-in-Chief of United States European Command and his line commanders? It would keep you out of trouble."

"Thanks for the free advice. But you know that anything less than the President's personal intervention at this point would not be appropriate, considering the gravity of the situation. Wouldn't you agree?"

Mapplethorpe knew he hadn't answered the question. But that wasn't the purpose of the conversation. He wanted McCormick to understand that from now on he, Mapplethorpe, would be managing the crisis. And he expected McCormick and the Chiefs of the services to support him completely. He also wanted to reemphasize the point that he expected to have access to all satellite intelligence. That meant control of NRO.

"All right, I'll make you a deal. I'll give you what you need. But in turn, I must know what you plan to do." McCormick knew he was asking for the moon. But it was worth a try.

"Of course." Each knew the other was lying. But that was par for the course in the management of a crisis.

"Switch to a STU-3. Secure," Mapplethorpe ordered.

Mapplethorpe turned the black plastic key on his STU-3 and watched the electrical panel along the top of the secured telephone: TOP SECRET/DOD, JCS/McCormick/SECURED. He pushed a black button on the panel. He could now converse with McCormick with the compelling illusion that they were protected from hostile electronic intercept. Mapplethorpe was not predisposed to believe that half of the electronic equipment he had to use during the course of a day really worked. But the game of maintaining vigilance during a crisis required that he act as if he believed that a shield of electronic security enveloped him and every other senior government official.

"DIA readings this morning from Big Bird and Close Look reveal a heavy concentration of Category I motor rifle divisions moving toward coordinates 307, 309, and 401," McCormick said.

"Why the hell didn't you tell me this morning?" Mapplethorpe realized how much he had underestimated the real threat to the 5th Squadron. Within minutes, if not an hour, they could be totally wiped out. He turned toward Shaw, asking by hand signals whether Gross was still on the TAC SAT. Shaw indicated that he had lost him.

Ignoring Mapplethorpe's question, McCormick replied, "According to the snapshots I've got here, they've sent in a full Category I motor rifle division, consisting of three motor rifle regiments and a tank regiment. What's really bothersome about these pictures though, is that unlike most Category I divisions, these divisions are fortified with three rifle battalions and one tank battalion. And unlike their regular tank battalion, this one contains three companies each of three platoons, with four tanks per platoon. And that's the good news."

"You're kidding me."

"I wish I were. You're sure you want to hear the truth?"

"Should I stand or sit?"

"My suggestion is to lie down. There's a caravan of men and weapons that looks as if it comes out of an epic film. The motor rifle regiment has its own artillery as well as an antitank battalion equipped with wire-guided antitank missiles. But that's not all. The regimental anti-aircraft batteries are equipped with four ZSU-23/4 tracked multiple cannon and four SA-9 surface-to-air missile platoons."

"What in God's name are they doing with surface-to-air missiles?"

"Tommy, I'm surprised that you're surprised. This is a big boys game. They're not playing around. These are serious folks. As best as we can count, each tank regiment of the motor rifle division contains three tank battalions of thirty-one tanks each, plus combat and service support, including a ZSU anti-aircraft battery. And the combat support unit contains a Frog battalion with four launchers, an artillery regiment with over fifty 122 millimeter howitzers, a multiple rocket launcher battalion with eighteen multiple rocket launchers, and an antitank battalion, plus reconnaissance, engineer, Nuclear Bacteriological Chemical defense, signal, and various other support units."

"What haven't they sent in?" Mapplethorpe asked, overwhelmed. This is not what he had expected. And time was running out.

"So far, they've kept all their nuclear crap under wrap. But our HUMINT tells us that may not be the case for very long," McCormick replied.

"What ever happened to their new political thinking—their new military doctrine of sufficiency? That they would use only the amount of force that was required to defend themselves adequately. Not more. Not less."

"Less, Tommy," McCormick said, knowing that the familiar form of Mapplethorpe's first name irritated him. "They could be using some of their nuclear babies."

"What do you think they are waiting for?"

"They're waiting to see if we use our Pershings, our Honest Johns, or Lances."

"How many do we have on hand that are operational?"

"Honestly?"

"Don't bullshit me, not now."

"I don't really know. Officially we have seventy-two Pershings on German soil; ninety Honest Johns in Greece and Turkey; and ninety-seven Lance missiles in Belgium, Germany, Italy, and Holland. One notch below Maximum Vigilance status. All on DEFCON TWO."

"How many of them can get off the ground without first blowing up our own ground crews around them?"

"Tommy, I never realized what a cynic you are."

"In twenty years of working with you and your people, Ronny, I've learned to acquire a healthy skepticism about your trajectory estimates."

"You mean you don't believe that the SSKP for each of our missiles is .96?" McCormick had to restrain his sarcasm. Everyone knew that the Single Strike Kill Probability ratio, a measure of the missile's ability to leave the ground, enter trajectory, and remain on course, was significantly less than 70 percent. But if the Air Force published that fact, it would be the end of any future missile programs, as well as the end of any other major Air Force projects. Truth was a panacea for those who could do very little with it. Only hard-worn skepticism, layered over with a thin veneer of self-delusion, could allow one to survive in the world of the bureaucrat, especially the military technocrat who had to create and defend numbers that had no correspondence to reality. But that was their livelihood. And as he would often say after a couple of drinks, "Don't ever fuck around with a man's bread and butter."

While listening to McCormick, Mapplethorpe flashed on the screen a slide, entitled "MC 14/3: NATO Nuclear Targeting."

Although NATO was no longer a viable force in Europe, its nuclear targets were identical to those of the U.S. military, which was no great surprise to him. Plans for both were developed by the same JCS Strategic Planning Group. But he had direct control of the tactical nuclear weapons in the European theater by having rerouted all the communications linkages from the NRO and the NSA through Baltimore.

Mapplethorpe had to know exactly what was available to him in the European theater. But only McCormick really knew what on that list was operational.

"Ronny, I've got MC 14/3 up on the screen. Let's take a walk through it."

"I can tell you right now that a lot of that is outdated. I just told you what we had and what was operational."

"I read you. Just indulge an old man."

"All right, old man, you've got it. But you owe me one big one." He wasn't kidding. One day he would draw down on Mapplethorpe's line of credit.

"It says that we have 2,250 nuclear artillery shells."

"We have about one thousand," McCormick replied.

"One thousand eight hundred fifty free-fall nuclear bombs."

"Six hundred fifty would be more accurate."

"What happened?"

"Rust. Deterioration. Poor maintenance."

"You mean SOP."

"Pretty much."

"What about the seven hundred Nike Hercules SAMs?"

Mapplethorpe was beginning to get the idea that he might be in charge of very little. Like all National Security Advisors who think they have more detailed knowledge than the bureaucracy, he resented having to rely on the Joint Chiefs. With the significant cutbacks in the military budget over the past ten years since the deterioration of the Soviet Union, and despite the successful Iraq War, less money was being appropriated to the care and feeding of the once new and exciting weapons of death.

"Tommy, we're just finishing the final touches on replacing the nuclear Nike Hercules with the non-nuclear Patriot missiles. But we've put in about 250 Patriots. Not very impressive."

"Four hundred antisubmarine weapons?"

"Forget them! We've literally deep-sixed them."

"Three hundred atomic demolition munitions, nuclear land mines?"

"There, I've got some good news for you. We still have a full complement of three hundred left."

"Well that's the first piece of good news I've heard in a couple of hours." Mapplethorpe paused. "You've already given me the read-outs on the Pershing, the Honest John, and the Lance."

"So, what are you going to do?"

"I don't know. Major Gross wants to use the SADM in order to stop the Russian advance. I've turned him down—at least for now."

"Don't do anything precipitously."

"What do you mean?"

"I think you know what I mean." McCormick realized that he had just hooked himself a deep-sea bass that was trying to break loose. He would let him go this time, but only because he was still at a disadvantage. But hopefully not for long.

"Thanks for letting me pick your brains. I won't forget it." From now on, Mapplethorpe thought, he would be more careful in the way he handled McCormick. He pushed a button and turned the black key, shutting off his STU-3 telephone.

Mapplethorpe nodded his head and Shaw cleared the room of the twenty staffers.

The two of them sat alone in the room and carefully watched the screen.

TOP SECRET. NO DISTRIBUTION. EYES ONLY.
NO FORN/NO CON/HUMINT/SIGINT
CODEWORD: OPERATION BALTIMORE.
ESTIMATED TARGET TIME: 72 HOURS

# CHAPTER

## 9

Not all bouillabaisse is fish soup.

Sometimes it can be an ungainly mixture of unusual people committing unnatural and immoral acts.

For Army Colonel Matthew "Zarb" Zarbitski, a compact, compulsive forty-two-year-old Special Operations Forces commander wearing a black beret, detailed from the 82nd Airborne Division, 18th Airborne Corps, to USSOCOM at MacDill Air Force Base in Florida, the bouillabaisse consisted of elite troops from five different operational forces. Not since the war in the Persian Gulf had so many elite units of the U.S. Armed Forces fought in an integrated capacity alongside one another. But could he blend them into one effective fighting machine?

He fired his Colt Commando in short bursts, trying to preserve his ammunition and maintain his men's morale while they were forced to keep their heads down. Dropped twenty miles behind Russian lines, he and his group of twenty-five were waiting for the retrieval helicopter, a modified Sikorsky UH-60A Black Hawk, to pick them up.

Zarb was worried. They were running low on rations and ammunition and could not hold out much longer. Pinned down by a Soviet RPK 7.62 millimeter amidst the insufferable bushes and trees on the outskirts of Wildeck, he was concerned that they had not yet completed their mission of reconnoitering the area for any advanced Russian troop movements, and were not well positioned to be a decoy for the impending assault on Spetsnaz headquarters.

Zarb motioned to Sergeant Walter Johnson, a handsome, black twenty-nine-year-old Army Ranger from Fort Benning, Georgia, to take a handful of men and work their way slowly along the perimeter of the trees toward the machine gun. At the same time, he instructed Lieutenant Robert Rovner, a City College of New York graduate who had been detailed from the First Special Forces Group, Green Beret, at Fort Bragg, North Carolina, to take the dual purpose light/heavy M60 7.62 millimeter machine gun and approach the enemy from his left.

Zarb would provide fire cover from his Colt Commando, a cut-down version of the famous Armalite assault rifle that was not very popular among his elite fighters because of its thunderous muzzle flash. It was considered too noticeable, especially during night fighting. But the sun was beating down mercilessly, so he ignored their complaints.

He and his remaining group of men crawled through the prickly underbrush, maintaining continuous radio communication with both Johnson and Rovner.

"Charlie Zebra, this is Wasted Juice. I've got the Big E spotted at about one hundred feet."

Johnson knew he was taking creative liberties with his call signs. But Zarb had already been warned about Johnson's compulsive need to improvise. "Never be surprised by the Big J" was his standard warning to all his commanders. He knew that he could afford to be cavalier because he was good. Better than good.

"Wasted Juice, this is Charlie Zebra. I read you loud and clear. Be careful! The Big E can have you cornered very quickly if you don't watch yourself." Zarb's warning was too late. He could see one of Johnson's men climb up a tree.

The Spetsnaz soldiers, dressed in green camouflage, turned their attention away from the men on the ground and directed all of their considerable firepower at the man climbing the tree.

From Zarb's point of view, Johnson was either stupid or heroic—he couldn't decide which. Probably heroic. Only a few minutes ago, all of Zarb's men were pinned down by enemy fire. Now the situation was reversed. Johnson had selflessly drawn the enemy's fire away from them.

"Reckless Rider, this is Charlie Zebra. Do you read me?"

Zarb didn't receive a response from Rovner. He only heard the rapid fire of the M60 machine gun. Somewhere out there on his left, Rovner and his men were making their way toward the enemy.

"Charlie Zebra, this is Reckless Rider. I'm fifty feet away from the RPK. My men are fanning out toward the target. Any good-night stories or kisses before we bid our dear Spetsnaz friends a fond adieu?"

From beneath the twisted folds of the bushes and trees, Rovner could see the burst of fire from the RPK. He knew he had to get to the RPK before Johnson took it out. Just a simple matter of interservice pride. By tradition, a Green Beret could never lose out to a Ranger. When he saw Johnson's man climb the tree, attracting the RPK fire, Rovner realized he had to act quickly.

Looking up, Rovner saw the modified Sikorsky UH-60A Black Hawk helicopter hovering above him. The big eggbeater in the sky. He knew then he only had a few minutes left before the colonel would start pulling them out of the area. He had to do something dramatic, and fast.

But it was too late!

The Spetsnaz commandos were advancing too quickly on his group. What the hell had happened, he wondered.

Johnson was pulling his men back toward the landing zone. The man who had climbed up the tree slid down quickly and started to flee. But too late. A bullet hit him, and he fell to the ground.

Suddenly, the sound of an RPK 7.62 millimeter machine gun was everywhere, firing 660 rounds per minute in what seemed to Zarb a harbinger of imminent defeat.

Poised with his Colt, Zarb sprayed the area in front of him, trying to provide fire cover for his retreating forces.

"Pull back!" Zarb screamed into the portable Combat Net Radio. "That means you two guys, Rovner and Johnson. Do you read me?"

The radio was silent.

The enemy had simply reversed Zarb's strategy, and before he could recognize it, he and his men had been lured into a trap.

"Shit!" Zarb was annoyed with himself. He should have known better than to take on this assignment. But maybe he should be blaming his unit as well.

They were supposed to be the elite of the elite. But they weren't fighting as a unit. They had no sense of coordinated action. Each soldier was acting like a cowboy without a sense of group cohesion or purpose.

Unlike the synchronous whirring of the rotary blades of the modified helicopter beating a steady whirlwind above him, Zarb realized that the history of special warfare was marked with this type of inefficiency, redundancy, interservice rivalry, and lack of coordination.

When Mapplethorpe had personally recruited Zarb from the 2nd Battalion of the 75th Infantry Regiment at Fort Lewis in Washington State, he was given what was then described as an impossible assignment—to create an elite group to assault and protect highly sensitive targets. The group would be responsible directly to Mapplethorpe. Even then, Zarb had serious misgivings about the undertaking. And now, as his group of twenty-five of the best men in the service were in full retreat, he knew that any doubts he had were vindicated. He had an undercooked bouillabaisse, each fish with its own tradition and prerogative.

For hostage rescue, he had the Special Forces Operational Detachment Delta, or Delta Force as it was popularly known. Based on the British 22nd Special Air Service Regiment model, Delta Force was designed to provide a surgical strike capability for any potential terrorist episode. Organized into Squadrons A and B, containing sixteen men each, Delta Force was composed of highly select men, chosen for their intelligence and self-reliance, renowned for their marksmanship: 100 percent hits at 650 yards and 90 percent at 1,100 yards. But if they were so great, wondered Zarb, then why did they blunder so magnificently in their one major attempt at rescuing the American hostages held captive in Iran, in Operation Eagle Claw?

Then, of course, Zarb had several hotshots from the U.S. Army Special Forces, the Green Berets, like Lieutenant Robert Rovner, who was quickly retreating toward him, firing his M60 machine gun. He was typical of the wunderkinds that he was getting from the Green Berets.

Zarb watched as the helicopter began to descend. Funnels of dirt, grass, and debris arose from the woods like a series of mini-tornadoes sucking the Black Hawk downward to the ground.

As Johnson and Rovner's forces pulled back toward the landing zone, the exchange of gunfire became more intense. Like the hordes of Chinese crossing the Yalu River during the Korean War, the enemy began to swarm the perimeter of the landing zone. In a few more minutes, they could literally wipe out Zarb's forces.

As long as the enemy was hiding in the forest, the Black Hawk and the two accompanying AH-1 Huey Cobra gunships would not be able to land. The Spetsnaz would destroy the helicopters and pick off the men trying to reach them. So Zarb's objective had to be to keep the enemy fire at a distance to allow his men safe access to the helicopters.

He needed some kind of marker placed on the enemy so that the gunships could identify them and strike without injuring any of his own men in the process.

"Reckless Rider, this is Charlie Zebra, do you read me?"

"Read you loud and clear, Charlie Zebra. We're trapped! I've got a couple of wounded kids here who have to be medivacked out."

"Can you place a marker on our friends crawling along the forest floor, so the boys upstairs can neutralize them?"

"Let's see what we can do, Colonel." Rovner switched over to Johnson. "Hey bro! Cover me!"

"One firefight, nice and easy."

Johnson opened up with a barrage of M10 submachine gun fire as Rovner and two of his men ran toward the enemy.

Rovner tied a couple of white phosphorous smoke flares to a Claymore antipersonnel mine and hurled it into the bushes. The area burst into a ball of fire. The Spetsnaz commandos came running out of the woods, screaming, their bodies ablaze.

Rovner opened fire with his machine gun and put the fleeing Spetsnaz soldiers out of their misery.

Following the direction of the white incandescent light, the two Cobra gunships swooped down like vultures ready to devour rotting carcasses and released four of their eight TOW missiles.

The screams became louder. The smoke became thicker and darker.

Rovner ordered his men to retreat back to the landing zone, covering their retreat with short bursts from his machine gun. "Let's get the hell out of here!"

The two Cobra gunships made another run over the burning area, opening up with their 20 millimeter cannons and releasing their remaining missiles.

A flaming sun of destruction rose above the horizon of dead bodies. The smell of burning flesh permeated the air.

Panting with fear and exhaustion, Rovner and his two men arrived at the landing site. At the same time, the helicopter started to take off with ten men on board. A second Black Hawk had just flown in and was hovering above waiting to pick up the remainder of the group.

"Come on, you guys, hurry up!" As Zarb tried to urge the remaining fifteen men forward, a Spetsnaz soldier armed with an RPG-22 broke through Zarb's perimeter of defense and fired an 84 millimeter shell right into the ascending helicopter. Within a moment's breath, the helicopter blew up. Only Johnson and Rovner survived intact.

The remaining men fell to the ground, five seriously injured. The few remaining opened fire—but only after the Spetsnaz had shattered their myth of invincibility. Zarb's men were no longer an elite unit. They would become only another group of American soldiers who had died in action in a location unlisted in high school textbooks; because according to official records, this firefight had never occurred.

As Zarb boarded the second Black Hawk helicopter, the pilot turned around toward him and gave him a classified message.

TOP SECRET/SENSITIVE/EYES ONLY/HAND DELIVER TO COLO-NEL MATTHEW ZARBITSKI. IMMEDIATELY WITHDRAW FROM GERMAN FIELD OF OPERATIONS. RETURN TO USSOCOM, MAC-DILL AFB, FLORIDA. ASAP. BY PERSONAL REQUEST OF PRESI-DENT DONALD WESTVIEW. FURTHER ORDERS TO FOLLOW.

# CHAPTER

## 10

A President's motorcade in Washington is like a Macy's Thanksgiving Day Parade in New York City.

If left up to President Westview, he would convert every one of his motorcades into a festive parade with him as a political Santa Claus who was both jovial and beneficent, dispensing patronage and political favors as if they were Christmas presents. Even more, he loved the whole notion of an impromptu press conference at any and all events because he liked to be seen in motion.

To Mary Dougherty, it presented a virtual nightmare to keep the President bound to his schedule and inside his bulletproof limousine. His motorcade was the focal point of a highly orchestrated procession of people, cars, and resources. And with the crisis in Western Europe, every event she arranged for the President had been thrown off schedule. She now had to contend with the worst of all situations—the imperatives of a predetermined schedule in total conflict with the President's own desires. In fact, the President seemed increasingly more whimsical about his time.

Normally, she would be advised of any changes in his schedule at least twenty-four hours beforehand so she could check out the background of everyone with whom he might be meeting. Today, she had been informed by Randy, the President's appointments secretary, that he would be headed to Saint Elizabeth Hospital, once the largest federal mental institution in the United States, which a decade ago had been deeded to the District of Columbia. But since she was given only a fifteen-minute warning, she was unable to check out anyone the President might be seeing. And of all places—a mental institution containing some of the sickest patients in the United States.

"Hold your horses, boys, Zorro is still on the front lawn holding a press conference."

Mary spoke into the flesh-colored microphone in the sleeve of her sport jacket. She was talking to David Brooks, a twenty-eight-year-old recruit who had joined the Secret Service six months before, and John Dobbins, a seasoned forty-three-year-old former Washington policeman who was one of ten black agents on the President's detail.

"Hey, boss, the cars are going to blow a gasket unless we start to move," Brooks replied.

Brooks was an attractive ex-Ranger who had served with the 2nd Battalion, 75th Infantry Regiment, Fort Lewis, Washington. He had just returned from his yearly Army Reserve duty. When asked what he did, he simply broke out into a sheepish grin and said that he had some sun and fun.

"Listen, hotshot, when you become the prez then we'll follow your advice." Mary didn't like his impudence.

Although she found him boyishly attractive, with his flaxen hair falling carefree over his forehead, Mary had increasingly less patience with his impetuous nature. He was sloppy. For someone who had been trained in Special Operations, including the martial arts, he seemed inordinately lax and carefree. Something was wrong, but she couldn't quite place her finger on it. There was a certain quality of inappropriate innocence mixed with a contrived smart-ass quality.

"Mary, I've got the motorcade lined up, headed southeast out of Pennsylvania Avenue," Dobbins responded patiently.

Dobbins was assigned to cover Brooks. He was responsible for making certain that Brooks was familiar with all the standard procedures required to protect the President. As far as Dobbins was concerned, Brooks was still significantly behind on the learning curve.

"How are we positioned right now, John?" Mary asked.

She was standing on the front lawn of the White House facing Pennsylvania Avenue, watching the group of reporters set up their klieg lights and TV cameras. She knew most of them by their first name. And those she didn't know were recognizable from their news shows.

Without consulting his advisors, the President had requested an impromptu press conference to discuss the deteriorating situation between the U.S. and the Russian Federation. But Mary couldn't concentrate on the content of Westview's message. She was too busy surveying the people around him, trying to spot that one person who might attempt something dangerous against the President of the United States.

Westview walked down from the circular driveway onto the front lawn and stood in front of the TV cameras, positioned like lemmings ready to fall off a promontory. His objective was simple: Appeal directly to the American public. Appear in control and sound reassuring. Above all else, avoid any confrontation with the press. Allow them to seem petty and peevish.

Mapplethorpe and Shaw stood in the distance, watching the spontaneous mini–press conference.

"Good afternoon, ladies and gentlemen. I know you are all anxious to hear some news about our problem in Western Europe. Let me share with you the latest information. Yesterday afternoon several divisions of Russian soldiers that had been stationed in the eastern part of Germany for the past several years as part of the 1991 Gorbachev-Kohl agreements on the reunification of Germany were ordered to return to Russia. They refused. Instead, taking matters into their own hands, they engaged in provocative military exercises against U.S. military units normally stationed in Germany. Unfortunately, as a result of overreaction on both sides, arising from misperceptions, misunderstandings, and poor communications, a crisis mounted rapidly.

"Let me just say that there is no reason to panic. Contrary to reports in the media, we are not, I repeat, not at war with the Russian Federation. Just the opposite, I think it would be fair to say that representatives from both countries are working around the clock trying to resolve this misunderstanding in a cooperative, harmonious way. We are extremely optimistic that we will be able to find a mutually satisfactory solution. I am in constant contact with Igor Zotov, the President of the Russian Federation."

"Mr. President?" Julia Bond, a well-coiffed, self-possessed CNN anchorwoman with a master's degree in political science, raised her hand.

"Yes, Ms. Bond?"

"Mr. President, first of all, I want to ask whether there has been a news blackout, like the one we had in the Iraq War?"

"No, Ms. Bond. Why do you ask?"

Westview glanced surreptitiously at Mapplethorpe, who, in turn, nodded his head. He knew the President was lying. Mapplethorpe was impressed by the President's performance. He sounded appropriately concerned, while at the same time projected a guarded optimism. The only thing that was missing was the truth. But it would take the journalists and the American public several days before they figured out what, in fact, had really happened. And then it would be too late.

"Because, Mr. President, we have heard absolutely nothing from either the White House or the State Department since this war—"

"May I remind you once again, Ms. Bond, that there is no war. There has been no major engagement of either U.S. or Russian troops. What we have at this very moment is a miscommunication of intent, which I assure you that I and my staff have been monitoring very closely. As a matter of fact, I have just gotten off the phone with President Zotov. He and I discussed our mutual concerns and explored several constructive ways of defusing the situation. In particular, we will request the Secretary General of the United

Nations to intervene as a mediator, and, if need be, be prepared to send a UN International Peacekeeping Force to Germany within forty-eight hours notice."

After years of managing the media in both domestic and international crises, Westview had learned several important lessons: Take control of a crisis as quickly as possible; make certain that the media projects him as the image of a statesman who is very much in charge of the situation; select carefully those lies you want to disseminate to the public in order to maintain the appearance of a self-confident, proactive crisis manager. Actually, he had not been able to contact Zotov. Nor did he have any intention of calling up the Secretary General of the UN. But it was true that he was committed to resolving the crisis—only it would be done his way!

"Mr. President," the anchorwoman picked up, "most Americans believe that this crisis is far more serious than you or your senior officials have portrayed. There are unconfirmed reports that you have placed our armed forces on Maximum Vigilance status. Is that right? And if so, why did you do it if this is not a serious crisis or if war is not imminent?"

"Ms. Bond, as I have just said, what we have at present is a problem between two old adversaries that arose from a serious misunderstanding between renegade Russian military units that tried to provoke a confrontation with some of our armored troops stationed in Germany. We are not at Maximum Vigilance."

"Are you, then, formally accusing the Russians of starting a war? And what has been the official German reaction to this crisis?"

"Ms. Bond, in all fairness to the other journalists present here, I will answer your question, then pass on to someone else."

"Fine, Mr. President!" Bond was impressed by the way Westview maintained his composure and was manipulating the press conference. Clearly, this was his game, and she doubted whether any of the journalists could wrest it away from him. However, her curiosity was piqued by his use of the word "problem," a word that spanned a range somewhere between "military provocation" and "major engagement." And that left the President a lot of room in which to maneuver with the truth.

"No! I have not either formally or informally accused the Russians of precipitating a war, because I don't believe that they want a war with us or anyone else. They have too many problems of their own at home to worry about anything other than fighting for their economic and political stability. So it is not surprising that Russian President Zotov has been unable to contain some of their more, shall I say, rambunctious military units from engaging in seditious activities both against the Russian Federation itself and some of its adjoining neighbors. As you well know, since the disintegration of the Soviet Union several years ago, the presidents of the different independent republics have had an extremely difficult time controlling their respective military units and security organizations. As a result of those long-standing problems, I have had a standing order, for some time now, to place our forces on DEFCON TWO in order to respond to any crisis as quickly as possible. As my doctor likes to say, 'An ounce of prevention is worth a pound of cure.'

"As to your final point, Ms. Bond, I and Secretary of State Chester Manning are in constant consultation with our German and European allies. And we are all in full agreement that this problem must be resolved as expeditiously and fairly as possible, and whatever transgressions have been committed will be addressed later, at a more appropriate time. For the moment, we all share one common goal—peace—at all cost."

Even Bond had to admit that she wanted to believe everything the President was saying. He sounded so confident, knowledgeable, and reassuring. But in some disturbing way, it was too smooth. Westview had a reputation of acting cool under stress. Some journalists even went so far as to call him the Ice Man.

"Any further questions?" Westview could feel the flush of success. He was sure that he had effectively co-opted the media with his well-honed media spin of good intentions, half-truths, wishful thinking—presented with a composed demeanor. By the time the media dissected his press conference, most of what he really intended to do would have already been implemented. And if not, then he would hold another press conference trying to explain "the insurmountable barriers" that led to his "inevitable failure."

Then in a contrite voice, he would ask for forgiveness from the American public, which he knew had been conditioned over the past several decades to tolerate almost any number of political transgressions, deceptions, and failures as long as the politician admitted his shortcomings and said he was sorry. He would then proceed to present another agenda of half-truths, wishful thinking, and unrealistic hopes.

And so it would continue, until the public or the media became fed up with his smooth evasiveness. But that rarely happened. Like his more formidable presidential predecessors, Westview knew that public inertia and indifference was his best shield against the truth.

"One last question, please." Westview felt comfortable pointing to Carl Bradford, a middle-aged freelance television and newspaper journalist who had a history of exasperating the President.

"Mr. President, is it true that Dr. Daniel Fitzpatrick, one of your senior National Security Council analysts, has been murdered in Tokyo?" Bradford usually waited until Westview finished responding to a previous question, then would insert a new question in an attempt to throw the President off-balance. As with most journalists, covering a crisis or an incident was simply another opportunity to play the game of games—who appears to be most knowledgeable and competent. It was a game of one-upmanship.

"I'm glad you asked that question, Mr. Bradford. Dr. Fitzpatrick was one of my most talented and dedicated national security experts, and he will be very much missed by everyone who knew him. I've called his family and extended my personal condolences to them. I also swore to them that I would stop at nothing to uncover the strange circumstances of his death. The Japanese government has also promised they will provide me with all the necessary assistance and cooperation."

"Any suspects yet?" Bradford asked.

"I'd rather not comment on that matter at this point in the investigation." Westview waved the journalists farewell and walked toward his waiting limousine, a stream of questions following in his wake.

Mary pushed aside the still unsatiated swarm of media vultures. Brooks opened the rear door of the bulletproof black limousine and the President entered.

"Dobbins, I want you in the lead car," Mary ordered. "Brooks, you'll cover my right flank. I'll be riding shotgun for Zorro." She watched the twenty men in her security detachment disperse to their assignments, and slid into the driver's seat.

Brooks sat quietly alongside her, his uncocked Uzi machine gun in his lap, scanning the road. Occasionally he glanced at Mary. He didn't trust her. She seemed to try too hard. But he found her slightly pugged Irish nose quite attractive.

Glancing in the rear-view mirror, Mary watched the President make himself comfortable. She barked commands to her subordinates making certain that a simple car ride from one end of the city to the other end didn't turn into a day of infamy, a favorite expression of hers. She pressed the accelerator, drove down the driveway, and waited a few seconds as the hydraulically driven steel antiterrorist barriers embedded along the front of the White House driveway descended slowly into the ground. The uniformed White House executive guards, with their crested brocaded officer's hats, held the metal gates open and waved her on.

The entire motorcade proceeded down Pennsylvania Avenue, past homeless men and women bundled together over metal gratings at Lafayette Park, directly across the street from the White House.

Mary was becoming inured to the hand-painted signs proclaiming everything from the imminent destruction of the world to the premature resurrection of Christ. Lafayette Park had become an incredible eyesore, filled with wooden placards and pup tents.

"Dobbins, this is Mary! What's holding up Zorro?"

"We've got a huge white tractor-trailer turning right onto Ninth Street. He's holding everything up," Dobbins replied.

"Use the gumball machine and let's pick up some speed. Otherwise, we'll never get to St. E's in time for the arrival ceremonies."

"What do they do? Give out Thorazine tablets as a welcome gift?" Brook's sarcasm grated on her nerves.

Although she was concentrating on the progress of the motorcade, she was preoccupied by two disturbing thoughts. Why, in the middle of a potentially earth-shaking crisis, does the President of the United States decide to visit a mental institution? And why does he insist on traveling by car when it would have been easier to have flown by helicopter directly from the White House lawn to either the Naval Station or Bolling Air Force Base? Each was only ten minutes from the hospital. When she thought about it longer, she realized that Westview always preferred the ceremonial trappings of a motorcade over boring helicopter flights. But why visit St. E's?

As the motorcade started to pick up speed, Mary relaxed. Her need to remain vigilant was directly related to how fast the caravan moved. At highway speeds of at least sixty-five miles an hour, she was less concerned about a possible attack from an assailant than with the possibility of an accident. But according to her inverse rule of security, the more vigilant she became, the less probable was a crisis. The air traffic over National Airport was a good example of what she meant. It seemed as if the more congested the sky became over Washington's main airport, the fewer the accidents that occurred. She often wondered why. And then one day the answer came to her. It was really quite simple. A situation recognized as potentially danger-ous forces one to be that much more careful. Therefore, the greater the perceived possibility of an accident or a crisis, the less likely it is to occur. Unfortunately, there were always exceptions to a rule. And she was afraid that she was heading into one of those exceptions at St. E's.

The motorcade turned right onto Ninth Street as a tractor-trailer moved out in front of them, forcing the procession to slow.

In all, there were seven cars in the motorcade. With sirens blaring and lights flashing, the two uniformed District officers, riding their Harley-Davidsons, led the way. Although Mary was their direct supervisor, techni-cally they reported to the chief of the Washington metropolitan police. So she had placed Dobbins in charge of them. In her mind all cops spoke the same language.

The rest of the motorcade consisted of an assortment of cars serving various functions. Right behind the two motorcycle policemen was a four-wheel drive Jeep Wagoneer carrying six Secret Service agents armed with Uzi submachine guns and sawed-off double-barreled shotguns. Mary was grateful she was not overseas. Otherwise she would also have to worry about the protocol car, containing a bevy of prima donnas, each one more demanding than the next.

Following another car, containing extra weapons and spare car parts, was the President's limousine. That was usually trailed by a follow-up car of Secret Service agents whose main function was to ride alongside the limou-sine, covering it from any potential assault as it turned corners. In back of the follow-up car was the control car with the White House Chief of Staff, a military aide carrying the mysterious black box from which the President could launch a nuclear attack, and one or two other allegedly indispensable aides. Hangers-on, as she called them.

Bringing up the rear was the support car, which contained the press spokesman, the official White House photographer, as well as a military medic and his requisite medical emergency kit—oxygen tank, complete surgical cut-down and suture kit. On an overseas assignment, Mary might be responsible for managing an additional White House car, followed by two more staff vans, two camera vans, two wire vans containing all the electrical equipment for the cameras, and two or more press vans.

"We're passing the National Gallery of Art, heading south across the mall at Ninth Street, beneath the underpass. Do you read me, Dobbins?" Mary was annoyed. There was no response. "Dobbins, do you read me?"

Because the Wagoneer in front of her was so high off the ground, she was not able to see either Dobbins's car or the uniformed motorcyclists in front of him. But it was often difficult to get effective communications going among the cars when passing through a tunnel or an underpass.

This tunnel was always dark. She could only see the Jeep in front of her and the follow-up car behind her. The motorcade barely moved.

"Papa Bear, this is Mother Hen. Do you read me?" Mary liked to call the two D.C. policemen Papa Bear because they were big and burly. Usually Papa Bear flashed their red lights in a dark underpass. It was a way of clearing the road. But this time there were no red lights.

Suddenly, there was a loud noise. It sounded like a burst of gunfire or a truck backfiring. A cloud of smoke exhaust filled up the underpass. She could barely see the Jeep in front of her. What the hell was going on?

Brooks looked at her as if to ask what now?

"Papa Bear, put those gumball machines on! Let's get the hell out of here!" she shouted into her microphone.

"Mother Hen, this is Papa Bear! That noise was simply the truck backfiring and spewing out some of its exhaust."

Brooks cocked his Uzi again. Just to make certain.

"Papa Bear! This is Mother Hen! Is everything all right?" Mary was having a hard time spotting either Dobbins or Papa Bear. She barely saw the white tractor-trailer truck speeding away from the underpass.

"This is Dobbins, boss. We're fine! For a moment there, we lost radio contact. The tractor-trailer had some exhaust problem, but it just left. We're moving out now at full speed to make up for lost time."

"Fine, Dobbins! This is Mother Hen signing off." Mary smiled with relief. The truck's exhaust backfire could just as easily have been the sounds of gunfire. Fortunately it wasn't. Her hyperacute response was one more piece of evidence to Mary that she should force herself to take a long-needed vacation.

Instead of continuing on to Route 295, she had the motorcade veer off onto the South Capitol Street exit, passing close to the dilapidated Washington Navy Yard where her father had once worked helping to build and refurbish battleships and aircraft carriers. But that was a very long time ago. And she had no desire to recall that painful period in her life.

They crossed the Frederick Douglass Bridge, spanning the polluted Anacostia River, which separated downtown Washington from the black ghettos of Anacostia.

Mary recognized the remnants of the World War II Quonset huts at the Anacostia Naval Annex. To her right was a row of three-story red-brick buildings surrounded by high metal fences cropped by barbed wire—Naval Station Washington, one of the many "disguised" centers in the Washington area, dedicated to analyzing aerial reconnaisance photographs. This was a more obvious location. In the other parts of town where they were doing similar work the facade was not as easily penetrated.

Farther down South Capitol Street, black alcoholics meandered about the street with bottles of cheap booze wrapped in brown paper bags, cheering the motorcade as it passed them by. It was a speeding distraction, much like an ambulance or police car headed for an emergency, without any particular relevance to their own lives.

"Mary, can we stop here for a few minutes? I'd like to get out and meet some of the folks," Westview asked.

By nature he was not a bigoted man, and he had never really learned to overcome his well-bred Northeastern guilt over the increasing disparity between those who were more fortunate, like himself, and those who were far less fortunate. In any case, he was a politician, and like all good politicians he had learned to appear reflexively concerned.

"Spare One, pull over to the side! We're making one of our PR guilt visits." Mary hated these impromptu stops. They were inherently dangerous. Unpredictable. Anything and everything could happen.

The motorcade stopped in front of a boarded-up, run-down movie theater. Westview got out of the car and shook hands with several of the derelicts sitting on the front stoops of the other boarded-up buildings near the theater. Like bees around a hive, the Secret Service agents from the motorcade swarmed all around the President and all over the block.

"Shit man, we got a snow storm comin'. I ain't never seen so much whiteness in all my born life." A tall, disheveled black man in his late forties, known in the neighborhood as Amos, started to swagger toward the President.

Mary became nervous. She physically interposed herself between the two men. Yet there was something familiar about the man. Had she seen him somewhere before?

"Dobbins, I need some help!" Mary shouted.

Dobbins walked over and frisked Amos.

"Hey bro, what's the problem? I ain't done nothin' wrong."

"Nobody said you did. Just think of me as your personal tailor, trying to fit you out for a new suit."

"Okay, bro! I like that!" Amos laughed.

Mary could always rely on Dobbins to handle a sensitive incident like this without appearing anxious or concerned, and without jeopardizing someone's life. He knew the tribal rites of his own people as well as she knew the customs and mores of those poor souls in Northern Ireland or the South End of Boston.

"Brooks, cover Zorro from across the street while I interdict this gentleman."

"Hi there! My name is Westview. President Donald Westview. What's yours?" Extending his right hand out in a clear sign of friendship, the President shook Amos's right hand.

"Prez, it's a definite pleshure to shake the hand of the man who calls the shots in these United States. But how do I know that you're the real prez like you say you are?" Amos tried to stand straight as he slurred his words.

More than at any other time in his life, he wanted to appear sober and, if possible, responsible. Within the fog of alcoholic distortion and euphoria, he wanted to command respectability. But the harder he tried, the worse it became.

"It's a pleasure to meet you, Mr. . . . ."

"Misteh Mastah . . ." Amos peered into the President's eyes. They were trying so hard to appear warm and caring. But Amos trusted his gut, as irritated as it might be, and his gut told him that there was something wrong with this man.

"I'm sorry, but I missed your name. You said Mr. . . . what was that again? Mr. . . . what?" Westview was trying hard to appear concerned.

"Mastah . . . you know like slave and mastah . . . that's what I am, the mastah. Do you read me?" Amos was suddenly flooded with feelings of rage.

"Mr. President, I think it's time for us to move on." Mary sensed the increasing hostility in this man.

"Please, Mary, I want to have an open field with this gentleman."

"That's right, Mary." Amos tried to put his arm around Mary's shoulder, but she threw it off.

"I wouldn't do that, bro!" Dobbins restrained Amos.

"Let the prez talk to a black man. He ain't nevah seen one. There ain't none workin' for the man. Except for you, bro! Anyway, didn't you hear what the prez said? Let him have an open field wid thiz gentleman. So he can take a better look at me. Right, Prez?"

"That's right," Westview replied as he indicated to Dobbins to let Amos go.

"Thiz iz one hip prez. But he ain't got much of a memory, does he, Mary?"

Mary quickly motioned several of her agents to move in and back Dobbins up. Something was about to happen.

Amos lurched forward and swung his right fist, knocking the President down. Mary and Dobbins pinned Amos down to the ground in seconds, whipping out their Smith & Wesson .38 pistols from their shoulder holsters, and pointing the guns at his head.

"Been here before, Mary, haven't we?"

"That was you . . ." Mary was hesitant to continue. She didn't want to say more than she had to. But she remembered him now.

"It's only fair, Mary. You know that."

Dobbins looked quizzically at Mary. He sensed there was a secret between them to which he should not be privy.

"It's all right, Dobbins! Let him go! I can handle him!"

"It make no difference that he be the prez. He knocked me out that night for no reason. You know that, Mary. You wuz there. It wuzn't fair. You know that."

"What's your name?" Mary helped him stand up while Dobbins looked at her with complete incredulity.

"They call me Amos. But my full name is James Erasmus Warner the third. Fancy ain't it?" With a clear sense of pride, he brushed himself off.

"Where do you live, Amos?"

"Everywhere, Miz Mary. Sometimes over the heat vents in front of the State Department. Sometimes near that building where you saw me last time."

She could see that Amos was harmless. He was one of the countless number of homeless who had become the urban gypsies of the 1990s. The Secret Service had a whole slew of names of homeless men, women, teenagers, and children who lived on the streets of every major city.

"The chief honcho wants to see you, boss!" Walking toward them, Brooks drew his Astra .357 and pointed it at Amos.

"Put that away, Brooks!" Dobbins said.

"Dobbins, who died and make you God?"

"All right, you two! Let's cut out the macho games!" Mary said.

"You don't need that, son. I ain't goin' to do anythin' that's goin' hurt anyone," Amos said.

"Sure, pops," Brooks responded. "Guys like you never hurt anyone. You just gave the President of the United States a slight, friendly type of tap on the face. Sure, you're harmless. Really harmless."

"Don't ride him, Brooks!" Dobbins shouted.

Mary watched the President pace up and down in front of the limousine, checking his watch.

"Sure, Dobbins. I'm going to take good care of him. Right, Amos?"

"Miz Mary, I don't trust this gentleman."

"Don't worry, Amos. Nothing is going to happen to you. Trust me. Isn't that right, Mr. Brooks?" Mary indicated to Brooks to put his gun away.

"Like I said, boss, the chief wants to see you right away."

"Dobbins, stay here! Make sure nothing happens!" Mary walked toward the President, glancing backward as Brooks pushed Dobbins aside and started to jostle Amos.

Dobbins reached out to grab Brooks.

"Dobbins, let Brooks handle that man," the President ordered. "If we don't get going, we'll be late for the opening ceremonies."

"Yes, Mr. President," Dobbins replied, looking at Mary for confirmation.

Reluctantly nodding her head in agreement, Mary accompanied Westview into the limousine as Brooks forcibly pushed a screaming Amos into a District police van while Dobbins stood helplessly by.

Mary wondered why they needed to take him away. He wasn't a danger to anyone. Amos was simply a helpless person whose pride had been hurt by none other than the President of the United States. If the President had apologized, Amos would have gone on with his aimless life.

For a minute, she felt a chill run through her body. It had been a long time since she had thought about her father. But Amos had reminded her of him. He had left the family when she was just a child. Neither she nor her mother knew what had happened to him.

Driving up Martin Luther King Avenue, Mary felt overwhelmed by the events of the day. The presidential security detail was normally a very hectic assignment, especially with an active President like Westview. But this day had been inordinately bizarre. In fact, the past few days had been a total parody of normalcy. First, a crisis breaks out suddenly in a region of the world that had known nothing but peace for the past ten years. Then, there was the murder of Daniel Fitzpatrick.

Now, the President of the United States, in the middle of a crisis, decides to visit a mental institution. And then this. A poor black man is carted away because he struck the man who ran on the presidential ticket of caring and compassion.

Mary was impatient for the day to end.


In several minutes, the motorcade pulled into the main driveway of Saint Elizabeth Hospital, four hundred acres of prime Washington land, bordered on the west by the Anacostia Freeway and abutting the Naval Annex. On the east lay Alabama Avenue and the Hebrew cemeteries. To the north was Suitland Parkway. Running north and south through the middle of the hospital grounds was Martin Luther King Avenue, a broad street, consisting of boarded-up buildings alongside a flourishing McDonald's. The history of the city lay here somewhere, under the rubble.

This was not Mary's first visit to the hospital. She had sent countless numbers of people here who had, in one way or another, threatened the President. They were either sent to Richardson Division if they didn't constitute a serious danger, or John Howard Division for maximum security detention.

Stepping out of the limousine, the President eagerly approached Dr. Juan Prince, the superintendent of the hospital, a handsome mulatto from the Dutch Caribbean island of Curaçao. He had trained in psychiatry at Howard University. Several of his principal deputies were standing restlessly alongside him.

"Juan, it's so good to see you again," the President greeted Prince warmly.

Mary was surprised by Westview's physical embrace of Prince. She could not recall any time during her three-year tenure on the presidential detail that Westview had ever met Dr. Prince. Yet they greeted each other as if they were close colleagues.

"I can't thank you enough for coming here to visit us, at a time when we know that you have far more pressing problems."

"Thank you for your kind words and warm reception. But let me say that nothing could be more pressing than the well-being of those less fortunate than ourselves."

Prince smiled warmly and nodded his head in silent approval. Yet something about him bothered Mary. Maybe his dark, chiseled features made him simply too handsome. Or was it his effortless, smooth manner, which seemed to command Westview's deference? She felt uncomfortable.

"Because we know that your time is extremely limited, we've designed a special tour for you," Prince said.

Surrounded by a small group of psychiatrists and nurses, Prince led Westview, Mary, and six Secret Service agents to an 1850s L-shaped four-story red-brick building sitting in the center of a lawn strewn with newspapers, bottles, and empty cigarette packages.

Although she had been at the hospital before, Mary was still unprepared for what she saw. Patients moved about the grounds as if they were automatons, walking past one another in a Kabuki of digitalized motions and distant stares. When they did interact, it involved a heated discussion or an argument over cigarettes—Do you have a light? May I have a cigarette? Give me that back, it's mine!

It seemed to Mary that reality for these patients was minute-by-minute survival. Only the here and now defined the currency of daily exchanges. None of them recognized the President, although one patient walked up to him and asked if he was Abraham Lincoln. That wasn't such a crazy question, thought Mary, because the similarity was striking—the long, thin face, the strong jaw, and the big ears. Only the beard was missing.

Why, of all days, thought Mary again, did Westview decide to come here? It was baffling.

Prince led the group into Richardson Division, one of the oldest complex of buildings at Saint Elizabeth. It housed two to three thousand patients, depending on the number of people that were being dumped out of the private hospitals in the Washington area on any given day.

It was the barbed-wire screens covering the windows that Mary found most appalling. It made the patients look dismembered. The only thing she could see from outside the building were patients' hands grasping the wire as if it were the last chance to assert their presence. And it was only through their incessant screaming that she realized that these people were, indeed, insane. It wasn't so much what they were saying. Most of it was innocuous threats, swearing, epithets, and reaffirmations of sanity. It was the fact that they insisted on screaming their presence to whoever walked by.

"This is the admissions office." Prince led them down a long corridor populated by milling patients, staring indifferently at the strange group of people walking past them.

"Do you have a cigarette?" A hunchbacked woman in her late sixties stuck her arm in front of Mary, who, for a split second, lost her composure.

"No, I don't smoke . . . never did."

"Do you have a cigarette?" The woman repeated the question to Mary as if she hadn't heard the response.

"I told you that I don't have any." Mary sounded angry.

"Now, Janet, don't bother this nice lady. She told you that she didn't have any cigarettes. So what do you say to her?" Prince placed his arm around the patient's shoulder. His soothing voice seemed to quiet her. Westview smiled at Prince, admiring the way he handled the patient.

"Okay, okay. No cigarettes. I won't ask for cigarettes. I promise. No more cigarettes." Janet looked agitated and backed away from Prince.

"That's okay, Janet. No harm was done," Prince replied.

"No damage was done. Right, no damage was done. I didn't do any damage. Did I?"

"No, of course not. No harm was done." Mary felt frustrated by her inability to communicate with the woman.

"Do you have any cigarettes?"

"Now, Janet, what did I tell you?" Prince was beginning to lose his composure.

"Juan," Westview said, then caught himself short. "Dr. Prince, I think we should get going. Otherwise the chief of my security detail will never forgive me. Isn't that right, Mary?"

"Yes, sir."

Mary felt queasy. She wasn't certain whether it was the smell of the unkempt patient, dressed in oversized clothing streaked with fecal stains, or whether it was the general odor of the ward, scrubbed down daily with carbolic acid and ammonia in an unsuccessful attempt to wash away the hidden pockets of urine.

"You don't have cigarettes, do you?" Janet grabbed Mary's shoulder.

"No, I told you, no." Mary shrugged her off. She adjusted her shoulder holster to make sure it was secure.

"Janet! Leave that nice lady alone!" Prince said, his voice firm. Janet stepped back, frightened.

He gestured the group toward a cleanly scrubbed examining room where a female was being examined by a physician.

"Lady, lady, can I talk to you?" Janet persisted, grabbing on to Mary's shoulder again. "Please, lady, can I talk to you?" She tried to pull Mary away from the group. "Please, lady. I have a secret. A real secret." She bent over and whispered, "There are soldiers here. But they don't look like soldiers. They are dressed like patients."

"Janet, I told you to leave that woman alone," Prince shouted.

"Now, I'm certain Mary can handle her," Westview said as he tried to sound reassuring.

Silently beckoning two blue-uniformed orderlies, Prince ordered them to take Janet away.

Mary thought about what the patient had just said about soldiers disguised as patients, and for a moment wished she could talk with her.

"Don't forget to bring cigarettes next time," Janet screamed down the corridor as the two orderlies dragged her away. Mary sensed that in one way or another, Janet would pay for her indiscretions, and watched as the orderlies took their less-than-compliant patient to a padded seclusion room.

"Let's see if we all can't fit inside here," Prince continued, acting like a tour guide at an amusement park, shepherding the hordes of gaping visitors through the poorly functioning turnstiles, helping them try to forget the scene that had just occurred.

Mary felt that the only thing missing was souvenirs and cotton candy. But the President seemed to be enjoying himself.

"Hey, boss, funny meeting you here," Brooks said after he walked up quietly behind her. "Don't worry, they'll take good care of her," he added, referring to the unpleasant episode with Janet. "They're pretty good here. This ain't no snake pit."

"Where have you been? And where's Dobbins?" As much as she hated to admit it, she was relieved to see Brooks. Despite the fact that she didn't trust him, she nevertheless felt calm when she knew his whereabouts.

"I had a couple of chores to do, remember? One of which was to leave Dobbins back at the caravan so that we wouldn't get into each other's way."

"Hello, Miz Mary," a familiar voice interrupted. It was Amos, the man who had attacked the President.

"What is he doing here?" Mary asked.

"I decided to bring Amos here over to St. E's for a little R and R. Remember, section 871 of the United States penal code states that someone who knowingly and willfully makes a threat to harm or kidnap the President is considered to have committed a felony punishable by five years in prison and up to one thousand dollars in fines. Since I know how much you like him, I decided to bring him over here for a rest cure instead."

"You're right. It certainly beats the slammer. At least here, he can get some medical help. Poor guy," Mary replied.

"What, are you kidding?" Brooks asked. "This guy is one lucky SOB. He did strike the President of the United States."

"What the hell would you do if the President had . . ." Mary suddenly realized that Brooks knew nothing about what had happened the night that the President had accidentally knocked Amos down. So she held her question and turned her attention toward Prince as he addressed the group.

"As you may know, we admit people to this ward who have been found to be a danger to themselves or to others. Also, if they evince psychotic behavior, we will admit them here." Prince was clearly in his element. He moved around the cramped room with ease.

Amos ignored the group.

"For our limited purposes, I want to show President Westview how we classify someone who has made a verbal or physical threat against him. And I would like to show what happens to them after they are admitted. As Ms. Dougherty and Mr. Brooks already know," Prince said, directing his little lecture to the President, "there are three basic classes of mental patients. Class I includes those patients who may make a threat against you, but whom the Secret Service determines pose no real danger to your well-being. The threat may have been misconstrued by a witness, made as a joke, or made under the influence of alcohol, which the person cannot later recall making."

"Is that the category you would put Amos in?" Mary wanted to know what would happen to him, since she wanted to see him released as quickly as possible. She had the distinct impression that the longer he was kept in the hospital, the worse it would be for him.

"No, I'm afraid not," Prince replied. "We'll get to Amos in a minute. We keep Class I patients for a twenty-four-hour period and quick alcoholic detoxification. Then we release them to the custody of their family or official guardian."

"What if they have no family, as is often the case?" Westview asked.

"Well, Mr. President, unfortunately the only thing we can then do is to release them to their own custody," Prince replied.

"Does that mean they go back to the streets?"

"I'm afraid so, Mr. President. Class II patients are those who threaten the life of the President, but are ultimately determined by the Secret Service to pose no real danger. Usually we admit them to this unit, but conduct an extensive investigation in cooperation with the Secret Service. From an intensive interview and past psychiatric history, we decide whether they constitute a serious danger to the President. If they do, then we put them in Class III. If we don't find them to be a danger, we release them into their own custody."

"What about Amos?" Mary asked.

"Thank you, Miz Mary. I appreciate your efforts on my behalf." Amos seemed to be enjoying the attention, and was hoping it would continue. For a brief moment, a bizarre idea flashed through his mind. If he struck the President again, he might receive even more attention.

"Amos constitutes a Class III because he made a direct physical strike against the President," Prince continued. "We have to incarcerate him against his own will and keep him in the hospital for a minimum of thirty days, to be reevaluated every thirty days until the . . ." Prince hesitated to pronounce the last few words.

"Until the end of my life, right?" Amos interjected.

Amos was beginning to feel a little nervous. The realization that he could spend the rest of his life in any one place, let alone Saint Elizabeth, began to scare him.

"With a Class III we develop a network of family, friends, neighbors, and co-workers whom we ask to help monitor the mental status of the Class III threatener."

"We call them spies," Brooks said facetiously.

Mary looked sternly at Brooks, silently reprimanding him for his insolence. But Westview broke out into raucous laughter, which started everyone else in the room laughing, including Amos.

It was a good note on which to end the presentation. While the visitors chatted informally with the doctors and nurses accompanying them, Prince silently signaled Westview and the two of them walked off down the hall. They approached seven male patients sitting together at the far end of the hallway. Westview indicated to Mary that he wanted her to step aside while he talked to them.

Mary walked over to the nurse's station and asked one of the nurses to see the clinical charts of the men in the hall.

Each had been diagnosed as Class III. Each had threatened to kill the President with a lethal weapon. The M16A2 (Armalite assault rifle), CAR15 (Colt commando carbine), and the M11 (Ingram submachine gun) were the weapons of choice. Mary was disturbed by the fact that these were all highly sophisticated weapons, used primarily by the U.S. Special Forces.

She stared at the remaining information: Admitting Secret Service Agent: David Brooks.

And all seven were born in Baltimore.

# CHAPTER
## 11

For Desaix, who had finally been been ordered by Manning to return stateside, the frenetic activity of the State Department Operations Center reminded him of the all-night brothels on Bourbon Street.

Attractive young people walked provocatively around. Junior-grade FSOs were always ready to welcome a senior official into the highly guarded inner sanctum, providing he had the proper credentials. Every effort was made to accommodate a "customer's" personal request. And everyone at the Op Center recognized Desaix. He was, as they say in New Orleans parlance, "a steady and welcome trick."

Calls from complete strangers would come in from all parts of the world demanding one or another type of service. Sometimes, it was a request to access a particular State Department official. More often than not, it was a call for help in the resolution of an international crisis.

Like the sex provided on Bourbon Street, nothing was or could be straight. Every request and resolution had a special twist to it. Whether it was the need to talk to a senior official or whether it was the help required to release innocent people from a terrorist seizure, these "professional kids," almost without exception, would find the right person to handle each difficult situation. That, of course, did not guarantee the outcome. Far from it.

But like good sex, Desaix felt it was more important to have the illusion of having had a good time than actually worrying about whether one did or did not, because the illusion of happiness lasted far longer than the actual memory of the experience. And so it was with international crisis management. According to Desaix's axiom: the truth of the moment was always tainted by the subsequent euphoria of success or the chagrin of failure. The consequences of a crisis were often assessed by those pundits or officials who made the first pronouncements on CNN, NBC's *Today* show, ABC's *Good Morning America*, or ABC's *Nightline*. Then came the judgment of the print media, particularly *The New York Times* and *The Wall Street Journal*. Collectively, they constituted what Desaix considered to be the front-line critics. The strategy, tactics, and outcome of the crisis may have been a great success, but if the media judged it to be a disaster, then that's the way it would be remembered. That, in part, explained why there were so many television sets strewn all over the Op Center.

"Welcome back, Dr. Clark. We've missed you. There's been a lot of excitement around here. I'd figured you would be part of it soon." Joan Fennell was a pleasant, heavyset, mid-career FSO-3 brunette, who, along with Ambassador Reginald Boynton, a supernumerary who was about to retire, ran the Op Center. Together they constituted the core of the permanent staff. The rest of the staff consisted of a dozen or so career FSOs who rotated through the Op Center every two years. Most, if not all, of their training came from OJT—on-the-job training.

So typical of the Foreign Service, thought Desaix, as he walked through the maze of telephone banks, fax machines, telecopiers, television sets, and computer terminals. Here was the State Department's incredible investment in the latest up-to-date equipment, but, as usual, they had forgotten to invest an equal amount of time, money, and effort into the training of the personnel who would staff the Op Center. State was lucky these kids were bright and eager, because they learned to use the equipment largely on their own.

"We've got a whole new bunch of recruits. Some fresh out of the Foreign Service Institute."

"Are they any good?" Desaix asked.

"Yeah, they're bright-eyed and bushy-tailed. They'll remain that way for the next twelve months, and then it'll be cynicism all the way."

Desaix eyeballed the new crop. He wished there were some dramatic ritual of indoctrination he could witness as they went from the sane, regularized order of their civilian life to the unstructured, haphazard frenzy of the Op Center. Like boot camp in the Marines, where the drill instructor would chew out the new recruits and inform them that they were about to enter the bowels of hell. But, alas, he realized that was misplaced romanticism.

He loved the cacophonous sound of the structured chaos in the room and, like a young boy following the screaming sounds of a fire engine, he turned his head from one end of the room to the other and back again.

"Call on line six!" A red-headed man in his mid-twenties, dressed in dungarees and a red plaid shirt, stood up in front of his computer terminal, with his phone raised.

How times have changed, thought Desaix. Years before, when he first started in the crisis management business, the de rigueur dress was the pin-striped suit. The full limits of informality extended to removing your jacket and rolling up your sleeves. That was it. There were very few women, blacks, or Asians. Now, as he looked around the rectangular-shaped room, over 50 percent of the people in the room could fit in some minority category. If anyone still thought the Foreign Service was the last bastion of WASP supremacy, they only had to look at the composition of the personnel in the Op Center.

Accompanied by Fennell, Desaix passed through another electronically secured door leading into a long, carpeted corridor. Midway down the corridor was an overhanging sign: S/S—O/CMS, CRISIS MANAGEMENT SUPPORT OFFICE.

"That's the new Secretary's Secretariat—Office of Crisis Management. We've revamped it since you were here a few months ago."

"Will I still recognize it?"

"Hopefully. But it's getting increasingly more restricted. Technically, I should be asking you what you are doing here, considering the fact that a Western European crisis is not your area."

He looked at her askance as if to question her assumption that a crisis occurring anywhere around the world would not be within his professional purview.

"You know what I mean. We got a bunch of hungry boys in the tank. And they don't seem too interested in cutting up any more of the pie."

"Thank God I don't like pie. I eat cookies."

"The cookie monster."

"Something like that."

"Anyway, I'll take you to the Sit Room. You can catch up on all the incoming and outgoing cables."

At the end of the corridor was a series of glass-enclosed rooms, each with a variety of people milling about. They entered the room marked TASK FORCE ONE/U.S.–RUSSIAN CRISIS.

The room was no bigger than twenty feet by thirty feet. In some ways it duplicated the look of the front office of the Op Center. A major part was taken up with a large mahogany table outfitted with a bank of unsecured telephone consoles, located under handwritten signs that designated the different agencies and departments involved in the management of the particular crisis.

At both ends of the table were places for the coordinator and deputy coordinator of the task force. Usually, the office director or the country desk officer was designated the coordinator of the task force, depending on whoever was available. In this case, the Russian desk officer had been given the honor of running the task force. Along both sides of the table were representatives from their State Department bureaus and agencies: Agency for International Development, Legislation, Public Affairs, Politico-Military Affairs, Diplomatic Security, Legal, and Consular Affairs. Occasionally, a representative from DOD or CIA sat on the task force. But in this case there were none. Too bad, thought Desaix, he would miss the intellectual cross-fertilization.

On the wall, at the far end of the room, a large blackboard was filled with a roster of names under three separate categories: Action Officer, Taskings, Deadlines. On top of the blackboard were three clocks, each one set to the three time zones involved in the crisis: Washington, D.C., Moscow, Greenwich Mean Time. On a table to the right of the coordinator's chair lay five different clipboards marked Incoming Cables, Outgoing Cables, Situation Reports, Press Releases, and Logs.

Alongside the clipboards were two conventional unsecured telephones.

One of Desaix's rules of crisis management mandated that, above all else, make sure that someone keep certain unsecured commercial telephone lines continuously open, even if it meant having someone read the entire Old and New Testaments in order to do so. All the other nonessential calls could be rerouted to other telephone extensions. Despite all the sophisticated satellites and electronic equipment, the most reliable form of communications during an international crisis was still the commercial telephone.

Off to the side, at the far end of the room, was a small glass-encased cubicle containing two STU-3 telephones. That was where the classified calls were supposed to be made. In truth, most of the calls, whether secured or not, were handled on the unsecured line. And the reason, as everyone knew, was quite simple. Once the unsecured lines were tied up it was very hard to get a secured call into the same place, because an unsecured line was required in order to get a secure call in. Circular reasoning, at best, thought Desaix.

Another one of Desaix's rules of crisis management dictated that one should never get lost in the details of managing a crisis, lest you lose the overview of the situation. Always delegate the responsibility of making a phone call to someone else—even if they don't know how to make it. You never want to spend your time making a phone call; you might lose an opportunity to make a crucial decision.

A corollary of that rule was to always appear and act as if you were indispensable. Which meant that reading incoming cables was one of the most important initial activities in which one should engage.

A second corollary required a complete and comprehensive list of pizza and Chinese food take-out services in the area, preferably posted on the blackboard for everyone's perusal.

As he looked around the room, Desaix recognized a few faces. Most of the FSOs staffing the task force were from the European bureau. By all rights, this was their crisis.

According to Desaix's rules of crisis management, all bureaucracies had a basic and inherent territorial interest in maintaining control over the management of their own crisis. Nothing less than the bureaucratic equivalent of genocide could force that bureau to relinquish control.

So Desaix walked stealthily into the room. But he knew it wouldn't fool anyone in the European bureau. As far as the others were concerned, the wolf was on the prowl.

"What can I do for you?" Joel Everett, the avuncular-looking coordinator with a rotund and deceptively pleasant face, looked up at Desaix.

"Just checking out what's been happening," Desaix replied.

"If you don't mind my asking, exactly who are you that would require me to allow you to read any pertinent information about the crisis?"

Fennell could see that they were headed into a direct confrontation. "This is Desaix Clark, Joel, the DAS for EAP," Fennell said, hoping her introduction would set a better tone.

In the old days, in the days before all of the glass-enclosed rooms and STU-3 phones, this introduction opened all sorts of doors. Now it generated bewilderment, or worse yet, hostility.

"Yes, how may I help you?" Everett would have liked to tell Clark to go fuck himself, but he would have to wait to see what this hotshot DAS thought he was entitled to.

"May I read the latest Sit Reps?" Desaix asked, having gone through this exercise of proving his entitlements many times before. As usual, he was becoming angry. He was getting too old to have to prove himself continuously.

"Yes, of course." Everett sounded more accommodating than he felt. But after a sixteen-hour shift, he was too exhausted to tangle with another DAS, even one from another bureau.

Reading over the Sit Rep, Desaix sensed that too many disparate pieces were not reflected in the neat narrative of events and bureaucratic counter-responses he was reading. Too many uncomfortable coincidences, he thought. The mysterious death of the top U.S. government Russian expert just at the moment when he would be most needed, by a bizarre use of hydrogen fluoride. The disturbing question of why the Russian Federation, in conjunction with the other independent republics of the Commonwealth of Independent States, would precipitate a major war in Western Europe, just at a point in their history when they were most vulnerable to defeat. After ten years of major U.S. and Western European financial assistance, everyone knew that their economy was still in shambles. Although they had already converted their state-controlled economy to a free-market one, they were still a basket case. A completely bankrupt ex-superpower.

There was very little left of the Commonwealth of Independent States. It was no more than a loose confederation of autonomous republics centered around the powerful Russian Federation. Although officially there was supposed to be a shared leadership, it was really the President of the Russian Federation who was de facto leader of the Commonwealth. He was the one who controlled the vestiges of the once formidable Russian military, GRU, and FSA. Where once the diktats of an inefficient centralized communist system prevailed, now there was a loose association of bickering independent states who reluctantly cooperated with one another on the basis of mutual economic and political benefit.

It just didn't make sense.

Why would the Russian Federation, in its completely debilitated, almost moribund condition, want to start a major war with an economically, politically, and militarily stronger country like the U.S.? Although Desaix had to admit that the U.S. economy was not all that great either; for some time now the GNP had grown at a conservative 2 percent per year. And for the past two years the other economic growth indicators had been completely flat. Some economists were even maintaining that there was another recession coming, as evidenced by the ever-increasing unemployment rate.

After reading the Sit Rep, Desaix handed it to Fennell to read.

"What's wrong with it?" Desaix asked provocatively.

"What do you mean?" Fennell had learned a long time ago that Desaix never asked an innocent question. There was always something behind it. But she wasn't a Russian expert. She was simply in charge of making certain that the Op Center functioned as well as possible. More often than not, it did. And she never examined anything beyond the point she had to.

"It looks too clean," Desaix said.

"Too clean?"

"A conflict breaks out for no apparent reason, and everything is described so neatly and precisely. It just never happens that way. Listen. '0557, Wildeck, Germany, M1A1 Abrams tanks from the 5th Squadron, 11th U.S. Armored Cavalry Regiment, respond to Soviet T-72 tanks racing toward them. Six BTR-60s move down the autobahn threatening U.S. position. Firefight almost ensues.' "

"So?"

"Crises don't have a precise chronology. They're usually quite messy. When they look too neat, there's usually something very wrong."

"Would you like me to make one up for you?" Fennell responded.

Everett had been following the conversation, just close enough that he didn't have to be accountable for everything that was being said.

Desaix read the Sit Rep out loud. " '0630, FLASH cable to Department of State. Reference: Major Russian Offensive. Notifications and Distributions of FLASH cable: Sec State, Dep State, Under Secretary of State for Political Affairs, and Assistant Secretary of State for European Affairs notified. Task Force organized. Department of State coordinates Task Force efforts with Interagency Crisis Management Group including CIA, DIA, DOD, JCS, NSA, White House.' "

Desaix couldn't look directly at Everett. He felt that incredible mix of emotions swell within him, usually signaling the rise of some form of self-destructive behavior coming on, where he often created situations that led to some form of gratuitous confrontation. Desaix had to be very careful about what he said or did now that the wave of what one of his ex-wives used to call Louisiana melancholy swept over him.

Watching Everett sit there, so self-assured, while people swarmed around him in a frenzy of busy activity, made Desaix feel both envious and angry. Why were they all here? True, this was their area of professional responsibility. But there was no reason why he shouldn't be here as well. He was a professional crisis manager. Someone who made his living and, more importantly, derived his professional identity from running international crises like this one. True, this was not his regional responsibility, but nevertheless . . .

He stopped himself for a moment. The truth was that no one in this room, or on the seventh floor, owed him even a phone call, let alone a formal invitation to participate. If this were the Far East or Asia, then he had a legitimate excuse to be part of the action. But this wasn't the Far East or Asia. And this was a realization with which he could not come to terms. He felt himself struggling with that demon within himself that his mama used to call his princely pride, that part of his personality that made him feel special and different.

He wasn't like those other people in the room. He had been in the business of crisis management way before anyone in this room had even joined the Foreign Service, let alone participated in their first crisis. Like in war, he had earned his obligatory Purple and Bronze stars. What about all those times he had been wounded while managing a crisis overseas? Or those times he was PNGd out of different countries? Shit, didn't that count for something? Didn't that entitle him to play in this game? Perhaps the biggest game of all. But he knew the answer. Every crisis was a new game, with different players and a whole new set of rules. And he had to start all over again.

He saw visions of Fitzpatrick's mutilated body on that shining metal table, and was resolved to play in this game. Perhaps the last one of the season. And if he could only find out about Baltimore, he had a strong gut feeling that the game could be his for the asking. But no one was going to give him an invitation to join. He would have to find his own, special way in. Perhaps Baltimore was the price of the ticket.

" '0700, Deputies' Coordinating Committee convened by General Mapplethorpe at the NSC. Fitzpatrick's office notified. Result: DEFCON TWO. Russian Amb, Deputy Chief of Mission, and Pol Con called in to see Sec State. Demarche made.' " Desaix appeared a little confused when he put the paper down.

"Is there something wrong?"

Fennell was solicitous of Desaix's feelings. She had learned to trust them in the past. She had seen him reverse an entire strategy simply because it just didn't feel right to him.

"Why would the Sec State call over the Russian Ambassador to make a demarche, when it should have been done by someone in the bureau?"

"He didn't call them. They called on the Sec State to make a formal demarche." Everett liked the fact that he could correct an entitled DAS.

"What? You mean they came here to protest what was described in the official Sit Rep as Russian aggression?"

"That's right. They marched all the way over here."

"Do we know what happened in that meeting?"

"No one was allowed in the room. Not even the Russian desk officer."

"Then who took the conversation notes?"

"Take a wild guess."

"No one," replied Desaix.

"You get the rubber duck."

"So there's no written record of the meeting?" Desaix asked.

"That's about right," Everett said.

Flipping through the rest of the Sit Rep, Desaix saw a large number of discrepancies. Increasingly, the ten-page Sit Rep seemed to portray a picture of Russian aggression matched by U.S. restraint and caution. Not surprisingly, Desaix felt that the narrative had been skewed in such a way that, whatever the outcome, there would be no doubt in anybody's mind that the U.S. had tried to do everything within its power to constrain the belligerent Russians. But what bothered him the most was the fact that there was a series of extremely sensitive meetings in which there were no other participants other than the Sec State and his Russian guest.

Even in a crisis, that type of behavior was quite unusual. If anything, there was a strong incentive in a crisis to leave as much of a paper trail as possible in order to cover one's bureaucratic rear end. Desaix was beginning to realize that this crisis was being held very tightly, restricted to only a few of the seventh-floor principals.

"What's this you have here in the Sit Rep about redeployment of certain Special Forces from the European theater back to MacDill Air Force Base? And why, within two hours, were they redeployed to unknown restricted areas?" Desaix was surprised to read about the withdrawal of any U.S. troops from·Germany at a time when they would be most needed. "What is an unknown restricted area anyway?" Desaix asked.

"Beats me," Everett responded with complete indifference.

"Would you mind finding out the answer for me? I certainly would appreciate it." Desaix was trying to control the rising swells of rage. Above all else he had to learn to wait his turn. It would come, if only he waited and avoided any major incidents.

"Hey, Major Trilling," Everett yelled out, "see if you can't help out Mr. Clark, our DAS for EAP. He's concerned about the redeployment of the SOFs." Everett introduced the short, taut Major Trilling to Desaix.

"You'll have to excuse me, but there are a lot of problems that I have to oversee," Everett said, then walked over to the Director's office and closed the door behind him.

"Desaix," Fennell said, "I've got to be leaving too. I trust that you will find your way around here. It's good to see you back." She gave him a tender squeeze on his arm, and slipped him a piece of paper on which she had written the combination for the doors to the Secured Video Telecommunications Conference where the Sec State and his minions were conferring.

"Thanks, Joan." Desaix turned his attention toward Major Trilling.

"Could you tell me what this means? It says that DOD has redeployed Special Forces away from a theater of operations back to MacDill Air Force Base, and then to certain, unknown restricted areas."

"Well, sir, to the best of my knowledge, it means that certain elements of our Green Berets, Rangers, and other highly trained troops will be moved out to highly classified staging areas."

"Don't they normally fly these troops right out of MacDill to Frankfurt? Why prestage them to restricted areas?"

"Again, sir, the only thing I can say is that a lot of this material is highly classified."

"In other words, Major Trilling, you don't really know, do you?"

"Well, sir . . ."

"Thank you, Major."

"Yes, sir."

# CHAPTER
## 12

**D**esaix left the task force room disgusted. He walked down the hallway to the overhead sign that read S/S—O/CMS, Crisis Management Support Office. He pushed a red button beneath a plaque that read SVTC, Secured Video Telecommunications Conference. When he had left a few months ago, they were just installing this thirty-million-dollar complex of sophisticated teleconferencing equipment.

Slowly, Desaix opened the first heavy steel door, which led to the second secured steel door. He pushed the numbers Fennell had given him, feeling as if he were walking through the bank vaults of Zurich. Stepping up to yet a third set of gleaming steel doors, Desaix was impressed by the irony of having all these new technologies for managing international crises. So far, he had seen nothing that would improve the quality of decision making.

Stepping up into what was often referred to in the overseas embassies as the tank, Desaix walked into a steel-encased room, surrounded by an electromagnetic field that prevented electronic penetration; before he could feel claustrophobic, he pulled open the last door and entered the sacrosanct arena where only the chosen few decide the outcome of a crisis, or in this case, the course of history.

The SVTC room was no bigger than an average-sized living room, with rich brown carpeting and a large mahogany console with six television screens placed on top of it. In front of the console was a camera videotaping the "actors" in the room. Desaix saw himself walk into one of the screens, past the official seal of the State Department.

Like all electronic tanks, the ventilation was terrible. It felt like a hot, sultry night along Bourbon Street. For a few seconds, Desaix felt that he might pass out.

"Look what the hot desert winds blew in," Paul Twitty announced. Twitty was the Under Secretary of State for Political Affairs. He was a sixty-seven-year-old flaxen-haired, rotund chain-smoker, whose Falstaffian comportment belied what was once a thin, caring, gentle person.

Where once discipline and judgment had been the hallmark of his personality, he had transformed himself into a grotesque physical parody of his younger self, a self-indulgent child, beset by unexplained temper tantrums and mood swings, hell-bent on living out whatever few remaining years of his life were left to him in vituperative explosions of self-destructive behavior.

Where once he spoke civilly, at times with great compassion and concern, Twitty now laced his language with the stinging barbs of his relentless sarcasm. Once discreet in his public appearances, Twitty now blustered about with a ferocious pomposity and bitterness that could do very little to hide the personal insecurity resulting from the fact that he was no more than the Secretary's factotum, an incidental, insignificant personage who was brought into the department as a legacy in order to placate Twitty's mentor, a wealthy, self-aggrandizing former Secretary of State.

"Hello, Paul. Hello, Mr. Secretary," Desaix said, trying to ignore Twitty and shaking hands with Secretary of State Chester Manning instead. He nodded to the other two people in the room.

"I'm glad to see you, Desaix. Welcome back."

"Thank you, Mr. Secretary. I'm glad I got back in time. It looks like things are jumping around here."

"I was sorry to hear about Fitzpatrick." Frank Young, the middle-aged Assistant Secretary of State for European Affairs, extended his condolences.

"Thanks, Frank. I appreciate it." Desaix liked the former Naval Academy graduate, who had spent the better part of his professional life in government in Commerce or as a staffer at the White House. He was one of those professionals who belied the popularly held notion that all bureaucrats were basically lazy and ineffective. Unlike Twitty, Young was secure enough in his own well-honed bureaucratic and political skills to welcome Desaix's participation in whatever crisis might be at hand. His sharp features and intimidating height contrasted the fact that he was extremely considerate and caring.

Desaix smiled at Judy Taylor, standing at the other end of the room. The svelte, attractive Assistant Secretary of State for Public Affairs was a political appointment made personally by the President. She always seemed to have a seductive smile on her face, forcing Desaix to recall the short but passionate affair they had a few years before, when she was an enthusiastic lobbyist for a major Washington public relations firm. If it were up to her, they would still be continuing the discreet liaison. But after six months of courting, Desaix had found her unduly possessive.

"Hello, Desaix. It's always good to see you." She let the words hang in the air for a second, as if she were subtly suggesting that it was still possible to rekindle an old flame.

"Good to see you again, Judy."

Right now, Desaix felt frustrated enough that he would not have minded spending a brief time alone with her, remembering how many hours he had spent with her. With Judy, it had been easier to try to fornicate away his personal problems, including a persistent dissatisfaction with himself and an unrelenting need for action, than to confront, analyze, or change them.

"What can we do for you, Dr. Clark?" Twitty asked, moving restlessly about in his chair in obvious discomfort.

"I don't need anything right now, Paul. But thanks for asking."

"Ladies and gentlemen, let's get back to work. Everyone is waiting for us," Manning interrupted, adjusting the knob on the screen in front of him. "We've got the President on screen one. He's about to come in any second."

"On screen two, we have Randolph Merck, Sec Def," Young said. He knew that Desaix liked to acquaint himself with all the players. The more input he had from all sides, the more effective he could be. But Young suspected that Twitty would do everything possible to make certain that Desaix would not be in the room much longer. Whatever good feelings ever existed before between Desaix and Twitty were no longer there.

"Larry Jenkins, the DCI, is on screen three. I presume you know which one he is," Twitty said, trying to annoy Desaix.

"General Ronald McCormick and some of his JCS staff members should be on camera four any minute now," Manning added, as he turned around toward Desaix, then stared at his bandaged right hand. "What happened?"

"I burned myself with some caustic chemical during Fitzpatrick's autopsy."

"Desaix, come on now," Twitty interjected. "We all know you wanted to get out of Tokyo as quickly as possible to where the action was—here. So you created your own walking papers."

"Paul, I think it's time for us to get down to business," Manning said, tactfully scolding Twitty. Manning knew how unnecessarily provocative Twitty could be.

"Before we begin," Twitty interjected, "don't you think it's a good idea for us to clear the room so that only those who belong remain?" Everyone in the room knew he was referring to Desaix.

"Who, specifically, should leave, Paul?" Taylor's patrician bearing made it quite clear that she feared no one in that room.

"I think with the President coming on shortly, we should just keep it to a minimum."

"I think we're just fine as we are," Manning said. "I'm certain that the President will be happy to see Desaix." Although Manning took some pleasure from seeing his senior officials jockey for bureaucratic advantage, Twitty never knew when to stop.

Taylor gave Desaix a nod of approval. She pointed to her wristwatch and mouthed the words, "What are you doing after this?"

Desaix simply smiled and wondered what his colleagues in the room would say about his concept of power: Contrary to popular misconception, power is a feminine and not a masculine trait. Real power consists of the ability to manipulate emotions, relationships, and attitudes. Therefore, first learn how to seduce a woman before even thinking about acquiring power.

Desaix watched with almost childish wonderment as all the principals appeared on the television screens. This was the first time he was participating in what amounted to a full CMG meeting, which by tradition was limited to cabinet officers and one deputy. Twitty had a legitimate concern when he requested that all nonessential personnel leave the room. But what appeared to be his personal animosity toward Desaix was so overwhelming that his request could not be given serious consideration.

"Mr. President, everyone is assembled. We've got DOD, CIA, State, and, of course, the NSC." Manning noticed that Mapplethorpe sat to the right of the President, close enough to signal those in the room that he was the second most powerful man in the country.

"I want to inform you that we have a new guest," Manning added.

"Desaix, it's always good to have you around," Westview said. "I'm sorry to hear about Fitzpatrick's death." Without pausing, Westview added, "And, of course, it's always a pleasure to see you, Ms. Taylor. It is Ms. Taylor, isn't it?"

"Yes, Mr. President."

Desaix was most impressed by Mapplethorpe's absence of visible concern when the President offered his condolences. Fitzpatrick had been Mapplethorpe's senior Russian expert. It was Mapplethorpe, over Desaix's protests, who had insisted that Fitzpatrick accompany the team to Japan. Desaix still had no idea why, in the midst of this crisis, Fitzpatrick had not been immediately recalled to the States.

"Gentlemen . . . and Ms. Taylor, I requested this emergency teleconferencing meeting so soon after this morning's White House Sit Room meeting because the situation is deteriorating faster than I had anticipated. Contrary to what I had announced in my press conference, I have been informed by General Mapplethorpe and Supreme Allied Commander Europe that both we and the Russians are now poised to use tactical nuclear weapons. However, under any condition, I cannot allow that to occur. Is that understood? We must stop this crisis from escalating. I've ordered Vice President Bonner to curtail his trip to the Far East and return immediately."

"Mr. President, you can be sure we will do everything we can to prevent that outcome," Twitty said, fidgeting in his chair as he spoke.

"I'm sure you will, Paul. But time is of the essence. I need a better reading on the situation as well as a course of action for the next few days."

"Mr. President, am I to understand that we are to change our marching orders from this morning's White House meeting?" Jenkins asked, then looked at a jet-lagged James Ball sitting next to him.

Desaix was jealous that Ball had been invited to this highly restricted meeting, and that his own presence was merely an accident. But drawing on his rules of crisis management, he realized that the most difficult part about managing an international crisis was actually getting oneself invited to participate.

On the TV monitor, Desaix watched as White walked into the DOD conference room and sat behind McCormick. A disturbing thought haunted him. If he, Desaix, had *not* been invited to this party, then why were both Ball and White there, when they had no apparent expertise in handling this type of crisis?

Suddenly, Desaix's own twin dragons of self-destructive behavior—envy and jealousy—began to rear their ugly heads. He tried to occupy his mind with self-proclaimed brilliant solutions to the present situation, but the more he tried to envision answers that might dazzle the President and his advisors, the more frustrated he felt. What if he couldn't come up with the solution that would impress everyone? He realized that uniqueness and creativity— two of his strengths—were also the underpinnings of his destruction. Sometimes he was much too eager to shoot from the hip, to provide a prescient but premature solution that no one was ready to accept, let alone implement. So he resolved to assume the least disquieting posture, that of the concerned psychiatrist. Attentive and solicitous, but above all else, saying nothing unless it was desperately required.

"Gentlemen," Westview continued, "I believe the key to unlock the mystery of this spiraling conflict resides in the understanding of Russian President Igor Ivanovich Zotov's personality. It might help us anticipate what he might do next, and shape those initiatives we might make." Westview seemed to direct his attention to Desaix as he spoke.

"One of the options that President Westview and I have been exploring for immediate implementation," Mapplethorpe said, "is a teleconference between the two Presidents to see if we can't straighten this situation out face-to-face, so to speak." Mapplethorpe hoped it wasn't apparent that it was he who had conceived of the teleconferencing mini-summit. For a moment, he thought the President looked miffed with him; but he was certain the annoyance would pass.

"I believe the Op Center is hooking up the necessary communication with the Russians just as we are speaking," Manning said.

"Thanks, Chet. I appreciate that." Mapplethorpe said. "Did they give us any indication of how long this might all take?"

"At best, only a few minutes," Twitty interjected, although he knew that might be unduly optimistic. But at worst it would only be several hours. Would his optimism alienate the Secretary, who was by nature more circumspect? Twitty still resented the fact that Manning had not asked Desaix to leave the room.

"In preparation for this meeting," Jenkins said, "I've asked James Ball, the Director of the Office of Scientific Intelligence, under which he also heads the Center for Leadership Analysis, to give you a thumbnail sketch of President Zotov. I will disavow Jim's hasty preparation, and add that, despite our extensive contacts with the Russian President, the Agency has very little information about him."

Nervously, Ball opened up a file marked TOP SECRET/SENSITIVE/ NO FORN/NO CON. THE PSYCHOLOGICAL PROFILE OF RUSSIAN PRESIDENT IGOR IVANOVICH ZOTOV.

A few years ago, Ball would have presented the biography of a particular world leader by simply showing a five-minute film, showing him engaged in some singularly nondescript activity, such as walking in his garden or working in his office. A sensitive part of the film would show that leader reviewing a line of elite troops. The film presentation idea had been specifically designed for a former President who had been a movie star himself, who conceptualized foreign policy as a series of close-ups and action shots. That was the only way that President could integrate the complicated national security material. If the CIA was good at anything, Ball had to admit to himself, it was particularly adroit at tailoring its material for the one and only customer who really counted—the President of the United States.

Fortunately, Westview was a strong patron of the Agency's Center for Leadership Analysis and enjoyed reading about the complexities of human character, particularly as it evidenced itself in unusual political behavior. Most other Presidents would read biographies in order to uncover some type of peccadillo—preferably sexual. But Westview normally liked to read about a world leader's particular style of handling a problem. So Ball quickly put together a pastiche of facts, observations, and speculations.

Only Desaix understood how much the Agency's psychological profiles were lacking in credibility and accuracy. The weekly magazines were frequently better in their assessment of world leaders. For one thing, the journalists had direct access to any world leader, irrespective of their political affiliation. Secondly, other than a basic commercial interest, journalists had very few preconceived biases about that leader, other than one or two general impressions.

"President Zotov has been described by those who have met him as being highly intelligent, incisive, unassuming, and practical," Ball began.

"I've met him on several different occasions, and that sounds just about right." Westview was eager to get to the main part of the analysis: how Zotov responded to stress, and most importantly his ability to play brinkmanship politics.

"Zotov was born during the Nazi invasion of Stalingrad, sometime in December of 1942. His birth was never accurately recorded and he dismisses any inquiry about it as vain and foolish. He is married for the second time, to a woman doctor, about fifteen years his junior. He has three sons from his first wife and one daughter from his present wife. Despite the fact that he is a family man, he is considered to be a ladies' man. We believe that he has an attractive mistress who works very closely with him. We also suspect that she works for the GRU."

"Don't they all," Taylor joked. Manning gave Taylor a stern look.

"Although he is perceived as low-key, he can be brusque, if not outright rude. However, he is known as a man of compromise, or 'pragmatic choices,' as he prefers to call them. He resents being cornered in any negotiation and will always insist on having some dignified exit. Like his predecessor, Boris Yeltsin, whom he most resembles, he was trained as a civil engineer, and he thinks in a systematic, concise, logical scientific fashion. However, unlike Yeltsin, he relies on his reasoning, rather than his emotions. He would prefer to analyze his way out of a problem. He is unlikely to initiate any political action without having thoroughly evaluated its consequences.

"Despite his seemingly conciliatory manner, he can be both dogmatic and authoritarian in his approach to political problems, particularly his nation's chaotic domestic problems. In foreign policy, we have seen a more flexible approach. Although publicly he espouses the merits of democracy and capitalism, privately he might be prepared to go to war in order to create a new Soviet Union with the Russian Federation as the center. He has been frustrated by the slow changes in the different republics, marked by ethnic violence, corruption, and severe economic shortages. Despite massive capital infusion from Western Europe, the U.S. and, particularly, Japan, the situation in all the republics has approached a state of chaos.

"He is a risk taker who seems willing to sacrifice his life to establish an expansionist Russia. His ascendancy to power through the turbulent Gorbachev and post-Gorbachev period of coups and countercoups was marked by a notable amount of risk taking, aligning himself with the first democratically elected president of the Russian Federation, Boris Yeltsin. He was initially trained at the prestigious Moscow University, joined the Communist Party, and then quit to work with Gorbachev and Yeltsin."

"Mr. President," Mapplethorpe interrupted, "I understand that in a few minutes Zotov will be coming on the air." Looking anxiously at Twitty, Mapplethorpe was concerned that Westview was not adequately prepared for the meeting with Zotov.

Young whispered something in Twitty's ear. "I've just been informed, Mr. President, that Zotov is ready to come on-line."

"Tell him that we have some technical problems to straighten out," Westview replied.

Young picked up the STU-3 and relayed the message to the Op Center.

"Go ahead, Jim," Westview urged.

"As you know, Mr. President, despite the ongoing deterioration of the Russian system over the past ten years, there has still been a continuation of overseas espionage, especially from the former Soviet bloc countries of Bulgaria, Poland, Romania, and Czechoslovakia. For the most part, many of the overseas operatives are singletons, working on their own, primarily for economic profit. However, Mr. President, there also has been increased state-sponsored sabotage, assassination, and acts of terrorism committed by certain elite units of the Russian Military Intelligence, particularly the GRU, as well as certain elements of Spetsnaz."

"I'm sorry to interrupt you, Jim," White interjected, "but our NSA intercepts and DIA assets in the Russian Federation corroborate this very distressing point. We have noticed an increase in terroristic activity, as well as in assassination attempts, directed against opposition leaders and ethnic minorities in the other republics not willing to take orders from Moscow. We have pinpointed a lot of the activity to elements of the Spetsnaz units of the Russian 107th Guards Airborne Division."

Merck fidgeted restlessly with his fingers. He was anxiously waiting for permission from the President to redeploy his tactical and strategic nuclear weapons and place them on-line before it was too late. "Sir, if I might add a precautionary note, since our meeting this morning the Russians have already begun to preposition their road-mobile SS-25 ICBMs away from their normal remote areas in Russia." Merck didn't have to add that the mobility of that system increased the survivability of the Russian land-based intercontinental missile force.

"Gentlemen, what you are telling me seems to complicate events significantly. Before we finish Mr. Ball's excellent profile, and before we talk with Zotov, I need a quick readout on our present nuclear deployment in Western Europe."

Before Mapplethorpe could open his mouth, McCormick stood up and flicked on his television screen an updated multicolored chart of U.S. weapon systems in Western Europe. This was his turn to shine, an opportunity to recoup the lost prestige from the morning's disastrous Sit Room meeting.

"Mr. President, what we have here is a nice mixture of weapon options that, with your permission, can be placed on-line within hours. At the bottom of the list, we have the eight-inch howitzer, based about forty miles south of Wildeck. We have about two dozen of them there. Each has a five to twenty kiloton capacity targeted primarily at Russian forces dispersed throughout the eastern part of Germany. A fair assessment would be that they have a fair destructive capacity with a very quick response time.

"Then, we have the FB-111A, based in England, with primary target responsibility for the major cities of Moscow, St. Petersburg, Kiev, Minsk, and Tbilisi. Along the same lines, we have the F-15 fighter jets stationed in the United Kingdom and Germany; again, not too far from Wildeck. The F-15, which I have personally flown, has a moderate destructive capacity with an extensive territorial coverage. Of course, we have the Lance missiles near Wildeck, carrying payloads anywhere from one hundred to two hundred kilotons, targeted against Russian troops both in Germany and the Commonwealth of Independent States. It has an extremely high destructive capacity and quick response time." McCormick stopped and looked around the room. "Any questions so far?"

No one responded. McCormick was more than happy to continue. "You know that we withdrew all the Pershings from the western part of Germany several years ago. We just have two major tactical nuclear weapons systems left in the U.S. The Minuteman II, with a 275 kiloton yield, a high destructive capacity coefficient, and a moderate response capability. It also covers Russia and the rest of the Commonwealth of Independent States. Then we have the 350 kiloton Peacekeeper, stationed in the U.S. and targeted against Moscow, Kiev, Minsk, and St. Petersburg. That's it for right now."

"Thank you, General McCormick. So we are ready to go, if we have to. Is that right?" Westview asked.

"For the most part, yes, sir."

"Good! Mr. Ball, would you mind finishing your briefing before we talk with Zotov. I would ask you to make it as simple as possible."

"Sir, if you don't mind," Mapplethorpe interrupted, "I think we really shouldn't keep the Russian President waiting any longer."

"Thank you, General Mapplethorpe, but I think we owe Mr. Ball the courtesy to let him finish," Westview replied.

"Thank you, Mr. President. I don't really have that much more to add to what I've already said, except that President Zotov doesn't like to be kept waiting—he becomes quite testy."

"One moment, please. Mr. Young, can you find out if our invited guest has walked away?" Westview asked.

Snickers broke out in the room. It seemed as if the President was playing a cat-and-mouse game with Zotov. Young picked up the STU-3. He nodded his head, indicating that Zotov was still on the line.

"Okay, please continue, Mr. Ball," Westview said.

"What makes Zotov quite unusual is the fact that he can mask his emotions. He is self-effacing and an extremely quick study. Unfortunately, he feels he must live under the shadow of his famous predecessor, Boris Yeltsin, who as you know, along with Mikhail Gorbachev died several years ago under extremely mysterious circumstances. Zotov has tried to harness runaway inflation, combined with a deep recession, as he deals with impending anarchy within his own republic. Economically, the country is almost at death's door. At least forty-five million Soviets live below the official poverty level. Eighty percent of the country is still on some form of rationing of either food or gasoline. New clothes and shoes are hardly available anywhere.

"The independent republics that constitute what once was the Soviet Union are at war with one another, in one way or another. Armenia and Azerbaijan have been fighting militarily each other for the past five years, despite repeated attempts by Moscow to forcibly impose law and order. Ukraine . . . Moldova has been completely crippled by ethnically inspired strikes. Georgians are once again fighting among themselves. CIA's net assessment is that Zotov would have to do something drastic to alter any of the above."

"Such as what?" The President appeared engrossed by Ball's presentation.

"Possibly go so far as announce martial law, disband the puppet government of the State Council, consisting of the leaders of all the republics. He could abrogate the current constitution and declare himself the new President over all the republics.

"There is a little-known provision in the constitution, section 110, paragraph 7, which, in effect, allows him to declare martial law first in Russia and then in the other republics for a period of no more than six months. That would give him the time to become another Stalin. All liberties could be suspended throughout all the republics. And the Russian Army, the FSA, and GRU could reign supreme once again. The old Soviet Union that was disbanded in 1991 would once again be reconstituted under a new name. The gulags and the psychiatric hospitals would again fill up with political dissidents.

"But in order to do all this, he would have to prove 'just cause,' such as a national security crisis or a danger to him that would threaten his leadership, and therefore the integrity of the Russian military and security apparatuses, normally required to maintain peace and stability throughout the Commonwealth in conjunction with the local militias."

Ball was wary of emphasizing the point about psychiatric hospitals too strongly. Desaix was the one who had negotiated some of the major agreements between the U.S. and the old Soviet Union to release incarcerated political dissidents.

"What, then, is your worst-case scenario?" Mapplethorpe asked impatiently, trying to anticipate the President's response, as well as speed up the briefing.

"A national catastrophe that would take either one of two forms: a revolution from below or a military coup from either the right or some other extremist group," Ball said. He waited for Jenkins to intercede, but he didn't.

"What about another populist revolution? How would it look?" Merck asked, wanting to hear the Agency's position before he espoused his own.

"It would look like this past winter's miners' strike in Russia," Jenkins interrupted Ball. As the DCI and the official spokesman for the Agency, he felt that he was obligated to respond. "The miners not only won all of their basic demands, but set up a series of strike committees that became the headquarters of local power. These committees were considered by most of the parliamentarians as 'another embryo of the people's power.' If a new wave of strikes from all the different sectors of the economy were to spring up across the country, as we think may be quite likely this summer, then the nationwide momentum for political change from below might prove to be a steamroller phenomenon. As we saw with the election of Yeltsin as President of the Russian Federation."

"Leading to civil war," Desaix finally interjected. "As Ball and Jenkins have already pointed out, Zotov might be extremely eager to invoke the Emergency War Powers Act, granting him full and absolute power over not only Russia but the Commonwealth of Independent States as well." Desaix felt exhilarated. He had just played his ace in the hole—presenting a worst-case scenario that would have to force everyone in the room, including the President, to seriously entertain his analysis and his presence.

But Desaix was still increasingly disturbed by the discrepancy between what he was hearing and saying and the apparent facts of the situation. Why would a country that was entering into the very situation that they had always feared—domestic chaos—be so eager to precipitate what could be World War III? This was real cognitive dissonance.

"Good point, Desaix," Westview said, pleased to see that Clark had managed to swim past the bureaucratic barracudas.

Desaix liked the President. There was a personal chemistry between them, in a relationship that actually went back to the early days of the administration when Desaix had saved the President from compounding the problem of a hostage situation by acting as his own negotiator. Westview had insisted on talking directly to the hostage-takers, inadvertently elevating the importance of both the terrorists and their demands. When Desaix was called in to take over the management of the crisis he had to literally kick the President out of the Sit Room to save the situation. But despite the unceremonious way Westview had been treated, he had appreciated what Desaix had done for him.

"Come and see me after this meeting, Desaix. I want to talk to you." Westview smiled. For the first time all day, he felt relaxed.

Twitty was obviously annoyed with Desaix's preferential treatment.

"Thank you, Mr. President. I look forward to it," Desaix responded, enjoying the fact that the envy level in the room had just risen markedly.

Ball interjected, "Sir, the second scenario of a Russian catastrophe involves a possible coup against the Russian President, executed by elements of the Russian military and the FSA." He paused to assess the President's reaction, but Westview remained silent. He then recapitulated the rumors about an impending coup in Moscow against Zotov.

"This time the rumors have a certain ring of legitimacy to them," Ball went on. "Yesterday's brutal assassination, which we can now confirm, of Zotov's executive secretary, Colonel-General Nikolai Pavlovich Kurasov, reaffirmed to many of the members of the State Council that some runaway elements of the GRU or Spetsnaz may attempt to kill Zotov next." Ball spoke quickly since Jenkins was giving him a sign to speed up.

"DIA reports increased anti-Zotov activity by some of the more extreme groups, like Pamyat, the ultranationalist group that has targeted the Jews as part of a Jewish-Masonic conspiracy to undermine Russian nationalism," Merck said. "Basically, these right-wing nationalist groups are anticommunists, and their Russophile sentiments overlap with a growing blue-collar yearning for the despotic simplicities of a new Stalinist era." Merck wanted to reaffirm both the unique value and independence of DIA, never quite forgetting that he was in a continuous friendly competition with the CIA. White and McCormick would never allow the Sec Def to conduct a multi-agency meeting with the President without having mentioned DIA at least once.

Westview interjected. "Let me simply reiterate a basic point. I want this problem solved as quickly and as efficiently as possible. Keep all defense systems on Maximum Vigilance status—DEFCON TWO. But no one, I repeat, no one is authorized to proceed one step forward without my approval."

"Mr. President, I've received word from the Op Center that the Russian President refuses to go on the air if he has to wait any longer." Twitty sounded impatient, as usual. Ever since Desaix walked into the room, he had been relegated to a second-string player. Somehow he had to regain the initiative.

"Fine, put him on the air, Paul."

"Do we know what we want to say, Mr. President?" Desaix asked, wanting to make certain there was a game plan. Zotov was notorious for turning his adversaries against one another if they seemed in any way fragmented.

"Don't worry, Desaix. I'll just improvise. I have a good personal relationship with him." Westview felt a little offended that Desaix would question his ability.

On the other hand, Desaix was not surprised. The ad hoc strategy was typical of the American negotiating style.

"Mr. President, Zotov is on the other line."

"Who will be taking notes for this meeting?" Westview asked.

"I will," Desaix responded with alacrity, although he knew all too well that the ignominious task of taking notes in any crisis always fell to the most junior member attending the particular meeting, usually a junior FSO. In this case, however, Desaix was certain to have been designated to record the detailed conversation. Traditionally, the U.S. President met with the Russian President alone, with only an interpreter from the Russian side and two note takers, an American and a Russian. But teleconferencing had changed all that. Now one could have as many people from as many locations in a conference meeting as permitted.

One saving grace, Desaix realized, was that whoever records the minutes of a historic meeting has ultimate control over what would eventually be written in the history books. He would be the source for anyone who wanted to use the historical notes, the first juncture of control in managing the crisis.

Desaix watched the sixth TV monitor as the scrambled picture of Zotov started to resolve into a clear image. Everyone in the room was quiet. "Penetrating" was the word that came into Desaix's mind. Zotov appeared far more impressive than Desaix had imagined. He seemed to fill up the television screen with a charismatic presence. The thick, wavy white hair softened the strong lines of his angular face. His deep dark brown eyes scanned the four television monitors placed in front of him. Desaix turned toward Taylor, knowing she would be impressed by Zotov's thick, sensuous lips.

There was an intensity of purpose that seemed to be etched along the furrows of Zotov's thick, clearly dyed black eyebrows. Looking more closely at Zotov's face, set against a completely blank red background, Desaix noticed that his right eye seemed to be twitching. But there was something both intelligent and warm in his face. Desaix couldn't quite put his finger on it. The more Desaix stared at Zotov's face, the more he saw a mischievous glint in both eyes. A pleasant troublemaker!

Without saying a word, a four-star Russian general sat down next to Zotov.

Desaix recognized the Russian general, but didn't say a word. So the son of a bitch had managed to get himself into the crisis management game, thought Desaix. Good for him! Now the game would have some interesting twists and turns!

"Good day, President Westview. It's good to see you again." Zotov's English was clipped, precise, and revealed only the minimal amount of the stereotypic Russian accent, with its broad, bloated pronounciation of vowels.

"It's good to see you too, President Zotov. I'm sorry that we must meet under such disturbing circumstances. But, hopefully, we can find a solution that will resolve our problems quickly . . ." Westview paused deliberately, and then emphasized, "Before they get completely out of control. Let me just add that it is extremely important that neither one of us overreact to the present situation. As you see, Mr. President, I have assembled my senior advisors. I want them to have a clear sense of our mutual desire to resolve this crisis in the the most effective way possible. In a complete spirit of mutual trust and cooperation."

"You could not have expressed my sentiments any more clearly. I'm sorry, but for security reasons, I'm not able to provide an equally impressive group of advisors. But I did bring along my trusted marshal, who is in charge of all the Russian Armed Forces and Commonwealth of Independent States militias, so he too can hear what is being said between us." Pausing to collect himself, he added, "You may already know that my closest advisor and friend, Colonel-General Nikolai Pavlovich Kurasov, was killed yesterday." Zotov lowered his head for a moment before he continued. "He was a close family friend as well as advisor. I am the godfather of his young children. Is that what you say in English? No?"

"Yes, we say godfather. And please, let me express our condolences. On behalf of myself and my staff. We know how close the two of you were. Let me also extend my greetings to Field Marshal Kulikov, whom I have previously met. And now, President Zotov, with regard to the matter at hand, I propose that we call for an immediate cessation of all aggressive actions on both sides. This way we can begin a cooling-off period to straighten out any problems we might have."

"I am in full accord with you." Zotov's face became a pleasant smile. "Our marshal will instruct his generals to suppress the renegade forces with force, if necessary, in order to prevent a war from breaking out between our two great countries—the United States and the Russian Federation."

Looking up at the TV screen at both Zotov and Westview, Desaix was amazed. What should have been a more heated discussion was turning out to be a series of pleasantries. Where were their emotions? Both men were known to possess equally strong tempers. So what was this crisis about? A few minor misunderstandings?

"Good," Westview continued. "Then I will order my Secretary of Defense to order a cease-fire."

"Thank God!" Zotov said, then paused. "I only have one request, President Westview."

"What is that, Mr. President?"

"I would like to have a direct meeting with you as soon as it can be arranged. In your country, if possible. As an amateur historian, I think I can learn some lessons from your own civil war of the last century, which will be useful in solving some current problems in our commonwealth."

"I will be happy to host your visit as soon as we know that a cease-fire is being implemented by both sides." Pausing, Westview added, "We can combine your interest in the Civil War, and our need for privacy, by meeting at Camp David."

"Fine, Mr. President. I will notify my staff. And, if you don't mind, I would also like to visit some of the Civil War battlefields I have never seen . . . like Richmond . . . Gettysburg . . . and the battlefields near Baltimore . . ."

If anyone had been looking at Desaix's face just then, he would have seen it turn ashen.

# CHAPTER

## 13

Like most Americans, Desaix felt like a tourist whenever he visited the White House. Of course, he felt the same way about Disneyland.

As much as he might want to believe in the Magic Kingdom, he knew he would have to walk away from it in order to return another day. Fundamentally, he was a kid at heart who never wanted to be disillusioned by life's coarse realities.

The fact that every President had stood, ate, or slept on the very spot that Desaix was standing never ceased to amaze him. It was a practiced innocence that belied a relentless cynicism. He could feel overwhelmed or infatuated, almost at will, much as he had at his lecture in Japan. On one level, he realized that he was using his enthusiasm as a psychological defense against his underlying mistrust and melancholia. On a deeper level, he suspected that he was afraid of committing himself wholeheartedly to any one person for fear of being disappointed when that person didn't live up to his high expectations. So he guarded himself against the inevitable disappointment by acquiring the fashionable habits of the world-weary cynic.

In reality, Desaix was far more idealistic than anyone might have imagined. Like his Protestant Huguenot ancestors, who had fled France in the late seventeenth century in order to seek religious freedom in Louisiana, he continuously sought within himself those feelings of spiritual redemption that might, one day, make him feel complete.

And like many of his post-Vietnam contemporaries, Desaix had an ambivalent relationship with both his country and his President. He felt grateful to have been born in a land of promise, but throughout his life he was never certain what it was that the country promised him other than the uncertainty inherent in a life of promise. His need to attain a multiplicity of professions, without achieving true excellence in any one, was a direct product of his uncertainties. So he became a psychiatrist, a strategist, and an international crisis manager. All in the name of the American promise and the American dream.

"Identification, please!"

He handed his State Department pass to the executive protection security guard sitting behind the transparent plastic shield in the protective booth at the visitor's gate.

"Social Security is 127-78-9023; birth date is 12/07/51."

The guard scanned the computer. With Desaix's Social Security number and birth date, he could access a wealth of information about him, including his place of birth, history of arrests, present government position, whether he was allowed to see classified material, and what type.

"Will you be handling TOP SECRET material?"

"Yes."

"Compartmentalized material?"

"Yes."

"What type?"

The guard smiled at Desaix. Both had played their little ritual of entrance without any problems. Desaix knew that the guard knew exactly what type of compartmentalized intelligence Desaix had access to. It was right there on that fluorescent screen. But according to proper protocol for handling classified material, one never admitted to which type of classified material one had access, ostensibly because the material was extremely sensitive. But the real truth was that the less one said about the nature of one's work, the more mysterious, and therefore more important, one invariably appeared. And in Washington, appearance was everything.

"I'm sorry to keep you waiting, sir, but there seems to be a glitch in the computer."

Desaix laughed. So much for modern computers.

Looking across Pennsylvania Avenue, Desaix wondered what kind of message the group of homeless camped out in Lafayette Park were sending to the networks about President Westview's domestic programs. There they were, sprawled over metal gratings on the sidewalk, hoping to be bathed by the vapors of warm exhaust streaming forth from the underbelly of the streets. What had happened to the President's rhetoric of a caring and committed nation? Was that simply campaign rhetoric? Or did the President really mean to rid the nation of this moral blemish?

Desaix was never one to pursue social causes. But ever since childhood, when his physician father and socialite mother lived with their brood of two sons and three daughters on Prytania Street in the fashionable Garden District of New Orleans, he was aware that he had lived a privileged existence. A maverick since childhood, Desaix had learned early on that he had to make his mark on a family that had made personal accomplishment and social responsibility the primary justifications for their existence. If his eldest brother, Gaston, was about to become a general practitioner, then Desaix would become a board-certified psychiatrist as well as a Ph.D. in international affairs, just to prove that he was that much better in order to attract the dutiful praise of an emotionally distant father. Throughout his formative years, scholastic competition, sibling rivalry, and sporadic outbursts of deviant behavior marked his relationship with most of his brothers and sisters. Only his youngest sister, Antoinette, an affectionate, sweet tomboy, provided him with the gentle kindness and understanding for which he thirsted and sought in his subsequent relationships with women. Although he was particularly close to his mother, a histrionic concert pianist who had given up her promising career to raise the children at the insistence of his strict, absent father, Desaix often found himself in the emotionally precarious position of acting more like a surrogate lover and husband than a son. Early on, he had learned to distance himself from the suffocating maternal emotions that were commonly identified as love, need, and dependency. He was, as honestly as he could describe it, a product of a typical upper-class professional American family—functionally dysfunctional.

Unlike the homeless beggars who made their morning and evening rounds up and down St. Charles Avenue, imploring callous residents for a night's shelter or a day's meal, Desaix had lived in the Corinthian-columned splendor of a "small cottage," with fourteen-foot ceilings bathed in patches of scattered sunlight. Unlike the fetid smell of the unkempt, Desaix could recreate in his mind the smells and sights of the family's crowded flower gardens, the waxen-barked crape myrtles with their airy blossoms of red, purple, pink, and white, nestled alongside the sweet magnolia.

"Sir, you can pass on through," the guard said. "Someone from the President's office will be waiting for you in the West Wing. If you have any question there will be enough people who can direct you to the proper place."

"Thank you."

"You're welcome, sir. Here's your visitor's badge. You are authorized to walk without any escort. Do you have any questions?"

"May I go to the bathroom without anyone watching me?" Desaix smiled, and glanced at the large A on his badge. Did that mean that he was an adulterer? he thought naughtily.

He walked leisurely down the well-landscaped path to the blue awning identifying the basement of the West Wing. He felt the sense of history reverberate through his body. Roosevelt, Truman, Eisenhower, Kennedy, Johnson, Nixon, Ford, Carter, Reagan, Bush, and finally Westview. It was that sense of being part of history, more importantly, of having influenced it, that excited Desaix. Goethe had called history "that ephemeral woman," and it was she who gave Desaix his raison d'être for remaining engaged with other people. Otherwise, he would have been happy to return home to New Orleans to retire, to practice medicine, or maybe even do what many doctors dream of doing—write a novel based upon his fascinating cases. But for Desaix, life had meaning only if there was an opportunity to have an impact on history.

Desaix was always surprised at how truly small the White House was. He walked down a short hallway decorated in the Federalist style. Darkly stained oak chairs and coffee tables stood by off-white walls, from which hung original oil paintings of pastoral views and cowboys riding herd over vast plains. The low, seven-foot ceilings gave one the impression that the building was little more than an expanded doll house.

As he turned the corridor, a group of Secret Service agents, standing guard in the hallway with plastic ear pieces and automaton-like manners, signaled him to approach the Oval Office.

"Hello, I'm Mary Dougherty, Chief of the President's protective detail. May I help you?" an attractive, compact woman in her mid-thirties asked in a matter-of-fact manner, trying to decide as she sized him up whether he was carrying a gun or anything else that could be harmful to the President. Something about him looked dissolute. His deep-set eyes seemed to absorb everything before him avidly. It made him sexy. For certain, he radiated a boyish mischief.

"Ms. Dougherty, if you look me over any more intensely, you offer me no other choice than to marry you. Not even my four wives ever looked at me like that!"

"You're . . . ?"

"I'm Desaix Clark, Deputy Assistant Secretary of State for East Asian and Pacific Affairs. I have an appointment with the President."

"Let me see." She carefully reviewed a list of names on her clipboard and shook her head with disappointment. "I'm sorry, but I just can't seem to find your name on the appointments list."

"I assure you there must be some mistake. I do have an appointment this afternoon with the President. They let me through the front gate."

"Quite frankly, they let a lot of people through the front gate."

Desaix liked this special agent. She had spunk. He tried to recall what seemed familiar. The way she talked. A husky, sexy quality about her voice.

"There's Ms. Newmann, the President's appointments secretary, walking toward us. She'll take you in to see him."

"Dr. Clark, it's good to see you again. The President will see you now," Randy Newmann said. The attractive Midwesterner led him into the Oval Office.

The room was as impressive as he remembered it. The fact that he had visited it several times before was completely lost to him. Each time was as if it were the first.

How strange, thought Desaix. Even in the latter part of a warm spring there was a fire burning in the fireplace.

"Mr. President, Dr. Desaix Clark is here to see you." Randy left the room as Desaix approached Westview.

"Good to see you again, my friend." Westview stood up and greeted Desaix warmly, taking his hand and shaking it firmly. It was only then that Desaix noticed the long, tapered fingers, and thought there was something wrong with them. They looked and felt too malleable. They seemed to be able to bend unendingly. In medical terms, they were hyper-reflexive. "Please sit down over here, next to me." Both men took their places at the famous oak desk.

"I'm glad to see you, Mr. President. I'd been hoping to get an appointment with you."

"Desaix, you can imagine how busy I have been over the past few days."

"I'm sorry I sounded so insistent." Desaix was concerned that the President looked pale, anemic.

"No, no, my friend. Remember, it's I who wanted to see you. I have something very important for you to do for me."

"Yes, sir." This was the very moment for which he was waiting.

"First tell me how you have been. I've heard that you've gotten yourself in a little bit of nasty trouble."

"Thank you for asking. Personally, I'm doing all right. I can't complain. But Fitzpatrick's death in Tokyo was quite disturbing. The way he was tortured . . . and killed."

"Yes, I was very sorry to hear about that. But I've requested the Japanese to spare no effort in tracking down the killers."

"That will be very useful."

Talking freely and seated sideways with his arm around the chair, the President was obviously pleased to see Desaix.

"You know, Desaix, I've been reading over some of your suggestions on media management—keep them isolated, maintain control, dole out the news in two-minute sound bites. I found it very useful in my last press conference."

"Thank you. Maybe next time I can be there in person in order to help you out."

"Yes, of course . . ." Westview paused. There was an irreverent quality about Desaix that had always amused Westview. He enjoyed talking to Desaix. But this time, he wanted to prime him with a little bit of flattery before he made his request.

"Was it true that you discovered Fitzpatrick's body while you were screwing one of those geisha girls in the hot tub?"

Desaix was surprised that the President knew the details of his sexual escapade, or even cared about it.

"I was engaged in some R and R."

"Nothing too strenuous, I hope." Westview laughed.

"Mr. President, the most disturbing part of Fitzpatrick's death was not the gruesome way he died, but the fact that there is some evidence to suggest that he was killed by an American."

"What do you mean?"

"There was an American who was waiting for us with a Sig Sauer P226. He clearly knew me and wanted to know whether I had killed Fitzpatrick. Then he asked me if I knew about Baltimore—"

"The city?"

"No. At least, I'm pretty certain it's not the city."

"What do you think he meant?"

"I think he was talking about some kind of code. Strangely, President Zotov made a reference to it in his discussions with you."

"What makes you think that?"

"Why would he make a reference to the city of Baltimore in the middle of discussions regarding safety measures to contain a conflict in Western Europe?"

"Maybe he was seriously interested in visiting the area after the problems were resolved."

"Possibly. But I doubt it."

"Then how do you explain the American who was waiting for you behind the wall, ready to kill you?"

"Again, I can't." Desaix was silenced by the question. How did the President know that the American had been hiding? Desaix hadn't mentioned anything about a wall. "The only way I can make sense of it is to assume that someone on either the U.S. or the Russian side does not want to resolve this crisis. Baltimore may be the code word for a plot to get rid of all those people who stand in the way. As our government's top Russian expert, Fitzpatrick either knew something he was not supposed to know; or else he tried to stop Baltimore. And as a result he was killed."

"Are you suggesting that an American Russian expert and the President of the Russian Federation were both involved in a conspiracy code-named Baltimore?" Westview was no longer smiling.

"Fitzpatrick was either working for the Russians, or President Zotov is on the U.S. payroll," Desaix replied hesistantly, sensing that Westview knew more than he was revealing.

Westview broke into a hearty laughter. "You certainly have a vivid and, may I add, fertile imagination."

Desaix didn't join in the laughter. He was still obsessing over whether either thesis was correct. The Russians were either on our payroll or someone high up in the U.S. government was on theirs. But why now? Détente had gone on so well for such a long time.

"And what would the motive be?" the President asked. "Every crime, or alleged crime, needs a motive." Westview enjoyed pitting his intelligence against Desaix's.

"You've got me on that one, Mr. President. I wish I could give you a plausible answer, but I can't. It just doesn't make sense on a lot of different levels. That's why I wanted to see you. Perhaps you could clarify some points."

"I'd be happy to help in any way possible." Westview enjoyed sounding gracious, particularly to a skeptic like Desaix, who, by his very nature, was distrustful of any form of altruism.

"How did you know that the man who held the gun on us was hiding behind a wall?" Desaix asked, sensing that Westview was playing some type of mind game with him.

"You are a suspicious fellow, aren't you?" Westview patted him on the knee in what Desaix interpreted as an incredibly paternalistic gesture. "That's good, I have some serious suspicions of my own."

"About what, Mr. President?" Desaix sounded annoyed. He felt as if the President was toying with him.

"Desaix, in exactly seventy-two hours there will be a coup attempt against me."

"What?" Desaix was shocked by the calm manner in which the President related the news.

"I only know that it will occur. But where, how, and when still remain the major unknowns."

"Who is organizing this coup?"

"Well, you're the crisis manager. That's what I want you to find out," Westview replied matter-of-factly. He watched as Desaix looked increasingly more incredulous and annoyed. Any minute now, he should explode, the President thought.

"Mr. President . . . thank you for your valuable time." Desaix stood up and started to walk toward the door.

"Where are you going, Desaix?" Westview jumped up and followed him.

"Mr. President, you and I have worked together in a lot of different crises."

"That's right! So?"

"So?" repeated Desaix angrily. "Please give me the benefit of the doubt that I know something about how you behave under stress. I've seen you choke with fear when a crisis was unraveling. At the same time, I've seen you gloat with delight when you managed it successfully. And now you asked to see me in order to inform me nonchalantly that someone is trying to overthrow you. Mr. President, you just sounded less concerned and less convincing than if you had just ordered a scoop of vanilla ice cream with nuts and raisins. You know me well enough to know that I don't enjoy playing games when an important issue is involved. Something else is going on. I don't know what it is, but I do know when I am being toyed with. You knew there was an American hiding behind the wall. I didn't tell you that. You either put all your cards on the table or don't play at all—at least, not with me. You're playing mind games . . . and I don't like it."

"You're right, Desaix. Please, forgive me," Westview said contritely. He led Desaix back to his seat. "Unfortunately, I took your advice too literally."

"What are you talking about?" Desaix was still fuming.

"Here, take a glass of water. Cool down!" Westview poured from the silver decanter. "You don't remember your own lessons, do you?"

"Please . . . Donald . . ." When Desaix was beyond the point of tolerance with anyone, he often called them by their first name.

"Don't you remember the first time we worked together? There were close to two hundred hostages held captive in a building filled with napalm. I had the choice of appearing tough and decisive by calling in the FBI SWAT team to rescue the hostages and risk the possibility of turning the situation into a blazing inferno where half the hostages could die. But I would come out looking like a hero. Or I had the option of using my manipulative skills to convince the terrorists to release the hostages because it would benefit their cause in the long run. In that case, I would have looked weak and indecisive. One was a high-risk option, the other one was a low-risk option. Remember?"

"Yes. So what?"

"The first lesson you ever taught me, Desaix, was do what your heart tells you to do. You said to me, 'If you don't believe in fighting for it, then don't do it. Test a man's passion, and you'll uncover his fortitude.' Remember?"

"Yes, I remember." Desaix smiled. He was surprised to see how much of an influence he really had had on Westview.

"How was I to know what Dr. Desaix Clark really felt about me or the presidency, unless I could uncover his emotions?"

"My word . . . my integrity . . . my professionalism . . ." Desaix replied defensively.

"All words, Desaix. Wasn't it you who taught me to go for the emotions and forget the words. Listen to what was not said. Uncover the affect and you'll know what someone really thinks and feels about an issue."

"So the student has become the teacher?" Desaix laughed.

"In a manner of speaking. I still have a way to go." Westview chortled. He extended his hand. "Still friends?"

"Friends!" Desaix shook his hand, reaffirming the continuing bond of their special relationship. "How may I help you, Mr. President?"

"Desaix, I'm really frightened." Westview leaned over toward him.

Desaix saw beads of sweat collecting on his forehead.

"Do you have any problem with my asking for patient-physician confidentiality?"

"What?" Desaix looked at the President skeptically. "Are we starting to play games again?"

"No, Desaix! I swear to you that what I am about to tell you requires the bond between a doctor and a patient that cannot be broken by law or unwillful confession."

"You are asking me to treat you as a patient?"

"You've been a teacher of sorts. Now I ask you to be my psychiatrist."

Desaix said nothing. He was incredulous. Could he really believe what he was hearing? The President of the United States wanted to become his patient so that he could invoke the inviolate doctor-patient privilege. A moral seal of ethics that could not be broken. A bond of confidentiality stronger than any TOP SECRET clearance.

Desaix was impressed that Westview had correctly assessed the only thing Desaix believed in, the basic integrity of the medical profession. Above all else, do no harm. By having taken to the Hippocratic oath, Desaix had committed himself to providing care for anyone, no matter what sins he or she may have committed. The mass murderer was entitled to the same medical care as a virgin nun. Neither one was to be judged by his or her religion, morals, or political beliefs. In the eye of the doctor, all people were created equal. And the only basis for discrimination was the pathology of the body or mind.

"On one condition," Desaix replied cautiously.

"Name it!"

"If I suspect that you are in any way trying to abuse that confidentiality by trying to co-opt me, I have the right to break that confidentiality."

"Agreed!" Westview replied cheerfully.

They shook hands. Then Westview sighed in relief and said, "Someone is making it look like I am going crazy."

"What do you mean?"

"Remember what I told you before you started to storm out of here, that in the next seventy-two hours there will be a coup attempt against me?"

"I thought you were kidding. It's not often that the intended victim knows exactly what will happen to him."

"I know that the coup will occur. The pretext of the coup will be that I'm crazy."

"How do you know that?" Desaix asked, intrigued by the idea that someone could be that sophisticated and Machiavellian to make a President of the United States appear crazy. Not an easy task, he thought.

"I know what you're thinking. Anyone who wants to be President has to be crazy, by definition. Right?" Westview laughed.

"It certainly entered my mind."

"Listen to me. I'm serious. I know this may sound crazy, but a lot of strange things have happened over the past several days that indicate to me that someone is trying very hard to prove I'm not competent to run this crisis or remain President." Westview's voice suddenly became conspiratorial.

"What evidence do you have?"

"I had been hearing rumors floating around the media that I am physically ill and have some undefined mental problem associated with that illness. Nothing more specific than that."

"Washington is one big rumor mill."

"I know that. But yesterday I had to visit Saint Elizabeth Hospital because of a long-standing commitment. The word went out to the press that my presence there was evidence that something was mentally wrong with me. Otherwise, why would I go all the way out there in the middle of a serious international crisis?"

"What else?" Desaix was still not impressed.

"I have a feeling you're not convinced of my suspicions."

"That's all they are, Donald. Suspicions. Nothing more." Desaix was becoming restless. He was beginning to wonder whether Westview wasn't playing with him again. He clearly knew more than he was saying.

"My informants in the Agency told me that both a Psychological Profile and Operational Code were ordered on me by some unidentified senior official. Specifically, they were ordered under code UMBRA, which as you know can only be authorized by me for use only in an international crisis. In this case, the request was made to see how I would respond to a hypothetical coup."

"Is there any way to find out who ordered it?" Desaix asked, suddenly starting to take Westview's concerns more seriously. Only a handful of senior officials knew about the Psychological Profiles and Operational Codes on world leaders prepared at the CIA. And Westview was correct. By law, only the President of the United States could order a profile on an American citizen for domestic use. Violation of that law constituted a serious criminal offense.

"I've tried to find out, but I got nowhere. All of a sudden I feel that there is almost no one I can trust. And I have little time to play Sherlock Holmes. But I do have certain suspicions."

"I hate to sound like a lawyer, but despite the fact that your evidence sounds increasingly more compelling, it is still only circumstantial."

"You are a tough man to convince, Desaix." Westview retrieved a folder from the top of his desk marked TOP SECRET/EYES ONLY/NO DISTRI-BUTION and took out a blurred photograph. "Here's a picture that was taken of Fitzpatrick. Over there is the rubber tube that was used to pump hydrogen fluoride into his eye."

Desaix looked at the picture, taken from above, at about the same location he had first encountered the man behind the wall. A nude man with tape over his mouth was being held down by two large men wrapped in white towels. One of the men looked like Richard White. But Desaix couldn't be certain. He felt sick . . . and ashamed. Fitzpatrick was being killed while Desaix was fucking his brains out in the room next door. There was a certain perversity to that idea. Eros and Thanatos. "So, Fitzpatrick uncovered the coup, and as a result he was killed."

"Fitzpatrick was assassinated in Tokyo by officers of USOCOM or Special Forces units under the direct command of Lieutenant General Richard White, the Director of the Office of Signal Intelligence at the NSA, who in turn, reported to General Mapplethorpe."

"Are you certain?" Desaix felt his adrenaline begin to pump as Westview's story became increasingly more credible. Now he understood why Mapplethorpe had insisted that Fitzpatrick and White accompany him to Japan, overriding Desaix's own objections. In Tokyo, White could kill Fitzpatrick with relative impunity. The circumstances of his death would remain forever murky. If it had occurred in the United States, it would have raised a lot more suspicion and publicity. So Desaix's trip to Japan was simply a vehicle by which government officials could commit a crime and get away with it. Or, at least, so far.

"What can I do to help?" Desaix asked, convinced by the photograph.

"I want you to find out where, when, and how this coup will occur, and to stop this insidious propaganda to portray me as crazy. We know that Mapplethorpe and White are involved. But that's all we know. I want to know who else in the executive branch, the military, and the intelligence community are involved. Do your magic. Try to ferret out as many of the conspirators as possible without their knowing that you know. Then at the right time we'll pick them all up."

"Why don't you pick up Mapplethorpe and White right now?" Desaix asked, wary of the facile words he was hearing.

"If I did, I would only be cutting off the head of the rattlesnake without knowing where the rest of the body was. I want enough information to ambush all of them at the right moment." Westview hoped that Desaix's skepticism was diminishing. "Remember, I only have seventy-two hours, if that. Their pretext for the coup will be that I'm crazy." Then Westview burst out laughing. "What if I really am crazy, Desaix?"

"Even paranoids have enemies."

# CHAPTER
## 14

Conspiracies breed even more conspiracies.

Like the mythical Gordian knot, there is no beginning or end, simply an endless tangle of innuendos and accusations, whispered in the shadows of suspicion and paranoia. And its attraction rests on the fact that it explains everything, but in fact reveals very little.

On the positive side, the notion of a conspiracy allowed Desaix to believe in something other than his own delusion of omnipotence. He didn't want the responsibility of having to uncover the Veritable Truth. It was a lot easier just to believe in a sinister plot. Then all he would have to do was identify the good guys and the bad guys. Unfortunately, Washington politics didn't operate that simply. There were just too many shades of gray.

"Oh, Dr. Clark, Secretary of State Chester Manning called to say he wants to see you in an hour," Randy said as Desaix walked out of the Oval Office.

"Thanks," Desaix answered, preoccupied. The President of the United States was fighting for his very survival by trying to prove he was not crazy. In the process, he risked the serious possibility of appearing crazy. Proving the unprovable was akin to swearing that ghosts did or did not exist. It was all really a question of what the philosophers called epistemology. How do we know what we know? And Desaix was in no mood for deductive speculations. So he would have to uncover and extract only the essential core of the conspiracy and discard the rest for some later time. Who was after the President and why? And how was this, if at all, connected to the mounting crisis between the U.S. and Russia?

"A penny for your thoughts, Dr. Clark?" A perky voice interrupted his thoughts.

"What?" Desaix looked up and saw Special Agent Mary Dougherty.

"At least I prevented you from walking into a highly restricted area," Mary said, pointing to a door marked MAINTENANCE CLOSET. "That's where we keep some of our most important national security equipment—the whisk broom and dust pan; a Eureka vacuum cleaner; and the all-important Glamorene Spray 'N Vac no-scrub rug cleaner and deodorizer."

"I was that close to danger, huh?" Desaix laughed as he realized the absurdity of the situation.

"Could you imagine what could have happened to you had you discovered the secret of X-14 stain remover?" Mary liked the lightness of Desaix's response. He clearly had a mischievous side to him.

"I fear to think what might have happened to me." Desaix enjoyed the fact that a normally restrained Secret Service agent would encourage this type of banter.

"For certain, we would have had to take your security clearance away."

"That bad?"

"Could be worse. If you found out that we used Swell dust, mop, and cloth treatment. Well . . . that's serious!" Mary accompanied him toward the door.

"It would take me some time to debrief you and find out exactly what you did or did not know. And then . . ."

Mary liked the way he smelled. He was wearing one of those softly scented colognes that suited both men or women. Clearly, he was not threatened by gender identity. "And then what?" she asked teasingly.

"Are you propositioning me, Ms. Dougherty?" Desaix bent close to her flushing beatific face.

She muttered, taking one step back.

"Is that a yes, no, or maybe?" Desaix smiled knowingly.

"That will teach me not to play with a shrink," Mary replied defensively. "Nowhere on our computers did it indicate that you were so bold."

"Yes, no, or maybe?" Desaix enjoyed provoking her to move from the shadows of flirtation to the blinding light of direct sexual confrontation. It was the quickest way he knew of culling the serious players. The ones who knew how to provoke, engage, and follow through.

"You don't leave a woman much room to maneuver, do you?"

"Sublimation and rationalization are highly overrated defense mechanisms; they can't offer you a cup of coffee." Desaix was in a hurry. He would be late for Manning, but he had to see if Ms. Mary Dougherty was as courageous as she thought.

"Come back at the end of the day. I'll be waiting for you. How's that?" Mary replied, pleased that she could regain her composure so quickly.

"I'm impressed." He opened the doors. "Dinner at seven. If I'm late, just wait. I'll be there. If not, call the State Op Center, they'll know where I am."


As Desaix approached the eight-story nondescript State Department Building, a behemoth taking up the entire block of Twenty-third and C streets, he noticed an increased number of security guards at the main C Street entrance. He wondered which foreign dignitary was in the building today.

Walking through the glass doors into the main foyer, Desaix felt immediately at home. He was surrounded by the familiar gray-granite walls draped with the flags of the United States and several foreign countries. In front of him was the large wooden information desk, staffed by volunteer Foreign Service officer wives. On both sides of the information booth were security guards and metal detectors through which visitors had to pass. Not unlike an airport.

Officials who worked in the building passed through subway-like metal turnstiles after passing their identification card through an electronic sensor. Not quite as elaborate as the CIA's alternating barricades, nor the NSA's tight electronic surveillance, but effective enough to deter someone who might want to rush the guards.

After his card passed through the electronic sensor, Desaix walked into one of the unmanned elevators and pressed the seventh-floor button.

The elevator stopped on the sixth floor. In terms of State's professional hierarchy, Desaix could expect to find most of the Department's Assistant Secretaries and Deputy Assistant Secretaries on that floor, one floor below the Secretary of State and his principal deputies' suites. Desaix's own office, which he had not visited since his return from Japan, was on the sixth floor, down the fifth corridor, which was painted red.

"I'll be damned, if it isn't Sigmund Freud himself!" Paul Twitty joked as he wobbled into the elevator, holding a wooden cane in his right hand, and an asthmatic inhalator in his left.

"Good afternoon, Twitty." Desaix pronounced his name with the sardonic tone of voice he felt matched the nature of Twitty's grotesque appearance and quaint last name.

"So you finally decided to do some work?" Twitty asked, placing his hand-carved cane beneath the NO SMOKING sign, and took out a pack of unfiltered Sobriani cigarettes. He lit one and inhaled the smoke with gusto. He would show the good doctor that despite rumors to the contrary, he was in fine physical condition.

"Old habits break hard, don't they, Paul?" Desaix smiled with a smug sense of superiority. He knew that his presence always forced Twitty into some passive-aggressive act of defiance.

"No, they don't, Desaix!" Inhaling the cigarette with the grand gesture of someone who has never had a second thought about his self-destructive lifestyle, Twitty added sarcastically, "And you, Desaix, have you gotten syphilis yet?"

"There is only one way to find out, Paul."

"You mean bend over and pick up the soap?"

"Yeah, something like that!"

They both started to laugh. Despite their differences, Desaix was one of the few senior State Department officials with whom Twitty could trade sexual banter, without feeling overly self-conscious about it. In some perverse macho way, Desaix was someone Twitty would have liked to emulate, in another life. But where Desaix jumped from one bed to another, Twitty simply hobbled between State Department meetings.

"You're going up to see the Secretary?" Twitty made a point of knowing whom the Secretary of State was seeing at any given moment. It allowed him to monitor the Secretary's concerns and get a fix on who was or wasn't popular with Manning. At State, like most of politics, information was power.

"Yeah, I have a meeting with Chet."

Both Desaix and Twitty knew that only a few people were allowed to address him by his nickname. And for some unexplainable reason that continually irked Twitty. Twitty had always suspected that Desaix and Manning must have whored around together sometime in the distant past, when Desaix worked on the President's election campaign. But that was only speculation. What wasn't speculation was that the closest bonds of trust in politics were forged in the bedrooms of Washington mistresses and courtesans, the unofficially anointed, those wealthy women who had more time and leisure than purpose in life. They were, as Twitty called them, power groupies, often identified in the Style Section of *The Washington Post* as fashionable ladies, who had been recently divorced or were about to be divorced. For the most part, they were seasoned women whose primary livelihood arose from their ability to act socially graceful and speak politically correct. And Twitty was jealous of the fact that Desaix and Manning were part of that social entourage.

When the elevator reached the seventh floor both men walked off in the same direction. A matronly secretary with blue-tinted gray hair sat in the rotunda leading into the Secretary's oak-paneled suite of offices. Her sole job was to make certain that anyone who approached the Secretary's office had an appointment with one of the principals working inside. If not, she was to call a security guard and have that person evicted, as gracefully as possible.

"Good morning, gentlemen! And, how might you both be on this fine morning?" she asked.

"Fine, thank you!" they replied in unison, still chuckling, as they walked past the blue-uniformed guards into a narrow, heavily carpeted corridor lined with paintings and photographs of past Secretaries of State and Deputy and Under Secretaries.

"Paul, I have a serious question for you." Desaix wanted to take advantage of the fact that Twitty was considered one of the State Department's most seasoned experts on Russia and Eastern Europe.

"Come on, Desaix. The last serious question you asked me was two administrations ago!" Twitty couldn't help the fact that he had a compulsive need to give Desaix a hard time. In part, he was still envious that Desaix could somehow waltz himself into the middle of this new crisis, without having paid any of the obligatory dues, and position himself as an essential player in its resolution.

"Twitty, do me a favor. Bust my chops some other time," Desaix said in a lowered voice as they passed the nonuniformed diplomatic security agents surrounding Manning's office.

"Okay then, what's your question? But remember, you owe me," Twitty said as they walked into one of the small elegantly appointed waiting rooms off the corridor.

"Paul, I'm perplexed."

"That's not unusual for you."

"Come on, Paul. You promised."

"Go ahead." Twitty liked the feeling of granting Desaix a favor. He just couldn't wait to extract his payment.

"You've worked with the Russians for over thirty years—"

"Thirty-five years, to be precise."

"You know President Zotov pretty well—"

"Extremely well. We used to go out drinking when he was Gorbachev's political hatchet man. Before he worked for Yeltsin." Twitty was enjoying this. It placed them back in the mentor-student relationship with which he felt extremely comfortable. From Twitty's experience, Desaix was most likeable when he was learning. And the ability to provide new and different information had always been Twitty's basis of garnering power.

"I don't understand it, Paul. The U.S., Russia, and the Commonwealth of Independent States have been at peace for almost a decade. Despite minor differences there has always been a spirit of cooperation . . ." Desaix checked his watch. He was already late for the Secretary's meeting. He picked up the phone on the coffee table, dialed Manning's office, and was relieved to find out that the Secretary was running a half hour behind schedule.

"I think I understand your question." Twitty was pleased to see that even Manning's prodigal son was not immune to being nervous about an appointment with the Secretary.

"You're wondering how it is that after almost a decade of peace we suddenly find ourselves, without any warning, at the verge of World War III."

"That's part of it. But why now? It doesn't make sense. We are two enfeebled empires that should be concerned with our deteriorating domestic condition. And that's the other part of my question. How is it that both we and the Russians have almost identical domestic problems at the same time?" Despite what Desaix thought of Twitty personally, he respected his almost visceral knowledge of the Soviets.

"You want me to be very frank with you?"

"Of course."

"The truth is I don't know," Twitty said, preparing himself for the receiving end of Desaix's infamous sarcasm.

"Come on, Twitty. You don't expect me to believe that. With Fitzpatrick gone, you are the administration's top Russian expert."

"Look what happened to Fitzpatrick," Twitty said, realizing that he was treading on dangerous ground.

"Are you intimating that he was killed because he knew something about events in Russia?" Desaix asked. He wondered whether Twitty was now playing some kind of mind game with him.

"Why would a Russian expert be sent over with you on a trip to Japan on a matter of secondary concern—in the middle of one of the most significant crises since World War II?" Twitty was beginning to have fun with Desaix. Maybe the time for retribution was at hand. He liked Desaix's perplexed look. For the first time in a very long time, Twitty had Desaix off-balance.

"I don't really know."

"That's right. You were the DAS in charge of the team, and yet you had no choice in whether you should take Fitzpatrick. Interesting isn't it?" Twitty inhaled his foul-smelling Sobriani, and took a deep breath from his inhalator. "Most unusual, wouldn't you say?"

For a moment, Desaix would have sworn that Sidney Greenstreet had just stepped out of *Casablanca.*

"Twitty, you know something that I should know, don't you." Desaix wasn't certain how much of what Twitty was saying was simply posturing.

"Let me put it this way—I know, or at least I think I know, more than I should as an Under Secretary of State. And for me that type of situation can be dangerous." Taking a deep breath on his inhalator, Twitty watched Desaix's haggard-looking face. "You know, Desaix, if you're not careful, pretty soon you'll end up looking like the portrait of Dorian Gray. I'm worried about you."

Despite the good-natured verbal jousting, Desaix was fast losing patience with Twitty.

"I appreciate your concern, but if you really want to help me out, Paul, please tell me about Fitzpatrick. How is that related to what's happening in Germany between the Russians and us?" The steady, monotonous sound of the Chippendale grandfather clock was annoyingly distracting. Desaix could feel time mocking his efforts to uncover what he felt should be a moment of truth.

"Desaix, what I'm about to tell you could be fact or fiction but it's up to you to figure out."

"Twitty, don't fuck with me! I'm in no mood to be played with."

"Someone high in the administration didn't want Fitzpatrick around while this war between the U.S. and Russia was being started."

"What in God's name do you mean while this war was being started?"

"I mean that this war was purposefully started. Otherwise, how could you explain the sudden transformation of what was once an incredibly friendly and cooperative relationship into what could potentially evolve into World War III?"

"Like any crisis, you could have had a miscalculation . . . a misperception on the battlefield. Exactly what Westview said. There could be any one of a number of ridiculous causes, but—?"

"But what, Desaix? Why do you, a sophisticated professional, question the probability of someone who supposedly is on the side of good and justice, like good old Uncle Sam and company, starting a war?" Twitty was certainly enjoying this tête-à-tête. It had been a long time since they had sat in the Secretary of State's office, not since back in the late 1970s, shooting the breeze, making all types of assertions, part fact, part fiction, part rumor.

Desaix now felt that Twitty was not playing with him. He was making too serious an allegation.

"Why would we want to start a war?" Desaix asked although he could probably enumerate the reasons himself if he had to. But all of it seemed absurd.

"To increase the President's popularity at a time at which it has been the lowest in his career."

"Oh, come on!" Desaix said, playing the devil's advocate. He was trying to ascertain how valid Westview's accusations implicating Mapplethorpe were. "Okay. So wars automatically increase any President's popularity. But that's so transient. No one would really want to start a war for that."

"I see that you have forgotten your American history," Twitty said, now sounding professorial.

Desaix was becoming progressively more anxious. Everything Twitty said led him back to the military. And to Mapplethorpe. It was Mapplethorpe who had insisted on Desaix's taking Fitzpatrick with him to Japan. It was Mapplethorpe who had refused to see Desaix upon his return from Japan and who tried to cut him out of the action loop. And Westview had specifically accused Mapplethorpe of fomenting a military coup against him.

"It's Mapplethorpe, isn't it?" Desaix asked with a resigned tone of voice.

"Once again, I ask you to recall American history." He slowed down his normally rapid-fire speech so Desaix wouldn't miss a word. "Prior to our official entrance into World War II on December 8, 1941, President Roosevelt realized that he had to build a public constituency in the United States in order to enter the war on the side of the Allies. So he decided to engineer a *casus belli*. On the legislative side, he illegally shipped a fleet of merchant ships to England under a newly concocted program called the Lend Lease Policy. Similarly, there is increasing evidence to indicate that Roosevelt forced the Japanese into attacking us at Pearl Harbor by denying them their necessary resources and ignoring obvious signs that would have warned the U.S. of the surprise attack."

"Come on! That's a lot of uncorroborated speculation."

"Believe what you want, Desaix. That's your prerogative. But remember the question you asked me. Why is the U.S. suddenly and unexpectedly at war with a close trading partner with which it has had almost a decade of peace."

"Yeah, but—"

"You tell me, Desaix. What do you think happened in Operation Desert Shield?"

"As President Bush reiterated repeatedly, we were there to stop the Hitler-like aggression of Saddam Hussein," Desaix answered halfheartedly. Twitty's arguments were compelling, but they pointed in a disturbing direction. Now they implicated President Donald Westview as the direct instigator of a potential Third World War, rather than Mapplethorpe, who had simply acted as an advisor.

"First, President Bush gave Saddam Hussein the signal, through his Secretary of State, James Baker, to invade Kuwait. Once Hussein invaded that small, helpless country, Bush set about building a military coalition that defeated Hussein's army in less than two months."

"So what?" Desaix asked impatiently. He didn't see the connection to the present.

"Then, after Bush had militarily defeated Hussein, he shifted U.S. policy one hundred and eighty degrees and decided to ignore this Middle Eastern Hitler in his systematic decimation of the Kurds, the Shiites, and even the Sunni Muslems in Iraq. The subsequent genocide of countless thousands of Iraqis was accomplished by the very weapons the U.S. had supposedly destroyed in the two-month war. And don't forget that this newly articulated policy of implicitly abetting Saddam Hussein was done in the name of nonintervention into the domestic affairs of a sovereign country. This rationale was conveniently provided to the U.S. public after we had just destroyed three-quarters of Iraq."

"What's the point, Twitty?" Desaix checked his watch for the last time. He was in a hurry to get out of the room.

"My dear DAS, the point is that every President has his own hidden agenda, in which he may have a perfectly reasoned scenario for starting a war without someone like you or your professional psychiatric colleagues having to invoke that wonderfully romantic, but completely irrelevant, concept of insanity. In the case of President Bush, he needed a major yet highly contained war that would distract the American public's attention away from the five-hundred-billion-dollar savings and loan crisis, a recalcitrant recession, and two sons who were receiving front-page news exposure on their alleged involvement in the S&L fraud. And it didn't hurt the stagnant U.S. economy to have two recently devastated countries in the

Middle East, Kuwait and Iraq, open for U.S. business. And then we had the added bonus of becoming the only superpower to have a permanent military presence in the Middle East for close to ten years, effectively controlling over 80 percent of the oil production capacity in the world."

"So what happened to Bush's concept of preserving democracy and stopping aggression?" Desaix couldn't help but ask the question with a certain note of intended cynicism.

"As you know all too well, it went the way of all well-articulated principles . . ."

"Flushed down the toilet of expediency and rationalization," Desaix said, then shook Twitty's hand. Desaix started to walk out of the waiting room.

"Don't forget, Doctor! As you just told me in the elevator, old habits die hard. And that applies to Westview as well." As Twitty watched Desaix enter Secretary Manning's office, he hobbled down the corridor in the opposite direction. "Don't forget to watch your back!" He was sorry he and Desaix were no longer good friends. But Desaix would need his help again, and at that moment, Twitty would be willing to forget all the real and imagined hurts that had separated the two of them. Twitty realized one truth about Washington: today's enemies might become tomorrow's friends.

Walking past the two diplomatic security agents, with their characteristic grim, impersonal expressions, Desaix shook Secretary of State Chester Manning's hand with both of his own.

"It's good to see you again!" Manning said, holding Desaix by both shoulders, examining him up and down as if he were a long-lost relative.

"I'm glad to be here with you, Mr. Secretary." Desaix always felt like his young son, or as Twitty and others sarcastically called him, the prodigal son. Much of the hearsay was true. Manning did treat Desaix like the son he never had.

A ruggedly handsome man in his own right, Manning still identified with his tall, swarthy DAS. In his mind, he felt that they resembled each other, if not in physical features, in more important ones. Both carried themselves with a self-assurance that bespoke a clear comfort with challenge, diversity, and uncertainty. Their personal bond of affection had been forged during Westview's last presidential race, when Westview was twenty points behind his opponent, a tough New England lawyer who had been successfully attacking Westview for his own commonly perceived wimp factor.

Taking advantage of Westview's inability to articulate a comprehensive domestic and foreign policy strategy, despite having served in the House and the Senate for over twenty years, his opponent capitalized on Westview's widely, if not accurately, perceived image of also not being too bright. Aware of his own problems, Westview called in his trusted and loyal friend to run the faltering campaign. Manning, in turn, asked Desaix to join him as one of his principal political strategists, after having met him at a symposium at MIT, where Desaix had discussed the use of psychiatry and psychological principles in the execution of foreign policy. After the symposium, both men struck up a casual but nevertheless caring relationship. From time to time, they visited each other. When Manning visited New Orleans, he would always stop by Desaix's apartment for an evening of the Big Easy.

When Manning needed help turning the polls around, he called in Desaix, who developed a picturebook strategy and game plan that allowed Westview to tie up his opponent in obsessional dilemmas he was unable to resolve. After Westview was elected, Manning asked Desaix to join him in any part of the State Department he wanted. To Manning's surprise, Desaix chose a DAS position in the East Asian bureau under the direction of another close friend, an Assistant Secretary of State who knew Desaix well enough to leave him alone to pursue those activites he enjoyed most—international crisis management, negotiations, and long-range strategic planning.

In return, his friend expected Desaix to keep him apprised of any major developments that occurred on the seventh floor during his own flights abroad—and perhaps to whisper one or two praiseworthy comments to Manning about his friend's deft handling of the complicated Far East situation. In truth, there was very little for the East Asian bureau to do other than manage the mercurial U.S.-Japanese relationship and the untoward consequences of the transfer of Hong Kong to the People's Republic of China. For the most part, the rest of the Pacific Basin countries had very few problems, other than those that dealt with a surplus trade balance and capital reserves.

Manning appreciated the fact that Desaix picked a State Department bureau and a senior-level position that put very few demands on Desaix. But, if the truth be known, he was pleased to have Desaix down in the bureaucratic trenches, providing him with an essential pair of eyes and ears.

"Come on in, Desaix!" Manning led Desaix through an unpretentious office with a worn leather chesterfield facing a wood-burning fireplace. Unlike the Oval Office, this one was less formal and intimidating. Manning had hung a few replicas of double-gauge shotguns on the wall opposite his oak desk as a reminder that he much preferred to hunt duck on his ranch in south Texas.

"Tell me, son, what the hell is wrong with your bandaged hand?"

"I had a minor accident when I was examining Fitzpatrick's cadaver in Japan." As Manning examined Desaix's left hand, Desaix noticed that Manning also had a small bandage covering the fourth finger of his left hand.

"I hope the hand's all right," Manning said.

"Not bad," Desaix answered.

"Come on in and make yourself comfortable here," Manning said. He closed the door on the other side of the room, at the far end of his desk, a door that led to a small room in which the previous Secretary of State would often retire when he wanted to get some rest during the day.

"It's good to see you, Chet. I'm sorry things didn't go too well in Tokyo. I've wanted to talk to you about what happened."

"Desaix, I'm sure you did the best you could. I don't have to tell you, but we perfectionists tend to be too harsh on ourselves. So let go of some of those mental reins in your head. I have a selfish reason for wanting you psychologically unencumbered."

"That serious, huh?"

"More serious than you would imagine."

"I'm all yours."

"As a psychiatrist, what would you say about a person who believed he was being persecuted?"

"If it's real, then I would say he had a problem. And I would want to know who is doing it and why he is being persecuted."

"And if the person were not actually being threatened?"

"Well, I would say he had a problem. And I would want to know why he felt he was being persecuted."

"You'd say that he was paranoid, right?" Manning pronounced the diagnosis as if it were a death sentence.

"Yes."

"And if that person was creating his own persecution? What would you say?"

"I'm sorry, Chet, but I don't seem to be following you."

"Desaix, let's say that this paranoid person was actually fabricating his own threats of persecution?"

"I'd say that he was sick." Desaix started to fidget in his chair. Manning was carefully leading him through a chain of logic that culminated in a conclusion he was reluctant to admit to himself.

"Would you say in lay terms that he was crazy?"

"It would depend."

"On what?" Manning realized he might be pushing him too hard. "Take it easy, son. I'm not trying to make you say something that isn't correct or goes against your sensibilities."

"I understand." Desaix knew that Manning was talking double speak. He wanted Desaix to stop hedging and arrive at some conclusion, preferably Manning's.

"Do you really understand, son? What I'm talking about here is strictly between you and me, right?"

"Whatever is said here doesn't leave the room." Desaix could now smell Manning's bourbon breath.

"Good. I don't want anyone, not Westview or anyone else, to know we had this converstion."

"Agreed."

"Then I want you to listen carefully to me. I'm going to say it as simply as I can. Donald Westview, the President of the United States, and the most powerful person in the world, is crazy. One hundred percent, certifiably crazy." Manning paused to ascertain Desaix's reaction. "Desaix, you understand what I am saying, don't you?"

"I hear it loud and clear." Desaix didn't react. He simply wanted a few seconds to process what Manning was telling him.

"Hard to believe, isn't it?" Manning asked, sitting back on the sofa.

"What makes you think he's crazy?" Desaix asked calmly, hoping to uncover a fallacy in Manning's reasoning.

"He's organizing a coup against himself," Manning answered, pleased that his political protégé had also learned to play the game with a poker face.

"What?"

"You heard me, son! Donald Westview, the President of the United States, and my closest friend, is organizing a coup against himself that will occur in approximately seventy-two hours."

"How do you know?" Desaix kept hearing Westview's own recent request to him to find out "where, how, and when."

"Why did the President of the United States personally order the immediate withdrawal of Special Operations Forces fighting covertly behind enemy lines back to the States?" Manning answered Desaix's question with a question as he picked up a classified paper.

"He wanted to diffuse the crisis."

"Let me read a cable that was intercepted.

"TOP SECRET/SENSITIVE/EYES ONLY/HAND DELIVER TO COLONEL MATTHEW ZARBITSKI, SPECIAL OPERATIONS FORCES COMMANDER, 82ND AIRBORNE DIVISION, 18TH AIRBORNE CORPS. IMMEDIATELY WITHDRAW FROM GERMAN FIELD OF OPERATIONS. RETURN TO USSOCOM, MACDILL AFB, FLORIDA. ASAP. BY PERSONAL REQUEST OF PRESIDENT DONALD WESTVIEW. ORDERS TO FOLLOW."

"So?" Desaix asked defiantly, hoping that Westview had a good reason.

"Son, didn't I teach you one simple lesson? Whenever you hear hoofbeats, don't think of zebras."

"I hear the hoofbeats, but I'm not sure they aren't some kind of artifact or simply noise."

"Okay, Desaix. I know better than to argue with you. Here, take a copy of this cable and check it out to make certain that your good friend here from Texas hasn't suffered some kind of heat stroke."

"Not likely."

"Thank you for having that much faith in me. But, son, this isn't a question of your believing me. On the contrary, I wouldn't have asked you to come and see me if it were that simple. Hell, don't you think that I know as well as you do that you're a natural-born skeptic. I want you to check out everything I am telling you. Better yet, check me out! Double-check me! If I'm wrong, I'll give you complete authorization to place me in a loony bin. But if I'm right, and you feel comfortable with what I told you, then like any good psychiatrist, I expect you to certify the President of the United States as one hundred percent crazy. Agreed?" Manning held out his hand. Desaix shook it.

"What happened to the Special Forces unit?" Desaix asked incredulously as he quickly glanced over the cable.

"I want you to visit Saint Elizabeth Hospital as soon as possible. That's where you'll find your answer to your question."

"Are you telling me that a Special Forces unit was redeployed from a battlefield to a former federal mental institution?"

"Yes."

"Chet, what the hell are you talking about? What does a redeployed Special Forces unit and Saint Elizabeth Hospital have to do with a coup and the President's sanity?"

"We're going to have to stop now, Desaix. I'm already running behind schedule. When you've checked out what I've told you to your satisfaction, come back and see me."

"So whom should I see next?"

Manning wrote a name and address on a piece of paper. "Go and see her. She knows all about him."

Desaix looked down at the piece of paper and shook his head in amazement.

# CHAPTER
## 15

Since the construction of the Commonwealth of Independent States, nothing had been more restrictive on the State Council than *demokratsia*.

Peering through the French windows onto Red Square, Russian President Zotov inhaled his filtered American cigarette with the grateful anguish of a man who could recognize that his time might be limited. Watching the handful of Ukrainian and Russian demonstrators marching around Red Square with hand-painted banners demanding an end to the fighting with the U.S. and an increase in economic aid, he decided how simple it was for them to march. Fifteen years ago they would have been arrested for trespassing within two hundred feet of the Kremlin. Some would have been sent to Lubyanka Prison, while others would have been sent to one of the many psychiatric hospitals for the criminally insane, like Moscow's Kaschenko Psychiatric Hospital. But those were the days of a bygone era when the Commonwealth of Independent States was still the Soviet Union. As he watched the demonstrators become unruly, emptying trash cans, shouting and waving obscenities in the direction of his office windows, Zotov shook his head sadly at the incredible sacrifices that he and his fellow citizens had to endure in the name of democracy and the free-market system. Without a doubt, the price for restructuring his country was prohibitive. And now there was nothing left. Even the room in which he was standing, the Council of Ministers, once the showcase of grandeur and splendor, looked shabby and frayed from years of no maintenance. Lenin's tomb, a few hundred feet below him, had been completely dismantled. Supplies were in such grave shortage that the red bricks that composed the tomb had been used for the construction of cooperative apartments on the outskirts of Moscow.

Zotov waited impatiently for the handful of members of the State Council to enter. No one who entered the Council of Ministers could be less than impressed with the size of the room, originally designed to accommodate the extravagant festivities of the czars. The ceiling, now covered with dark oak panels, once contained one of the most impressive rococo decorations of cherubs and archangels in all of Russia. But now one couldn't help smelling the stale, musty odor, or noticing the cracked ceiling, frayed upholstery, discolored velvet curtains, and broken windows. There was simply no money left to do the necessary renovations. For the tenth year in a row there was still a trade imbalance. That was the rationalization offered for actively continuing the negligence. The reality was far different. The truth was there was too much economic and political instability in each of the republics to attract significant foreign capital.

So this dilapidated room, awash in fetid air, was the recently reconstructed mausoleum for the New Political Thinking.

My God, he wondered how he could even maintain the pretense that he was running a government. There was nothing left—not even the illusion that once they had been a great superpower.

All that remained were a handful of the military, FSA, GRU, and civil service. The rest of the comrades had defected, body and soul, to the concept of free enterprise and entrepreneurship, awaiting their big kill. Russian Orthodoxy had been replaced by the atheism of communism, which, in turn, had been co-opted by the crass commercialism of capitalism. But could materialism really substitute for spiritualism? Zotov thought not. For the Russian soul needed to share in the collective angst of a persecuted experience. Without anyone out there to blame for their misfortunes, the Russian citizen would be forced to point to himself. And that was inexcusable. As a Russian, he could never assume that he was fully responsible for his own actions. What would be next?

"Gentlemen, how are you doing?" Nicholas Pugo, the sixty-three-year-old Director of the FSA, walked into the room.

"My dear friend. Or should I still call you General?"

"Please, Igor, I was a general many years ago. I am now the Director of the FSA."

"I should tell you, before I forget. Marshal Kulikov will not be attending this meeting. He left a few minutes ago."

"Why?" Pugo sounded angry. "Has one of his whores given birth to another one of his illegitimate children?"

"Now, now! Even you must admit he is one of our best military strategists in a crisis."

"As far as I'm concerned, he is one of our most prolific fornicators!" Pugo tried to disguise the bitter taint of jealousy. "Where did he go?"

"He convinced me to preposition him at our underground facilities at the Russian National Command Authority, outside of Moscow. He felt that he should be there, personally, to manage the crisis."

"Clever fox! What does he know that we don't?" Pugo had a very hard time trusting his ex-adjutant, whom he had always considered to be a sneaky, manipulative schemer who would sacrifice his own mother for professional advancement.

"Enough petty jealousies, Pugo! Tell me what new programs you have instituted to inform our citizens that we are, indeed, a democratic society?"

"This past week alone I renewed our informants column, which allows our good citizens to write in and complain about any abuses that our security forces may be committing. We have also created a new television series with a German company and an American distibutor to dramatize case histories taken from the once closed files of the KGB."

"So that is what we have become, an extension of Hollywood?"

"Zotov, these are new times. We need new approaches to new problems. And more hard currency."

"No, my friend, these are not new solutions to new problems. These are quick but ineffective approaches to some very old problems, which, like old sores, refuse to go away."

"Ah, you must be in your Russian mood—cynical and frightened." Pugo felt comfortable talking to his friend of thirty years in a mildly provocative manner. Ever since he was third secretary of the Soviet Embassy in Hungary, Pugo and Zotov had become close friends. They had met on a Communist Party junket to several Eastern European countries. Even then their personal relationship presaged the division that would one day exist throughout the entire country. Pugo was Byelorussian. Zotov was Russian. Pugo felt like an outsider in the government and was jealous of the fact that both Zotov and Kulikov were pure Russians. But now the situation was different. Pugo was no longer desirous of becoming a Russian. It was déclassé.

"Take a look outside the window. Tell me what you see." Zotov hadn't moved from his position behind the drapes.

The crowd below was becoming increasingly unruly. Garbage cans were being thrown at the militia and police who were positioned around Manezh Square.

For Zotov, there was an air of unreality about the scene. Here, in front of the Kremlin, he was witnessing the same scene that Czar Ncholas II, Stalin, Gorbachev, and Yeltsin had witnessed over the past hundred years. But the situation seemed worse than ever before. At least in the past there was always a new revolution giving rise to a new ideology. But now there was no ideology left—despite what the Americans thought.

Zotov ran the Russian Federation, the largest and most important of the republics, on the basis of tattered theories of democracy and capitalism, wishful economic thinking, and a series of uninspired rallies. He had never forgiven Gorbachev, one of his intellectual and political mentors, for having continued the damaging cult of personality that had thrown the entire country into such a total state of chaos and anarchy.

Only one thing could save Russia and the remaining republics from collapse. It was the only thing left. Not an ideology. Not a religion. Not even a cause. He had to have a legitimate reason to invoke paragraph 7 of section 110 of the Commonwealth of Independent States, allowing him to mobilize all his troops and declare a state of emergency.

But he needed a legitimate excuse.

The crisis in Western Europe, unfortunately, was still not serious enough for him to invoke paragraph 7. If he heated it up any more, he ran the risk of precipitating a nuclear war. Something nobody wanted. Not even the most jingoist of his military officers. And President Westview had just informed him that the Americans were willing to de-escalate the crisis almost immediately. If they meant what they said, then there would be no reason for him to invoke paragraph 7 of section 110 at all. But at least now he had taken full advantage of the opportunity to mobilize his armed forces without creating any major concerns among the Presidents of the other republics.

Pressing his thin, tapered fingers to the bridge of his nose while closing his eyes, he recalled the famous words of the father of the latter-day KGB, Count Felix Dzerzhinsky, who said, "Trust is good, but control is better."

It couldn't be more clear to Zotov. He had to control the outcome of events. He could not allow events to govern his behavior. It was the complete absence of this understanding that had led to the personal destruction of Gorbachev and the devastation of all of Mother Russia. And for that, he could never forgive Gorbachev. Gorbachev had ignored Dzerzhinsky. But Dzerzhinsky had not forgotten Gorbachev. Complete trust had led to complete chaos and self-destruction.

Only regaining control could rectify that mistake. And it was up to him, Zotov, to correct the mistakes of the past.

"My friend, your mind was wandering once again." Pugo was worried about Zotov's increasingly distracted appearance. He had good reason, and he was concerned.

Zotov didn't notice the group of men who had walked into the room while he faced the window. Perhaps he didn't have to. He could smell them, a pack of hyenas, waiting for the kill.

"Good day, how are you?" The beefy-faced Yuri Primakov, the Minister of Interior and Chairman of the Council of the Commonwealth, placed his arm around Zotov's shoulder.

"What do you think?" Zotov said, already knowing what Primakov thought. It wasn't very difficult to figure out Primakov. For him, the combination of fear and force was the panacea for all social injustices and ailments. The problem was that Zotov was never sure who was to be frightened and who was to use force.

"I don't know," Primakov answered. He accepted the fact that he always had to lie to Zotov. He was simply continuing the time-honored, cherished Russian tradition of vranyo—lies. A tradition that even glasnost could not destroy. His father and grandfather and great-grandfather had practised vranyo. It made life bearable even in these times of openness and New Political

Thinking. But, most importantly, it allowed Primakov to lie to Zotov while knowing that Zotov was aware that Primakov was lying to him. For centuries this was the accepted practice that allowed Primakov and his peasant ancestors to lie to the authorities without losing face. It did no one any harm, as long as the rules were followed.

"What do you think?" Because he was from Kiev, the capital of Ukraine, Zotov really wanted to hear Primakov's assessment of what he was witnessing in the square below.

The crowds had gotten larger and more boisterous in their demands for ending the potential war with the U.S.

"I see you've brought in the elite army units to control the crowds," Primakov said. "Isn't that being a little heavy-handed?"

"Maybe. On the other hand . . ." Zotov didn't want to complete his thought. It might reveal more than he wanted.

"Ah, I see."

"What do you see, my friend?" Zotov asked. He didn't like Primakov's coy innuendos.

"That you ask me questions for which you don't really want answers."

Primakov knew how to annoy Zotov.

"Well, I see you are serious." Primakov paused. "Let me see. What do I see? Well, I see pretty much the same thing you do, Mr. President. I see a lot of trouble for all of us in this room, unless we do something quite imaginative and, most importantly, effective, in order to subdue what may become a riot. It is a riot, is it not, President Zotov?"

"What difference does it make what we call it?"

"I think you know quite well!"

"Idiot! This is a riot, and you and I know that it is a riot."

"If you say so. But you don't have to justify the use of elite military troops. It is your judgment call. Not mine."

"Yes, Yuri Dimitrovich. You've made your point. Now let us get down to the business of the day."

Zotov sat at the end of the stained oak table. Seated around the table were his Chief of the Army, the Director of Special Operations, the Minister of Defense, the Foreign Minister, and the Director of the FSA, about half the normal number of members attending his regular State Council meetings. But this was the Plenipotentiary Planning Group of the State Council. The counterpart of Washington's Crisis Management Group. These were the people to whom Zotov would entrust the management of the crisis with the U.S.

"Igor Ivanovich, perhaps you can summarize for us your teleconferencing with the Americans?" Pugo asked, acting as Zotov's executive assistant.

"Before I talk to you about the meeting," Zotov said, "please give me an update on the investigation of the murder of my beloved assistant and colleague, Colonel-General Nikolai Pavlovich Kurasov."

"Unfortunately, we have very little new information, although I think we are now developing an important lead. It was picked up by one of our female agents. But I don't want to discuss this any further at this time." Pugo was always concerned about potential leaks from the military.

"Don't you trust your own colleagues?" General Boris Yershov interjected. He was Deputy Commander of the Russian Army, a fifty-eight-year-old, who, unlike many of his younger military colleagues, was in top physical shape. He was part of that dying breed of men who belonged to what was once called the Polar Bear Club. Men who dared to swim in the icy waters of the Moscow River during the winter months. Zotov envied his perpetual ruddy complexion and light tan. Ironically, Yershov refused to swim in the river during the summer months because he claimed that he was a purist. Polar bears were rarely found in the water during summer.

"The fact is," Pugo said, "that I trust and value my military colleagues so dearly that I don't want to reveal any inadvertent confidences. One never knows these days what constitutes a military secret. So with total respect to my comrades in arms, as well as those who serve with only pen and paper, I remain respectfully reticent until I deem it to be the proper time."

"I understand, you . . . weasel." Yershov barely whispered the final word.

"I'm sorry. What did you say?" Pugo asked, furious, wishing to embarrass the general in front of his Planning Group colleagues.

"All right, gentlemen," Zotov continued, "now that we've performed our obligatory ritual of spilling a little blood at the beginning of every session, let us discuss my television meeting with President Westview. I can summarize it by saying it was short but very productive."

"What do you mean, Mr. President?" Primakov asked, determined to be noticed. He had not been originally invited to this meeting and was enraged that he had to intrude himself into it by insisting that one could not discuss civil order without the very man directly responsible for it, the Minister of the Interior.

"In short, my dear Primakov, had you been in the room with me, you would have seen right away that the chemistry between me and President Westview was extremely good. We both agreed to call a halt to this insane military escalation. So as of this moment, I inform you, Leonov Vadim, my Minister of Defense, to order all your field commanders, as well as any special units, to stop fighting. Furthermore, any renegade units should be dealt with severely."

"What are you saying?" Vadim asked. This forty-six-year-old apparatchik, who had become the youngest Minister of Defense in the history of the Russian Federation, was a Harvard classmate of Randolph Merck, the U.S. Secretary of Defense.

"You heard me! I want all military units presently engaged in combat with the U.S. to stop fighting immediately."

"Are you certain this is what you want? May I remind you that we did not start this war. And as a major superpower, we have an obligation to defend our homeland, our prestige, and our integrity."

"And how do you propose to do this? By fighting your way into oblivion?" Zotov was becoming increasingly more impatient with his new breed of whiz kids, patterned after the American model of the Ivy League–trained bureaucrat whose primary interest was to create a name for himself, with the eventual eye of returning to the private sector so that he could capitalize on his government contacts. Zotov called him, and others like him, his revolving door apparatchiks.

"Mr. Vadim, President Zotov is right, you know," Yershov said, then paused as he monitored Zotov's restless expression. He concluded that it was safe to continue. "We are presently in a very unusual position of strength vis-à-vis the U.S. We will have, within a very few hours, one-quarter of our Russian ground forces committed to a confrontation with the Americans. Let me—"

"General Yershov, did you or did you not hear me order the Minister of Defense to cease and desist any and all combat—immediately? Yes or no?" Zotov's voice rose in intensity. He was clearly becoming angry. Insubordination was intolerable.

"Please, let me finish, Igor Ivanovich. Remember, we are now part of a new democratic society. This is no longer the Russia of old. We all have a duty and a responsibility to hear each other out." Yershov waited what seemed to be minutes until Zotov nodded his head for him to continue. Yershov stood up and, holding a military chart, continued in a less plaintive tone. Pointing to a hastily designed map showing Russian and U.S. troop deployments around Wildeck, Yershov cleared his throat and puffed up his shoulders as if he were about to make a high school commencement speech.

"As I mentioned before, we are in the unusual position of making a counteroffensive blow that would knock out the major U.S. thrust. I'm bringing in three motorized rifle divisions, including seven hundred artillery pieces, mortars, and multiple rocket launchers; seven hundred T-72 tanks; three hundred fixed and hand-held SAM launchers; 650 anti-aircraft artillery pieces; five hundred surface-to-surface missile launchers; 2,200 armored personnel carriers; and 45,000 Category I troops. The U.S. strength is less than one-third of ours. We can at this point outman and outgun them. We will never have an opportunity like this again. It is our one and only chance to defeat our arrogant friends. All I have to know is on which of our flanks they will be mounting their assault."

"And if we don't defeat them, my dear general, then what?"

"Well, Mr. President, we would simply bargain for peace. As we are doing now."

"And how would you propose that we pass this war plan through our legislators?" Zotov asked. "They would never accept this. Furthermore, they would place you under house arrest because you would have revealed yourself to be a dangerous, bellicose old man who cannot be trusted to maintain the new social order. Don't you understand, my dear old friend, that your job is never to fight a war, but to look as menacing as you possibly can. And then, from time to time, you are to review the troops."

"Then, my dear President, you can have my resignation, for you have no need of a military man, but a cute puppet dressed in a general's uniform."

"Now, now, General, let's not become too hasty," Zotov replied defensively, realizing that much truth lay beneath Yershov's words.

Vadim rose with a broad smile reminiscent of an American politician ready to deliver a speech, and motioned Yershov to sit down. "As most of you know I have spent quite a few years in the United States and there probably isn't a part of the States that I haven't toured." Vadim sounded unusually patronizing, an annoying habit most Russian friends attributed to the years spent abroad.

"Please, Vadim, spare us the Cook's tour," Zotov interrupted. "We would all appreciate it." He lit another in an endless chain of cigarettes.

"Yes, sir." Vadim sounded more like the little boy he always imagined himself to be. "But the Americans are basically good people. Their primary concern is to make certain they receive their weekly paycheck on time and have enough money left over after they've paid for their basic necessities to buy a six-pack of beer and rent several videotapes for their Japanese VCRs. My point is really quite simple. If you want to understand the Americans as they are now, then look back to what we Russians were like in the 1970s. The Americans of the future have become the Russians of the past. The Americans are just the way we were. They are afraid of risk and uncertainty. All they ask for is to be taken care of by the government or the multinational corporations. Unlike us, they have become extremely conservative and almost reactionary. Thanks to perestroika and glasnost, we Russians have broken through the age-old shackles of mental servitude. We and our former allies in Eastern European have become the risk takers and the entrepreneurs. We no longer want the state or anyone else to take care of us. We Russians have become the individualists that the Americans once were. Even their movies no longer belong to them. They are now owned by the Japanese or the Germans. The U.S. has become the economic battleground for the Japanese, the Italians, and the Germans. Where once the Japanese were the primary buyers of Treasury bills, Germany now owns over 55 percent. In short, where once Japan owned America, Germany is now in charge. In many ways, my dear friends, the Americans have become irrelevant to the future. But we, in turn, are the future. So why waste all our valuable energies and resources on such a wasteful, unproductive activity as war? As the Minister of Defense of the Commonwealth of Independent States, I second President Zotov's motion to stop this insane war immediately."

"Thank you, Mr. Minister of Defense," said Zotov. "I would like to stop this war for precisely the very reasons you have just stated. But I would like to remind you that our economy has been deteriorating for the past ten years as well. We too are primarily owned by the Germans—our gas, our oil, our industrial complexes. If you remember your World War II history, you know that the United States prospered after that war. But for a long time since then, their economy has taken a downhill turn."

"So why not fight them and defeat them if they are weak?" Yershov asked, optimistic that Zotov would eventually follow his advice and allow him to make a major military counteroffensive.

"For that reason alone, I will not engage the U.S. on the battlefield," Zotov answered. "If your enemy is weak, then why not leave him that way? Why give him the pretext to become stronger or more belligerent? I'm not that foolish. Nor can they provoke me into that position. At least, not as long as I am alive." He ground out his cigarette in the ashtray.

The noise outside was becoming insufferable. The screams of women and children were so disturbing that both Pugo and Primakov simultaneously stood up to close the windows.

"Leave them open! It smells like a gymnasium in here," Zotov said, then lit another cigarette and inhaled deeply.

"But does it have to be a noisy gymnasium?" Primakov asked, watching his troops brutally round up the demonstrators and haul them into paddy wagons. What is going on, he wondered. He hadn't ordered such violent behavior.

"Suppose the Americans refuse to stop fighting?" Yershov asked as he put away his charts. For the first time in a very long time he had been overruled by Zotov. Perhaps there was no longer any trust between them. He flinched as he heard the sound of gunshots. "What is that?"

"AK-47M rifles and RPK light machine guns," Zotov replied matter-of-factly. "The sooner you gentlemen can sit down, the quicker we can dispense with the meeting."

Neither of the men sat down.

"Come over here, quickly, Igor Ivanovich!" Pugo was clearly upset.

Everyone at the table stood up and accompanied Zotov to the window.

It looked as if the elite units of the army were fighting the Spassky guards stationed along the Kremlin grounds.

A canister of CN tear gas flew in through the open window. The room quickly filled with the irritant. Everyone started to cough. Zotov covered his face with a handkerchief.

Bursting into the room, a young lieutenant announced breathlessly, "We're under siege. It's a coup!"

# CHAPTER

## 16

The difference between a coup and a military exercise is intent, surprise, and proficiency. The Russian Army was known for none of these.

"Over there!" Pushkin shouted to the Spetsnaz soldiers fanning across the grounds of the Kremlin. He fired 660 rounds per minute from his RPK light machine gun toward the French windows, careful not to hit anyone. He simply wanted to scare the State Council members and send a clear signal that he was quite serious about his intentions.

"Sir, there are two T-72s rolling down Kremlevskaya Quay. If they come around the corner they will outflank us from our rear. What do you want us to do?" asked Spetsnaz Captain Marat Vartanian, a twenty-nine-year-old heavyset Armenian. He was part of the 8,500 man division of Vozdushno-Desantnyye-Voyska elite airborne troops that Pushkin had recruited for Shield, the secret organization dedicated to overthrowing the incompetent Russian government and resurrecting the failing economic and political regime under a right-wing military dictatorship. Normally, he would have been part of Vysotnik or Raydoviki, the Russian equivalent of the British SAS or the American Rangers, rescuing hostages or engaging in special operations.

"Take the two 50 millimeter M-41 mortars and place them at both ends of this building. When the T-72s turn around both corners into Red Square toward us, we will give them a surprise party."

Pushkin fired his RPK to provide cover, as Vartanian ran to his platoon huddled around a jeep. Pushkin knew that his time was limited. If he couldn't get through the Kremlin doors and capture Zotov by 0200, exactly one hour from now, he and his men would be in very serious trouble. Within the hour, Yershov would be able to mobilize several divisions.

Crouched behind two overturned burning black Volgas, Pushkin directed a group of his soldiers to provide fire cover for him as he dashed toward Basil's Cathedral, three hundred feet away, kitty-corner from Spassky Tower, one of the three principal entrances to the Kremlin. The other two entrances, Trinity Tower and Borovitsky Tower, were located on the opposite side of the building, facing Alexander Gardens.

When he reached Basil's Cathedral, he fired at the soldiers guarding the entrance to the tower. If he could only get rid of them, he could clear the way for his men to enter. Once inside, it would be simple to reach the Council of Ministers chamber.

Bullets from the Tower Guards' AK-47Ms screeched overhead. Pushkin thought it particularly fitting that the church, built by Ivan the Terrible in the sixteenth century to commemorate his conquest of Kazan, should be the scene of the second coup against a democratic regime in Russia.

He fired his RPK at two young guards, who fell to the ground in a pool of blood. Pushkin was sorry to have killed fine young Russian boys who should have been fighting alongside him. But he had no other choice. He had to get to the Council of Ministers chamber, and they were in the way.

He motioned to a group of his Spetsnaz soldiers hiding behind the burning Volgas that it was all right for them to run across the cobblestone street and join him.

But as they started to cross Red Square, a 7.62 millimeter PKM machine gun located on the second floor of the Kremlin burst out in a flame of bullets. Two of his soldiers fell onto the cobblestones. Writhing in pain, they screamed for medical assistance.

Under ordinary conditions, Pushkin would have brought along a cadre of medics. But this was not a classic Spetsnaz operation behind enemy lines. Instead he had been ordered to undertake a bare-bones coup.

Had he not spent his last two waking and sleeping days—mostly sleeping hours—with Tamara, he might have thought through the operation more thoroughly. But how could he turn down two days of passionate lovemaking? That would have been asking too much of him. To die for glory and country was one thing. But to die without love—now that would not have been consistent with his noble ancestral tradition of duels and scandalous behavior. Tamara had completely thrown off his sense of disciplined, meticulous planning. She was incredibly sexy and passionate. Certainly a worthy love partner.

"Give me some fire cover!" Pushkin issued the order to his Uzbeki captain with the gold front tooth.

"Give the colonel some protection!" the captain shouted to his men.

Under cover of bursts of light machine gun fire, Pushkin ran to the wounded soldiers. "Are you all right, boys?"

"Yes, sir! I'm fine," responded the ruddy-faced boy with a broken leg. "But I'm afraid that my friend has a really bad chest wound. I'm afraid—"

He was interrupted by a burst of PKM machine gun fire coming from that same second-story window.

Pushkin concluded that if he didn't get these soldiers out of range of the machine gun, all three of them would die. Unfortunately, the Uzbeki captain needed him along the corner of Basil's Cathedral to provide cover.

Pushkin pulled out a hunting knife from a leather sheath on his belt, cut the boy's pants, and exposed the broken bone. He tore the pants material into several long strips.

"Brace yourself! This may hurt. But it will allow me to carry you back to your pals."

"Yes, sir!"

The second lieutenant covered his head as bullets kicked up stone fragments around the huddled men. He released a muffled scream as Pushkin tied his hunting knife tightly against the fracture to provide some support for the leg.

Looking straight into the chest hole of the other soldier, Pushkin could see an impaired lung, flailing in and out, bathed in blood and covered with fragments of torn tissue and broken bones. The soldier was in respiratory distress. Life for him, at best, could only be a few more minutes long.

Pushkin could do little more than wrap a strip of material around the soldier's gaping chest wound.

As he assessed the situation, he became distressed. T-72 tanks were turning both corners of the Kremlin. None of the 50 millimeter shells his men were firing seemed to stop them. In a few minutes he would be trapped between the oncoming tanks and machine gun fire.

Pushkin flung the screaming second lieutenant over his shoulder in a fireman's hold and carried him to the temporary safety of his group.

"Get him in a stretcher and take him over to the hospital on Prospekt Marx."

Before he could return for the second soldier, a 155 millimeter T-72 tank shell came screaming into the middle of the square, completely pulverizing the body of the boy with the chest wound. As blood and flesh splattered the air, Pushkin turned his head aside and threw up. Surprisingly, on such an occasion, he was thinking of Tamara. They had argued half the night as he tried to dissuade her from joining him. She no longer wanted to work for the GRU. The poem *Eugene Onegin* came to mind for a minute as he thought of her:

> I remember the wonderful moment
> When you leaped into my eyes
> Like a fleeting mirage,
> Like a spirit of pure beauty.

"Are you all right, Colonel?" the captain asked Pushkin, who seemed dazed.

"I'm fine, Captain. Just trying to figure out our next move."

"I have a suggestion. Misha, come over here!" The captain liked to call his men by their first name.

"Yes, Captain!" A blond-haired, lanky Russian, no more than nineteen years old, stood up straight, fearlessly.

"Where's your baby doll?"

"I've got her right here!" The private raised the hollow tube of his already loaded Sagger antitank missile.

Pushkin was proud. His men showed a lot of initiative. "Burp your baby, Misha, I think she has a lot of gas." By anthropormorphizing weapons, the captain allowed his men to develop an extra-special attachment to them.

Misha put the tube on his right shoulder and fixed the sight coordinates to two thousand meters, two-thirds its normal distance. Through the range finder, the approaching T-72 looked like a surrealistic metal behemoth slowly approaching with the deliberate intention of devouring all in its path.

Feeling the captain tap him on his metal helmet with the go-ahead signal, Misha slowly squeezed the trigger. The 120 millimeter missile exited the tube and followed a straight trajectory right into the barrel of the T-72.

The tank blew up with all the incandescent splendor Pushkin normally associated with the traditional May Day celebrations in Moscow. But that was before glasnost and perestroika.

"Open fire and follow me!"

Pushkin ran toward the gate with the captain and his men trailing behind, their RPKs, PKMs, and AK-47Ms ablaze.

From the perspective of the tower guards, Pushkin's onslaught resembled a blazing holiday cake, thrust unceremoniously into their collective faces. The guards withdrew behind the heavy wooden oak doors of Spassky Tower.

"Damnit! Misha, bring your baby with you. We're going to blow down this door. Or better yet, maybe we should enter through Borovitsky Gate, the tourist entrance."

"Radio communication informs me that all the entrances have been sealed off," the captain said. "I think you should let Misha burp his baby again. I don't have much time. The Defense Minister has called in air cover. Five Mi-24 Hind gunship helicopters should be appearing momentarily." The captain couldn't afford to have his men standing out in the cold, totally exposed.

"Do we have any RPG-7s?" Pushkin asked. He wanted to make certain that he had an anti-aircraft missile on hand if one of the Mi-24 gunships appeared.

"I've got one flanking our rear. Just in case they decide to shoot our asses off."

"Then tell Misha to burp the baby," Pushkin said as he scanned the darkening late afternoon sky. He checked his watch and saw that it was 0130. He had thirty minutes left to blow down the door and find Zotov. After that, he had fifteen minutes more to implement his escape plan.

For the second time, Misha placed the Sagger on his shoulder, and when he felt the captain's two knocks on his helmet, pulled slowly on the trigger. The 120 millimeter missile hit the door straight on. But nothing happened. To everyone's amazement the door remained completely intact. Those sons of bitches Solario and Ruffo, thought Pushkin, the fifteenth-century architects who designed the Kremlin, had constructed an impregnable fortress. That was one variable he hadn't even considered. He could never have imagined that a fifteenth-century oak wood door could withstand the impact of modern-day weapons. It was impossible, unless someone had purposefully reinforced the door. And only one person could have ordered that—Zotov.

In the distance, from a southwesterly direction, an Mi-24 Hind gunship approached. A second T-72 tank was starting to turn the far east corner, pointing its cannon toward Pushkin's group.

"Sir, we can either retreat back across Red Square, where our armored personnel carriers are waiting for us. Or we can scale these walls. We've brought a few grappling hooks and rope."

The captain seemed confident, reaffirming the basic tenet of Spetsnaz training: they were required to be proficient in the martial arts, swimming, flying, parachuting, mountain climbing, marksmanship, soccer, wrestling, and horseback riding. That was how many of the Russian-sponsored sports teams and events could operate as a front for Spetsnaz soldiers, who used these teams as a jumping-off point for their spying activities.

Pushkin ordered the soldier in charge of the climbing equipment to put it into place. Tanks and gunships were getting so close that the captain swore he could smell the gun powder in their barrels. The T-72 blasted its first round of shells. Three Spetsnaz soldiers fell quietly.

Pushkin was left with less than two dozen men to storm the Kremlin. So he decided to deploy his men into three groups. Two groups of three men each were to stop the tank and the helicopter. The remainder would scale the stone walls. Pushkin would have to rely on the Uzbeki captain to coordinate the defensive actions while he tried to get into the Council of Ministers.

"We've only got a few minutes to reach the parapets a hundred feet above us. Secure both my flanks."

Pushkin and six Spetsnaz soldiers started to shimmy up the ropes that had been fired over the precipice from a launcher. He could imagine himself riding with Genghis Kahn, attacking the fortresses dotting the steppes and countryside of thirteenth-century Russia.

He climbed the wall against the fire from the Spassky guards. They started to shoot down from the precipices with their AK-47Ms and AKS-74s. A few seconds later the Mi-24 opened up with its 25 millimeter cannons.

Four Spetsnaz soldiers screamed as bullets ripped through their bodies. They released their grip on the ropes and fell to the ground.

"Knock out that goddamn helicopter!" Pushkin screamed at the captain while he fired his RPK upward. Two guards fell to the ground.

This scenario was not what he had anticipated. His plans had included a surprise assault on the Spassky Gate, intended to swiftly overwhelm the limited number of guards. Why had he lost the element of surprise, he wondered. He checked his watch and saw that he had only fifteen minutes left.

The Mi-24 Hind helicopter was swooping down on them, with its cannons blazing away, when the captain tapped the Spetsnaz corporal on his shoulder. The corporal pulled the trigger on the RPG7 and both men watched the missile hit the underbelly of the Mi-24.

The helicopter burst into an incandescent ball of fire, forcing a second helicopter to bank sharply to avoid being destroyed. But the second rocket blew it up; its debris falling onto the advancing tank in the square.

The captain moved his men away from the tank's direct line of fire, and sought refuge behind the stone walls of Saint Basil's Cathedral. He knew that the tank commander would be very reluctant to fire on such a holy relic and national monument.

The captain was wrong. The stone wall started to crumble in front of him.

"Misha, come here!" When he appeared, Misha had already set the Sagger upon his shoulder. Looking through the range finder, he could see that the tank was approaching very cautiously. He felt like a young David to an oncoming Goliath.

"Two thousand meters . . . fifteen hundred meters . . . one thousand meters . . ."

He was holding back until the last moment possible to release the 120 millimeter shell. He had to feel the exact right moment. Like a matador, who had the power to kill the bull at any time, he wanted to do it with grace and refinement and perfection.

"Fire the goddamn thing! Otherwise, we'll all blow up." The captain saw the T-72 less than four hundred meters away. "What the hell are you waiting for?" He banged on Misha's helmet more insistently. He fired. Pushkin hoisted himself over the parapet. He fired his RPK into the darkening late afternoon sky in vain, and bowed his head in a gesture of gratitude and admiration. They were the true heroes of this enterprise.

The fifteen Spetsnaz soldiers who had climbed to the top of the parapet with Pushkin pulled the pins from their ten-year-old East German grenades and dropped them on top of the T-72. The tank exploded into bellowing clouds of flame and smoke. The smell of cordite permeated the air.

Pushkin rushed across the parapet and kicked open the metal door that led down the staircase to the main hallway to the Council of Ministers. He had exactly five minutes left, but these were the most dangerous minutes left. The last passage he and his men had to traverse.

"You two, work the halls! The rest of you stay behind me. Avoid any major confrontation. I want to get to the Council of Ministers chamber quickly. Remember why we're here. We want Zotov. That's all!"

Pushkin was anxious. The taste of victory was near. He had no doubt that his men would follow him all the way. It was part of the credo of both the Shield and the Spetsnaz. But, more importantly, he was their spiritual and strategic leader.

Two Spetsnaz soldiers moved quickly down the richly carpeted hallway, opening doors as they went by.

Pushkin followed closely behind. But he felt uneasy. All of a sudden it seemed too easy. Spassky Guards were nowhere in sight. Finally, they reached the impressive set of large oak doors. The chamber of the Council of Ministers.

Pushkin turned the newly polished brass doorknobs. The door wouldn't open. He fired his RPK and kicked it open. He and his men rushed into the room at precisely 0200.

# CHAPTER
## 17

Like politics, strange bedfellows make exactly that—strange bedfellows.

Emotional compatibility may simply be another excuse for being unable to tolerate diversity and uncertainty. Passion, on the other hand, refuses to recognize the requirements of conformity and predictability. It exists for its own reasons, and may disappear as suddenly as it appeared. One of the crucial determinants of a successful relationship is symmetry. Who is on top of whom, or as the Russians say *kto/kovo*, may well determine the outcome of a passionate liaison, or as a matter of fact, any relationship.

Assistant Secretary of State for Public Affairs Judy Taylor nervously paced the plush carpet of her three-hundred-dollar a day suite at the Kalorama Guest House, an elegantly refurbished mansion opposite Lafayette Park, two blocks east of the White House. It was one of those Washington hotels that specialized in offering discreet service, which, in the parlance of the arbiter of local fashion, the Style Section of *The Washington Post*, meant that prominent officials or personalities could have an afternoon tryst without anyone at the front desk wondering why someone would pay a full day's rate for only a few hours occupancy.

She didn't like having to wait for *him*. It reminded her of the basic inequality in their relationship. True, he was important. Very important. But she did not consider herself unimportant. In fact, she was quite important to those men who knew her well.

Choirboy, on the other hand, made her feel important only because she was with him. Anyone who was with him, by definition, was important. Yes, Choirboy was fun. Maybe more than fun. But he didn't bring out in her what Desaix did. Seeing him today had reminded her how it felt to be totally in his focus. She reflected for a moment, uncertain whether the feelings she had were nostalgic or simply restrained passion. It had been almost three years since she had terminated their five-year relationship. They had met at one those fashionable Georgetown dinners, where only a thinly sliced piece of undercooked roast beef and raw asparagus were served. But the hours together following dinner had more than made up for the meal's inadequacies.

Checking her watch, she saw that Choirboy was already twenty minutes late. That meant there would be twenty minutes less play time between them. It was strange that he hadn't called to tell her he would be late. That wasn't like him. Unless, of course, he had gotten tied up in one of those very hush-hush meetings.

Damnit, she thought, how much longer should she wait?

As she picked up the bottle of Dom Perignon in the black ice bucket and started to unwrap the green and black metal foil, there was a knock at the door.

Moving away from the curtained French doors that overlooked the metal-wrought veranda and fire escapes, she walked quickly toward the door.

"All right, Choirboy, where the hell have you been?" Opening the door, Taylor gasped at who was standing there. "What are you doing here?"

"Gratitude for what you've done for me; appreciation for what you could do for me; and a remembrance of times past." Handing her one long-stem red rose, Desaix leaned casually against the door frame.

"How did you know where I was?" Taylor asked nervously.

"It was really very easy," he lied. "I asked the White House telephone operator to call your office and find out where you had checked out to for the next several hours. They called your office, which normally would not reveal that type of information. But because it was the White House asking that question, your secretary was completely intimidated."

Desaix neglected to add that Manning had told him exactly where she would be.

"But . . . you . . . can't . . . come . . ." For the first time in years, she was totally flustered. Only Desaix could make her feel that way.

"Are you certain that I can't come . . ." Desaix paused, knowing that his teasing double entendre would not be lost on her. He added seductively, "Come in . . . of course . . ."

"Don't put on that Cajun charm of yours." Taylor glanced at her watch and opened the door. "What the hell! A girl's got to have some fun, right, Desaix?"

"Particularly a girl who is used to having fun. And is being stood up by her date." Desaix knew how to play on her hedonistic impulses. "Are you going to let me in?"

"I don't know, Desaix. Since you seem to know so much already, what would you say that I should do?"

"Is that my price of entrance?"

"It depends on whether I like the answer or not."

"Your heart tells you to greet an old friend. Your mind tells you that Choirboy—isn't that what you call him?—is about to come, so to speak. The answer is really quite simple."

"What do you mean?"

"You let me in, and you get two for the price of one. Just think. The anger you feel toward Choirboy will be displaced onto me in the heat of passion, and we will get reacquainted in the nicest of ways. How could you resist?"

Without waiting for her response, he pushed the door open and locked it behind him.

"What are you doing?" Her voice cracked. Her throat felt dry.

"Don't worry! Choirboy will be delayed for at least two hours." Desaix took the bottle of Dom Perignon and drew the cork out slowly.

"How do you know?"

"How do I know what?"

"How did you find out about Choirboy?"

"Someone told me."

"No one would tell you this, except—"

"It's someone as close to the President as you—maybe even closer."

She remained silent. Instead, she extended her glass and watched the champagne effervesce to its brim.

"I'm nosy," he said. "You know that. Did you forget that I was in the business of learning people's secrets?"

"And exploiting them." Taylor's hand started to shake as Desaix approached her. She could smell his wonderful mixture of aromatic colognes. For her, he was a walking love potion. Her body broke out into goose bumps as she recalled the tactile trails of love he had imbedded in her the last time they were together.

"Have I ever exploited you, *Milkshake*, the nickname that I originally gave you? Doesn't Choirboy call you that too?"

He nuzzled his face against her head, and ran his tongue along the nape of her neck. When she began to breathe more rapidly, he trickled some drops of champagne down her neck and slowly started to lick it off. He could feel her body begin to melt into his.

"How did you know about Choirboy?" she asked, halfheartedly trying to pull back from him.

But her words were barely intelligible.

"I saw the way you both were playing with each other during the teleconference. It didn't take a shrink to see there was something going on. Once I figured that one out, it wasn't too hard to hear you shout out his name as you were opening the door."

"Very good, Sherlock!"

Looking slowly around the room and out through the French doors, Desaix marveled how much this room and building reminded him of one of those elegant cat houses on Bourbon Street. But then, a lot of hotel rooms held that same distinction.

Desaix began to open her blouse, slowly, purposefully, as if each pearl button would reveal a hidden treasure. Once unbuttoned, he caressed her pendulous breasts with his tongue.

"You're a bad boy, Desaix," Taylor purred as she ran her long, tapered fingers through his curly brown hair and pressed her body against his. It felt taut, familiar, and comfortable.

Desaix undid the catch on her bra and trickled more champagne over her breasts, licked it up, slowly, gently. He unzipped her skirt and gracefully slipped it off her. She, in turn, undressed him.

They stood in front of each other, naked. He placed her gently on the end of the Victorian bed, her long tanned legs hanging over the edge in eager anticipation. Spreading her legs slightly apart, he spilled a few drops of Dom Perignon onto her mons pubis and gently placed a wet, warm kiss on the triangular area of tight, curly hairs. She smelled and tasted as succulent as he had remembered.

As he traced the delicate folds of her labia with his tongue, he recalled their time in Cap d'Antibes, lying languidly on the rocky beaches of the Grand Hotel, making love with the abandon of lovers whose only concern was the next moment of mutual pleasure. That sun-drenched day she had tasted of suntan lotion and salty seawater. How vividly he could recall the azure brilliance of the Gulf d'Antibes, lapping over their bodies, as they struggled to meld into each other under the scorching noon sun.

Taylor pulled Desaix upward with a sense of urgency, until he covered her body with his. As he entered her, she clasped him with the passionate embrace of a woman who knows she is only a moment away from complete release. "Oh, my God! Desaix, hold me. Oh, baby, I want you! You're the only one who can make me feel . . . Oh, my God! Hold me!" She clasped Desaix's torso toward her as her body erupted into spasms of contractions.

Stroking her forehead, Desaix felt that old feeling of tenderness and compassion well up again. She had been his mistress on and off between his second and third marriages. Or was it his third and fourth? "Hold on, beautiful! Take your time. This is just a little thank-you present for helping me out in the Op Center."

Like most good lovers, they were both compatible and incompatible at the same time. Their sex together was wonderful, as was their overall companionship. So what had gone wrong? Possibly nothing. That was the basic problem. Beneath all that sexual passion was a substratum of fondness, respect, and caring, but no deep love or cry for mutual dependence. By disposition, they both were loners who wanted to connect only intermittently and selectively.

Judy laughed and said, "You are wonderful, Desaix. You know that, don't you?"

"My more modest, shy side would question that assertion and ask, 'Is that right?' "

"Stop playing games!" She smacked him playfully on the back, and pushed him off her. Then she rolled over on top of him.

"Desaix, has anyone told you that you are an evil man?" Nuzzling his nose with hers, she playfully licked his lips.

"Someone once told me that on the beaches of Cap d'Antibes. She said that a truly evil man was one who made you realize that anything was possible. There were no limits for him; only the ones he imposed on himself."

Desaix ran his fingers delicately along the sides of her body, and could feel her body undulate, as if she were seeking another moment's satisfaction. She ground her pelvis into his and became excited to realize that she could arouse him so soon again.

"You don't give up, do you?"

"Me? Are you kidding?" Desaix ran his fingers over the crevices of her back.

"I can feel it again, Desaix. You're acting like a bad boy. And you know what happens to bad boys, don't you?"

"I only know what happens to boys who don't act bad from time to time."

"Like who?"

"Like your friend President Donald Westview, aka Choirboy."

"Oh, I see! It's serious time now. Well, what makes you think that Choirboy is so virtuous?"

"Well, his nickname for one. That certainly connotes something about his character."

"You're fishing again, Desaix. I know that cute baiting technique of yours. It hooked me in the first time you tried it." She rolled off him and poured herself a glass of champagne.

Desaix pulled her back onto the bed, and finished the champagne in her glass. "Maybe I'm getting a bit jaded or worn, but—"

"Shut up, Desaix! Sometimes you don't know when to stop talking." Tipping the remaining contents of the glass onto his body, she kissed him passionately.

This time he grabbed her by the shoulders, and mounted her from the rear, in a furious ride that culminated in a mutual release that left them both completely exhausted.

"It always amazes me how you can read my thoughts and know exactly what I want when I want it."

"Sweetheart, don't flatter me. I wish I could tell you that I'm Svengali. But I'm not. I'd just like to be."

"Uh oh. I'm in trouble when you start using that poor Southern humble pie routine on me. I think our time's up—at least for today."

Taylor stood up abruptly and threw back the covers. "Sometimes, lover boy, you don't know when to stop. You know me well enough to know that if I had wanted to tell you something about one of my lovers, all you had to do was to stay around long enough so I could have time to smoke at least three cigarettes. Then I would have told you more than you ever wanted to know."

"All right, so I'm gauche. Give me a break. I'm just a poor—"

"Enough! Don't spoil the great afternoon." She got up to dress.

"Take it easy, Milkshake. I'm not here to do anything more than what you and I have been doing for some time. Certainly, before there was ever any such person as Choirboy."

"Peace!" Taylor extended her right hand out in a gesture of friendship.

"Peace," Desaix responded by pulling her toward him and holding her around the waist. "This afternoon has turned out to be a pleasant surprise for me."

"Ditto for me," she said as she started to run her hands over his body. "Do you know that I like the way your body feels?"

"What do you mean?"

"Oh God, you are something else!"

"No, I mean it. What do you mean that you like the way I feel?"

"Simply that! I like the way your skin feels. It's smooth and silky—like when you want something from someone."

"Are you calling me an opportunist?"

"That would be too polite."

"This whole thing started because I made an offhanded comment about Westview," he said. He drew her back toward him and caressed her face. "Let's not spoil an afternoon because of something stupid that I said. We've always been able to rise above our differences. Anyway, I owe you for what you did for me this afternoon."

"Forget it! I owe you a lot more than that. What about all those times you made feel alive when I had no reason." She kissed him gently on the lips and ran her hands through his hair. "You've always been gentle and kind with me. Maybe the only man I've known who has been like that with me. Too bad we couldn't be a steady diet for each other."

Their conversation was interrupted by a knock at the door.

"Who could that be?" Taylor finished dressing quickly and started to walk toward the door.

"Wait a minute!" Desaix finishing adjusting his standard pin-striped charcoal State Department suit with its requisite red tie. "What if it's Choirboy?"

"He never comes unannounced. Usually a Secret Service agent comes in to check the place beforehand. Then she discreetly leaves, trying to leave the impression that this is a normal, routine outing for the President."

"Is her name Mary Dougherty?" Desaix asked.

"Yes it is. Short, attractive, no-nonsense. Don't tell me you've got something going with her?"

The knock at the door became louder and more insistent.

"Take it easy! Who is it?"

"The hotel manager."

"What do you want?" Judy asked.

"I have an important message for Ms. Judy Taylor."

"I'll be right there."

Before she got to the door, the door knob turned.

She was pushed back violently by two well-dressed men firing Star Model Z-70 9 millimeter submachine guns with silencers. Taylor absorbed the initial barrage of bullets.

"Choirboy . . ." was the last word she murmured.

Covered in her blood, Desaix crashed through the French doors.

# CHAPTER
## 18

Even in danger, a middle-aged male can run only as fast as his biological limits allow. To say the least, Desaix was not a physical fitness devotee. His physical exertions were limited to the minimum requirements of lovemaking, which provided less than adequate cardiovascular toning for a man of his age, no matter how much he enjoyed it.

When Desaix crashed through the glass French doors onto the antiquated fire escape, he barely missed the hail of 9 millimeter bullets.

Covered with glass debris, blood on his clothes, a cut on his right hand, and wounds on his face and chest, Desaix ran down the wobbly wrought iron steps pursued by two gunmen sporting short-cropped haircuts and black inexpensive suits, looking like FBI agents but acting like Special Forces.

His only hope was to flee down four levels to the street, where he could get lost in the crowd.

His heart raced as bullets ricocheted all around him. If he slowed down for even a fraction of a second, he would be dead. And he was losing his wind rapidly.

The barrel of the first gunman's Z-70 submachine gun was almost over his shoulder. Desaix stopped dead in his tracks, turned quickly around, knocking the barrel of the gun aside, and then grabbed it. He thrust the gunman forward, forcing him to tumble down one flight of stairs.

Shifting his finger to the uppermost trigger indent of the Z-70, Desaix opened fire.

He missed!

Rolling sideways on the metal platform, the gunman pulled out a stainless steel double-action .380 Walther Model PPK/S and started firing.

Desaix was trapped in a crossfire. Both gunmen had their sights trained on him. One of their bullets would find its target soon.

Fear of death won out over fear of mutilation as he crashed through the window of an empty room from the fire escape, one floor below. He hid beside a huge Edwardian armoire, catching his breath.

He waited for the gunmen to follow him through the window. But all he could hear was an eerie silence. The gunfire had stopped. And there was no movement on the fire escape.

It gave him a moment to think. What in God's name was happening? Fitzpatrick and Taylor were both dead. Why Taylor? Perhaps she was simply a target of opportunity. Or was Westview the primary target? Or was he, Desaix, the real target? He wondered who besides Manning knew he was here. He hadn't told anyone where he would be. Maybe he had been followed. But by whom?

The doorknob to the room started to turn. Desaix checked the safety latch to see if it was locked. The sound of the creaking door competed against the rapid beating of his racing heart. Now he could hear someone moving on the fire escape. So that was it. They were setting up a crossfire. He quietly moved over to the other side of the door and hid behind it. If he were lucky, Desaix could surprise at least one of the gunmen.

The baby-faced killer crouching at the ledge of the window sighted Desaix, pulled the trigger of his PPK/S, and smiled as he watched Desaix fall to the ground. But he relaxed too soon.

Grabbing his wounded left shoulder with his right arm, Desaix slammed the hotel door on the pock-faced gunman entering the room. His submachine gun practically fell into Desaix's arms. The unarmed gunman raced down the carpeted hallway.

"Stop, before I fire!"

The man froze in place. Desaix held the submachine gun in his right hand as he approached the pock-faced man. The EXIT light cast a morbid red shadow over them.

"Who are you?"

"John Doe."

"Why do you want to kill me?"

"My name is John Doe."

"Your friend isn't going to be too happy with the fact that you've been caught."

When the gunman reached into his jacket pocket, Desaix opened fire. The youth fell to the ground with his hand still in his pocket.

Desaix crouched against the wall, waiting for the baby-faced gunman to appear. But all was silent. He dragged the dead man onto the landing beyond the exit door and examined the contents of his pockets: a small vial in his jacket had the familiar smell of hydrogen fluoride. The gunman was probably going to swallow it, thought Desaix, to avoid being interrogated.

But why hydrogen fluoride again? Could Westview be behind this, just as

Manning had warned? Or was this part of the coup against the President, just as Westview had predicted? The hydrogen fluoride seemed to implicate Westview. But the fact that only Manning knew that he was here pointed Desaix's suspicions to him. Or better yet, were both men dupes of someone else? Like Mapplethorpe?

Desaix examined the scanty contents of the man's leather wallet and found a plastic identification card.

Name: John Doe.

Status: Psychiatric patient, Saint Elizabeth Hospital, Richardson Division.

Attending physician: Dr. Juan Prince.

Place of birth: Baltimore, Maryland.

Suddenly, bullets whizzed by him. Desaix tried to return the fire, but his gun was empty.

He threw it down and ran down the hotel stairwell. As he had hoped, he was able to clear the alley and melt into the crowd of tourists gaping at the historic buildings.

Desaix was bleeding from his right hand and left shoulder as he walked leisurely to the park across from the hotel. But for the moment he was inured to the pain of both wounds.

How ironic, he thought, that if he were seriously injured or killed no one except his four ex-wives would benefit from his sizeable life insurance policy. Too bad for Milkshake. She always needed more money than she could put her hands on. Who, better than she, would have appreciated proceeds from someone whose life was both heroic and decadent? A debauched Don Quixote. That's what she once called him. She was perhaps the only one of his loves who appreciated his picaresque character. She was indeed a kindred soul. And he would miss her. They had been comfortable lovers. In a world where love bore the unfair burdens of unrealistic expectations and fantasies, they had had something very special between them.

By this time, the entire block surrounding the hotel was covered with police, ambulances, and other emergency vehicles. He had to avoid them. Otherwise he would be picked up and booked as a criminal suspect. At this point, he couldn't afford the luxury of being incarcerated by the police. He had too many assignments to complete.

Running down several blocks and then crossing Dupont Circle, Washington's rough equivalent of Greenwich Village, Desaix walked quickly past the familiar musical ensemble of Rastafarians, with whom he would banter on a casual Sunday. Mr. Joe headed this group of menacing-looking Jamaicans, who, with their hair in dreadlocks and their gentle, humorous manner, played their drums and guitars in a sensuous reminder of their homeland.

"Hey mon, you ain't lookin' so good, today. You gotta lotta blood abawt you. Yo're gonna need one of us healers, you know."

"Thanks, Mr. Joe, but I'm just a sloppy eater."

"You'll see, mon. No mon is an island, and no island is complete without us. You like that, mon?"

"I like that, mon." Desaix looked back toward the direction of the hotel. The second gunman was nowhere to be seen.

But as he approached his three-story brownstone at the corner of New Hampshire Avenue and Nineteenth Street, he spotted him sitting in the front seat of an unmarked black Ford Torino, clearly waiting for him. The question now was how to get to the surgical kit in his apartment. The emergency room of George Washington University Hospital, only seven blocks away, wouldn't afford him the protection he needed. Somehow he had to distract his assailant so he could get into the apartment.

Warily, he walked back to the Rastafarians. Desaix explained what he wanted to Mr. Joe and gave him a hundred-dollar bill.

Taking their instruments, Mr. Joe and his Rastafarians crossed the street and approached the Torino.

"Hey mon, wat you want to hear?"

"Buzz off!" replied the gunman.

"Hey mon! You don't have to get so attitudinal. We are Third World oppressed musicians trying to make an honorable existence."

Mr. Joe started to play his bongos, loudly, provocatively, blocking the gunman's view of the entrance to Desaix's brownstone.

"Listen, I told you once before, buzz off!" The gunman looked all around for signs of Desaix. There were none. "I'm waiting for someone to arrive. Could you step aside, please." He paused. "Do you dig me?"

"Do we dig you, mon?" Mr. Joe repeated the question in an infectious singsong pattern. Raising his arms as if he were about to conduct a symphony, he brought them crashing down on his drums, parodying the simple sentence "Do we dig you?" by creating a nonsensical sound around it in a reggae format. "Boys, let's show this gentleman that we dig what he says."

The five-man band started to play and sing.

"Come on, get out of my way!" the gunman yelled, pulling out his weapon and pointing it at Mr. Joe. "Get the point?"

"You are a man of great persuasion, and, I suspect, equally strong conviction."

"Don't fuck with me. I'm in no mood."

A member of the group standing at the corner signaled Mr. Joe that Desaix had just entered his building.

"Gentlemen, I think our presence is no longer required. Our newly found friend here has had sufficient exposure to our talents."

"So long, boys. I'll recommend you for my next social event."

"Hey thanks, mon. We're deeply appreciative. And for a few extra dollars, I think we can provide you with all the information you may be looking for."

"What do you mean?"

"If I'm not mistaken, you are not exactly waiting here to win the lottery. Ain't that right?"

"What is it your business what I'm doing here?" He began to reach for his gun again.

"I like to think of myself as a man of opportunity. An entrepreneur of information, so to speak. You got to know something about somebody, and I'm the man to get that information for you."

"Yeah sure. Next time, buddy. Now buzz off! I don't have the time for you."

"That's too bad, mon, because I'm convinced that I've got exactly what you're lookin' for." Mr. Joe was using the top of the Torino as a drum.

"How do you know what I'm looking for?"

"Try me," Mr. Joe said as he rubbed his thumb and first two fingers together, indicating that like almost everything else in life his information was for sale.

"How is this?" the gunman asked as he flashed a ten-dollar bill.

"In the free-market system, we would say that is not a very competitive offer. The man you're looking for gave me one thousand percent more than that. So I would say that in order to be competitive, you would have to offer at least two thousand percent more."

"Two hundred dollars. How's that?"

"That would be mathematically precise, and emotionally quite rewarding." Mr. Joe took the money and held it up to the sky, examining it carefully. "Looks to me like the proper currency."

"Well?" the gunman was clearly impatient.

"The man you're lookin' for—a tall, dark-complexioned man with black curly hair, came right by here, just as we were talking. As a matter of fact, he engaged our services, much as you have just done, to make certain that you were preoccupied with our scintillating presence."

"Cut the crap! Where did he go?"

"He went into that tall apartment building at the end of the block. He probably went into one of those doctor's offices."

"How do you know?"

"Hey mon, you don't have to be a brain surgeon to know when a man is bleeding all over the sidewalk."

"What do you mean?"

"He was covered with blood, mon. His right hand. His left arm."

"That's him, all right. Which way did you say he went?"

"Down there!" Mr. Joe pointed toward the end of the block.

The man sped off without even a word of gratitude.

"You see, gentlemen, we have just made a double hit on the same piece of information. In the world of finance, we call that leverage."

Like wandering minstrels, Mr. Joe and his band strolled back to Dupont Circle to continue to play their music and trade on information.

As Desaix opened the door to his apartment, he realized he hadn't spent much time there lately. When he had first moved in he had committed himself to decorating it with original lithographs and oil paintings from the early German Abstract period. But the furniture was starting to look a little shabby and the room had a dusty layer.

Desaix dug out his surgical kit from the drawer, sat down at a table, and started to cleanse his wound with iodine. He felt like passing out. The pain was excruciating, far more than what he had experienced two days before in Japan. As he was about to place the first suture through the wound in his left shoulder, there was a knock at the door. He picked up his gun and walked cautiously toward it.

No one was on the other side of the peephole.

The bell rang again.

"Who is it?"

"Mary Dougherty."

Desaix opened the chained door slightly. He saw it was Mary and let her in. As he closed the door, he fell down.

"Hey, cowboy, you're not doing too well." Mary examined his wounds. She managed to drag him over to a frayed couch. "You need a doctor. You've lost a lot of blood."

"Believe it or not, I am a doctor." Desaix felt foolish lying on the couch.

"I know. But you know the old saying, 'A doctor who treats himself has a fool for a doctor, and a fool for a patient.' "

"Why are you here?"

"When I got to the Kalorama and heard the description of the man who fled, it sounded too much like you to be a coincidence."

Desaix grabbed the bottle of iodine from her, but she took it back.

"Here, let me do that. In my previous incarnation, I was a nurse."

"And now Mary Dougherty is Chief of the Presidential Detail. Pretty impressive career development." Desaix nodded his head in approval.

"I've gone from the care and feeding of the sick to the care and feeding of one privileged man. Who knows, maybe he is also sick." Mary cleansed the area around the wound. "I would say that you are currently giving a home to a bullet."

"You seem to know your weapons pretty well," Desaix said, wincing with pain.

"I should. They take good care of me, if I take good care of them."

"Pretty much like men?" Staring at her, Desaix found her attractive in a provocative sort of way.

"Not even close, Doctor. Guns often turn out to be more reliable than men. Now hold still. This is going to hurt." She picked up the skin on one side of his shoulder with a pair of tweezers and started to clean the wound.

"Holy shit! What did you do?" Desaix grabbed on to her strong arm.

"I'm cleaning the wound," Mary replied.

"But will I have any shoulders left when you're through?"

"Don't worry! You can always add some pads. Give you kind of a Joan Crawford look." She opened up the surgical kit.

"What are you doing now?" Desaix's stomach was swirling with nausea. For him, this was the worst of all possible situations. He had to depend on the kindness of a stranger.

"I'm going to suture you up. Any complaints?" Mary appeared self-assured, almost cavalier.

"Yeah . . . I mean . . . what . . . the . . . hell . . . do . . . you . . . know . . . about suturing someone?" Desaix was unsuccessfully trying to resume control of the situation.

"You're using too much energy, asking me too many questions." Slipping her hands into the white talcum-powdered gloves, she threaded a hooked surgical needle with number four cat gut.

"You can't do it! You're not a doctor," Desaix barely blurted out.

"And you're a doctor, but you can barely lift your head up from the pillow. So what good does your medical degree do for you at this moment in time? Anyway, I was an emergency room trauma nurse. This kind of stuff is kid's play."

"All right! But just be gentle."

"If nothing else, I am extremely gentle. You can ask the guys who work for me. I only bust their hump twice a day. They don't think that's too bad."

She injected 2 percent novocaine into the folds of the wound, numbing Desaix's shoulder, so she could proceed quickly with the next step, piercing through the swollen folds of tissue.

"Oh shit!" screamed Desaix, who felt comfortable revealing his pain in front of her. The needle felt as if it were ripping his flesh. Dougherty hadn't injected enough novocaine. But he didn't have the heart to tell her. She was trying so hard to help him.

"Am I hurting you?" Mary asked.

"It's not you. The needle has been filed down too much."

"I'm sorry."

Desaix closed his eyes and tried to block out the excruciating pain.

Mary looked around the living room as she continued to suture. It was what she might have expected from a bachelor with a TOP SECRET security clearance—a carelessly disheveled home. In clear defiance of State Department rules, Desaix had brought home all types of classified papers and left them strewn around the apartment. She wondered what type of information was contained in them.

"Oh, Jesus! This thing really hurts. Are you certain you know what you're doing?" Despite his provocative question, he was impressed by her quiet self-confidence and assertiveness.

"Here, you want it?" She pulled the needle through the final sutures and handed him the gleaming steel clamp.

"Tough, aren't you?" Beneath her take-charge exterior, Desaix sensed a vulnerable, caring woman.

"Maybe . . . maybe not. You're the shrink. You tell me. Am I tough, or is this simply a show that I like to put on from time to time when I don't have anything better to do?"

"For an answer to that question, I'd have to charge you my professional rate." Pausing to watch her bandage him, he added, "Anyway, I'm glad you're here."

"Thanks. That's the nicest thing anyone has said to me all day. Maybe even all week." Wrapping the bandage around his shoulder, she was impressed by his wiry physique. Despite the rumors about his Big Easy lifestyle, he seemed to keep himself in relatively good shape.

"It sounds to me that you've been starved for some TLC."

"Now you're getting a little too personal."

"Excuse me. I wasn't aware that I couldn't ask my physician any personal questions."

"This is strictly a professional relationship."

"So where do I pay the bill?"

"In due time. For the moment, let's say you owe me." She finished bandaging up his shoulder. The bullet had ripped through his flesh but had not lodged deeply in him.

"*Avec plaisir.*" He watched admiringly as she finished bandaging his left shoulder. "Where did you learn to patch and sew like that?"

"I told you I was an ER nurse." She held his right hand. For a man of his height, she thought, he had unusually small hands.

"That doesn't really answer the question, does it?" He watched as she prepared herself to clean the wound.

"What do you mean?"

"ER nurses can't do half of what you did. You acquired your experience somewhere else."

"You're very observant." She started to anesthetize the reopened wound of his right hand.

"That's a polite way of telling me to mind my own business, isn't it." He liked looking at her. She was attractive, irreverent, and tough.

"At least for now." Taking a deep breath, she paused as she began to cleanse the wound with the iodine.

"If you don't mind my asking you again, why are you here? And how did you know I was here?" Desaix had to distract himself from pain.

"That's two questions."

Mary enjoyed the bantering. It had been a long time since she had verbally sparred with a man and didn't feel as if she were intimidating him. She could sense that Desaix was trying to engage her in order to find out what made her tick—what she thought and why. And it wasn't because he was a trained psychiatrist. It seemed particular to his own personality.

"Okay," he answered. "I'll break it down into two simple parts."

"Never mind. I get the point." She paused again. "Listen, I'm not trying to change the conversation, but is this a chemical wound?"

"Yes, hydrogen fluoride. The same chemical that was used to murder Fitzpatrick."

"And now Judy Taylor is dead," she added hesistantly. It was clear to Desaix that Mary was trying hard not to show how upset she was.

"Why was she killed?" he asked her. The pain of his throbbing hand reminded him of how gruesomely both Fitzpatrick and Taylor had died.

"They weren't after her. They were after you."

"How do you know?"

"She was never a threat to the President." Turning her head ever so slightly away from him, she felt strangely embarrassed by what she was about to tell him. "As you well know, she was extremely discreet in all her liaisons. She was simply waiting for their weekly afternoon rendezvous."

"Weekly? Isn't that a bit risky?"

"You tell me, Doctor. Self-destructive behavior is your field of expertise. Not mine. I simply serve by standing and waiting—not analyzing."

The fact that Westview had a mistress was clearly no surprise to Desaix. It was simply the continuation of a long and dishonorable tradition of American Presidents who were sexually active.

After a while, neither the press nor the public cared anymore. The truth was that sex and politics, whether domestic or international, were inextricable. They lived in an unholy synergy of convenience. And Desaix, better than anyone else, could appreciate, and more importantly, enjoy that synergy. Desaix sensed that Mary tolerated what she saw, but in no way condoned it. Good for her, he thought. There was one virtuous person among the two of them—for right now at least.

"You seem to be lost in deep thought. Want to share some of those brilliant ideas?"

"Yeah, I was thinking of the long and illustrious history of our more sexually active Presidents."

"Must be quite a long list?"

"Enough to make the American public think twice about double standards when it comes to electing their public officials."

"Is that a fancy way of saying that you're scared shit of what might happen to you if these boys ever catch up to you?"

"Maybe. What you were telling me was that whoever killed Taylor was really intent on killing me and not her. Is that right?"

"Let me put it this way—you're not wrong, as far as I know."

"Why do you put those qualifiers on?"

"Because the truth is that I don't really know. I have no hard facts to support the argument one way or another. Worse yet, I don't really know who they are." Mary finished bandaging him and paused to monitor his facial reactions.

"Would it surprise you to find out that the man I killed was a patient at Saint Elizabeth Hospital?"

"Was he born in Baltimore?"

"Yes, as a matter of fact. How did you know?"

"Was his doctor listed as Dr. Juan Prince?"

"Right again."

"Did he use a Star Model Z-70 submachine gun?"

"What the hell is going on, anyway?"

"Have you told me everything you know?"

"Yes, to the best of my knowledge. Why are you asking me these questions?" Desaix wondered whether Mary knew about what Westview had just told him—that there was to be a coup against him. But he didn't feel comfortable enough with her to ask. Why should he? Just because she helped him? He would simply have to wait and see what she did before he would consider revealing Westview's secret. Anyway, she might be part of the coup. She might even want to see him killed. Perhaps she was trying to co-opt him.

Desaix's principle of survival surfaced: trust is a habit just one emotional high away from complete addiction.

Mary placed her index finger to her mouth, requesting silence. She pointed to the hallway, indicating that someone was walking outside, down the carpeted hall toward them.

Desaix was impressed with her abilities. The more he studied her body, the more he sensed that she radiated an almost masculine sense of confidence. She was decisive and opinionated, as well as nurturing. He wondered what she would look like in a negligee. Watching her swivel her hip to the side so that she covered the entrance of the door with her 9 millimeter Beretta, he wondered how well she could move in bed. Would she insist on being on top?

"Stop staring! It won't help either one of us out too much right now."

"Are you as good as I think you are?"

"I can shoot the bull's-eye at seventy-five feet away. Is that what you mean?"

"Yeah! That's precisely what I mean." Desaix enjoyed the smart-ass retort to what he knew was his inappropriate, sexist comment. Another of Desaix's rules of life was applicable: one smart-ass deserves another smart-ass. Perhaps, he had found his match.

The footsteps stopped abruptly outside the door. There was the sound of a click as if someone were cocking his gun.

Very slowly, Mary reached for the doorknob. Without a moment's hesitation, she swung the door open and started firing. A burst of semiautomatic fire was returned.

Jumping back, she pressed herself against the wall and pushed Desaix away from the doorway. The burst of semiautomatic gunfire shattered the contents of Desaix's apartment.

Mary realized that she and Desaix were outmanned and outgunned. Two men stood at the door firing Star Model Z-70 submachine guns. In a few seconds they would be inside the apartment.

Grabbing Desaix by the arm, Mary raced to the other side of the small apartment. She crashed through the front window, followed by Desaix.

This time, however, there was no fire escape to break their fall onto the sidewalk.

# CHAPTER
## 19

Like amyl nitrate, both a coup and lovemaking have certain aphrodisiac-like properties.

Tamara's fully clothed body rested against the alabaster column. She didn't want to let him go. She would have liked every part of him buried in her. The tighter she held him, the more she realized that he was, in fact, hers. Only she could spoil him like this. Who else would use her multipurpose GRU identification card to pass through all the checkpoints in order to meet her lover in the midst of a raging battle? Maybe her mother was right. She was man crazy. Or maybe she was just plain crazy.

"My foolhardy beauty . . ." Pushkin caressed her frightened face. He had trusted her with his life. Against all his best intuition and military professionalism, he was thinking with his heart. Not the heart of the poet he had imagined himself to be, but with the heart of the lover he was becoming—as improbable as it seemed in the midst of this chaos.

Other than the men he had personally recruited, she was the only other person to know anything about the coup. Days before, in a moment of passionate lovemaking, he had asked her whether she was willing to die with him. As most lovers are wont to answer in the heat of passion, she answered that she would be willing. When he had called her on the promise, she thought he was crazy. But she had arrived, and now was trying to make love with the sound of gunfire in the background.

Pushkin felt the confluence of love and history converge in one moment and in one place. Here in the Kremlin, in a sixteenth-century anteroom next to the august chamber of the Council of Ministers, he had achieved what even his own ancestor was not able to do. A moment of silent passion.

She loved the sensation of having his big hands over her body, although she felt a little intimidated by the fact that the President of the Russian Federation was next door.

"My spirited one." Pushkin repeated the first words of love she had spoken to him, only days before.

Unlike previous relationships, Tamara had become an instant obsession to Pushkin. Most of his liaisons ended in a few days. But Tamara would be different. He could tell. An intelligence professional who could easily compromise him (he became excited at that notion), she had succumbed to him like an innocent schoolgirl.

As he stroked the back of her neck, tenderly running his fingers down the sinuous tendons of her shoulder, he realized that their relationship was in the process of transforming from one in which he had been the hunted to one in which he was the hunter. For him, this had greater implications than the outcome of the coup. Bizarre, he thought, that history took a back seat to love.

"You can be so gentle." She pulled him toward her, once again.

Like all women who feel complete when their lover is with them, she wanted to implant the memory of his tender caresses into her mind and body for as long as possible. It was a particularly feminine gift that Pushkin envied—the ability to retain the sensual imprint of the moment within the very core of their bodies, to be recalled at the proper time.

"You are crazy, you know," Pushkin said, holding her face in his hands. Her voice was making him lose his concentration, while something within him insisted on his releasing her.

A knock on the door interrupted them.

"Yes?" Pushkin laughed when he realized that he sounded inappropriately official.

"Captain Marat Vartanian! It's urgent, sir!" The sounds of gunfire outside the door became increasingly louder.

"Come in, Captain!"

"Yes, sir!" The heavyset Armenian walked into the room. From the corner of his eyes, he watched the beautiful woman arrange her wrinkled military blouse and skirt. Vartanian finally blurted out what he had come to say. "The Spassky Guards are starting a major offensive. They've captured one of our 50 millimeter M-41 mortars, allowing their T-72 tanks to approach the Kremlin without any resistance. We only have a few minutes to evacuate our position and head for the landing site."

"Okay, let's go!" Pushkin grabbed his machine gun and started toward the door.

"What are you doing?" Tamara had a hurt, angry expression on her face. "So what am I? A fish? Are you just going to leave me here to die in these shallow waters?"

"Please, sir, we must leave now." Vartanian had very little patience for the New Russian Woman, a hybrid of American women's liberation and

Russian *mujeek*. They belonged at home, taking care of babies or old men. They shouldn't be a nuisance.

"Come with us! Give my nightingale your AK-47." Pushkin kissed her on the lips and handed her Vartanian's rifle. "Are you certain?"

"Am I certain? How can you ask? I signed my death warrant when I decided to fall in love with you."

She took the rifle, adding, "Don't worry, Captain Vartanian, I know how to use this."

"Yes, Major! I understand."

A blaze of RPK light machine gun fire threatened them as they slid along the walls toward the Council of Ministers.

"How good of you to come," Zotov said, resting both of his feet on the conference table, smoking a Pani cigarette. He looked like the CEO of a major Fortune 500 company who had just been informed that his diamond-bedecked wife was running away with the Romanian chauffeur.

Pugo, Primakov, and Yershov paced nervously about the room, mumbling profanities to themselves. Misha had taken the other four members of the PPG away and locked them into a small room nearby. They were neither valuable nor dangerous enough to keep with them or to spare men to guard them.

Pushkin knocked Zotov's feet off the conference table with the butt of his gun and jerked him to his feet.

"Come on, lazy bones. We've got to get out of here."

Bullets fired from Red Square shattered the remaining windows.

"Just give up, Colonel Pushkin. My men will be grateful to end this mess and let bygones by bygones," Zotov replied with the smug self-confidence of someone keeping a secret.

Pushkin beckoned to Vartanian. "Give me some fire cover as I pull Zotov out of here. Take that T-72 out before they take us out with one of those cannons."

"Sir." Misha ran into the room, dragging his Sagger antitank missile. "Three platoons are headed down the hall! What do you want us to do, sir?"

"Misha, set your baby up here. Take out that T-72! And then follow us downstairs to the basement."

Pushkin motioned Tamara to cover the door, while Misha ran back into the hallway to pick up 120 millimeter single-shot casings.

"Captain, take a handful of men and set up a cross-fire of two PKM machine guns in the hall. Give me a few minutes lead time, then follow me down. Remember we're headed toward Khodinka."

"The Central Airfield?" Zotov was impressed with Pushkin's planning. He had even left enough time to engage in an afternoon tryst. But that was no surprise to Zotov or anyone else who had ever worked with Colonel Casanova.

"That's right, Mr. President."

"You'll never get to it—there are too many guards."

"We'll see." Pushkin knew it was a long chance. But it was his only way to get out of Moscow. Khodinka, or the Central Airfield as it was currently known, was a large field of grass. In the past, it had been publicly known as the rehearsal ground for the Red Square military parade. But secretly it had been planned as a point of escape for members of the Politburo if they were ever confronted with a situation such as this. The subway line at Sverdlov Square Metro, under the Kremlin itself, went from Mayakovska Station to Byelorusskaya Station to Dinamo Station. The last station was Central Airfield. From there, the members of the Politburo could take a helicopter or plane out of the city. But that was before the democratic revolution of 1991.

A 125 millimeter shell blasted through the windows and Pushkin pushed both Zotov and Tamara to the ground, covering them with his body. The room became a maelstrom of broken glass, jagged-edged wooden boards, and mounds of plaster. The relentless sound of semiautomatic gunfire augmented the sense of chaos.

The Spassky Guards rushed down the hall, encountering a heavy barrage of gunfire from Vartanian and his soldiers. There was no doubt in Vartanian's mind that there soon would be hand-to-hand combat if they didn't get out of their indefensible position quickly.

Zotov lay beneath a block of cement, surrounded by an expanding pool of blood.

Tamara seemed dazed, but all right.

Pushkin tried unsuccessfully to lift the cement block. He checked Zotov's vital signs and realized that Zotov was rapidly descending into a state of shock. His pulse was rapid and thready. His respiration was labored. "Captain Vartanian, come in here, right away!" Pushkin screamed into the hall, while he twisted a tourniquet around Zotov's right leg to stop the bleeding coming from the artery running down the back of his leg.

"Yes, sir!"

Vartanian and Misha were covered with powder burns and debris. "Marat, Misha, help me get this column off Zotov."

"I don't understand, sir. If we leave him as he is, he won't be any good to anyone. Our objective will have been accomplished. The coup will be over."

"Don't argue with me. This man is more valuable to us alive as a hostage than dead. So get this goddamn piece of cement off him. Trust me when I tell you that if he dies like this, we all die."

"I don't understand," Vartanian said, turning toward a frightened Misha, who simply shrugged his shoulders. Vartanian looked around the room and gave a loud whistle. "Pugo, Primakov—all dead."

"Don't count them out yet. They may be simply dazed. But I don't care whether they are alive or not. Zotov is my principal concern. Do you understand that?"

Carrying her AK-47 toward the remnants of the twisted metal door,

Tamara discarded whatever doubts she may have had about joining Pushkin. It dissolved into a hail of bullets.

"Misha, bring little baby over here!" Vartanian marked a big cross on the concrete boulder.

"If you don't think that you can do it, tell me, Misha." Pushkin could sense that Misha was nervous.

"You're right, sir. I'm not sure I can do it without killing the President."

Pushkin grabbed the Sagger, carefully aimed it a few inches above the cross, and fired. Just as he had hoped. The concrete shattered, freeing Zotov's leg.

"I'm going to carry him over my shoulder. You two, with Tamara, cover my back and flanks."

They all rushed into the hallway in a burst of fire and raced down the staircase to the basement, where they suddenly encountered Yershov.

"Drop your guns!" Yershov yelled. "I have over twenty soldiers armed with semiautomatics." Yershov appeared disheveled but in control.

Pushkin nodded to Tamara, Vartanian, and Misha to drop their weapons.

# CHAPTER

## 20

The American soldier's basic disposition is to avoid conflict, whenever possible. Failing that, his preference is to engage in what has been euphemistically called "a police action" or "special operation," such as Korea and Vietnam.

But nothing in his character or training predisposes him for turning against his own government. The American soldier neither understands nor accepts the basic premise of a coup, of a conspiracy against one's fellow officers and the fundamental precepts of democracy. Something in the notion of free will and free choice forces him to recognize that conspiratorial betrayal in the guise of a better government is inimical to the American way of life.

That's why Colonel Matthew Zarbitski felt distinctly uncomfortable in civilian clothes. Riding in an unmarked white tractor-trailer, he and sixty of his elite troops were following a smaller white van boldly marked: FLUORIDEX FUMIGATORS/VERMIN ARE OUR BUSINESS. Seated in the front were Lieutenant Robert Rovner and Sergeant Walter Johnson.

The caravan of four unmarked trucks and two marked cars proceeded slowly through the run-down neighborhoods of Anacostia, turning right from Suitland Parkway onto Alabama Avenue toward Martin Luther King Avenue and Bolling Air Force Base. The men in it felt conspicuous. But most of the people loitering about in the streets considered it with as much interest as they might give to an elaborate delivery for one of the neighborhood fast-food restaurants.

"Lieutenant Rovner," Johnson said, "get this! I spend the better part of my adult life trying to get away from this neighborhood. And now look at me—riding in civvies in a pest-control car. Now how am I going to explain this to my mama?"

"No offense, Johnson, but this place really looks like a shit hole."

"Hey, Lieutenant, it's okay if I say that. But it's not the same for someone like you."

Swerving the steering wheel to avoid hitting a little boy crossing the street, Johnson turned toward Rovner, "See what you made me do?"

"Take it easy, Johnson. This place may be a shit hole, but it's a lot better than the place I came from."

"Don't bullshit a bullshitter."

Johnson had to admit to himself that Anacostia did indeed resemble something close to the aftermath of the World War II Dresden bombing. Even after the twenty years since he lived there the city had still not fixed the crater-sized potholes. Children raced mischievously around the littered streets as if this were their playground. Abandoned cars acquired the communal acceptance of a religious icon—adorned with colorful graffiti, broken windows, and bare, rusted chassis. These were the de facto symbols of a decaying urban culture enshrined in the natural liturgy of the streets—the pulsating music of rap, rock 'n' roll, and salsa. Somewhat ashamedly, Johnson felt very much at home on these streets. So he was genuinely hurt by what Rovner had just said. Had they not been such good comrades at arms, he would have slugged him.

"You don't believe me, do you?" Rovner asked. He was a well-built, medium-sized man who liked to tease Johnson because as a kid who grew up in the slums surrounding Pelham Parkway in the Bronx, he had been used to the ritual taunting that occurred among the different ethnic groups. Even in the 1990s, there was an unspoken state of tension among the Jamaicans, the American blacks, and the first-generation elderly blue-collar Jews who were increasingly displaced by the influx of Vietnamese, Hong Kong Chinese, and Koreans. The son of once proud grocers, Rovner had very quickly found himself without a profession or a family inheritance when his father, in a short-sighted move, decided to sell his small grocery store to a family of Koreans from Pusan. He never forgave his father. But, on the other hand, he would never have joined the military, at a time when it was cutting back in manpower, if his family's business had not been yanked from beneath him. In a perverse way, he was grateful to these new immigrants for jolting him out of complacency.

"Listen, Rovner, I only give a shit about one thing. Don't fuck up on me when I'm going into action. Do you know what I mean?"

"Since when did I ever let you down?" Rovner felt hurt that Johnson might even consider the possibility that in some way or another he had fallen short. Together they were an incredibly effective fighting machine.

"Take it easy, Rovner. No accusations have been made or intended."

"That kind of talk can easily be misconstrued. Do you know what I mean?"

"Hey, listen, Lieutenant, I'm just trying to do my job, navigating our way out of this hellhole. Why the hell we're screwin' around in this neighborhood is beyond me."

"There's Bolling Air Force Base. Dim your lights."

The MPs at the gate stopped the convoy. Rovner handed the MP a piece of paper.

"Excuse me, Lieutenant, may I please see your orders?" Examining the paper carefully, the black MP turned toward Johnson. "It's not clear from your orders why you are here."

"We're here to pick up some supplies, and load some on helicopters that will be arriving," Johnson replied. "What you've got in your hands is an executive order signed by National Security Advisor General Thomas Mapplethorpe. You can check what I'm saying by calling the number on the bottom of the page."

The guard took the paper and placed a call to the White House. After a few minutes of conversation with Colonel Sonny Shaw, the guard waved the procession on through the gates.

Out of sight of the gate, Johnson led the caravan onto an old runway. He stopped his van in the middle of a field, jumped out and walked over to the tractor-trailer.

"What happened back there?" Colonel Zarb asked, his cocked 5.56 Colt Commando Carbine lying at his side.

"A slight administrative problem," Rovner replied.

"Is it taken care of?"

"I would say so."

"Do you share that assessment also, Sergeant Johnson?"

"Yes, Colonel, I do."

"Good. Now pull your van out of the way and radio the Cobras to start flying in. We're already running behind schedule."

"What if we meet with resistance?" Rovner asked.

"You know what you have to do, Rovner. How many times do I have to go over that?"

"Well, sir, I just want to make sure everything is in sync."

"Just take your designated positions without incurring any collateral damage. Nothing should stop us from achieving our objective. We have a lot to accomplish in forty-eight hours." Zarb was growing impatient with Rovner. "Johnson, I want you to have the empty trucks head for the warehouse and load up on those canisters of hydrogen fluoride. Then head on downtown— around Fourteenth and H streets."

"Yes, sir. I understand," Johnson said, then saluted and returned to his van.

"Rovner, I want you and my men to help me secure this base."

"I'm ready!"

Zarb and Rovner headed the tractor-trailer filled with soldiers to the dilapidated control tower, while Johnson and the other vans pulled up to the warehouse marked WARNING: DANGEROUS/TOXIC CHEMICALS.

With his men dispersing across the crater-filled airfield, Zarb recalled nostalgically how impressive Bolling Air Force Base had once been—long before the infamous cuts of the Bush administration, when the military budget had been slashed at least 30 percent. During World War II, Bolling Air Force Base had been used as a transit point for ferrying the Pentagon brass back and forth from the European and Pacific theaters. After the war, the base fell into disrepair as both D.C. commercial airports, National and Dulles, became popular. However, for want of a comma in some appropriations bill, Bolling Air Force Base was inadvertently saved from total razing. For the most part, it was currently being used as a temporary billeting quarters for military personnel and as a chemical storage facility. Among the several chemicals that were being stored there, hydrogen fluoride was in greatest supply. It was the chemical of choice by most military bases both to eradicate vermin and for the manufacture of semiconductors for military purposes. Bolling Air Force Base had become a way station for matériel and personnel like many other "closed" facilities.

Perhaps this coup, thought Zarb, could revitalize the impressive military force that had once existed. But even Zarb had to admit to himself that it might be wishful thinking.

But the objective was clear. To hide and be ready to act at the appropriate time. He and his men had to secure the base as quickly as possible with the fewest number of casualties. The real importance of Bolling was its close proximity to Saint Elizabeth Hospital—the second staging area for Project Baltimore.

From both locations, they would be in a perfect position to receive more men and matériel in order to disperse and quietly secure other strategic locations including National Airport, Dulles International Airport, Langley Air Force Base, Andrews Air Force Base, the National Military Command and Control Center in the Pentagon. After that they would secure vital communications satellites and international links at the CIA and NSA, and the coaxial cables in downtown D.C. that controlled the broadcast transmissions of the major television networks, CNN, Western Union, MCI, ATT, and Public Broadcasting. Then would come the White House Special Operations Center itself. Other assets would be quickly secured once these strategic pylons were firmly in place. Zarb wasn't certain that this plan was one hundred percent realistic because he wasn't part of the planning team. His job was to put the plan into effect—and *that* he was certain he could handle.

Zarb, Rovner, and five men fanned across the garbage-ridden field, hitting the ground each time searchlights were aimed in their direction. For the most part, they had been lucky. As expected, they had encountered no resistance.

"Over there, sir," Rovner said, pointing to a large rusted light tower. Three men were standing guard.

What were they doing there, wondered Zarb. Why were guards, heavily armed with M3 Browning submachine guns, on a defunct base? Perhaps his intelligence had been faulty. DIA reports designated the airfield as one with minimal security requirements. He hadn't planned on having to take out so many MPs. This was not his style. Killing counterinsurgents was one thing, but getting rid of your own boys, some of whom he may have trained, well, that was another story. But worse yet, what if other intelligence assessments he had been given were equally faulty? Intelligence had been his bête noire for some time. How many men had he lost because DIA and CIA combined could not give him an accurate reading of a situation? He was in the business of securing military objectives and not wasting assets—particularly human assets. He would try to take the MPs out without harming them. But that might not be possible. Fuck, he thought. He didn't like this coup business at all. There was something unsavory about having to turn against one's own troops. It wasn't American!

"Rovner, take three men and try to get inside the tower. I'll cover you," Zarb said as he checked his watch. "We've got exactly five minutes before the Cobras fly in. The last thing I want is a major firefight. The neighborhood reporters will be climbing all over our ass."

"Got you, sir!"

Rovner motioned three of his men and ran with them toward the control tower.

The brightly lit moon worked against them, and the MPs opened fire.

Damnit, thought Rovner, the guard at the gate had forgotten to pass on his okay to these MPs.

Zarb was the first one to see the ominous-looking armored personnel carrier moving quickly toward him. From its sleek low outline and external fuel tanks, he knew that it was a full-tracked M113A3 APC, armed with a .50 caliber machine gun.

The APC opened fire, spraying the area in front of him with a hail of bullets.

Zarb and his men were trapped. Their only hope was to remain there, splayed out on the wet ground until Rovner and his boys got to the top of the tower and knocked out the APC.

Zarb could taste the dirt kicking into his face. Some coup, he thought. Half of his men were preparing to become fucking fumigators. The other half were hiding in the mud or scaring away MPs. This was a hell of a way to run a war—even if it was only a small one.

But the truth was that Zarb, like many of his men, was addicted to the idea that they were going to war. Any kind of war, as long as it increased his adrenaline and allowed him to have a focus in his life. Preparing for battle allowed him to maintain and rationalize a rigid standard of discipline and exercise. Whatever else could be said about war, Zarb knew that it was the only thing that made him feel totally alive.

Rovner, on the other hand, had very little desire to feel alive in this way. He simply didn't want to die without having seen some significant action other than the street fights he grew up with. He'd rather fight here than spend his life in some factory welding sheets of steel.

Rovner ran up the circular metal tower stairs, cocked his Ingram submachine gun, and was ready to release thirty-two rounds of 9 millimeter bullets. Encountering a red-haired MP, he paused. His instructions were to seize the tower with a minimal cost of human lives.

The MP also paused.

Rovner wanted to pull the trigger. But something stopped him from doing it. What was it? Was it the fact that he had never fired on another American soldier? Or that he really wasn't certain what he was supposed to do? There was something very wrong about the concept of this coup. It didn't make much sense to him. His orders were to implement Operation Baltimore and facilitate the overthrow of President Westview. He and the other soldiers had been assured that the President would not be harmed. They were told that the coup was necessary for national security. Something was terribly wrong. Or he simply didn't understand what was happening.

A burst of gunfire erupted. Even while he was trying to make sense of things, his body knew what had to be done. When the red-haired MP tumbled down the circular stairs, Rovner felt sick. This was the first American he had ever killed. Hopefully the last. But no sooner did he mount four more steps than he confronted two more MPs.

More gunfire. The MPs followed their comrade down the stairs.

Accompanied by his three men, Rovner rushed up the stairs to the top of the tower. There were no guards left.

From the rusted metal walkway, Rovner saw the APC racing toward Zarb. Rovner and his men opened fire with his Ingram submachine gun and sprayed the APC. Zarb and his men started to fire as well. The combined firepower pierced what had seemed like an invincible aluminum envelope. Their bullets tore up the 275 horsepower engine. The APC blew up, bursting into flames.

Men dressed in battle fatigues fled the APC, their bodies ablaze. The stench of burning flesh was unbearable, but there was very little either Zarb or Rovner could do. The point of no return had been reached. As if tied by an unspoken bond of compassion, both Zarb and Rovner opened fire simultaneosly and mowed down the human torches. As they fell to the ground in grotesque postures, the charred bodies looked as if they had been created by Hieronymus Bosch.

The Special Forces men turned their heads aside.

"Secure the perimeters and clear the area."

"Yes, sir!" Rovner paused.

"Well, Lieutenant? Is there something wrong?"

"I don't know, sir. I know this is a hell of time to say what I'm about to say. But, sir, I've got to get it off my mind."

"Go ahead, Rovner. I think I know what it is you want to tell me."

"I just don't feel right about what we did." Without any warning, Rovner started to weep.

"It's all right. I know what you're feeling. I'm feeling the same way too." Zarb's eyes began to swell with moisture.

"I've never done anything like that. How the hell can we go around killing our own men? They aren't my fuckin' enemies. I don't even know who my enemies are."

"That's all right, Lieutenant . . . that's all right." Zarb patted Rovner's back.

The six men with them nodded their heads in silent agreement.

"What am I going to do, Colonel? I can't continue like this."

"Take it easy on yourself. It's not easy killing our own boys. But the only way I can think about it is to think of them as the enemy."

"But they're not. You know it. I know it. These guys know it. What in hell are we doing, Colonel? I just don't understand it. We're not fighting communists. There are no more of them around. We're not fighting fascists. They're not around. So who the hell are we fighting? Tell me, Colonel. Because if I can't justify it to myself, how am I going to justify it to these guys?"

"I just don't know. I don't have a good answer. But right now, let's just clean up this mess and bring in the Cobras. If nothing else, we have a time schedule to meet."

"Fuck the time schedule."

"I told you that I can understand your frustration, but there is very little we can do about it right now. Furthermore, Lieutenant, I have to remind you that you volunteered for this assignment. I didn't force you, remember?"

"Yes, sir."

"Then let's do our job and get the show on the road. We've got only a few minutes before the choppers come in."

Rovner and his men dragged the charred bodies to the edge of the landing strip and covered them with tarps. From the distance, they could hear the whirring sound of the Cobra gunships. Against the moonlit sky they looked like alien predators flying in formation, ready to descend on their prey.

"All right men, clear the landing zones," Rovner said. He counted six gunships. Where the hell were they when he needed them. At least their presence would have helped him and his men depersonalize the violence. Maybe the deaths of these soldiers, lying under the tarps, could have been made more palatable. Maybe not.

The helicopters descended in a ballet of swirling debris. For a brief moment, Rovner forgot the horror of a few minutes ago.

Seven groups of fifteen men dressed in civilian clothes disgorged from the mechanical whirling dervishes.

"Colonel Zarbitski, I'm Captain Victor Moon, 2nd Battalion, 75th Infantry Regiment, from Fort Lewis, Washington."

Moon, a thirty-two-year-old crewcut preppie from West Point, had all the enthusiasm and vitality of a U.S. Army Ranger who believes he is privileged to participate in a moment of history.

"I want you to deploy your Cobras according to plan. This is Lieutenant Rovner. You will coordinate all your activities with him. Is that clear?"

"Yes, sir!" Moon said, though he felt a twinge of discomfort. He had never had to report before to a lieutenant, particularly one who wasn't a Ranger. But Colonel Zarbitski was one of their own—a trained Ranger, home-grown and nurtured at Fort Washington. He could trust him.

"I want you to pick up some of our boys at Saint Elizabeth Hospital and fly them on to other destinations," Zarb ordered.

"Excuse me, sir, but did you say Saint Elizabeth Hospital? Isn't that a mental institution?"

"Yes, it is, son."

"Do we really want men who are—?"

"Crazy?" Zarb asked, impatient that some of the men in this elite of elite units lacked a certain imagination. Why not station men at Saint Elizabeth Hospital? That would be the last place anybody would look for them.

"Well, sir, that's not exactly a place one would think of recruiting an elite unit of men," Moon said as he nervously looked at Rovner for support—though none was forthcoming. He had challenged the colonel. Now Moon was on his own.

Screaming sounds of police sirens suddenly broke the crackling sounds of gunfire. Four District police cars raced beyond the gates to the airstrip. With guns drawn, eight policemen cautiously stepped out of their cars.

"What can I do for you officers?" Zarb asked, quickly evaluating what it would take if the situation got out of hand. He concluded that he and his men would meet very little resistance.

"We've gotten several calls from people in the neighborhood that there has been more than the usual sound of street gunfire. We're here to find out exactly what the disturbance might be."

The black sergeant looked uneasily at all of the weapons. He concluded that something was going on. But he didn't know what it was. The question was whether he wanted to find out.

"We apologize for any disturbance we may have caused."

"Anything we should know about?" Having once been an MP, the sergeant knew that a full-bird colonel would only tell him enough to justify his having called in four squad cars.

"There was a minor munitions explosion in the warehouse. Nothing serious. We've got everything under control. Thanks for coming by, though."

The last thing Zarb wanted to do was kill some cops who were simply doing their jobs.

"As long as you're sure it's under control," the sergeant said, then ordered his men to put away their guns.

"Yes, Sergeant, it's under control."

As the police sergeant drove away from the base, the Cobra gunships were revving their engines. Something was definitely going on. Something strange and dangerous. But the colonel's excuse would do. Who was he to question whether ammunition was stored on the base. As far as he knew, ammunition hadn't been stored there since World War II. In fact, nothing had been stored there since the Vietnam War, some thirty years ago. What the fuck, he thought, it was none of his business.

"Let's get the hell out of here," Zarb ordered, "before the entire police force descends on us. Get the choppers out of here." Zarb and his men headed toward three different gunships. "Don't forget, we've got exactly forty-eight hours. Good luck!"

The six AH-1S Cobra gunships lifted off with civilian-dressed men, fully armed.

Sergeant Johnson filled his two dozen spray canisters with hydrogen fluoride and drove the white minivan through the front gate of Saint Elizabeth Hospital. He was followed by the unmarked white tractor-trailer.

The guard waved him through without inspecting the contents of either vehicle. Fumigation of certain empty buildings was routinely done in the evening to avoid disturbing the patients.

The grounds were just as he had remembered: the shrubbery was well groomed but the walkways were littered with cigarette papers and empty beer and alcohol bottles. He was surprised to see patients walking around the hospital grounds in the dark. He certainly wouldn't have the courage to do that. They looked strange. Not because they were crazy, but because they moved stiffly, with an android-like quality. Guiding the caravan of trucks to Richardson Service, he felt as if he were entering a different time dimension. The patients looked as if they were a herd of the homeless, penned up in the corral of red-brick Civil War buildings.

As a child, he remembered stories that went around his neighborhood that "they" were doing "terrible things" in that hospital. Rumor was that patients were subjected to all types of mutilation experiments and amputations. The irony, as Johnson knew all too well, was that St. E's had been initially constructed as a Civil War hospital where Union soldiers had their arms and legs amputated. Almost one hundred years later, the hospital became the bastion for frontal lobe lobotomies, where the nerve cells in the front of the brain were purposefully destroyed by the insertion of an ice pick through the patient's eye socket.

Johnson had an aunt who had been admitted to St. E's diagnosed as an intractable schizophrenic. Recalcitrant to all types of psychotropic drugs, the aunt finally received a pre-frontal lobotomy. After the operation she was extremely compliant in her behavior. But she also walked around the house in a zombie-like state, fearful to move her body in any way that might anger some imaginary group of gods. He was always told that she was special. From time to time, she would suddenly fall down to the ground, kicking and screaming, flailing her arms about in a spasm of blind fury. Once he tried to put his hand in her mouth in order to prevent her from biting off her tongue. Had his mother not pulled his hand away, he would have lost several of his fingers. So he had vivid memories of his aunt as the lobotomized woman who almost ate his fingers.

Dr. Juan Prince and Roger Cordonnier, a brawny man with an accent, were waiting for him at the rear entrance of Richardson Service. Johnson had worked with both the doctor and Cordonnier in several other select operations that had required off-line military and medical expertise. He and Prince had worked well together, several years earlier, in organizing the overthrow of one Latin-American dictator and one Far East dictator. But this was the first time that a psychiatric hospital was being used as a forward base for reprocessing and prepositioning military men.

To a military operative, off-line meant that there was no longer any need for the formal bureaucracy. Over the past ten years, both the State Department and the Defense Department had been gradually dissolving as focal points for legitimacy and manpower in foreign policy and defense. Some foreign policy was conducted in Foggy Bottom. But, as in the Kennedy, Nixon, Ford, and Bush administrations, most of the crucial decisions were made at the White House via the NSC.

In the same way, the Department of Defense was only a skeleton of what it once was. With 5 to 10 percent decreases yearly over the last decade, it was a miracle that anything was still left at Defense. Except for a few major military installations, primarily those that housed elite combat units, there was very little left of the former four-hundred-billion-dollar budget, except the Ranger school, the Green Berets, several divisions of Marine units, the SEALS, and several other elite military units. That was it. What was once a standing military force of two million men was now a confederation of elite combat units working outside the normal chain of command—off-line.

Still, Johnson felt a strong sense of pride serving his country in this most unusual of missions. As trite as it sounded, his was not to ask, but simply to dare and die. Although he could say very little about what he did, he knew that his family was proud of him.

Sixty well-dressed, fully armed men stood at attention before Prince and Cordonnier.

"You're five minutes late, Johnson. What happened?" Prince sounded impatient.

"A slight delay, Colonel Prince—a few skirmishes here and there which forced me to return back to the base to see what had happened. Nothing serious." Johnson admired the suave, self-contained professional who was a colonel in the Army Reserve. He just didn't trust him. Prince didn't seem to allow for any margin of error. Johnson suspected he must be hell on his staff. Demanding. Hardly ever satisfied.

"If we would have waited any longer, some of my patients would have gotten suspicious," Prince responded with irritation in his voice and ordered his men onto the vehicles.

Johnson couldn't get over the irony that one of the most elite fighting units in the U.S. military was being billeted in a psychiatric hospital connected by 140-year-old Civil War–constructed tunnels and conduits to Bolling Air Force Base. He wondered, Why didn't they use the tunnels to transfer the men from the base to the hospital?

"You got enough fumigating equipment?" Cordonnier asked, checking the canisters of hydrogen fluoride in the back of the van. He usually considered himself calm and cool in difficult situations. But ever since the afternoon's chase of Desaix Clark, he felt uncertain and suspicious. Things weren't going well. He had never lost a partner before, at least not so early in the game. This Desaix was one clever son of a bitch.

Cordonnier could hear his employer interrogating him. Why had he failed in killing Desaix? Worse yet, how did an experienced freelance operative accidentally kill the President's mistress? And how the hell was he going to explain the fact that Desaix was on the loose with knowledge of an impending presidential coup?

This time his directions were simple: don't let Colonel Zarbitski fuck up on target acquisition. And most importantly, Cordonnier's part of Operation Baltimore had to go smoothly. Without any hitches. And within twelve hours. Not very much time to create the critical mass of panic that he needed, but on the other hand, Rome was not burned in one day either.

"Hey, doc, what have we got coming toward us? It looks like one of your schizophrenics is sleepwalking," Cordonnier said. He didn't like when his operational responsibilities had to dovetail with Prince's psychiatric responsibilities. Although he had to admit that there was no better cover than a mental institution. If the coup were discovered by patients, it could always be denied. By definition, the patients were crazy. So how could one believe them? Who would ever think of looking in a mental institution to uncover the nerve center of a coup? Except perhaps for Dr. Desaix Clark.

"Amos, what are we doing here so late at night?" Prince said, clearly angry. "Stay away from the trailer, Amos!"

"What's all the commotion?" Amos asked. "I can't sleep none." He looked around suspiciously as the men mounted the trucks.

"Nothing, Amos. There's nothing going on." Prince could see that he would have a hard time convincing Amos to go back to bed. Damnit, he thought, he should have doubled his dose of Stelazine.

"Doc, you can't convince me that I'm not seeing what I know I am seeing."

"I would never try to do that. You know that very well," Prince replied.

"Is everything under control?" Cordonnier asked, now visibly distraught.

"Everything is fine," Prince said, though he could not disguise the discomfort in his voice.

"No, doc," Amos continued, "this ain't like this morning when you tried to convince me that I hadn't seen the President of the United States running out of an apartment house in the middle of the night. Not only did I see him, but I saw that lady he was with. The one who protects him. You know, the one with the hearing aid. And I know damn well that the President hit me in the face. No one can convince me differently. Not even you."

"You're absolutely right, Amos. Everything you said happened just the way you said it happened. But for now you have to get to bed." Prince took Amos's arm and tried to lead him back to the ward. But Amos was resistant.

"Are you certain you don't need any help?" Cordonnier asked, starting to reach for his gun.

"Everything is just fine. Tomorrow morning Amos will feel a lot better. Everything is under control. I assure you."

"You better be right. We've got too much at stake."

"What's he talking about, doc?"

"Amos, these men are making a late-night shipment of supplies to the hospital. That's all."

"I count a pretty good number of men. You know, doc, I used to deliver groceries at all hours of the night to one of the big supermarkets. Sometimes I would need help to unload the truck. But that was like a few men. Maybe two or three. They were union, you know. So we couldn't afford any more."

"Yes, I know, Amos. Let's talk tomorrow."

"Dr. Prince, we're holding up the convoy. You better get rid of him. Now." Cordonnier was starting again to pull his gun out of the holster.

"You see, doc. Even this guy called it a convoy. Nobody moves groceries in a convoy. I'm not that crazy. And I've been in the war, you know. The unpopular one. I certainly ain't stupid either."

"Amos, please!" Prince was having a hard time moving Amos into the building.

"Let me help you, doc," Cordonnier said, as he stuck his Sig Sauer 245 against Amos's right temple.

"You see, doc, I ain't that crazy, am I?" Amos laughed that nervous laughter that many people tend to associate with the insane. A combination of righteous indignation mixed with cackling.

"No, you're not that crazy, Amos. As a matter of fact I'm not sure that you're crazy at all."

"Is that a Sig Sauer 245?" Amos was on a roll. For the first time in a very long time he felt good about himself. The psychiatrists in those other state institutions would tell him that he would be healthy once he felt good about himself. And just at the moment of death, he did. No one could take that feeling away from him. That was all there was to that. Jeez, how simple. Too bad he never had a gun pointed at his temple before, he thought.

"Old man, listen to the doctor. Otherwise, this will be your last night of insanity."

"You mean this is my first and last day of sanity. And for that I can't thank you enough." Amos was ready to hug Cordonnier, who instinctively pulled away from him.

"You're crazy, old man."

"That's why I'm here. What's your excuse?" Amos said. He grabbed the barrel of the gun and pressed it even more tightly against his right temple.

"You don't believe that I would pull this trigger?" Cordonnier asked Amos, looking to Prince for some assistance. But none was forthcoming.

"Pull it!" Amos said. "At least I would have died in combat. You can't fool me. This is some kind of military operation. I've been watching you admit these guys onto the unit all day and night. Who the hell do you think you were fooling? Certainly not the inmates in Richardson Service. You got to be crazy to think that you're pulling the wool over our eyes. Wait till they hear about this." Amos broke out into resounding, robust laughter. A clarion call of his impending sanity.

The sound of a gunshot, into the air, silenced his laughter. Knocking the gun aside, Prince caught a frightened Amos as he fell back into his arms.

"What the hell are you doing, Prince?"

"Making certain you don't do something stupid. Get on that van," Prince said, furious with Cordonnier.

"Come on, you guys, we got to get the hell out of here. As it is we're running late," Johnson shouted from the truck as he started to move the convoy out.

Cordonnier looked at the departing vehicles and at Prince, holding Amos. Unable to contain his frustration, he struck Amos across the face before jumping into the departing van.

"I wasn't wrong, was I, doc?" Amos asked, caressing the bruise on his face. He felt proud. He had finally been vindicated. Violence was not imaginary. He had been struck across the face—not once, but twice. Now he knew that something bad was about to happen.

"Come on, Amos, let's go back to bed. Tomorrow, I'm going to transfer you out of here." Prince knew that the only reason Amos was still alive had to do with the simple fact that a dead patient attracted all sorts of unwanted attention as well as creating serious administrative problems.

"Thanks, doc. You don't have to worry about me. I'll be okay. Believe me, I know how to take care of myself."

"I know that. But it's still a lot smarter for me to get you out of here as soon as possible."

Prince led Amos back into the sanctuary of Richardson Service. He recalled the aphorism he had once seen posted on the bulletin board at the CIA: Paranoids really do have enemies.

Let's hope it's over soon, thought Prince. The plan was simple. Part PSYOPS. Part urban guerrilla warfare. Part simple destruction. The crucial ingredient of Operation Baltimore would be a critical mass of frightened and rampaging disenfranchised citizens who would endanger the safety and well-being of the rest of the city. Cordonnier's objective was to create chaos and disorder that would overwhelm the normal capacity of any urban police force. In response, Westview would have to deputize the National Guard and regular military units through the legal process of *posse comitatus* in order to maintain law and order. At the same time, the President would invoke martial law, giving him extraordinary and unusual executive powers. Everything would be set in motion.

# CHAPTER
## 21

For Desaix, a crisis had the same natural rhythms as the exuberant, foot-stomping, hand-clapping Cajun music he was weaned on. In moments of personal crisis, he would put on a record by Clifton Chenier, king of zydeco, just to hear the accordian, amplified by the clatter of the frottoir, a metal washboard played with thimbles or spoons, and remind himself that there was still a raw, vital street-party spirit out there that he hadn't yet tapped into.

Desaix knew all too well that a crisis manager could ignore the facts of a given crisis. In many cases, a decision maker's value system might not allow him to accept the outcome. Or he might suffer from what some academicians call psychological rigidity. Or he might be constrained by bureaucratic politics.

No crisis manager could, however, ignore power or the abuse of that power. The notion of an imminent coup was something that Desaix could contemplate, analyze, interpret, strategize, or develop option papers for. But the fact that he was in the middle of such a coup made him that much more wary, uncertain about where to direct his attentions. In the world of intelligence analysis, Desaix knew that one could often discover the truth by a comparison of the lies. And in this case, the most obvious candidate for *coupmeister* was, of course, General Mapplethorpe.

In a developing Third World country, it was always the chief military advisor to the President, or the colonel in charge of the military and security forces, who was the immediate suspect as the instigator of any coup. In a democracy, there were no logical candidates. Military and intelligence chiefs were clearly not above reproach, but neither was the local banker free from suspicion.

However, when the troops are storming the ruler's residence, there is a certain validity and immediacy very few can deny. And when one becomes a moving target, the message is clear: DFWP—Don't Fuck With Power. Especially when you ain't got it.

Already, there had been two real attempts on his life, and the one aspect of government that he knew well was that the Mapplethorpes of the world never, but never, acted on their own. The gunmen probably worked for Mapplethorpe, who in turn was taking directions from someone else. That was the customary hierarchy of a military coup.

Desaix recalled one period in the Iran-contra affair when a Marine lieutenant colonel initiated a whole series of international transactions where arms were being sold to Iran in return for release of American hostages in Lebanon. A direct violation of American foreign policy. It was clear to anyone who had been following the criminal trials of those involved in the cover-up that the lieutenant colonel was allegedly acting at the behest of his superiors— the National Security Advisor, a not too bright former Marine colonel himself, and the possibly demented President. In fact, it was almost an axiom of Washington politics that no one working in the government ever took an initiative on his own or implemented a plan without the imprimatur of someone else above him. This was true of almost every administration since World War II.

Desaix had to take stock of where he was. He and Mary had been fortunate that the jump to the ground from his second-story apartment had been cushioned by the building's awning. Next time he might not be so lucky. As a matter of fact, he had a clear sense that his luck was running out. It was only a question of time. More than ever, the sense of urgency propelled him onward. He could feel the flood of adrenaline flush away whatever fear he might have been willing to admit to himself.

"Would you please sit still."

Mary sat next to him in her sparsely decorated home in Georgetown, cleaning out his bleeding shoulder and hand wounds with hydrogen peroxide.

"I feel like a total, helpless cripple. Why is it every time we're together, you seem to be coming to my assistance? This does not look good for a man, particularly a shrink, who prides himself on independence."

"Well, Doctor, have you discussed your problem of dependency with your shrink?" She walked across the whitewashed floors of her modern living room and turned on her stereo. "A little zydeco music to make the healing go faster."

Then taking a roll of gauze, she wrapped it around his right shoulder, timing her movements to the lilting music.

"That's Clifton Chenier. How did you know he's my favorite?"

"Mine too! It's a classic. I got one of his last recordings on Arhoolie Records of—"

"Live at St. Mark's. *On va le danser comme il faut.* We're going to dance it the way it should be." Desaix rose before she could stop him and danced

Mary around her living room with the exuberance of a native son of the Louisiana bayou who grew up with the carnival chants and street-party spirit of this country-western, bluegrass, French patois.

"It looks like you're healing mighty fast."

"Come on, tell me, how did you know that he was my favorite?"

She didn't reply. She simply gave him one of those all-knowing smiles.

He liked her low-key, seductive manner. There was no way she would tell him—of that he was certain. So he would have to play the game—the one he invariably won. Chase and hunt.

Mary liked the feeling of his arms around her waist. It had been a very long time since she had enjoyed the touch of a man. Certainly, even a longer time since she had danced with anyone, except . . . But, in his presence, she couldn't even mention the name to herself.

"What's the matter? You know where I come from in New Orleans, c'est défendu to look like that. Make me look bad. It say to everyone that je ne peux pas faire heureuse ma femme. Tu comprends?" He mimicked the singsong pattern of the Cajun speech.

"I think that may be the problem."

"What's that?"

"That you would know how to make me happy. Probably very happy. But I'm sure you would know how to make most women happy, including Ms. Taylor."

"Hey, that's hitting below the belt—so to speak."

"I'm sorry. I think I'm just a little jealous."

"Would you care to explain that one?"

"Forget it!"

"No! What in God's name did you mean by that?"

"Girlish infatuation." She pulled away from him, feeling embarrassed.

"Come here!" Desaix pulled her back toward him.

"No! Leave things as they are."

"What the hell are you talking about?"

"Nothing!"

"Come on!"

"No, let me go!"

"Something is wrong." He followed her into the antiseptic white kitchen with all the modern conveniences, which one could see were rarely used.

"Do you want something to eat?" She opened the refrigerator, took out a can of beer, and tossed it to him.

"Thanks! But you can't buy me off that simply. Certainly not with one can of light beer."

"Well, what does it take? A full dark beer? Hard liquor?"

"What makes you think that I drink?"

"Guys like you always drink. Come on, who are you kidding?"

"Wait a minute! Are we talking about you? Or are we talking about me?"

"Does it really matter?" Suddenly, she felt as if she couldn't breathe.

Emotional claustrophobia. If she were smart, she would run out of her house as quickly as she could. But she was not too anxious to act smart. At least not yet.

"Listen, was I mistaken? Or did you not come on to me?"

"Truthfully?" she asked.

"Yes," he replied. Desaix let her go. He was becoming increasingly frustrated. Something was very wrong. And he was arrogant enough to presume that it had nothing to do with him.

"Of course," she said, "I find you extremely attractive. I'm sure that many women have already told you that."

"Let's put it this way, I'm not surprised. If that's what you mean."

"That's precisely what I mean." Opening a bottle of beer, she nervously guzzled it down.

"Then what's the problem?" He grabbed the bottle out of her hand.

"Hey, wait a minute, what the hell are you doing?" She tried to grab the bottle back.

"I'm kind of funny. If someone's talking to me, I expect them to talk to me. Otherwise, I get this uncomfortable feeling that I'm being ignored. And that's something I have a real problem with."

"Damnit, can't you understand it? You're the shrink. Can't you understand that I'm having a hard time dealing with you—for whatever reason."

"I don't understand. You come out of nowhere like Bat Woman. You save my life, you patch me up, then you tell me that you have a hard time relating to me. It doesn't compute."

"I want to work with you. You have some valuable information and insights that I can use."

"So you want my mind and not my body?"

"If that's the way you want to phrase it, then I'll accept it."

"Okay, I think I understand." Desaix laughed as he drank his beer, handing back hers. "Maybe you were right when you said that guys like me tend to drink. I think now you can understand why."

"I'm sorry." She wanted to caress him—to comfort him. She knew that she had just hurt him.

Desaix felt increasingly uncomfortable in her presence. It wasn't simply the issue of her physically rejecting him. This wasn't the first time it had happened. It certainly wouldn't be the last time. But he had finally met a woman who had the same determined, opportunistic streak that he possessed. And evaluating it from the opposite side, he found it to be both offensive and destructive.

"Are we still friends?" Mary extended her hand.

"Yeah, sure. Why not?"

"Now don't tell me that I'm going to work with a pouting, downtrodden, rejected, dejected Lothario? Can't we just be professional colleagues, simply trying to help each other out?"

"You mean like . . . friends?" Desaix smiled. She had a good sense of humor. He would enjoy playing with her without having to dominate her sexually. For him, it would be a new type of game. But more importantly, he would need her professional help. She had access to the White House and the National Security Council at a time when he was potentially persona non grata.

"Are you up for a trip to a mental institution?" She took her .38 Smith & Wesson and the wireless telephone she referred to as her electronic umbilical cord, and led Desaix down the two flights of stairs leading to her garage.

"So you think my problems are that serious?"

"Yeah! If we don't find out what is at the bottom of these killings and attempted killings, you and I may be in a deep mess."

Desaix followed Mary into her black Ford Torino, and they sped off in a southeasterly direction toward Saint Elizabeth Hospital.

"Remember that man who was killed in the hotel who carried ID as John Doe, that patient of Dr. Prince?" Desaix asked. He wondered whether he was in one endless cartoon, flipping between one improbable madcap adventure and another.

"The one who was supposedly born in Baltimore, Maryland?" Mary drove the car with the aplomb of a sports car driver who could bank the corners with the least amount of effort.

"How do you know?"

"I saw his medical records at Richardson Service, when the President visited. Mind you, the President, pressed as he was for time during a major international crisis, still had the time and desire to visit several recent psychiatric admissions to St. E's."

"Did he happen to know those patients?"

"I don't know, but he did seem extremely friendly."

"He's a friendly sort of guy, isn't he?"

"I'm beginning to think there is a hell of a lot going on behind the scenes where little guys and gals like myself are not allowed to play. I'm certain if he could have avoided it, the President would have preferred not to have taken me along, but that would have raised too many unanswerable questions for him and me." She hoped for some empathy from Desaix. "But what made the game even more interesting was the fact that a group of these recently arrived, obviously physically fit patients were all admitted under the protective custody of my Secret Service unit."

"What's so strange about that?"

"I didn't know anything about them."

"So?"

"A cockroach doesn't walk on the floor toward the President without my knowing about it. In this case, however, it turns out that they were all admitted by David Brooks, a hotshot special Secret Service agent assigned to the President Protective Detail—over my personal objections. Up until last week he had been an Army Ranger in the 2nd Battalion, 75th Infantry Regiment."

"And where, may I ask, was he last week?"

"Good question."

"Could it have been, by any chance, Japan?"

"Yes, as a matter of fact, it was."

"How are you so certain?"

"Being the suspicious daughter of suspicious Irish parents, I checked Immigration and Customs. They informed me that he had entered the U.S. with a Japanese multipurpose visa."

"Sneaky, aren't you?"

"I would prefer to call it aggressively suspicious." Mary drove through Anacostia and onto the hospital grounds.

As far as Desaix could see, the Anacostia area was still strewn with the rubble of self-hate: broken beer bottles, cannibalized automobiles, and twisted baby carriages.

It had been a long time since Desaix had visited St. E's. The hospital had always been an ignominious repository of the terminally insane; the ones for whom psychotropic drugs and psychotherapy had little, if no, relevance. It had been the way station for the criminally insane, the intractable catatonics, and a World War II traitor, the poet Ezra Pound.

Desaix had trained at an institution not too dissimilar from St. E's. At his venerable Massachusetts Mental Health Center, a Harvard Medical School affiliate, located in a similarly impoverished black ghetto in the South End of Boston, Desaix had learned that education in psychiatry consisted primarily of watching, listening, and living long enough to be able to refute everyone on the basis of the fact that you were older and knew better.

Saint Elizabeth Hospital, like most present-day psychiatric hospitals, was basically a money-losing proposition, where the homeless were parked for a few days until they determined that they were well enough to return to the streets. Interestingly enough, while they were in the hospital, they were officially diagnosed as schizophrenic. But as soon as they returned to the street, they were immediately classified, for administrative purposes, as homeless.

As Mary and Desaix walked through the dingy yellow corridors of Richardson Service, Desaix recognized that characteristic odor, the "back ward smell," the one that made him gag. It was, as best as he could determine, a mixture of urine, dried vomit, and incredibly pungent cleaning fluid, carbolic acid.

"Something wrong?" Mary asked. She had resumed her no-nonsense role and was intent on seeing all the John Does, those who were listed as being born in Baltimore.

For Desaix, Richardson Service probably held the secret of the recent killings, and possibly the presidential coup.

"May I help you?" The heavyset black head nurse radiated a clearly defiant attitude. Her manner informed Mary and Desaix that she was not only the protector of her patients, but she was literally keeper of the ward. No one entered without her personal permission. Desaix knew the type well. Every psychiatric ward had a head nurse just like her.

"Yes, we'd like to see Dr. Prince," Mary replied.

"May I ask what this is in reference to?" The nurse stood fast in front of them, blocking any movement forward.

Desaix could see down the corridor into the main rec room, where most patients would normally spend their day in some form of catatonic stupor.

"I'm Mary Dougherty, Chief of the President's Protective Detail. I want to see several of your patients. I understand that a few have been admitted to this ward under the name John Doe." She pulled out her ID and showed it to the nurse, who appeared unimpressed.

"I'm afraid that I am not allowed to comment on the status of any patient without Dr. Prince's authorization."

"We know that, that's why we're here to—"

"I'm sorry, it's a little unusual for you to be seeing the doctor and patients at such a late hour. Why don't you come back—"

"It may be unusual, but I do have the legal right to examine any medical chart if I deem that the individual may be a potential threat to the safety of the President of the United States." Mary put away her ID. She was, however, ready to pull out her .38 Smith & Wesson to circumvent this bureaucratic problem.

"Ms. Dougherty, I don't dispute your legal right to enter this ward. But I can insist that you come at a time that is convenient for both the patients and the doctor."

"Not to speak of your own convenience, of course," Desaix interjected.

The nurse gave Desaix a dirty look, but refused to respond to his snide comment. She turned back to Mary.

"I'm afraid the answer is still no, Ms. Dougherty."

Desaix realized he and Mary would have to find another way to get the information they needed. They were definitely going nowhere by being polite. "Come on, let's go" Desaix said and turned around.

Quizzically, Mary followed him down the unguarded darkened hall to their left. Just as they turned the corner, a lone figure jumped out in front of them from one of the dormitory rooms. Both Mary and Desaix froze in their steps.

"Afraid, Miz Mary? Hey?" As the figure approached them, Mary started to reach for her gun.

"A gun isn't going to do you much good, at least not in this place. It's against the law to carry a gun on a ward. Of course, it's against the law to kill a patient. Or anyone, for that matter."

"Amos, is that you?" Mary asked.

"Yes, but how did you know?" Amos sounded disappointed.

Mary relaxed and said, "Don't worry. I won't tell anyone that I guessed your identity." She knew the game.

"Please don't tell them! These are mean folks around here."

"What do you mean?" Desaix asked.

"Who's that man next to you, Miz Mary? Is he one of those Secret Service types? Or is he one of those military types?"

"Military types? What do you mean?" Desaix asked, trying to sound concerned and caring.

"Who is he, Miz Mary?" Amos took a step backward.

"He's a doctor who is working with me."

"As a matter of fact, Amos, I'm a psychiatrist," Desaix said.

"Are you here to punish me for what I said about those soldiers?"

"What soldiers, Amos?" Desaix asked, gently taking him aside into an empty room, away from the main corridor.

"Those soldiers that Dr. Prince said didn't exist. I saw them loading up there onto that big white truck. If Dr. Prince wasn't there to save my life, that ugly man with the big gun would have killed me. You know Miz Mary, it's a hell of a lot more dangerous in here than on the streets. You should never have brought me here. It wasn't fair. You know that, Miz Mary."

"Tell me about that man who was ready to kill you with the big gun."

"He was just a big white man with an accent."

"Where did he go?"

"He went with all the other soldiers into that white truck."

"Amos, can you remember if there was anything in that truck besides a lot of soldiers?"

Amos started to laugh. He laughed even harder at Desaix's expression of disbelief. "Don't worry, doc, I ain't crazy. At least, not the way you think."

"I'm sure you're not. As a matter of fact, you are the most sane guy I've heard all day long."

"Do you really mean that?" Amos was beaming with pride.

"You can trust him, Amos. He doesn't bullshit. Believe me." Mary's comforting smiles belied her concern that Amos would be in very serious trouble if they didn't get him away from here. He simply knew too much. So far nothing happened to him because he was a patient who had been brought in by the Secret Service. And if anything strange had happened to Amos, Prince would have to answer too many embarrassing questions. But time was running out.

"I believe you, Miz Mary. Except as I've said before, you did make a mistake."

"Amos, let's get back to the truck. What was in that truck?" Desaix was growing impatient.

"Well, it was funny. They had all these cans of something or other. Something that could kill roaches and rats."

"How do you know that, Amos?" Desaix was impressed by Amos's acuity of observation. He was also beginning to wonder about the reason for Amos being committed to St. E's.

"That what was funny. They were carrying cans of bug stuff. I'm not crazy! I saw it written on the side of the van—fumigators."

"Probably hydrogen fluoride," Desaix whispered as he heard the sound of footsteps in the corridor. "Quick, let's get out of here!"

"Follow me," Amos said, leading them down a dark corridor toward the staircase.

"Stop! The three of you!" the nurse shouted, accompanied by three armed guards.

They ran down the staircase toward the basement of the building, through a maze of old lead pipes and frayed electrical wires. Desaix was amazed how much debris had accumulated over the past century and a half. There were old broken baby prams, hand-cranked washing machines, even a turn-of-the-century black buggy.

Suddenly Amos collapsed.

"Are you all right?" Desaix asked. Other than the fact that he was out of breath, there did not seem to be anything very much wrong with him.

"I'm okay, doc. I'm not in bad shape for a man who has spent most of his life on park benches and beneath bridges."

"You're doing fine, Amos. None of us can do any better." Desaix was concerned about the sound of guards coming closer.

"Can you continue?" Mary asked, helping Amos to his feet. "Which way?"

Amos pointed down the long hallway. "Follow me."

Suddenly Desaix realized the full absurdity of the situation. Two professionals, whose lives were being threatened by killers, had placed themselves at the mercy of a person society had labeled totally incompetent of taking care of himself, let alone two other people. The gods have a sense of humor, he thought.

"This way!" Amos said, leading them through an even darker tunnel, no bigger than the width of a human body.

Desaix wondered whether Amos had made a serious mistake. "Where are we, Amos?"

"Don't worry. A few more feet and we'll be there."

"Where's there?" Desaix asked, incredulous that he had allowed a psychiatric patient the opportunity to determine his fate.

"Doc, have some confidence in me. Isn't that what you guys tell us?"

Mary and Desaix laughed silently.

"It's over there. But be very quiet and very careful. You'll see why."

In the distance, the narrow tunnel merged into a large, well-lit cemented area that looked like any major river tunnel.

Desaix proceeded cautiously. He saw sophisticated air vents, emergency halothane fire extinguishers, and metal doors leading into other tunnels.

"This is where they came from."

"Who?"

"The soldiers I saw tonight. They came from here. But they left from the hospital."

"How do you know, Amos?" Mary asked. The tunnel had broadened so that it was now large enough for cars—or trucks.

"Once when I was walking around St. E's, I discovered this here tunnel."

"We were told by DOD of a labyrinth of tunnels beneath the city," Mary said. "But no one I knew ever saw them or took them seriously. The tunnels were supposed to be used as civilian shelters during a nuclear attack." Even as Mary spoke, she was now convinced that these tunnels had been dug by DOD for reasons other than the ones she had heard. She realized that if the city were to erupt into a state of civil disorder and the streets were blocked, military troops could move through these tunnels and around the city completely unhampered.

Mary, Desaix, and Amos walked cautiously along a metal catwalk.

"These are canisters of hydrogen fluoride," Desaix said, realizing he had uncovered something truly dangerous.

"Let's get out of here," Amos said, "before it's too late. I don't feel right not seeing anyone here." Amos started to open the metal side door.

"Too late, Amos! It's a pity no one listens to people like you." A familiar voice from the shadows reverberated throughout the tunnel.

"What in God's name are you doing here?" Mary asked.

The last memory she had before she fell to the ground was of the blazing barrel of an Uzi submachine gun.

# CHAPTER
## 22

**M**ilitary firing squads the world over differ only in their intended victims and the number of bullets it would take to kill them. But their raison d'être is always the same—expeditious execution. Pushkin had learned this lesson early in his professional career. But in a moment's hesitancy, the winning edge of decisiveness could vaporize.

"Three . . . two . . ." Yershov sounded smug as he started the countdown. Finally, Yershov thought, this Spetsnaz upstart and his mistress would pay for their indiscretions. What insolence, he thought, that Pushkin could seriously consider holding him and his colleagues prisoner in some dilapidated closet in the Kremlin from which they had easily escaped.

"Wait!" Pushkin interrupted. "Do you mind, General Yershov, if I lay President Zotov down on the ground. He is becoming increasingly heavy, and you may accidentally shoot him while trying to shoot us. Now you wouldn't want that, would you?"

"No, you're right, Colonel Pushkin. We wouldn't want to accidentally kill the very reason you and I are battling each other. Would we?" General Yershov motioned to his men to relax their grip on their weapons.

Pushkin lay President Zotov carefully on the ground and listened to his chest to make certain he was still conscious. He glanced at Misha and Vartanian, who had laid down their weapons. They were outnumbered five to one—a compelling reality.

"Now that all the proper civilities have been observed, may we proceed with our execution. We still have some other loose matters to tidy up. Unfortunately, your remaining troops have overwhelmed the Spassky Guards. So the longer we procrastinate, the more difficult my job becomes."

"Why hurry, General? The advantage is completely on your side. I'm certain there are things you would like to know, and I may be able to provide."

Yershov was confused. Too much was going on at one time. The imperatives of an immediate execution were clear, but the need for clarity of the entire situation might be more important.

"Please, General Yershov, my name is Major Tamara Popov, I am with GRU, military intelligence. I was sent to report on the activities of Colonel Pushkin. I think it is very important that you let me tell you in private what it is that I have uncovered." She walked toward Yershov, imploring him with her plaintive, seductive eyes.

"I am aware of your mission, Major Popov, but I am afraid that you have compromised yourself as well as the military in your collusion with Pushkin." Yershov nodded to his men, indicating that they should raise their weapons once again.

"But please, Major, are you going to tell us all what it is that you have uncovered about your lover?" Yershov was clearly sarcastic. "Are you going to tell us how good he is?" The soldiers started to laugh.

"What I was going to say is that he is a hero. A genuine hero, who is involved with a group that is dedicated to preventing Mother Russia from becoming totally destroyed by our present government. He is not acting alone—"

"Enough! Don't say anymore!" Pushkin grabbed her arm and pulled her back toward him. If he had had a pistol at that very moment, he would have shot her.

"Don't pull my arm!" she shouted. Pulling away from Pushkin, she shoved him against Misha, who, in turn, grabbed Yershov by his collar while Pushkin grabbed the general's gun and opened fire. In the confusion, Tamara picked up Misha's Sagger antitank gun and pulled the trigger, barely missing Pushkin and Yershov.

Ten Spassky Guards fell to the ground.

Vartanian picked up his 7.62 millimeter RPK machine gun and opened fire. Four more Spassky soldiers toppled over.

The remaining Spassky Guards opened fire with their weapons.

Black smoke and the smell of gunpowder permeated the blood-stained walls of the darkened tunnel.

"Come on! Let's get out of here!" Pushkin shoved Yershov forward. "Vartanian, take Zotov! Let's keep moving toward Khodinka!"

"You're making a big mistake! My men are everywhere, including the Central Airfield."

Pushkin picked up an AK-47 and pointed it at Yershov's head.

"Your men may be waiting for us, but you won't be there to greet them unless you help us. And I won't provide you with any fancy countdowns." Pushkin dragged him along the blood-soaked cobblestoned floor.

Vartanian flung Zotov over his shoulder. How was it, he wondered, that as a wounded man loses blood, he becomes increasingly more heavy. It was a strange law of biophysics. Wounded bodies make dead weights.

Tamara covered Pushkin's rear as the small group advanced slowly through the pitch dark tunnel.

If Pushkin's memory was correct, there were a number of paths. None of them could be anticipated in the dark. And now it was almost impossible to see anything other than the immediate three feet ahead. Only iridescent tracers from the guard's semiautomatic bullets provided the necessary light for their advance. If a time-lapse photograph could have been taken of the bullets streaking through the air, it would have looked like the tail of a bright fragmented comet, streaking against the black sky.

"Damnit!" Pushkin yelled as a bullet grazed his forehead.

"Ah, the gods are paying you back for this nefarious deed of yours." Yershov laughed.

Pushkin responded by whacking Yershov in the back with the butt of his AK-47.

"General, just keep moving! And keep your mouth shut!"

"That's fine, Colonel. But which of the tunnels do you suggest we take right now? There is, if you look ahead, a fork in the road. One road goes to the right—to the sewerage. You can smell it, can't you? To the left, the road seems to go on endlessly. Which way do we go, my commander?"

"Let's take the one that seems to go nowhere. Because, if nothing else, it smells better." Pushkin turned around to his group. "How are we doing?"

"Colonel, we have to get out of here fast! They're only a hundred feet behind us!" Vartanian was clearly carrying the brunt of the advance. Zotov lay slung over his right shoulder as lifeless as an old Persian rug.

We must get him some help, thought Pushkin. The coup will succeed only if Zotov remains alive.

Tamara was completely preoccupied covering their rear flank. As the flashes of gunfire illuminated her intense face, she looked like the classic image of a World War II partisan fighting the Nazis—beautiful, committed, and very Slavic.

Pushkin would have liked to make love with her at this very moment.

She turned around and nodded her head to him, as if she could read his thoughts. He smiled. She had an uncanny intuition that resonated with his feelings. Just a while ago, she had created a commotion to divert the attention away from him and what he was about to do. Without any signals from him, she simply knew that the time was opportune. He liked the fact that, like all true lovers who have penetrated each other's souls, they worked extremely well together.

"Daydreaming, Mr. Poet?" Yershov laughed. "Love and war are not very compatible. You can only do one at a time. However, from what I have heard of your escapades, it seems as if you are quite a talented individual."

"Keep moving!" Pushkin shouted, neither amused nor flattered. If the general didn't watch himself, he would not survive the day. Pushkin had not expected or needed to capture the general. It was fortuitous. Perhaps, Pushkin thought, he might serve as an insurance policy when the time was right.

Suddenly, Pushkin decided to change his plan. He pushed Yershov in the opposite direction, down the foul-smelling path. As he took a few steps, he felt the cold water swirl up to his knees. It smelled like a combination of a sewage plant and a crematorium of decaying bodies.

"What are you doing? I thought we were heading in the other direction?" Yershov refused to move.

"Move on, General! Otherwise, you will spend your last breath in this stinking hellhole."

Yershov breathed heavily. He was not looking forward to wading through all the sludge, a combination of human excrement, sewage, and oil spills.

The sound of gunfire subsided.

"Do you hear that?" Pushkin pushed the general forward.

"What the hell are you talking about?"

"No more gunfire. Interesting isn't it?"

"I don't know what you're talking about."

"You don't?" Pushkin grabbed Yershov by the neck and shoved the general's face into the stinking liquid.

"What are you doing to the old man?" screamed Tamara.

Lifting Yershov's head from the sewerage, Pushkin yelled at him, "Tell them, old man, why I am about to drown you."

"I don't know what you're talking about." Yershov could barely speak. He gasped for air while he tried to prevent himself from vomiting.

"You don't, huh? We'll see!" Pushkin pushed his head once more into the dark, cold sewerage. Bubbles of air floated to the top. Yershov struggled to get his head above water.

"Pushkin, let him live!" Tamara ran toward him, and grabbed Yershov.

"General, are you going to tell your GRU agent why I am about to kill you?" Pushkin looked angrily at Tamara.

"What are you talking about, Pushkin?" Tamara said, leaning against both Misha and Vartanian for support. She felt faint.

"Speak, old man! Otherwise, this will be your last breath of putrid air." Pushkin grabbed Yershov's flaxen white hair and yanked back his head. It reminded him of a scene from Titian's famous The Head of St. John the Baptist, where a decapitated head is being delivered on a silver tray.

"You never had a chance. You were set up," Yershov started to sputter. "I can't . . . I can't . . ."

"Who set us up?" Pushkin started to submerge Yershov's head into the effluent once again. "Who set us up?" Pushkin yelled.

General Yershin stuck his tongue out. And in the tradition of World War II partisans who refused to divulge any secrets during their interrogation by the enemy, he bit down hard and quickly. He fell into a pool of bright red blood, as he hemorrhaged from his mouth.

His tongue wiggled around the sewage, like an overgrown tadpole.

# CHAPTER
## 23

Confronting death, either willfully or unwillingly, acts as both an antidote to life's more boring moments, and a nanosecond of realization that one's life may not, in fact, be worth saving.

At times, Desaix courted the vagaries of death in the same courtesan manner that the mulatto *poule de luxe* on Bourbon Street invited that ominous well-dressed stranger into her boudoir. Eager to serve, she was at the same time frightened of the consequences of the pleasure that she might give him. Would he pay her? Or beat her?

As one might expect, Desaix invited the confrontation with death as a challenge to his sense of inviolability. But even for Desaix the situation was close to intolerable. Waves of anxiety and nausea overcame him. He watched helplessly as Mary lay on the ground, writhing in pain, bleeding from her right leg.

Amos lay face down in a pool of highly Thorazined blood. As best as Desaix could make out, this disheveled man who had warned of life's dangers had paid the usurious price of being frighteningly sane in an insane world.

"Well, Dr. Clark, we meet again!" David Brooks stood defiantly in front of him, cradling his Uzi.

"By now I should at least know you by name. We always seem to meet in strange places." Desaix recognized Brooks's voice from their first encounter in the attic above the room in which Fitzpatrick died. "So this is where you stored the hydrogen fluoride?"

"It's as safe a depot as any!" Brooks chortled.

"Has the U.S. government gone into the pest-control business?" Desaix wondered whether President Westview knew what one of his trusted men was doing.

"You could say that." Brooks felt extremely cocky.

"Whom would you say are the pests you are empowered to eradicate?"

"Oh, come on, doc! You must be kidding!" Brooks was becoming impatient—with himself. What was he waiting for? Why didn't he just pull the trigger and get the whole thing over with? Was it his fascination with Desaix and his legend as a famous international crisis manager and infamous womanizer? There were a lot of questions he would like to ask Desaix.

Desaix looked around the vast loading area of the tunnel as Brooks hesitated.

About twenty feet away were seven steel canisters marked FLAMMABLE. Two hundred feet to his left, a group of soldiers dressed in camouflage and wearing red berets were loading canisters of hydrogen fluoride onto trucks marked PROPERTY OF U.S. MILITARY.

Desaix wondered who the hell was behind this whole enterprise? Mapplethorpe? Was this part of the conspiracy about which President Westview spoke? What did they intend to do with all that hydrogen fluoride? Or was this what Manning had warned him about?

"Before you pull that trigger, could you tell me why?"

"You mean could we play twenty questions?"

"Hey, Brooks! The general is on the phone." A lieutenant standing next to the trucks held up a telephone receiver. "He wants to talk to you!"

"Tell him I have important business to finish here."

"Which General? Mapplethorpe? Is he behind this?"

Brooks didn't answer, then said, "I bet you really want to play now, huh? It's getting more interesting, isn't it?"

"David, do you realize what you are doing?" Mary painfully reached out toward Desaix. "It's not going to be too long before the President figures out that you and Mapplethorpe are behind this coup. It's crazy! Call it off!"

"We have to get her to a hospital," Desaix said, as he gently lifted up her skirt to examine the wound on her right thigh. He tore a piece of cloth from the bottom of the skirt and wrapped it around her thigh to stop the bleeding.

"Finish up your physician act," Brooks said, "but don't think you'll get third-party insurance reimbursement for it."

"Try to move your foot," Desaix told Mary, ignoring Brooks as he ran his hands down her right leg trying to determine if anything else had been injured.

"Oh, it hurts!" Mary screamed, pushing his hand away. "It's killing me, up here, around my thigh! Not down there!"

"Okay, kids. Time is up! No more fun," Brooks said, pointing the Uzi at them.

Mary pushed Desaix's hand up around her thigh over her silk panties and manuevered it up to the hollow of her back. She pressed it close against her.

Desaix felt what appeared to be the outline of a leather holster. Now he understood what she wanted him to do.

"Stand up, Desaix. I want the privilege of killing you face-forward. I too have some professional pride. I've never yet shot a man in the back."

"Is that what they taught you in the Special Forces?" Mary asked, shifting her position so that Desaix could unfasten the holster.

Before Brooks realized what was happening, Desaix rolled away from Mary and opened fire with her "drop gun," a "Saturday Night Special." Thank God, thought Desaix. Like most law enforcement officials the world over, Mary carried an illegal pistol hidden on her body.

Brooks dropped to the ground, his Uzi firing haphazardly.

Desaix dragged Mary behind an embankment of rubber tires to survey their situation. He concluded that there was very little chance of their leaving the tunnel alive unless he could create a diversionary tactic.

The tunnel had exploded with the sound of the Uzi's ricocheting bullets. It sounded as if a microphone were attached to the barrel of a cannon. Desaix shot at the handful of Special Forces soldiers rushing forward to help the dying Brooks. They fired back with semiautomatic weapons. Desaix could barely hear Mary talking to him. It was as if it were a conversation between the deaf and the mute.

"Leave me here!" Mary said. "It's the only way you're going to get out alive. You've got to tell the President what is happening. You've got to warn him that Mapplethorpe and Brooks are behind a coup against him."

"Forget it. I can't leave you here. Somebody's got to take care of you."

"Give me my gun." Mary tried to sit herself upright.

"Boy, would I love to give you a gun. But there's one problem. We only have one. The only way we can get out of this place is to create a distraction so we can get to those trucks at the loading zone."

"Please, just leave me here! You have a better chance of getting out yourself. Even if these guys capture me, they won't do anything more than put me through the psychological hoops." Mary grimaced with pain, not believing a word she was saying, but hoping that Desaix did.

The tunnel had become an inferno of black choking smoke and semiautomatic fire. Desaix tore more strips of cloth from her skirt and stuffed them in the inner tubes of three of the tires that were shielding them. Then he took a matchbook from his pocket and spread the matches out in an orderly pattern inside each of the three tires. He had created a makeshift detonator.

"What are you doing?" Wracked with pain, Mary grabbed the tires and yanked herself toward him.

"Goddamn, it! Get your precious ass down!" Desaix said, pulling her down, embarrassed that his sexual reference might make her feel uncomfortable. Although she appeared tough, there was a sensual vulnerability about her. The swept-back pageboy haircut, the taut body with its boyish proportions, the sure-footed stride with its athletic bounce. He nonetheless found all of this extremely attractive, even inviting. Was it any accident, he· thought, as he watched soldiers running around the truck loading zone, prepositioning themselves for an assault on them, that he was wondering about Mary's sexuality.

Maybe she was bisexual? That notion excited him. In the same way he was addicted to both physical and mental danger, he was also addicted to sexual excitement, sometimes without discretion. When he was feeling generous with himself, he described his condition as a genetic or familial abnormality. When he was feeling less charitable, he knew that it was part of his dark Huguenot side. In either case, there was a definite sense of inevitability about his sexual curiosity that he had learned to accept.

Suddenly, the firepower coming at them increased. The tunnel sounded as if the bowels of hell were about to rip apart.

"Hurry up, Desaix! We don't have much time!" Mary crouched alongside him as he prepared to ignite the tires.

Drawing Mary toward him, he felt her body tense up, and then relax. Well, thought Desaix, maybe there is some hope here.

"What the hell are you grinning about?" Mary pressed herself against him, reassured by his presence.

"Just some private thoughts, nothing more."

Letting her go for a moment, Desaix struck a match and watched the inner rim of the tire burst into flame. But it was too weak to ignite the rest of the cloth.

"Quick, give me the gun!" Mary said, then took several bullets out of the chamber and banged the tips with the gun handle until they broke apart.

"If you don't mind my reminding you," Desaix said, "the goal of this exercise is to kill those guys down there before they kill us."

"Here!" She handed him a palm filled with gunpowder. "Pour it over that little streak of light that you call a fire. And juice it up."

"And why do I get the honor of possibly blowing off my hand?"

"Don't you remember your manners, Dr. Clark? A Southern gentleman always volunteers his own life before risking the lives of women and children. Don't tell me that chivalry is dead."

He poured the gunpowder into the tire and watched as the simmering fire burst impressively into flames, increasing the swirl of suffocating black smoke already in the tunnel.

"Are you ready?" Both of them rolled the burning tire fireball into the group of soldiers. Covering their mouths with their clothing, Desaix and Mary pressed tightly against the wall of the tunnel, holding each other as they rushed past the now screaming soldiers toward the loading ramps, where two unarmed soldiers were still loading canisters onto the idling truck.

He pushed Mary into the cab and jumped behind the steering wheel, slamming the truck into gear while pressing his foot all the way down on the accelerator.

Trailed by a hail of bullets, the truck sped away from the tunnel.

"Not bad for two cripples," Mary said. Her face tightened as she squeezed her right thigh with both hands, trying to stop the bleeding.

"Don't look now, but we have some company behind us." He placed his hand on top of hers and was delighted to discover that she didn't pull it away.

As the truck emerged from the smoke-filled tunnel, Desaix could see one military jeep filled with four Special Forces soldiers on his tail. He raced through the stop signs, almost hitting several patients absent-mindedly crossing the street.

"Look at this!" Mary found a piece of paper on the front seat. She read out loud, "PROJECT BALTIMORE. *Fourteenth and U Street*: Fumigate Todman Projects. Two hundred twenty units. One thousand two hundred tenants. *Thirteenth and T Street*: Fumigate Shaw Smith Projects. Five hundred units. Two thousand five hundred tenants." She looked up at Desaix, uncertain of its meaning.

But Desaix's attention was riveted on two problems. How was he going to get rid of the military jeep quickly closing in behind him? And how the hell was he going to get through those closed steel gates of the hospital without killing themselves or some patients?

The eight-foot red-stone wall that surrounded Saint Elizabeth Hospital had been constructed on the paradoxical premise that the public had to be kept at a safe distance in order to protect the patients from harm. At that time, it was a very progressive approach to mental illness. The real danger lay not with the patients, but with the public.

Desaix glanced at the side-view mirror, and saw that the jeep was gaining quickly. Any second, they would be the perfect target. One blast from the machine gun mounted on the front of the jeep and there would be little, if anything, left of them. What an insane world, he thought. Here he was, racing around a mental institution in a stolen U.S. military truck, threatened by U.S. Special Forces, because he was trying to prevent a coup against the President of the United States. No one in his right mind would believe this scenario. Not even if it was contrived by some perverted novelist who had been nurtured on the tortured writings of the British spymasters, splashed with a dash of that daffy English children's classic *The Wind in the Willows*.

"Desaix, be careful!" Mary screamed as the truck careened against the stone wall, shooting sparks of fire and smoke into the air while emitting a horrendous shriek of metal crunching under the sheer weight of immutable stone. Wiping away the broken glass splattered across his face, Desaix hugged the stone wall, driving it like a sound and light festival on the Fourth of July.

Mary ducked low in the cab, and grabbed Desaix tightly around his waist. This was the first time since childhood she felt totally vulnerable, abandoned, and afraid. Or that she let it be apparent to anyone other than her mother.

Unable to turn the wheel fast enough, the driver of the jeep smashed right into the gate and exploded in a billow of mounting yellow flames.

A group of mental patients congregated around the burning Jeep that had been left behind, helpless to do anything but wonder if Hollywood had not finally intruded into their daily lives.

"Where are we going?" Mary sat up quickly and brushed off glass and debris. In ten years of Secret Service work, she had never come so close to death. For her, whatever constituted unnecessary risk was, by its very nature, inappropriate, gratuitous, and, quite frankly, foolish. And it was her job to make certain that the inherent danger of any situation was never actually realized. Even the appearance of danger was an admission of failure. Both personal and professional. But this time it seemed different.

"What is the name of the superintendent of this hospital? The guy that Amos claimed was behind this army plot?" Desaix asked, as he steered back toward the hospital grounds, through an underpass beneath Martin Luther King Avenue. He followed faded signs that led to the main administration building.

"Dr. Prince." Mary waved the piece of paper she had been reading, surprised that they were still alive. "What about this list of addresses? I think tracking them down would tell us a lot about what's going on. These must be the places where Brooks and his boys were going to deliver their canisters of hydrogen fluoride. And look what it's called—Project Baltimore. Sound familiar?"

"That's precisely why I want to pay a visit to Dr. Prince. I think he's knee-deep into this. I'd be willing to bet he knows who's in charge, who else besides Mapplethorpe and Brooks is involved, and what the objective is. And, most importantly, how much time we have left . . . if any." Desaix stopped the truck in front of a large white building.

"Do you think this is a smart idea?"

"Listen, why don't you stay in the truck, and wait until I come back. It will only take a few minutes." Desaix scanned the campus for evidence of more troops. For the moment, it looked safe. It seemed as if everyone on the hospital grounds was watching the burning jeep.

"Hey, remember, I'm part of this duo," Mary said, getting out of the truck and defiantly hobbling up the stairs.

"You're right. I know it seems crazy to stop here at this moment, but there's too much left to find out. Are you okay?"

"I've felt better, but I'll make it." Desaix held the glass door to the building open for her. As he expected, this late the building was empty. Only an ancient janitor lay asleep in a corner of the hallway.

"I think Dr. Prince's office is down here somewhere," Desaix said, taking Mary's arm to steady her. "What I don't understand is why St. E's should be the center of all this military activity. And why an elite unit of Special Forces should be garrisoned in this hospital, of all places. It doesn't make sense unless . . ." Desaix paused as he struggled to open Prince's locked office door.

"Unless Prince is very much involved in this coup. But how could he amass so much power? And why would he plan a coup against his friend?"

Mary couldn't forget how deferentially the President had treated Prince.

"Mary, I need your shoe for a moment."

"What?"

"Your shoe. I need your shoe." Desaix ran his hand over her curvaceous ankle before he took the low-heeled shoe from her right foot. He was surprised to see how small and dainty her foot was. There was something extremely delicate about this woman who looked and acted so tough.

He slammed her shoe against the glass door and reached through the broken pane to turn the doorknob.

The first thing he noticed as he entered was that the usual smell of cleaning fluid, so characteristic of hospitals, had been replaced by the aroma of a very expensive men's cologne. Aramis or Polo.

He looked around the darkened room. It was befitting for the superintendent of a four-thousand-bed hospital. At one end of the room was a large mahogany table bracketed by two unfurled full-sized flags—a frayed United States flag with fifty stars and a crisp, new Public Health Service flag with the distinct emblem of two intertwining anchors. At the other end of the room was a group of padlocked metal file cabinets standing beneath a row of autographed photographs.

One of the pictures showed President Westview warmly embracing Dr. Prince. Desaix was intrigued by the barely legible inscription: "To my dear friend and savior, Dr. P. Affectionately, Wes."

"What are we going to do now?" Mary was no longer aware of the throbbing pain in her leg. She was overcome by a combination of fatigue and incredulity.

"How the hell am I going to get this cabinet open?" Desaix tugged on the padlocks. The cabinet drawers were alphabetized, presumably containing files of Dr. Prince's patients. With so little time left, Desaix was betting that whatever he was looking for was in one of those cabinets.

"Unfortunately, I don't have any more of those magic bullets," Mary said, her nerves jangling. "Try this." She pulled a bobby pin out of her hair and handed it to Desaix.

"You're a walking arsenal. What the hell am I supposed to do with a pin?"

"Here, let me try!" Mary bent the bobby pin, slid it into the lock, and jiggled it around.

"Is this what they teach you in the Secret Service?"

"If you can't think like a criminal, how are you supposed to apprehend one?" Mary worked the pin along the grooves of the cylinder. When she heard the expected click, she looked up at Desaix and smiled. With one dramatic pull downward, she removed the padlock.

"Excellent work, Agent Dougherty. Now help me look for a file marked confidential, or anything that might be related to Westview." He handed Mary a stack of files.

They both riffled through the files. Nothing unusual appeared.

"It's got to be here!" Desaix said, frustrated, as he slammed the cabinet shut.

"What is it exactly that you're looking for? I don't think we have much time. I can guarantee you that this place will be swarming with our friends from the Special Forces."

"My instincts tell me that this Dr. Prince must have a file of some sort on President Westview."

"Why?"

"Because there is something going on between this shrink and the prez. Something that goes beyond friendship. Something that might entail a therapeutic relationship. Why does a President of the United States leave his Situation Room in the middle of a world crisis to visit a psychiatrist? Believe me, no politician wants to be seen anywhere near a psychiatrist during normal times, let alone during a crisis. And how do you explain the fact that Special Forces units dedicated to the President's overthrow are being warehoused in the very hospital his close friend Dr. Prince runs?"

"What about Special Agent David Brooks? Where do you place him in this conspiracy?"

"He's only a henchman." Desaix flipped through folders, discarding the worthless files on the floor. "For Mapplethorpe and . . ."

"And . . . ?"

"That's exactly what's not clear to me. Somehow, Prince is involved. Otherwise, none of this could have taken place here. But it's Westview's presence here yesterday and his unusually strong relationship with Prince that bothers me."

"Are you saying that Westview knows about this coup?" Mary asked, distraught at her own conclusion. Why would her boss be interested in overthrowing himself? Vice President Allison Bonner would be next in line of succession, although everyone in government agreed it was best to keep the Vice President on overseas trips as often as possible—far from Washington. "It just doesn't make sense."

"Maybe . . . All we know right now is that President Westview warned me of an impending coup against him. All evidence points to Mapplethorpe, Brooks, Prince, and elite units of the Special Forces. For the moment, that's all I know. For all I know, you may be part of this conspiracy."

"Right!" Mary pointed to her injured right leg. "And I just love the sight of blood, especially my own." She paused, indignant at his accusation. "Well, as a matter of fact, you might be part of this conspiracy for all I know."

"That's the beauty of trying to solve a political crisis—anything and everything is possible. You can't rule anything in, and you can't rule anything out."

"Just like love—a floating crap game. Trust becomes an expendable commodity," Mary said.

"I'd say that's a bit harsh," Desaix replied, "but I like the analogy. Just like the most impassioned lovers, who will say almost anything, including boldfaced lies, in order to sustain the passion of the relationship, politicians and crisis players will do it all the time—say and do anything to achieve their goals."

"And what might they be?" Mary asked. She had given up going through the files, and now through the window she could see the movement of soldiers rushing around the grounds.

"Lovers and crisis players like to play the game—to feel the rush."

"Then there is no hope for any goodness or genuine concern in this world?" As Mary spoke, the soldiers in the corridor became audible.

"On the contrary, I still strongly believe that only through a weird combination of self-deception, faith, and hope can one get through this entire mess called life, or as I like to identify it, this continuous state of crisis management."

"Desaix, we'd better get out of here, now!"

"Wait a minute! I think I have something here. Look!" Desaix waved a copy of a file marked "Z."

"Z? That's not a name."

Absorbed by what he was reading in the chart, Desaix ignored her.

Mary scanned Prince's office. From her previous visits to the hospital as part of the White House advance team, she knew that many of the offices and buildings had more than their obvious exit or entrance. Built during the Civil War, Saint Elizabeth Hospital had countless numbers of hidden passages, secret stairways, and tunnels that were all used to run an effective underground slave railroad.

She was hoping that Prince's office had just such an egress.

"Listen to this! Patient Z is a tall, thin man in his early fifties with specific characteristic features: Extremities are long and thin. His arm span is greater than his height (ninety-five inches versus sixty-five). The lower segment measurement (pubis to sole—forty inches) is in excess of the upper segment (pubis to vertex—twenty-five inches). The patient has the characteristic arachnodactyly, pectus excavatum or pigeon breast, dolichocephaly, a long, narrow face and high-arched palate. His weakness and reduplication of ligaments and joint capsules lead to double-jointedness in his hands and knees, and with recurrent dislocation of the hips, patella, and other joints." Desaix thought about Westview's unusually pliable handshake, and broke into a broad smile. "Christ, it's him, all right!"

"Let's get out of here! Take the damn file!" Under the faded blue and red Bokhara rug in the middle of the floor, Mary discovered a trap door with a rickety wooden ladder.

"Listen! The patient's vision has become progressively poor because of his ectopia lentis. There are increasing signs of cognitive deficiency as a result of his incipient organic brain syndrome, secondary to cardiac insufficiency due to a deteriorating ascending and abdominal aorta. The patient complains of severe abdominal and chest pain, particularly after sexual intercourse."

"Z stands for Zorro, the Secret Service code word for President Westview!" Mary whispered as she pushed him down the ladder in front of her.

"Dr. Prince has been treating President Westview for what amounts to a lethal illness characterized by a deteriorating mental condition."

"What's he got?" Mary slammed shut the door above her and locked it.

"Marfan's syndrome," Desaix shouted to her, as they raced through the moist, dark dirt tunnels beneath Saint Elizabeth Hospital. "The same disease that Lincoln had . . . before he was assassinated."

# CHAPTER
## 24

History is like a restless mistress who refuses to involve herself with the daily concerns of her paramour. She is more intent on experiencing the grand sweep of the moment by enhancing whatever passions may be available to her—be it jealousy, envy, or resentment. And so, love eventually becomes equated with struggle. And rebellion evolves into the panacea for the forlorn and injured. Everything else is of secondary importance. Only rage and revolution become the natural, if not perverted, expression of that original pristine love.

And the mistress must either become legitimate or irrelevant.

So too, history must become a force either to contend with or ignore. Like that very same restless mistress, events in Russia could no longer await the safe arrival of Pushkin, Zotov, or Popov. The fact that they were struggling for their own survival was completely irrelevant to the viability of independent republics.

Likewise, the inordinate amount of repression and supression that followed was simply a measure of the fear that pervaded what remained of the Russian citizenry. Since the brutal times of Ivan the Terrible, the Russians had feared only two conditions: disorder and chaos. Both were expressions of the inability of the Russian soul to master its own destiny. So if a Russian was required to feel passion, best it be regulated by political or ideological diktats.

No true Russian could care that trudging through the waste and sludge of Moscow's sewerage system was the potential salvation of what remained of the country. The simple fact was that no true Russian could tolerate to see his empire, let alone his country, crumple in front of his eyes without trying to do something about it.

While the demonstrators were protesting in Manezh Square alongside the Kremlin, Tamara, Pushkin, Misha, and Vartanian, who was still carrying Zotov, were wading through the sludge beneath the Kremlin walls on their way to Khodinka, the Central Airfield. From there they would be able to proceed by helicopter to the underground bunkers of the Russian National Command Authority, some fifty kilometers outside the center of Moscow, under the command of Field Marshal Kulikov.

Pushkin had not spoken a word since General Yershov had bitten off his tongue. A true partisan, he thought. Yershov killed himself rather than reveal a secret that might have compromised several other people's lives. How lucky for everyone that he had never trusted the general from the beginning. Otherwise they too would have been dead by now.

The sound of rapid gunfire had markedly subsided. Perhaps they had been effective in killing most of the Spassky Guards who had been chasing them. But he couldn't be certain about that, or anything else. Certainly not Tamara!

"Colonel Pushkin, how much farther do we have to go? Zotov is beginning to weigh a ton." Although Vartanian had come from strong peasant stock, his legs were beginning to stiffen under the dead weight that was draped over his shoulders.

"Not much farther, Vartanian. Maybe a few more minutes. That's all!"

"That's all! Ha! A few more minutes are all I need before I join our dear friend Zotov here."

"You're turning into such an old woman!" Stooping under his fifteen-pound Sagger antitank gun, Misha also felt he had only a few more minutes left inside of him. Part of the problem was inhaling the putrid fumes of the Kremlin sewerage. It's true, he thought, all politicians are full of shit!

"Old woman, my ass! You pansy!" Vartanian was not in a mood to banter with anyone, let alone one of his subordinates.

"Let's end this! You sound like the old hags at the marketplace," Pushkin shouted, remembering the first time he met Tamara.

She walked behind him, feeling the chill of his silence toward her. Testing the fragility of the moment, she extended her graceful fingers and ran them gently through Pushkin's curly black hair. Ever since that moment when Pushkin shoved Yershov's head into the sewerage, she had felt betrayed. He had accused her of being a GRU spy, implying that she was sent to spy on him. And knew more than she had revealed.

While that was true, it was irrelevant. The only thing that mattered now was that she loved Pushkin. And Pushkin loved her. She hoped.

At least he didn't pull away from her hand. Maybe he had forgiven her. Oh, my God, she said to herself, how complicated love is. Why is it so intertwined with betrayal? And why did she have to fall in love with a man whose principal profession was working within the shadows of truth?

Not that she was Miss Innocence.

As he knew all too well, she was a GRU agent on assignment to follow him and report on his activities. But wasn't it clear to him, she wondered, that from the moment she dared to risk her life to see him at the very beginning of the coup, that she wanted to remain with him not just then, but for all time? At that very moment, she had betrayed her own profession to be with him. He must know that! She hoped.

"So, Mata Hari, what type of secrets will you seduce out of me this time?" he asked. His insincere laughter resonated like an accordian in an echo chamber.

Tamara turned him around and kissed his face with the fervor of a teen-ager. Sloppy and overenthusiastic. "Forgive me! Forgive me! I spoke such foolishness in order to save us."

She felt sorry for the lines of fatigue that creased his dark, intense face. But as her mother always told her, brave men were allowed to look tired. And had the right to demand everything from everyone.

"Colonel Alexander Lvovich Pushkin, I order you to tell me that you love me, despite my stupid, treacherous behavior."

"And if I don't? Then what will you do?" Pushkin had a mocking, quizzical expression.

"Then I will refuse to go forth."

"Really? And if I order you? Then what?"

"I will simply lie down here and engage in passive resistance."

"Wait, gentlemen! We have an insurrection within our own insurrection. What should we do?"

"Do as all true Russian men do, Colonel."

"And what is that, Vartanian?"

"Spank her! And let's get on with it. My back is killing me!"

"What say you, Misha? Do you agree with your superior?"

"Sir, I have the greatest respect for both you and Major Vartanian. I feel fortunate that I don't have to make such decisions as my two superiors must do."

"Well, Major Tamara Popov, you have heard the valuable opinion of my men. One says that I must spank you. The other says that he is unable to assume the responsibility for such heinous acts that I may be about to commit." Pushkin looked at Tamara as if he had never seen her before. How really beautiful she is, he thought. So Russian. So majestic! Tall. Well proportioned. Long blonde hair. Blue eyes. She reeked with vulnerability and, most maddening of all, unspoken sexuality.

"So, my handsome colonel. What is you decision?"

Suddenly a round of 7.62 millimeter RPK light machine gun fire ricocheted around the tunnel, and Misha, who had shielded the embracing lovers, fell into the sewerage, dead.

Vartanian put Zotov down and shot off a round from Misha's antitank gun; the gunfire in the distance subsided.

"Oh, Misha!" Pangs of guilt swept over Tamara. Had it not been for her momentary procrastination, he would still be alive.

Rushing forward, Pushkin led Tamara and Vartanian, with Zotov back across his shoulders, through the maze of tunnels toward the history museum. He knew from the red markings on the tunnel wall that they were passing below Lenin Central Stadium, in which he had played when he was on the Cosmos soccer team. Like many other Russian amateur and semiprofessional athletic teams, membership was a convenient cover for dozens of Spetsnaz soldiers to travel all over the world, playing soccer while at the same time collecting intelligence from the host governments.

As they passed beneath Moscow State University, Pushkin thought he heard semiautomatic fire ahead of them.

Then he saw what he had been looking for—three bright red letters— KCA, Khatinka Central Airfield, inscribed alongside a rusty metal ladder that led upward through a narrow hole to the surface.

"Colonel, how are we going to get Zotov through this narrow hole?"

Pushkin looked around the tunnel to see if there was anything they could use to tie and haul the body up.

"Tamara, you're the clever one in this group. What do you recommend?" Pushkin's voice had an edge of sarcasm.

Without a word, Tamara pulled Pushkin's frayed leather belt from around his waist and indicated to Vartanian that he remove his belt as well.

"Pushkin, you climb the ladder, and pull Zotov up."

"Yes, Major!" Pushkin snapped smartly to attention.

"Vartanian, you push from the bottom!" He too snapped to attention and saluted.

"And, my dear major, what will you be doing?" Pushkin started to climb the ladder, holding the belt with his right hand. When he felt secure, he pulled Zotov's body up the ladder, rung by rung, while Vartanian pushed from below.

"I'm going to be the project manager, supervising both of you." Tamara smiled. What had started out as a sarcastic challenge from Pushkin had turned into an impressive performance.

Both Pushkin and Vartanian were exhausted and soaked with perspiration when Zotov finally reached the top of the ladder. Pushkin felt Zotov's slow, steady carotid pulse, thankful that he was still alive. Having lost a lot of blood, he was in a state of shock. Pushkin knew he had to get Zotov to the Russian National Command Authority before time ran out. Without Zotov, Project Baltimore could quickly unravel, with dire consequences for Russia and the world.

Thinking this made Pushkin wince. How could the destiny of a country as great as the Commonwealth of Independent States depend on the fortunes of one man? It wasn't right. It wasn't fair. No one man should be able to determine the destiny of a nation. That type of personalized diplomacy should have gone out with Gorbachev. Didn't anyone yet realize that societal reforms instituted by one individual could never survive without the support of institutions?

So why had Zotov suddenly become so important? As President of the largest republic, he had only as much power as the Presidents of the other individual republics allowed him to have, according to the 1991 Treaty of the Commonwealth. The liberals in the State Council had opposed Zotov's increasing authoritarianism, which had started some ten years ago when he allied with Gorbachev. On the other hand, the conservatives in both the Council of the Republics and the Council of the Commonwealth blamed Zotov for the continuing disintegration of the political, economic, and social systems in the Commonwealth of Independent States since Gorbachev's time. And Zotov, his life on a thread, wasn't able to provide any answers.

Jamming his shoulders up against the manhole cover, Pushkin found that it would not budge.

General Yershov had been right. The remaining units of the Spassky Guards were waiting for them. They had sealed the manhole to trap them in the sewer, knowing that sooner or later they would die from exhaustion, hunger, and thirst. On the other hand, the alternative was possibly worse. If they managed to get themselves out of the tunnel, they would encounter soldiers waiting to decimate them as they exited.

"Vartanian, load up that Sagger! Shoot a hole through that manhole cover! It's the only way we're going to out of here."

"Are you certain, Colonel?"

"Remember what General Yershov said? They would be waiting for us as soon as we left this rat's nest. Do you have any other ideas? I am open to any suggestions. I have a very important man dying right here. And I've got to get him to Commonwealth National Command Authority before we and the Americans blow each other up."

"What if we continued and exited through another manhole?" Tamara was eager to heed Yershov's warning.

"That would be fine, except we're supposed to have a helicopter waiting for us. Just above our heads."

"Does it sound like a helicopter up there?" Tamara was insistent, and Vartanian was beginning to share her concerns.

"Colonel, Major Popov may be right. It may be wiser to emerge through a manhole from which General Yershov's troops don't expect us. At least we'll have a fighting chance to survive. If we go up this manhole, we know we can expect an ambush."

"Here I am trying to bring back some law and order to our great Mother Russia by returning our noble President Zotov. But what do I confront among my very own men? Insurrection and questioning of authority. Two very uncharacteristically Russian behaviors. I am very disappointed."

"In whom are you disappointed? In you or us, my dear disillusioned colonel?" Tamara was beginning to feel untypically maternal. "Does your decision have to do with the fact that you may not want to bring Zotov's body down and then lug it back up another staircase?" Tamara grinned. She was beginning to understand her brave, resourceful warrior. Basically,

Pushkin liked to work as little as possible. If there were two solutions to a problem, he would choose the simpler one. It was no accident that the first time they met and made love he had postponed a major meeting of his Spetsnaz co-conspirators.

"Let me and Major Vartanian take over the arduous task of carrying the President."

"Major, you have the genius of being either insurbodinate or extremely insightful."

"Or both!" she replied with a clear sense of cockiness.

"Whatever we're going to do, we must do within five minutes. That is when the helicopter is supposed to pick us up."

"And what about the ambush?" Tamara asked.

"After our extensive analysis, I have decided that as we have been fortunate this far, there is no reason to expect those fortunes to change. We will continue as planned." He recalled one of his grandmother's sayings: "God favors those fools and *mujeeks* who don't know any better."

"Then let us go! Before it's too late." With the anticipation of breathing fresh air, Vartanian began to feel nauseated.

"Vartanian, bring the Sagger up here! Let's see what it can do."

"Are you crazy, Pushkin?" Tamara had seen this type of desperate behavior in soldiers who were about to complete their missions. There seemed to be an unconscious need to accelerate the endgame scenario to a conclusion—whatever that conclusion might be.

Vartanian loaded the Sagger and handed it to Pushkin, knowing that if Pushkin fired the gun in such close quarters he risked serious injury to both himself and Zotov.

Pushkin realized his error.

"Here, take it!" He handed the gun back to Vartanian. Tamara looked relieved. "You stay down there at the bottom of the ladder. Fire it when we are in place."

Pushkin shielded Zotov's body with his own, pressing both of them tightly against the side of the tunnel. Vartanian had a clear shot at the manhole cover. But if he were off by ten centimeters, both Pushkin and Zotov would be no more than a fond memory.

"Don't worry, Colonel! If I miss, I'm going to have to deal with Major Popov, and that's not a prospect I look forward to."

Tamara smacked him affectionately on his back.

Vartanian took careful aim and squinted through the infrared night finder, making certain that the cross hairs of the nightscope covered the manhole. Slowly, he squeezed the trigger. Heavy metal fragments of the cover bombarded them as smoke swirled around in a cyclone of disorder, swept aside by the rush of fresh air that greeted them.

"Is everyone all right?" Pushkin brushed off the dust and metal from his uniform. He checked Zotov carefully. His primary cargo was still alive!

"I'm fine," Tamara replied.

"Same here, Colonel!" Vartanian responded vigorously.

"Then let's get out of here, quickly! By now, every Spassky Guard in Moscow knows our location." Pushkin pushed Zotov through the manhole and climbed out after him.

As Popov and Vartanian emerged, they heard a barrage of gunfire and a loud scream.

Please, God, thought Tamara, spare Pushkin.

Tracer bullets arched across the cool, dark moonlit night sky with the grace of a steel ballerina pirouetting across a stage of mayhem. About two hundred feet from the manhole, Tamara saw an Mi-24 helicopter descending onto an open field that, in more halcyon times, would have been used as a soccer field. With Zotov over his shoulder, Pushkin was staggering toward the helicopter. The Mi-24 provided fire cover against the approaching Spassky Guards, using the dual 50 millimeter cannons mounted on the sides of its bloated camouflaged belly.

"Hurry up, both of you!" Pushkin's normal stentorian voice was drowned in the din of gunfire. As the helicopter started to lift off, Pushkin reached out to Tamara, who extended one hand to him and the other hand to Vartanian. The Mi-24 lifted off with both Tamara and Vartanian hanging from Pushkin's powerful right arm. Pushkin ached as never before.

"My hand is slipping!" Vartanian screamed.

"Grab my ankles!" Tamara screamed back. She felt like a rubber band being stretched to the limit, afraid that any second she might snap.

The helicopter rose quickly and banked sharply to the right to avoid the ground fire.

Vartanian let go of Tamara's hand.

"No!" Tamara screamed and managed to hook his sliding body beneath his shoulders with her feet.

Vartanian grabbed her hips. How befitting, he thought. A decorated, combat-tested Spetsnaz soldier, dying halfway between the ground and the air. Not quite infantry. Not quite paratrooper. Simply Spetsnaz, the elite mongrel. It seemed so perverse. A veteran of conflagrations in Afghanistan and the Baltic states, here he was, in the middle of a crisp, cool Moscow night, being shot at by his own countrymen while hanging on to a woman, who, in turn, was dangling from a helicopter. If he didn't know better, this could have been a scene from the Moscow Circus. But they were no bears doing some foolish tricks. Only foolish humans.

With the help of others, Pushkin slowly drew Tamara into the helicopter. Vartanian held solidly on to her legs as she sat inside, feet dangling from the open door, hands grasping the leather halters on the side of the door.

Vartanian could feel the clear definition of her leg muscles. Under other, less dangerous circumstances, he would have found the situation erotic. Or comical. Or both. But for the moment he had to comfort himself solely with the notion that she would not let go of him. Thank goodness the ground fire was no longer able to reach.

"Hold on! Don't let go! Pushkin is sending down a harness!" Tamara yelled loudly.

Vartanian could barely hear her. The sound of the wind whistling past him made him feel as if he were in a wind tunnel.

"When the harness comes alongside, take hold of it." Pushkin hoped that Vartanian could hear him. He turned the winch at the side of the open door and unraveled a two-hundred-foot steel cable. But the combination of both the high wind and high speed of the helicopter made it hard for Pushkin to position the harness.

Vartanian reached out with his right hand and tried to grab it. But as he did, he could feel himself slipping down Tamara's leg.

"Oh, my God!" For a very brief second, Tamara thought she was losing him. The more she tried to squeeze him close, the more his hands slipped. She concluded that the gods were either testing or teasing her.

"I'll try it once again!" bellowed Pushkin. "But this time, let the harness hit you before you grab for it."

Vartanian nodded. He knew he could not hold on much longer. Both of his arms were ready to detach from their shoulder sockets. Finally, Pushkin snapped the cable so that the harness hit Vartanian's chest.

"He's got it!" Pushkin screamed with delight.

Vartanian grabbed the harness with his right hand, while he held Tamara tightly with his left. One wrong movement and he would find himself splattered one thousand feet below. Carefully, he drew up his legs so that he was able to place first his right foot, and then his left, into the harness. Finally, he let go of Tamara's legs.

It worked! Within a few seconds, he was seated on the floor of the helicopter, hugging his companions.

The Mi-24 banked toward the left, heading in the direction of Gadanya Forest, seventy-five miles northeast of Moscow.

The Russian National Command Authority was composed of a series of underground concrete facilities in and around Moscow, built several hundred feet below the surface, to accommodate the senior members of the Russian power elite during wartime conditions. The deep underground facilities contained everything from a fully staffed hospital to plush dining facilities and sleeping quarters. Designed some fifty years before to withstand a direct nuclear hit, its concrete walls were eighteen feet thick, able to withstand a 7 psi (pounds per square inch) pressure detonation, equivalent to four Hiroshima atomic bombs.

Since the Russian National Command Authority had been created to protect thousands of the Russian leadership from a nuclear attack, many of its underground facilities had been located directly beneath the ministries in Moscow. In time of war or high military alert, the leaders were required to leave their offices and descend into a series of concealed passageways. From there, they could either ride a subway car specifically designated for their use or walk through a series of subterranean passageways to this underground city for the power elite. Once there, the Central Committee, the Council of Deputies, the Ministry of Defense, the FSA, as well as many other state ministries would remain sheltered while the commonwealth converted itself into a wartime posture.

Built immediately after World War II, these underground facilities were expanded during the Korean War, the Vietnam War, and the U.S. war against Iraq. All the while, the facilities had afforded the then Soviet leadership the opportunity to survive a nuclear strike while still directing the war effort. To enable this, the installations had a highly effective life-support system, capable of protecting the occupants against both chemical and biological warfare, and a highly developed communications system, which allowed the leaders to transmit and receive crucial messages to and from their battlefield commanders.

From these installations, the military leadership could operate fifty space systems for both military and civilian uses, including the manned space stations, Mir and Salyut, and reconnaissance, launch detection, navigational, meteorological, and communications satellites. The most important, the radar ocean reconnaisance satellite (RORSAT), the electronic intelligence (ELINT), ocean reconnaissance satellite (EORSAT), and the global navigation satellite system (GLONASS), provided highly accurate positioning data for military use.

Seated in this expansive underground facility, Field Marshal Alexander Kulikov, once Commander-in-Chief of the Warsaw Treaty Organization and now the newly designated Chief of the General Staff, watched the radar screen as the Mi-24 approached.

"The helicopter pilot requests permission to land," Master Sergeant Gregory Becheroff, the Georgian radio operator, shouted into the crowded room of fluorescent radar screens and computer terminals.

"Of course . . . of course . . . give them immediate permission to land." The man with the smiling eyes was eager to see President Zotov, as well as his protégé, Colonel Pushkin.

"Yes, sir!" Becheroff yelled into the radio microphone. "Immediate . . . repeat, immediate permission to land." He turned to Kulikov. "Emergency medical assistance is requested for President Zotov."

"Of course—permission granted. Get all the doctors needed out there as quickly as possible. Tell Pushkin that I want to see them all as soon as they arrive."

Before Becheroff could transmit the message, Kulikov was out of the Control Center, racing up the concrete stairs to the landing pad. Without any formalities, he rushed over to the helicopter and watched intently as Pushkin helped the medics place Zotov on a stretcher. The medics inserted an intravenous tube into Zotov's arm and attached a catheter to his penis.

"Spetsnaz colonels are nothing but braggarts and cowards," Kulikov shouted at the top of his lungs and spread his arms out to embrace Pushkin.

"And all marshals are ingrates and armchair generals who suffer from venereal disease." Before Pushkin could complete the insult, Kulikov grabbed him in a tight bear hug with such passion that it frightened Tamara. Surprisingly, she found herself jealous of such an open display of affection between the two men. Yet only Russian men could be so overtly affectionate with each other without having to worry about being accused of some sexual perversion, as might happen with the British or the Americans.

"General . . ." Pushkin muttered.

"General? What do you mean, 'General'?" Kulikov pointed to his colorful row of medals. "Marshal, my dear friend. Marshal. Several days before your successful uprising at the Kremlin, I was a general. Today, I am a marshal." Before he could be introduced, he walked over to Tamara.

"You didn't tell me that you would be bringing along such a Russian masterpiece," Kulikov said, taking Tamara's hands into his own. "What a delicate specimen."

"This is my dear colleague and companion, Major Tamara Popov, GRU. Without her invaluable help, we would never have made it here safely."

"I am certain that she helped you . . ." Kulikov added with a licentious smile, "in many different and important ways."

"A pleasure to meet you too, Marshal Kulikov," Tamara replied sardonically as Kulikov walked over to congratulate Vartanian.

"And this strapping major, I presume, is the one who flew outside the helicopter while his ingrate colonel sat comfortably inside."

"Yes, sir!"

"You mean to agree with me, Major, that your superior is an ingrate?" Kulikov could barely contain a laugh.

"No, sir. Of course not. Colonel Pushkin is not an ingrate. As a matter of fact, he's a very courageous . . . noble—"

"That's okay, son. I know all about your illustrious colonel." He grabbed Pushkin by the shoulder and they walked over to Zotov's stretcher. "It's serious, isn't it?"

"I'm afraid it is, sir. He sustained quite an initial injury. And then he's lost a lot of blood." Pushkin was delighted that Zotov had made it to the headquarters still alive.

"Can he talk?"

"I don't think so," replied one of the medics.

"Zotov, can you hear me?" Kulikov was distressed by the sight of his good friend lying on the stretcher. So listless. So close to death. The last time he had seen Zotov, he was his robust, mischievous self, playing his usual pranks. Zotov particularly enjoyed handing out explosive cigars.

"I'm afraid he can't hear you," the medic said. "But give him a little time."

"Come with me, my friend! We have a lot of important work to do."
Kulikov led Pushkin to the Control Center, motioning Tamara and Vartanian to follow them.

Although Pushkin was knowledgeable about electronic warfare, he was
still surprised to see the panoply of advanced technology packaged in that
claustrophobic room. Despite the current popular image of the Russian
republic as a Third World country, when it came to the needs of her own
military, she was still a superpower. And this room was strong evidence of
that.

"My friend, we have certain matters to attend to, without our patron. We
must make certain decisions for Zotov that he is not able to make on our
behalf."

"Yes. I agree." Pushkin could feel the adrenaline rush through his veins.
Having been privy to Project Baltimore from its very inception, Pushkin
knew exactly what Kulikov meant.

He, Pushkin, was about to be given the chance to determine the outcome
of Russian history in a way that few, if any, people would ever have. It was
one thing for him to carry out the orders of the President of the Russian
Federation, but it was a completely different, if not more frightening, experience to act as the President. In conjunction, of course, with the President's
principal ally and friend—Marshal Kulikov.

"According to Project Baltimore," Pushkin began, "Zotov was to announce the invocation of section 110, paragraph 7 of the Commonwealth
Constitution, overriding section 73. In effect, this would allow the President
of the Russian Federation to invoke emergency war powers and call in both
the military and the FSA to take complete control of every major state-run
office and operation." Pushkin blurted out the provisions of the plan he had
rehearsed for several months.

Tamara was surprised to see how much Pushkin was enjoying his role.

"It would also forbid the secession of any republics from the Commonwealth of Independent States," Kulikov added, relishing the thought of
fighting those insolent Ukrainians.

"How do we go about step one without the President actually being here?"
Pushkin asked.

"Ah, my friend! Now, you will see the miracle of modern technology. It's
called computer digitalization. Using only the computer and some samples
of his normal speaking voice, we can re-create Zotov's voice as if he were
right here in the Command Center. We had tapes prepared for such a
contingency."

Kulikov motioned to a soldier sitting in front of what looked to Pushkin
to be four very sophisticated tape recorders, and ordered him to turn them
on.

President Zotov's voice boomed through two loudspeakers, hanging on
the wall.

My dear citizens, as you know, our country has been in a state of civil unrest for some time. As President of the Russian Federation, I had hoped that with the passage of time this civil unrest would improve. Instead, the very opposite has happened.

Yesterday morning, I and several members of the State Council were brutally attacked, in the Kremlin itself, by renegade elements of our elite Spetsnaz units. An attempted coup against the presidency and the Commonwealth of Independent States was successfully aborted by the honorable Spassky Guards of the Kremlin.

As a direct result of this failed coup, and the increasing civil unrest in Moscow, and in the Russian Federation, Moldova, Georgia, and Ukraine, I have no other alternative but to rescind section 73 of the Commonwealth Constitution, which allows each republic to secede from the Commonwealth of Independent States at its own discretion.

I have been authorized by the State Council, the Council of the Republics, and the Council of the Commonwealth to invoke section 110, paragraph 7 of the constitution, granting the President of the Russian Federation absolute and complete authority to maintain civil law and order by whatever means are deemed necessary in a given situation.

As a result of this newly invested power, I have asked the Russian Armed Forces to take immediate actions to insure that there will be no further demonstrations of civil unrest.

Similarly, in order to avert a civil war from which we Russian people would suffer for years to come, I have ordered our various security agencies, as well as the elite units of the armed forces, to take over the management of the central authority of each of the republics. As of this moment, and for the foreseeable future, the civilian authorities will play a consulting role. There will no longer be any civilian authority in any of the independent republics.

In order to alter the economic depression in which we have found ourselves, as a result of the failure of perestroika and glasnost, I have ordered the recentralization of several industries. Strategic private enterprises will be socialized until further notice.

I know that all these measures sound drastic. But if they are quickly and efficiently enacted, we will save the Commonwealth and, in time, relax the restrictions.

I deliver this message to you with a heavy heart. I am sad to report that we are presently engaged in a potentially dangerous war with the United States. And in order to fight this war effectively I have no other choice but to enact these measures.

I promise, as your elected President, to terminate this war as quickly as possible so that our valiant Russian soldiers do not fight one more minute than they have to.

I ask you, my fellow citizens, to pray for me and for our collective salvation.

Thank you. And bless you all.

"Well, what do you think, my dear Pushkin? In a few minutes, we will transmit this broadcast all over the Russian Federation and the remaining republics in the Commonwealth of Independent States. At this very moment, our troops are moving into positions of power and control." Kulikov beamed with pride. "Not bad for a man who is still in a coma."

"Amazing!" Pushkin noticed Tamara's angry facial expression. She was trying to tell him something.

"Thanks to your courageous actions and to the technology of computer digitalization, we true Russians, the military and security organizations, are now able to regain, once again, the power and control that was taken from us during those 'lazy days of perestroika and glasnost.' " Kulikov slapped Pushkin on his back as if he were an important American politician.

"And now, we must finish Project Baltimore," Pushkin added warily.

"Of course . . . of course . . . Project Baltimore. That has always been our primary objective." Kulikov's face was warm and smiling, but his eyes were cold. His reply was unconvincing.

"Tomorrow, we'll finish the rest," Pushkin said as he felt a cold chill run down his back.

He recalled the image of General Yershov biting off his own tongue after warning Pushkin of a possible betrayal.

When will they turn against me? he wondered.

# CHAPTER
## 25

President Westview paced the busy bullpen of the Operations Center at the Alternate Military Command Center at Fort Ritchie, Maryland, some eighty miles northwest of Washington.

Westview truly believed, without any arrogance, that it was divine destiny for world leaders like himself and Zotov to provide noble, restless men of action a clear purpose in life by allowing them to serve the specific interests of a world leader. But it was also a measure of the talent, or perhaps genius, of a world leader to articulate his personal interests into an ideology that would encompass the vox populi—the voice of the people.

For Westview, the voice of the people was best articulated by moral imperatives that had little correspondence with reality. A unilateral aggressive act was explained as a "justified intervention." An act of war was a "police action." And since it was America's destiny "to support democracy and freedom the world over," any confrontation was a moral joust between "good and evil" with America, by definition, always on the side of "truth and justice."

Westview had studied the lessons of President George Bush and Secretary of State James Baker, how they had brilliantly manipulated world opinion and sentiment against an intransigent tyrant, Iraqi President Saddam Hussein. Westview was prepared to incorporate certain elements of their successful rhetoric into his forthcoming speech to the nation.

If only the gnawing pain in the middle of his abdomen would stop, he could focus on the memo Mapplethorpe had prepared. Westview recognized, ironically, that these lessons drew very heavily on Desaix's now infamous

TOP SECRET memorandum entitled CRISIS MANAGEMENT: THE ART OF MANIPULATING AMERICAN PUBLIC SENTIMENT IN ORDER TO JUSTIFY U.S. INTERVENTIONS THE WORLD OVER.

Desaix's basic precepts were too important to be ignored: (1) Restrict media coverage; (2) Co-opt/manage TV images; (3) Never mention or show U.S. casualties; (4) Focus news coverage on high-tech weapons—portray nonbloody image of war; (5) Emphasize moral high ground; (6) Express low expectations for political/ military outcome; (7) Hide behind a bodyguard of lies in all press briefings. So Westview had used them to advantage over the past six months. Too bad Desaix would never know just how right he had been, thought Westview.

The continuous bustle of people around him, shouting information, barking orders, and monitoring computer terminals gave Westview a warm sense of comfort. He was the one who was making it all happen.

Secretary of State Manning, National Security Advisor Mapplethorpe, Chairman of the Joint Chiefs McCormick, Secretary of Defense Merck, and Director of Central Intelligence Jenkins moved about the cramped Command Center as the President reviewed the memo.

"Gentlemen, time is running out! I have exactly twenty minutes before airtime. I need a Situation Report and some suggestions about what to put into my speech."

They walked together into a safe room, a metal-encased room surrounded by an electromagnetic field that deflected any electronic eavesdropping. But, unlike the Situation Room in the White House or in the State Department, the room was designed to accommodate no more than eight people, seated around a truncated rectangular mahogany table. Worst of all was the ventilation. Every scent of cologne and sweat lingered in the room.

Maps of Western Europe and the Commonwealth of Independent States were spread over the walls with colored push pins scattered over them indicating the disposition of U.S. and Russian forces. Thick curved arrows pointed in the direction of the eastern part of Germany, illustrating the major U.S. thrust of attack against the Russian forces.

"First of all, let me start by saying that the Germans have been screaming foul." Manning spoke with a characteristic calmness that irritated almost everyone but the President.

"Chet, what's their particular beef?" Westview smiled.

"The German Foreign Minister has practically been camping out in my office at State, protesting the presence of troops that could lead to . . ." Manning broke into a German accent, "unkontrollable vorfair."

"Serves the krauts right for being a bunch of candy-assed chicken shits during Desert Shield." Years later, General McCormick had still not forgiven either the Germans or the Japanese for refusing to send direct military assistance to U.S. ground and air troops in the Persian Gulf.

"Well now, General, that's not the type of respect that we want to show to one of our closest NATO allies, is it?" Secretary of Defense Merck spoke, somewhat tongue-in-cheek. He was simply mocking the well-known underlying anti-German sentiment in the room.

For the past ten years, Germany had become a "voracious economic monster, coasting along on America's sweat and blood," a phrase DCI Jenkins had coined several years ago in one of his National Intelligence Directives. Unlike the Japanese, who were now one of two major economic superpowers in the world, Germany had not demonstrated any desire to become a responsible member of the international community. Even when the Persian Gulf crisis threatened their vital oil supplies, Germany's immediate, almost reflexive response was to continue to break UN embargo sanctions against Iraq and to provide technical assistance to Saddam Hussein's nefarious gas warfare machinery. Many of the senior U.S. government officials felt that a unified Germany had not changed in character from a Nazi Germany.

No one in the room, including the President, was shedding any tears for the impending devastation of Germany. If anything, there was an unspoken pleasurable sentiment that the Germans might finally receive a long-overdue comeuppance.

Over the past several years, many prominent and influential economists had argued that the poor economic condition of both the U.S. and the Commonwealth of Independent States was due to the unremitting strength of the unified German economy. It was close to impossible for American industry to compete directly with the European Common Market, of which Germany was the leader.

"Tell the Foreign Minister that we'll be happy to stop the war as soon as he gives us some of his soldiers and planes," McCormick added boisterously.

"By the way, where has he been hiding his army and air force?" Manning asked, curious to find out the answer so that he could apply some critical leverage on the Germans.

"CIA analysis shows that the damage to the German military and industrial complex would be over 30 percent," Jenkins answered smugly. "That's without using the majority of their armed forces and planes, hidden away in the different mountain regions of Germany." Of course, bomb assessment damage was an art and not a science. The margin of error could be quite great. But he didn't choose to share this information with his colleagues.

"You're talking about an army and air force one-quarter the size of ours," Merck replied matter-of-factly.

"That's what happens when you decide to dedicate your economy to making money, and decide to assume a neutral posture," Manning added. "Just like Switzerland."

"At 30 percent rate of damage, there would be nothing left of Germany or her economy in three days of fighting." Westview smiled broadly.

"If one didn't know any better, Mr. President," Mapplethorpe said in a somber tone, "one might say that this potential war between the U.S. and the Russian Federation could have been started for the very purpose of getting rid of the German threat."

Everyone in the room laughed except Manning. "Was that supposed to be a joke, Mapplethorpe?" Manning sounded furious.

"I apologize. I admit that it was in bad taste." Mapplethorpe was having a hard time portraying any sense of embarrassment. But he did wonder why Manning was so inappropriately defensive.

"Gentlemen," Westview said, "before we divert ourselves from the main discussion, let me add that I have been in contact with most of the leaders of Western Europe. Everyone wants to see this situation resolved as quickly as possible. And that includes the representatives of the European Common Market, the Perm Five of the UN, the General Secretary of the UN, and the GATT 7." Westview was clearly irritated with this discussion. The conversation was becoming disconnected.

"And don't forget the Pope. He wants immediate cessation of all hostilities, which he is prepared to monitor, along with the UN International Peacekeeping Force." Even as Manning spoke, he realized that the scenario was totally unrealistic.

"Let me summarize the German situation, as best I understand it," Westview continued. "Please correct me if I'm wrong, Chet, but in a few days the Germans will call for a UN resolution that will demand the immediate withdrawal of all troops. My sense is that it will pass extremely fast. So, gentlemen, we have exactly two days, if that, to restrain, if not subdue, the Russians. Is that clear?" Westview always had the ability to reduce the complexities of any problem by referring to it as "the situation."

"That's right, Mr. President. We have two days, at most, to obtain our objective." Manning looked at Mapplethorpe, who was squirming in his chair.

"General McCormick, how's the crisis as of today?" Westview checked his watch, a typical restless gesture. He had only ten minutes before going on the air.

"Which crisis, Mr. President?" McCormick replied.

"What do you mean, General?"

"The crisis in Germany or the one at Bolling? Elite units within the Special Forces, commanded by a Colonel Matthew Zarbitstki, are staging some sort of action at Bolling." McCormick's voice was angry and insubordinate. "I found out about all of this, literally just before I came here, Mr. President. And when I asked around, I was told in no uncertain terms that Special Operations Forces troops were under the direct command of General Mapplethorpe."

"General McCormick, what is it that you want to know?" Westview asked indignantly.

"To put it simply: what is going on?"

"Ronald, may I remind you that the President is your Commander-in-Chief," Mapplethorpe interjected brusquely.

"Right, General Mapplethorpe," McCormick replied facetiously, emphasizing the word "General" as if he were some kind of paper soldier.

"I thought you had been informed of the situation," Westview said. "But, be that as it may, since the war in Iraq, the Special Operations Forces at MacDill Air Force Base have been under the direct command and control of the President, or his duly appointed surrogate. In this case, it happens to be General Mapplethorpe." Westview's tone was matter-of-fact.

"Yes, sir," McCormick said, getting the uncomfortable feeling that he was getting the bureaucratic runaround. But above all else, he was still a military man. And that meant he was supposed to follow orders.

"General McCormick," Mapplethorpe interjected, "contrary to what you might have thought, your boss, Secretary of Defense Merck, had been informed, just like everyone else in this room, a couple of hours ago. Isn't that right, Randy?" Mapplethorpe was a master of these bureaucratic games. He knew how to make certain that some senior official appeared accountable. Whether they were or weren't was completely irrelevant.

Looking around the table, Merck realized he had just been placed in the hotseat. And he knew he was being judged for only one thing right then— his personal loyalty to the President. Would he side with his Chairman of the Joint Chiefs or would he side with the President of the United States? A wrong decision and it could be the end of his political career. But as in all decisions where political viability was involved, truth was a commodity one could little afford. Only the truth of the moment really counted. Was he or wasn't he with the President?

Westview waited.

"General Mapplethorpe is absolutely correct. I received the plans for the deployment of Special Operations Forces late last night. I didn't have time to clear it with you through the bureaucracy. And I don't have to tell you how cumbersome it is. So I simply called Mapplethorpe back on the phone early this morning." Merck paused to assess McCormick's reaction before he continued. "I was going to tell you before this meeting. But I never got the chance."

"Does that answer your question, General McCormick?"

"Yes, Mr. President."

"Now, could you give me a thumbnail sketch of where we stand." Westview was pleased with the way Merck had handled himself. He definitely had a future.

"To summarize very quickly, I would have to say that at this point in time both we and the Russians are headed for a major confrontation, if something isn't done to stop it quickly." McCormick turned toward Merck. "Would you agree with that assessment, Mr. Secretary?"

McCormick had learned his lesson well, Mapplethorpe thought, as he looked smugly at Westview.

"Yes, I do. The only thing I would add is that we're on DEFCON TWO, and I want to know if we should go to DEFCON ONE, Maximum Vigilance.

"I think we should remain at DEFCON TWO," replied Mapplethorpe.

"Before I make a decision, I want to hear something about what has been happening in the Russian Federation." Westview was concerned. According to plan, he was to have heard from Zotov by now. Just agreeing to end the war, as they had done a few hours ago in teleconference, was not sufficient. What if Zotov were double-crossing him? It was possible. Russians always had trouble with trust. Not to say that he himself didn't.

"As you know, Mr. President, our intelligence assets are very limited in that area."

"Goddamn it, Jenkins! Is there any time or place when your intelligence assets aren't limited in one way or another? What the hell is the American public spending all those billions for?" Westview screamed out his words as a pain shot through his abdomen. "And what's happened to President Zotov? Where is he?"

"Sir," Jenkins responded nervously, "as you know, we've been spending most of our funds for spy satellites and aerial reconnaisance. Very little money is designated for human assets."

"Is this your goddamn way of telling me that you don't know what the hell's happening over there? Or that you don't know where Zotov is?" Westview was finding it difficult to control his anger.

"Don, I think you should take it a little easier on Jenkins and McCormick," Manning interjected. "We're all trying to do the best job possible, given the limited time and incredible constraints." This was the first time Manning had ever called the President by his nickname in a meeting. But he felt that Westview might respond to a soothing reminder that he was flying off at that handle.

"Chet, mind your own business. When you become President, which I am certain you will someday, then you can call the shots. But, right now, I AM THE PRESIDENT!"

Mapplethorpe didn't like the tenor of what was going on, and was tempted to cut the meeting short, before it got completely out of hand. But he was afraid to alienate the President.

"Thank you for reminding me, Mr. President," Manning replied somberly.

For a moment, Westview wasn't certain whether Manning was being facetious or not. But he really didn't care. He assumed that their long-standing relationship would endure this minor difference in opinion. If not, then what value was there in their friendship?

But an unanticipated consequence of his flare-up was the bond of support that seemed to coalesce around the group. Though unspoken and unattended, alliances were being formed. That was part of the unconscious bonding that frequently occurred among policymakers during a crisis.

Certain Presidents used this group cohesiveness to motivate their advisors into action. Franklin D. Roosevelt would openly pit his Secretary of State against his Secretary of War, in the hopes that, on their own, they would form an alliance against the President that would make them even more innovative and productive. John F. Kennedy pitted his National Security Advisor against his Secretary of State and Secretary of Defense. Of course, the master of purposeful group manipulation was Lyndon Johnson. He never ceased to pit the principal Secretaries in his cabinet against one another.

President Bush, differing from his predecessors, and despite a friendly and inviting countenance, would brook absolutely no dissension or appearance of disloyalty.

Westview was aware of his place in history. But at this point in time he knew he was experiencing a great deal of stress. And there was very little he could do about it.

"Where are we, Jenkins? No, more importantly, where is Zotov?" Westview was feeling desperate. He had been unable to reach Zotov through their direct television satellite connection or famous hotline.

"We have some intelligence to suggest that after an unsuccessful coup in the Kremlin, Zotov was taken by elements of the Spetsnaz through the underground tunnels of Moscow." Jenkins looked around the room, waiting to see if anyone else's knowledge supported him.

"INR at State seems to corroborate Jenkins's analysis," Manning said, then winked unobtrusively at Jenkins. "Some of my more experienced analysts think that Zotov may have been taken to the Russian Command Authority, about seventy-five miles northwest of Moscow."

"How the hell do we get in touch with him?" Westview asked, alarmed. Whatever he decided to do in the next few hours depended on his ability to reach Zotov.

"DIA tells us that Marshal Alexander Kulikov is the man in charge of the Russian Command Authority. He's a tough-assed reactionary who believes that Russia should have returned to a military dictatorship a long time ago. He also believes that the U.S. is the inveterate enemy of the Russian Federation." McCormick watched Westview's reaction carefully.

There was none.

Westview realized that his troops were circling the campfire against him, and that his advisors were like lemmings. If one fell off the precipice, the others would follow suit.

"Mr. President, General McCormick brought up the issue of tactical nukes. What do you want us to do?" Merck tried to minimize his previous impression of his having been obsequious.

"What about the nukes, Mr. Secretary of Defense?" Westview sounded increasingly more testy.

"I just want to know our standing orders as of this moment," Merck said calmly.

"What were your standing orders before this moment?"

"No first strike."

"And?"

"We use tactical nuclear only if the Russians use gas, biological, or nuclear weapons against us." Merck felt defensive, like a graduate student being questioned during orals.

"Then, Mr. Secretary of Defense, one might infer that nothing has changed in that policy. Is that clear? Or will we need an Executive Order?"

"No, sir!" Merck responded with the brisk attentiveness of a private standing at attention.

"Then I think we've covered everything." Westview sounded tired. He found it increasingly hard to run group meetings.

"Before we adjourn for the day, Mr. President," Mapplethorpe interjected, "I would like to be certain that we are all on board with the state of preparedness of both our command and control systems and strategic weapons systems." Mapplethorpe was trying to salvage the final vestiges of an alert President, not yet besieged by fatigue and stress. He wanted to leave the impression with the Crisis Management Group before they left the meeting that the President was still very much in charge. Mapplethorpe didn't want to wake up the next day and read on the front page of *The Washington Post* that some very senior unidentified administration official felt that the President was cracking up. He recalled the image of President Nixon asking his National Security Advisor to get down on his knees and pray for salvation. The very next day, *The Washington Post* openly questioned Nixon's mental competency. Mapplethorpe had to avoid that at any cost.

"I think that's an excellent idea, General Mapplethorpe."

"Thank you, sir." Mapplethorpe beamed in the face of scowls of contempt from the rest of the group for this obvious ass kissing. "All right, gentlemen, let's start with MEECN."

"The Minimum Essential Emergency Communications Network, our two-way hardened teletype link between SAC headquarters and the Minuteman silos, is fully operational," responded General McCormick.

"GWEN?" Mapplethorpe asked, shooting his question across the table toward Merck.

"The Ground Wave Emergency Network, with its eighty relay stations and their four-hundred-foot transmission towers, is fully operational," Merck responded as if he had rehearsed the answer.

"AFSATCOM?"

"The Air Force Satellite Communication System is fully operational and linked up with MILSTAR's [Military, Strategic, Tactical, and Relay Network] three polar and four geostationary orbit satellites—all prepared for automatic evasive action in case of attack," McCormick responded with renewed vigor.

"ERCS?" Mapplethorpe asked with the childish enthusiasm of a choirboy reading his catechisms.

"The Emergency Rocket Communications System is a bit antiquated, as you already know," Merck responded. "The system consists of old Minuteman III ICBMs with radios fitted in their nose cones. Because of its age, we're putting it on standby till we get a signal from the President that orders us into a nuclear second strike. Then we would launch the ICBMs and let them broadcast launch orders to the other missiles still in the silo for half an hour."

"And what about Looking Glass?"

"As far as I know, the Boeing 747 SAC Airborne Command Post took off from Ellsworth Air Force Base in South Dakota about half an hour ago. That is, if your elite, hotshot Special Operations soldiers haven't expropriated that either." McCormick couldn't resist being provocative. He waited to see who would pick up the bait.

No one did, to his dismay. He was itching for a fight.

"Well, that's about it, Mr. President. Everything seems to be okay," Mapplethorpe said, ignoring McCormick's steely-eyed gaze.

Westview took a deep breath, trying to minimize the chronic pain in his abdomen. Then he spoke quietly but firmly. "You're fired, General McCormick, for insubordination to a superior officer."

"Please, Mr. President! General McCormick didn't mean what he said!" Merck protested, standing up to demonstrate his allegiance to his general.

General McCormick stormed out of the room.

"Randy, I appreciate your loyalty to a subordinate," Westview said, "and I'm certain that General McCormick does too. But I have no other recourse than to dismiss him. I will make a public announcement to that effect in a few minutes."

"Mr. President, am I to understand that a public announcement means that you have already chosen your new Chief of the JCS?" Merck was astounded. He was only a few seconds away from resigning.

"Every wartime commander must have contingency plans," Westview replied. "And every Commander-in-Chief has the right and duty to designate a new wartime cabinet."

The tension in the room was palpable. The next question was apparent to everyone. Who would be next?

For the first time, Mapplethorpe was taken by surprise. This was not a scenario that the President had ever discussed with him. And yet it was very clearly thought out beforehand. Uncharacteristically, Mapplethorpe started to perspire. All he could think of was who would be the next Chief of the JCS.

"Mr. President, does that mean you have chosen your next Chief of the JCS without consulting your Secretary of Defense?" Merck asked.

"That's right, Randy!" Westview stood up and walked over to the maps on the wall.

"Well, sir, I have no other choice but to resign as your Secretary of Defense," Merck said, then scribbled something on a piece of paper, stood up, and extended his hand in a conciliatory gesture.

Westview didn't bother to turn around as Merck hesitated a moment and then walked out of the room.

Two down, everyone in the room thought. How many more to go? One thought permeated the minds of several people in the room: The President of the United States is crazy.

# CHAPTER
## 26

Secretary of State Chester Manning stared silently through the brown-tinted windows of his black Cadillac limousine. Driving through the Catoctin Mountains of central Maryland into Washington, he felt completely isolated from the pristine beauty of the rolling hills covered with large, imposing oak trees. He placed his left hand against the window, as if he might be able to pull down one of the hanging branches.

It had been such a long time since he was able to enjoy nature, to hunt quail and deer on his ranch in Texas. He recalled the many times he and Westview would rise at four-thirty, in the freezing cold of dawn, lay quietly in the duck blind, camouflaged with shrubbery, and entice the ducks to float toward them. At the appropriate signal from Manning, Westview would start shooting with his double-gauged shotgun. After Westview had killed his quota of ducks, Manning would begin, always making certain that Westview had killed more ducks than he.

Those were the days when deception and calculated slaughter were part of the accepted ritual of playful camaraderie. It was a time when their friendship was not based on some implicit quid pro quo. They were just truly inseparable and for all practical purposes they were like brothers. Competitive. Jealous. Playful. Mischievous. Theirs was above all a bond of personal friendship and family ties. Three generations of intermarriage, mutual friendships, and patrician upbringing had been interwoven in their lives.

And no major drama had challenged their thirty-year friendship. Although both had gone to the same boarding school, neither one had either saved the other's life or salvaged the other's academic career from ignominy. Theirs was a friendship that evolved effortlessly. Perhaps too effortlessly.

There was never any question as to whose career was the more important of the two. Since childhood, both had playfully agreed that Westview would become the President of the United States and Manning would be his Secretary of State. That was just the way it was. Neither one had ever questioned the assumption that Manning might not want to be Secretary of State—or that he might have harbored quiet ambitions of becoming President himself. It had always been assumed that Westview would climb up the executive ladder of politics while Manning would garner the requisite political assets through the legislative route. The unspoken agreement, however, was that Manning's ambitions would always remain subordinate to those of Westview's. Neither one had dared to question that assumption for fear of disrupting the thirty years of unspoken beliefs upon which their relationship was based.

In many ways, though, Manning was the more talented of the two in the art of making it happen, the art of doing whatever one had to do to complete a task. It was Manning who had corraled the necessary delegates at the convention to nominate Westview as the Republican presidential candidate. Unbeknownst to Westview, Manning had to dredge up some unsavory material about several of the Texas delegates. Of course, this was simply part of making it happen—at whatever the cost.

But over the last few years, their relationship had become increasingly more strained. It bothered Manning that Westview had become erratic, unpredictable. Witness today's sudden emotional outbursts.

At the same time, Manning sensed that Westview felt threatened by Manning's increasingly independent power base.

As he passed a dilapidated farmhouse, Manning's fears for their relationship faded into the recesses of nostalgia. He chuckled to himself as he recalled those duck hunts. It was a time when they each could enjoy the other's company without having to worry about the consequences of their actions. Disregarding local ordinances, they killed as many ducks as they wanted. The pond belonged to Manning, and he didn't have to acquire permission to hunt there. Not even the game commissioner, who had the right to fine each of them, dared to intrude on their frolic.

After the day's hunting, they would bring in some of the local women who were eager to meet Easterners. They didn't have to fear being indiscreet. The women they picked up were only interested in having a good time. And neither he nor Westview was in any position of importance. Simply aspiring politicians, just beginning their climb. Their collective ambitions were the lubricant that provided the necessary momentum to overcome life's accumulated frictions. They merely devoured whatever impeded their progress. But now there were no more hunts or games—at least, not in the woods. Instead, the game had shifted to the parlors of Georgetown, the corridors of the East Wing, and the seventh floor of the State Department.

Where once the game elicited the ticklish delight of group play, it had now transformed itself into a pattern of self-absorption and self-aggrandizement. Both he and Westview were consumed by their respective ambitions. Playing the game of politics was no longer fun. Wheeling and dealing. Manipulating. Making trade-offs. That was hard work!

Natural beauty took second place as the Secretary's caravan of cars raced down Massachusetts Avenue, the elegant broad, tree-lined thoroughfare bracketed by the Vice President's mansion and imposing three-story embassy chancelleries. The cars pulled into the semicircular driveway of a distinctly unimposing two-story squat concrete building that seemed out of place amidst the historic homes.

The diplomatic security agents rushed out of their cars to assume their normal positions. A slight, pleasant-looking Oriental with shrewd eyes greeted Manning as he stepped out of his limousine.

"Mr. Secretary, it's a great pleasure to see you, again! Please excuse the informality!"

"It's good to see you, my friend!" Manning embraced Yutaka Imai, the Deputy Foreign Minister for Political Affairs. "We have much to talk about!"

They entered the Japanese Embassy, arms linked, as the dawn awakened.


Lieutenant General Richard White seated President Donald Westview in front of the television camera in the soundproof studio of the underground Alternate Command Center at Fort Ritchie.

"Well, Dick, does it meet with your approval?" Westview asked teasingly.

White's face broke into a wide-toothed childish grin. "Yes, sir! It's beyond my wildest dreams or expectations." White could hardly contain himself. The hell with it, he decided. Why shouldn't he be happy? But he needed a few moments to savor the incredible news.

"Have you informed James Ball, at the Agency?"

"Yes, sir. Same reaction as mine." White thought about how fortunate he and Ball had been for having gone with Desaix to Tokyo. At the time, they were both upset at having to go along. But had they not gone, none of this would have happened.

Westview had expected White's response. He had just asked White as a way of checking on his credibility. A minor point. But as President, he must always remain vigilant, especially with his closest advisors, lest they see themselves not as advisors, but as the President's surrogate—or perhaps his replacement. That was precisely the problem with the cabinet he had just summarily dismissed.

They had taken too many prerogatives upon themselves. They had forgotten who, in fact, was the President of the United States. They had confused the opportunity to provide advice as substitute for acting as the implementers of that advice. And recently, they hadn't even been able to provide the necessary information he had requested. But in all fairness to them, he had asked them questions he knew beforehand they were not going to be able to answer.

His mind turned quickly to the basic points he did want to make. Times are tough, but with faith in God and in ourselves, together we can defeat our enemies.

Desaix's memorandum was very clear—the President of the United States should always assume the moral high ground by invoking very strong images and principles of morality and religion. Funny, he thought, that a man like Desaix would provide that type of advice. He was sorry now he had brought Desaix into it.

Prince had called Westview to tell him that Desaix now had his medical and psychiatric file. What a goddamn pain in the ass that Desaix could be, thought Westview, as he hooked his microphone to his tie.

"Mr. President, in exactly five seconds you will be on the air. Please watch the red light." White was excited. Soon he would hear his name mentioned in front of an audience of two hundred million people.

"You're on the air, Mr. President!"

Reading from the TelePrompTer, Westview looked into the television camera with the flashing red light.

My dear fellow citizens. I am talking to you this evening in order to keep you abreast of the unusual events that have occurred in Germany between the U.S. and the Russian Federation.

I call it unusual because for the past ten years the United States of America and the Russian Federation have been working together as partners in helping to create a new world order of peace and prosperity. However, certain renegade units of the Russian Army that were stationed in Germany have refused to return to Russia as originally planned. Instead, they have tried to precipitate an incident with our military troops stationed in Germany in order to force both the United States and Russia into an unconscionable war.

Let me assure you that I am doing everything possible to find a just and fair solution to this situation. I have asked the Secretary General of the United Nations, as well as key allies, to help us mediate this crisis initiated by several disgruntled Russian generals.

Let me assure you of another thing. Under no condition will I use nuclear weapons, even if our Russian adversary makes a first strike.

I will, however, retain the right to retaliate by any other means that I deem appropriate.

Since its ill-fated experiments with perestroika and glasnost, the Commonwealth of Independent States has been gradually returning, with the help of their military and security apparatus, to its old totalitarian ways. As Americans we had hoped that the experiment in freedom that had taken place in the Soviet Union during the late 1980s would have taken hold and been allowed to flourish, as it has in the rest of Eastern Europe.

Unfortunately, that does not seem to be the case. A secretive elite group of Russian military officers has been in the forefront of trying to return Russia to the old ways of totalitarianism as a way of trying to stop what they perceive to be the continuing deterioration of their society.

It is my intention, as the leader of the free world, to do everything possible to prevent this from happening, in a peaceful, internationally acceptable way.

In order to insure that I have the best possible talent to resolve this crisis, I have brought several new people into my cabinet. As Secretary of Defense, I have appointed Lieutenant General Thomas Mapplethorpe, who will resign his military commission in order to comply with the law that requires that only civilians can be Secretary of Defense.

As my new National Security Advisor, with direct responsibility for managing the crisis, I have appointed Lieutenant General Richard White, who is presently Director of the Office of Signals Intelligence Operations at the National Security Agency.

As the new Director of the Central Intelligence Agency, I have chosen James Ball, presently the Director of the Office of Scientific Intelligence at the Central Intelligence Agency.

Chester Manning, my long-trusted friend and colleague, will remain as Secretary of State and will be appointed the new Chairman of the Crisis Management Group.

I have informed both the Speaker of the House and the Majority Leader of the Senate of my choices. Because of the unusual circumstances they have assured me of their immediate confirmation by Congress. In the meantime, my appointees will be serving as acting heads of their respective departments.

There is no question that these are the finest public servants that I could have chosen at this point in time.

As a final word, let me add that as Americans we are a community of conscience. We know it is our duty and obligation to keep the flame of justice and right burning the world over.

Ours is a life of freedom and choice. And so if it be necessary, as free men and women, we will go forward to fight a just and moral war, armed with a trust in God.

God bless you all.

# CHAPTER
## 27

When Desaix and Mary emerged from the underground Civil War tunnel, they found themselves on an empty, garbage-strewn parking lot in Anacostia, several blocks from Saint Elizabeth Hospital. They walked a few blocks to a major traffic artery, hailed a cab, and headed for Mary's apartment.

Sitting next to each other in the back of the cab, each reflected silently on the day's events. In a perverse sense, each had endured a parity of injury, sustenance, and betrayal. Desaix had been shot in his left shoulder. Mary had been shot in her right thigh. Each had nursed and bandaged the other. Each had provided nurturance and succor to the other. They had experienced more in their few hours together than most would experience in a lifetime.

Desaix was still in a state of disbelief over a psychiatric hospital being used as a staging area for covert military operations. While he was no great moralist, the use of such a facility for a military purpose was a violation of the basic sanctity of medicine. Hospitals were the sanctuary for the sick and the infirm.

The fact that a psychiatrist was an integral part of all of this was almost less disturbing to Desaix than the simple idea that Prince would allow his patients to be placed in danger. Like Amos, these patients were helpless; they had to rely on their alleged benefactor to protect them from any potential harm. So much for the Hippocratic oath.

As much as Desaix had spent years trying to rid himself of responsibility for patients—in his dual professional career as psychiatrist and crisis manager—he would never compromise the well-being of those patients he had decided to treat. Even when he flew overseas, he always made certain that another psychiatrist covered them.

Then, of course, there was the matter of the President's file. How the hell did this fit into all that had been happening over the past two days? Was this military coup Mapplethorpe's way of trying to get rid of a President who could become psychotic? Was Prince the President's psychiatrist? Or was he simply hiding Westview's medical records from someone else? And if he were the President's psychiatrist, which seemed likely, then how and why was he involved in a coup against him?

In contrast to Desaix, Mary felt betrayed by both Brooks and the President. But she was reluctant to say anything to Desaix about her feelings. She still had a lot of reservations about him.

On the positive side, she was impressed by his vitality, intelligence, spontaneity, and resourcefulness. He was clearly committed to his convictions. But she was having a hard time discovering exactly what those convictions were. He wanted to uncover the perpetrators of the coup and try to stop them. He also seemed committed to being part of ending the U.S.-Russian conflict in Germany. But there was something too effortless about the way he encountered and maneuvered around danger. It was almost as if he were having a temptestuous affair with uncertainty and imminent death. Desaix went beyond the standard definitions of courage and bravery.

From her ten years experience in the Secret Service, she recognized action junkies like Desaix, who would find life intolerable if there wasn't the potential of danger just around the corner. Unfortunately, that type of addiction was infectious. If she stayed around him too long, she might end up like him. She wondered if he had any insights into his own behavior. Was he running away from something—depression, boredom, rejection, fear?

But beneath Desaix's psychological tempest of activity and defiance she sensed a gale of gentle care and nurturance. She could still feel his fingers roaming over her body, healing her wound and reassuring her that everything would turn out for the best, if only she kept the faith in both herself and him. Together they could confront the mounting odds against them. Like all gifted healers, he seemed to empower her with the feeling that the resolution to any problem or crisis resided within her. At one and the same time, he made her feel both special and accepted. Something she had not felt for a long time.

Mary closed her eyes and rested her head on Desaix's shoulder, but her mind was feverishly at work. What happened to David Brooks? From the day he was assigned to the Presidential Protective Detail, at the insistence of President Westview, she had nothing but distrust. He was one of those cocky gunslingers, reeking with self-confidence and contempt for everyone else.

Clearly, he had been placed in Westview's detail to keep an eye on the President. But who was behind Brooks?

Nothing made sense.

When the cab pulled up to her two-story Georgetown town house, she looked around the empty street. No unusual cars. No strange faces.

"Is it safe?" Desaix asked jokingly. At this point, he had very little energy left to take any precautions. He just wanted a little bit to eat, a very hot shower, and a few hours of sleep.

"It depends on whether you trust me or not."

For the first time in their relationship, he was taken aback by the seriousness with which she responded—almost as if she were unconsciously going out of her way to warn him about something. Her reaction was the same as when he had made his first sexual overture toward her. She had pulled back with a contemptuous expression. Yes, there was definitely something strange about her. At one and the same time, beckoning and repelling him.

Years of training forced Mary to nudge Desaix to the side of her front porch. The door was ajar.

With her gun raised upward, she kicked the door completely open and stepped inside, poised to fire. The living room looked like the aftermath of a tornado. Almost nothing had been left intact.

Mary picked up a broken piece of sandstone with a sigh. "This was a hand-carved statue made in Zimbabwe. It was given to me by a very dear friend who knew how much I loved African art."

"I'm sorry. It's all my fault. If you hadn't brought me here, none of this would have happened." Although Desaix felt contrite about the extensive damage done to her house, he knew that she was not completely blameless. It was she who had sought him out at his apartment. As a matter of fact, she had never given him a convincing answer to how she had known where he was after the shootout at the Kalorama Guest House. She told him that through the police radio channels she had picked up that there had been a disturbance at the hotel, and surmised that he was in trouble. Subsequently, she tracked him down through the State Department Op Center.

But it didn't make complete sense. Something was missing. A piece of information. An unmentioned source. A hidden agenda.

But right now he was too tired to think.

"Let's see if they left anything in the refrigerator." Mary stepped over several pieces of broken furniture and limped into the kitchen. Her thigh was starting to hurt again.

"Before we do anything else, let me fix you up before you start to hemorrhage on me. Or we'll both be in trouble."

"Oh, stop worrying! I'm not a hemophiliac," she said from the kitchen, where she was busy preparing sandwiches.

Although they seemed to be getting along, something about her didn't seem right to him. He decided to look around, in the noble pursuit of trying to get to know her better through her possessions. Desaix had an aunt in New Orleans who once told him that if he looked into a woman's boudoir, he'd learn a hell of a lot more than if he made love to her. So he decided to experiment with his aunt's wisdom.

He was surprised to see an Edwardian walnut dresser and armoire in Mary's bedroom. Although no expert in antique furniture, he had always associated the heavy, tall Edwardian pieces with masculine taste. He rifled quickly through her clothes, not knowing what to expect.

"How do you like your peanut butter?" Mary asked from the kitchen counter.

"Smooth or chunky. I don't care," he yelled back. He quickly and quietly went through her dresser drawers. One for sweaters. One for leotards, tights, swimsuits. One for lingerie. There were a few scarves and earrings scattered here and there. Nothing of significance. Until Desaix came to a neatly folded pile of silk underwear, under which he found a stack of glossy Polaroid pictures, images that Mary would not want to place in a family album. There were pictures of her in different nude poses. Clearly, he thought, she was a closet exhibitionist. From the various suggestive positions, Desaix inferred that she was posing for someone with whom she had a very close and trusting relationship. But that other person was not evident. He quickly riffled through the pictures.

In one photograph, Mary's body was splayed over a bed, her fingers caressing her thick sensuous vulva, almost inviting the photographer to make love to her. In another picture, Mary was bent over a chair, spreading her vaginal lips with her fingers, seeming to invite the photographer to enter her from the rear.

The picture that excited him most was the one that showed her crawling on the carpeted floor, tongue extended in a highly suggestive manner. Reflected in the full-length mirror of the armoire was a naked leg.

The next few pictures showed Mary wearing black stockings and high-arched shoes with stiletto heels, holding a short black whip. She had a playful, teasing expression on her face. Again, Desaix saw the hint of a limb in the reflection from the mirror. But the next picture stopped him cold. There it was. Just what he had suspected. Mary was lying on a bed with an unidentified woman on top of her. They were, in what the New Orleanians called, *la position soixante-neuf*. Each one was performing cunnilingus on the other one. Desaix could recognize Mary's face easily. But there was something familiar about the other woman as well. Her long torso, her pendulous breasts hanging over Mary's abdomen, the cut of her hair.

The photos of lesbian love made Desaix extremely excited. Especially when he finally recognized the other woman—Judy Taylor, the deceased Assistant Secretary of State for Public Affairs. A woman who had once been his lover, and with whom he had made love less than twenty-four hours ago.

He put down the pictures and lost himself in his feelings. He was aroused not so much by the identity of the lovers but by the thought of how tender women could be with each other when they were making love. The idea that two women were trying to bring complete and unrestricted pleasure to each other through the nonromanticized instruments of tenderness, compassion, caressing, and kissing was truly the erotic aspect of lesbian love. He envied a woman's ability to employ those emotional faculties with which he felt uncomfortable—empathy, patience, compassion, and tenderness.

He had no patience for men who boasted of their sexual prowess, for theirs was frequently a simplistic, if not brutal, concept of sex, celebrating the act of love as a misbegotten series of increasingly more rapid and forceful penetrations. The harder, the faster . . . the better! Similarly, he disliked making love to those women who had grown up with the classic male-dominated notion of eroticism, which consisted primarily of phallic penetration and dominance.

Desaix had learned to respect the fact that, for the most part, women preferred the company of other women, both as friends and as lovers. But the ultimate paradox of lovemaking was that although a woman could make wonderful love to another woman, it in no way precluded her from making just as wonderful love to a man. As a matter of fact, the women with whom he had had the most fulfilling sexual escapades were those very same women who had had, at one point or another in their life, a woman lover.

He recalled how, from the outset, Judy Taylor was willing to be as flexible as he wanted her to be. She was almost too compliant. Too giving. Judy responded in the prescribed fashion of heterosexual love. One for him. One for her. And then one for the both of them, together. The de rigueur mode of heterosexual lovemaking in the late 1980s and 1990s, the ethos of a mutually dependent generation of the 1990s, a direct visceral reaction to the me-ism of the hedonistic 1980s.

It was only when he purposefully threw Judy off-balance during their lovemaking, by responding in unexpected gentle ways, that he allowed her to feel completely uninhibited. He insisted that she allow herself to be selfish. Only then could he enjoy himself in her presence.

It was she who taught Desaix that a mature, experienced woman can have equally good sex with a man or a woman, without having to pigeonhole herself into any commonly accepted pathology. Judy was, as she often proclaimed sarcastically, a woman for all seasons. Freud would have been fascinated by her. Polymorphous perverse sexuality was her mother's milk, so to speak. And she was proud of it.

The next Polaroid shot proved that point. Judy was bending over Mary and kissing her breasts while an unidentified man stood behind Judy, entering her from the rear. Desaix could see a portion of the man's penis entering Judy, while he held on to her buttocks with his left hand. The only identifying characteristics were a marriage ring on his wedding finger and a pinky ring with what looked like a crest.

Ménage à trois. Troilism! He wondered whether the photographer who took the picture didn't make this arrangement a ménage à quatre. And who could that be? God bless Judy, thought Desaix. She never did believe that the sexual act should be restricted to simply two people.

Hearing Mary walk toward the bedroom, Desaix stuffed the last photograph into his pants pocket and closed the drawer.

"Did you find anything interesting?" Mary asked, holding a tray of sandwiches and cold drinks.

"No. I was looking for some lingerie that I could use to bandage up your thigh. It's still bleeding." Desaix sounded calm and collected. When caught in the middle of an immoral or illicit act, he thought, admit to nothing. Compose yourself. Lie like crazy. Then go on the offensive. "A peanut butter sandwich. I love it. With or without nuts?"

"What the fuck were you doing in my dresser drawer?" Mary's hands started to tremble.

"Well, to tell you the truth, I'm a transvestite—"

"Cut the bullshit, Desaix! You're a goddamn liar! Did you get to see what you wanted?"

"I don't know what you mean." Desaix walked toward her, trying to decide how he was going to calm her down.

"Were you titillated?" Mary was straining to steady the shaky tray.

"What do you mean?" Desaix held her arms, to stop her trembling.

"Let go of me!"

"Calm down."

"Calm down! Are you fucking nuts?"

"Big deal—a couple of photos. So what? I've got a whole bunch of them at my place." He stroked her arms gently. "Just take it easy. We've been through a lot together."

"Take it easy? You goddamn sanctimonious son of a bitch!"

"Listen, I'm sorry. I didn't mean to upset you. I was looking for some smooth linen to wrap your thigh. So help me God! That's the honest truth!" Keep lying, he told himself.

She broke out of his grip, and threw the tray down on the carpeted floor. "Don't patronize me!" she shouted, as her whole body started to shake.

"I'm not patronizing you! I'm simply trying to say I'm sorry. It was a stupid thing for me to have done. I'm sorry." He tried to embrace her.

She pulled away from him. "Who the fuck do you think you are to come in here and rifle through my drawers? The FBI? The Secret Service? The Agency?"

"Does it matter that I'm only a misdirected Deputy Assistant Secretary of State for East Asian and Pacific Affairs?" He reached out to her again. But she wouldn't let him touch her.

"Funny! Real funny!"

"Are you angry with me for what I did, which I admit was not totally above board? Or are you angry with me for what I found out?" His voice was soothing as he started to approach her once again. He knew she felt humiliated, but he wanted her to understand that, instead of his being repulsed, he was turned on. As a matter of fact, the more they fought, the more ardently he wanted to make love to her.

"Let me ask you, as a shrink . . . you are a shrink, right?" she asked.

"Yes, I am a shrink." He allowed her the opportunity to demean him.

"As a professional who is supposed to understand people's motives and peculiarities, what would you say about your behavior—rifling through a woman's dresser, looking through her most intimate garments and mementoes?"

"I would say it's inexcusable and reprehensible."

"Inexcusable and reprehensible?" She paused to catch her breath. "You sound like a goddamn truant officer."

"What do you want me to say?"

"That you are FUCKING SICK!" she screamed.

"Maybe you're right! I could never complete my analysis because my training analyst felt I was too filled with pathology and too resistant to change."

"Great! Now you're going to give me a fucking diagnosis of your sickness. You are SICK! Do you know that, Doctor! YOU ARE FUCKING SICK!"

"If it makes you feel any better, then I will tell you I am sick. I won't argue the point."

"Good! Now get the hell out of here!" She pointed toward the door.

"Do you really want me to go?" Desaix asked plaintively.

"Yes, I do!" She seemed bewildered by his patently absurd question.

"Okay! Do you mind if I call the Op Center and tell them where I'm going to be." He paused, purposefully looking sheepish. "Just in case something might happen to me."

"What a goddamn manipulator you are! You really are shameless." Mary started to pick up the sticky sandwiches.

"I plead guilty. I am a manipulator. I am a deceiver. I am a trespasser on private property. I am everything you say I am. But I also care a lot for you." He bent down to help her, not sure what had made him say that. It was true he cared about her. But was it because they were struggling? Or because he knew he could never really have her. The more he wondered, the more excited he became.

"When does someone like you ever play it straight?"

"What do you mean?"

"You know exactly what I mean."

"It's a good question. I don't know."

"Even when you make a comment like that, it gives me the creeps." Mary stood up and threw the pieces of broken glass in the wastebasket.

"So there's no hope for me? Is that it?"

"Hope? Shit! You are so hopeless, you make Peter Pan look prematurely gray."

"So I have to grow up."

"About two eons worth of time!" She pushed him away as he tried to approach her.

"So I'm immature, and you're . . ." He hesitated, realizing that he was about to put his foot in his mouth.

"I'm what?" she asked with a defiant smirk.

Desaix didn't answer. There was something comical about the whole situation. Here they were, arguing as if they were two lovers. And what was it that he had uncovered? A few pictures of herself and Judy making love. So what? "I would say that you've turned out to be a very pleasant and interesting surprise," he said cautiously, starting to approach her.

"A surprise? Or weird, unusual, and perverted?" But she didn't stop his approach. Something inside her told her to trust him. Contrary to her own defensive expectations, she believed him when he said he was pleasantly surprised.

"You know what the real problem is with you?" he asked, standing in front of her, gently stroking her face with his right hand.

Reflexively, she pulled away. "What is the real problem with me, Doctor?" Anger was a lot easier to handle than the flush of excitement she was feeling.

"Your real problem is that you don't appreciate how wonderfully unique you really are." When he tried to stroke her face again, she didn't resist his overture though he felt her tremble at his touch.

"Unique, as in unicorn? Or unique as in deviant?" Her voice softened. She could feel herself relaxing.

"Unique as in special. Unique like someone who deserves to be loved in very special ways." His face was flushed with anticipation, and he made no effort to hide it.

"Why do I feel that I'm being handled right now? Subjected to the famous Desaix approach?" She paused to catch her breath. "Why do I have this terrible feeling that I know what's about to come next?"

"Did Judy ever tell you about me?" Desaix couldn't resist asking the question.

"Please don't!" Mary wasn't sure what she was feeling. Did she really want to push away from him?

"I think it's both beautiful and extremely exciting that you and I could have loved and been loved by the same person." Without a doubt, the notion that he and Mary had both made passionate love with Judy excited him beyond any other erotic fantasy. He hoped he could convey the excitement of that image to Mary.

"Don't! Please don't! You've done enough emotional damage for one day." Mary turned away from him.

"I miss her too!" Desaix took Mary's hands and led her toward the bed.

"No! I can't talk about it!" She pulled away from him. "I just can't!"

"She loved you, and you loved her. She loved me, and I loved her. It's not a very complicated equation." Desaix started to unbutton Mary's blouse. She wasn't wearing a bra.

Mary held her breath.

Gently stroking her pear-shaped breasts with the tips of his fingers, he felt her nipples become firm at his touch. Slowly, he placed her breast into his mouth and tenderly sucked her small brown nipple. He then ran his tongue along the nape of her neck as he removed her blouse. Her body shuddered and her skin broke out in goose bumps. He lay her down on the disheveled bed, and with an effortless motion, careful not to hurt her wounded thigh, he pulled off her torn skirt and panties. Her arms stretched out to receive him. She was naked on the bed, trembling with the excitement of anticipation.

Desaix undressed himself and simply lay along side of her, admiring the taut, petite, slightly tanned body. He ran his fingers up and down her body lightly, watching the goose bumps appear and disappear.

"Mary, close your eyes and try to imagine that the hand that is touching you is the same hand that made love to Judy. Think of her as I make love to you." Desaix whispered, "Don't be afraid to tell me what you like or don't like."

Her body relaxed beneath his fingers. While he gently sucked her nipples, his fingers made their way down her body, resting seductively just above her mons pubis. He paused, and lifted his fingers ever so slightly just above the tuft of brown curly hair. Desaix watched her rib cage rise and fall as she started to breathe more deeply, more rapidly. She was beginning to pant in expectation of what he was about to do to her. Her arched pelvis invited his fingers into her.

Desaix's fingers descended into the scented ruffle of pubic hair. He felt her pelvis reach up to him. The farther down his fingers descended along the thick folds of her vagina, the more slow and gentle his touch became, lifting each of the labia, teasing it ever so lightly with a pinch of his fingers. Approaching the clitoris with his fingers, he paused and raised the hood above the swelling organ so that he could have better access to it. He lowered his head and blew gently over the clitoris, awakening it to the possibility of imminent engorgement and discharge. He too was becoming erect. But he had learned a long time ago that he would not intrude his desires upon her, at least not until she was satisfied first.

What excited him most was the thought that he was about to satisfy her— the way she could best enjoy it.

As his tongue entered her vagina, she moaned with pleasure, pushing her pelvis into his face, gyrating so that not one part of her vagina would be forgotten, and waited, impatiently.

Quickly, he thrust his tongue in and out of her, counterpointing her increasingly more rapid and circular pelvic motions. He knew that she was beginning to lose conscious control of her pelvic movements, and realized her body was literally his now. He could do with it whatever he wanted. But for the moment, his only concern was for her to come over his face, discharging her sweet vaginal fluids into his mouth.

*A little harder! A little faster! Oh my God! I'm flying away!* The words raced through her mind. *Please don't stop! Don't hesitate, not even for a moment! Oh, Judy! Oh my God! Don't stop! Please, don't stop! I'm shaking all over! I can't keep control of myself! But please don't stop!*

Convulsing with joy, Mary pulled Desaix up toward her, intertwining her body with his. Even the pain in her thigh couldn't take away the pleasurable intensity of the moment.

Desaix wrapped his body around her, letting her contract with the feeling of safety and warmth she must have experienced with Judy.

In his own way, Desaix knew he had just made love to two women.

"Are you all right?" he asked after she buried her head in the nape of his neck and started to sob.

"Yes," she answered very softly.

"You'll miss her, won't you?" he said stroking her hair.

"Yes, very much." She looked straight at him with tear-filled eyes. "I was jealous of you . . . because you were the last one to have made love with her." She wiped the tears away, but discovered that she couldn't stop crying.

"It's more than just Judy, isn't it?" he asked.

She took her index finger and ran it slowly over his face.

"Is it a schizophrenic's face or a sociopath's face?" he questioned

"Maybe a little bit of everything. But what I see right now is a very caring, tender man who, despite the fact that he can be very wily and dangerous, was extremely considerate with one very scared woman."

"How do you know that being considerate isn't part of this wily character's modus operandi?" He held her face in his hands, and gazed into her eyes. They were softer, less wary. The evening's residue of anger and humiliation had disappeared completely.

"Because I'm beginning to think you're a big phony."

"What?" Desaix raised himself upon his elbows, indignantly.

"I think you take great pride in looking and acting tough." She clenched her fist and tapped him with it. "But anyone who can make love as tenderly as you do can't be all that bad."

"Would you believe that I really care about you?" he asked, surprised at how easy it was to make that statement.

"Yes, I do believe that you like me. And I'm going to tell you a little secret. I like you. Perhaps more than I should."

"Is that why you were crying?"

"Are you always so smart?"

"I try hard to be," he said, realizing he was entering unfathomed waters, that he had pierced her psychological defenses. She was extremely vulnerable, and so potentially dangerous to herself—and others. At this point in their relationship, she might become dependent and needy. And that would be a pivotal point. He felt his own body tense up at the thought of an unspoken requirement for continuous emotional sustenance.

"I'm not frightening you, am I?" She stroked his cheek, sensing a change had taken place.

"No, not at all." He was lying, and she knew it. "Why do you ask?"

"I don't know. I just have this feeling that you're pulling back from me." She was beginning to feel anxious. It was the same old pattern. Once she revealed any emotional vulnerability, she became prey to her own fear of losing control, and projected all types of fears on the person to whom she was closest.

"Mary, we're just beginning what could be a wonderful relationship. Be easy on yourself. It's going to take time for us to really get to know each other."

"But it's not fair. You've just made me feel totally content. What can I do to make you feel the same way?" She kissed his neck, his chest, and worked her way down his torso. She could sense his body tense up. "Is there something wrong?"

"No, so why don't you just come back up here and relax." He pulled her toward him and held her head in his hands. "Mary, please understand that I am genuinely happy just to be with you. I'm not an emotional or sexual accountant. You don't have to try to satisfy me because that's what the sex manual prescribes. Trust me, we'll have a lot of other opportunities together."

What he really wanted to say, but couldn't, was that she would have to learn how to make love to him so that it didn't feel to him as if she were mechanical. But now was not the time.

"That's not fair! I don't like the fact that you can tell me when and what I should or shouldn't do—especially when it comes to lovemaking." She pulled away from him and rolled over to the other side of the bed. She was hurt and confused.

"I didn't mean to hurt your feelings. Maybe we should stop while we're still ahead."

"Jesus, is this what happens when a woman opens up to you?"

"What do you mean?" Desaix sat up and started to dress himself. He realized he may have made a mistake and penetrated her defenses too quickly. What was coming out was the underlying rage that was an inherent part of her loosening self-control and her fear of becoming dependent on him.

"What do I mean? Look at me, damnit! I'm lying here naked, having just been made love to by a man who has mind-fucked me with the fantasies of a past woman lover. He, of course, is above any need for sexual release. At least not from a person like me. Right?" Without waiting for an answer, she continued, "So what does this sensitive, patient, understanding lover do? Take a guess?"

"What?" Desaix wanted to avoid an argument. She was trying to force him to say what he had been thinking.

"Oh, come on, Desaix! Don't be so fucking patronizing!" She stood up and started to dress. "He acts like a sexual martyr, sacrificing himself on the altar of helping the handicapped and the sexually deviant. Like me."

"Please, Mary! Let's stop now, before one of us says something that he or she doesn't mean."

"Dr. Desaix Clark, for your information you already crossed that line when you informed me that my noble sensitive male lover was in no way in need of fulfilling his own sexual desire. He was too noble, too caring to impose his needs on this inexperienced sexual novice." She strapped on her gun. "Hey, lover boy! You want to know how to make a woman feel shitty— tell her that you don't want her to make love to you! That really does wonders for her ego."

"I'm really sorry! I wasn't thinking! You're right!" He reached out for her, but she pushed him away.

"Look, let's forget it." She picked up the phone, took a deep breath, and called her office at the White House. "Do I have any messages?" she asked the voice on the other end.

The White House night switchboard operator told her that the President's office had been looking for her all day.

"Thank you." She looked at Desaix with a frown.

"What is it?"

She waved Desaix to be patient while she dialed the President's office. "Hello, Randy, this is Mary. Fine. The President's been looking for me? Who else?" She turned to Desaix and covered the phone. "Westview wanted to see you as well." She listened for a moment. "Okay, right away. Tell him I'm on my way."

"Me? Why does he want to see me?" Desaix suddenly realized that he hadn't called his office all day.

"Apparently he was briefed about our little escapade at St. E's, and wants us to get over there ASAP." She hung up the phone.

Desaix immediately picked it up again to call State's Op Center, which normally kept track of his whereabouts twenty-four hours a day.

"Are we getting a little competitive here? First my phone call, then your phone call?" she asked, needing a little revenge.

Desaix ignored her comment as he held the phone. "Secretary of State Manning? Please leave an electronic message that I will be able to sit in his meeting with Yutaka Imai at 9:30 in the morning. And who else? Call Yutaka Imai and tell him I can see him sometime during the day, and that I'll call him back tomorrow. Thanks!" He hung up.

"You're one busy little beaver, aren't you?" For a moment there she could see that she was getting to him.

"Truce!" He crossed his fingers high in the air as if warding off an evil spirit.

"We still have to work together, don't we? Or do we?" Mary decided to go on the offensive. She just couldn't let him leave the room with that smug, sanctimonious air. Before anything else could proceed, she had to rectify her hurt pride.

"Let's go then. You don't want to keep the prez waiting for us."

As he walked toward the door of the bedroom, she stopped him and kissed him passionately on the lips. "Let the President wait! God knows how many times he's kept me waiting." She started to unbutton Desaix's shirt, and unbuckle his pants. Before Desaix knew it, she was on her knees fellating him. Her determination surprised him and excited him. He barely had time to wonder how he felt about this aggressiveness before she brought him fully erect. When he was sufficiently excited, she lay her compliant partner on the bed and mounted him. Rocking gently back and forth, she felt increasingly excited as Desaix closed his eyes, arched his back, and moaned. A wonderfully satisfying moan.

"One for me! One for you! And next time, one for us!" Mary laughed mischievously after it was over.

"That was wonderful!" Desaix kissed her passionately, grateful that she had persevered. Now he knew they really had a chance to endure as a couple. She was a fighter. "Mary Dougherty, you're one hell of a testimony to Irish fortitude."

"I'm a testimony to no one and nothing." She dressed herself.

Desaix followed her example. "Just for the record, and for my compulsive need to stick my nose into everybody else's business, who the hell is that man in the photograph? And who took the picture?" Desaix received no answer as he followed Mary downstairs.

"Be a good boy, Desaix, and don't ask me any more naughty questions. It spoils the fun." She leaned over and gave him a kiss on the cheek before walking out the door. "By the way, lover boy, if you have no intention of using it as a sexual aid to stimulate your fantasies, don't forget to give me back the photo with the Holy Trinity."

"Of course!" Desaix replied unconvincingly as they arrived downstairs and walked toward the cab. For a moment, Desaix could have sworn he was with Judy Taylor.

They sped around Washington Circle, in front of the emergency room of George Washington University Hospital, heading down the large, empty streets of Pennsylvania Avenue, populated by the occasional homeless person camped along the grates in the sidewalk, wrapped in the protective covering of shredded blankets and cardboard boxes.

"Wouldn't you like to stop off at the ER and get that wound sewed up?" he asked. Although the wound wasn't as serious as he initially thought, he still wanted to make certain it was properly cared for.

"No, I'm fine, but thanks for the concern," she said as they continued racing down Pennsylvania Avenue. Driving up to the low-lying cement barricades surrounding the distinctive spear-shaped black metal gates of the White House, she stopped to assay the situation.

"Is it Westview in the picture?" Desaix was still preoccupied with the identity of the third person in the photograph.

"Please, Desaix! Now is not the time!"

"It's got to be the President! He loved Judy. Judy loved you. And you were in charge of guarding the President. So you knew all his comings and goings. QED. The third person has to be President Westview!"

"Desaix enough!" She pulled up to her designated space and parked the car. Where the hell were Dobbins and Smith, she wondered. They should have been on the graveyard shift. Instead, there was a whole new group of Secret Service agents and executive security guards she didn't recognize at all.

Desaix and Mary walked up to the guard house.

"Yes, ma'am? May I help you?" the thin, polite executive security guard asked.

"I'm Mary Dougherty, Chief of the President's Protective Detail. I have an appointment with the President."

"Yes, ma'am! May I please have your identification badge so that we can check it out." Without pausing to hear her response, he turned toward Desaix, "Sir, may I see your identification, please."

"This gentleman's with me! He is a Deputy Assistant Secretary of State. I can vouch for his clearances."

"Yes, ma'am, I understand. But I still must insist on seeing his identification."

Desaix pulled out his State Department badge and handed it over to the guard, who took both badges and gave them to an agent seated in the guard house. He, in turn, punched their identification numbers into a terminal. It took several minutes for him to receive the response to clear them through.

"Ms. Dougherty and Dr. Clark, you may go in through the Seventeenth Street exit." The guard snapped to attention.

Mary and Desaix walked through the side door of the West Wing, passing a series of agents, each of whom checked and rechecked both of their credentials. Mary knew none of them.

Nowhere in the West Wing of the White House could Mary see evidence of her Secret Service agents.

# CHAPTER
## 28

As they approached the oak doors of the President's office, Randy Newmann ran up to Mary.

"At last, a familiar face," Mary said.

"Mary, where have you been? We've all been worried about you! Every hour on the hour, the President had asked me where you were." Randy hugged Mary while nodding to Desaix. "The President is waiting for you too."

"What's happening around here? I don't recognize anyone. Where are my Secret Service agents?" Mary knew that Randy would tell her as much as possible without compromising her boss's trust.

"You've still got a few more minutes before you have to go in," Randy said, checking her watch. "We've just come back from the Alternate Command Center at Fort Ritchie. It's been crazy. Everything is topsy-turvy. The President, I'm sure, will tell you all about it. But we have a whole new team on board. The President has made a clean sweep of everyone and everything, including the Secret Service."

"It almost looks like a coup," Desaix replied with a smile.

Desaix's axiom: always, but always, be nice to secretaries, and assistants. For they represent the true hidden power of any system. A pleasant word, a box of chocolates, a bouquet of flowers, and an uncondescending attitude were the basic commodities influencing secretarial power.

"Why don't you mention that to the President, Dr. Clark. I think he would find that quite amusing. He wants to see you alone." Randy led Desaix into the Oval Office and closed the door.

Desaix was surprised to see the President pacing nervously around the room, his body shaking with anger.

"Where have you been? I've been waiting for you." Westview said, then motioned him to sit down, dismissing all formality.

"You seem angry, Mr. President," Desaix spoke in a soothing tone.

"Very perceptive of you, Dr. Clark!" Westview's face was transforming into a grimace of disgust.

"What's wrong?" Desaix asked in a silky tone of voice. Above all else, Desaix wanted to avoid a confrontation. For reasons he could not yet fathom, Westview was clearly looking for a fight. Whether it was anger displaced from someone else, or from some other frustrating situation, it was something that Desaix had to uncover during this new therapeutic relationship.

"What's wrong? You dare to ask me what's wrong?" Westview asked as he grabbed a glass of water and gulped it down as if it were an elixir of rage.

"Donald, it would help me and you if you explained what it is that's making you so upset."

"What the hell do you call someone who reveals your confidences?"

"Mr. President, what are you talking about?" Desaix tried to eliminate any trace of defensiveness in his voice. Westview reminded him of those countless patients he called the help rejectors. These were patients who initially had come into his office desperate for help, and, as soon as they received the requested help from the doctor, they rejected it by abruptly terminating the therapy session. On the surface, this type of behavior seemed illogical and self-defeating. But in reality, it was a means by which the patient was able to reestablish control of his own life while at the same time throw the powerful helper into a state of helpless confusion.

"I got a call from Manning, who told me that you saw him yesterday, and told him that you thought that I was crazy because I thought there was a coup being plotted against me."

"That's interesting," Desaix said, not wanting to appear defensive. Yet at the same time, he wanted to see how far he could push Westview into revealing the full extent of his anger.

"Interesting?" Westview parodied Desaix's response. "Typical shrink talk."

"I'm sorry that you don't like my response."

"Let's just cut the psychobabble!" Westview drank another glass of water. "Did you or did you not tell Manning that you thought that I was crazy?"

"No, I did not!"

"Did you or did you not tell him that I had withdrawn several Special Forces units from Germany during a skirmish in order to preposition them at Saint Elizabeth Hospital for some future coup against me?" He paused to catch his breath. "A coup engineered by me against me."

"No!" Desaix was beginning to see a subtle pattern to Westview's questions. They all contained elements of projection, a psychological defense mechanism that allowed a person to absolve himself of responsibility for his own negative feelings by projecting them onto someone else.

"Did you or did you not tell him that I had stored canisters of hydrogen fluoride at the hospital to use to instigate urban riots?"

"I think you know the answer to that."

"Do I?" Westview grabbed a classified cable from his cluttered desk and threw it at Desaix. "Does that look familiar?"

Desaix glanced at the cable and pulled out a folded copy of Manning's cable from his suit pocket. He compared them. They were identical. Both cables informed Colonel Zarbitski to withdraw his Special Forces troops from Germany ASAP. By personal order of President Donald Westview.

"Well, Dr. Clark, how do you explain the fact that you have a copy of that highly restricted cable?" Without waiting for an answer, he continued in a rushed, manic tone of voice. "You weren't supposed to have a copy of that cable. The fact that you do is already incriminating."

Desaix listened attentively as Westview spun his paranoid web. Clearly, he had been talking to Manning, who must have revealed the substance of their conversation. Everything that Westview was accusing Desaix of was precisely what Manning had provided as evidence of Westview's insanity. Or did Westview simply reverse everything that Manning might have told him and projected it onto Desaix?

But one more disturbing possibility entered Desaix's mind. Had Manning set him up? And if so, why? The two essential ingredients of a paranoid fantasy—suspicion and projection—were beginning to dominate Desaix's own thoughts.

"With all due respect, Mr. President, what difference would it make if I either admitted or denied your accusations?" Desaix refused to act defensively. If he did, it would open a Pandora's box—to no useful purpose.

"Very clever, Dr. Clark! Very clever!"

"What would you like me to say?" Desaix was trying to draw out Westview. If he had only wanted to accuse Desaix of betraying a trust, he wouldn't have asked to see him. There was something else behind these accusations. But what? A cry for help? A need to reestablish personal control over his fragmenting mind? Or was it a setup?

"Tell me that I'm wrong!"

"If that's what you want to hear from me, then why subject me to this harangue?" Desaix asked, offering him an opportunity to be conciliatory.

"Oh, no! I know your mind games!" Westview's voice started to crack.

Desaix poured Westview a glass of water from the pitcher. He took it without saying a word. "Mr. President, when you first called me into this office, I told you then that I don't play mind games. And I certainly don't appreciate it when others play games with me."

Without responding, Westview continued to answer his own question. "What all of this means is that you have been spreading malicious rumors about me in an attempt to portray me as certifiably crazy."

"To what purpose, Mr. President?" Desaix asked. He sensed that he was coming closer to attaining Westview's original mandate: find out who, why, and when a coup is being fomented against me.

"Who was it who said that I was certifiably insane?"

"I don't know," Desaix replied calmly.

"Are you telling me that I'm imagining it?"

"No, I'm simply saying that I did not say it."

"Then who did?"

"I think you know who might have said those things against you." Desaix decided to resume the offensive.

"Who? I don't know what you're talking about."

"I think you do. All these accusations have been nothing but a poorly veiled attempt at testing my loyalty to you . . . or to that other person." Desaix stood up and started to walk toward the door.

"Wait a minute, Desaix!" Westview pressed the intercom button. "Randy, show him in!"

Westview carefully watched Desaix's reactions as Chester Manning walked into the room.

"Greetings, gentlemen!" Manning said cheerfully.

"Sit down, Chet."

"Thank you, Donald." Manning nodded to Desaix.

"I asked you to come over here in order to meet with me and Desaix. I was extremely disturbed by rumors that Desaix had been assigned by you to find out whether or not I was crazy. Is that right?"

"Donald, ever since childhood, I've thought that you were not always all there. If you know what I mean," Manning joked, feeling perfectly at ease.

"Don't give me that good ol' boy routine! It doesn't work on me." Westview became noticeably more agitated. "This isn't funny, Chet."

"What would you like me to say in front of Desaix, Donald? Just say the words, and I will repeat them verbatim." He smiled cryptically. "Desaix is no fool. He will form his own opinions about you, and I am certain about me. Whatever you may or may not want me to say will make very little difference to Dr. Clark. Isn't that right, Desaix?"

Desaix didn't respond. He wanted to see the psychological struggle between Westview and Manning play itself out without his intervention.

"Answer my question, Chet!" Westview repeated. "Did you or did you not instruct Dr. Clark, your protégé, to find out whether I was certifiably insane?"

"Donald, ever since we were kids, when you were wrong, you always went on the offensive. And your hostile tone of voice suggests that you are trying to make me look bad for something that you may have done."

"Don't play shrink with me, Chet! I already have one shrink too many as it is." Westview glanced at Desaix. "As your boss and Commander-in-Chief, I order you to tell me whether or not you ordered Desaix to find out if I am crazy."

"Take it easy, Mr. President. All I did was ask Desaix to fulfill his professional obligation as a psychiatrist because I was concerned. My instructions to him were very simple. Try to make sense out of a behavior pattern that appeared to me to be both inconsistent and self-destructive."

"Self-destructive?" Westview repeated the word as if he were being asked to swallow poison.

"Donald, what would you call a President of the United States who was trying to organize a coup against himself, only to expose it later on?"

"What the hell are you talking about?" Westview was losing his patience.

"Oh come on, Donald! If you want to play charades with me, then you're wasting everybody's valuable time." Manning stood up, ready to leave. "What the hell do you call your recalling of elite Special Forces units from a field of combat in Germany to a mental institution in Washington, D.C.? Rational? Logical? What in God's name were they supposed to be doing there? Handing out Thorazine . . . or grenades?"

"So it was you who gave Desaix that restricted cable!"

"Of course it was me! What the hell am I supposed to do when I see that kind of order? Laugh or cry?" Manning was disturbed. He sounded personally offended. "You may or may not believe this, Donald. But for over thirty years I have cared and worried about you. There were times that you could be absolutely lucid and brilliant. But there were other times when you were irrational, erratic, and volatile. When we were young, climbing our way to the top, your unusual behavior was considered interesting, quaint, and peculiar. But now that you're the President of the United States, you can't afford to appear interesting or peculiar. We're in the middle of a major international crisis, on the brink of World War III. And what do I uncover from sources? My best friend has ordered Special Forces units redeployed to St. E's to promote urban riots." Manning paused to catch his breath as he walked toward the door. "Of course I asked Desaix to help me out. If your best friend had broken his leg, what would you do, Donald? Call a wet nurse? No, you would do exactly what I did—call a doctor. Well, it happens that my best friend has serious emotional problems. Whom would you want me to call for help, Donald? General Mapplethorpe or Dr. Desaix Clark?"

Desaix felt trapped by the paranoid realities of both men, each trying to convince the other that theirs was the ultimate truth. At least this would allow him some point of reference from which to judge their subjective realities. Unfortunately, in a case of folie à deux, where there were two mutually conflicting realities, truth could only be measured in terms of relative lies.

"I'm sorry, Chet. Please forgive me." Westview rushed up to Manning and embraced him. Manning pointed to his own head, indicating to Desaix that he thought Westview was crazy.

"Good-bye, Mr. President! If you want my resignation, I will have it on your desk as soon as possible."

"No, Chet. I need a trusted friend who can speak his mind freely."

"So long, Desaix. Take care," Manning said as he walked out.

Westview sat down at his desk. "I'm convinced now. He's the one who's plotting the coup against me." He pushed the intercom button. "Randy, please ask Mary to come in and join Desaix and me."

"I think Manning does care about you," Desaix said, concerned by Westview's agitated state.

"I don't think so, Desaix. Secretary of State Chester Manning wants to be President of the United States. And you must help me to stop him!"

# CHAPTER

## 29

The law was very clear about the legal limits of the sacrosanct doctor-patient privilege, thought Desaix. If a patient threatens someone's life, the psychiatrist was legally required to report it to the authorities as well as the intended victim. Otherwise, the psychiatrist could be considered an accomplice to the patient's intended act of violence. But to whom would he report his patient, the President, wondered Desaix, who was completely taken aback by what he had just heard.

"You wanted to have me killed?" Desaix asked, expressing a suspicion he had been harboring since his near fatal encounter with Brooks at St. E's.

"That's right," Westview replied calmly.

Mary remained silent, tongue-tied for the first time in her professional life.

"That's right. I ordered your assassination." Westview cracked his knuckles, and deliberately looked away from each of them. He was trying to compose his thoughts. He wanted to be certain there would be no misunderstandings. With Desaix as his psychiatrist, there should be very little room for clouded thinking or confused statements.

"Why?" Desaix spoke calmly, but with a growing anxiety. He tried to separate his personal concerns from those that belonged to the province of psychotherapy.

"Because . . ." Westview paused.

"Yes, Mr. President?" Desaix pressed him, trying to break through the President's resistance. He studied Westview carefully, noting the tendency of his mind to meander.

"Oh, I hate the word 'assassination'. It makes things sound so brutal, so coldblooded."

"Are there any other terms you prefer?" Desaix was hoping Westview would free-associate so that he could understand how the President visualized murder.

"Operationally speaking, it's an assassination. But somehow I prefer to say the word 'death.'"

"Why?"

"It has a less threatening quality about it."

"What I think, Mr. President, is that you're trying to avoid being direct with me or with yourself. If you keep wandering around the central issue, we are not going to get anywhere. For the third time, Mr. President, why did you order my death?" Desaix was now brusque. Westview seemed to be playing a cat-and-mouse mind game.

"You were a nuisance!" Westview's reply was direct, but stated with a certain warmth in his voice.

"In what way was I a nuisance?" Desaix asked, not sure whether he should laugh at Westview's response. The President, however, was telling him the truth. It was important that Desaix understand what underlay Westview's concept of nuisance.

"You were sent to Japan because no one in the administration, including myself, wanted you anywhere near the White House during this international crisis. Everyone I spoke with had a well-articulated reason why you would be more of a hindrance than an asset. Quite frankly, although you are perceived by many of my senior advisors as incredibly bright, you are also a royal pain in the ass."

"Well, I certainly can't argue with that," Desaix replied nonchalantly. "I have been called worse."

I'm sure you have, thought Mary.

"But, Mr. President, is it your normal practice to kill every one of your pain in the asses in this administration?" Clearly, Westview's response had been flip, short of the mark. What was he hiding?

"No, Desaix, it's not my normal practice to order anyone's death. But in this case I felt I had no other choice." Westview looked somberly at Desaix with an expression devoid of any sense of guilt.

"I'm trying to understand why you would order my execution and then, two days later, invite me to the White House to become, shall we say, the President's analyst?"

"Sounds crazy, doesn't it? Maybe that's prima facie evidence that I do need a psychiatrist," Westview said, smiling inappropriately.

Desaix didn't respond. Was Westview in fact playing games with him? Was he stalling for time? Or was he indeed mentally ill? Desaix's mind raced through several psychiatric diagnoses—sociopathic personality, paranoia, Organic Brain Syndrome. He looked at his watch. In a few hours, he would have to see the Secretary of State.

"I ordered David Brooks to kill you because he convinced me that you were involved in a coup against me. Hopefully that answers part of the question."

"I'm not sure it answers the two questions I asked you," Desaix said. He never liked convoluted answers, and this one sounded like it could be the basis of a four-part TV mini-series.

"In other words, you don't believe me." He turned toward Mary. "You've known me for quite a long time, Mary. Do you believe me?"

"Mr. President, I can only say that I would like to believe you. I presume from the message you left on my machine that you knew that Desaix and I had a terrible experience with David Brooks."

"Yes, I was told that he almost killed both of you. That's precisely why I came to the conclusion that he was not working for me, but for them."

"What do you mean 'them,' Mr. President?" Mary asked, confused.

"I'm not totally clear who 'them' is. I think it's Manning, but it may be another group of senior advisors along with some elite units of the Army—all dedicated to overthrowing me." Westview was beginning to look distraught.

"Do you mean Project Baltimore?" Mary asked, handing Westview the list of Washington addresses marked Project Baltimore that she had found in the Army truck at St. E's.

"So you found out about Project Baltimore? Thank God! For a moment I was afraid you would think I was really crazy." Westview quickly glanced over the paper. "I can't tell you how grateful I am that you found this. It proves my suspicion that General Mapplethorpe is behind it all. His right hand is David Brooks, along with his adjutant colonel, Sonny Shaw, and Colonel Matthew Zarbitski. And I'm certain all of these people report directly to Chester Manning."

Desaix was becoming increasingly wary of Westview, especially after their preceding meeting. First, Westview sets himself up. Then Manning is supposedly trying to oust him. Now it's Mapplethorpe. The size, composition, and nature of this coup in Westview's mind was continuously changing. It looked as if Manning might be right.

"Mr. President, exactly what is Project Baltimore?" Mary asked, confused.

"Project Baltimore? That's a good question. I wish I could tell you about it. But I only know a limited amount. Even then, I'm not certain that I know what's relevant."

"Well, please tell us what you do know. Otherwise, Mary and I can't help you, if that's what you want." Desaix was aware of a sudden change in Westview's emotions. His speech and manner seemed frenetic. Only a few seconds before, Westview had been calm and collected. Now, why did he suddenly appear jumpy? Desaix again ran through a list of possible diagnoses. Because of Westview's extreme fluctuations in mood and concentration, Desaix suspected that in addition to Marfan's the President had some type of Organic Brain Syndrome, resulting from a lack of oxygen to his brain. But Desaix was wary of labeling him at this point.

"Of course . . . of course . . . I want you both . . . to help me. That's why you're here." Westview paused and looked anxiously at Mary and Desaix. "Have I said anything wrong? Is there anything you don't understand? What can I tell you that will convince you that I need your professional help, Dr. Clark?" Westview was noticeably agitated.

"What's bothering you, Mr. President?" Desaix realized that Westview was flooded with anxiety and was having a hard time concentrating on what he was saying.

"Nothing . . . absolutely nothing! What should be bothering me? Do you think I look bothered?" Westview's eyes bulged with fright.

Mary was having a hard time looking straight at him. Westview appeared out of control, helpless. Pitiful was the word that came to her mind.

"We were just talking about Project Baltimore, then you became extremely agitated. What went through your mind at that moment?"

"Desaix, I'm trying to understand what you're saying to me. Believe me, I'm trying very hard. But something upstairs in my head won't let me focus."

"Desaix, maybe we should stop here for a moment," Mary said, becoming upset as she watched the President lose control over his emotions. It reminded her of when her father went on his biweekly drinking binges— yelling, screaming, then begging for forgiveness.

"No! You can't stop now!" Westview exclaimed. "We don't have much time left! We're going to war if I don't get to talk to President Zotov!" Westview broke into a cold, clammy sweat. The pain in his stomach was more intense.

"Mr. President, would you like to lie down and rest?" Desaix took Westview's hands into his. He could feel Westview's pulse racing. He was in tachycardia. If he became any more anxious, he might go into cardiac arrest.

"Please, don't make me rest. Not now. Time is too short. I can handle it. Believe me. I've been in a lot more pain. This is nothing. Once, Dr. Prince gave me both Demerol I.M. . . . and some sedative. And I could tolerate the pain."

"What pain? Where do you feel the pain, Mr. President?"

"I'm all right. I'm all right. We must continue! Otherwise, we will all be victims. Please!" Westview withdrew his hand and grabbed his stomach.

"Does your stomach hurt, Mr. President?" Desaix was concerned that with Marfan's syndrome Westview had a good chance of having his abdominal aorta, the main blood vessel feeding his lower limbs, dissect and rupture. Similarly, this connective tissue disease could compromise the other parts of his cardiovascular system, his skeletal system, his nervous system, and his eyes.

"No!" Westview shouted. Staring anxiously into Desaix's penetrating eyes, Westview realized his lie was transparent.

"Please, Mr. President. Why don't you lie down?" Mary asked. She took his shaking hands and tried to lead him toward the couch.

"No, Mary. I want to sit here. If I lie down, I might fall asleep. And not get up."

The intercom phone rang. Mary picked it up, listened, and then covered the mouthpiece. "Randy wants to know if you want to talk to General White, who says it's urgent."

"Tell her to hold all visits and phone calls until we've finished here." Westview waved the phone away.

"General White at the NSA? The one who accompanied me to Japan?" Desaix asked, surprised to hear that White would have direct access to the President.

"The very same one. While you two were cavorting around town," he said, adding a touch of levity, "I appointed him my new National Security Advisor."

"What happened to General Mapplethorpe?"

"I fired him! And appointed him my new Secretary of Defense. Sounds crazy, doesn't it?" Westview broke out into laughter. "Maybe I really am crazy."

"Not if you knew what you were doing." Desaix recalled the old punchline to a tasteless joke involving a mental patient, "I may be crazy, but I'm not stupid." Clearly, if Westview was crazy, there was a method to his madness.

"I fired Mapplethorpe, Jenkins, Merck, McCormick, and Manning."

"You fired Manning?" Desaix looked bewildered. Then what was he doing at the earlier meeting?

"Yes, I fired him, then reappointed him back to State and Mapplethorpe as Sec Def. Now I can keep a close eye on both of them. But the rest have been replaced by White and Ball at the Agency."

"Ball? The same one who went with me to Japan?" Desaix was suspicious. Why should the two officials on his expedition to Japan be selected for cabinet positions? Neither White nor Ball were very senior within their own agencies. Was this simply a coincidence or was there some connection between the appointments and the negotiation mission to Japan? If Westview had tried to kill him, Desaix, was Westview also involved in Fitzpatrick's death?

"Why did you fire Mapplethorpe?" Desaix asked.

"Because he tried to kill you, Mary, and me," Westview replied very matter-of-factly.

"What evidence do you have for that?" Mary asked, stunned.

"Several days ago, when I met with the Crisis Management Group, I asked one simple question. How, in God's name, did this war get started? And do you know that no one could answer that question? Especially my National Security Advisor, General Thomas Mapplethorpe. He was the one who also insisted that Desaix be sent over to Japan at a time when I said we needed you here. He didn't want you here at all. He was afraid you might take over the entire action. So he rigged it bureaucratically for you to go with his Russian expert, Fitzpatrick, who was to keep tabs on you and make certain you remained there. But Fitzpatrick started to complain about his assignment."

"Is that why he was murdered?" Desaix sounded angry.

"Partly. He was also becoming a nuisance, sending back-channel communiques every day."

"Your administration has a nasty habit of dealing with nuisances by exterminating them," Desaix added sarcastically, suspicious of the President's answer.

"You're right! Except I didn't realize that this was a nasty habit that Mapplethorpe himself had acquired. I had direct intelligence that Brooks was really working for Colonel Zarbitski."

"So, why did you insist on my taking him into the Protective Detail?" Mary asked with a combined sense of curiosity and vindication.

"I have no one else to blame except myself. Mapplethorpe had convinced me that I could no longer trust my Secret Service because they were poorly trained and, if you excuse me, led by a woman with limited experience. So Mapplethorpe placed Brooks, who in turn brought in a whole group of Special Forces soldiers, who were, as you both now know, warehoused at St. E's with the full knowledge and consent of Dr. Prince."

"Mr. President," Mary asked, "are you saying that under Project Baltimore, Mapplethorpe is trying to mobilize a military coup against you by using the very people who were supposed to protect and serve you?"

Manning had been both right and wrong, thought Desaix. The President had ordered the Special Forces troops and the hydrogen fluoride to St. E's. But Mapplethorpe had been able to manipulate an already wary, frightened, and paranoid President by convincing him that there was an impending coup against him. He had him convinced that the most effective way to be protected was to go off-line and avoid the normal bureaucracy. Then Mapplethorpe brought in the very people who were going to commit treason. No wonder Westview had suspected Manning, Desaix, and Mary as potential threats to his personal security. Given the President's paranoid disposition, and his sense of imminent death, he could have been manipulated to believe that anyone wanted to kill him.

"So Project Baltimore was the code word for it all," Mary said. "But Mr. President, I'm still not clear how this coup was to take place."

"Fitzpatrick was murdered by Brooks, under Mapplethorpe's direct orders, because he had uncovered the plans for the coup while he was in Japan. He tried his best to warn me, but, I didn't . . . believe . . . him," he said, his voice cracking. "That was only the beginning. As a result of the macabre way he died, I initiated my own investigation, without anyone knowing about it . . ." Westview saw the hurt expression on Mary's face and realized he was admitting he hadn't trusted her.

Desaix gave her a comforting glance, but it didn't work. She turned away.

"I discovered that Mapplethorpe had stockpiled a huge supply of hydrogen fluoride at St. E's." Choking on his words, Westview continued, hesitantly, "All of this was being done, of course, with the full consent of Prince, who threatened to reveal my medical condition to the public if I tried to interfere."

Desaix could see that Westview was having a hard time coming to terms with what he thought Prince had personally done to him.

"Why do you think Prince was willing to help Mapplethorpe?" Desaix asked.

"You should tell me, Dr. Clark!" Westview's voice sounded inappropriately angry. "Isn't it true that psychiatrists score highest on tests measuring the need for power? Higher even than politicians like myself!"

Desaix realized that Westview's anger at Prince was being displaced onto him. That was simply the way the mind worked when it didn't want to directly confront the object of its anger. "Yes, Mr. President, psychiatrists, as a group, have a tendency to score the highest on the Authoritarian Personality Scale. On standard psychological tests they have the strongest need for power."

"See! You psychiatrists have a greater need for power than we professional power brokers. Ironic, isn't it?" Westview paused to take a drink of water. "Is it any wonder that Prince's collaboration with Mapplethorpe is for power? The need to be in the center of action. The need to feel as if you are wheeling and dealing. Just like you, Desaix." Westview didn't even try to hide his tone of moral superiority.

"What, then, is the objective of Project Baltimore?" Desaix asked, reluctant to continue. It was clear to him that any issue highlighting the President's sense of vulnerability would precipitate another angry outburst.

"The objective of Project Baltimore? Haven't you been listening to me? What the hell have we been talking about all this time?" Westview stood up, extremely restless. "The objective is quite simple: to create a state of national and international emergency that would justify the use of the military to take over all civilian functions. Once they have a de facto military occupation of the country, Mapplethorpe can bypass the Constitution, the Congress, the press—all by having tricked me into invoking a state of emergency."

"How could Mapplethorpe force you to do something you don't want to do?" Desaix knew that he was stoking Westview's rage.

"How? You're asking me? The foremost crisis manager is asking me how a trusted military advisor, as well as a trusted cabinet of senior officials, can blackmail me, the President of the United States?" Westview poured another glass of water from the pitcher on his table. He drank it down rapidly and broke into a spasm of coughing. Recovering from the cough, he continued. "Contrary to what most people think, the President has very little direct power to do anything but go to the bathroom. My strength is my ability to persuade. Persuade my cabinet, the bureaucracy, and Congress to do what I think they should have done in the first place."

Desaix felt that Westview was trying to manipulate him into believing that a President was not responsible for his actions. This type of externalization of responsibility was not unusual in paranoid disorders. The paranoid person would frequently portray himself as a victim who has been taken advantage of by his friends or family. So he projects his own malevolent intentions onto those who are closest to him. Then he doesn't have to take any responsibility for his own feelings. At the same time, the paranoid pesonality hopes to elicit feelings of pity from his doctor.

"Mr. President, are you telling me that you had no part in developing or implementing Project Baltimore?" Desaix wanted to assess the internal consistency of the President's allegations. Were they simply paranoid delusions with no basis in reality, were they based on fact, or half-truth, half-delusion?

"No, Desaix!" Westview replied. "I had a lot to do with Project Baltimore. That's why I feel so terrible about what I've done." Westview choked back his emotions. Appearing distraught was a humiliating experience for him.

Desaix recalled Manning's last gesture to him, indicating that the President was crazy, and was increasingly impressed with Manning's courage to sacrifice both his professional status and long-standing friendship with the President in order to make him realize that he needed professional help—ASAP.

"Maybe we should stop for a little while," Mary said, concerned that the President was under too much mental pressure.

"Thanks, Mary. I'm all right. I understand that Desaix is trying to help me. Why do you think I called both of you over here? Just to tell you that I think I have a renegade National Security Advisor and a treacherous Secretary of State? Hell, you know that better than I do!" Westview paused to take another drink of water. The pain in his stomach had subsided, and he felt more energetic.

The last point had not been lost on Desaix. Both Mary and he had passed through a baptism of fire. Only now was Westview assured that he could trust them. And for both a politician and paranoid personality, trust was a hard-earned commodity.

"No, I will assume full responsibility for the crimes I unwittingly initiated. As you may know, the Vice President, the Speaker of the House, President pro tempore of the Senate, and the major congressional leaders are currently out of the country for a variety of worthless purposes. That was no accident. There is a plan to have them executed at the proper time, as well as me, and God knows who else."

"That's insane! Absolutely insane!" Mary exclaimed, uncertain whether she could believe him and this incredibly improbable scenario.

"I know, Mary. It sounds like the rantings and ravings of a madman. But that's another reason I needed to talk to you, Desaix. You would understand ruthless ambition."

"I appreciate your trust in me and Mary. Please continue." Desaix was skeptical. Open gratitude from a paranoid patient was always suspect.

"After my unsuccessful meeting with Manning, I am now, more than ever, convinced that both of you must help me to stop Project Baltimore before the situation goes completely out of control. Manning, Mapplethorpe, and their cronies had convinced me that if we precipitated both a domestic and international incident that we were able to manage, the United States could pull out of its economic, political, and psychological slump. If we precipitated political unrest at home, just serious enough for us to justify the use of military force, I, as President of the United States, could use the period of unrest to consolidate and increase my power. And if we precipitated a minor incident in Germany against the remaining units of the Russian Army, I could mobilize the people in this country to back me, which would further increase my popularity at the polls."

"So Project Baltimore was a blueprint for the U.S. to return to economic and political supremacy?" Desaix's voice was subdued. He was convinced that what Westview had just told him and Mary sounded grandiose, suspicious, and irrational. On the other hand, it had to be taken seriously. The question for Desaix was how to stop this madness, real or imagined, from continuing any further. But first he had to uncover its source. To whom did Project Baltimore really belong? Was it Mapplethorpe or Manning, as Westview claimed? Or was it Westview's clever deceit, disguised as madness, in order to be exposed by the President at some later more convenient time—just as Manning had hinted?

"How do you think I can help you, Mr. President?" Desaix asked, uncertain whether Westview was using him for his protective shield of professional confidentiality. Or whether he really needed him to help unravel what seemed like a paranoid nightmare. And Desaix's vanity wouldn't let him believe it was simply a question of substituting his presence for that of Dr. Prince's. Then again, he wouldn't put it past Westview to play on his vanity as well as his need for action.

Both he and Westview knew all too well that these were Desaix's character flaws. Despite Westview's ranting and ravings, he was still counting on the fact that Desaix liked hanging around the locker room of the crisis management game.

Mary felt as if she were watching a game of tennis as intentions, memories, distortions, emotions, and questions flew back and forth between Desaix and Westview. And as in tennis, at any particular time, it was hard to say who was winning.

"How can you help me? That's a good question, Desaix," Westview replied thoughtfully. "Our country is moving toward chaos. And if I don't act quickly, the world is on the road to war." Westview chuckled out loud. The task of helping him bordered on the ridiculous.

"Are you sure there isn't anything more I can help with?" There was something very important that Westview had forgotten to mention to Desaix. Marfan's syndrome certainly had consequences for Westview's performance as President.

"Isn't that enough?"

"Yes, of course. But there is one issue that neither you nor I have discussed."

"Would that be your fee?"

Mary smiled. Desaix frowned. He wouldn't let the President off with a cheap joke.

"Okay, it's not your fee. So what are you getting at?" Westview was honestly puzzled. He had mentioned everything from ferreting out conspirators to stopping a major war. What else was left?

"It's an issue that's been with us all along, but we haven't really talked about it."

"And those are the ones that are of greatest interest to a shrink, isn't that right, Desaix?" Westview started to pace again, resting his hands on his stomach.

Mary shook her head in disapproval. She thought there might be an element of sadism in Desaix's relentless probing.

"What are you doing with your hands, Mr. President?"

Westview looked down at his hands.

"Does your stomach hurt?"

"It has been hurting me for quite a while. But you and I know that there is really nothing I can do about it."

Desaix was impressed by Westview's ability to deny his illness. It was clearly a fact of his life, and he had learned to live with it for so long that he didn't really understand how impaired he could become. Typically, patients with Marfan's syndrome went into pulmonary failure as a result of cardiac insufficiency. Or they suffered from emotional outbursts, mood swings, and organic psychosis as a result of the decreased oxygen entering the brain. The most treacherous of all outcomes could be sudden death from a dissecting aortic aneurysm, a faulty blood vessel tearing apart, whether in the chest or in the abdominal region. It was believed that while Lincoln was President he suffered from cyclical mood swings and protracted periods of melancholia and indecision, very likely due to Marfan's.

From Desaix's medical point of view, Westview was suffering from an abdominal aneurysm that was slowly tearing itself apart, ready to burst. It was only a question of time before it would completely rupture and throw Westview into shock. In short, he was a walking time bomb.

"Didn't Dr. Prince discuss an operation with you?"

"He did. But the risk is too great."

"What about the risk of not having it done?"

"Listen, I asked you to be my doctor, not my mother. Or is that too much to ask of you?" Westview began to raise his voice.

Desaix realized that he had hit a core of mixed emotions. Why would Westview become so angry over a matter that pertained to his well-being?

"What gives you the right to ask me, or even suggest to me, that I place my life on the line for some physician to play God with?" Slamming the glass of water on the desk, Westview watched indifferently as pieces of glass flew all about him.

Mary rushed up to help him, brushing the fragments of glass off him.

Westview stared straight ahead, motionless, like a child who was about to be reprimanded.

When she was through, Mary led him over to a chair and sat him down. But suddenly Westview collapsed in his chair.

"Desaix, what's wrong with him? He won't respond. Mr. President, talk to me! What's wrong?"

Desaix took the shade off the lamp on a side table and passed the lit bulb in front of Westview's eyes, checking his pupils' reaction to the bright light. "Oh, shit!"

"I can barely feel his pulse!" Mary shouted.

Desaix grabbed Westview and threw him onto the carpeted floor. He pressed his ear onto Westview's chest and listened carefully for heartbeats. There were none. He ripped Westview's shirt wide open, and slammed his fist against his chest. "We've got a cardiac arrest! Call the White House surgeon, STAT! Tell him to bring a CPR tray! And not to mention a word to anyone!" Placing both of his hands over each other, Desaix pressed methodically down on Westview's sternum. "One, one thousand. Two, one thousand. Three, one thousand." Desaix stopped the heart-pumping action to breath into Westview's mouth. "Hurry up, Mary! I need you to breathe into his mouth while I pump on his chest."

After Mary left a short message for Dr. Hugh Barnett, the White House physician, she rushed over to help Desaix. She stuck her fingers inside Westview's mouth to check for obstructions or loose dentures. Then she began to breath into his mouth in synchrony with Desaix's chest pounding.

"I get no pulse!" Desaix felt Westview's right carotid artery.

"What are we going to do?" Mary's eyes were riveted on the motionless body of the President of the United States.

"It's what we're not going to do that will be important. No one, but no one, is to know what just happened." Desaix kept banging on Westview's chest, still hopeful that the heart might revive itself.

"Are you crazy?"

"Maybe."

At that moment, Desaix wondered what it would feel like to be President of the United States.

# CHAPTER
## 30

General Mapplethorpe, accompanied by Colonel Shaw, showed their new identification passes to the civilian security guard at the southwest entrance of the Pentagon.

As Mapplethorpe surveyed the line of black government limousines, with their twisted turkey-neck reading lamps in the back seat, parked along the area marked OFFICIAL VEHICLES ONLY, he made a mental note of who would be waiting for him in the tank—Jenkins, McCormick, and Merck. The only car missing was Manning's.

If Mapplethorpe had been a scholar of Italian literature, he could have compared his descent through various metal detectors and guard stations into the bowels of the Pentagon as the real-life analogue of Dante's Inferno— the further he descended, the greater the sins he encountered. Fortunately for Mapplethorpe and his colleagues, he was too unimaginative to understand poetry, and too practical to appreciate a moral metaphor. For him, the Pentagon was exactly what it was intended to be—a five-sided, run-down government building that housed the nerve center of the four-hundred-and-fifty-billion-dollar military war machine, and a corps full of potential retirees at the level of full-bird colonel and above.

Like any weekend during crisis, all of the Pentagon parking lots were filled. Mapplethorpe's rule of thumb to measure the severity of a crisis seemed to be working: count the number of employee cars in the parking lots and the number of pizza delivery vans. The greater the number of cars and vans, the more severe the crisis.

For over fifteen years, the Pentagon had been Mapplethorpe's home before going to the NSC. The drab green, gray, and brown peeling walls were a welcome reminder that he was back, but this time as a civilian Secretary of Defense who was still addressed as general.

An impressive title and position, he thought, as he jaunted down E corridor to the basement tank, an ultrasecret sealed room where the other ex-cabinet officials were waiting for him. But the title of Secretary of Defense was exactly that—a title with little substance, particularly now during Project Baltimore, when all military action was being coordinated from the White House and the Old Executive Office Building. Ironically, what should have been the command and control center was being bypassed by none other than himself, for fear that Project Baltimore's execution would be bogged down in military red tape.

In a way, Mapplethorpe had predetermined his own fate. It was he who had made certain that whoever became Secretary of Defense or Chairman of the Joint Chiefs of Staff would inherit a position with little power. That's the way Mapplethorpe had designed it. And that's the way President Westview had wanted it. A centralized military command and control center at both the White House and Fort Ritchie.

Westview, that son of a bitch, thought Mapplethorpe, as he pulled opened the final metal door into the tank. It was Westview's plan all along to get rid of him when he implemented Project Baltimore. Once that was accomplished, the President had no further need for him. He would have served his purpose. As a reward, Mapplethorpe would receive the honorific title of Secretary of Defense, a position that would allow him to leave the military with dignity and a thirty-year pension. As well as insure his silence.

"Good day, gentlemen," Mapplethorpe began. Jenkins, Merck, and McCormick were already seated around the oak table.

"Greetings, Mr. Secretary," Merck said, smiling hesitantly, unable to hide that edge of hurt.

"Is Manning coming?" Jenkins asked.

"I don't know, Larry. I didn't see his car outside. We'll just have to wait and see," Mapplethorpe replied.

"Well, this is your nickel, Mr. Sec Def. Would you like to tell us what this meeting is all about?" Merck asked, then looked around the table for support, making certain he was articulating a collective impatience.

"Remember, General, you are now talking to civvies, no longer bound by the codes of this country to which we've formerly sworn our allegiance," McCormick said. His sarcasm had only intensified since the meeting at Fort Ritchie.

"Ronnie, I don't have to remind you that you are a four-star Air Force general with a thirty-year pension coming up any day now."

"Why thank you, Tommy! I didn't realize you were in the retirement planning business," McCormick replied, not enjoying being reminded that he was captive to a system that had just officially rebuked him.

"All right, let's cut it out, boys," Jenkins interjected. "We're not here to scrap over some bureaucratic turf. Those battles are all over. And lost. Let's just get down to business, though my instincts tell me that we should not be meeting like this."

Before business could be discussed, the door to the tank room opened up, and Manning entered.

"Greetings, gentlemen."

"Welcome, Chet," McCormick said. "Pull up a chair, and take out a deck of cards. I think we're going to play five card stud." McCormick was genuinely pleased to see him. It made him feel comfortable to know that Chester Manning would be part of any meeting that Mapplethorpe convened. He was the only one whose political instincts and judgment McCormick trusted completely.

"Well, Tommy, we're all here now. It's your show," McCormick said, trying to provoke him.

Mapplethorpe paused to collect his thoughts, and then proceeded deliberately. "Thank you for coming here on such short notice. I've asked you here because I am very concerned about the meeting we had with the President at Fort Ritchie. I was, and still am, concerned about what seemed to me to be his extremely erratic behavior. Does anyone disagree?" Mapplethorpe looked around the room.

"Erratic is an interesting word, Tommy," Manning said, sounding genuinely intrigued. "But that's the kind of word that's filled with all kinds of connotations. Do you have any particular one in mind?"

"Yes, I do."

"Well, don't be coy, son. What are you trying to get at?" Manning asked, forcing the issue faster than Mapplethorpe had anticipated.

"You've known the President for a long time, Chet. Didn't you think that his behavior was peculiar . . . strange . . . ?" Mapplethorpe was clearly having a hard time saying exactly what he meant.

"Now, General, you certainly must have a better word in mind than strange or peculiar. Quite frankly, I often find my own behavior kind of peculiar. But that's no crime. Or at least I don't think that's a crime." Manning was having fun playing with Mapplethorpe.

"Come on now, Chet! Have you ever seen your friend seem as erratic as he was at that meeting?" Mapplethorpe wasn't going to be intimidated by Manning.

"I've seen him howl at the moon after a whole night of poontang! I've seen him crawl on all fours when he was drunk as a sot. I've seen him choke a man till he turned blue just because he called him crazy. Is he crazy, then? Yeah!"

"That's not what Mapplethorpe means, and you know it, Chet. So stop screwing around." Jenkins was becoming impatient with Manning's games.

"So what precisely is General Mapplethorpe trying to imply? That President Westview is crazy? As in insane?" Leaning forward, Manning looked intimidatingly at Jenkins. "If that's what he means, he sure as shit better have some clinical proof and a real professional to make that pronouncement. Otherwise he's practicing medicine without a license. And that's a crime in this country!"

"All right, Chet, all right," Merck interrupted. "Let's assume you're right and the emotional outburst we all witnessed was just an aberration. Then explain how the hell we are going to get out of this war?" Merck wanted to get to the bottom line. He still wasn't certain why he was there.

"What is it that you would like to do, Mr. ex–Secretary of Defense?" Manning asked. He enjoyed reminding Merck that he no longer had the legitimacy or mandate to implement anything.

Except for one very important fact. Merck had always represented, on an unofficial basis, the black constituency of the President's public support. That was something a political animal like Manning could never ignore.

As Westview's loyal friend, Manning needed to fathom what the disgruntled, recently dismissed members of his friend's cabinet were planning and channel it into something constructive. Or torpedo it, if it presented a problem.

"First, Secretary Manning," Merck said, "I think that we can all agree that the President acted in a peculiar fashion. Whether he's acted like that in the past in a whorehouse or a bar is of little importance to me or, I suspect, anyone else in the room." Merck scanned his colleagues to make certain he was talking on behalf of everyone there. "But in my opinion, our President seems to have problems. I'm not certain what's wrong with him, but I am convinced that if he continues to behave in the same way he acted toward us yesterday, this country is in trouble."

"Could you be more specific?" Mapplethorpe asked. "I think it would help everyone here to articulate what you think is the problem."

"Look, I'm not the one who convened this hush-hush meeting. And may I remind you that we all had a helluva time getting in. We no longer belong to the august group of senior officials in this administration."

"I know that. And I appreciate your coming," Mapplethorpe said, trying to be conciliatory.

"I refuse to be treated as a member of some therapy group. May I remind you that I'm not the one whose competence is being questioned."

"I agree with Randy. Westview's judgment is the issue."

"Jenkins is right on." McCormick leaned back in his chair.

"All right, gentlemen. Your point has been made," Manning responded defensively. "So what do you want to do?"

"I might as well say what's on my mind." Merck looked directly at Mapplethorpe and Manning, both of whom were still part of the administration. "The President has to go."

Both McCormick and Jenkins agreed with Merck. The three of them looked at Mapplethorpe, who sat quietly.

"I'm in agreement!" Mapplethorpe responded in a resounding voice.

The group waited for Manning.

"Business as usual, Mr. Secretary?" Merck asked. "Everyone lays their cards on the table while you listen and wait. It's your turn now."

"I'd like to find a constructive way to deal with this problem," Manning responded cautiously.

"What does that mean?" McCormick asked.

"It means that if the President has a problem, that is, *if* he *really* has a problem, I want to find a constructive way to deal with it. I'll sit here as long as you accept the fact that I don't subscribe to making quick judgments." Manning paused before making his next point. "If you don't want me here, then just tell me, and I'm out." He looked around the room, realizing he had just placed the group on the defensive. If they wanted him out, he would leave. But no one could say that they hadn't been warned about his objections.

"What should we do?" Merck asked aloud. He was taking Manning at face value.

"Invoke the Twenty-fifth Amendment of the Constitution," Mapplethorpe said quietly.

"The Twenty-fifth Amendment?" McCormick asked, incredulous.

"Yes, the Twenty-fifth Amendment," Mapplethorpe replied, "describes in detail what is to be done when the president is disabled. It can be invoked by the Vice President *and* a majority of *either* the principal officers of the executive department *or of such other body* as Congress may by law provide, to transmit within four days to the President pro tempore of the Senate and the Speaker of the House of Representatives their written declaration that the President is unable to discharge the power and duties of his office. Thereupon, Congress shall decide the issue, assembling within forty-eight hours for that purpose if not in session. As provided elsewhere in the Constitution, the line of succession includes, in order of priority, the Vice President, the Speaker of the House, President pro tempore of the Senate, and the Secretary of State."

Immediately, Manning understood why it was so important to Mapplethorpe that he attend this meeting. Mapplethorpe needed a co-conspirator. At least one of those people in the line of presidential succession—and preferably someone who was intimately involved with Project Baltimore. But Manning didn't understand why Mapplethorpe needed the other members in the group. Westview had already divested them of any power or authority. They were really of no political value.

"Could you believe that Vice President Allison Bonner would be next in line?" McCormick chortled. "Little Lord Fauntleroy? The pock-faced wonder from the suburbs of Poughkeepsie, New York, and purgatory? Shit, man! No way this country would support the VP. Everyone knows that he's the President's best insurance policy against any assassination attempt."

"Ron is right," Merck interjected. "Even if the President walked around the White House in the nude and masturbated all day long, this country would never accept Bonner as President." Whatever Mapplethorpe had on his mind did not seem very well thought out. And this type of thinking was not only sloppy but extremely dangerous. If anyone outside the room got wind of this conversation, Merck feared they could all be implicated for treason.

"Tommy," Manning said, "I must admit that McCormick and Merck have a legitimate point. My good friend Don Westview, as crazy as all you folks might think he is would never in a million years dream of anointing that pubescent wonder of hyperactivity as president of anything, except West-view's Northeast fan club." Manning paused to catch his breath. "Hell, man, if you can even locate Little Lord Fauntleroy, somewhere out in the boonies of the Far East cavorting with those two other brain surgeons, the Speaker of the House and the President pro tempore of the Senate, then give me a call."

Mapplethorpe broke out into a high-pitched laugh, which reminded Manning of a jackass in heat.

"Tommy," Manning continued, "you can't tell me that you called us to discuss some half-baked idea that you're going to get the President out of the White House on some trumped-up charge of insanity, just because you got your four stars a little tarnished, and he demoted you from National Security Advisor to Sec Def? I can't believe that anyone in this room is capable of this type of mutinous behavior. I, for one, do not want to have anything to do with this kind of foolish thinking or talking." Manning stood up to leave. Too bad Desaix wasn't here to witness this scene, he thought.

"Please, sit down, Mr. Secretary. You're right." Mapplethorpe quickly stood up and blocked Manning's exit from the room. "You know me better than that, Chet!" He placed his arm warmly around Manning's shoulder and led him back to his chair.

"No one here is talking about mutiny. The reason I called this meeting was to discuss the options that were available to us, if for whatever reason the President of the United States became incapacitated."

"Tommy is right, Chet," Jenkins said, disturbed that Manning would consider leaving the room without having first arrived at a consensus. But he was far more upset by the fact that if Chet left, Jenkins would be the only civilian left in the room who represented the interests of a nonmilitary organization. Despite the fact that they all had been demoted, Jenkins, like everyone else, knew they were still extremely influential with their organizations and constituencies.

Although Ball was the new DCI, Jenkins would still work very closely with him. That was simply the way of the national security bureaucracy. For that reason alone, Jenkins wanted to make certain he would have a bureau-cratic ally in Manning.

"All right, Larry. Tell me how Tommy is right," Manning said, sitting down. "As I understand the Twenty-fifth Amendment, you need the approval of the Vice President and a specially designated committee of Congress. If something should incapacitate the President, whoever is next in line of succession automatically takes the oath of office."

"Exactly!" seconded Jenkins. "When Nixon resigned, Ford took over the very same day."

"Now imagine, for hypothetical purposes only," Mapplethorpe said, "that the President of the United States, the Vice President, the Speaker of the House, and the President pro tempore of the Senate, were all incapacitated. The Secretary of State would be next in line to become the President of the United States." He looked from man to man. "Well, what do you think?"

"Think of what?" Manning asked, really wanting Mapplethorpe to repeat the question.

"You're just trying to bust my chops, Chet!" Mapplethorpe replied. "You, as you well know, would technically be next in line to become the President of the United States."

"Unfortunately, I've been aware of that fact for most of my tenure at State," Manning replied smugly. "The chief of my protective detail continuously reminds me of that fact. So what?"

"So what? At this very moment, this country needs someone like you— someone who has the confidence of Congress; the confidence of the people; is impeccably honest and rational; and has the maturity and the depth of experience to resolve this potential catastrophe with the Commonwealth of Independent States." Mapplethorpe sensed that he had a chance to reverse Manning's cynicism, which for a professional politician was simply a mask for unlimited ambition. Once that ambition was mined, all types of dreams and plans could be conjured. Mapplethorpe was playing the role of the magician who sotto voce asked his participants on stage to cooperate with him in fooling the audience. His real problem was determining whether Manning was part of the magic show or part of the audience.

"Tommy, you really surprise me," Manning said. "You're beginning to sound like a local ward leader recruiting me for a congressional race."

"Chet, the only thing I ask you to think about is the possibility that we may have to invoke the Twenty-fifth Amendment very soon. And we have heard very clearly in this room that the others cannot really be considered viable candidates for the presidency." Looking around the room, Mapplethorpe saw everyone nod their head in agreement. Not bad. This was the first consensus he had been able to achieve all day long. Long live Manning for President! he thought.

"Tommy, it's crazy! Even if I wanted to agree with you guys—which by the way, I haven't done yet—what, in God's name, makes you think that you could place me next in succession?" Manning was determined to see how far he could play out this presidential scenario. But he knew he could not continue to act too coyly, not with this group of barracudas. They would suspect that something was wrong; the more he protested, the less credible he would appear.

Unlike, say, the Council of the Cardinals, upon the death of a Pope, when the Cardinals were in the process of anointing a new papal candidate, it was mandatory that the Cardinals assume a posture of humility. Of course, the opposite was true in American politics, especially presidential politics. If one were too humble or self-effacing, it was a signal to the political community that one wasn't to be taken as a serious candidate. The rules of the game mandated a modicum of humility, not a surfeit. Manning, always sensitive to the nuances of the political process, consented to play along, although it may have been against his better judgment.

"What would happen to the VP, the Speaker, and President of the Senate?" Manning asked, not expecting to receive a coherent answer.

"Don't worry about that," Mapplethorpe responded matter-of-factly. "That's my problem." He paused to look around the room, and added with a Cheshire grin, "Or should I say that it's our problem, gentlemen. Are we all agreed, then? That the Twenty-fifth Amendment will be invoked, and that the line of succession will be activated so that Manning will be next in line for the presidency."

"You've got my support," Merck said, then stood up.

"Ditto," McCormick replied.

"Count me in too," Jenkins said as he started to walk out of the room with Manning and McCormick.

"Whatever you think you've just decided," Manning told them, "I'm totally against everything that you and your cohorts have just said. And I will renounce and prosecute any acts of violence perpetrated against any government official."

"Sure, Mr. Secretary. I understand and fully agree with your concerns," Mapplethorpe replied.

How naive they were, thought Manning as he left the room. Their scenario lacked one crucial element—a written letter of support, approving the Secretary of State's actions.

When the tank door closed, Mapplethorpe looked upward, toward the soundproof ceiling.

"Did you get the entire conversation, Shaw?"

"Yes, General."

"Then edit it and get it to Prince as quickly as possible."

Mapplethorpe checked his chronometer watch. "We'll need it by the ten o'clock news."

# CHAPTER

## 31

The Russian National Command Authority at Gadanya Forest, seventy-five miles northeast of Moscow, resounded with the drunken jubilation that one could only encounter in Tbilisi, Georgia, on the anniversary of Stalin's birth or death, depending on one's particular sentiments.

"To the miraculous recovery of my dearest and oldest friend, President Zotov of the Russian Federation, and to his loyal Spetsnaz soldier Colonel Pushkin! I drink to both of you! My dear friends!" Field Marshal Alexander Kulikov raised his glass of wine.

"And to my dear Marshal Kulikov, whose Russian hospitality is both gracious and dangerous." Raising his long-stemmed wine glass, President Zotov laughed with the gratitude of a man who has been forcibly turned back from the doorsteps of death.

Neither the urinary catheter leading from Zotov's shriveled penis to a transparent plastic bag hanging on the side of his wheelchair, nor the bandages around his head and arms prevented him from reveling in this moment.

Everyone in the Operations Center of the National Command Authority was both pleased and surprised to see that Zotov could recuperate so quickly. That was a good omen for the future. No matter how modern and sophisticated a Russian might think he was, he would always be a prisoner to centuries-old superstitions. And throughout history, nothing mattered as much as the health of the leader, whether he be Peter the Great, Czar Nicholas I, Mikhail Gorbachev, or Zotov.

"To our courageous President Zotov, who returned to us from the living dead so that he could share this fine bottle of Georgian Tsinandali wine!" No one was more relieved than Pushkin to see that his efforts to save Zotov's life were not in vain. Now they could proceed with the rest of Project Baltimore.

"Thank you, my dear courageous friend!" Zotov turned toward Tamara and Vartanian. "To your brave and beautiful comrades-in-arms, without whom there would be no President Zotov! To your health!"

The twenty technicians and soldiers in the room raised their glasses and drank in unison as if they had rehearsed their collective enthusiasm.

"My dear friends," Kulikov began, "I would like to assure you all that as long as there remains one beautiful woman like Major Tamara Popov or one fine glass of Tsinandali wine, which was cultivated by my ancestors in Kakhetia province, I swear to you that there will always be a Russia." Kulikov toasted both Zotov and Tamara in one broad gesture. As far as Kulikov was concerned, the only thing missing from this much needed merriment was the music of the Steppes, the relentless sound of balalaikas, the Gypsy violins, and the clapping hands urging the musicians to play on. But he could wait until this godforsaken crisis was over. And then, how he would make up for it. He hadn't been made a marshal just because he could successfully conduct a war. More importantly, he knew how to create a memorable party.

"If I drink any more of this fine wine, my friend," Zotov said, "I won't be able to tell you the difference between what's in my urine bag and what's in my glass." Zotov patted the side of his wheelchair.

"What difference does it make after a few drinks? Both fluids look alike. And who knows, if you were a diabetic, they would both taste alike. Anyway, it's all going out the same hole." Kulikov roared with laughter.

Pushkin smirked. He felt left out of the bantering, which he understood, all too well, properly belonged to old friends who had shared each other's personal and professional lives since childhood.

Tamara could see that Pushkin looked a little remorseful; he was being displaced by Kulikov. After only one day of rest, he was already restless. Fortunately for him, a young Spetsnaz lieutenant approached Kulikov with a flimsy piece of paper.

"Now let's get back to work!" Kulikov bellowed. "I have just been informed that we are now ready for a systems check on our state of preparedness."

Pushkin's sullen face broke into a broad smile.

Winking at him, Tamara also smiled. She wanted him to know that she understood. But beneath her smile was that sad feeling of emptiness that she and every Russian woman dreaded—that feeling that she was about to lose her loved one. Not to the glory of war. Or to the sanctity of work. But to the avoidance of emotional responsibility through action, alcohol, or sex. The Russian male had become a master at avoiding responsibility and at displacing blame onto everyone but himself. Especially onto their women. All sins and deficiencies could be traced to the woman of the household.

"Marshal Kulikov, we're ready for our State of Preparedness countdown!"

the Georgian Op Center technician Becheroff yelled from his computer terminal at the bottom of the pit, in front of a brightly lit outdated map of the Commonwealth of Independent States.

"Mr. President, are you ready?" Kulikov asked Zotov.

Zotov was more than ready. He was beaming with pride. Project Baltimore was proceeding as anticipated. Of course, there were a few minor problems. For one, the crisis was mounting in tension. But for that, he had to talk directly with President Westview, whom he had been told was not immediately available.

"Let's begin," Zotov said as he wheeled himself alongside Pushkin and took his hand firmly.

Vartanian and Tamara huddled together like a brother and sister who had been abandoned by their parents. They were like waifs at a Saint Nichol's Day festival in the company of distant family relatives.

"Maximum Vigilance Status!" Becheroff shouted. "Four Command and Control mobile posts on railroad cars have already departed from their original base of operations."

"I see the Command and Control post moving from Kazan toward Sukhumi," Kulikov said, with a bewildered expression on his face.

"Yes, sir! Fully operational and in continuous communication with us." The Georgian coordinated his communications efforts with ten other Op Center technicians sitting at computer terminals at the same work station.

"Good. Use secured channels to tell them they have been tasked for the dual preparation of a U.S. missile strike and riot control in Georgia."

"Yes, sir!" Becheroff said, though he flinched with discomfort. He felt sorry for his countrymen who would incur the burden of Zulikov's wrath. He recalled how ruthlessly former Foreign Minister Edvard Shevardnadze, one of the major proponents of autonomy for the individual republics, had cracked down on his fellow Georgians when they refused to disavow their desire for independence in 1990. It had taken Georgia too long to recover from that trauma. Eventually they became independent and, as expected, ungovernable.

"Marshal Kulikov, we have a pre–Maximum Vigilance of minus one with the Command and Control car headed from Neperopetrovsk to Petrozavodski on Lake Ladoga." Becheroff shouted his information, but with a certain hesitancy in his voice. He had learned the hard way, that in war it was not good to be the bearer of bad news. Russian marshals and generals had a nasty habit of confusing the bearer of bad tidings with the nature of the news itself.

"Why?" Kulikov's impatient voice resounded through the Operations Center.

"Why? Sir, I don't know why." Becheroff sounded frightened of what might happen next. He didn't want to be the one to tell Kulikov, the preeminent crisis strategist, what every technician in the crisis management business had known for a long time—that the entire Russian system, unlike the American, was antiquated. Secured communications were carried over modified commercial telephone lines rather than optic fibers. The computer software had been developed by talented Hungarian computer systems experts—before there were any hard currency transactions in Russia. It was a combination of lack of money and bureaucratic incompetence that accounted for their dilapidated crisis management system. Everyone was apprised of the poor state of Russian preparedness. But, like all good Russians, the senior officers wanted to believe what they wanted to believe.

*Vranyo.* Telling someone something that both you and he knew to be a lie. But neither one wants to admit to the other that, in fact, both are in a collusion of not even wanting to know the truth. Russian crisis management had fallen victim to the unspoken virtues of *vranyo*—the denial of reality. But who could argue with vodka and *vranyo* as the legitimate salvation of the Russian soul.

"The third Command and Control railroad car was already heading eastward from Hkaberovsk toward Vladivostok," Becheroff continued.

"What state of Maximum Vigilance was it in?" Zotov asked eagerly. Vladivostok was the easternmost port of what was once the Soviet Union— their major warm-water port to the Pacific Ocean. It was the culmination of Peter the Great's dream of having a Pacific port for landlocked Russia.

"A state of minus two away from Maximum Vigilance," Becheroff replied.

"A state of minus two?" Kulikov roared. "What is going on here? Don't we have any rail cars other than the one from Kazan that is in any condition to deal with a crisis?"

"Yes, sir! We do, but, unfortunately it's still missing."

"What do you mean missing?" Zotov asked, disturbed to hear that something that might affect his capability was either not functioning or not available. "Where did it go? It just didn't disappear!"

"Well, as a matter of fact . . ." Becheroff tried but was afraid to continue.

"Well, as a matter of fact, what?" Kulikov asked angrily.

"I don't know how to tell you this . . ."

"What is it, my young Georgian friend?" Zotov asked, placing his hand comfortingly on Kulikov's shoulder, silently asking him to reconsider his inquisition.

"The Command and Control rail car that was leaving Stavka from Irkutsk is missing." Becheroff's voice started to crack. He was beginning to sound as frightened as he felt.

"Missing? How do you lose a rail car?" Kulikov asked, looking desperately at Pushkin and Vartanian.

Without exchanging a word, they knew that it would be up to them to do all the dirty work needed to find the missing train.

"I don't know, sir! The rail car was signed out to General Kranich. That's all we can see on this computer," Becheroff replied defensively.

"That whoremonger! He's probably running a cat house on that train.

And while he's fucking his brains out, we are left extremely vulnerable,"
Kulikov screamed. But the louder he screamed, the more impotent he felt.
There was nothing anyone in that room could do. There probably were other
generals who were doing the same thing. For all he knew, all of his remaining
generals might have annexed the remainder of the Commonwealth of Independent States into different business sectors.

My God, Kulikov thought. How many of his generals had become entrepreneurs, selling arms to warring ethnic factions within the Commonwealth.
Russia was becoming more like Lebanon—a wasteland of conflicting political, ideological, and mercenary interests bound together by only one common element—making money. He knew quite well that his Georgian field
commanders were selling vintage AK-47 rifles to the international black
market, making certain to be paid in hard currency. The transaction would
take place in the early morning, before formal fighting broke out between
the Russian Army and local criminal gangs seeking political and economic
dominance. Then, after each side had depleted most of its ammunition, one
or the other would declare a cease-fire and take stock of what weapon systems
were still available. Kulikov knew all too well the unwritten rule of this
Commonwealth of Independent States civil war. Whichever side had the
preponderance of ammunition at the end of the day would sell the other side
the day's surplus. This way the warring factions could continue another day's
fighting.

The new mercantile warfare of the twenty-first century was really a vestige
of past Soviet involvement in the murky waters of the Middle East, the
misbegotten invasion of Afghanistan, and the ethnic rivalries within the
disintegrating Soviet Union. If he were truly cynical, Kulikov might believe
that the only real reason for trying to keep the Commonwealth of Independent States together was to provide his field commanders an opportunity to
garner a decent living. So it was no real surprise to Kulikov that the mobile
Command and Control Center on the Stavka train from Irkutsk was missing.

"Marshal Kulikov," Zotov asked, "have we completely coordinated our
strategy for an integrated counteroffensive against the U.S. if we need one?"
He wanted to be assured of maximum military preparedness, particularly if
the war extended into a massive exchange of ballistic missiles.

"Yes, sir!" Kulikov pointed to the words inscribed in bold red letters on
the chart alongside the map—TEATR VEONNYKH DEISTVII. He added
with authority, "I have put my finest three armies at Moscow, Venitza, and
Smolensk on Maximum Vigilance status."

"Good. What else?"

"We are in complete coordination with PVO STRANY at their own
underground National Command and Control Center sixty miles southwest
of Moscow."

"Do we know what the PVO STRANY plans are concerning a potential
air and ballistic missile war?" Zotov asked.

"We are coordinating a comprehensive early-warning radar coverage that would detect any ballistic missiles fired from the U.S. or their Trident submarines," Kulikov answered, nodding toward Becheroff, hoping to be relieved of further discussion of the early-warning system. That should be left to technicians.

Picking up on Kulikov's nonverbal invitation to speak, Becheroff pointed to the map of the commonwealth with a red flashlight pointer.

"At present, we are coordinating coverage of our early-warning radar and Crisis Management Systems in Irkutsk, Minsk, Novgorod, Pechora, Sary-Shagan, and Krasnoyarsk with the Cosmos 3228 and Cosmos 2164 satellites. We are experiencing problems with one or two other satellite ground stations, but we are addressing these at the moment." Becheroff sounded out of breath. It was his fault he felt so debilitated. Had Becheroff not been so good, Kulikov would not have used him almost exclusively. Ironically, Becheroff had made himself indispensable to the effective control of most Russian crises managed from the Russian National Command Center.

"If we are attacked by the U.S. Air Force, can we defend ourselves?" Zotov asked, expecting the little Georgian technician to reply honestly.

"Given all the factors, I think we would have a very good chance at early detection of a surprise air attack," Becheroff replied defensively. "We can pick up their Stealth bombers and F-111Es with the PVO STRANY. The laser weapons at Sary-Shagan and at Samipalatinsk can intercept the American ICBMs."

"Tell me, my dear Georgian friend," Kulikov asked with an avuncular tone of voice, "what are the real chances of one of their missiles penetrating our Space Defense System?"

"Less than one in ten!" Becheroff answered with a strong sense of conviction.

"Are you certain?"

"Well . . ." Becheroff stammered.

"Well, what?" Kulikov asked.

"It depends on whether they have fratricide among their missiles or whether they send in decoys." Becheroff reaffirmed his conviction that only one in ten missiles would pass through what the Russians called their iron curtain.

"What about our offensive capability?" Pushkin was primarily concerned with the damage that the Russians could inflict.

"That's a good question, Colonel Pushkin," Becheroff replied. He sensed that Pushkin hadn't liked his condescending tone of voice. But he didn't know why he had to answer a mere colonel's question, when he had been responding to questions from a president and a marshal.

"And the answer, Master Sergeant?" Pushkin asked in an equally patronizing tone. He wasn't going to let this little Georgian get away with insolence. Not to a true Russian.

"The Strategic Rocket Forces are on Maximum Vigilance status. They have mobilized their rail mobile missile units, ready to fire at will. Our

SS-21s, SS-23s, and the other ICBMs at Imeni Gastello, Dombarovskiy, and Zhangiz Tobe are also on Maximum Vigilance status. They are ready to fire at a command from President Zotov." Becheroff was now feeling exhilarated by the information he was passing on to such an important group of functionaries. He was even beginning to believe his own rhetoric.

"Have you thought of any countermeasures, Sergeant Becheroff?"

"Of course, Colonel Pushkin. We at the Russian National Command Authority always develop a very elaborate countermeasure strategy. We divide that strategy into three parts. The first part is intended to disrupt and confuse the American crisis management and early-warning systems. We would ignite flare gases from several oil refineries near all of our missile sites, which would confuse their KH-12 photo reconnaissance satellites."

"Very ingenious, Becheroff."

"In truth, Mr. President, we decided to use that technique when we saw how effectively it was used in the Iraqi war."

"Too bad. I thought we had a monopoly on ingenious strategies. Maybe the next strategy," Zotov said, smiling.

"The second phase of our strategy was completely developed by us. In this phase we would deploy nuclear space mines from our Cosmos 2262 satellites, specifically targeting the American polar and geostationary orbits of MIL-STAR."

"Excellent, Becheroff! Excellent! Now that's a plan worthy of any brilliant Russian."

"Finally, we would sabotage designated ground-based American communications assets, particularly the satellite control facilities at Sunnyvale, California, and the PBX telephone switching exchanges in San Francisco, California; Fairview, Kansas; Hillsboro, Missouri; Lamar, Colorado; and Lyons, Nebraska."

"Very thorough. Very impressive, Becheroff," Zotov exclaimed as he praised the now distracted Becheroff, who had just turned his attention away from his audience to an alarming piece of information on his computer screen.

"Is there something wrong, Becheroff?" Kulikov asked, annoyed. A master sergeant in the Russian Army was supposed to give his complete attention and respect to his President at all times, thought Kulikov. There was absolutely no excuse for any other type of behavior. He made a mental note that at a more appropriate time and place he would reprimand Becheroff.

"Marshal Kulikov," Becheroff began, "our Soyuz satellite is picking up increased U.S. military activity near Wildeck, Germany. But I can't make it out."

"What do you mean, Sergeant Becheroff?" Zotov asked in a loud commanding voice, reminding everyone in the room that it was he, and not Marshal Kulikov, who was the real Commander-in-Chief of all the Russian forces.

"Mr. President, there seems to be an increased movement of M1A1 Abrams tanks toward our T-72s. There also seems to be an increased activity of APCs heading toward the autobahn in our direction." Becheroff cursorily examined the satellite photos handed to him by his Op Center colleagues before handing them to Pushkin, who, along with Tamara and Vartanian, carefully examined them. Their faces revealed extreme concern about what they were seeing.

"I think the Americans are trying to sweep around our easternmost flank in order to cut off a potential retreat," Pushkin spoke authoritatively.

"Or," added Vartanian, "the Americans might be doing what they did in their lightning victory against the Iraqis—cut off the access for any potential reinforcements from our elite Spetsnaz units held in reserve."

"Major Vartanian, I am afraid you may be right. And, if you are, we will be in very serious trouble." Kulikov examined the photos. "And what do you think, Major Popov? Isn't this your specialty—military intelligence?"

"Sir, I am GRU . . ." She hesitated to say any more, lest she get into trouble. "But I would have to agree with both Pushkin's and Vartanian's assessment. The Americans may be trying to swing around our flank and cut off both our supplies as well as our troop reinforcements."

"Just like a woman to agree with her lover!" Kulikov roared, but noticed that Tamara didn't find his comment particularly funny.

"But what if that were a military feint to the east in order to distract our attention away from the main thrust of their forces in the west?" Aiming his remark at Kulikov, Zotov sounded concerned for the first time. "Where is their famed 150,000 man U.S. 7th Army Corps? If they are massing to the west of our troops, then this increased movement of U.S. troops toward our eastern flank is nothing but a military trick to draw our attention away from the main thrust."

"I think President Zotov is right," Kulikov said, always impressed with his friend's self-taught knowledge of military strategy. "Becheroff, can you give us the answer from your photo satellite readings?" Kulikov appreciated the fact that in many ways the ability to interpret satellite photos was more of an art than a science. The proper reading of those photographs required what the marshal called "an old man's wisdom"—years of experience. A documented history of trial and error. This was not a game for amateurs or novices. Too much was at stake.

"Unfortunately, because of extensive cloud cover and poor weather all over Western Europe, I am unable to tell you anything further. I'm afraid that the weather complicates the situation."

"That leaves us with our basic all-purpose, on-ground, human intelligence provided by our favorite human asset," Kulikov said, staring at Pushkin, who broke out into his noted smile.

Pushkin knew it was up to him now.

"You have exactly twenty-four hours at most," Kulikov said, "to acquire a copy of the U.S. AirLandBattle Plan and find out where the main thrust of their attack will be!"

"Yes, sir!" Pushkin snapped smartly to attention. As he left the room, he looked wistfully at Tamara. He might never see her again.

Shaking nervously in the back seat of the dilapidated green taxicab, Julia Bond held firmly on to the videotape.

She had received this mysterious package from a "reliable senior official" only a few hours ago. After having viewed it on her own VCR, she was rushing to the CNN studios.

A sudden bump from the car behind jolted her out of her numbness. "What happened?" she asked the driver through the back window. All she could see were the bright headlights of a car clinging closely to the taxi's rear bumper.

"I don't know, ma'am!" the taut, lanky black taxi driver replied in a clipped British accent. Unlike many of the Ethiopian refugees who decided to open a restaurant, Ermyas had bought a medallion to drive a cab. It gave him more time to pursue his passion—political science.

The car bumped the taxi again.

"Jesus! What the hell is going on?" Bond clutched the videotape more tightly.

"I must stop now! Otherwise, that crazy person will destroy this cab."

"Please, don't stop! Whoever is bumping us wants to kill me. I'm sure of it."

"As you say, ma'am. I think that life will become a lot simpler once I lose that car." Ermyas swerved off the Whitehurst Freeway and drove as fast as he could between the rusted steel girders supporting the road over the cobblestoned streets of Georgetown.

"Thank you," Bond said, then passed him a fifty-dollar bill. "There's more where that comes from, if you get me safely to the CNN building on Mass Avenue, near Union Station."

"Ma'am, I am impressed with the evidence supporting your argument."

Ermyas looked for a place where he could turn off and hide, but it didn't take very long to realize that he was not going to get rid of the car behind him. Having fought for Eritrean independence in his homeland, he had learned well the barbaric lessons of vengeance and violence. Even if he were to stop and discharge his lovely passenger, his own life would be in serious jeopardy. He had, without any choice, become both an accomplice to a murder and a potential victim. But that was the unpredictable way of the world. So he rationalized.

This time the taxi was jolted from the right.

"Please, speed up! Otherwise, that car will knock us off the road."

"Ma'am, someone doesn't like us," he said, looking into his rear-view mirror. "Hey, you're that anchorwoman on CNN, aren't you?" Ermyas swerved his taxi to avoid being hit by the other car, which he could now identify as a Ford Torino.

"Yes," she replied. "Please, drive faster." Bond braced herself by spreading her arms across the back seat.

"Then my service is at your command, ma'am. My name is Ermyas." He smiled warmly.

The taxi and the pursuing Ford now drove side by side. The driver lowered his window. Bond could see two soldiers wearing red berets and khaki camouflage uniforms sitting beside the driver.

"That is not a friendly-looking man," Ermyas said, suddenly turning his steering wheel, trying to squeeze the Ford into hitting one of the steel girders. He was formulating his plan of attack from remembering the countless number of chase scenes he had seen on TV. If nothing else, he was now in his first high-speed chase, hopefully for a good cause.

Sparks flew into the air as the two cars raced side by side.

"Hold on tightly, ma'am!" Flooring the accelerator, Ermyas could feel his ten-year-old taxi gag before it surged forward. When he was just a few inches in front of the Ford, he swerved to the right and crashed against the Ford's left front fender.

Bolts of sparks flew into the air as if a subway car had just been derailed from its high-voltage third rail. The sound of crumpling metal frightened both of them. Bond felt as if the cab had just been broken open by the largest nutcracker in the world. As her head hit the side window, Ermyas hit the windshield, and like Bond, he started to bleed from his forehead.

The badly damaged Ford sat, immobilized.

"Are you okay?" Ermyas asked, surveying the remainder of his taxicab. The right side of the cab was seriously damaged. Cotton padding from the seats was strewn all over the insides.

Getting up from the back floor, Bond felt as if she had just been in a ten-round boxing match. And she was the loser.

She ran her hands over her body. Nothing seemed broken or punctured.

"I think I'm okay," she said. "I just feel like I've just been shaked and baked. Are you all right?"

"Yes, ma'am. A little shaken up too, but I'll be fine." He pushed his foot down on the accelerator, and although bolts and screws rolled around, at least he still had an engine, and the cab moved. Ermyas turned onto a street without cobblestones to avoid further damage.

"Oh no!" Through his rear-view mirror, Ermyas saw a twisted headlight rushing toward the cab.

Bond braced herself for another onslaught of knocks and bruises.

Ermyas turned off the road and drove alongside the Potomac. He slowed down considerably so that the Ford could catch up.

"What are you doing? They're almost on top of us again!"

"Trust me!"

The damaged Ford started to bump them from the rear. It kept ramming the back of the taxicab, which kept slowing down.

Ermyas turned the steering wheel sharply to the left, hoping that the Ford would miss the cab, override the banks of the river, and land in the Potomac.

Instead, the Ford caught the cab on the left bumper and forced it in a counterclockwise motion that pitched the taxi over the embankment, straight into the murky, freezing waters. The swirling currents sucked the car downward into a whirlpool of death.

Watching the taxicab's tail light disappear and the last bubbles of life rise to the surface, Roger Cordonnier turned toward the soldiers seated alongside of him and grinned.

Ms. Bond and the videotape were completely neutralized.

# CHAPTER
## 32

**A**s a distinguished board-certified cardiovascular surgeon, Captain Hugh Barnett, MD, USN, with his staff of three attending surgeons, one internist, five OR/ICU nurses, three physician's assistants, and two medical technicians, was able to perform any surgical operation. Sequestered in a distant corner of the White House, the totally self-contained White House medical facilities boasted three state-of-the-art operating rooms, each consisting of a heart-lung machine, which even allowed Barnett to perform open-heart surgery on the President. Although Barnett was on twenty-four-hour call, no one, including himself, thought that trying to revive an incapacitated President would ever be a real possibility. Most of Barnett's time was spent treating everyday ailments for which the White House personnel didn't want to visit their local physician. Not since the attempted assassination of President Reagan, back in the early 1980s, was there a need to utilize this operating room.

No wonder doctors were totally unsuited to work with others, thought Desaix, as he watched the mild-mannered, forty-eight-year-old Barnett carefully thread the cardiac catheter into President Westview's flaccid right arm. Most physicians were accustomed to assume full responsibility for all their actions, and as a result, had very little tolerance for group meetings and decision by consensus. Similarly, doctors were not trained to be overly concerned about the sensibilities of others. For Desaix, there was no such thing as miscommunication. One either did or did not understand the imperatives of the moment. It was not open to interpretation. One either knew what to do or what not to do. Temporizing a decision as a way of gaining a better understanding of the situation was simply out of the question. Time was a demanding taskmaster—it was not a matter of convenience.

With the flick of the surgeon's wrist, Barnett could determine Westview's fate, as well as that of the nation—and, possibly, that of the world. From that standpoint, Desaix had to admit that he was jealous of Barnett. One wrong decision or one missed opportunity and no group of gods on Mount Olympus could do anything to rectify that mistake.

Whatever else might happen, Desaix was determined to keep the President's condition secret. It would allow him to maneuver with a maximum amount of flexibility and a minimum amount of interference.

Standing alongside Barnett was Lieutenant Commander Neva Moser, USN, an attractive, petite woman, holding two defibrillator paddles over Westview's bare chest, ready to pass, if needed, three hundred and fifty volts of electricity through the President's body.

Dressed in a green scrub suit, Mary stood in one corner of the high-tech operating room, along with two attending surgeons and two scrub nurses, fearful that she might be more of a hindrance than a help.

Moser handed Barnett the two defibrillator paddles. He held the paddles close to the President's chest, waiting for them to charge up to their full capacity. Only the reflexive responses of Barnett's well-rehearsed motions would determine whether or not the President of the United States would live or die. Or worse, remain in an intractable coma.

"Clear the table!" Barnett ordered. He placed both paddles on the President's chest. "Okay, Neva, give me the juice!"

Westview's body jumped in the air as the bolt of electricity raced through his body in a desperate attempt to awaken it.

"Flatline, Doctor!" Moser exclaimed as she watched the EKG monitor trace its deadly signature.

"Juice me, Neva!" Barnett said, placing the paddles on the President's chest again. "Clear the table!"

This time, Westview's body looked as if it were being raised off the metal operating table by some hidden electromagnetic force.

"Still a flatline, Doctor."

"How about intracardiac calcium to prime the heart?" Desaix asked almost sheepishly, reluctant to interfere.

"Good idea. Neva, get me five cc's of calcium chloride in a size seven syringe. STAT!" Barnett nodded to his fully suited operating staff to be ready to lend him a hand.

"Here, Doctor. A gauge seven syringe with five cc's of calcium chloride." Handing Barnett the syringe, Moser, like most well-trained OR/ICU nurses, repeated the doctor's order as a way of counteracting the possibility of a mistake.

Barnett glanced up at Desaix, who had been hovering around Westview's body, before he inserted the metal needle into the fourth left intercostal space, directly over the heart. Pulling back slowly on the syringe, Barnett watched the bright red blood flow from the left ventricle of the heart into the potentially life-saving solution of calcium.

Then he quickly plunged the needle forward and pushed the five cc's of calcium chloride directly into Westview's heart muscle.

"Let's zap him again," Barnett said, then grabbed the paddles and placed them on Westview's chest.

Once again, the body jumped. If it weren't so serious, Desaix would have broken out laughing.

"Doctor, we're starting to get ventricular fibrillation," Moser said, watching as the white lines on the EKG terminal formed little blunted peaks on what was once a flatline.

"Ten cc's procaine amide."

"Yes, sir." Moser injected the medication into the IV bottle of 5 percent D5W.

"Ventricular tachycardia. It looks a little better."

Desaix relaxed a little. Although Westview was still in danger, at least he was starting to develop arrhythmias, which could be treated.

"Push another bolus of 5 percent procaine amide," Barnett said.

"Normal sinus rhythm." Moser was almost gleeful. A cheer broke out in the OR.

Mary raised her arms in a sign of victory.

But as far as Desaix was concerned, this was only the beginning of their problems. Westview had a dissecting aneurysm, and within a short time he would be hemorrhaging.

"I think we should type and cross-match the President's blood," Desaix said. "Neva, what's his hemoglobin and hematocrit?"

Moser walked over to the analog spectrophotometer, which could instantaneously read out a patient's blood picture. "Hematocrit is twenty-four and dropping. Normal standardization is forty to fifty-four. Hemoglobin is seven and dropping. Normal standardization is fourteen to eighteen."

"As I feared, he's losing a lot of blood," Desaix said, wondering whether Barnett knew about Westview's Marfan's syndrome. It was not unusual for a President to keep an unusual medical condition to himself. Very few of Kennedy's personal physicians knew anything about his congenital adrenal insufficiency, Addison's disease.

"Neva, quickly hang up two units of bloodtype O negative!" Barnett ordered. "Then get the blood bank to send over five units of the President's prefrozen plasma!" Moser took two units of whole blood from the freezer in the operating room and handed them to Barnett, who piggybacked them onto the IV bottles.

Mary felt awkward. There was very little she could do to help out. And she felt subtle nonverbals from Moser that made her uncomfortable.

The two surgeons and nurses dispersed themselves to different parts of the OR, preparing themselves for what would be a major operation.

"Desaix, how did you know that the President was losing blood?" Barnett asked, beginning to formulate in his own mind the plans he needed to put into place in order to move the President out of the White House and into Naval Bethesda Hospital.

"From his precipitous drop in blood pressure, accompanied by a sudden cardiac arrest." Desaix knew that this was not a real answer to Barnett's question. But he needed a bargaining chip. And information could be a very useful chip. If he played his cards correctly, Desaix suspected that he could get what he wanted—President Westview remaining in the White House under a shroud of complete secrecy. Only Dr. Hugh Barnett, whom he had known only slightly before this episode, could make this possible.

"Desaix, I'm asking you as one doctor to another. How did you know that the President was bleeding so severely? Remember what you told me when I first asked you what had happened?"

"Yes, I remember." Desaix was playing unfairly, and he knew it. A man's life was at stake and he was holding back on vital information that could possible save him. In the world outside of power and politics, Desaix could be brought up on charges of unethical professional behavior. But when it involved the destiny of the country's security, Desaix felt he was entitled to take certain liberties.

"Desaix! This isn't some kind of political game!" Barnett said, then looked toward Mary for help. "The President's life is on the line. You told me that Westview had been talking to you and Mary and then suddenly went into cardiac arrest."

"Don't you have his medical history?" Desaix replied in a righteously indignant tone of voice. He wanted to grab the high moral ground as quickly as possible.

"You know damn well that the White House physician is the last one to know anything about the President's medical condition. Most Presidents keep their personal medical histories to themselves, and share them only when they have a desperate need to. They usually treat the White House physician as nothing more than an extra burden that the Secret Service has imposed on them." Barnett did another cursory physical examination on Westview. He was conscious of Desaix's watchful eyes, as if he were being examined by a medical board to determine whether he was fit to become a surgeon.

"So what did you find out from your medical exam?" Desaix knew he couldn't play this game of who-knows-what much longer. Time was running out. One way or another, Westview would have to have an operation. He watched as the OR staff prepared for major cardiovascular surgery, turning on the heart-lung machine, priming it with three units of whole blood.

"Bilateral hyperelasticity of both extremities combined with a subluxation of the corneal lenses," Barnett answered.

"Does that tell you anything?" Desaix was not surprised that Barnett didn't immediately know the diagnosis. Although an extremely competent surgeon, Barnett was not known to be a sophisticated diagnostician. Surgeons, in general, were primarily cutters and sewers. That's what they did best.

"It tells me I wouldn't want to operate on him."

"Why?" Desaix asked.

"Because if his extremities are any indication of some underlying connective tissue disease, then it would be a mess trying to put him back together. I'm not sure any of his tissue or skin would hold together."

"What if you had no other choice but to operate on him?" Although Barnett had described the condition, he still couldn't identify it. But in all fairness to Barnett, Marfan's syndrome wasn't exactly a household word. And the likelihood of Barnett having treated a similar case was almost one in a million.

Barnett and Neva wrapped Westview in a hypothermic blanket, trying to lower his body temperature so he could survive another cardiovascular shock to his system.

"Time is running out, Dr. Barnett." Checking his watch, Desaix realized that he only had an hour left before his meeting with the Secretary of State.

"That's right, Dr. Clark. We have a patient who is rapidly dying because we don't know exactly what his condition is. So maybe I should remind you of the Hippocratic oath." Turning toward Neva, he added, "Call Naval Bethesda and tell them to prepare the presidential suite. Then call the White House communications office and ask for a helicopter to take us to the hospital."

"Yes, sir," Neva replied, picking up the telephone.

"Not so fast, Ms. Moser!" Desaix ordered.

Mary and the other support staff in the OR were startled by Desaix's peremptory order. But she felt she knew him well enough to suspect that he wasn't playing any games. Certainly, he was concerned about the President's well-being. But she suspected that he was even more worried about the war in Europe and the intended coup. Having observed his style over the past two days, she came to the conclusion that he would stop at nothing to attain control over the situation.

"What should I do, Dr. Barnett?" Neva felt trapped.

"Let's hear what Dr. Clark proposes," Barnett said as he injected five cc's of a beta blocker into Westview to maintain the regularity of his sinus rhythm. Palpating the abdominal region, he detected some rigidity, indicating that fluid was leaking into Westview's abdominal cavity. If something didn't change soon, Barnett would be dealing with an internal hemorrhage and be forced to perform an emergency laparotomy. And that would be a nightmare.

"I need forty-eight hours of complete silence," Desaix said. "No one, but no one, other than the people in this room, the rest of your OR staff, and

Randy Newmann, the President's appointments secretary, is to know the condition of the President. As far as everyone is concerned, the President is incommunicado because he is totally preoccupied by the war."

"May I ask why?"

"You may. But I may not respond."

"What am I supposed to do if the President starts to rupture internally?" Barnett asked, concerned that he would have to assume full responsibility for the President's death. It was too scary to contemplate.

"You'll operate on him right here! You have three of the best-equipped, most modern operating rooms in the world. You have two outstanding surgeons and one internist to assist you. And in addition to Ms. Moser, you have an additional ten OR/ICU support staff specifically trained for this type of situation. You are better equipped than most of the major hospitals in this region, including your beloved Naval Bethesda. You're simply implementing the mandate that was created over ten years ago when this special medical unit was created in the White House."

"Okay, you've made your point, Desaix." Barnett looked hesitantly at Neva, the two other doctors, and the two nurses—all nodded their heads in approval. "What's Westview's diagnosis?"

"Here's the deal. I'll give you the diagnosis, which will make life a lot simpler for you because you'll know exactly what to do. You keep him here— pre- and post-op for the next forty-eight hours. During that time, neither you, Neva, nor anyone else in this room will talk to anyone about the President's condition or what transpired between you and me."

"And after the forty-eight-hour period?"

"After that, you can do whatever you deem appropriate. If I won't be able to resolve some of the major problems in the next two days, it won't really matter what you will or won't do."

"What makes you so sure I will stick to our bargain?"

"From everything I've heard, I think that you are a man of your word."

"One professional gentleman to another, right?" Barnett added with a sardonic smile.

"Yes, but just in case you have a memory relapse, Mary Dougherty, in her official capacity as Director of the President's Protective Detail, will see that you keep your word." Desaix turned toward Mary for confirmation.

"Dr. Barnett knows that the Secret Service, by statute, must be present at any and all medical procedures that may be performed on the President of the United States," Mary said. Although she had some qualms about the ethical nature of what Desaix was doing, she was impressed by the way he was able to maneuver Barnett into a position of compliance.

"And if I need any further personnel or equipment, what do I do then, Dr. Clark?" Barnett asked, though he knew that it was futile to continue the discussion with Desaix. He would only be boxing himself further into a corner. It was a no-win proposition for the moment.

"Do what you normally do. Fill out your request in triplicate and hand it to Mary. She will take care of it."

Desaix beckoned Mary to accompany him as he walked to the door, then turned back to Dr. Barnett. "He's got Marfan's syndrome with a dissecting abdominal aneurysm," Desaix said. "He needs an operation STAT! I'll be back in a few hours to check on the President's condition."

Outside of the operating suites, Mary put her arm around him.

"You are a brilliantly charming stinker," she said. "I'm not certain that if I were a member of those medical ethics committees that I wouldn't pull your license to practice medicine. But I do know that had President Westview been privy to your discussion with Barnett, he would have appreciated your strategy. As despicable as it may have been."

"Mary, would you believe me if I told you that I don't really enjoy manipulating someone like Barnett. He's a decent, competent fellow."

"I believe that you believe that you are not as evil as people think or wish that you might be."

"Thanks. I'm glad someone understands me." He wanted very badly to nuzzle her. "But Randy's next. She's going to be crucial if we want to keep this whole thing secret."

"Let me handle her. She trusts me," Mary said, before leading him into Randy's office. There was something dangerously infectious about having witnessed Desaix effectively manipulate the President's personal physician.

"Mary! Dr. Clark! My God, how I've been waiting for you to come!" Randy rushed around her cluttered desk and hugged Mary. Her eyes were red and swollen from crying.

"He's going to be all right, Randy. We've just been with him and Dr. Barnett," Mary said.

"Oh, thank God, thank God," she said, bursting into tears of gratefulness. "Are you certain that the President will be fine?" Randy clearly needed the kind of assurances only Mary could provide.

"It depends," Mary replied.

"On what?" Pulling back, Randy looked startled.

"Well," Mary replied, "it depends on whether you care enough about him."

"Mary, what on earth are you talking about?" Looking hurt, she turned toward Desaix for an answer.

"I know that you care a lot about the President," Mary continued.

"Yes, I do!"

"So the real issue is how much you really like him," Mary said, hoping that she wasn't overplaying her hand, even though Randy was biting the bait.

"Mary . . . I just can't believe you'd say that."

"You're right. I'm sorry. I think we've all had an emotional shock. Please, forgive me."

"All right, but what are you driving at? What can I do to help?"

"Have you told anyone at all about his condition?" Desaix asked, concerned that his plan may have already been compromised.

"No, I did just as you instructed me to do. I've told everyone, including General Mapplethorpe and General White, only that he was not available."

"How did they respond?"

Randy buzzed the front office to hold all calls; otherwise they would never finish their conversation. She hoped that her gesture would also lend credence to her ability to deal with the issues of silence and secrecy.

"What did they do?" Desaix continued, trying to arrive at the extent of Mapplethorpe's persistence.

"The same things that you do, Dr. Clark, when I won't let you talk to the President."

"You mean they became incredibly obnoxious?" Desaix replied goodnaturedly.

"That's putting it mildly! Mapplethorpe has assigned a Navy captain to call me every hour on the hour. Can you believe that! A Navy captain?"

"Randy, listen to me very carefully," Mary said, surprised at the seriousness of her own voice. "The President needs to rest now. But he won't get that rest if he has interruptions."

"I understand. I won't let anyone disturb him, even if I have to body-block anyone who tries to barge in."

"That's great, Randy. But I'm afraid that may not be enough," Mary replied.

"What do you mean?"

"Do you have any idea why the President wanted to see me and Desaix in the middle of the night?" Mary was pleased with how well she was leading Randy, ever so subtly, down the path of compliance.

"No, but I know that he wanted to see you very badly because he insisted that I track you both down, no matter where you might be." Looking at both of them, Randy flushed with embarrassment when she suddenly realized that she had accidentally discovered them both at Mary's house.

"He needed our help," Mary said, certain that the emphasis on the word "our" was not lost on Randy.

"Why?" Randy stood transfixed, like a child who was just about to be read a fantastic story.

"He wanted our help because . . ." Mary paused to emphasize its dramatic importance, hoping Desaix would pick up on the cue.

". . . because a group of people are trying to overthrow the President," Desaix interjected, making certain that Randy would not lose the full implication of what he was trying to tell her, since much of his plan depended upon her willingness to keep every advisor away from Westview. It was a difficult task to ask of anyone, let alone a wholesome Midwestern young woman whose very credo was apple pie and honesty.

"What do you mean?" Randy asked, totally taken aback by the news. She sank into the overstuffed armchair. Her face blanched. "Who would want to overthrow President Westview?"

"I am not at liberty to fully explain it to you," Mary said, "but the simple fact is that the President was aware that a military coup was in the offing for some time now, led by none other than General Thomas Mapplethorpe."

"What?"

"That's right, Randy," Mary said. "We have hard evidence that Mapplethorpe is directly responsible."

Randy knew that despite Westview's personal misgivings about Desaix, he never questioned Desaix's professional judgment or performance. When his advisors would complain about Desaix being an uncontrollable loose cannon, Westview would laugh knowingly and reply that "not one of those ingrates minds calling Desaix when they need someone to cover their collective asses." The President trusted Desaix's personal loyalty to the office of the presidency implicitly. So whatever Desaix had to tell her or request from her had to be taken seriously.

"You will have to trust Mary and me when we tell you that under no condition should he or anyone else, other than us, Dr. Barnett and his OR staff, know about the President's condition."

"No one is to visit him. Including his own wife," Mary said, though she knew that Mrs. Westview would be less of a problem than anyone realized. She spent most of her time away from Washington at their Palm Beach estate. When she wasn't busy tending to the demands of her servants, she was shopping at the fashionable Worth Avenue stores or watching the polo matches at the Palm Beach Polo Club.

"I understand. But even if I am willing to do what you are asking, I don't know how to. It's close to an impossible task. There's the war . . . and the riots . . . and . . ."

"Don't worry, Mary will help you," Desaix responded with a smile. "I think the best excuse you might use after you've exhausted the one about the President's being too busy is to say that he's resting quietly because he has a slight flu. This way you don't have to lie too much, and that's one excuse that elicits sympathy and deters further inquiry. I've got to get going, but I will be back soon."

"Thanks, Dr. Clark. I will try to handle this." Randy returned to her desk and phoned for the telephone messages she had just missed.

Desaix drew Mary over to a side corridor, avoiding the people who were beginning to arrive at work. "Thanks for winging it. Now, here's my plan. Let's work under the cover of Mapplethorpe's military coup."

"What do you mean?"

"Come on, Mary. You know what I mean," Desaix admonished her. "You're going to have to ride a very tight rein on both Barnett and Randy."

"Yes, sir!"

"Do nothing to disrupt Mapplethorpe's plan. We're going to use it as our camouflage. By now, I suspect that he's taken over control of the media as well as the government's communication system, so that the potential for news leakage concerning the President's medical condition is drastically minimized."

"Ah, so you admit that there are certain advantages to a military coup?" she asked facetiously.

"Definite advantages. And you and I are going to exploit every one of them." Desaix checked his watch, afraid he was running behind schedule.

"I want you to use your most trusted Secret Service agents to guard the President. Make certain that no one gets anywhere near him. Or that Barnett gets any fanciful ideas."

"Got it!" Saluting him, she added with a broad smile, "What else my Grössen Oberführer?"

"Take as many men as you need and go over to the Old Executive Office Building, to the Baltimore Room. As unobtrusively as you can, try to retake Mapplethorpe's central communications system. At most, he may have twenty people in there. Look for any incriminating documents."

"What about collateral damage?" She rubbed her injured thigh, reminding herself of the possibility of killing people. This was very serious business.

"Are you up to it?"

"I think so. Anyway, when it's all over, you can reward me with a trip to a lovely inn I know on Martha's Vineyard. We'll both need a rest and the Captain Dexter House in Edgartown is the place to get it."

"You got it!" he said, smiling. Then he wondered if the Captain Dexter House was a place she and Judy Taylor had gone together. But right now that was the least of his worries. "Once you've taken it over, make sure you get to me."

"Where are you and Woody Woodpecker going to be?" she asked, pulling him more closely toward her. "I guess I should be more respectful toward you, shouldn't I?"

"Yes, you should! Is this the way you are with your own team of agents?"

"Hell, no. I would kill anyone who tried some smart-ass attitude like that with me." She smiled. "But look how much I've improved since I've been around you."

"You've become a wonderful partner." They affectionately rubbed noses.

"How about lover?" She bit her upper lip.

"That too."

"I'll keep reminding you of that."

"Right now I've got to get over to Manning's office; otherwise, my name is deep shit. Then, I want to see some of my newly appointed friends at the Agency and maybe even the NSA. I've got to find out what they know about all of this mess."

"You're going to see Ball and White?"

"Yeah. Listen, I hate to break up a swell party, but I've got to get going." As he said it, he found it hard to leave her.

"Listen, cowboy. Do me a favor."

"I'm listening."

"I'm serious, now." Mary's face turned from an impish expression to an extremely concerned one. "Be careful."

Desaix handed in his visitor's badge marked with the large letter A, and walked through the turnstile in the bulletproof booth on Pennsylvania Avenue. As usual, he was late for his 9:30 A.M. appointment with Manning and Imai.

Reflecting on the meeting between Westview and Manning, Desaix wondered what further evidence Manning might have to buttress his argument that the President was crazy. Did it involve Imai?

Walking past two diplomatic security agents, with their characteristic grim, impersonal expressions, Desaix shook Secretary of State Charles Manning's hand. This time there were no Band-Aids. But he noticed rashes on the fourth and fifth fingers of his left hand. Probably contact dermatitis from the rings.

"Come on in, Desaix! I have a friend here who has been waiting to see you."

Desaix didn't say a word. Only one image rushed through his mind, but it was so absurd that he immediately dismissed it. He was trying to imagine the two gold rings on the left hand of the man in Mary's photograph.

Desaix's head was spinning. Should he ask him what Judy was like in bed? Christ, he thought, Judy really got around. Westview. Mary. Himself. And now Manning. But maybe he was jumping to conclusions a little too quickly. Just because Manning wore rings on his left hand, like the man in the picture, didn't necessarily mean he was the same person. On the other hand, it didn't exclude him either. Only one person could corroborate his suspicions—Mary Dougherty.

As he opened the door, Manning's guest stood up and smiled broadly.

"Kanbanwa, Yutaka Imai," Desaix said, smiled warmly, stood up, and bowed.

"Kanbanwa, Dr. Desaix Clark." Imai shook Desaix's hand firmly.

"Why didn't you tell me you were coming? I would have met you at the airport."

"I'm sorry, my friend, but I left only a few short hours after your flight. My departure from Tokyo was almost as sudden as yours."

"I knew that you would be happy to see each other," Manning said, beaming with delight as if he had arranged a successful blind date.

"What brings you here?" Desaix paused, unable to resist his next thought. "Were you upset with our negotiations?"

"Oh no! Not at all!" Staring at Manning, Imai added, "On the contrary,

I was just commending you to the Secretary for your professional handling of a most difficult situation, both in the negotiations as well as in that tragic incident with Fitzpatrick."

Desaix nodded his head in gratitude. He knew that Imai was only telling part of a story. Something was missing. Imai hadn't come eight thousand miles, in the middle of a mounting international crisis, to inform the Secretary of State that one of his senior officials had done a good job. At the same time, Imai hadn't flown to the U.S. in order to discuss their negotiating impasse over stationing the 9132 Mobile Radio Unit on the island of Kyushu. He could have done that by sending a message through the Japanese Embassy. So why was he here?

"Yes, Desaix, Imai has just been telling me what an admirable job you did in Tokyo under the most trying situation," Manning said, then paused. "I know how upset you were with Fitzpatrick's mysterious death in the—"

"Geisha house, sir," Desaix interjected.

"Yes, geisha house. Thank you for helping me out."

Desaix nodded his head. What a hypocrite, he thought. Manning knew those geisha houses quite well.

"I'm sure that you are still wondering what brought me over to the United States in such an urgent manner?" Imai bowed his head, recognizing the fact that Desaix was purposefully being kept in the dark.

"I always assume you have extremely good reasons for whatever you do," Desaix said, suddenly realizing there was a silent collusion between Imai and Manning.

"Thank you, my friend, for your undeserved trust in me." Imai removed a small envelope from the inside pocket of his brown suit jacket and handed it to Desaix. Manning watched intently.

Carefully opening up the tightly sealed package, Desaix sensed that what he was about to see would definitely be a surprise. He was beginning to feel uncomfortable with both men hovering around him, eagerly awaiting his response.

"My God!" Desaix exclaimed after he opened it. The package contained a stack of three-by-five glossy pictures of Fitzpatrick being tortured by a group of men. "That's David Brooks!"

"Correct. President Westview's handpicked special agent. In reality, a Special Ops technician who specializes in intelligence . . . and unusual interrogation methods." Manning's tone was as somber as Desaix had ever heard it.

Each photograph became progressively more gruesome. The pictures showed Fitzpatrick being forcibly pushed into a bucket of what appeared to be a toxic fluid, presumably hydrofluoric acid, because the subsequent picture showed Fitzpatrick's necrotic wound in the right eye. Eventually, Desaix had to turn his head away from the final picture of Fitzpatrick, lying on a floor of wooden slats, with scratch marks of presumably dried blood stretched all the way from one nipple to the other and a gaping hole where his right eye had been.

Looking up at Imai, Desaix could barely speak. He wasn't certain what exactly bothered him. Clearly, the pictures underlined the cruelty of Fitzpatrick's death. But Desaix had seen Fitzpatrick's mutilated body at the morgue in Chuo-Ku prefecture. It was not a pretty sight then. So by now he should have accustomed himself to the sight of the tortured body. There was something else. Maybe it was the fact that someone had been ordered to take those pictures during Fitzpatrick's torture. But who? And why?

"Take a closer look at the men on both sides of Brooks," Imai said as he handed Desaix a magnifying glass.

Desaix examined the picture of Brooks holding Fitzpatrick's head in the vat of acid. He moved the magnifying glass carefully across the paper, as if he were looking at a pathology slide beneath a microscope. But, in this instance, there were no macrophages or microbes to discover. It was a little more sinister. He was looking for people he would know. Desaix was impressed by the sheer number of people involved in Fitzpatrick's torture. But where were they when he was looking for witnesses? Only two days ago, he had been told there were none. Now it looked as if an entire assembly had been invited to this macabre party at the geisha house.

"Desaix, my boy, I know that this is not easy for you. But take a careful look at the face to the immediate right of Brooks." Manning began to pace the small Bokhara rug in front of the coffee table.

"No, sir. It's not easy for me. But I'm just a little bit confused about how these pictures suddenly appeared, when only two days ago I was told by Imai and the Prefecture Chief of Police that there was no evidence or any culprits." Desaix realized that he was embarrassing his friend Imai, but there was too much at stake.

"I'll be happy to answer that question for you. But first, my friend, try to identify the face that Secretary Manning suggested to you." Imai sounded impatient.

Why is Imai so eager for me to identify those pictures? wondered Desaix. What was his agenda? He moved the magnifying glass more slowly this time and stopped at the outline of a taut, lean man with short-cropped hair. "General Richard White!"

"The newly appointed National Security Advisor to President Westview," Manning spoke with contempt in his voice. "And who's that on the other side of him?"

Examining the blunt features of the stocky man, Desaix was reluctant to speak. It couldn't be!

"Can you guess, my friend?" Imai asked in a soothing voice.

"No, it's not possible!" Desaix clearly recognized the face. But it couldn't be!

"James Ball. Former Director of the Office of Scientific Intelligence, and the newly appointed Director of the CIA," Manning said, as if he were a Greek chorus, making certain that Desaix would not miss the obvious implications of his statement.

"Ball and White! It's just not possible! They were in the rooms next to me!" Desaix recalled the photograph that the President had shown him, ostensibly incriminating Mapplethorpe, White, and Ball. It showed a nude man with tape over his mouth, allegedly Fitzpatrick, being held down by two large men wrapped in white towels. One of them looked like White. The other may have been Ball. Both of the men reported to Mapplethorpe, according to the President. But this photo showed evidence of five men, not two, torturing Fitzpatrick. Desaix was confused. He wondered which photo was the real one? Who took it? And why? For the moment, he wasn't going to say anything until he could sort out all the contradictory pieces of evidence in his mind.

"No, my friend," Imai said somberly. "You *thought* that they were in the rooms next to you. But in fact they were in Fitzpatrick's room, torturing him."

"Why didn't I hear any noise?" Desaix was trying to assimilate all the information as quickly as possible. Brooks. White. Ball. And there were two other men present in the room. They were standing to the sides of White and Ball. Their faces were blurred. One was clearly an Oriental. The other seemed to be a shorter, more compact version of White.

"Dr. Oda Nobunaga, the forensic pathologist whom you met in Tokyo, concluded from the autopsy blood reports that Fitzpatrick was given a sedative beforehand so that he would remain quiet. Dr. Nobunaga also suggested that Fitzpatrick was given a tranquilizer to diminish the extent of pain that he might feel."

"How considerate!" Desaix replied facetiously. He recalled Dr. Nobunaga—short, cherubic, incompetent. It was Nobunaga who had insisted that Fitzpatrick was killed with a gun. At the time, Desaix had been annoyed by his blatant error in diagnosis. Now Desaix wondered, Had he been purposely misled?

Desaix repositioned the magnifying glass on the Oriental face. It wasn't easy to detect any distinct features. But the more Desaix stared at the photograph, the more he imagined that the person was none other than Nobunaga himself.

Looking up at Imai's smiling face, Desaix decided to say nothing. For some reason, it was clear that neither Imai nor Manning expected him to detect the identity of Nobunaga.

"Our police were unable to make an identification of the two other people in that picture, other than the fact that one of the men was Caucasian and the other Oriental," Imai replied matter-of-factly.

"Imai, are you certain that no one could identify either of the two?"

Desaix watched Imai closely, hoping he was wrong about his worst thoughts.

"Desaix, I wish that I could say I knew the identities of the other two people in that picture. But we have an old Japanese expression that says that all Orientals look alike." Imai broke into a high-pitched, child-like laugh.

Manning simply smiled. "Frankly, I think that fuzzy picture of the Occidental reminds me of Colonel Sonny Shaw. I can't tell you why, but it just does." Manning looked quizzically at Imai, as if he were waiting for a response.

"Clearly, I was shown those pictures so that I might reach some conclusion. What is that you want me to conclude?" Desaix put the picture in his jacket pocket. Added to Mary's picture, Desaix felt like a walking bombshell. One photograph implicated Manning in some type of ménage à trois. And the President's photo implicated Mapplethorpe, White, and Ball in the heinous crime.

On the other hand, Imai's picture clearly implicated Brooks, Shaw, Ball, and White, as well as Westview or Mapplethorpe. Possibly even both. But with Nobunaga in the picture, there seemed to be a greater dimension to this murder. Did that mean that Imai knew about it? Beforehand or only afterward? And who else was involved in this conspiracy of murder? Was it part of the planned coup against the President? Did it have anything to do with this precipitous crisis against the Russians? Was it any accident that two countries with similar domestic crises would have almost identical military coups, attempted at approximately the same point in time, against two faltering leaders? How did this all relate to Twitty's warning about Westview's hidden agenda to precipitate a war? Could Zotov also have the same hidden agenda? And what about Westview's own admission that he was trying to start a war? Was it possible that Westview had been coordinating his strategy with Zotov all along? Christ! Desaix thought to himself. He had more inconsistent observations, facts, and questions than even he was comfortable with.

"I asked you here because I wanted you to see the same evidence that Imai showed me."

"As soon as our police were able to obtain these pictures, I flew here to show them to Secretary Manning personally," Imai said. He was having trouble reading his friend's flat facial expression.

"What does this all mean?"

"Think about it, Desaix." Manning gripped Desaix's shoulders tightly. "I think these pictures are quite incriminating."

"Of whom?" Desaix wanted Manning to answer the questions that he was trying to get Desaix to answer.

"I think it's self-evident. Don't you?" Manning sounded annoyed. Desaix wasn't responding in a predictable manner. "I asked you to find the necessary evidence to prove that Westview was certifiably insane. So far, you've seen the restricted cable, the Special Forces at St. E's, the canisters of hydrogen fluoride, and you've witnessed his bizarre behavior in our meeting with him at the White House. It's my opinion that this picture proves that Westview was directly responsible for Fitzpatrick's murder. I asked Imai to fly all the way here to vouchsafe for the validity of this photograph, which is certainly the most definitive piece of evidence to certify the President as insane."

"Please, not so fast, Mr. Secretary," Desaix said. "What I see is a lot of people in our government involved in the murder of Fitzpatrick. For reasons that are still unknown."

"That's true, Desaix. But don't you find it strange that most of the members of your negotiating team were, in one way or another, involved in Fitzpatrick's death? Including two principals who have since been promoted to major cabinet positions?"

"Mr. Secretary, let me understand this correctly. Are you telling me that you think President Westview ordered the murder of Fitzpatrick?"

"Yes!"

"And what about Mapplethorpe?" Desaix looked at the impenetrable expressions on both Manning's and Imai's faces.

"We have strong evidence to suggest that it was Mapplethorpe who carried out the President's instructions. Everyone in that picture worked directly for the President under the supervision of Mapplethorpe." Manning looked disturbed. He couldn't seem to elicit the astonished, disturbed response he had expected from Desaix.

"Everyone?" Desaix asked.

"Yes, everyone!"

"Including the unidentified Oriental?" Desaix asked as he scrutinized Imai's face, although it betrayed nothing.

"Most probably," Imai said, then added, "even though we can't identify him."

"Why would the President want to kill his own senior expert on Russian affairs?" Desaix asked, now feeling anxious. He was beginning to sense that real betrayal was at the crux of both Fitzpatrick's murder and the current crisis.

"That's why I called you in. I would like you to find out why the President and his National Security Advisor would want to have Fitzpatrick brutally tortured and murdered."

"Why me, sir?"

"Because you're close to the President," Manning replied hesitantly, realizing that the answer was not good enough for Desaix. "He trusts you as a professional. And so do I."

"And you want me to declare the President of the United States insane," Desaix replied hesitantly, mindful of Imai's presence.

"If, in your professional opinion, that's what you feel is appropriate."

"Then you, as the Secretary of State, would somehow have the Vice President invoke the Twenty-fifth Amendment of the Constitution to activate the constitutional line of succession. First the Vice President. Then the Speaker of the House. Then the President pro tempore of the Senate. And then . . ."

"The Secretary of State," Imai said, nodding his head in silent approval.

# CHAPTER
## 33

**W**hen Manning urged Jenkins to come downtown for a meeting with McCormick and Merck, Jenkins knew his life was in danger.

Manning was suspicious that Mapplethorpe had set up and recorded the secret Pentagon meeting for the sole purpose of creating the necessary pretext to "accidentally" eliminate this "dangerous cabal" of disgruntled ex-cabinet officials.

So Jenkins carefully checked his car for any plastique hidden beneath the car's carriage or along the metal rim of the hubcaps.

"Daddy, what are you doing?" Lynne, his spunky eleven-year-old daughter asked. She ran up to him and hugged him.

"Come on in, sweetheart!" her mother interrupted. "Daddy is busy right now." Mrs. Jenkins was an attractive middle-aged woman who had always been supportive of her husband's career. Like many of the women who had married into the Agency, she had learned to live a life of obligatory paranoia. Although it wasn't easy, there was an element of unpredictability and danger that she and Larry had learned to tolerate without having to take out the inherent stress and tensions of his dangerous job on each other. It had taken years of marriage counseling, which had been arranged by the newly enlightened Agency, staffed by sensitive, caring mental health workers. The "New Agency" had helped to keep her marriage intact. For that, Mrs. Jenkins was extremely appreciative. In the old days, it was expected that a station chief would have been married and divorced at least once. Previous DDIs and DDOs had a typical history of twenty-year marriages, filled with emotional *sturm und drang*, terminating when the husband announced he had been having an affair with his secretary, which required him, by some solipsistic logic of self-preservation, to divorce his wife, break up the family, and marry his secretary, in order to maintain his job security and TOP SECRET clearance. All that changed after Larry Jenkins became the DCI. If nothing else, he had brought marital harmony back into the spy business.

Mrs. Jenkins knew to ask or say very little when he began to check his prize possession—his new Lexus sedan. His tinkering was usually a sign that something was very wrong. And she had learned through extensive counseling to respect the way he handled his professional fears and concerns.

"Sweetheart, I'm just checking for some loose bolts. You know I pamper my Lexus almost as much as I pamper you!"

Jenkins stopped to give his daughter the big hug she wanted. He looked lovingly at his wife.

"Larry, are you certain you want to drive downtown? Why don't you use the subway? It will get you there much faster." Mrs. Jenkins turned away, unwilling to let him see the tears welling up in her eyes. She was trying not to show him she was worrying about his silent preoccupation.

"Mrs. Jenkins, since when did you become my travel agent?"

"Okay, you're right, Larry." Mrs. Jenkins really didn't want to go back inside yet.

"Daddy, can I go with you?" Lynne held tightly on to her father.

"Not today, baby!" Jenkins suddenly felt guilty that he hadn't spent any significant amount of time with her in the past several months. He had been busy, staffing out the HUMINT, ELINT, and SIGINT requirements for the White House and the National Security Advisor. And now Mapplethorpe had turned against him. The ad hoc meeting at the Pentagon was a classic first-year exercise in setting up a client the Agency wanted to turn against.

The next step was obvious to Jenkins—to publicly discredit him, Merck, and McCormick. Then Mapplethorpe could create a series of spontaneous accidents, which would receive very little news attention or public sympathy. It would be a convenient way to get rid of an embarrassing thorn in Mapplethorpe's side. Larry had no doubt that McCormick, Merck, and even Manning were in the same dangerous situation.

"Please, daddy. I want to go with you!" Lynne only knew enough about what her father did to impress her sixth-grade friends. She knew that he worked in some area of the government that dealt with secrets and traveling. But she was smart enough never to ask her father a question when she knew that he might lie to her.

Mrs. Jenkins ran into the house as the phone rang. Her momentary departure gave Jenkins the opportunity to hold tightly on to Lynne and speak to her in a way that he knew would alarm his wife.

"Sweetheart, you know that I love you very much, don't you?" He looked around his front lawn and house. No one was watching them. No unusual cars. No unusual trucks. No telephone workers fixing the telephone wires.

For the moment, Jenkins concluded, he was safe. More importantly, his family was safe. Mapplethorpe wouldn't be stupid enough to hurt his family. That would be gratuitous and unnecessary. And, if nothing else, Mapplethorpe was a man of sparse motions and actions. "I know that you want to go with me. But right now I have to meet with some very important people who aren't going to be bringing their children with them. So I don't think you'll enjoy sitting around some stuffy office, waiting for me to come out."

"All right, daddy. But next time, you promise to take me?"

"I promise, sweetheart."

Lynne covered her father with wet kisses she called slurpies and then ran inside the house.

"Larry, that was Chet Manning on the phone," his wife said, standing at the door. "He insisted that you take the subway downtown and get off at the Foggy Bottom exit. He said that he would have one of his men waiting for you. And that you would recognize him."

"Well, you were right. You are a great travel agent." He walked up toward her and gave her a farewell hug.

"I'm not too bad at making your arrangements, am I?"

"No. Apparently you and the Secretary of State think alike. That's quite a compliment." Jenkins was relieved that his wife would be comforted by the notion that the Secretary of State was concerned enough for his safety that he made a special phone call.

"Please, be careful, Larry. I never liked Mapplethorpe. He's a snake." She hugged him again, then gave him one of those kisses that she usually reserved for his two-week trips abroad.

"Bye, baby. If you don't hear from me in the next couple of hours or so, don't worry."

"I know, I know. Get going. You'll be late." She pushed him away, indicating that she wasn't worried.

"Take care." He slid into the driver's seat, pressed his foot down on the accelerator, and headed toward the Friendship Heights metro station in Chevy Chase. He parked his car and walked quickly toward the escalators leading down to the trains.

The station at Friendship Heights, located on the border of Washington and Maryland, was always in some state of disrepair. So it was not unusual for him to see a group of workmen dressed in coveralls fixing the escalator that he and only two other people were riding on.

A young girl, about his daughter's age, stood immediately in front of him, while an elderly woman was way above him, at the start of the escalator's descent.

Suddenly the young girl started to cry. The escalator steps in front of her had disappeared, flattening out into a grinding mesh of gears and interlocking metal parts. She tried to jump over the gaping hole, but couldn't. The girl fell into it, screaming.

Pieces of torn flesh and blood splattered Jenkins's recently pressed suit, as he too fell into the bowels of this newly constructed meat grinder.

Randolph Merck pulled his fifteen-year-old Datsun 280Z quickly out of the driveway of his million-dollar Federalist house in Chevy Chase. He was already late for the hastily arranged meeting with Manning and company. He drove down Western Avenue and stopped at the stop sign before entering Chevy Chase Circle, which he always found hazardous to navigate.

He was preoccupied with the impending meeting, wondering whether it really had any value. There were so many other things that he could be doing. But Manning had advised him not to do anything without first coordinating with the group. So for reasons that he himself did not understand, he acquiesced to Manning's request. Perhaps he needed their support more than he realized. The fact that the prior meeting had been taped was really not a surprise to him. That was standard operating procedure for all meetings held in the tank, whether they were official or informal.

He watched the traffic at the circle, thinking that today he would enter it aggressively and force the other cars to accommodate themselves to him.

But he had some trouble. A black Ford Torino would not let him cut into the circle. It hugged his car, keeping him at the outer edge of the circle and exposing him to the dangers of the five different streets feeding into the circle.

Shit, Merck thought, if I didn't know any better, I would think that whoever is driving that car is purposely trying to prevent me from entering the circle.

As he moved away from the Ford, Merck looked into his rear-view mirror. For a moment he thought he recognized the driver, a big man, looking like a parody of a professional wrestler who had been in the ring one too many times.

Merck made a right onto Connecticut Avenue, one of the broad boulevards leading to downtown Washington. Weaving in and out of traffic, he made a left onto Porter Street, past Adas Israel Synagogue, the house of worship for most of the Jewish members of the last three administrations, and a quick right turn into the synagogue's parking lot. He pulled into a space flanked by cars, and turned around in his seat to see if the Torino, which he had spotted ten blocks back, was still following him.

Nothing. Perhaps he was too jumpy.

He started his car again, and put it in reverse. CRUNCH! His car plowed into the driver's front door of the Torino.

Suddenly a bullet whizzed by Merck's head as he tried to get out of his car. There was no doubt now in Merck's mind that the man driving the Torino had been sent to assassinate him.

As Merck glanced around the parking lot, he realized that the only safe sanctuary was the synagogue itself. If he could get into the building, he had a chance of calling Manning for help and hiding until the police came.

He opened his door and ran into the synagogue through its back entrance, down carpeted corridors, toward the main sanctuary. The last time Merck had been here was as a guest at a bar mitzvah. He had been impressed by the large size and simplicity of the sanctuary, with its large rectangular windows, etched with overlapping Stars of David. In contrast to the Jason Memorial African Episcopal Church that he and many of the other black members of the administration attended, Adas Israel was a relatively unassuming, if not prosaic, house of worship.

Merck wondered, as he ran to the front of the sanctuary, whether the rabbi, like several clergy he knew, worked closely with the District police and the national security agencies of the federal government. Of all the synagogues in the District, Adas Israel probably could yield interesting intelligence, with so many high-ranking government officials as members. As Merck knew all too well, no religious congregation in Washington was exempt from working closely with the national security agencies. Georgetown University, a Jesuit-run Catholic university with a distinguished graduate school for foreign service, was a recruitment hotbed for potential CIA agents, as well as a sanctuary for retired CIA, DOD, and State Department operatives, who would teach one or two courses on U.S. foreign policy for the prestige of being an adjunct professor.

It was no secret that the Vatican had the most professional and extensive intelligence network in the world, next to Israel's Mossad. Of course, they had close to two thousand years to perfect it.

So it was ironic that Merck might meet his final destiny in a house of worship, a place that he had learned to revere and fear since childhood. While he had been taught since his Communion that the Jews were Christ killers, Merck had become sophisticated enough to learn that each religion had its own designated scapegoats and dirty secrets, all designed to maintain the myth that God does not betray man.

Only man betrays man.

Merck huddled between the seats of the sanctuary as his killer walked quietly around its rear, searching for telltale signs of Merck. His only hope was to distract the gunman and flee through the door on the side of the raised platform that contained the Ark with the Torah scrolls.

Christ, wondered Merck, didn't any of the Jews in this congregation pray during the weekdays? He picked up a thick black book, inscribed as the Haftorah, and flung it to the other side of the sanctuary, forcing his assailant to fire in the direction from which the sound came. Merck fled through the door, ran down a long corridor, and sneaked into an empty office.

"Send the police to Temple Adas Israel! This is an emergency!" Merck screamed into the phone.

"I'm sorry, Mr. Secretary. I think that you're a little too late," Cordonnier said. He wore a broad grin, and held his 9 millimeter Beretta firmly.

"Tell Mapplethorpe that he won't get away with this."

"How do you know it was Mapplethorpe who sent me to find you?" Cordonnier laughed. "And they told me that you were smart."

"Who else would want me dead?" Merck asked, moving slowly around the desk with his arms raised in the air.

"It depends on the motive, Mr. Secretary." Cordonnier motioned him forward through the door.

"Don't call me Mr. Secretary. You know I'm not the Secretary of Defense anymore." Merck was pushed into a room marked Mikvah, which contained what seemed like a small swimming pool.

"Okay, Your Honor. Will that do?" Cordonnier paused to admire the pool. "It seems as if Jews like to swim. Or maybe it's for secret baptisms." Cordonnier laughed.

Merck wondered if he had been wrong. Who else besides Mapplethorpe would want him executed?

"It's never too late for a little religion, isn't that right, Your Honor?" Roger Cordonnier enjoyed the notion of making this assassination creative. Mixing religion into his work might sanctify its importance. He compared himself to a general calling in the military chaplain to bless him and his troops on the eve of battle. A most apt analogy, he concluded.

"Before you kill me, tell me who ordered my death." Merck had an obsessive need to know. That was his nature.

"I'm afraid that I must maintain the confidentiality of my client. Just like a priest or a doctor. If not, you wouldn't respect my professionalism. And that, Mr. Secretary, is all I really have in this line of work."

"May I help you, gentlemen?" A heavyset man wearing a red skullcap suddenly walked into the room, surprising both Cordonnier and Merck.

Merck quickly jumped Cordonnier as he turned toward the rabbi. As they struggled over the gun, it went off.

The rabbi fell to the ground, muttering, "*Shema Yisroal, Adonoy . . .*"

Merck fell backward into the ritual Mikvah pool. He would never learn who had ordered his death, in a house of worship where the children of Abraham, Isaac, and Jacob asked for forgiveness, once a year, for the sins that they did and did not commit.


Three-star Air Force General Ronald McCormick rarely trusted regularly scheduled commercial airflights.

As a result of the severe economic recession in the early 1990s, many domestic airlines had gone into voluntary bankruptcy in order to protect

themselves against their creditors. As a result, many of these airlines had to
cut back on their experienced pilots, mechanics, and flight attendants.

So more often than not McCormick would rather drive, or buy a ticket
on a train, bus, or rickshaw, than fly one of the airlines. And now that he
had been fired from the armed forces, he no longer had his customary
privilege of flying whatever plane he might want to in the formidable arsenal
of the U.S. Air Force.

But this time he had no choice but to fly Penn West, the commuter special
between Harrisburg, Pennsylvania, and National Airport, if he was to be on
time for the meeting with Manning, Merck, and Jenkins.

Boarding the twenty-seat modified DeHavilland four-engine commuter
plane did not give McCormick any great sense of comfort. It had been over
twenty years since he had been on a turboprop. The best that he could say
for them was that if they encountered any mechanical problems, the pilot
could shut off the engines and simply glide down to the ground.

As the plane approached National Airport, McCormick could hear the
sound of trouble developing in the landing gears. They would not descend
into proper position. The pilot, a woman with only five years of flying time,
decided to pass the airport several times in a futile attempt to lower the
wheels. But it seemed as if her well-intentioned maneuvers only compounded
the problem. Her co-pilot, an even less experienced man in his early twen-
ties, suggested that she talk to one of the five passengers on the flight, a
three-star Air Force general. Possessed of more fear than pride, the pilot
introduced herself to McCormick, who felt flattered by her request for aid.

Futilely going through routine procedures for dislodging the landing
wheels, McCormick radioed the Pentagon Sit Room, located at the National
Military Command and Control Center, to explain the situation.

On the other side of the phone sat Colonel Zarbitski, who had been
waiting for just such a distress call. Zarb's men had radioed in prior to the
plane's departure that their job had been accomplished. He needed no further
instructions. He knew exactly what to do.

Zarb ordered an antiquated Huey helicopter to fly beneath the belly of
the four-engine DeHavilland in an attempt to create enough air turbulence
to dislodge the four wheels. It was a trick that the general himself had
perfected during his tour in Vietnam, when he was responsible for helping
to bring down crippled aircraft.

McCormick watched the Huey take off from the Pentagon heliopad, only
a half mile north of National Airport. It rendezvoused with the crippled
plane midway, at two thousand feet above ground.

But as the helicopter flew beneath the belly of the plane, the DeHavilland
started to shake unremittingly.

Something is wrong, thought McCormick. The Huey is flying too close
to the plane. The air turbulence will either destroy the plane or force it to
the ground through an artificially created downdraft.

The pilot watched McCormick's maneuverings, unable to convey her feelings of inadequacy. There was nothing she could think of doing. Radio communication had been lost for the past ten minutes and the plane was running out of fuel. Without landing gear, McCormick would have to rely on the ability of the DeHavilland to glide down onto the George Washington Parkway in the middle of rush hour traffic.

The plane shook with an incredible vibration, straining every bolt and seam to its maximum tensile capacity.

The whirring sound of the helicopter's rotorblades drowned out the screams of the four passengers as the plane dived nose first toward the roadway. McCormick shook his head in disbelief. What an irony, that the gods would let him perish so ignominiously in a plane crash, only a few hundred feet from his office at the Pentagon.

# CHAPTER
## 34

Despite the fact that Desaix had the highest levels of security clearances, the CIA treated him as if he were a registered agent for a hostile country.

Standing impatiently in the reception room at the newly renovated headquarters at Langley, Virginia, Desaix was reminded of his typical dentist's office visit, waiting for his annual checkup. There were the characteristic brown Naugahyde couches and glass-covered coffee tables, littered with all sorts of popular soporific magazines. Even the smells of the building were the same, for the highly polished marble floors, buffed twice a day, reeked of a phenol-based cleanser.

One strange, possibly insignificant, act haunted Desaix, against the background of all the accusations and confrontations he had encountered regarding Westview's sanity. Some unidentified senior government official had ordered a Psychological Profile and Operational Code done on the President of the United States. Desaix wanted to know who had ordered it and why. And he suspected that the answers were highly relevant to deciding whether the President was actually insane.

He waited while a pleasant Southern matron with blue-tinted hair verified his identity, taking her time, completely disregarding the significance of his blue identification card, which officially authorized him access to the most sensitive types of intelligence data, including TOP SECRET, Signal Intelligence, and Electronic Intelligence. According to his clearances, Desaix was allowed to know everything—from whether a world leader had colon cancer to whether he was corrupt, to whether it would take money, power, or sex to co-opt him. But standing in front of that nice lady, filling out paperwork that included home address, telephone number, and Social Security number, Desaix felt like Peck's Bad Boy.

Like most visitors to the Agency, Desaix was assigned to an anonymous secretary from James Ball's office. Today, the secretary sauntered into the room, made a few pleasantries about the weather, and perfunctorily inquired whether he had been to the Agency before. When he reminded her that she had accompanied him on several previous visits, she giggled with the same childishness she had on those previous occasions.

She placed him in the middle of a turnstile-like apparatus, slipped her identification card into an electronic sensor, and waited until it flashed the bold red letters, CLEARED. As far as the Agency was concerned, Desaix belonged to that completely indifferent secretary as long as he remained in that building. If he had to go to the bathroom, she would stand outside the door and wait for him. It always amazed Desaix that the Agency had managed to convert a simple visit by a senior official in the administration into an infantilizing experience of uncommon proportions, so that the visitor was duly informed, in no uncertain terms, that he was an unwelcome interloper, who was not only not to be trusted, but for the most part should be best handled as if he were a toddler who had just been deposited at a local day-care center.

Once CLEARED, Desaix proceeded up a white-marble staircase, past a bronze wall-hanging that commemorated the valor of past CIA and OSS agents who had died in the service of their country. Outside in the courtyard, Desaix could see an aqua cylindrical metal statue with hieroglyphics-like writings that contained a secret message no one had yet decoded.

Then came the most crucial decision of the day: would he be led to the right or the left side of the L-shaped building? If he went toward the right, he was visiting the Deputy Director of Operations, or the covert side of the house. There no one, but no one, talked in the hallways. On that side of the house, he would typically encounter the hard-drinking, womanizing undercover operatives who had spent the better part of their professional careers in the backwater areas of some Third World country.

If he went to the left, he was going to the analytical side of the Agency, the "softer" side of the house, considered a repository of liberals, mushy-headed thinkers, and Walter Mitty dreamers who had spent the better part of their professional careers reading technothrillers and writing precooked, unimaginative reports.

In a perverse way, Desaix called this decision Mengele's Dilemma, after the notorious Dr. Josef Mengele, who arbitrarily determined the fate of Auschwitz concentration camp detainees by pointing his finger to the right or to the left while humming Mozart.

"This way, please." The secretary pointed to the right side of the building, which meant that Ball was still in the process of moving his office from the covert side of the house to the overt.

They rode up the elevator to the third floor where they walked down a long asceptic corridor, bereft of any furniture or boxes. Desaix walked into the crowded Office of Scientific Intelligence, affectionately known as the Office of Sluts and Nuts because it contained sensitive psychological material relating to every world leader's mental state and sexual habits. Desaix was greeted warmly by James Ball.

"Congratulations!" Desaix said as he gave Ball a hug, which made all the secretaries giggle.

"It's good to see you, Desaix. I meant to call you, but I've just been so busy, as you can well imagine."

Ball's ruddy face, blunted features, and warm blue Irish eyes gave him the appearance of someone who himself had led a dissipated life. But as Desaix knew all too well, nothing could have been further from the truth. Ball was an ambitious, ascetic workaholic who had sacrificed his personal life for his profession. With only two ex-wives and no children to worry about, he had focused his complete attention on achieving his one goal—professional advancement.

"What brings you to these hinterlands?" Ball closed the door, slumped down into his well-worn leather sofa, and placed both feet on his cluttered cocktail table.

Desaix could see that Ball was feeling cocky. His problem was going to be how to confront Ball without having him panic or feel trapped into a vicious circle of denial, recrimination, and stonewalling. Desaix would need Ball's assistance to obtain some very important information for which only he had access, including Political Profiles, Operational Codes, and National Character Studies.

"First, I want to congratulate you on your appointment. It certainly was a pleasant surprise."

"Thanks. It was a surprise for me too," Ball replied, as he suddenly became more wary. Certainly, Desaix didn't come to congratulate him. He could have done that by phone. But he knew Desaix, so he knew that he would not have to wait long. Desaix wasn't the kind of person who liked to waste either his own or someone else's time.

"Jim, you and I go back a long way, to the time this office was doing nothing more than elaborate puff pieces for the Sec State and the President. Without me in the system, you didn't have anyone who really understood your products or knew how to use them."

"Would you like something to drink? Coffee? Tea? Southern Comfort?" Ball asked, sensing that Desaix was trying to call in some old debts.

"Remember how I used to warn you and your people that without someone like me at State to read and interpret your political profiles, you were simply wasting your time?"

"Uh huh. As I recall, to quote you precisely, 'We were like Beethoven, writing a brilliant symphony for people who basically couldn't even read music.' " Ball paused for a response. "Did I get that one right, Desaix?"

"I'm glad to see that you have a good memory."

"Desaix, you and I agree that I owe you. So how much are you calling in?" As a twenty-five-year bureaucrat who needed five years till he could collect his pension, Ball did not have to be reminded that his viability in the government depended almost exclusively on his ability to pay back favors.

"What happened in Japan?"

"I don't know what you're talking about." Ball tried not to appear defensive. He didn't want to provide Desaix with an excuse to probe any further than needed.

"Jim, throughout our ten-year relationship, you and I have always treated the other with respect. Don't change that now."

"I don't know what you're getting at. I'm in the process of moving into the big office upstairs—" Ball jumped up excitedly. "My schedule is so crammed that I can barely take a shit. But you asked to see me, and I make time to see you. So, please, don't lecture me about respect and Auld Lang Syne!" Ball started to crack his knuckles.

"Damnit, man!" Desaix stood up. "I came up here, promising myself that I would treat you with the utmost dignity and respect because I wanted us to work together on some pretty important issues—like finding out who ordered Fitzpatrick's murder." Pausing to assess Ball's ashen face, Desaix decided to continue his line of attack—strike hard, fast, and deep—before Ball could compose himself.

"Take it easy, Desaix!" Ball stepped back, frightened that he might get hit.

"Listen, goddamn it!" Desaix grabbed Ball by his collar and rammed him against the wall. "Fitzpatrick was tortured by you and White. You stuck his body in a vat of hydrogen fluoride acid as a way of making certain that the message of his ugly death was not lost on someone. Whom did you want to scare? Me? The President?" He raised his arm as if he were going to smack Ball across his face, beginning to feel that adrenaline rush of starting to go out of control.

"You're crazy! I didn't kill Fitzpatrick!" Ball pushed Desaix away.

"I have SIGINT and HUMINT information that tells me different!" Desaix pulled the incriminating photograph out of his pants pocket and handed it to Ball.

"Who the hell gave you this picture?" Ball's face flushed red.

"Someone!"

"Someone? Who the hell is your source? If nothing else, I always considered you an intelligent person." He held up the picture and waved it in front of Desaix's face. "But this photograph is one giant step for forgery and one tiny step for your alleged acumen."

"What the hell do you mean?" Desaix asked. This was not the reaction he had expected from Ball. He had imagined a scenario in which Ball confessed to all sorts of conspiracies, and then, as atonement, would plead with Desaix to help him entrap the true culprit—Mapplethorpe. And even provide evidence against the President, if he were involved, assuming Manning and Imai were right.

"What's wrong with the photo?" Desaix questioned, suddenly feeling stupid that he had been trapped into believing a picture could be definitive evidence of anything. It was no secret to anyone who knew or worked with Desaix that he was intimidated by most modern technology, let alone modern intelligence techniques. All of his colleagues at NSA, CIA, and State knew how much Desaix hated to work with computers, photographs, and recording devices. As Ball had once said, "Desaix had a brilliant mind for the fourteenth century, before the advent of the printing press or gunpowder."

"Desaix, the question is not what's wrong with the photo," Ball continued in a softer tone. "The real question is what is right with the photo."

"I don't get it."

"It's very simple. This photograph is a montage of pictures that were selectively cut and pasted together into one desired image. The only thing that belongs in this photo is Fitzpatrick's body."

"How do you know?" Desaix was already trying to figure out who was trying to pull a fast one over him. Ball, or Imai, or Manning, or all three?

"It's not very hard to figure it out. But if you don't trust me, I'm perfectly willing to call in one of our satellite reconnaissance experts who deals with this kind of thing every day. He'll tell you right away." Ball waited for Desaix's response.

"Okay, call him." Desaix wondered what Ball would really do.

Ball pushed down his intercom button. "Please send me down one of those experts in the photo recon lab, ASAP!"

"Yes, Mr. Ball," the secretary's voice answered through the intercom.

"Are you telling me that you had nothing to do with Fitzpatrick's death?" Desaix asked, confused. Then who killed Fitzpatrick? He had been certain it was ordered by Mapplethorpe. All the circumstantial evidence pointed to him—Brooks's death, Fitzpatrick being on Mapplethorpe's staff, the President's personal confession, the Secretary of State's intimation. And now this photograph.

A knock on the door interrupted his thinking.

"Sir, you wanted to see me?" A young man with glasses walked into the room.

"Take a look at this photograph. Tell me as much about it as you can."

The young man took out a magnifying glass and pored over the photograph reverentially.

"It's a two-day-old photo made with a high-speed Leica with highly light-sensitive film. Whoever took this picture, or pictures, wanted to leave the impression that the picture was taken at night, in what looks like the vestiges of a wooden tub . . . or possibly some type of hot tub." The young man spoke in a matter-of-fact tone, never once looking up.

"You said picture or pictures. What do you mean?"

"Subject to further examination and certain laboratory procedures, I would conclude from the way that the dark lines cut across some of the figures in the picture, as well as the different textures of skin on the different people, that this photograph was a compilation of several different photos."

"How many different pictures?" Ball smiled at Desaix.

"Give me twenty-four hours, sir, and I will be able to tell you."

"Thank you. I don't think that will be necessary."

The technician walked out of the office as quietly as he had entered.

"Well, Desaix, what are you going to do now that you've lost one of your prime suspects?" Ball couldn't restrain his tone of self-righteousness, even though he could see that Desaix was stunned by the revelation that the photograph was a forgery.

"I don't know. I'm sorry. I was wrong."

Ball was surprised that Desaix didn't even question the possibility that the photograph might, in fact, not be a forgery. Now it was Ball's turn to have some fun with Desaix.

"You know, in my business the last things an intelligence operative has any faith in are documents and pictures . . ." He paused to emphasize the point, "or an alleged expert." He had wanted to go on, but he couldn't control his laughter. For the first time in years, he had Desaix hanging with enough uncertainty that he would question his own name.

"Please, do me a favor, Jim. Don't mind-fuck me now. That's the last thing I need." He walked anxiously around the cluttered office. "I see that the President knew what he was doing when he appointed you DCI. With your creative, sadistic temperament, you're going to be great. Please accept my apologies."

"Thank you. From the master of mindbenders, I would say that was one hell of a compliment." Ball was uncomfortable with the pity he felt for Desaix. He had never seen him so totally immobilized by uncertainty.

"I just don't understand it!" Desaix said, furious with himself. How had he let himself be set up by Manning and Imai? And why would they do this to him? What did they have to gain from allowing him to think that both Ball and White were involved in the murder, ordered by none other than President Westview himself? Was Manning seriously thinking of trying to force the President out of office so that he would have a chance to be in the line of succession? If that were true, then someone would have to eliminate the first three contenders—the Vice President of the United States, Speaker of the House, President pro tempore of the Senate, all of whom were in Japan for the next two days. And how did this fit in with President Westview's allegations that Mapplethorpe had convinced him to stage a coup against himself?

Too many unanswered questions swirled around his head. There was only one thing to do, according to everything he had ever learned. When a crisis overloads its crisis manager with too much contradictory information, he knew he had to return to basics. Like the catechisms he had to recite at parochial school. Trust intuition, not information. Go with your affect, not your intellect. Appreciate the emerging contradictions as part of the organic nature of a rapidly evolving crisis, no matter how confusing it might all appear. Never become persuaded or seduced by any part of the information, no matter how convincing it may appear, because it may be nothing more than an attempt to acquire some false sense of certainty and hope. Learn to tolerate the anxiety of uncertainty and contradiction without coming to premature conclusions.

"Desaix, what can I do to help you out?" Ball asked, interrupting Desaix's thoughts. Ball could now afford to feel magnanimous. In the game of bureaucratic one-upmanship, he had won.

"I need to go through some of your files: Psychological Profiles, Operational Codes, National Character Studies."

"You name them, and they are yours. Did you need me or any of my assistants?"

"Maybe. Is Damon Perkins around?"

"I'll get him for you." Ball pushed the intercom button and asked for Perkins. "He prefers that we go over to his shop. He claims that it's a lot easier for him."

"No problem. Thanks. I appreciate this." Desaix concluded that he may not have needed the photograph to blackmail Ball into co-operating with him. Although his initial instinct was to press him further for answers, Desaix decided to wait until after he had read the profiles. He had gotten what he wanted all along—unrestricted access to the most sensitive data-banks in the entire government. It was in those files that Desaix's intuition told him he would find the key to Project Baltimore.

Desaix and Ball walked down the hall to an office called the Center for the Study of Leadership Analysis, where a distracted, disheveled man in his late forties sat working in front of a desktop terminal.

"Dr. Damon Perkins, this is Dr. Desaix Clark, DAS for EAP."

"We've already met," Desaix said. Perkins, an intense, bright eccentric, didn't even bother to look up or shake Desaix's hand. He simply beckoned Desaix to sit down alongside him. Perkins was completely engrossed by what he was doing. And when he wasn't working on the computer, he shifted his attention to a crossword puzzle that never left his side.

"I'll leave you two alone. Damon, give Desaix whatever he needs." Ball walked back to his office. He had some very important calls to make—especially one to the NSC. General White owed him one. For the moment, Desaix had been neutralized by the high-tech photographic mumbo-jumbo. But now he had to find out how Desaix had obtained that photograph. Too many people could be hurt by it.

Ball felt comfortable leaving Desaix with access to his shop. Perkins would act as an effective brake on anything that Desaix wanted that seemed unusual or incriminating.

"What's an eight-letter word for mistrust?" Perkins asked, turning toward his crossword puzzle.

"Betrayal."

"I like that." Perkins smiled cryptically at Desaix.

"Something funny?" Desaix asked. He knew that Perkins was considered strange by many people. There was a disconcerting aura about him, something akin to the stereotype of the mad scientist.

"You must have really scared Ball," Perkins spoke with mischievous delight.

"Why do you say that?" Desaix asked. Although Perkins was eccentric, Desaix liked him. There was something childishly appealing about him.

"He never allows any outsider to enter this shop. We're considered *verboten*." For the first time, Perkins looked directly at Desaix. "Where would you like to begin?"

"With the Operational Code of President Igor Ivanovich Zotov. Then I'd like to compare it with the Operational Code of President Donald Westview."

"Any particular focus?"

"I want to see how compatible they are in terms of their political operating styles. I also want to know how they might settle any major differences there might be between them."

"Like a war?" Perkins replied sarcastically.

"Like a war," Desaix answered, sensing that Perkins was a lot shrewder than he appeared to be, with his contrived persona of the absentminded professor.

"Let's start with the Psychological Political Profiles first. Don't you agree?" Perkins punched in the code word UMBRA. Then he split-screened Westview's and Zotov's Political Psychological Profiles, marked by the bold lettering: TOP SECRET/NO FORN/NO CON/HUMINT/ELINT/NO DIS/ EYES ONLY.

Desaix scanned the screen. The information that he was reading was of the highest degree of sensitivity. The warning labels on the screen couldn't be more clear. No foreigners or contract workers were allowed to read it. No paper copies of this analysis were allowed to be made or distributed. And the Psychological Profiles were based on information culled from human and electrical intelligence. On a computer terminal sitting next to the first, Perkins put up a screen marked OPERATIONAL CODES: ZOTOV/WESTVIEW.

"It's not so bad, with all this modern technology," Perkins said, smiling. He was clearly enjoying the role of a showoff. And he always enjoyed the company of what he called competitive intelligence, something he felt was drastically missing at the Agency.

"Can you imagine what the old man could have done with all this technology?" Desaix asked, almost certain that he already knew the answer.

"He probably would have said it was completely unnecessary—" Damon had once briefly met Nathan Leites, the eccentric inventor of the Operational Code, a method of analysis which examines the way a world leader would approach a crisis situation.

"Or completely self-indulgent," interjected Desaix.

From a historical perspective, Freud had developed theories that tied behavior to unconscious drives and motivations. Reduced to its simplest form, sex and aggression were viewed as the underlying pistons for man's sublimated behavior.

Similarly, knowing whether a political leader believed that the world was primarily composed of forces that promoted harmony or conflict was an important variable in predicting if that leader might use war as an instrument of his foreign policy or, alternatively, call in the United Nations to mediate potential conflicts.

Also, by studying a political leader's attitudes about how history was shaped, whether by individuals or collective forces, Desaix could predict what course of action that leader might take in an extremely confusing and chaotic situation. He could predict whether that leader would resort to totalitarian measures of repression or more conciliatory, collegial, democratic approaches.

In short, the Operational Code, complemented by a Psychological Political Profile, was always a valuable tool for thinking systematically about a political leader when Desaix was required to make an assessment about present and future behavior. For Desaix, the code was the very basis of crisis management decision making. Only by knowing what a political leader might or might not do, could a crisis manager decide what was or was not feasible in terms of realistic strategies and tactics.

The Operational Code and the Psychological Political Profiles were the bricks and mortar of the Office of Sluts and Nuts. Damon's professional raison d'être was tied up with whether he could produce the analysis requested by the White House, DOD, and the State Department. But he was well aware that Desaix Clark was one of the few men at State who was qualified to understand his particular, immodest brand of genius. For ten years they had known about each other's existence, used each other's information, but had never worked together.

Damon's basic suspicions about Desaix's motives and integrity gave way to an overwhelming need to demonstrate to Desaix how clever, ingenious, and perceptive he really was. He couldn't wait to begin.

Working on two computer terminals at once, Damon asked his program to summarize data from the Psychological Political Profile and other classified sources of information, and to display it in the format of the Operational Code. By typing in key words, the program would produce a concise comparative analysis of Westview and Zotov.

The format for the Operational Code came up first.

OPERATIONAL CODE/
PSYCHOLOGICAL POLITICAL PROFILES:
CLASSIFIED TOP SECRET/UMBRA/NO FORN/NO DIS/
HUMINT/ELINT/EYES ONLY.

## THE NATURE OF POLITICS AND POLITICAL CONFLICT

### 1) Politics

Philosophical: Does harmony or conflict characterize the political universe?

Instrumental: What is the best approach for selecting political goals? Moralist/ideological versus pragmatic/problem-solving?

### 2) Opponents and Allies

Philosophical: What is the fundamental nature of the political leader's opponents' operating style?

—Zero-sum game versus cooperative bargaining.

—Confrontational.

—Confrontation avoidance.

—What is the basic character of the political leader's allies? Do they work in concert or do they work autonomously?

Instrumental: What is the optimum way for a political leader to manage an opponent? Or an ally?

—Direct discussions and negotiations.

—Indirect manipulations.

—Primarily covert action.

—Two-track diplomacy (overt and covert).

—Emphasize domestic or foreign policy priorities.

## SHAPING HISTORICAL DEVELOPMENTS

### 3) Control of History

Philosophical: Does the political leader believe that the course of historical developments is determined by an individual or a collective body?

Instrumental: How does the political leader calculate personal and political risks?

—High-risk strategies versus low-risk strategies.

—Rational/intellectual versus emotive/irrational.

—Inner-directed versus outer-directed.

—Close-minded versus open-minded.

## 4) Predictability

Philosophical: Is the political future predictable?
—What are the major forces that impact on the future?
—How uncomfortable is the political leader with uncertainty?
—How important is control? How far will he go in order to maintain control?
Instrumental: How does the political leader advance his own interests? His country's interests?
—Will the political leader lie, deceive, betray in order to achieve both his personal and his nation's goal?
—Will the leader subordinate his personal goals to that of his nation's?
—Should the political leader negotiate from a position of strength, parity, or weakness?
—Does the political leader think from a strategic point of view? Or tactical?

## 5) Power

Philosophical: How important is power to the political leader?
—Does he see power as a zero sum game?
—Does the end justify the means?
Instrumental: Does the political leader share power?
—Does the political leader believe in an open versus closed style of acquiring power? Or using power?
—Does the political leader utilize the bureaucracy or does he circumvent it?
—Is the political leader sensitive to domestic law and to international law? Will he circumvent it?

## 6) Optimism

Philosophical: Is the political leader basically confident that he can achieve his personal/political goals?
Instrumental: What are the best methods of achieving his goals: Intervention versus nonintervention.

## 7) Political Weaknesses

Philosophical: Does the political leader perceive any personal/political weaknesses?
Instrumental: What does he do to correct it?
—Does he assume responsibility for it? Or does he blame it on others?
—Blame it on circumstances beyond control?

Desaix was impressed by Damon's personal improvements on the standard format for the Operational Code. He had added sections on power, optimism, and weakness.

"What do you think?" Damon was eager for positive reinforcement.

"You're missing one section. Maybe two," Desaix replied.

"Which ones?" Damon reread the menus.

"You need a section on the political leader's history of medical and mental illness." Desaix tried to speak in a nonjudgmental tone.

"You have a point there, Desaix."

"And I would add a category on sexual proclivity and how that might affect a leader's performance. Witness JFK." Desaix knew that he didn't have to spell out Kennedy's sexually promiscuous lifestyle, played out within the confines of the White House.

"Well taken! Well taken!" Damon was thrilled to be working with his main institutional client. He would happily add whatever was required.

"Okay, Damon. Time's running out. Let's see what we have here."

"I'm going to consolidate a great deal of information on Westview and Zotov so that we can easily compare their responses."

Within a split second, the screen was full, and Desaix was trying to discern patterns of behavior that might explain why both Zotov and Westview had mirror-image domestic and foreign policy problems.

| OPERATIONAL CODE | ZOTOV | WESTVIEW |
|---|---|---|
| **1) Politics** | | |
| —philosophical | conflict | conflict |
| —instrumental | pragmatic | pragmatic |
| **2) Opponents and Allies** | | |
| —philosophical | cooperative | cooperative |
| | confrontational | confrontational |
| | works with Allies | works with Allies |
| —instrumental | direct negotiations | direct negotiations |
| | two-track diplomacy | two-track diplomacy |
| **3) Control of History** | | |
| —philosophical | individual | individual |
| —instrumental | high-risk strategies | high-risk strategies |
| | rational decision maker | rational decision maker |
| | inner-directed | inner-directed |
| | close-minded | close-minded |

**4) Predictability**

| | | |
|---|---|---|
| —philosophical | predictable future | predictable future |
| | leader determines future | leader determines future |
| | fears uncertainty | prefers uncertainty |
| | fears chaos | prefers controlled chaos |
| | high need for control | high need for control |
| —instrumental | personal concerns supersede national goals | personal concerns supersede national goals |
| | high lying, deception, betrayal | high lying, deception, betrayal |
| | only rules from a position of strength | only rules from a position of strength |
| | views personal and national destiny as one and the same | views personal and national destiny as one and the same |
| | works from long-range sophisticated strategic plans | works from long-range sophisticated strategic plans |

**5) Power**

| | | |
|---|---|---|
| | does not share power | does not share power |
| | conspiratorial | conspiratorial |
| | closed circle of advisors | closed circle of advisors |
| | can betray advisors | can betray advisors |
| | end justifies means | end justifies means |
| | personal power must be absolute | personal power must be absolute |
| | circumvent bureaucracy | circumvent bureaucracy |
| | domestic and international laws must be circumvented in order to achieve political end goals | domestic and international laws must be circumvented in order to achieve political end goals |

## 6) Optimism

| —philosophical | extremely self-confident | extremely self-confident |
| —instrumental | strong interventionist political leaders believe he will prevail over all difficulties | strong interventionist political leaders believe he will prevail over all difficulties |

## 7) Political Weaknesses

| —philosophical | uses personal weaknesses to political advantage | uses personal weaknesses to political advantage |
| —instrumental | women, alcohol, and paranoia: aware of their weaknesses highly manipulative no basic loyalty to anyone but his own ambition | women, alcohol, and paranoia: aware of their weaknesses highly manipulative no basic loyalty to anyone but his own ambition |

"What do you make of it?" Damon had rarely seen two world leaders with such similarities.

"There's almost complete parity of operating styles between them. Except for the predictability variable, they are mirror images of each other." Desaix was both excited and surprised by the results. It was as if he were viewing a sophisticated CAT scan of two minds, operating exactly alike. "The parity of operating styles tells me that Zotov and Westview could work extremely well with each other. My intuition tells me that there could even be collusion."

"How did you pick up the collusive element?" Damon asked.

"Examine the concordance among variables like cooperative, direct negotiations, two-track diplomacy, high-risk takers who act proactively in individualistic, secretive, even conspiratorial fashions."

"I see. But that doesn't make them conspirators."

"Look at these other congruous variables. Both have an extremely high need for control. They are pragmatic, yet confrontational. Plus their collective personal well-being supersedes the needs of their nation. They are, in effect, willing to do anything necessary to attain their goals. Lie. Deceive. Betray."

"It sounds to me like two shrewd politicians."

"Two shrewd politicians who find themselves at the same moment in time in exactly the same domestic and international situation that, if successfully resolved, would benefit them personally and politically. Tell me those aren't ingredients for major collusion."

"Well, you have a point there."

"Damon, it's all here in your goddamn Operational Code. You're a genius!" Desaix felt like planting a big kiss on his forehead.

"But what about Zotov's fear of uncertainty?"

"It's right on the mark. It may differ from Westview, but it's consistent with the Russian national character." Desaix spoke excitedly. "I remember when we had our first Policy Planning Bilateral Strategic Talks with the Russians in the late 1980s, when they first discussed the concept of perestroika and glasnost. I suggested that before they rush into anything, they should look at the history of their own character, which showed, as you remember, that as Russians they were fearful of anything called democracy or freedom." Desaix was certain that Damon was acquainted with these classic observations.

"But if Zotov and Westview are in collusion, why would they want to start a war against each other?" Damon asked.

"If you have two world leaders with severe political problems in their respective countries, as Westview and Zotov do, what would you expect them to do that might be a quick fix?" Desaix was being rhetorical. "They could sit down and agree to do something that would benefit both of them. Tell me, Damon, from your knowledge of history, what one thing have world leaders consistently done in order to deflect attention away from complicated domestic problems?" Desaix was becoming increasingly excited as he realized that as he spoke he was unraveling the mystery of the sudden, seemingly unprovoked outbreak of war.

"Traditionally, world leaders have always precipitated a war outside their borders to solidify domestic public opinion behind them," Damon replied.

"Right! Whenever a world leader is in domestic trouble, the least costly, most expeditious thing he can do is start a war. It allows him to mobilize to a wartime economy. Soon factory output increases, unemployment decreases, and formerly discontented citizens support their leader.

"Look at Hitler. He started World War II in order to return the German economy to its pre–World War I prosperity. Or look at more recent tyrants like Saddam Hussein, Qaddafi, and Hafez Assad." Desaix was beginning to appreciate the significance of Westview's confession about the riots. It also fit in neatly with Twitty's warning that the war was started for reasons not immediately consistent with the conventional analysis of Russian and U.S. misperception and miscommunication. There was no misunderstanding or miscommunication between Zotov and Westview. On the contrary, their apparent need for a domestic coup and an international crisis had been agreed upon beforehand by both Presidents. And that's what Project Baltimore was probably all about, a mutually agreed upon blueprint for a plan that would assure their respective political survival. Each leader must have agreed to provoke their respective crises so that they could resolve them at the right time and appear to the world as heroes and statesmen.

But the frightening question that came into Desaix's mind now was the endgame scenario for the U.S. and the Russian Federation. If anything went wrong, neither leader might be able to prevent the war from escalating.

Desaix felt on edge. Conspiracies always made him that way. They were like a bouillabaisse of deceit and betrayal, filled with truths, half truths, tortuous circles of logic and violence. And there only one way to defeat a conspiracy—unravel it through dogged perseverance.

"I'd like to see a couple more Op Codes. Do you mind?" Desaix asked.

"Who's next?" Damon was pleased to continue the meeting. In the past, his only professional satisfaction was an occasional back-channel word of gratitude from Desaix, or an appreciative letter from the trainees at the "farm" in Williamsburg.

"Let's work on the Op Code of General Thomas Mapplethorpe," Desaix said matter-of-factly.

"What?" Damon almost fell off his swivel chair. "You know that the Agency is forbidden by law from collecting any information on an American citizen. Not to say anything about doing a Psychological Profile or Operational Code on a senior U.S. government official. That's a felony."

"We just constructed an Op Code on the President of the U.S."

"According to the Federal Regs 14–78 of the National Security Act, you are allowed to collect classified data and construct a Top Secret Op Code on the President of the United States if, as an Agency analyst, you deem that it is essential for the complete evaluation of how U.S. decision makers should handle a particular foreign relations problem or world leader," Damon said, ashamed to have to play the bureaucrat.

"General Mapplethorpe is a senior administration official who is involved in the management of a major foreign relations crisis. Right?"

"Well, you do have a point. We can certainly make a case for requesting the Psychological Political Profile because of the impending war. But if the Agency turns down our request, they may initiate an internal investigation. That could mean prison sentences for both you and me."

"Does that mean that you're with me?"

"I'm with you." Damon punched in the code needed to access the highly classified profile. "Here's a summary of Mapplethorpe's data."

"Let's see what you have there." Desaix didn't have to explain that he knew all about those "nonexistent" highly secret profiles of selected domestic officials. He was certain that Mapplethorpe was one of them, because he remembered that the President had asked him once how someone would go about analyzing Mapplethorpe's personality, given the "proper data." To Desaix, that meant that the President too was interested in developing a profile on Mapplethorpe.

He watched the computer screen as Mapplethorpe's personality emerged.

## PSYCHOLOGICAL/POLITICAL PROFILE: GENERAL THOMAS MAPPLETHORPE, NATIONAL SECURITY ADVISOR. TOP SECRET. NO DIS/NO FORN/NO CON/ EXTREMELY SENSITIVE/EYES ONLY.

*Summary:* General Thomas Mapplethorpe was the fourth of five children of a modest carpenter and his ambitious wife who doted on her frail son. At his mother's insistence, he went to West Point, where he was in the top 5 percent of his class.

His father deserted the family early in Mapplethorpe's life. His mother worked three jobs. There is strong evidence to suggest that Mapplethorpe never overcame the psychological trauma of his father's abandonment.

Dominated by the presence of a strong mother and four sisters, Mapplethorpe had no male role model after whom he could pattern himself.

He was accused in high school of being effeminate. Caught by his mother dressing up in her clothes, she sent him to a private military academy.

It is believed that at one point in his schooling he was emotionally distraught about personal conflicts and saw a psychiatrist. He was diagnosed as a borderline personality with the capacity to distort reality. He was capable of withdrawing into a world of fantasy, paranoia, and delusions of grandeur and omnipotence.

He has a history of visiting male brothels. He was officially reprimanded by his superior officer, Lieutenant Donald Westview, for having propositioned his male tech-sergeant. Officially, he has denied any homosexual activity. A copy of that reprimand is missing from his file.

Psychological history suggests strong homosexual tendencies and major sociopathic traits: lying, cheating, duplicity, and betrayal. He is extremely meticulous, oriented to detail, and an extremely good organizer.

Married briefly, twenty years ago. No children. Lives alone. No substance abuse. Work occupies his life. Believed to have a secret male lover—his adjutant, "Sonny" Shaw.

"That's quite a history!" Damon blurted out. "Now you know why you're not supposed to have access to these files. They're filled with information that has very little bearing on his political operating style."

"Don't you think that if Mapplethorpe is a closet homosexual, it is relevant to the way he conducts himself politically? Psychologically, I would think that he would overcompensate for his effeminate traits by acting super-macho."

"You might be right. But so what?"

"Well, if Mapplethorpe feels he has to hide his homosexuality from public scrutiny, he becomes a target for blackmail."

"Aaaah! I see what you mean." Beneath his compassionate liberal exterior, Damon was a homophobe who only understood homosexuality through the prism of antiquated psychiatric theories. He had never had the interest or time to be friends with a homosexual, and tried to reason away the issue by personally supporting antigay legislation.

Both men scanned the screen carefully.

"Let's see if we can get an Operational Code for Mapplethorpe," Damon said, as he cleared the screen of the profile. A moment later they were analyzing the information splayed out on the Op Code format.

"As we might expect from a military man who has been in the bureaucracy," Desaix said, "Mapplethorpe sees the world in terms of conflict versus conflict avoidance. He takes a pragmatic approach to problems, rather than an ideological one. But uncharacteristically, he believes in a confrontational mode with a zero-sum game approach."

"No, I think it's the other way around, Desaix."

"What do you mean?"

"In my opinion, Mapplethorpe demonstrates an incredible ability to be brutal with whomever he perceives to be a subordinate or an enemy. Look down here, you can see that he personalizes most relationships. So if you work for him or with him, and you're not his boss, he can really screw you over."

"A high authoritarian factor," Desaix replied.

"Extremely high. He has the characteristic pattern of someone who shits on his subordinates and sucks up to his superiors. But I see a strong potential for dealing with his international adversaries, like the Russians, in a sensible, pragmatic way, through negotiations rather than war. Look how high he scores on his desire for covert diplomacy. Look under the heading of opponents and allies. He's just like every good National Security Advisor since Kissinger. They all cut secret deals while taking a completely different public stance. I suspect he serves Westview quite well."

"In what way?"

"Like Westview, Mapplethorpe has a strong need to exclude the bureaucracy and work secretly. But he is completely loyal to his boss. Unlike Westview, his ability to tolerate uncertainty and chaos is extremely low. He shows very little initiative. Also unlike Westview, he will subsume his own personal interests to that of his country or boss."

"It sounds to me as if he is a loyal, trustworthy technocrat who will do whatever his boss orders him to do. Even kill," Desaix replied.

"I agree with that interpretation. Like Westview, he seems to love power. But he isn't as sneaky or duplicitous."

"So your point is that, above all else, Mapplethorpe is extremely loyal to Westview?"

"That's correct. He's a loyal military technocrat," Damon replied.

"Thanks. I think you helped me solve something that has been bothering me."

"What is that?" Damon asked.

"Nothing major. Just a small point about the degree of initiative and loyalty Mapplethorpe would exhibit." Desaix paused for a moment, hoping he was right in his feeling that he could trust Damon not to relay their conversation to Ball.

"I've been wondering, Damon, do you think it possible for Mapplethorpe to have initiated a military coup against Westview?"

"What?" Damon was as surprised by the question as Desaix thought he might be.

"There are some people who believe that Mapplethorpe is leading a military coup against Westview. And that he got rid of Jenkins, Merck, and McCormick in order to make way for your boss and White."

"But we just agreed that his Operational Code and his Psychological Political Profile shows no proclivity whatsoever to intiate anything on his own. Especially not anything that is in any way different from his boss. In that way, he is very conventional and predictable. That's why I was surprised to read that he was a practicing homosexual. It just doesn't fit."

Desaix knew Damon was right. It didn't fit. But it all began to make sense to him anyway.

Westview had lied after all. He—not Mapplethorpe—had initiated both the coup and the crisis with the Russians. Mapplethorpe was merely the instrument of Westview's will.

Desaix wondered about the other ways Westview had lied to him. For a professional who was supposed to be smart, Desaix felt like a horse's ass.

"Let's do one more person," Desaix said.

"Who?" Damon asked.

"Secretary of State Chester Manning."

# CHAPTER
## 35

How is President Westview doing, Dr. Barnett?" Mary felt sorry for the exhausted White House surgeon. He pulled off his green surgical mask in the cluttered changing room, consisting of little more than two wooden benches in front of two broken metal lockers.

He and his surgical staff had operated on the President for over five hours, replacing his ruptured abdominal aneurysm with the latest artificial Dacron artery.

"He's all right." Barnett was resentful of Mary's intrusive presence. "Are we free to go now? Or are we still under house arrest?"

"I don't blame you for feeling the way you do. This is not the way I would have wanted things to turn out either." Mary nodded her head in silent greeting as Neva walked in.

"Are his vital signs stabilized?" Barnett asked.

"So far so good, Dr. Barnett." Neva felt uncomfortable under Mary's stare.

"I repeat. Are we free to go?"

"I can't make that decision. You heard what Dr. Clark told you," Mary said, trying not to sound too defensive.

"Clark is not your boss, damnit! And stop calling him doctor." Barnett accidentally pulled off a few of his buttons as he tried to close his shirt. He was afraid of what he might do if he didn't restrain himself. And being exhausted didn't help.

"But, he is a doctor, Doctor," Mary replied.

She tried not to notice as Neva rubbed a white milky lotion over her dry arms. Slowly. Methodically.

"Damnit, Mary! He's no more a doctor than I'm a captain of an aircraft carrier." Barnett finished dressing himself in his standard navy whites.

"Dr. Barnett, we've got a major national security problem and Dr. Clark is trying his best to resolve it as quickly as possible."

"Keeping me and my staff hostage in our own operating room is not what I would call a creative, appropriate solution to that problem." Approaching Mary, Barnett brought his face defiantly close to hers, testing the limits of his confinement.

"Don't, Dr. Barnett! Please!" Mary reached inside her blue blazer, and released the snap on her shoulder holster.

"You wouldn't dare use that on me!"

"Dr. Barnett," Neva interrupted, "I think it's time for you to debride some of the necrotic tissue along the suture line. Remember, you asked me to remind you to cut out those overlapping flaps of skin immediately after the operation." Neva pulled Barnett away from Mary and led him toward the recovery room.

Mary left the highly restricted surgical unit, guarded by her hand-picked Secret Service agents, and discussed the problems of maintaining tight security around the West Wing of the White House with two of her youngest, most loyal agents. They had entered through a passageway from their home base at the Treasury Department, right next door.

If everything had gone according to plan, her agents were now positioned outside of the White House, around the West Wing, blending unobtrusively with the Secret Service agents placed by the President.

Entering Randy's office, Mary noticed a clutter of boxes containing briefing books, options papers, and memoranda. Randy seemed to be arguing with Mapplethorpe and Shaw.

"Randy, I have placed some twenty telephone calls over the past six hours, requesting an audience with the President . . ."

"I know, General Mapplethorpe, I know," Randy answered testily.

"Each time, you informed me that he was not feeling well. I figured that he must be quite sick, resting in bed upstairs. But neither his wife, friends, or cabinet officers have seen or heard hide nor hair of him." He seemed not to notice Mary, and continuing in a menacing tone of voice he asked, "What's going on?"

"I've told you, General Mapplethorpe. The President has given me specific orders that he not be disturbed by anyone. Anyone!"

Mapplethorpe was livid. He had checked all over the government and could detect no trace of Westview. No one—White, Ball—had seen the President.

"That's fine, Randy! But how did the President actually communicate that message to you? On the phone? In person? Over the transom?" Mapplethorpe wanted to strangle her.

Mary quietly summoned two guards through the portable microphone attached to the sleeve of her jacket. They stood outside Randy's open door, their L9A1 9 millimeter Browning automatics cocked.

"General Mapplethorpe," Mary spoke forcefully, "I think that Randy has made it quite clear that neither she nor the President is available to speak with you!" She walked slowly toward Mapplethorpe, brushing Shaw aside with a subtle twist of her shoulder, forcibly interposing herself between Randy and Mapplethorpe.

"I'm certain that when the President is ready to see you, he will." Mary spoke defiantly, staring straight into Mapplethorpe's beet red face.

"What in God's name are you doing here?" Mapplethorpe asked her, barely able to contain his anger.

"I don't know what you mean, General. Is there any reason why the Chief of the President's Protective Detail shouldn't be attending to the needs of her charge?"

"You're not supposed to be here." Mapplethorpe glanced quizzically at Shaw.

"Might I remind you that the Oval Office is only ten feet due north of here," she replied smugly. "And, my assignment, as designated by the Treasury Department and reaffirmed by Congress, is to protect the President at all times." Mary realized she was playing a dangerous game. Shaw looked as if he were ready to attack her. And Mapplethorpe was no fool. He knew that Randy and Mary were purposely hiding something.

Sensing the increased tension in the room, Randy became even more visibly anxious. She would have liked nothing better than to leave the room or bury herself in a pile of busywork. The stress of collaborating with Desaix and Mary was becoming a no-win proposition for her. Whatever she said or did would invariably antagonize someone. Without President Westview to protect her, Randy felt completely vulnerable. She suddenly realized that as of this moment she was working not for the President of the United States— but for Dr. Desaix Clark.

"Things have changed, Mary, since you and Desaix have been away," Mapplethorpe replied.

"In what way, General?" Mary asked ingenuously.

"Come on, Mary. Don't play games with me. It's neither convincing nor becoming." Mapplethorpe tried to end-run Mary and get into the Oval Office.

Mary resisted, using all her strength to push him against the wall. "May I remind you that I am in control of the President's Protective Detail until he, personally, fires me." Running her hand through her hair, she felt extremely proud of the fact that he could not intimidate her. "No one who has any authority over me has informed me that my Secret Service functions have changed." Mary watched as her two Secret Service agents moved quietly into the office and positioned themselves on each side of the door.

"The Presidential Protective Detail of the Secret Service has been transferred from Treasury to DOD. It has been placed under my control," Mapplethorpe announced. He knew that Mary was too sophisticated a bureaucrat to be intimidated by that statement. But that wasn't necessarily so for her agents. And if he didn't acquire immediate control of her unit, he would find himself in direct conflict with her.

"That's very interesting, but not very convincing," Mary replied. "According to my mandate, I have both the legal right and moral obligation to remove any obstruction or potential problem from the vicinity of the Oval Office."

"I hope you realize what you are doing," Mapplethorpe said as he and Shaw walked to the door. At this point, they had to avoid as many internal problems as possible. Attracting attention was the last thing they wanted.

Mary pulled a 9 millimeter Beretta from her shoulder holster and pointed it directly at Mapplethorpe. She couldn't let them go this easily. Mapplethorpe might be her only ticket into the Baltimore Room. And a direct confrontation with Mapplethorpe would probably be the only way for it to happen. It was now or never.

"Mary!" Randy screamed, alarmed that there might be violence in the Oval Office.

"It's okay, Randy," Mary said, then directed the group toward the door. "Call Desaix at Ball's office. Tell him that I'm on my way to Room E at the Old Executive Office Building, accompanied by my gracious hosts. Tell him to meet me there as soon as possible."

Randy picked up the telephone, relieved to see everyone leave the room. The remaining two guards allowed her a measure of sanity. But she felt numb, as if she were living through a surrealistic dream designed by a Hollywood scriptwriter and a madcap political psychiatrist.

Mary cautiously negotiated their way down the long carpeted corridor of the West Wing. She walked immediately behind Mapplethorpe and Shaw, her gun, hidden from sight by her jacket, pointed at their backs. As they walked, more of her agents joined them. By the time they crossed Old Executive Lane, eight agents accompanied her.

A tall, handsome man in his late thirties, dressed in full combat gear, sauntered up to the group as they entered the Old Executive Office Building. Mary's men tightened their grips on their Browning automatics.

"Tom! Sonny! Where are you going?" Colonel Zarbitski scanned the group, most of whom he did not recognize. "What's going on here?"

"This is Mary Dougherty, Chief of the President's Protective Detail," Mapplethorpe replied hesitantly, hoping that Zarb would pick up on the anxiety in his tight voice.

"Nice to meet you, Mary. I've heard some good things about you from the President," Zarb said, appropriately friendly.

"I'm just showing Mary and some Special Ops officers the Baltimore Room."

"I thought that was off-limits to everyone but you and Sonny?"

"Mary has been given special clearance by the President," Shaw replied in an uncharacteristically flat voice.

"So you finally found him!"

"Yes. He has been incommunicado for the past twenty-four hours because he hasn't been feeling well. But his doctors tell me that he will be up and about within a day."

Mary pressed the Beretta firmly into Mapplethorpe's back. Time was running out.

"It's good to see you," Mapplethorpe continued, pausing to add, "don't be a stranger. Come and see us soon."

"Take care," Zarb said, watching Mapplethorpe and his entourage proceed through the side door of the Old Executive Office Building. When they disappeared inside the building, he summoned his deputy on his portable phone.

"Make sure that the entire building is surrounded. I don't want a cockroach leaving without my knowing about it." Zarb barked the command. "Make certain that no one, and I mean no one, does anything without my specific instructions!"

"Yes, sir!" Zarb's deputy said, an eager Army Ranger who would have walked barefoot through the Mojave Desert without a canteen of water if Zarb ordered it.

Zarb had become suspicious the moment Mapplethorpe said the President had given Mary permission to enter the Baltimore Room. Since the beginning of the project, there had been one inviolate rule—no one except his immediate staff was allowed in that room.

Positioning himself behind a concrete embankment, Zarb kept a close eye on the windows in the Baltimore Room. At the appropriate time, he was confident that Mapplethorpe would transmit a signal through them. But above all else, he had to make certain that in the process of rescuing Mapplethorpe nothing untoward would happen to Mary. Ironically, if any harm did come to Mary, it might mean his career, if not life.

"Where did you get your men from?" Mapplethorpe asked, as he punched in the sequence of buttons that would open the door of the Baltimore Room.

"Don't worry about them. I can assure you that they are completely loyal to me." She turned to her men before the door opened. "Secure the room! Try not to harm anyone! And wait for further instructions!"

Her Dirty Dozen burst into the room, forcing the twenty-odd people working there to raise their hands in the universal sign of capitulation. Two technicians dropped beneath their workbenches, only to feel embarrassed later on that no one else in the room had cowered.

"Mary, I'm certain you've informed your merry band of marauders that they are committing an act of state treason, for which they will be punished according to military law?"

"I'm certain they will consult their lawyers when the time is appropriate.

Thank you for your concerns," Mary said as she nudged Mapplethorpe into the room, her gun snugly nestled in the curve of his back.

The infamous Baltimore Room looked a lot less imposing than she had imagined. It was a larger, more cluttered version of the White House Sit Room. The most impressive part was the rotunda ceiling, part of the building's original charm. The room was filled with computer terminals, telecommunications equipment, electronic gadgets, and cryptic signs and unintelligible writings plastered all over the walls. For the most part, it looked like a messy teenager's bedroom.

"General, I'd like a copy of Project Baltimore." Mary spoke quietly but forcefully.

"Project Baltimore?" Mapplethorpe asked with an annoying sarcasm. He turned to Shaw. "As my chief of staff, do you know anything about a Project Baltimore?"

"Let me see," Shaw said, assuming a pensive demeanor. "Yes, as a matter of fact, I have heard of Project Baltimore."

"Then please inform our gracious hostess what you know about this project. God only knows with a prosaic name like that it couldn't be all that important." Mapplethorpe had decided to keep Mary preoccupied until Zarb could build up an effective strike force to seize the building, which would normally take thirty minutes.

"To the best of my memory," Shaw said, "Project Baltimore involved a major U.S. government financial commitment to maintain the harbors and ports of the city of Baltimore. I think the project involved something to do with our mothballed fleet docked there." Shaw chuckled, resolved to have some fun.

Checking her watch, Mary realized she was losing valuable time. She had not been fooled by Zarb's nonchalance. He had been too compliant. Too acquiescent. If he were true to form, Zarb would attempt an assault on the building very soon.

"Gentlemen, I genuinely appreciate your collective sense of humor. But unfortunately I am not in a mood to laugh." Mary's voice sounded angry. "I will give you precisely five seconds to produce a copy of Project Baltimore."

"What are you going to do? Shoot us all?" Mapplethorpe asked sardonically.

"Four seconds . . ." she continued.

The room became completely still. No one moved. Not even Mary's men.

"Oh, come on, Dougherty! Give up this silly game of Dungeons and Dragons!" Mapplethorpe said.

"One second . . ." Mary screwed an Italian-designed silencer onto the barrel of her 9 millimeter Beretta.

"Wait a minute! What happened to three and two?" Shaw suddenly realized she might not be joking.

Mary aimed the gun at Shaw's right kneecap. She fired with pinpoint accuracy.

Shaw screamed, clutching his blood-drenched pants. He reflexively stood up, trying to appear strong, but buckled over onto the floor.

"Sorry, Sonny. I forgot to tell you that I never learned to count very well." Mary slowly aimed the gun at Mapplethorpe, and pulled the trigger.

Screams filled the room. Mapplethorpe remained standing. Mary had purposely missed him.

"Next time, General, I won't miss. Trust me," Mary said matter-of-factly.

The message was not lost on any of Mary's men. Their boss was, in the parlance of the Special Ops soldiers, one tough bitch.

Mapplethorpe walked to the front of the room, lifted up a chart on U.S. troop deployment in Germany and began to open an old Mosler wall safe. "Would you please have a medic attend to Sonny's wound?"

He would give her what she wanted. But in a few minutes, when Zarb stormed the room, he would take it back.

Mapplethorpe handed her a thick black book marked SENSITIVE/TOP SECRET/EYES ONLY/NO DISTRIBUTION: PROJECT BALTIMORE.

Mary flipped quickly through the pages, concentrating on the section titles: OBJECTIVES, TIMING, COUP, COUNTERCOUP, ENDGAME. One thing was clear to her: this book was the evidence for which Desaix had been looking.

And others would kill to possess.

Only the sound of automatic gunfire ended Mary's concentration as she watched her deputy fall face downward into a pool of blood.

Zarb had begun his siege.

# CHAPTER
## 36

Desaix was depressed. The more he delved into the background of his colleagues, the more uncertain he felt about his ability to analyze their behavior or intentions correctly, let alone manipulate them. It was strange, Desaix thought. This time, increased knowledge didn't necessarily lead to a greater feeling of mastery over a problem. As a matter of fact, it seemed as if the converse were true. The more Desaix learned, the more he realized how little he had known all along.

Feelings of inadequacy and vulnerability suddenly overwhelmed him, forcing him to retreat into a protective cocoon of silence. Within that self-spun shroud, he was able to convince himself that he didn't hear the haunting words that he had dreaded since childhood—*stupid, awkward, incompetent.*

*Competency!* The very shibboleth of his existence. How he hated the word. He felt like vomiting that very moment. Desaix long ago decided that the only human trait that was both universally admired and feared was *competency.* Only a man who could perform better than anyone else in a given endeavor could truly be independent of others. Such a man could, by virtue of his well-deserved uniqueness, float above the frighteningly restrictive laws of normal behavior that dictated the conduct of the rest of mankind.

Without realizing it, Desaix had found himself tumbling about within a vicious circle of unrealistic expectations and disappointing results. The more of this crisis he tried to manage, the more inadequate he felt. Information and knowledge should be a source of control. But the more Desaix learned about Project Baltimore, the more confused and sad he became. The natural Cajun bravado was dissolving into a cauldron of uncertainty, disgust, cynicism, and despair.

He felt like the disillusioned little boy who had celebrated Halloween in New Orleans, eager to partake in the festivities that re-created the legend of the ghost of Marie Laveau, the Voodoo Queen. According to legend she had sallied forth from her tomb on the eve of All Saints' Day and made her way down Rampart Street to the cottage on St. Ann Street where she dispensed her mysterious potions and presided over ritual dances in the backyard. As long as Desaix was part of this ritual, he was able to both enjoy and master the fear inherent in celebrating the macabre. But as he grew older and was forced to put away his jazzy red mojo bag of magical herbs, he found himself rationalizing the gaudy appearances of Halloween as an ersatz religious holiday with its roots in the traditions of Roman Catholicism practiced by the French and Spanish settlers who had brought slavery to Louisiana in the eighteenth century. Cajun magic gave way to professional rationalism. Consequently, emotional investments in the mysteries of the unknown became perceived as cynical manipulations by crass commercial and power interests. In time, Desaix learned to believe in nothing but his own abilities—a burdensome task, indeed, which eventually led him down the path of cynicism, disgust, and despair.

So it was no wonder that for the moment Desaix felt completely manipulated.

"Desaix, are you listening to me?" Damon asked, concerned that his colleague had tuned him out.

"Yeah, I hear you," Desaix lied. He hadn't heard one word that Damon had told him for the last five minutes.

"Manning's Operational Code. Remember?" For a brief moment, Damon sensed that Desaix was frightened by what they had read.

"Now that we know we can get into the files, let's merge the Operational Code format with Manning's Psychological Political Profile."

"Right. Just take it slow."

Damon pushed the appropriate keys on the computer and the screen filled up once again. Unlike the other Op Codes, this format was specifically requested by the client.

## OPERATIONAL CODE/PSYCHOLOGICAL POLITICAL PROFILE OF CHESTER MANNING/CLASSIFIED TOP SECRET/ UMBRA[U]/NO FORN/NO DIS/HUMINT/ELINT/EYES ONLY.

### THE NATURE OF POLITICS AND POLITICAL CONFLICT

#### 1) Politics:

Philosophically and operationally, Manning is the master of maintaining a political style that incorporates both conflict and harmony at the same time.

As a successful businessman and three-term congressman from Austin, Texas, Manning was known for his ability to maintain an image of harmony, cooperation, and consensus while working behind the scenes to enhance his personal and professional power. During this period, his principal administrative assistant and backroom operative was the current Vice President of the United States, Allison Bonner.

After graduating number one in his class at the University of Texas Law School, Manning was made an associate professor of law. His mentor, John Fawn, dean of the law school, considered Manning to be exceptionally talented both academically and managerially.

Dean Fawn dismissed Manning from the law faculty when he uncovered an elaborate plan by Manning to have him deposed several years before his intended retirement. Several weeks later, Fawn died mysteriously in a hunting accident. [U]

As a real estate developer, Manning created a series of companies and limited partnerships in which several of his general partners were indicted for tax fraud and extortion. Manning was cleared of any wrongdoing and subsequently acquired his partners' financial interests.[U]

Manning donated a large portion of his sizeable fortune to charities and social causes. He has received several "Man of the Year" awards.

In politics Manning has had many political mentors.

Manning perceives politics in a practical, problem-solving way. Although he espouses the basic values of democratic idealism, trust, decency, fair play, and team effort, he believes in no ideology.

For the past five years, Manning has been on the payroll of Keiretsu, a Japanese corporate group, paid covertly through a middleman working for the Deputy Foreign Minister, Yutaka Imai.

Although Manning believes in a strong protectionist trade policy, there is evidence to suggest that he has been covertly providing the Keiretsu with the necessary assistance to dump their goods in the U.S.[U]

On several occasions, Congressman Manning was accused by German manufacturers of supporting legislation that favored Japanese interests over German interests. Publicly, Manning has denied any anti-German sentiments.

### 2) Opponents and Allies

Manning's basic philosophy is that there are no permanent allies or enemies. There are simply personal or national interests, which vary over time.

His political profile reveals a history of making and turning against personal and professional allies. He has been nicknamed by his congressional colleagues the Stealth.[U]

He views the world as a zero-sum game of winners and losers. A winner one day can be a loser another day. His ability to roll with the punches has proven very effective in his political campaigns. As a congressman, he always had a strong constituent support.

His basic style alternates between confrontation and conciliation. He believes that the only effective government is an authoritarian one, where one man rules through effective manipulation of public symbols. He feels that democracy is inefficient and unwieldy.[U]

## SHAPING HISTORICAL DEVELOPMENTS

### 3) Control of History

Manning believes that the world is ruled by a small elite of like-minded leaders whose vested interests are easily discernible.

He believes that most world leaders are motivated by power and historical impact. The lubricants to achieve power are money, force, terror, intimidation, and sex.[U]

Manning believes that major world leaders should work closely together to maintain their own domestic power base and to enhance their international prestige. Alliances can and should shift as needs change.

Manning's concept of a personal historical destiny is Darwinian: he believes that only the fit survive. He feels that a few very special people with a clear sense of their own historical destiny are chosen through a natural political process of self-selection to lead.

### 4) Predictability

Manning believes that individual personalities determine the course of history. A leader must be comfortable with uncertainty, learning how to harness it with the right blend of control and laissez-faire.

A leader must have a specific strategy in mind and know how to implement it, always working from a position of strength. His personal interests must always appear to be subordinate to the common good.

### 5) Power

For Manning, acquiring and maintaining power is the essence of a political leader's existence. He must share power only to the degree that it is necessary to accomplish his goals. The end justifies the means.

A political leader has a mandate to circumvent laws if necessary. For the most part, real power is acquired through covert methods.

### 6) Optimism

A political leader must be optimistic about his political destiny. He must be able to convey it in public speeches and appearances.

Courage and optimism are essential ingredients for a successful politician.

### 7) Weaknesses

A politician's weaknesses must never be revealed. However, it is important to uncover and manipulate the weaknesses of other leaders.

"Impressive, isn't it?" Damon stated with childish delight.

"Very!" replied Desaix, stunned. He didn't even know where to begin. It was all there. The entire explanation behind Fitzpatrick's death and Project Baltimore.

But the information made sense only on one condition—that it was accurate.

"I bet you're wondering how the Agency got all this information?" asked a familiar voice behind them.

Desaix turned around in his swivel chair, surprised to see White standing alongside Ball.

For a moment, the tall, lanky National Security Advisor and the short, ruddy faced DCI looked like a couple of hillbilly farmers on TV, advertising some product that required the aura of natural, down-home authenticity.

"It's the White and Ball show!" Desaix said sarcastically. Over their shoulders, on a small wall shelf, he noticed the concealed TV camera that had monitored him and Damon.

"Surprised, Desaix?" White grinned smugly.

"You could say that." Desaix heard some movement in the hallway. "Sounds like you brought an army with you."

"Just a few security guards to make certain that no sensitive intelligence suddenly disappears from this office." Ball sounded uncomfortable with his threat that Desaix wasn't going to leave the office with his new knowledge.

The information incriminated both White and Ball—one way or another. Especially in Fitzpatrick's death. Manning was right, even if he was a double-dealer. White and Ball were directly involved in the torture and murder of Fitzpatrick. Just as the photograph had shown. Or . . . had it?

"Aren't you wondering how Dr. Perkins here did such an excellent job on the Psychological Profile and Operational Code of our eminent Secretary of State?" Ball smiled.

"Thank you, sir!" Damon preened. "I'm very honored by your appraisal of my work."

"Don't take too much credit for it. Remember, Perkins, we did provide you with extremely sensitive HUMINT," Ball replied curtly, hoping that the message of humility would not be lost on Desaix.

"All the sensitive information that you just read on Manning, Westview, and even Zotov was provided by a highly secret joint task force of the CIA and NSA." White walked slowly toward Desaix.

"As a matter of fact, two unlisted members of that task force are standing right in front of you," Ball said, flanking White.

"White and you," Desaix replied with cynical enthusiasm.

"How incredibly perceptive of you, Desaix," White added.

"It helps to be analytically oriented." Desaix laughed.

"If I may speak on behalf of my partner," White said, "we are certainly great admirers of your intuitive and analytical talents. That's clearly what brought us together for this propitious occasion." White reeked with sarcasm, although Desaix picked up an underlying tone of resignation rather than hostility.

Ball and White circled Desaix like hungry jaguars ready to pounce on a startled gazelle.

"Have I committed any errors of which I am not aware?" Damon blurted out nervously.

"No, you've been fine, Damon," Ball said as he placed his thick, beefy hands on Damon's shoulders. "Just relax and enjoy the show."

"How did you get this information, Jim?" Desaix asked, beginning to wonder if he hadn't been purposely set up by Ball in a very elaborate, sophisticated campaign of disinformation. Not too dissimilar from the misinformation Manning had tried to use against him with that doctored photograph. Desaix had already convinced himself, based on what he considered his infallible intuition, that Ball was right—the photograph was fake.

"I'm not at liberty to say," Ball said, looking quizzically at White for permission to continue.

"You don't expect me to believe that. It says right there on the document that you were using human intelligence, signal intelligence, and satellite. If this document has any validity . . ." Desaix paused to see if he could provoke Ball into a defensive posture, ". . . then I would have to conclude that you had a very high-level informant who knew Manning extremely well."

"Yeah . . ." Ball waited to see what conclusion Desaix would come to.

"I would say someone who had been a friend of his throughout his entire career. Someone, I would say, like a childhood friend. Someone who had been like an older brother . . . a hunting partner . . . a political colleague . . . a very close personal friend . . . who knew him extremely well." Desaix carefully watched both Ball's and White's facial reactions. There were none.

This game of trapping the hunters was going to be more difficult than Desaix had imagined.

"What makes you think there was only one information source?" White asked. "Profiles and codes are always based on a composite—academicians, lobbyists, business partners . . ."

"Consistency of observations over a period of time. A very definitive profile—information that was 'suggested' more strongly than usual. Somebody was very eager for me to see this—and have no doubts."

"Why is it so important for you to know who the source or sources are?" Damon asked ingenuously. "Aren't my analyses sufficient?"

"Of course, your analyses are sufficient," Desaix replied, mindful of Damon's extreme sensitivity to criticism. "But when you brought up the Psychological Political Profiles and Operational Codes on the screen, I noticed that the necessary information on Westview, Zotov, Mapplethorpe, and Manning was readily available. You never once had to check your sources or cross-index a conclusion. It was already formatted for you."

"Christ, what do you expect?" Damon asked defensively. "I've been working on their analyses for the past year, preparing for several forthcoming meetings."

"I know that. And I was duly impressed." Desaix reiterated his unconditional support of Damon. "But I was equally impressed by the existence of Manning's analysis, in light of the fact that doing a profile or Op Code on any U.S. citizen, except the President of the United States, is strictly prohibited by law."

"So?" White asked, trying to be provocative. "Don't tell me you've suddenly decided to become a Boy Scout?"

"No, you don't have to worry about that." Everyone in the room laughed, including Desaix.

"So what's your point, besides the fact that it's illegal?" Ball asked matter-of-factly.

"If you notice the notation on the bottom of many of the paragraphs on Manning's file, you see the letter U in brackets." Desaix pointed to the printout.

"U in brackets is designation for code UMBRA. You know that. We know that," White said, exasperated.

"Don't get so nervous, Richard," Desaix responded in a soothing voice.

"Don't fucking patronize me, Desaix! Like you did in that Japanese morgue!" White shouted, shocking both Damon and Ball with his anger. "Listen, I've got a group of guys outside who are pacing the hallway, just waiting for you to come out."

"Are you threatening me, Dickie?" Desaix asked, then realized he was provoking White, hopefully into a confrontation where he would inadvertently reveal his intentions.

"No, he's not threatening you, Desaix." Ball answered for him, physically blocking White's access to Desaix. "Are you, General White?"

"No! Damnit! I am not threatening you, Dr. Clark!" White shouted. "Hell, I don't think there is a man in this room who would dare to threaten the infamous Desaix." Reaching his hands out toward Desaix, White continued, "We're all too fucking scared of what the bogeyman might do to our minds. That's what you want us to say, isn't it, Desaix? Like the rest of this frigging administration, we're all too scared to find out what you know about us that we may not even know about ourselves."

"Enough! Richard, get a hold of yourself!" Ball shouted.

Damon sat quietly in his chair, realizing that Desaix was creating a conflict between Ball and White with only a few provocative statements and innuendos.

"Code UMBRA is given to extremely sensitive intelligence that is specifically requested for or by the President of the United States. Isn't that right, General White?" Desaix asked in a seemingly deferential tone of voice.

"UMBRA is UMBRA! Everyone in this room knows what it means!" White said, trying to calm himself down. He disliked playing mental games with Desaix. It was a waste of time and energy as far as he was concerned.

"Damon, do you take me for a fool? You didn't put code UMBRA on either Westview's or Zotov's files," Desaix said. "They were obviously routine profiles done in anticipation of our government's needs. But Manning's was different. Who would request it? Especially knowing that it was a potentially illegal request? That profile is something quite out of the ordinary—on all counts. Isn't that right, Damon?" Desaix asked.

Gazing at Ball for approval, Damon replied hesitantly, "Yes."

"A request for a profile on a current Secretary of State? There is only one person who could have legally ordered that profile—President Donald Westview. Correct, Ball?"

"Yes!" Ball replied.

For a moment Desaix felt like Sherlock Holmes, who, in the final scenes of his movies, pieces together all the missing elements of the murder.

But he was also playing for time, trying to solve another question in his mind. Was Manning's Operational Code valid? Or was it a setup to entice him into initiating some dangerous action against Manning?

More importantly, if Manning's Operational Code was valid, Desaix would be one step closer to figuring out who provided the sensitive intelligence upon which that code was based. And why. With those answers, Desaix could develop the strategic point around which he could build his plan to stop the coup and the war.

"Wasn't it also true that he was the person who ordered you and Perkins to develop the Operational Code?" Desaix asked.

"That's correct," Ball replied.

"Now comes the question that will separate the bullshit from the truth." Desaix could feel the tension in the room. "President Westview was the sole informant for Manning's profile and code, wasn't he?"

"You know that I could have you killed for finding out the answer to that question," Ball replied threateningly.

"I know that you could do to me what you did to Fitzpatrick!" Desaix replied.

"If we wanted to torture you and then kill you, why would I have allowed you to see Manning's code?" Ball asked defensively.

"In the beginning, I thought that you were trying to set me up. The same way that Manning set me up with that phony photograph incriminating you and White in Fitzpatrick's murder. But if that were the case, I wouldn't be here discussing the code with you and White, now would I?"

"Yeah? Well, how do you know that you'll be getting out of this building alive?"

"I don't know, Richard. You could still have me killed. I know that and you know that. But I may be the only person, other than Westview, who can prove that neither you nor Ball were involved in Fitzpatrick's murder." Desaix paused to assess their reactions. There was a palpable sense of relief in both of their faces. "That's why you let me work with Damon, Jim! It was your way of testing out whether, after seeing Manning's code, I would arrive at the conclusions that both you and Richard know to be the truth."

"And what is that, Desaix?" asked Ball.

"Chester Manning and Yutaka Imai were the only ones directly responsible for the murder of Daniel Fitzpatrick."

"How did you figure that out?" White asked, sounding pleased.

"When we were at the morgue examining Fitzpatrick's mutilated body, I discovered that he was killed by hydrogen fluoride. Not by a 9 millimeter bullet as Dr. Oda Nobunaga, the forensic pathologist close to Yutaka Imai, wanted me to believe.

"Remember how annoyed you were with me at the morgue, Richard?" Desaix asked.

"Yeah, I thought that you were acting like a patronizing smart-ass, making all kinds of problems for us and the Japanese."

"I was." Desaix smiled. "I wanted to be particularly insufferable with Dr. Nobunaga."

"Why?" Ball asked.

"One of Japan's top forensic pathologists doesn't make that kind of error— confusing a bullet wound with an acid wound. A first-year medical student doesn't make that mistake. So the question that kept on bothering me from that day on was why Nobunaga and Imai went to such lengths to convince me that Fitzpatrick died of a bullet wound. They knew I would detect the error immediately. The answer came while I was dressing the acid wound on my hand. Nobunaga wanted me to believe that the killer was someone in the American government who would eventually use hydrogen fluoride for other nefarious purposes."

"You thought that we did it?" White asked.

"Yes. Both Manning and Imai wanted me to believe that both of you were responsible for killing Fitzpatrick under the direct orders of Westview, through Mapplethorpe."

"Why?"

"The simple answer, Richard, is that they wanted to involve me with them in certifying President Westview mentally incompetent, so that following the constitutional line of succession, Chester Manning would become the President of the United States."

"But that means that the Vice President, the Speaker of the House, and the President pro tempore of the Senate would have to be incapacitated or dead," White said, his sudden realization frightening him. "You're talking about the murder of . . ."

"That's right, General!" Desaix replied calmly. He realized that he had co-opted them. "We have, at best, twelve hours in which to stop an insane war and prevent three assassinations. But if you would, let's go back to the basic plan of Project Baltimore."

"I hate to sound naive, but what is Project Baltimore?" Ball asked.

"Jim, please. If you want to work together, which I think you do, then please grant me a modicum of intelligence. It will help toward establishing a relationship based on trust." Desaix was trying to coax a confession from them as to their complicity.

"You're fishing, Desaix." Ball laughed. "I know when you're certain about something. And when you sound like a peacock in mating season."

"I agree with Jim," White added. "You're just trying to find out what we know about Project Baltimore so that you can inform on us." White sensed Desaix's vulnerability.

"Let me ask you, then, whom would I inform?" Desaix asked. Desaix thought, who were they afraid of? And why?

"You don't know?" Ball asked, surprised.

"I think you're afraid of what Westview might do to you," Desaix replied. "You're afraid that the same thing might happen to you that happened to Jenkins, McCormick, and Merck. He might fire and replace each of you with someone else."

"Fire? Hah! That's the least of our worries! Why don't you try something like . . . murder?" As White spoke, he realized that Desaix really hadn't understood the full extent of their fears.

"What are you talking about?" Desaix asked, confused. "Weren't they summarily fired?"

"Yes, each was summarily fired. But they were also murdered through what appeared to be accidents. Why do you think Jim and I walk around with bodyguards? To take care of you, my dear friend?" White was surprised that as much as Desaix might know about Project Baltimore, he still didn't know enough.

"Well . . ." Desaix replied smilingly.

"Don't flatter yourself! I understand that Special Agent Brooks may have had trouble getting rid of you and Mary. Believe me, Jim and I would not make the same mistake," White said sternly.

"What happened to Merck, McCormick, and Jenkins?" Desaix asked.

"You must have been quite a busy person to have missed the big news of the day," Ball replied. "Jenkins was found mangled in an escalator. Merck was found dead in a synagogue. And he isn't even Jewish. McCormick died in a freak airplane accident. All within the past six hours."

"And you think that Westview ordered it?" Desaix asked.

"Who else would want to get rid of them? Could it be that he was fearful that they might reveal Project Baltimore, which, if they had, would seriously compromise him?" Ball asked.

"Maybe someone wanted to make it look as if the President had created these accidents," Desaix answered.

"Like Manning!" White declared.

"That's exactly right." Desaix replied. "Look at your own Operational Code on him. On the surface he works collegially. But in reality he sets you up in order to turn against you. If you think about Project Baltimore and his modus operandi of betrayal, I wouldn't be surprised to learn that he, along with Mapplethorpe, had suggested the plan from the outset, ostensibly to boost the President's sagging popularity. But that was the manifest content of his intentions. In the guise of a trusted friend and advisor, he encouraged the President to accept a contrived coup, concocted by Mapplethorpe and himself. The coup was intended to give Westview the necessary pretext to order our army to intervene in civil affairs." Desaix paused. "Voila! By exposing his own coup, Westview regains much of his sagging popularity. It doesn't really matter that a few civil liberties are lost during this potential self-created crisis. My suspicion is that Mapplethorpe, Manning, and the President had agreed beforehand to scapegoat Jenkins, Merck, and McCormick as the culprits in this self-created coup against the presidency."

"The tape that was made of the secret Mapplethorpe meeting at the Pentagon. That's the key!" Ball turned to White. "You'll remember, Richard, that no mention was made of either Manning or Mapplethorpe's presence. Convenient omission, wasn't it?"

"You're right. There was no mention of Manning."

"What tape?" Desaix asked.

"Never mind that. What about the war?" White realized that Desaix had a better grasp of the mess they were in than he had suspected.

Damon sat mesmerized, absorbing the intricacies of a plot that he found ingenious.

"The controlled beginning of World War III is an integral part of Project Baltimore," Desaix said, but then stopped, exhausted, not knowing how much of what he had just spun out was fact and how much was fiction. He was hoping that the reaction of the men standing across from him would give him a clue.

"How do you know all this?" White asked provocatively.

Desaix was silent, reluctant to reveal that he had relied on some of Westview's own revelations during their all-night psychotherapy session. Patient confidentiality was still part of his professional code of ethics. But that was in the past. Desaix knew that now he needed Ball and White's help. As DCI and National Security Advisor, their sources of global intelligence and bureaucratic coordination were indispensable to stopping Manning and the full madness of Project Baltimore. Was that worth violating his professional standing? Whenever that question had come up in the past, the answer had always been a resounding no. Ironically, his psychiatric professionalism was the only part of him left with any vestige of integrity.

An unimpeachable source, so to speak, Desaix thought to himself, realizing how his poor pun could have unconsciously revealed the source of his information.

"It sounds like 'trust me or tough luck'," White remarked derisively.

"If you can't trust your own instincts or intuition, Richard, what have you got left?" Desaix replied, content for the moment that his vague answer would suffice.

"He has a point, Richard. Instincts and intuition. That's what all these fancy studies and memos are really all about, whether it's the Operational Code, Profiles, or highly sensitive intelligence. They are all just a different way of packaging information that relies on our instincts and intuition to evaluate it properly." What Ball didn't say was that despite all the fancy paraphernalia of the intelligence community that he had at his disposal, he didn't really trust it.

"If Desaix is right, we have to trust the person who is giving us the information, as well as sensing whether that information is consistent with our own assumptions about life."

"Christ, Jim! What's gotten into you? You're starting to wax poetic. Just when I expect it least." White laughed.

"As I was saying, before I was so pleasantly interrupted, besides Project Baltimore's domestic side, it has an equally Machiavellian component in the international arena."

"Which, I presume, includes an agreement between Westview and Zotov about when and where the war would start?" White didn't really care whether Desaix agreed or not.

"Richard, in this matter, I'll defer to you and Jim. Both of you were intimately involved in setting up the agreements between Westview and Zotov," Desaix replied.

"How did you know that?" Ball asked.

"I didn't. Not really. Not until you told me about the agreements. I had suspected that only Westview, Mapplethorpe, Manning, Merck, McCormick, and Jenkins knew." Desaix paused, adding a somber note, "But now three of them are dead. That leaves Mapplethorpe, Manning, and Westview. And, of course, you two."

"No, there was one more," Ball added sadly.

"Fitzpatrick," replied Desaix. "Of course. I should have figured it out. He knew all about the agreement between Westview and Zotov, but was probably completely against it. Right?"

"You're just beginning to scratch the surface," White added.

"Fitzpatrick was against the notion of any prearranged war between the U.S. and the Russian Federation."

"Keep going!" White said, as he realized that Desaix was working off intuition and instinct, and not hard intelligence.

"How did you know that there was a prearranged agreement?" Ball asked.

"Pretty much from comparing Zotov's and Westview's Operational Codes. Except for one important variable, they were very much alike. Westview sought out chaos, while Zotov feared it. Other than that, they are mirror images of each other. Both men are confronted with domestic problems. Stagnant economies. A military-industrial complex that has been rapidly dwindling. Internal domestic unrest." Desaix paused. "What better way to get rid of domestic problems than to create a real external threat that would force the citizenry of each country to consolidate its efforts and support its failing political leader? But now we must find a way to stop this madness, because contrary to plans, it is going to be impossible to measure and manage a war like this."

"It's very kind of you to attribute your insights to my Operational Code," Damon said, "but having worked with you now, I somehow think you're holding back some information."

"Yes, you're quite right, Damon. There was one other variable that I used—the National Character Study. But instead of going to a computer, I did it in my head. I was bewildered by the fact that the U.S. and the Russians have had years of peace. Then, suddenly, without cause, there is, one, a war, that, two, escalates incredibly rapidly, without, three, any of the diplomatic noises that one would normally expect. That in and of itself was strange. But what was more bewildering was, four, the fact that this particular war did not seem to be in the national character of either nation." Desaix conveniently forgot to mention his unimpeachable source.

"What do you mean?" Ball asked.

"Russians tend to be extremely fearful of anything that smacks of chaos. Especially war. It was highly unlikely that the Russians started the war, as Westview stated publicly."

"Why?" White asked.

"Because when a nation begins a war it has to have a very clear idea of what its strategic and tactical objectives are. Considering the fact that Zotov and Westview have almost identical political styles, I also assume that they would have similar political objectives, which, in this case, not only had a domestic component, but also an international one—the complete destruction of Germany!"

"What?" Ball and White asked simultaneously.

"Yes, that was the other equally important objective of this prearranged war—the destruction of a powerful economic and political competitor— Germany." Desaix suspected that both Ball and White were dramatizing their surprise.

"It can't be!" White said.

"Why not?" Desaix replied. "Just look at the map. The entire war is being fought almost exclusively on German soil. Strange, isn't it?"

"It sounds convincing to me," Damon interjected.

"It should, Damon. If you look at your own Operational Code on Manning, what you see is a Secretary of State who despises the Germans and has been on the Japanese side for over five years."

"So?" White demanded.

"So Manning convinces President Westview and General Mapplethorpe to join with the Russians in precipitating a controlled war between them in order to devastate Germany. Having seen Imai, I suspect the Japanese will provide the necessary funds to wage this war. What is a mere hundred billion dollars to pay to two allies—the U.S. and the Russian Federation—to permanently destroy an economic enemy? Both the U.S. and Russian economics would flourish, Germany would be weakened, and the Japanese would retrieve their billions by funding the reconstruction of a devastated Germany. Again, just like after the war with Iraq."

"Very interesting," Ball said.

"What's far more interesting, Jim, is that both you, Richard, and Fitzpatrick were sent to Japan to negotiate that agreement between the U.S. and the Japanese." Desaix had finally unraveled all of the elements of the Gordian knot. But he needed to keep on talking and thinking.

"What if you are right, hypothetically speaking?" White asked.

"Well, hypothetically speaking, I would say that Fitzpatrick was killed by Manning and Imai's henchman, Dr. Nobunaga, because he was going to publicly reveal the plan. After having uncovered Project Baltimore, which we agree Fitzpatrick had opposed from the very beginning as a Trojan Horse from which Manning would carry out his own coup against Westview. In short, Manning was running a coup within a coup."

"You mean Manning had suggested Project Baltimore to Westview in order to further his own personal political interests?" Damon asked, incredulous.

"Yes, my dear colleague. It's all right there in your Operational Code. Manning has had a consistent, long-standing history of turning against friends, allies, and political mentors—with, of course, the help of Yutaka Imai and the Keiretsu."

"I swear, neither Ball nor I had any idea of what Manning was doing," White said plaintively.

"I know that. That's why I told you that I didn't think that either one of you killed Fitzpatrick. Only two people suspected Manning of duplicity—of hiding his coup within another coup—and that was Fitzpatrick, who paid for his discovery, and President Westview, who purposely kept me away from Project Baltimore so that I wouldn't get involved in any of Manning's machinations."

"Why did he do that?" Ball asked.

"Westview knew from our previous collaborations that he would need me to smoke out Manning's coup within a coup. He suspected that Manning would use Project Baltimore as cover for his own personal ambitions because it was Manning who had suggested Project Baltimore from the very beginning. He knew that in time Manning would try to co-opt me into working with him against the President. Westview knew his friend well, as evidenced by the information that he provided you with for Manning's Operational Code, so he kept Manning as close to him as possible—making certain to keep a watchful eye on him.

"Westview knew my standard operating procedure is to always examine CIA and NSA files. He knew that even if he didn't get a chance to see the code, I would."

"But why did Manning give you a photograph that incriminated both of us?" Ball asked.

"At first, I thought it was intended to incriminate you both. But once again, he was banking on the fact that I would find out that it was a fake. What he wanted to do was to throw some doubt into my assessment of your information. If the photos were doctored, presumably by the Agency, then why wouldn't you also doctor the codes and profiles? He thought that he could throw some clouds of suspicion over my conclusions. In short, Manning was trying to co-opt me through the use of old PSYOPS techniques of disinformation against both of you, while at the same time trying to discredit the source of your intelligence for the codes, President Westview, by trying to convince me that he was mentally deranged. Manning and Imai hoped to implicate Westview as an incompetent and irrational President who had to be removed through the invocation of the Twenty-fifth Amendment."

"It sounds to me like Manning knows you extremely well," Ball said.

"I agree. I guess we're fortunate that you were able to see through the deception," White added.

"No. You're just lucky that President Westview was able to co-opt me first," Desaix replied.

"What do you mean, Desaix?" Damon was concerned by the frightening implications of that statement.

"An addict, whether he continuously craves action or heroin, doesn't really care what his supplier's intentions are as long as he is assured of a steady supply."

"So you're really saying that either man could have co-opted you," White said with a tinge of self-righteous contempt.

"We'll just have to see about that, won't we?" Desaix said.

# CHAPTER
## 37

Depending on the circumstances, a hospital can be a sanctuary for the infirm and lame, or a repository of unimaginable torture and grotesque horror.

Ironically, the perception of pain, rather than pain itself, is the determining variable. It determines whether the patient is looking toward the hospital experience with entitlement or fear.

Unfortunately, both Mary Dougherty and Walter Johnson were not very lucky.

Both were admitted to Saint Elizabeth Hospital on the same day, at virtually the same hour. Mary was admitted as an involuntary patient under the care of General Thomas Mapplethorpe, whereas Johnson was stationed at St. E's for psychological reprogramming under the supervision of Dr. Juan Prince.

Both were soon to learn that one must never interfere with nature's second law of thermodynamics, the law of entropy—that all natural states have a tendency to disintegrate into chaos and disorder.

Be they nature, man, or politics.

Lieutenant Commander Neva Moser, USN nurse, draped herself in a green surgical disposable paper gown and approached the naked female patient lying uncomfortably on the metal examining table.

The patient's muscular feet were fastened to brightly shining stirrups. Standing squarely in front of the patient, the only thing that Neva could see was exactly what countless obstetrician/gynecologists see in their daily office practice—a tense face rising awkwardly above a white sheet, and completely exposed female genitalia. The rest of the setting was also typical. An overly bright fluorescent ceiling light. A convex mirror positioned to allow the patient to observe the examination. A standing tray of highly polished steel clinical instruments, twisted into different bellowing shapes and sizes, looking like metal androids from a distant planet.

"Well, Mary Dougherty, isn't it a surprise to see you here?" As Neva spoke she picked up a translucent pair of talcum-powdered surgical gloves from the instrument tray. She carefully inserted her small, thin fingers into the gloves, marking the final effort with a sudden snap of the rubber.

Neva felt pleased with herself. Events were unfolding just as Mapplethorpe had predicted they would. A piece of cake, she thought.

Standing quietly behind Neva were Mapplethorpe and Shaw, successfully retrieved hostages from Zarb's brilliant assault of the Old Executive Office Building. They had worked with Neva before, interrogating an assortment of political informants, agents, and double agents.

To Mapplethorpe, Neva was an outstanding example of the armed forces volunteer of the 1990s, dedicated primarily to career advancement in a system where self-selected groups took care of one another. Mapplethorpe had long ago observed her unique talents when he had been hospitialized at Bethesda Naval Hospital for a minor illness.

Like most other medical officers, Neva had been routinely assigned intelligence functions as part of her normal military duties. Trained at an advanced intelligence school at Fort Meade, she was quickly spotted as someone who could be an effective interrogator. So it was no accident that she had been assigned by Mapplethorpe as Dr. Hugh Barnett's assistant to maintain a covert surveillance of President Westview's activities.

Despite Neva's knowledge of the President's whereabouts, Mapplethorpe had made a decision that he didn't want to waste valuable time trying to recapture the President from Mary's tight security around the surgical recovery room while Westview was still unconscious.

"What's going on?" Mary tugged at her leather arm and leg restraints, and finally realized it was useless to struggle any further. She recalled her last moments of resistance in the Baltimore Room when Zarb had tear-gassed the building and subdued her and her men by force. Now she realized that when they had been blindfolded, they were transported to St. E's.

And Neva was to be her interrogator, Mary concluded.

"Don't worry, Mary. I will be as gentle as possible. If you feel any discomfort, please don't hesitate to tell me." Neva radiated that rehearsed professional warmth that Mary recognized from visits to her own gynecologist.

"Neva, what are you doing?" Looking into the convex mirror, Mary realized that she would see everything that Neva was doing. She also saw both Mapplethorpe and Shaw standing behind her. "Christ! Don't tell me we're going to have a gang bang!"

"I told you not to worry. Just take some deep breaths and let them out slowly. That way you'll feel a lot more relaxed and it will be easier for me to examine you." Neva felt that her soothing voice would have a calming effect.

"Mary, Sonny and I are simply here to observe Neva's technique. She's reputed to be a master at what she does." Mapplethorpe spoke with a wry smile on his face.

"Of course, we wanted to make certain you were repaid for your kind hospitality." Sonny stood uneasily on his hastily bandaged leg, already concerned that the procedure might take too long. He still had a lot to do before completing his role in Project Baltimore.

"Mary, I'll be explaining to you everything that I will be doing as I proceed. Again, please don't be afraid to ask me any questions that you may have." Neva inserted the cold metal clamp into Mary's vagina and began to widen the opening.

"Neva, please let me go. There's nothing that I know that you don't already know." Mary felt Neva's fingers gently stroke her labia.

"Now, that doesn't feel bad? Does it?"

"Please, Neva. Don't do this," Mary replied quietly. "You're wasting your time. I can't help you or Mapplethorpe."

Neva ran her finger up and down the thin folds of Mary's vagina. "If you were excited, instead of fearful as you are now, these glands would discharge a liquid which allows for better lubrication." Neva squeezed Mary's labia minora between her fingers.

"Christ! That hurts!" Mary shouted.

"Oh, I'm so sorry," Neva answered in an obviously sarcastic tone of voice. "But I had to make certain you didn't have any evidence of gonorrhea. You know, given your active bisexual sex life, I would be remiss if I didn't make sure that you had no cyst or abscess, secondary to a gonococcal infection."

"You know damn well I don't have gonorrhea!"

"That's what they all say, my dear. But you can never be too certain. You know what I mean. Precaution is the better part of valor."

"Stop playing games, Neva! What do you want?"

"I personally don't want anything from you. I simply want to take good care of you. That's all." She inserted the index and middle finger of her left hand forcibly into Mary's vagina. "Why did you try to take over Room E? Was it to learn about Project Baltimore?" Neva decided to begin with the questions to which she already knew the answer.

Mary screamed as she felt Neva's fingers probe her vaginal walls, reminding her of the series of male gynecologists she had left because they were either too awkward or too brusque.

"Mary, I can complete this examination much more quickly if you would work with me, and not against me." Neva shoved her fingers more deeply into Mary's vaginal cavity until she could feel the blunt, rounded edges of the highly sensitive cervix. At the same time, she placed her right hand on Mary's abdomen, pressing forcibly downward.

"Oh Christ, Neva, please! That hurts!" Mary broke out into a cold sweat and watched helplessly as Mapplethorpe and Shaw began to smile.

"Who told you to break into Room E?" Neva asked as she shoved her gloved right hand farther into Mary's abdomen, several inches above the pubic symphysis. She pushed Mary's uterus downward as she pulled the cervix upward with the fingers of her left hand. "We call this a bimanual pelvic examination, to see whether you have any signs of pregnancy."

"Neva, please!" Mary screamed. "I don't know anything about Project Baltimore!" The more Mary tried to pull her hands out of the leather restraints, the bloodier her wrists became.

"I really have to check for signs of pregnancy—softening of the cervix or uterus. It would be negligent of me if I didn't do a complete vaginal. Can you imagine my embarrassment?" She forced both her hands more deeply into Mary's reproductive organs. Neva was actually concerned that she might accidentally injure the uterus if she weren't more careful.

"Mary, why did you take me and Sonny hostage?" Mapplethorpe asked uncomfortably.

"I thought you could give me an exclusive VIP tour of the Old Executive Office Building."

Shaking their heads in disapproval, neither Mapplethorpe nor Shaw said a word. They would leave the matter for Neva to handle.

"Mary, for the sake of our friendship, think carefully about the question I've asked you." Neva picked up an obstetrical forceps, consisting of a pair of fenestrated metal blades, each connected to a shank and handle. She held it up high enough so Mary could see its reflection in the mirror. Mary needed to know exactly what was going to be inserted into her vagina. It amplified the psychological terror of the experience. Interrogation 101.

"Mary, dear, this is a multipurpose Elliot forceps, which is often used by obstetricians to pull recalcitrant babies from their mother's womb. Frankly, I don't blame them for not wanting to leave."

She inserted the forceps carefully into the vaginal introitus, and turned the screw, increasing the distance between the ends of the clamps, stretching the vaginal canal.

"O . . . h . . . h . . . h . . . h . . . h . . . h!" Mary felt as if her insides were about to explode. "Please . . . p . . . l . . . e . . . a . . . s . . . e!"

"Can you believe that with this forceps, or the Tarnier's forceps, I can deliver an eight-pound baby? Yet with you I can barely deliver a simple, straight answer. Now, how can that be possible?" Neva was starting to get a little nervous, fearful that she might permanently damage Mary's vaginal wall.

Mary could barely tolerate the pain. She felt as if she were being completely disemboweled. She started to writhe around on the examining table, pulling on the restraints.

"Who sent you there? How did you learn about Project Baltimore? How much do you know about Project Baltimore?" Neva was beginning to sweat. Mary's high-pitched screams were becoming intolerable. She couldn't expand the forceps anymore without inflicting permanent damage.

"No one sent me there!" Mary tried to maintain her lucidity. The one thing she could not afford to do was to pass out. Then she would be completely at their mercy.

"Mary, you wanted to see Project Baltimore! We know that! That's not so hard to admit, is it?" Neva suddenly jerked the forceps out of Mary's vagina.

Mary felt as if her vagina had been sheared in half.

"Oh, I'm so sorry," Neva said sarcastically.

"You bitch!" Mary screamed, despite the fact that she felt grateful that the forceps were no longer inside of her.

"Really, Mary. I'm so sorry for whatever pain and inconvenience I may have caused you. Please forgive me." Not expecting an answer, Neva picked up a six-and-a-half-inch twenty-two-gauge spinal needle, passing through a five-and-a-half-inch thumb ring, with a trumpet-shaped opening. It was an instrument that facilitated the entry and direction of a spinal needle when a paracervical, pudendal, or perineal anesthetic block was indicated.

"Oh, my God! Not that!" Mary screamed out as she stared at the stiletto-tipped edge of the spinal needle. "Neva, don't!"

"Oh, Mary. You make me feel like such an insensitive professional with those screams of pain." Neva inserted her left index finger into Mary's vaginal opening, feeling for the ischial spine, a bone that was the standard landmark for a pudendal anesthetic block.

"No, Neva! I beg you! Don't!" Mary screamed as she felt the long thimble being inserted into her vagina.

"Now take it easy, Mary. You're becoming hysterical. I'm only doing what millions of women have already experienced before you with the delivery of their babies." Neva inserted the syringe, filled with five cc's of 1 percent procaine, into the needle guide.

"Don't!" Mary started to breathe rapidly and deeply. She was becoming lightheaded, blowing out all her carbon dioxide.

"This funny-looking needle guide is called the Iowa Trumpet for reasons I really don't recall. Now, I insert this spinal syringe, filled with a strong local anesthetic, through the Iowa Trumpet and guide it gently into its home, right here at the base of your pelvic bones, called the ischial spine."

Mary's perineum exploded into a broad circle of excruciating pain. It felt as if Neva were tearing the ligaments away from her vaginal orifice.

"Now, Mary, listen to me carefully. I don't want you to forget anything that I'm doing. And, please, ask me any questions that you may have. I want you to feel as if you are part of this gynecological procedure. I feel very strongly that you should have a sense of control over your own body. That way, you and I are not working at cross purposes."

Pushing slowly down the syringe, Neva had to look away from Mary's face blanching with fear and fixed in a grimace of excruciating pain.

"Oh come on, Mary. It's not all that bad." She withdrew the Iowa Trumpet and reinserted the spinal needle in the opposite side of Mary's vaginal introitus. Feeling for the ischial bone on the left side, she inserted the spinal syringe into Mary's perineum and pushed slowly down on the syringe.

"Please, enough!" Mary could tolerate the pain itself. What she could not tolerate was the terrible uncertainty of the damage that was being inflicted on her body.

Where the hell was Desaix, she wondered. She had told Randy to call him at the Agency and tell him to return as soon as possible. He knew she would have problems with Mapplethorpe and his cronies.

"Oh, Mary, you can't imagine the miracle of modern medicine," Neva said as she pushed down on the syringe once more.

Mary felt like throwing up. But if she did, she ran the risk of aspirating her own vomit. And then she would die from asphyxiation.

"Now listen carefully, Mary. What I'm trying to do is prevent you from feeling any further pain. Ironic, isn't it? I have to inflict pain in order to prevent it? It's one of those uncomfortable paradoxes of life that we should simply accept without delving too much into its significance."

"It was Desaix who sent me there. He wanted me to find the plans for Project Baltimore." Mary tripped over her words, fearful she might not have enough time to complete her thought.

"That's a lot better!" Before Neva withdrew the syringe, she jabbed it several times around the medial sections of the perineum, having failed to properly identify the ischial spine.

"He wanted me to find out when the U.S. and Russia would begin the war in Germany."

"And also according to Project Baltimore, how is the war to be terminated?" Neva asked, trying to test Mary's veracity.

"Why ask me?" Mary replied, relieved that the anesthetic was taking effect. She was beginning to feel numb in her pelvic region.

"Ah, I see that your uncooperative, negative attitudes are returning. Well, I think that I have a solution for that." Neva picked up a long, thin tube and held it in front of Mary. "I'm holding a Hegar's dilator. I am going to insert this cervical dilator very gently into your vagina. I have already prepped it with a solution that will prevent any spread of infection."

"Thanks! Am I supposed to be grateful?" Looking straight at them, Mary saw the disappointed looks on both Mapplethorpe's and Shaw's faces. Clearly, they had expected more impressive results. Suddenly, Mary's strategy became obvious to her. If she could only hold out a little bit longer they would become annoyed with Neva and order her to stop.

"Now, I insert this cervical dilator to expand the size of your cervix so that I might insert another, more important instrument." Holding the upper lip of Mary's cervix with a tenaculum forceps, Neva gently inserted the dilator. "Please tell me if you feel anything?"

"It hurts! Damnit! It hurts!" screamed Mary.

"I probably didn't block the peritoneal nerves well enough. Such a pity.

Now, I am going to insert a serrated curette deep into your uterus so that I can determine whether you have any abnormal growths, such as a tumor, or a fetus." Neva performed a four-quadrant and vault curettage with the newly sharpened curette.

"You're performing a goddamn D&C! Oh Christ!"

The scraping sounds of the D&C instruments reverberated throughout the operating room. It sounded like chalk screeching across the blackboard.

Even Mapplethorpe clenched his teeth.

"Who sent you to my office?" Mapplethorpe was impatient with Neva's slow, methodical interrogation.

"Desaix!" Mary screamed as Neva scraped her uterus more vigorously. The pain in her groin was unbearable. Only now did she really understand what Mapplethorpe wanted from her. He never believed that Desaix had been instrumental in sending her to the Baltimore Room.

"Here we have a little bit of a blood clot," Neva said, holding a piece of endometrial tissue in the air. "My God! How dreadful to think that I might have to take a biopsy of your cervix." She moved the Hegar's dilator around the increasingly larger cervical hole.

"A . . . h . . h . . . h . . . h . . . h . . . h . . . !" Mary screamed. The room was starting to spin around.

"Mary, I don't want to have you in more pain than is necessary," Mapplethorpe said. "All I want to know is who sent you to my office. I know that Desaix was interested in obtaining a copy of Project Baltimore so that he could incriminate me in some sort of conspiracy. But you and I know that is not what I am talking about!"

"Desaix!" Mary yelled his name in a desperate attempt to ward off the name that Mapplethorpe was really looking for. Mapplethorpe was far shrewder than she had imagined. She had to hold on. Otherwise, he would kill her.

"I think, Ms. Moser, that our patient needs more curettage." Shaw watched Mary squirm like a helpless animal sent to the slaughterhouse.

Neva increased the pressure on her curette, digging it more deeply into the increasingly thinner walls of Mary's endometrium.

"Westview!" Mary uttered, hoarsely. "It was Westview who sent me to get the book!"

Nodding his head, Mapplethorpe ordered Neva to continue the D&C.

Blood started to flow out of the uterus.

"Oh, my God!" Neva panicked. "She's starting to hemorrhage! We've got to stop!"

"Mary, just give me the name of that one person to whom you have been reporting all of the President's activities." Mapplethorpe needed that one piece of evidence. Then Project Baltimore would be complete.

"O . . . h . . . h . . h . . . h . . . D . . . e . . . s . . . a . . . i . . . x!" Mary felt Neva's fist slam into her uterus in what she suspected was a desperate attempt to stop the hemorrhaging.

"It's not Desaix . . . it's not Westview . . . who is it, Mary?" Mapplethorpe's somber voice receded into Neva's panicked cries for help.

Mary's eyes closed as her mouth opened into a silent scream.

# CHAPTER
## 38

Hands raised in the air, Lieutenant Jaime Rodríguez of the 5th Squadron, 11th U.S. Armored Cavalry Regiment, walked away from his M1A1 Abrams toward the group of Spetsnaz soldiers hiding in the German woods.

"Do you speak English?" Rodríguez, a twenty-five-year-old Puerto Rican tank commander, asked a blond-haired colonel, who seemed inordinately pleased to see him alive.

Rodríguez was excited. Despite the fact that he was taken captive, he could practice speaking Russian, an opportunity he did not have in college.

"How do you feel?" the colonel asked with barely an accent as he sent a few of his men to check out the tank.

"I think I'm all right." Rodríguez examined his uniform, and concluded that he was intact. "I see that you speak English." Looking around, he realized he was the only one who hadn't run away before surrendering. That stupid greenhorn major had sent him as the lead tank of a major assault with a crew that was inexperienced and frightened.

"Yes. I do speak English. But I'm afraid not very well," the colonel said, extending his hand in a gesture of friendship.

"I'm Lieutenant Jaime Rodríguez. Nice to meet you." Rodríguez shook the hands of all the Spetsnaz soldiers who were milling around him. It was a convivial atmosphere, as if Rodríguez were at a cocktail party for foreign graduate students. This was not the image he had carried of the ruthless Spetsnaz, experts in all the martial arts plus additional esoteric forms of killing.

"It is so good to meet you, Lieutenant Jaime Rodríguez. I am Colonel

Alexander Pushkin. These are my men." Pushkin was pleased to see that there was at least one survivor.

"Is that your real name, Alexander Pushkin?"

"Yes. Are you a real Hispanic-American?" Pushkin asked, offering him a piece of black bread from his backpack.

"Yes, I am the proud descendant of native-born Puerto Ricans who emigrated to the United States when I was four years old." Rodríguez was taken aback by the Russians' warmth. Now he was certain that the war had been a mistake. These soldiers no more wanted to fight than he did.

"Would you like something to drink?" Pushkin beckoned to a large, heavyset soldier who was drinking from a bottle of Stolichnaya. "This is my right-hand man, Major Vartanian."

"Armenian?" Rodríguez asked.

"Yes." Vartanian was proud that his first contact with an American soldier was so successful. This minority person seemed smart, despite American propaganda to the contrary.

"And this is Major Tamara Popov. A courageous and fearless fighter."

"It's great pleasure to meet you," Tamara said, less comfortable than Pushkin was with her broken high school English. She extended her hand in a genuine gesture of friendship. But, all she could see was a quizzical expression on Rodríguez's face.

"Ah, I think I understand," she said as she pulled off her red beret, shook her head, and allowed her long auburn hair to fall onto her shoulders.

"*Caramba! Que chica bonita!*" Rodríguez exclaimed, stunned by Tamara's Slavic beauty.

"Please. Give me translation, if you please." Tamara liked Rodríguez's gentle face.

"Excuse me, Major. But I just said how lovely you are." Rodríguez wondered what his commander would say if he knew that he was fraternizing with the enemy, and wishing he could proposition a Russian major in the middle of a war.

"Thank you, Lieutenant Rodríguez. We Russians would be insulted if you did not take notice of our beautiful women," Pushkin replied with a broad smile.

"Colonel, are you named after the famous Russian poet?" Rodríguez asked him. Although most of his college years were spent in politically correct courses, Rodríguez had taken an opportunity to amass a considerable amount of knowledge about the Russians.

"Do you know him?" Pushkin was surprised that anyone considered to be a second-class citizen by his own countrymen should have any knowledge about a Russian writer, let alone one who had lived over a hundred years before.

Rodríguez stood with the bottle raised high in the air, and recited a verse of Pushkin's in a voice that he was certain could be heard over the distant sounds of war:

> "As long as there is one poet here,
> My name will ring throughout all Russia,
> Every tribe of the land will call to me,
> The proud descendent of the Slav, the Finn,
> The savage Tungunz, and the Kalmuk of the steppe."

The living Pushkin was elated. He clapped so hard that he nearly exhausted himself.

Tamara embraced Rodríguez. "Call up President Zotov and tell him that we no longer fight the Americans. He recites Pushkin by heart. How can he be our enemy?"

This time Pushkin raised the bottle of Stolichnaya:

> "Time was, when our youthful feast
> Glowed and hummed, bedecked with roses,
> When the clink of glasses rang in answer to our songs,
> And we sat in serried ranks."

Rodríguez concluded the verse:

> "All that had changed. Our tumbling merriment
> In time grew calmer, like ourselves . . .
> We laugh less now, at the end of every song,
> We often sigh, and sometimes do not speak at all."

Everyone who was watching the small celebration grew silent. Rodríguez had inadvertently injected a somber note into the pleasantries. The reality of war finally set in.

Pushkin remembered that he had had a specific mission. Retrieve the AirLandBattle Plan, and uncover the direction of the U.S. armored thrust. Only then could the Russians prepare an appropriate trap.

"Well, Lieutenant Rodríguez, now that the party is over what are we to do with you?" Pushkin asked officially.

"What you mean, Alexandrovich?" Tamara asked. "Mr. Rodríguez is Russian friend. No?" Tamara grew concerned. Pushkin had many masters, including his own sudden mood swings.

"I'm afraid I won't be able to help you out on that point, Colonel." Rodríguez felt the jovial, collegial ambience suddenly switch. Funny, he thought. The Russians weren't all that different from the Latinos. Both could befriend you one second, and kill you the next.

"There might be one way in which you could save yourself," Pushkin said, staring into Rodríguez's firm face as he spoke, knowing all the while that he was wasting his time. Rodríguez was too proud. There was no way he would cooperate. There were too many cherished loyalties that Rodríguez would have to betray, despite the fact that those very same loyalties might have just betrayed him. That was the very nature of all hierarchies, be they military or civilian.

Pushkin recalled the pained expression on President Zotov's face when they last parted. Perhaps, like Rodríguez, he had been betrayed.

"Jaime, if I may call you that. You were the lead tank of the armored assault against our flank. Is that right?" Pushkin didn't expect an answer. There really was only one thing to do with Rodríguez. But he was certain that Tamara would try to stop him. She had developed an immediate liking for Rodríguez. He couldn't blame her. No Russian could blame how she felt about this bright and handsome prisoner.

"I was in an M1A1 Abrams tank that was captured by you and your people. That's all I can admit to," Rodríguez said, trying to appear relaxed as he answered questions that he knew might lead to his incarceration or death. But if he wasn't prepared for the inevitable now, when would he be? Wasn't that why he had been preparing himself with the teachings of Husserl, Heidegger, and Sartre? *Being and Nothingness.*

"You are very calm," Pushkin said as he cocked his antiquated AKS-74.

"No, Alexandrovich! What are you doing?" Tamara rushed toward Pushkin as he opened fire, hoping to thwart his aim. But she was too late.

Rodríguez fell to the ground.

"Why did you kill him?" Tamara screamed. "He was a simple soldier just like the rest of us. He meant us no harm."

"I had my orders," Pushkin said, then dismissed the Spetsnaz soldiers surrounding them. He didn't need any witnesses to this lovers' spat.

"Orders! What orders?" Tamara asked angrily.

"I had to find out whether the Americans were going to attack us on our eastern or western flank." Pushkin searched Rodríguez's clothes and found a piece of paper in his pocket.

"And you got your answer by killing him?" She sounded cold.

"He was unwilling to cooperate with us. I had no other choice." Waving the piece of paper, Pushkin was elated. "It's here. The Americans will attack us on our western flank."

"You didn't even bother to interrogate him. Why?" She watched as Pushkin dropped his rifle on the ground and approached her.

"Tamara, what is wrong with you?" He held her in his arms, confused by her overreaction. Something else was bothering her.

"You kill a man in cold blood and then you want to be affectionate with me. I can't!" Tamara pulled away from him.

"What are you talking about? It was I who had to restrain you from making love in the middle of the Kremlin."

"That was then. Now is now."

Standing behind her, Pushkin folded his arms around her. "Something is wrong. Please tell me."

She started to cry. Pushkin turned her around toward him and pulled her closer to him.

"I have my orders too," Tamara said as she pulled out her pistol and shoved it into his stomach.

"Why did you wait so long?" Pushkin didn't resist. His eyes glistened with pain.

"You knew all along, didn't you?" Tamara's hand started to shake. She wasn't sure she could carry out her assignment.

"Don't be afraid, my loved one. It had to be someone. Why not you—Zotov's mistress, as well as the trusted GRU agent who reports directly to the Russian General Staff? And let us not forget that you had to make amends to Mother Russia for the sins of treason that your grandfather Lieutenant Colonel Yuri Popov committed."

"How long have you known?" Tamara's voice started to crack.

"Probably from the very first moment I fell in love with you at that vegetable market, standing alongside the zucchini."

"It was broccoli, not zucchini," she replied, tears running down her cheeks.

"Pull the trigger, my love. It was inevitable. If not you, then it would have to be Misha, Vartanian, or someone else who would stalk me for the rest of my life. But one way or another, they would get me." Pressing her closely to him, he whispered, "I love you, Tamara. Nothing can change that. And I know that you love me. That's all I have ever really wanted. The rest of my life has simply been an exercise in waiting for you."

"I can't." Her hands shook so badly he had to hold the gun steady.

"You must. From the very beginning of the coup, Zotov and I knew he would have to betray me. He had no other choice. I was the instrument that would bring him to power. Therefore, I would have to be gotten rid of, lest I turn against him, which, quite frankly, I would have. Even then, if I were successful in replacing Zotov with Marshal Kulikov, I would have been eliminated at some later time by Kulikov. So, you see, my love, whichever way I look, the ending is always the same. Betrayal."

"Sh . . . h . . . h . . . h . . . Stop talking!" She wanted to drop her gun. But he wouldn't let her. "Run away! I'll shoot in the air. No one will know the difference."

"Pull the trigger, my loved one."

"I can't!" As she struggled to pull away from him, the gun accidentally fired, and he fell to the ground. Her eyes filling with tears, Tamara cradled his blood-stained body in her arms and tore up the piece of paper he held in his hand.

With guns pointing, the Spetsnaz soldiers rushed toward her.

"Vartanian, phone President Zotov and inform him that the Americans will attack us on our eastern flank," she said firmly, as if she hadn't committed the ultimate act of revenge—treason. For that alone, her lover would have been proud of her.

But without her saying a word, Vartanian understood what he had to do. He opened fire with his RPK light machine gun and watched her body slump over that of his trusted friend and commander.

# CHAPTER
## 39

**M**ary's unrelenting screams frightened Walter Johnson.

Along with the unbearable stench of urine, feces, and vomit, Johnson felt as if he had been consigned to a sewer. Even the ghettos of Anacostia never reeked as badly.

Incarcerated in a stuffy cell, no bigger than his own pullman kitchen, Johnson was afraid that if he didn't leave St. E's soon, he too would end up like that woman, cursing and screaming her lungs out in a state of unremitting pain.

When the rusted steel door to the isolation room opened up, Dr. Prince and Zarb strolled into the cell. Several armed guards waited outside. Ironically, most of the isolation rooms at St. E's had been constructed so that there was always an ample amount of sunlight streaming in through small windows. Perhaps, thought Johnson, a hundred and fifty years ago there was an assumption that mental patients would do best if they were exposed to sunlight. That, of course, was of little consolation to Johnson, who despite the fact that he had volunteered for this special assignment still felt both frightened and apprehensive.

Prince, like Zarb, had a particular expertise in PSYOPS, using psychological means to break down the defenses of an individual in order to make him compliant to the will of the interrogator.

Even Johnson knew that it was simply a matter of knowing which technique to use and how much psychological pressure to apply before the individual cracked up.

In six months at Fort Bragg, North Carolina, the home of psychological warfare, Johnson had learned, all too well, that the basis of PSYOPS was fear, intimidation, and terror coupled with the promise of relief. He had learned several techniques of interrogation, including the Chinese technique of *hsi nao*, brainwashing, which broke down a man's psychological defenses through intimidation, forcing him to incorporate a suggestion that could be used to avert the terror of punishment.

Johnson, like the other PSYOPS soldiers, had been programmed to become an effective, disciplined killer, immune to distractions and hardships. Through the process of hypnosis, he could be reprogrammed to redirect his lethal expertise. He had left Fort Bragg one of their best and the brightest.

"Well, how are you doing today, Walter?" Zarb asked cheerfully, as if he were a physician on his daily hospital rounds.

"Fine, Colonel. Just fine," Johnson lied. But he didn't want to reveal any signs of weakness. Otherwise he was finished.

"I'm certainly glad to hear that," Zarb replied.

"Remember, Walter, anytime you want us to stop, just tell us," Prince said, as he carried his black bag and walked over to the window. "Zarb, there's nothing here to cover the window. We've got a hell of a lot of light streaming into the room."

"You'll have to do the best you can," Zarb replied. "Do you see any electrical outlets?"

"Walter, is there anything that we can do to make your stay a little more comfortable?" Zarb was concerned that this exercise might be too strenuous, even for Johnson.

"No, sir. I'm just fine, thank you, Colonel," Johnson said, impressed with their kindness. But he knew that would change very quickly.

"Walter, we want you to put this headset on." Zarb held it out to him.

"Am I going to be listening to that noise?" Johnson had been through this experiment on brainwashing once before. To say the least, it was extremely painful.

"I'm afraid so." Prince strapped the earphones on him and tightly secured a woven black bag over Johnson's head. Then he ripped off Johnson's shirt. "Now, place your hands above your head. All the way up!" Prince shouted.

Johnson refused, realizing that he was entering the painful part of the experiment. Zarb picked up a black rubber hose, and struck Johnson across the chest.

Johnson buckled over. Suddenly he realized why this unique mission was considered a masochist's delight.

"That's what happens when you can't play a child's game like Simon Says!" Prince exclaimed. He turned a little round knob on a portable, miniaturized amplifier.

"Now you are going to hear noise that will sound like a helicopter landing," Zarb said. "All I want you to do is listen to the instructions on the tape, and to my questions. Don't move or bring down your hands. If you do, then I will have to do this nasty thing again. And we don't want that? Do we?" Zarb asked provocatively. His concerned tone had transformed into one of sadistic delight.

"All you have to do is listen and answer some easy questions. That's not too bad, Walter, is it?" Prince asked in a mocking tone and slammed the truncated rubber hose against the wall for effect.

All that Johnson could hear at that moment were the screams of the woman in the next room. There was no doubt in his mind that she too was being tortured. What irony, thought Johnson. Instead of using the hospital to cure and heal, it was being used as a political tool. Here was the great U.S.A. employing the same punitive procedures the Soviet Union did fifteen years ago, when the then KGB was using psychiatric hospitals to incarcerate political prisoners under the fake diagnosis of "sluggish schizophrenia."

"I think you will be interested to know that the procedure we are employing with you is called the KGB Starka Position, a gift from our adversaries," Zarb said perfunctorily.

The noise that came through Johnson's headset was exactly as Zarb had described. It sounded as if a helicopter were approaching, closer and closer. All Johnson could hear was the whirring sound of rotating helicopter blades. If truth be known, there was an extremely calming quality to the helicopter's noise, and to seeing nothing but black. If nothing else, the noise obliterated the screaming coming from next door. For a moment Johnson relaxed and forgot Prince's clear admonition. He let his raised hands drift down toward his sides.

WHACK! The rubber truncheon struck his shoulder.

Johnson didn't utter a sound. He had made up his mind that he would not give either Zarb or Prince the necessary excuse to stop the experiment because he was in too much pain.

*Relax!*

Johnson screwed up his forehead, trying to discern the word that he had just heard.

*Thump! Thump! Thump!* The sound of whirring helicopter blades became increasingly louder.

Johnson placed both his hands over the earphones, as if this motion could stop the sound. Zarb struck him with the truncheon.

*Relax! Let go of your control! Let us take over for you! You will feel much better!*

Zarb was not surprised to see that Johnson could tolerate so much pain. He had picked the best.

Once again, Johnson dropped his hands to the side.

WHACK!

Prince didn't really enjoy this, no matter how it appeared. It was too crass. Too unsophisticated. Too one-sided. Interrogation should present a challenge to the questioner, not some simple variation of a Pavlovian behavioral circuit—question, pain, response. But the purpose of the KGB Starka

Position was not to break down the prisoner, like *tote trakt,* the "silent floor." *Tote trakt* was developed by the West German police to break down the psychological resistance of the terrorist group, the Baader-Meinhoff Gang. In the "silent floor," the prisoner was placed in an empty room, painted completely white, inducing a state of total sensory isolation and psychological disorientation. As a result of this sophisticated procedure, the prisoner would be induced to commit suicide.

That was not Prince's intention here. Instead, he needed a quick psychological transformation. Playing on Johnson's naturally supressed anger toward the two authority figures beating him, Prince wanted to use that hatred to transform Johnson into an effective operative. And a hybrid variant of subliminal persuasion and autohypnosis should do the trick. For a man who had spent years earning the reputation of expert in PSYOPS, Prince knew that Johnson's reprogramming was just a matter of time.

Zarb, one of Prince's protégés, had been instrumental in the creation and execution of Operation Tintinnabulation during the Vietnam War, which involved the use of two C-47 aircrafts called Spooky, equipped with mini-guns, and Gabby, fitted with several loudspeakers. During its initial phase, Gabby employed a frequency-pulsating noisemaker designed to harass, confuse, and keep the enemy awake during night hours while Spooky provided air cover. During its second phase, the harassing noise continued, but emphasis was given to the use of *chieu hoi* tapes that encouraged defections. Psychologically, the first part of the tapes was used to eliminate the feeling that the night could provide security to the target audience, while the second part was designed to reinforce the enemy's desire to run from the irritating situation.

Neither Prince nor Zarb were amateurs in the business of interrogation. But both soon realized that changing some of Johnson's thought patterns in such a short time in order to succeed in his special mission was definitely going to be more difficult than either one of them had expected.

Johnson stood against the wall, arms raised, shaking his black-hooded head back and forth. He listened to the whirring helicopter blades become increasingly louder. At eighty-three decibels, his head was bursting. He felt as if the sound was going to rip his head apart, splitting it into tiny fragments of bone and gray matter. He could no longer help it. He reached for the headset to rip it off.

WHACK! WHACK! Zarb hit him several times, even more forcefully than before.

"A . . . h . . . h . . . h . . . h . . . h . . . !" Johnson screamed and banged his head against the wall.

Suddenly, the whirring noise stopped. It was replaced by a comforting, reassuring voice.

*Don't fight. Relax.*
*Let yourself enjoy the pleasures of the moment.*
*Precious Silence. Struggle means Defeat.*
*Listen to what your heart is telling you.*

*Trust your basic instincts.*

Johnson rested his head against the wall. His hands dropped to his sides. His body took on all the signs of relaxation.

Prince started the hypnotic suggestions in a dulcet voice.

"Walter, let all the tension in your body disappear. Let all that anger and rage that you have toward both of us leave your body, never to appear again."

Prince watched as Johnson started to sink down to the floor in a state of complete relaxation. "The annoying helicopter sounds are no longer in your head. Those terrible people who are trying to hurt you by beating your back are also gone. But all these disturbances can return unless you do something about it. Do you understand?"

"Yes," Johnson said in a lackadaisical voice. "I understand."

"Would you like to cooperate with me, Walter?" Prince asked in the friendly voice of an elementary school principal talking to a student helper.

"Yes."

"Yes, what?" Zarb interjected.

"Yes, I would like to cooperate with you," Johnson replied.

"Then I want you to tell me, who is it that you want to kill?" Prince asked in a concerned voice.

Prince looked at Zarb, who nodded his head in approval. It seemed as if things were proceeding according to plan.

"I want to kill . . ."

"Who?" Zarb asked, impatiently.

"Who?" Johnson replied, repeating Zarb's words as if he were in a confused state.

"What is your mission? Whom did you intend to kill?" Prince tried to contain his frustration, concerned that he might break the induced hypnotic trance.

"I can't," Johnson said, shaking his hooded head back and forth, as if he were possessed by demons.

Prince turned up the amplifier, attempting to jolt him out of his unconscious resistance.

"A . . . h . . . h . . . h . . . h . . . h . . . !" Johnson screamed as he grasped his earset.

W . . . h . . . h . . . a . . a . . . c . . . c . . . k . . . ! Zarb beat him across the back.

Jumping up, Johnson staggered into the wall, completely disoriented.

*Don't struggle. Relax.*

*Use the anger effectively. Don't let the anger get the better part of you.*

*Give up your control.*

*Let your friends help you.*

*They care about you.*

*Trust them. Relax.*

Once again, Johnson assumed a relaxed position

"Sorry about that, Walter," Prince added, eager to continue.

"I was . . . upset . . ." Johnson replied contritely.

"By what, Walter?" Zarb asked in a concerned, paternal tone of voice.

"I don't want to kill," Walter replied.

"We don't want to kill anymore." The professor lied. Johnson was being reprogrammed to become a freelance, singleton assassin. His previously programmed mind set was as a group-oriented Special Ops soldier, dedicated to obtaining specific objectives by killing in a disciplined, military fashion. While the hypnotic suggestions might be against Johnson's free will, it was still consistent with his basic instinct for revenge against the dominant white authoritarian system. Prince had previously suggested to Johnson as part of Project Baltimore that it was the white man who would be responsible for the incineration and destruction of the inner-city ghettos. Therefore, it was Johnson's moral obligation to save his black sisters and brothers from the evil deeds of the "boss man." For Zarb and Prince, it was an incredible confluence of circumstance and people. Their work was facilitated by the time-honored axiom of PSYOPS that a programmed killer can always be a reprogrammed killer.

*You are now in control of your own actions, Walter.*

*Trust your basic instincts.*

*You want to seek revenge for all your black brothers and sisters who have suffered, and were about to be killed by them.*

*Only you know who they are.*

*When you see them, you will know what to do.*

*First, you must stop that woman's screams.*

*After that you will proceed to visit the MAN, Himself.*

"How are you feeling, Walter?" Zarb asked in a mellifluous voice.

"I feel very relaxed," Johnson responded in a monotone.

"Good, I will now take off the black hood. Please, don't be frightened by the bright sunlight. You are to do nothing different from what your instincts tell you to do." Prince removed the earphones and hood.

"Thank you." Walter covered his eyes as he tried to adjust to the light. For a moment, he was disoriented.

"Are you certain you are all right?" Zarb asked, concerned.

"I think . . . I'm fine," Johnson said, through his movements and speech patterns were stilted, deliberate.

Just as they are supposed to be, thought his programmers. Both Prince and Zarb were pleased with their results. They had created a psychological Frankenstein. They were now certain that if Johnson followed the images and instructions conjured in his mind, he would accomplish their mission.

"Where are you going, Walter?" Zarb asked.

"I must find out who is hurting that poor woman who is screaming next door. She may be a black sister who is in trouble!"

"You may do as you wish," Zarb replied, saluting Johnson as he left the seclusion room.

"Don't forget, Walter. Listen to what your mind is telling you to do," Prince shouted.

"Yes, sir!" Johnson said, then walked absent-mindedly past the armed guards, one of whom made a hand sign to his colleagues indicating that he was crazy.

One compulsive thought ran through Johnson's mind—stop that woman's infernal screaming! Images of frightened black women and children running out of their burning tenement buildings flashed in front of his eyes.

He passed a group of well-dressed Special Ops soldiers in the hallways, and watched a group of disheveled patients dressed in stained gray hospital pajamas try to engage the soldiers in desultory, if not incomprehensible, conversation. There was something sad about the scene although he wasn't certain exactly what it was. He walked down the crowded corridor, following the scream, which no one else seemed to hear or mind. The screams led to a room marked OPERATING ROOM.

Johnson needed to get inside that room. But he had to get past two guards to do it. He wondered what the best approach would be. Direct confrontation? No! They could easily kill him. Diversionary activity? No. They looked too serious to be easily diverted from their task. The truth? Why not? At worst, they would push him away, treating him as a mental patient.

"Excuse me, guys," Johnson said as he stood before the two young guards. "Do you mind if I go inside?"

"Would you mind telling us why?" The soldier was obviously having difficulty restraining his laughter.

"I would like to kill the people who are making that lady scream," Johnson said, smiling.

"Well, sir, I'm afraid I can't let you do that!" Both soldiers laughed loudly.

"Why?" Johnson assumed the role of a confused schizophrenic, asking the question innocently.

"Why?" One guard doubled over in laughter.

"Why not?" Johnson repeated the question.

"Why not?" Both soldiers roared, finally able to release the pent-up tension of having to maintain the semblance of sanity in a setting that was definitely abnormal.

Johnson was right. The truth was far more devastating than any stratagem he might otherwise have devised. Even he found the situation mildly amusing. But unlike the soldiers who were devastated by the unintended humor of the situation, Johnson's thoughts were on the CAR15 carbine rifle he lunged for and successfully grabbed from one of the soldiers.

The laughter stopped abruptly as the two young soldiers slumped down to the ground, their heads bludgeoned by the rifle butt. Checking their carotid arteries, Johnson made certain they were still alive. Then he barged into the operating room.

"What the hell are you doing in here?" Mapplethorpe asked.

Shaw went for his side holster. But before he could pull out his Beretta, Johnson opened fire, killing everyone in the room except Mary Dougherty, who was so groggy from pain that she could barely understand what was happening.

"Come on, miss, let's get out of here!" Johnson said as he pushed aside the dead bodies and unstrapped Mary.

"Who are you?" Mary asked, disoriented.

"I'm Master Sergeant Walter Johnson, Special Operations Forces."

"Where are you taking me?" She tried unsuccessfully to break away from his firm grasp, wondering all the while who had sent him.

Without any further words, Johnson lifted her up and carried her to a small conference room in which Zarb and Prince were seated. He gently placed her on the sofa opposite them.

"Welcome, Mary," Zarb greeted her as if she were a returning heroine from the wars.

"We've been expecting you," Prince said, then rushed to her side and started to give her a cursory physical exam.

"What is going on here?" Mary was still groggy and in pain, but more confused by their warm reception. "Colonel Zarbitski, I don't understand. Only a few hours ago, you stormed the Baltimore Room, released Mapplethorpe and Shaw, and helped them bring me here. To be . . ." She stopped, not wanting to relive the pain of the last few hours.

"I had to do it, so that neither Mapplethorpe nor Shaw would become suspicious," Zarb replied.

"Suspicious of what?" Mary asked. She noticed that Prince was talking on a portable telephone.

"I think you know!" Zarb replied cryptically.

"I just called Randy to tell her that you were safe and in relatively good condition. She's going to reach Desaix at the Agency," Prince said, relieved. "Try to relax until the ambulance arrives."

Mary settled deep into the sofa. A chill crept through her body as she glanced at the solicitous Zarb and Prince. She was beyond exhaustion.

"Johnson, you executed the first part of your job extremely well. Now complete the rest of the assignment," Zarb ordered.

# CHAPTER
## 40

As a nation, the Russians have learned to accept military defeat as an act of God, intended as a lesson in humility, pointing the way to greater tolerance for pain, destruction, and sacrifice.

Napoleon's defeat of Czar Alexander and the formidable Cossack warriors at the Battle of Borodino proved to be the beginning of the end, not of Russia, as one might have expected, but of France, a much more experienced conqueror. So each Russian knew from the swaddling days of infancy that defeat was a necessary precursor to victory.

For Marshal Kulikov, standing alongside President Zotov at the Russian National Command Center, studying the reports of what had become one of the largest tank battles in recent times, this was no time for flag waving. It was a time for clear analytical thinking, and answers to some very difficult questions.

"How could we have lost over one thousand T-72s?" Kulikov asked.

"I don't know!" Zotov said, ashamed to have to make this admission to the elite group of military commanders, officers, and technicians hovering about the two principal leaders of what remained of the Commonwealth of Independent States.

"What do you mean, President Zotov? How could you not know?" Kulikov asked indignantly, making certain that his righteous tone would not be lost on his audience of professional combatants.

Zotov was aware from the collective reaction that the younger officers were particularly turned off by the marshal's impertinence.

"You yourself heard Major Vartanian's final broadcast. He said that the main U.S. forces were attacking our eastern flank," Zotov said.

"How do you explain the fact that only minutes after Colonel Pushkin's man transmitted his message to us, the Americans' 7th Armored Division attacked our completely exposed western flank? An extremely unusual set of circumstances, Mr. President. Isn't it?"

"I will admit that it is an intelligence failure," Zotov answered, annoyed by the drift of the conversation and the tone of the marshal's voice, both of which were clearly accusatory. At some point, Zotov would have to set limits. Otherwise each of them would end up saying something that could be harmful to Project Baltimore.

"An intelligence failure?" Kulikov asked, storming over to Becheroff's computer terminal. He slammed his fist down on the mainframe. "This piece of garbage gives me intelligence failures. I've got metal garbage flying over the earth telling me things that are incorrect, or telling me nothing, because there are too many clouds, or too few clouds, or no clouds." Walking back toward Zotov, he brusquely pushed aside several army generals. Kulikov wanted to make certain there would be no doubt in anybody's mind that he was not at fault in a military debacle that lost close to sixteen hundred tanks in six hours.

"What about all the Cosmos and Soyuz satellites above? Why couldn't they tell you what you wanted to know? Those only cost us billions in hard currency," Zotov asked, determined to go on the offensive.

"Mr. President, I just explained to you that too many clouds covered the designated sites. That is an admitted intelligence failure. But what we have with Pushkin's brilliantly wrong observation is a catastrophe from which we may never recover."

"May I remind you, Marshal," Zotov said, "that Colonel Pushkin, Major Popov, and Major Vartanian were brave soldiers who gave their lives for their country. They are genuine war heroes."

"As a military leader, I do not need dead war heroes with faulty military intelligence. I need live, active, efficient analysts who can tell me accurately the one thing I want to know."

"What is that?"

"Which is what way a goddamn army of close to a million men would turn at a crossroads," Kulikov answered as he paced about the crowded Operations Room in the underground bunker. "That's not a very difficult assignment to accomplish." Kulikov laughed inwardly at the absurditiy of the situation. The outcome of entire battles and wars almost exclusively depended on the judgment of only a few key people.

"Are you implying that I am to blame?" Zotov decided to confront Kulikov directly.

The tension in the room mounted quickly. The circle around the two political contenders seemed to tighten. No one had any doubts that whoever emerged from the confrontation would rule whatever remained of the commonwealth. And if history was true to form, Russian generals abhorred losing their military armament.

Many in the room remembered the reaction of the Russian generals during the Iraq War as they witnessed over one thousand of their tanks destroyed by the U.S. Army in less than one hundred hours. They felt both furious and completely impotent, and had vowed that such a debacle would never occur again. Yet here they were, less than ten years later, having lost over fifteen hundred of their finest tanks. But this time they could not blame the Iraqis. They had only themselves to blame. Was it a failure of civilian leadership or was it a military miscalculation? That's what would be decided between Zotov and Kulikov.

"For whom was the great war hero of Spetsnaz, Colonel Pushkin, working?" Kulikov asked. He knew that he had just lobbed in the opening salvo in their contest for power.

"As you know, Marshal, he was working for the Russian Army."

"Hah! We haven't had him on our roster since you had him detailed to Project Baltimore, which if my memory serves correctly, is the basis for this insane war." Kulikov watched as the President squirmed in his seat.

"Marshal Kulikov! You're insubordinate!" Zotov said, then stood up and waved his arms, as if ordering his troops to rid him of this menace.

"Insubordinate! What happened with Pushkin? Was he instructed to deceive us? Or was he simply incompetent?"

"Neither!" Zotov exclaimed.

"Then how could you place your faith in a man who proved to be so incredibly wrong?" Kulikov asked. "For a man who was in intelligence for most of his professional life, I find it difficult to believe that this could have been such a blatant intelligence failure! Pushkin was right there on the ground!"

"So was your goddamn agent! How come she didn't communicate anything back to us that would have contradicted Pushkin's last message?" Zotov asked. He had taken a calculated risk, revealing something so TOP SECRET that it was known only to a few people in the Operations Room. He was prepared for the gasps of surprise.

"She was lovestruck," Kulikov replied. "You saw how she begged me to send her to the front. What can I expect from a GRU agent who has fallen madly in love with her intelligence target? If anything, I blame you for not having informed me sooner that she had become ineffective." Kulikov knew he was playing dirty. Major Popov was his operative, working directly for the Army High Command through the GRU in order to keep a watchful eye on a man no one in the Soviet military hierarchy trusted—Colonel Pushkin. What Kulikov could never reveal was that Tamara had also been recruited by him to be Zotov's mistress.

Perhaps the game had been played too well, thought Kulikov. Pushkin had also been recruited by Kulikov to work with Zotov, and then turn against him. So he had served two masters: Zotov and Kulikov. But Tamara had effectively served three masters—Zotov, Pushkin, and Kulikov—with one objective. As a shrewd intelligence operative, Pushkin should have concluded that Tamara worked for Zotov, and he might even have suspected that she also worked for Kulikov. But what difference did it really make now, thought Kulikov, when the outcome was all the same—deceit, betrayal, more betrayal, and death. What a pity they had to die. He would miss them.

But Kulikov's one objective throughout—to save Mother Russia by reinstituting a military dictatorship—was too close to his grasp to be lost in misguided sentimentality.

"So now," Zotov exclaimed, "I am to be blamed for what you and your cronies had ordered her to do all along—compromise Pushkin through sex so that the GRU could keep a constant surveillance on his activities. And, I might add, on my activities as well!"

The entire room remained silent. There was something ludicrous, thought Becheroff, about two leaders hurling accusations at each other, trying to determine who was better, more competent, or more moral, particularly when everyone knew that the entire system was based on duplicity, betrayal, and nonaccountability. For the President to call the marshal deceptive, or vice versa, was to state the obvious.

"Please, President Zotov," Kulikov asked, "would you be so kind as to tell me and these patient people around us what it was that you and President Westview had agreed to in Project Baltimore? Did you both agree to destroy all those tanks? Or was it just a few hundred? Was it only Russian tanks? And tell us please, Mr. President, at what point were we the Russians, or the Americans, to stop this war, which you know never made any sense to our generals?"

"Project Baltimore was based on the assumption that neither side had an overwhelming fighting capacity—or desire. We agreed that we were to fight a war that would entail a minimum of casualties. Just as the Americans had done in the war with Iraq. They had fewer than one thousand dead."

"Yet as of this moment, we have sustained close to three thousand dead and another one thousand wounded. And your good, trustworthy business partners have sustained only one thousand deaths and about half the number of wounded. Was this the type of agreement that two wise men made to insure their political future?" Kulikov asked, outraged. Since it was clear the Americans had gotten the better part of the deal, he sensed that everyone in the room felt disgusted by Zotov's betrayal of his countrymen. All Kulikov had to do now was to push the point a little bit further that Zotov had been duped.

"We made an agreement," Zotov said, "so that the peoples of both countries could, once again, feel like an international superpower. And improve their economic lot!" Zotov's statement came out sounding more defensive than he had wanted.

"So the best way to improve the Russian economy is to kill its workers and destroy its matériel and resources?" Kulikov asked sarcastically. "Is this some new form of Marxist-Leninist economics?"

Those soldiers who were not too angry snickered loudly.

"I admit that I may have made a very serious mistake," Zotov said, realizing that the only thing he could do at this point was damage control—cut his losses by admitting his errors.

"I'm afraid, Mr. President, it is too late for repenting. I am ordering my soldiers to place you under house arrest. The Military High Command will take over immediately!" Kulikov motioned to several of his personal bodyguards to remove Zotov from the room.

"I protest! But I am also a realist, so I will go quietly. My only warning to you is to stop the war now, before we enter a full-scale nuclear catastrophe. You have exactly two hours to establish voice communication with President Westview." Zotov seemed to be pleading with the entire group as he was being escorted from the room.

"Sergeant Becheroff!" Kulikov ordered, wasting no time, as he acknowledged the sporadic applause from his admiring entourage.

"Yes, sir!" Becheroff replied.

"Place our Strategic Nuclear Rocket Forces on Maximum Vigilance status. Prepare a two-hour countdown!" How ironic, thought Kulikov. Zotov had ordered Pushkin to stage a fake attempt on Zotov's life in order to stabilize a government that was rapidly deteriorating. But thanks to Pushkin's perfidious nature and treachery, a real military coup had been successful without having had to fire a shot.

"*Boshen Daragoi!*" God be praised! Kulikov said, then spat on the ground to ward off the evil eye of a potentially jealous fate. He still believed in the old Russian superstitions.

# CHAPTER
## 41

**S**irens screaming, lights flashing, the military ambulance raced down Martin Luther King, Jr., Avenue as children threw stones and broken bottles at it. As one might have expected from the extensive troop movements in and out of Bolling Air Force Base and Saint Elizabeth Hospital, anything that had to do with the military now had a negative connotation. These children of Anacostia saw U.S. military personnel and matériel as part of an elaborate game of provocation and confrontation. An American variant of the Palestinian intifada.

"Christ, I feel like a pin in a bowling alley," Desaix said, holding Mary's hand tightly as she lay strapped down on the stretcher. Thank God, he thought, Randy had found him at the Agency. Desaix looked at her with a tenderness he rarely allowed to surface. "At least now I don't have to chase you around to make love to you!"

"I almost hate myself for telling you," Mary said, "but throughout the last few horrible hours I spent half of my time worried that I would never see you again. Never get to say good-bye." Mary looked up at Desaix's perspiring face. She wondered what he thought when he looked at her tortured body.

"I missed you terribly," Desaix whispered in her ear as he nuzzled her neck. As Desaix kissed her neck, he could feel her start to calm down. Gently, he stroked her disheveled hair. She never looked more beautiful to him than she did now. He held her tightly, wishing she would finally realize how much he really wanted her.

Mary folded her arms around his waist, grateful for having someone to love her for everything she was or feared she might not be.

Desaix tightened his grip, afraid he might somehow lose her if he relaxed his hold. "Now, Mary, you have to listen to me. I'm going to be extremely serious right now."

"You are telling me that you are going to get serious just at the moment that I might meet my maker?"

"I can forgive almost anything. I can forgive sex with another man, woman, or beast. I can forgive your falling out of love with me. But the one thing that I can't forgive is deception and betrayal."

"Deception and betrayal? Like what Westview and Manning did to those people who had served them well?" Mary stared at him, trying to determine why he had suddenly turned so cold.

"You know what I mean."

"Or the story you gave the TV reporter as we got into this ambulance? That I had been abducted by Mapplethorpe in his attempt to neutralize the President's Secret Service so that he could attempt a military coup?" She kissed him, hoping to regain the warmth of the previous moments. "Is that what you mean by wanting me to play it straight with you? The same way you play straight with the people around you?"

"There was a reason for my having done that. And you know it."

"Yes, it's called disinformation. An old propaganda technique used to manipulate the news to suit your own purposes." She pulled him closer to her. "But even if you don't want to admit to yourself that you're a grand manipulator, I can accept you as you are."

The ambulance sped across a bridge, bouncing over potholes.

"Oh, my God! It still hurts. Did she do any permanent damage?" Mary said, moaning and holding her abdomen.

"No, sweetheart. Both Prince and the Army doctor who checked you out said that you had been badly bruised. But he didn't see any evidence of any permanent damage." Desaix lied. Neva had created a hemorrhage in the wall of the uterus, which had sealed itself off. It would take some time before it could heal—if it ever did. There was also some question of whether the cervix had been torn. But Desaix didn't want to frighten her.

"You know, Desaix, I could swear that you're lying."

"What makes you say that?"

"Your eyes. Something in them tells me."

"All right. I lied. The doctor told me that you were about to die any second now. And the best thing I could do to improve your health would be to make incessant love to you . . . until the very last minutes of your life." He kissed her arms.

"Please don't!" Mary pulled his head up to her face. "Not here. Not now." She held his beaming face in both her hands. "Not when we have at least two major crises to resolve almost immediately."

"What do you mean?" Desaix asked, ignoring her protest as he continued kissing her shoulders.

"According to the time table on Project Baltimore, at least those parts I was able to read before Zarbitski took me hostage . . . in exactly one hour, we have to have President Westview ready to talk with President Zotov. Otherwise the . . . war . . . will . . . go to . . . nuclear . . ." Mary paused to catch her breath but drew him closer to her body. She started to cry.

Desaix cradled her head in his arms, affectionately licking away her tears.

"I hate being so helpless just at a time when everything is spinning dangerously out of control." Mary's eyes swelled with tears.

Mary's head swarmed with contradictions and paradoxes. A lover, who by admission and history was a grand manipulator, turned out to be considerate, caring, and dependable. A job, that used to be the most important focus of her life, seemed no longer within her ability to perform, or *care* about! She started to giggle, like the child she was never allowed to be, as Desaix caressed the nape of her neck with his tongue.

"Are you listening to me?" she asked him, as they lay side by side, folded into each other.

For Desaix, the sense of urgency that had been there only minutes before had miraculously disappeared. The crisis of the hour had magically transmuted into the contentment of the moment. Was it possible, Desaix wondered, that he was learning to accept the moment as a measure of happiness, and not simply as a measure of time that he had to fill with action or diversion? Could it be that taking care of Mary Dougherty was far more important than taking care of the limitless problems of some amorphous concept called the world? He held tightly on to her as the ambulance raced through burned-out ghettos. After a passionate kiss, they released each other, each wondering what the future held.

Turning onto Pennsylvania Avenue, the ambulance slowed down as it approached the entrance to the White House. When the back doors opened, the driver greeted his occupants with a cheerful salutation, "I hope the ride wasn't too bumpy!"

Desaix helped Mary walk out of the ambulance. She refused to sit in a wheelchair. He then instructed the driver to wait there for them. He held Mary tightly around the waist and walked unabashedly down the narrow hallways of the West Wing, toward the medical unit.

"Oh, I'm so glad you're back!" Randy rushed over to greet them. "Mary what happened to you? Are you all right?"

"A little bit bruised. Otherwise I'm fine. Thanks for tracking down Desaix for me. If it wasn't for you and Desaix, I might not be here." Mary hugged Randy and smiled at Desaix.

"How is the President?" Desaix asked.

"He's much better," Randy replied. "There's a whole new medical team in there taking care of him. This time they're from Walter Reed Army Hospital, per your telephone instructions." As Randy turned back to her office, she added, "I'm certain he will be happy to see the both of you!"

"How did you know it was Neva?" Mary asked Desaix, as they approached the medical unit.

"First of all Randy called me. But from the very beginning," Desaix replied, "I suspected Neva was working directly for Mapplethorpe after I had discovered a letter in her personnel file from the general commending her for her professional services rendered during his brief hospitalization at Bethesda Naval Hospital. I also became suspicious when I read that she had been stationed at Fort Meade, an advanced intelligence school. But there was nothing I could do until I had evidence, which you inadvertently, but graciously, provided me. I'm only sorry at how much pain it cost you."

"But how did you know about her?"

"About six months ago, when the President and I were working together on a hostage siege, I did my standard background check on both his White House physician and chief nurse. He panned out. She didn't. Remember, it's part of my job to check up from time to time on the President's health so that I know whether he's mentally and physically capable of managing a crisis. Otherwise I would have to end up taking care of him and the crisis."

"Despite my assurances to you that I thought they were top-notch?" Mary asked, feeling foolish. As much as she wanted to believe that he trusted her, she saw more and more clearly that ultimately he trusted no one but himself. Maybe that was something she would never change.

Pushing through the unguarded doors of the medical unit, they saw President Westview walking the corridor, dragging an IV pole in one hand, and leaning on the arm of a black Army orderly with the other.

"Mary! Desaix! How wonderful it is to see you again!" Westview moved slowly but firmly. He looked better than Mary had seen him look in a very long time.

"It's good to see you, Mr. President." Desaix shook his hand vigorously. He was genuinely happy to see Westview, despite the fact that he had caused Desaix so many problems.

"I think you will be happy to know that I just ripped up my letter to the Vice President granting him the authority to take over the government while I was under anesthesia. I'm still in charge. What do you think of that?" Westview was puzzled by Mary's silence. "What's wrong, Mary?"

Her gaze was fixed on the orderly who was propping up Westview.

"What's wrong, Mary?" Desaix asked, equally concerned by her blanched face.

"Nothing. I just feel a little queasy." But something was wrong. What was Johnson doing here? She recalled how callously Johnson had killed Mapplethorpe, Shaw, and Neva. Was murdering the President the second part of the mission that Zarb had reminded Johnson of? She tried not to panic. She wanted to scream and warn them, but if she even gave them a hint of what she was frightened about—

"Oh, how rude of me," said Westview. "I want you two to meet my indispensable right hand, without whom I would not be standing here in front of you both. When he arrived earlier in the day from Walter Reed, I was still bedridden. But look at me now. I want you both to meet Master Sergeant Walter Johnson."

"Hello, Sergeant," Desaix said, then shook his hand.

"Nice to meet you, sir," Johnson replied.

"Good to see you again," Mary whispered, barely able to get the words out of her mouth.

"Pleased to meet you, ma'am. Are you feeling okay? I could call the doctor if you would like," Walter responded calmly.

"Mr. President, Mary informed me that we must get you on a conference call very soon with President Zotov," Desaix said, bewildered by Mary's behavior. "Isn't that right, Mary?"

Mary knew if she did anything precipitously the President was a dead man. How would she warn Desaix without giving everything away?

"Yes, Mr. President. We must get on the hotline as quickly as possible," she said, smiling nervously as Walter looked implacably at her. But she could see from his clenching jaw that he was becoming nervous too.

"So you both know about Project Baltimore?" the President asked. He looked a little bewildered. He held more tightly on to Johnson's arm.

"Yes, Mr. President." Desaix said. "Don't you remember the conversation that you and I had the night before your operation? You admitted to the mistake of having created Project Baltimore." Desaix realized that Westview was having some recent memory loss, which was not an unusual occurrence after a major cardiovascular operation. If he had the time, Desaix would have done a complete neurological examination himself. But there was no time. They had exactly one hour to track down President Zotov.

"Of course, of course. We talked about Project Baltimore. I told you that I was disappointed in what I had created. Right?" Westview looked confused, afraid of saying the wrong thing.

"That's right, Mr. President." Desaix nodded his head in agreement, but he had no doubt that the President had some form of mental dementia. Westview felt compelled to fabricate and to conceal the fact that he couldn't remember what had happened. That Westview recognized both him and Mary was a good prognosis. But the real question was how long the President would manifest this dementia. Desaix was reluctant to entertain the one other possible diagnosis because its prognosis was far more serious.

"Walter, do you think you could help us take the President to the Situation Room?" Mary knew she had to stall for time until she could figure out how to separate Johnson from Westview. Somehow she had to signal Desaix about the potential danger.

"Yes, ma'am!" Johnson said, then tightened his grip on the President's arm and led him forward. Johnson's instincts told him to distrust Mary. She would try to neutralize his attempt to kill the President. And Dr. Prince wouldn't like that, after he had gone to the trouble of having Johnson assigned to Westview's aftercare staff.

"Just wait a minute, Sergeant Johnson," Mary said, placing her hand over Johnson's arm. "Don't you think you are being just a little rough with the President? Just like Neva was with me?"

"Neva? Oh, yes. I understand." Johnson's mind swirled with people and events, but he was having difficulty sorting them out.

"Neva? Wasn't she my nurse, Mary?" Westview asked, as if he had heard her name for the first time.

"Yes she was, Mr. President. And, Sergeant Johnson, this wonderful soldier, whom I affectionately call the Manchurian Candidate, was instrumental in my safe release. For that I will be eternally grateful."

Mary looked at Desaix as she spoke, hoping he had picked up on her reference to The Manchurian Candidate, a novel and movie about a brainwashed American prisoner of war sent by the Chinese communists to the U.S. to assassinate a presidential candidate.

"Ah, yes," replied the President. "Did we ever meet before?"

"You're meeting him now!" Desaix said, after immediately understanding Mary's reference.

As Desaix tried to figure out how to physically separate Johnson from his prey, Johnson realized he had to make his move. He released Westview's arm and grabbed his throat.

"Stay back! Both of you!" Johnson shouted.

Desaix knew he had to work quickly. The President couldn't breathe, and started to turn blue. But if Desaix jumped Johnson or yelled for help, he risked panicking Johnson into immediately killing Westview. Johnson released his grip on the President's throat, took several steps backward, dragging the President with him.

Mary turned to Desaix. "He's the one who saved my life at St. E's. Do you think that is enough of an emotional bond to use to talk him away from the President?"

"We'd better try it—and pray that it works," Desaix replied.

"Okay, I'm ready."

"Here's some advice: personalize the relationship; form a bond of trust quickly; remind him how he had saved your life; and suggest to him that what he is doing now is going against helping you out. Okay?"

"Yeah!"

"Just talk sweet, and scramble his brain."

Mary approached the anxious sergeant slowly, talking as she walked. "Sergeant Johnson, please listen to me! Stop what you are doing!" Mary felt foolish. Her words didn't alter Johnson's tightening grip on Westview one iota.

"Sergeant Johnson, don't you know me? I am Mary Dougherty. You saved my life. You are my dear friend. You killed those evil men—Mapplethorpe and Shaw—because they were hurting me. Because you are my dear friend, you killed the woman who was torturing me. But now you are trying to kill the President, who is also my dearest, closest friend. He has never hurt me. It isn't fair if you hurt him. He is a good man. He is my friend. So he is your friend. You can't hurt anyone who is my friend and your friend."

It's all so confusing, thought Johnson. How could he complete his mission and kill the President if Westview was Mary's good friend? And his good friend?

Mary and Desaix watched as Johnson started to loosen his grip on Westview's throat. It's working, thought Desaix. Mary had successfully substituted her thought pattern for Johnson's, establishing a highly personalized, if contrived, relationship between them. Johnson was finding it difficult to overcome the artificial cognitive dissonance she had created by insinuating a logic that was contradictory.

But Desaix couldn't take the chance she would not be totally successful. As Johnson's hand relaxed, Desaix rushed forward and pried the President from him.

Westview sank down into a chair, exhausted and shaken.

Mary took his pulse and increased the flow of D5W dripping from the intravenous bottle into his arm to counteract any potential fainting. Then she placed her arms around a very confused Johnson. "Who made you do this, Sergeant Johnson?"

"I don't remember," Johnson said somberly.

"Was it Colonel Zarbitski?" Mary asked.

Johnson was silent for a while. Desaix could almost feel the effort he was making to think clearly. "Yes. It was a colonel." He spoke in a depressed monotone.

So far so good, Desaix thought. Now comes the hard part: to use Johnson's guilt at almost having killed Mary's friend as the basis for reprogramming him.

"Sergeant Johnson, was there another man as well?" Desaix asked as he stood behind Johnson, hoping Johnson would associate the idea of mental relaxation with Desaix's voice, presence, and suggestions.

"Yes, his name was Dr. Prince. He kept asking me questions while the colonel beat me with that rubber hose. They covered my head with a black hood."

Johnson's voice became increasingly angry. Desaix could see Johnson's muscles tense up at the thought of his interrogation.

"Now it's your turn to get back at the people who hurt you. The people who tried to make you turn against your friends—and Mary."

Johnson didn't respond, although he appeared to be listening to Desaix.

"Relax," Desaix continued. "Just let all the tension in your body drain out through your arms and legs. Roll your eyes upward and close your eyelids. Let yourself totally relax." Desaix knew that his hypnotic suggestions were working when Johnson visibly relaxed. "Imagine a balloon attached to the end of your right hand. Now imagine that balloon slowly rising in the air, pulling your hand slowly upward."

To both Westview's and Mary's amazement, Johnson's right hand started to rise, as if an invisible force were pulling it upward.

"That's good, Sergeant Johnson. You may now lower your hand to your side."

Johnson's hand came down as easily as it had risen.

"Now that you feel totally relaxed, allow yourself to feel your basic, good impulses. Those impulses that allowed you to rescue Mary."

Johnson remained standing, eyes closed, the tension lines in his face noticeably softened. He felt a peace within himself that he hadn't felt in a long time. Mary must not be hurt, he thought. She is my friend.

Desaix picked up the wall telephone and dialed the President's office. "Randy, please call White and Ball and tell them to come over here ASAP. Make sure to tell them to bring over their two friends. They'll know who I mean."

"Desaix," Randy replied, "they're already waiting for you in my office. They were worried that they were late for a meeting you were supposed to have had with them ten minutes ago."

"Good. Just keep them there. Tell them that I'll see them in a few minutes."

"Who was that?" Mary asked when Desaix hung up the phone.

"It was Randy. We've got some visitors Johnson and I must see."

"Is there anything you want me to do?" Mary asked. She started walking the exhausted President back toward the medical unit. "I'll get Westview checked out, just to make sure nothing serious happened."

"When you finish, take him to the Sit Room and see if he can't find Zotov. But don't let them begin any formal dialogue until I get there. Okay?"

"Yes. Understood." Mary blew him a kiss with her hand.

Desaix turned his attention back to Johnson. "Sergeant Johnson, I have an important job for you to do when you open your eyes, which will help Mary . . ."

# CHAPTER
## 42

**D**esaix looked up as Ball, White, Zarb, and Dr. Prince walked into the Oval Office.

"Please sit down, gentlemen," Desaix said.

"I see that the office of the presidency becomes you," White said sarcastically.

"For better or for worse, that's true, at least for the moment. Crazy, isn't it?" Desaix leaned over in his chair, focusing his attention on his supposedly new allies.

"Well? Have you come to any decision yet?" Desaix paused to assess the situation. "Are you with me or against me?"

"Dr. Clark—" Zarbitski began.

"Please, Colonel Zarbitski, I'm an informal man, call me Desaix, unless you have a medical emergency. Then you have the right to call me doctor."

Everyone in the room laughed.

"Okay, Desaix. Dr. Prince and I are not really sure what it is that you want of us."

"General White, I thought you told me that you had made yourself perfectly clear to them." Desaix stood up and started to pace the room. "I'm disappointed."

"Wait a minute, Desaix. I told you that I would try my best to convince them to ally with us. I didn't promise you that they would agree." White was testing Desaix, whose posturing was so far not sufficient to intimidate anyone in the room.

"Do you feel the same way, Jim?" Desaix asked, wondering whether he had the makings of a mutiny on his hands even before any one of them had pledged loyalty to him.

"Desaix, I believed everything you told me back at the Agency," Ball said. "It was impressive. It was convincing. As we drove to St. E's to help you with Mary, I explained to both of my colleagues that you had very persuasive ELINT interception data obtained from the Baltimore Room that could implicate us all as co-conspirators with Manning. A coup within a coup, as you called it. I also explained to them that Manning would eventually turn against every one of us who helped him from the very beginning of Project Baltimore." Ball paused to see if his colleagues had anything to say. "I also conveyed your offer that if we turn against Manning, all would be forgiven and forgotten. That as a pragmatist you knew you needed our collective help to stop the war and dismantle Project Baltimore."

"Well?" Desaix asked warily.

"But that was then. This is now. Nowadays, allegiances change quickly. You know what I mean?"

"And what about you?" Desaix looked at Prince, who didn't bother to respond. The indifferent expression on his angular face told Desaix everything he wanted to know.

"So, gentlemen. As I understand your answer, you are basically telling me to go fuck myself, that you would rather take your chances with him than with me," Desaix replied calmly, but ran his hand nervously through his hair.

"Oh, come on, Desaix," White interjected. "Let's not get too dramatic about this. We're all big boys. We have no basic dislike of you. Why should we? So far, you've been quite charming and amusing. In fact, downright entertaining. But in the long run, what does it really mean whether a political leader has an Operational Code that explains why and how he acts." White stood up and walked toward Desaix. "In a world of nonaccountability, who really cares whether a President did or did not start a war. The only thing that the history books really care about is whether that President *won* the war. And it doesn't matter whether it cost the U.S. public one man or one thousand men. We play to win."

"I appreciate that, coach," Desaix replied, frustrated that even when he was trying to be practical, understanding, and even magnanimous, he still could not convince them to join him. Irrational self-interests always seemed to prevail.

"Both Jim and I are genuinely impressed with the way you deduced your way through the jungle of personalities, motives, and malfeasance," White said. "But that was then. Now is now, as Ball so rightly pointed out. You, better than anyone else, should know that there are no permanent personal loyalties. There are only shifting allegiances and national interests." White felt avuncular and hoped he was coming off that way to his audience.

"So is this a 'can't we be friends despite our differences' speech?"

"That's human nature, Desaix. You should know that better than anyone else," White continued. "What difference does it really make that Presidents Westview and Zotov would start a war that would benefit both of them personally and politically—as long as the U.S. and the Russian Federation would also benefit. Don't you remember that old adage: the business of U.S. foreign policy is business? So what if the Japanese decide to back us? This time. Next time those slanty-eyed motherfuckers will back another country."

"But I think what irks you the most," Ball interjected, "is the fact that the ultimate political opportunist, Chester Manning, was smart enough to suggest and implement Project Baltimore—merely to advance his own political ambitions."

"Admit it," White said. "Even you, a first-rate opportunist, who has a lot of convincing NSA ELINT intercepts behind him, have to admire a sneaky, thieving cocksucker like Manning, who would set up his own friend. But quite frankly, the game isn't over. How do you know that Westview won't have the last laugh on all of us? You don't know that. I, certainly, don't know that. So while the game is still in flux, my colleagues and I have come to the conclusion that we will serve whoever offers the highest bid. Just like you, Desaix."

"It's nice to know what good company I'm in," Desaix chortled.

"The only difference between you and the four of us, Desaix, isn't the fact that we've all lied, and cheated, and killed in order to remain players in this goddamn game. Because you and I know that you have done all of that—and then some. The real difference, after all is said and done, is that you care."

"Richard, I must say that's one hell of an indictment," Desaix replied sarcastically.

"But if you really cared as much as you think you do," White paused to emphasize the point, "you wouldn't have let your good friend Fitzpatrick go to Japan with you. I've seen you throw people off your delegation when you didn't want them. And it didn't matter whether they were ambassadors, movie stars, or political bigwigs. They were off."

"But not Fitzpatrick," Ball said, buttressing the accusation. "You knew something was wrong the moment Mapplethorpe insisted you take him. Did you stop him from going? No. You were too busy feeling sorry for yourself because you had to be there when all the action was on the other side of the world."

"So what happened to your good friend Fitzpatrick?" White asked rhetorically, as if he were on a tag team of moral indignation. "His presence, and eventual demise, created the very thing that you craved—a crisis. But not just any crisis. Because you're too special to handle a humdrum crisis like a hostage negotiation or a flood. No, my friend, you needed a tripleheader—the Triple Crown—a domestic turmoil, an international war, and, best of all, an insane President. That's what your good friend Fitzpatrick gave you, because you just didn't care enough to say one little word—nothing!"

"Are you guys finished?" Desaix asked, trying to appear calm. He wanted to hear what else remained of their pathetic, morally hypocritical lecture. But White's last remarks about Fitzpatrick hit a raw nerve. Desaix felt his back stiffen and a surge of blood rush into his head—that same sickening feeling he felt when he saw Fitzpatrick at the morgue.

"I don't know, Desaix. I really don't know. I wish that I could say that we were finished." White paused, concerned for the first time that Desaix was irritated with all of his rationalizations. "Maybe it's a testimony to you, but no one who has ever met you is ever really finished dealing with you. You're a bad habit that no one can get rid of. It's a pity. So, if you would, please give us some time to tell you whether we're finished with you or not."

Zarb and Prince sat silently on the couch wearing placid faces of indifference. Whatever alliance Desaix thought he could make with White and Ball clearly was not possible. Despite all the convincing evidence, including the doctored photos and the nondoctored NSA intercepts that had been retrieved from the Baltimore Room, Desaix realized he was on his own. None of them would side with him against Manning. Or against anyone else, for that matter. Theirs was a simple game of political opportunism. Whoever was in the lead would receive their support. It was as simple as that. It was completely irrelevant whether it was Westview, Manning, or Desaix.

"Thank you, Richard, for your frank response," Desaix replied as coolly as any man could who was being insulted as a prelude to an execution. "In short, you're telling me that each of you will ally with Manning, Imai, and Project Baltimore. You will support the coup within the coup. Manning will become President, and you will all sell out our country, the Commonwealth of Independent States, and Germany to Imai and his Japanese industrial colleagues."

No one responded.

"Well, I appreciate the honesty of your silence. I take that as a compliment."

"I'm truly sorry that things have not worked as you hoped, Desaix," Ball said, "but we feel that we're doing what's best . . ." Ball felt guilty, hoping that it wasn't apparent. The decision that the four men had made at St. E's was intractable.

"Frankly, gentlemen, I think we should be leaving," Zarb spoke in his clipped artificial military politeness as he stood up.

"Well, if you must," Desaix said as he pressed the intercom. "Randy, would you please have one of the White House limos take these four gentlemen wherever they want to go."

"We're all going to the Pentagon," White replied smugly. His strategy of directly confronting Desaix had worked beautifully. He had outpsyched the shrink.

Desaix held the door to the office open as they left. "I appreciate your having come to see me on such short notice. I'm sorry we can't find a way to work together, but I understand that none of this is personal. Good-bye and good luck!"

"I don't trust him," Prince said as they headed down the hall. But no one was listening to him. The unspoken collective thought was that in a moment of victory a certain amount of compassion for Desaix was required. Not bitter cynicism.

The chauffeured Cadillac Brougham limousine pulled up just as they stepped outside the White House. One of the Secret Service agents milling about ran to open the back door for the four of them. As the limo passed the gates to the White House grounds, the door locks automatically snapped shut and the chauffeur closed the glass divider between the driver and the passenger seats. He turned very slowly toward the men in the back. "Which way would you like to get to Hades, gentlemen?"

"Oh, shit! It's Johnson!" Zarb exclaimed, regretting having left his gun behind, as protocol required, when they had arrived at the White House.

The Cadillac Brougham, plated WHITE HOUSE ONE, drew shouts and applause from strolling tourists, who could now return home with a good story for their neighbors. The limo crossed the mall, L'Enfant Plaza, and entered the slow-moving traffic on Route 395. Its occupants' screams and supplications could not be heard through the fortified bulletproof glass windows. Their wildly waving hands, fingers bloodied from trying to punch their way through the plexiglass that separated the two halves of the car, could have been mistaken as handwaving by the populace.

Johnson, oblivious to everything but his mission, crossed the highway divider at just the right moment and slammed directly into a U.S. military tanker-trailer marked DANGEROUS CHEMICALS: FLAMMABLE.

The ensuing explosion could almost be heard seven miles away—all the way to the Situation Room in the basement of the White House.

# CHAPTER
## 43

**M**ary sat in front of the telecommunications console in the White House Situation Room, having difficulty setting up the teleconferencing link between Westview and Zotov. Westview sat beside her, going over a manual marked TOP SECRET: PROJECT BALTIMORE. He was trying to determine the precise means by which he was supposed to contact Zotov at Russian headquarters.

"How are things going?" Desaix asked as he entered the Sit Room.

"We're having some problems accessing them," Mary said. She glanced at the clock on the wall. They had only twenty minutes to contact Zotov before the world went beyond the point of no return.

The sound of endless sirens outside reverberated through the room. The explosion of a few minutes ago had created chaos for the D.C. police and fire department.

"What in God's name is that?" asked Westview, as he riffled through the section marked ENDGAME.

"I have a sneaking suspicion that you will have to appoint a new National Security Advisor and DCI," Desaix's said as he tried to imagine Johnson's final act of revenge.

And now there was practically no one left, except for Cordonnier, to carry out either Westview's Project Baltimore or Manning's coup within a coup. All the other players were dead: Mapplethorpe, Shaw, Johnson, Zarb, Dr. Prince, White, Ball, McCormick, Merck, Jenkins.

"That leaves only my dear friend, Chet Manning." Westview spoke reflectively, as if the deaths of both White and Ball were part of a grand design.

"Yes, it does, doesn't it," Desaix said, suspecting for the first time that the President was not as disoriented as he had initially thought him to be.

Mary pushed several buttons that would connect her with the National Military Command Center. Nothing worked.

"Mapplethorpe probably rerouted the circuits through Room E." Desaix sat down at the console alongside Mary.

"Nice to be working with you again, Dr. Clark." Mary smiled and rubbed her thigh against his.

"The pleasure is all mine. Believe me," Desaix replied.

"By the way, I think we should send the Vice President a brief Sit Rep," Westview said as he started to draft a TOP SECRET cable.

"I think that's a good idea, Mr. President," Mary added. "Put a cautionary note in about the need for tightened security measures. Especially his need to avoid any public ceremonies."

"That's an excellent idea."

"Thank you, Desaix," Mary replied good-naturedly. "Now I wonder if you could help me with this telecommunications linkup?"

"Let's see . . . normal telecommunications travel through an antiquated series of commercial wires and microwave systems from the Western Union Building on Wisconsin Avenue." Desaix was thinking out loud, trying to figure out the system of fiber optic linkages into which he would have to connect. "From there, the transmission would travel to New York City, where it would be relayed through underground and underwater telecommunications cables connecting Canada, Iceland, England, Scotland, Denmark, Finland, St. Petersburg, and finally Moscow."

"I never knew you were into electronics," Westview said as he finished the cable and placed it in a vacuum tube that would be sent by a messenger to the State Department for restricted handling and transmission overseas, completely bypassing the seventh-floor principals. Including Manning.

"I'm not," Desaix replied. "It's just part of the basic blueprint for the crisis management communications system I helped develop several years ago."

"Very impressive, Mr. Systems Manager." Mary laughed.

"Jesus. We have only ten minutes left," Desaix said. "I'm going to transfer our transmission through the Alternate Command Center at Fort Ritchie. From there, it will be beamed up to a passing WWMCCS satellite, where it will be bounced even higher up to another passing satellite. This satellite would be a Russian Molyna transponder in a geostationary orbit. From there the message should be downlinked to an antenna farm north of Moscow, as well as to the Russian General Staff headquarters at Stremski Fortress in Moscow's seventeenth military district."

"You genius, you," Mary said as she saw the red light flash, indicating that linkage between the White House and the Russian National Command Authority was complete.

A thick voice with a heavy Russian accent boomed through the Bose speakers hanging over the console. "Welcome. We have been expecting your transmission." The voice paused for a moment. "Please wait. I will get Marshal Kulikov."

"We want to talk to President Zotov," Desaix said, then turned toward Westview. "Something is wrong."

"Something may have happened to Zotov," Westview replied.

"Then I think it would be best if I handled this matter, as long as Zotov will not be speaking to you," Desaix said, determined to make the best of an unfortunate situation. With only voice communication, neither side could see who was or was not in their respective Sit Rooms. Fortunately, the White House Sit Room did not have a functioning television conferencing capability like the one at State. Thanks to Mapplethorpe's having messed up the entire telecommunications system.

"Why, Desaix?"

"First of all, as President, you shouldn't have to speak to anyone lower on the pecking order than Zotov. Second, if I can say that you are not available at crucial times in this negotiation, I have added room to maneuver tactically. I can always delay the Russians by telling them that I have to first check with you before I can agree to anything."

"Fine! But I won't let you give away the family store!" Westview replied.

A voice came over the speakers in English. "Good day. I'm Marshal Alexander Kulikov. President Zotov is not available. You will be dealing with me. To whom am I speaking?"

"My name is Desaix Clark. I am a senior official in the Department of State. President Westview also is not immediately available, but he can be reached at any time."

"Mr. Clark, what exactly is your title?" Kulikov's imperious voice had a sardonic edge to it.

"I am the Deputy Assistant Secretary of State for East Asian and Pacific Affairs," Desaix said. His blood flowed with adrenaline while he waited to hear Kulikov's response. Here he was in the White House. It had taken all the resources and guile he had. But here he was—back in the game. Managing the crisis of crises. The ultimate contest of wills. His against Kulikov's. Just two mortal people determining the fate of billions of people around the world.

That was the strange irony. The more serious the crisis, the fewer the number of people involved in the final outcome. Over the past quarter decade, as a result of improved communications, increased information technology, and a shrinking world, crisis diplomacy had become increasingly more personalized and less bureaucratic. Each successive President relied more and more on his own personal relationship with world leaders to resolve international problems.

President Bush had been the epitome of viewing international crisis management as one large Rolodex. If a Mideast crisis erupted, he simply picked up the phone, called Shamir, Assad, Mubarak, and King Hussein, and resolved the problem without any help from State, CIA, JCS, or even his own NSC. "Face-to-face" meetings and "phone-to-phone" discussions had become the modus operandi of crisis diplomacy in the 1990s. More than ever, the outcome of world peace depended on the psychodynamics of one world leader. Frightening, thought Desaix. But incredibly exciting. Especially if the role of a world leader was his.

"Pardon me, but this is just not acceptable. I cannot be negotiating with a junior official. If I must deal with the State Department, why am I not talking to Secretary of State Chester Manning?" Kulikov sounded angry.

"I can appreciate your concern. But I assure you that I am completely authorized to negotiate the end of Project Baltimore." Desaix shrugged his shoulders. He covered the microphone with his hand and turned toward Westview. "Is there any specific code word that only you and Zotov would have known that I can offer? So he knows I represent you?"

"Let me see." Westview leafed through the manual. "Yes. The code is that 'The President of the United States has stopped all currency trading. Especially trading the yen.' "

"What if he doesn't accept your bona fides?" Mary asked, worried that in precisely five minutes a nuclear war could erupt.

"We'll have to wait and see what does happen," Desaix replied somewhat cavalierly. From his previous experience negotiating with the Russians, he knew that they always liked to open negotiations with a verbal offense, questioning the legitimacy of the meeting or the integrity of the opponent. It was business as usual, with their primary objective to assume control of the negotiating process as quickly as possible.

So far, Kulikov was true to form. "I am sorry, but I must insist on speaking with the President of the United States or the Secretary of State."

"Then, General—"

"I am not a general! I am a marshal of the Russian Army!" Kulikov announced. He was annoyed and spoke brusquely.

"All right, Marshal Kulikov. Then we have nothing to say to each other," Desaix replied.

"What in God's name are you doing, Desaix? Are you crazy?" Westview whispered in his ear.

Nodding her head in agreement, Mary pointed to her head, making the point that she too thought he was crazy.

"Trust me, Mr. President," Desaix said, covering the microphone with his hand.

"Are you kidding? This isn't some game," Westview answered. He was beginning to panic. He envisioned what history would write about his presidential tenure. "I don't want to be the first and only American President to have been responsible for the nuclear destruction of the United States. Do you read me?"

"I think the message is coming across loud and clear," Desaix said, though he was vexed. Now he had two negotiations about which to worry. One with the Russians. The other with the President of the United States.

"What is going on over there?" shouted Kulikov. "I have an uncomfortable feeling that you Americans are not taking this situation very seriously."

"Should we begin our discussions, or will you insist that I am too insignificant to talk to?" Desaix asked, opening up his negotiating offensive.

"How can I be certain of your legitimacy?" Kulikov said more soberly.

"The same way that I must be comfortable with yours," Desaix replied.

"What would make you feel comfortable?" Kulikov asked.

"I will give you the specific code words that are intended to stop this war. In turn, you must give me the proper response. Is that clear?" If Kulikov responded positively, Desaix had effectively positioned him on the defensive.

"Please proceed, Mr. Clark."

Mary wiped her hand against her forehead, showing her relief.

"The President of the United States has stopped all currency trading. Especially trading the yen." Desaix spoke the words slowly enough so that Kulikov would have no problems understanding them.

For a few seconds there was complete silence. Both Mary and Westview were visibly nervous. Desaix seemed unduly calm, almost annoyingly so, thought Mary.

"The President of the Russian Federation has also stopped all of his currency trade," Kulikov replied.

Westview shook his head. "That's not correct, Desaix," he whispered.

"I'm sorry Marshal Kulikov, but I am unable to confirm your response."

"Are you calling me a liar?"

"I have said nothing about who you are or what you are. But I am afraid you are not empowered to negotiate with me or any other representative of the United States government." Desaix glanced at the clock. They had exactly three minutes left. "In the meanwhile, you have wasted extremely valuable time."

"That is impertinent!" Kulikov shouted.

"Perhaps. I have been called worse," Desaix laughingly replied.

"The correct response is that the President of the Russian Federation is selling the yen short and buying long on the deutsche mark."

"He's right on the mark," Westview whispered.

"That's correct, Marshal," Desaix replied.

"Are we in business, Mr. Clark?" Kulikov asked.

"Yes, we're in business, Marshal Kulikov." The tension in the air diminished markedly. "Within thirty seconds, both sides must cease any and all hostilities."

"Agreed," Kulikov replied.

"Immediate withdrawal of all forces to the positions they were in before the fighting started," Desaix said.

"We are in accord."

"The United Nations International Peacekeeping Force will be sent over to Germany within the next forty-eight hours to monitor the compliance by both sides."

"We have no problems with that provision, Mr. Clark."

"Good. Now that we've settled most of our major differences, I think we should end these negotiations and allow our ambassadors to iron out the minor details." Desaix knew that it was standard Russian negotiating practice to drag out negotiations in an effort to extract as many concessions as possible. And they were good at wearing down their opponents.

"Mr. Clark, there is one extremely important issue that we have not yet addressed." Kulikov paused to add emphasis to his point. "It has to do with the problem of reparations. As an ally in this venture, or should I call it a folly, we Russians are extremely sensitive to the fact that we lost almost three times the number of men and matériel in a war that we created for each other's benefit."

"Yes, Marshal?" Desaix asked, impatient to hear his demands.

"It seems only fair and just that your government reimburse ours for the matériel and men that we lost in this war, and also what you owe us for close to ten years as part of your 'generous aid package'—something you've never fully paid. We calculate that to be about one hundred billion dollars."

"What if we refuse?"

"That would be completely inconceivable, Mr. Clark. May I remind you that we are still a very powerful nation, sufficiently large enough to cause you and the world community serious problems."

"I don't imagine that you are trying to threaten us, are you?" Desaix asked. He knew that was precisely what Kulikov was trying to do. An old ploy. During the post–Cold War period, whenever the Russians felt threatened, they would strike out and threaten their perceived enemy. A way of warding off their own fears. Just like children.

"Let me repeat my point again, Mr. Clark. For reasons that you and I know quite well, our Presidents decided to enter into an alliance in which one side would start the war while both sides pledged to maintain maximum restraint. The loss of fifteen hundred T-72 tanks compared to a paltry loss of five hundred M1A1 Abrams tanks is something we must resolve immediately."

Silence and tension prevailed in the Sit Room.

"There is absolutely no agreement, Mr. Clark, without this reparations provision."

Desaix turned toward Westview. "What do you want to do?"

"He has a point." He paused. "How did I know that . . . their . . . military . . ."

"Are you all right, Mr. President?" Desaix asked as he looked closely at Westview. Westview's eyes were slightly glazed. His fingers twitched nervously. His body slowly rocked back and forth in his chair. Oh my God, thought Desaix. He's becoming paralyzed by the stress of it all.

". . . I didn't realize . . . that their military was much . . . less effective than anyone . . . had . . . imagined." Westview stammered as he tried to stand up, but had to hold on to the back of his chair to steady himself. "I miscalculated . . . this . . . whole . . . war . . . How . . . did . . . I . . . know . . . we . . . would . . . create . . . so . . . much . . . destruction . . . for . . . which . . . we . . . could . . . never . . . pay . . . The . . . Japanese . . . they're . . . supposed . . . to . . . help . . . us . . . out . . . But . . ."

"Desaix. What should we do? He's falling apart," Mary said as she tried to comfort Westview.

"Mr. Clark, so that you understand that we are not kidding, as you Americans like to say, I am, as of this moment, officially canceling our previous agreement to stop the war if we cannot agree on reparations. And furthermore, to make it quite clear to you that we Russians will not accept a second-class status, I have just ordered our nuclear rocket forces on a Maximum Vigilance status of sixty seconds."

Desaix felt as alert as he had ever been. Russians tended to overplay their endgame, a frequent tactical move in a negotiation. But then again he couldn't be certain. "Wait a minute, Sasha!" he shouted into the microphone. "You're not going to tell me that you're willing to escalate this war over an issue of money."

"What do you think Project Baltimore was all about? Money," Kulikov announced somberly, adding, "fifty-five seconds . . . fifty-four seconds . . ."

Mary was confused. Who was *Sasha?* Desaix had been speaking to Kulikov.

"He's bluffing! I know the Russians, Mr. President!" Desaix said to Westview.

"Money . . . we . . . don't . . . have . . . the . . . money! . . . I . . . made . . . a . . . mistake . . . Project . . . Baltimore . . ."

"Forty-nine seconds . . ."

"Mr. President, what do you want to do?" Desaix asked.

"Desaix, he's in no condition to make any decisions," Mary replied.

"No, I'm . . . still . . . the . . . President . . ." Westview said angrily. "No, . . . one . . . no . . . one . . . can . . . take . . . that . . . power . . . away . . . from . . . me . . ."

"Forty seconds . . ." Kulikov continued counting.

Desaix could see that Westview could no longer be expected to make any rational decisions. His head rolled from side to side on his shoulders. His mouth opened to speak, but no words came out. He was totally disoriented.

"Mr. President, will you give me the authority . . ."

In his condition, Desaix could involuntarily commit the President to St. E's with the psychiatric diagnosis of Organic Brain Syndrome secondary to Postoperative Cardiovascular Surgery. Westview was technically insane. In his position as President, he was becoming psychotic as well as becoming a danger to himself and others.

This was the first time in history that a President of the United States could be officially declared mentally incompetent. Although this was not the first time that the destiny of the world was decided by two or three advisors covering up for a physically or mentally ill President. In fact, a psychoanalytic analysis of one hundred years of the presidency would be an eye-opener at the very least. It was common knowledge that many previous administrations had been run by an elite group of advisors who gained control in a crisis. Once again, history was repeating itself with President Donald Westview, and Dr. Desaix Clark had effectively become the new President of the United States—if only for a few seconds.

"Thirty-five seconds . . ."

"Desaix, this is your call," Mary said as she watched Westview break into a cold sweat.

*"No, damnit! I will not give you any authority! I am still the President!"* Westview screamed.

"You have exactly thirty-four seconds left," Kulikov said.

Desaix quickly scribbled out a note and handed it to Westview, who looked at it and turned red.

*"No! I will not resign as President! This is a conspiracy! You did this, Desaix! You created this entire crisis so that I would resign!"*

"Please, Mr. President, Desaix is only doing what's best for you and the country." Mary tried to calm him down.

"Thirty-two seconds . . ."

"Oh no, Mary." Tears welled up in Westview's eyes. "You too? You're part of this whole conspiracy. Did Manning co-opt you too?"

"Mr. President, you know better than that. We're just trying to help you."

"How? By forcing me to resign? That's not going to help me. That's going to help you, Desaix, and Manning." Westview felt trapped. His mind was racing. He had to stop Mary and Desaix before it was too late.

"Thirty seconds . . ."

"Marshal Kulikov," Desaix said, "we don't want to escalate this war. No one will win if there is a nuclear war. There's been enough destruction on both sides."

"Mr. Clark, please tell your President that I am not President Zotov. My constituency of military generals is unified and wants me to continue this war until you agree to the economic reparations that we are owed."

"I want to talk to Kulikov! Give me the microphone, Desaix!" Westview shouted as he grabbed for the microphone.

Desaix pulled the microphone away from him and turned off the SPEAK switch. The President suddenly appeared calmer, more rational. But this all could change at a moment's notice, without any warning, given his mental condition. *Should I take the chance?* Desaix thought. *At risk was world peace. But at least this way, neither the President nor anyone else could accuse him or Mary of having been part of a conspiracy.*

"What do you think, Mary?" Desaix asked. He wanted her to be part of the decision. She nodded her head in agreement.

"Twenty-five seconds . . ."

Desaix handed the microphone to Westview and switched on the SPEAK button.

"Marshal Kulikov . . . this . . . is . . . President . . . Westview . . ."

"Where is Mr. Clark?"

"He's busy."

"How do I know that you are the President?"

"Marshal . . ." Westview paused. He was annoyed by the question.

"You have twenty seconds left . . ."

*"I am the goddamn President of the United States! I don't have to prove that to you or anyone else! Do you understand me, Marshal . . . ?"*

"President Westview, I want you to sign this letter of resignation," Desaix said, grabbing the microphone away from Westview. "Mary, help me out!"

*"I am the President! I am in charge here! I don't have to prove that to anyone! Including the Russians!"*

Mary tried to restrain Westview.

"What's happening?" Kulikov asked. "Who was that?"

"It's Mr. Clark again, Marshal. That was one of the President's security advisors. Completely disregard him. He was just trying to stall for time."

"I appreciate your honesty. Unfortunately, your negotiating game cost you five seconds! You have exactly fifteen seconds left."

"Mr. President, you must sign this letter of resignation!" Desaix demanded.

*"No! This is my war! My negotiation!"* Westview tried to break out of Mary's armlock.

"If you don't sign this," Desaix said, "you will be known in history as the American President who allowed a limited regional war started for purely selfish reasons to escalate into a nuclear holocaust because of mental incompetence. Please resign, for health reasons. Whatever happens, it will be completely my responsibility."

Westview suddenly calmed down. Mary loosened her grasp around his arms.

"Ten seconds . . . nine seconds . . ."

"And if I don't sign it?" Westview asked, sounding rational for a moment.

"I will launch a preemptive nuclear strike," Desaix said, as he began to push several of the buttons that allowed him to activate the appropriate nuclear codes, the release messages, the authenticators, and the Permissive Action Link System.

"That's blackmail!"

"Perhaps, but at least someone is in control of the crisis."

"Control is what this has been all about? Hasn't it?"

Desaix didn't respond.

"Six . . . five . . ."

"And if I do sign it?"

"Three seconds . . ."

Desaix's fingers were poised on the last button. He looked at Mary, her blue eyes filled with tears.

"Two seconds . . . one second . . ."

# CHAPTER
# 44

Martha's Vineyard, a tiny island harboring several distinct New England towns, was the perfect refuge from the flotsam and jetsam of life on the mainland.

Actually, the Vineyard was more than a refuge. For those denizens who populated it during the summer, it was another country, where the code of conduct and dress was dictated by nothing more pressured than the weather. For those who lived on the island year-round, it was particularly suited for eccentrics, inveterate drinkers, and hopeless lovers.

On that particular day, the bright sun glistened over the sea, and the white cusps of rugged waves rolled ruthlessly into the bone white sands of the unlittered beaches.

Holding her in his arms as the waves rolled over them, Desaix gazed into Mary's bright blue eyes.

"What are you looking at, sailor?" Mary laughed as she spat water out of her mouth.

"I am looking at you, Ms. Dougherty!" Desaix said, then kissed her firmly on her moist lips. "If we stay in the water much longer, I'm going to become completely waterlogged!"

"Okay, sailor! First one to shore receives endless back rubs with suntan lotion and gentle caressess—until she dies from blissful exhaustion." Arching her muscular shoulders, Mary started swimming toward shore.

Desaix watched her bob up and down with the waves, looking like a mermaid emerging from the kingdom of Neptune, forcing her way into the world of the mortals.

"I didn't realize that you were such a weak swimmer!" Mary teased him as he rubbed her dry with an oversized beach towel bought at a discount sale off-season.

"I try to concentrate on perfecting my other, less visible, physical activities," Desaix joked as he gyrated his pelvis. He felt wonderfully carefree and adolescent.

"I think your swimming needs improvement, not your stroking."

Desaix grabbed her by the waist and pulled her down on the sand.

"I adore you. Do you know that, Dr. Clark?" Mary spoke in a mock Russian accent. "You're my James Bond. A secret agent of the heart and mind."

"But how do I really know that it is you who I really love, and not some other person by the name of Mary Dougherty?" Desaix parodied the conversation he had had with Kulikov.

"By the way, how did you know that both our and their nuclear systems would not work?" Mary asked nonchalantly.

"Remember all the problems that you and I were having in the White House Sit Room, trying to set up the telecommunications system with Kulikov?" He delicately worked some suntan lotion into her chest as he spoke.

"Of course. Mapplethorpe screwed up the entire electrical and communication systems when he transferred it from the White House to the Old Executive Office Building . . . And could you make sure that the suntan lotion is spread evenly? I don't want to look like a spaniel."

"Yes, Madam Pasha!" He continued spreading the cream. "Have you ever heard of Desaix's Axiom?"

"No! Is it some kind of neurological disease of the mind? Or is it one of your profound insights?" Mary laughed.

"Desaix's Axiom, one of many, of course . . ."

"Of course. Rub a little more to the right."

"As I was saying, Desaix's Axiom states that, in any given crisis, systems and people will tend to break down when you least expect them to."

"So never expect them to perform well, and they will never disappoint you."

"Something like that," Desaix replied defensively.

"Then by the process of exclusion, you become the all-knowing, all-perfect repository of knowledge and performance. My . . . my . . . my . . . What an incredibly difficult burden for such a mortal like yourself."

"Is this gang-up-on-Desaix Clark day?" He put down the lotion and covered her with sand.

"Oh Christ, Desaix. Look what you've done." As she brushed the sand from her body, she leaned over and turned up the sound on their portable TV set.

"What's the matter?"

"Shhhhhh!! I want to hear what that reporter you talked to at St. E's has to say about the Summit!"

"What is she going to say that we don't already know?" Trying to pry her away from the TV set was a lost cause, so Desaix sat down alongside of her.

> The U.S.-Russian Summit will convene this afternoon in Geneva under the auspices of the Secretary General of the United Nations.
>
> Attending the conference will be the five permanent members of the Security Council—England, France, China, the U.S. and the Russian Federation. Members of the European Common Market will be attending as observers.
>
> Senior administration sources believe that a just and favorable cessation of hostilities between the U.S. and the Russians will be formally concluded by tomorrow evening.
>
> Thanks to President Donald Westview's deft handling of the crisis between the U.S. and the Russians, a nuclear holocaust was averted. Soon after all combat ceased yesterday morning at five o'clock, President Westview announced his resignation of the presidency because of an undisclosed medical condition. Vice President Allison Bonner was immediately sworn in as the forty-second President of the United States upon his return from Japan.
>
> President Bonner wasted no time organizing an international financial consortium led by Japan and the European Common Market countries to underwrite war damage reparations for the Commonwealth of Independent States and Germany.
>
> Although the Russians are believed to have lost close to three thousand soldiers and over fifteen hundred tanks, senior Russian officials are optimistic that a new Russian commonwealth will emerge. When asked what this commonwealth would consist of, recently elected president Alexander Kulikov said, "The Russian people are now united under the flag of a constitutional democracy that will be supervised by a military tribunal that promises to relinquish all power once political stability has returned and financial prosperity has been obtained."
>
> In short, it appears that the Commonwealth of Independent States will return to an autocratic regime, not unlike the ones that the Russians have previously overthrown.
>
> As one high-level official explained to this reporter, "The Russians have historically had an abhorrence to freedom, democracy, and capitalism. To them it meant only one thing—chaos. So they are returning to a regime that suits their national character."
>
> Attending the summit will be U.S. President Bonner, who has had extensive experience in dealing with the Russians as a Senator on the Senate Foreign Relations Committee. He is accompanied by his newly appointed Vice President, Chester Manning, and Secretary of State Paul Twitty, previous Under Secretary of State

for Political Affairs, who will be negotiating the details of the armistice agreement with the Russians, represented by President Kulikov and his new Foreign Minister and former boss, President Igor Zotov.

At present, former President Westview is hospitalized and is in stable condition at Walter Reed Army Medical Center for an undisclosed illness.

On a minor yet intriguing note, an Israeli counselor, Roger Cordonnier, has been declared persona non grata by the State Department for what has been called "behavior unbecoming a diplomat." He left the country earlier today. The Israeli Embassy in Washington has called charges that Mr. Cordonnier was a freelance ex-Mossad agent under contract to the State Department both "slanderous and absolutely preposterous."

Locally, District of Columbia police have ruled that the car accident that killed National Security Advisor Richard White and Director of the Central Intelligence Agency James Ball, as well as three other unidentified passengers, was an accident. They have ruled out any foul play or terrorist activity.

That's today's news. Have a good day!

Mary turned toward Desaix.

"You're the so-called senior administration official aren't you?" Mary asked as she lay down on the towel, beckoning him toward her.

"As well as the person who supplied the background information on Westview, Twitty, Manning, Kulikov, and everything sandwiched in between."

"Are you trying to tell me that you made all of this up and then fed it to the news media?" she asked. Playfully throwing sand at Desaix, Mary was incredulous.

"No, of course not. That's preposterous. Any journalist worth his or her salt would clearly check all their sources. All I did was to put a certain spin on the news that they reported." He lay on top of her, running his fingers through her wet hair. "Let's just say I managed the news so that I could limit the perception of the amount of damage that our dear President had created."

Throwing him off her, Mary poked him in the chest with her index finger. "Why the hell did you protect those guys, especially Manning? Why didn't you tell the truth?"

"Wow! Hold on a minute!"

"What's the matter? Did I say anything wrong?" She caressed his furrowed brow.

"No, you didn't say anything wrong. On the contrary. You asked me the most obvious question of all. Why didn't I blow the whistle on Manning and Westview? Why didn't I tell the world about two self-serving politicians who were willing to sacrifice a whole nation—no, why not make it a whole world—in order to play out their political ambitions? Why didn't I talk about their venality, their duplicity, their grandiosity? Not to mention the number of people both of them killed?"

"That's a good start." Mary added playfully, "Are you remaining silent because the new President may have bought us with attractive job offers?"

"You tell me," Desaix said angrily. "You know better than that."

"You have to admit that an offer to be President Bonner's next National Security Advisor is no small matter."

"No, it's no small matter. But I still haven't accepted the job."

"I'm sorry, but I didn't mean to sound sanctimonious. It's not as if I'm so innocent, either. Being offered director of the entire Secret Service is a dream come true."

"It may have been your dream, but you didn't work for Manning because of it, did you?"

"What in God's name are you talking about?" Mary asked, pulling away from him, startled by his question.

"If I were to say anything about Westview's or Manning's activities, I would have to reveal your involvement in the whole matter. And that's what both Westview and Manning were counting on. And they were right. The allegedly debauched, decadent Desaix who had more wives and mistresses than King Farouk would eventually fall in love with, of all people, a lesbian!"

"Christ! What's got into you? Please don't say something that you will regret later." Mary stood up, furious. She looked as if she could kill him.

"Mary, don't you see? Both Westview and Manning had my ticket from the very beginning of this goddamn mess."

"You're really something. Now I have the privilege of getting to see your remorseful, self-pitying side." Mary started packing up her beach ware.

"Mary, you better than anyone else knew that I was being set up from the very beginning." He watched her turn her back on him. "What an irony that a trained psychiatrist, a so-called expert on human behavior, considered a master manipulator by some, should be the one who was outmanipulated by the three people he cared most about—Westview, Manning, and, worst of all, you."

Desaix grabbed Mary by her shoulders and held her firmly.

"Let me go, Desaix." Pushing him aside, she yelled, "You're feeling goddamn sorry for yourself because there is no more goddamn crisis to get your adrenaline up and your jollies off. Well, I'm sorry for you. Maybe I can take a few naked bathers hostage here on the beach so you can practice your goddamn crisis management."

"Maybe you're right," Desaix said, remorseful. He tried to touch her, but she pulled away.

"Get off my case. And what's that crap about my being a lesbian? Aren't you the sicko who gets turned on by two women making it? Aren't you the great lover who's into troilism and all those other esoteric-sounding sexual practices?"

"That's exactly what I'm trying to tell you," he said, holding her by the shoulders. "Listen to me, damnit! I'm trying to tell you something that's extremely important to you and me—if you want us to have even a prayer of a chance to be together."

"Oh, I see! You're telling me all this because you love me."

"That's right. Why would I have kept silent if not for the fact that Manning had ordered you to spy on Westview and report to him all of the President's activities, even the more gruesome details, like hearing how the President made love to one Judy Taylor, your lover, and the President's mistress?

"You knew from the very beginning that I was set up by Manning. Who else but a childhood friend like Manning would know that the President had this potentially fatal disease, Marfan's syndrome. And that it also happened to cause erratic mental behavior.

"Manning was a shrewd politician who could always smell an opportunity to advance his own political career, regardless of whom he might have to fuck over or kill. Including his best friend Westview . . . with whom he shared Judy Taylor!

"So he convinced his best friend to concoct a scheme called Project Baltimore, which was ostensibly intended to solidify Westview's political base and bring peace and prosperity to our country after a decade of recession."

"Let go of me!" Mary tried to pull away from him.

"No, damnit! You're going to listen to me! That's the least you owe me," Desaix shouted, holding her even more tightly.

"I don't owe you anything. You dug your own grave. I didn't have anything to do with it." She stopped struggling, waiting to hear what else Desaix had to say.

"You see, the beauty of Project Baltimore was that Manning was able to slip in his own coup within Westview's self-contrived coup. A coup within a coup. He used Zarb, Prince, Cordonnier, and you to implement those plans. He even convinced his former legislative assistant, Bonner, to give him the authority to act on behalf of the Vice President, as well as the Speaker of the House and the President pro tempore, to give him the legal authority to declare Westview incompetent. Afterward Manning would have gotten rid of them had we not requested tighter security while they were in Japan. But the President suspected his friend. The Operational Code analysis he ordered was only one way to see exactly how his best friend might play out his own game. Westview knew all along that you were working for both him and Manning, because, like myself, he wondered how Manning knew about all of his activities. But I still don't understand how Manning got you to compromise the President using Judy Taylor."

"It was Judy who introduced Manning into our relationship in the first place. And he, in turn, introduced Judy to Westview," Mary said.

"At least you had a reason. I had none, except my own overinflated narcissism." Desaix let go of her, picked up a sealed white envelope, and handed it to her. "Here, take it."

"It's a little too late for a Valentine's Day card."

"Take it. Do with it what you want." Desaix watched her carefully as she opened the envelope.

Mary stared at the color photograph of herself, Judy, and Manning.

"I'm sorry. I took it from your dresser. From that point on, a lot of the pieces fell into place for me. You see, I never really understood why Manning wanted me to go to Japan when he did—right in the middle of a war, at a time when he would need me the most." He paused to wipe away the tears from Mary's eyes. "He wanted to make certain that Fitzpatrick was out of the way of Project Baltimore. So he and Westview agreed to send Fitzpatrick with me to Japan where he had very little to do, except boil over with anger.

"Both Manning and Westview were afraid that Fitzpatrick would go public with Project Baltimore, which he violently opposed. Worst of all, for Fitzpatrick, he suspected that the entire project was a subterfuge for Manning's megalomaniacal ambitions.

"So Manning ordered his longtime partner Imai and the cherubic Dr. Nobunaga to kill him, using, of all things, hydrogen fluoride, the very chemical that Manning knew would be used in Project Baltimore. You see, Manning and Imai wanted me to believe that the death was executed by Mapplethorpe, Shaw, Brooks, and, eventually, Westview, so that after co-opting me, Manning would have me declare Westview insane, evidenced by his medical problem and the fact that he could create such a dangerous, self-destructive plan as Project Baltimore in the first place. I mean, how crazy can one get, reasoned Manning.

"Suspecting Manning's potential for treachery, Westview sent Brooks over to Japan to uncover the murderer. But instead, Brooks realized that I had accidentally uncovered one of the key elements of Project Baltimore—the use of hydrogen fluoride to create civil panic and chaos."

As Mary listened, she stared at the photograph.

"So Brooks recommended to Westview that I be assassinated. Failing that, Westview saw that I could serve a far greater purpose, which, ostensibly, was to uncover the perpetrators of Project Baltimore, whom he already knew because they were all his accomplices.

"But the real reason that Westview sucked me in, by playing on my insatiable need for high-stakes action, was the fact that I would be able to smoke out Manning and provide the evidence that Westview was looking for against him. Like all good politicians, Westview was both unable and unwilling to confront his friend in this act of treachery. Westview found it quite convenient when Manning ordered the executions of Jenkins, McCormick, Merck, Mapplethorpe, and Shaw. It allowed the President to start over with a clean slate and eliminate anyone who knew anything about Project Baltimore. But I didn't put it all together until I realized it was Westview who took this picture of the three of you—Judy, you, and Manning. Manning had ordered you to strike up a relationship with me so he could keep a tab on my activities."

"I'm sorry, Desaix," Mary said.

"I think you are. But at this point, there is very little I can be certain about. Including you."

"You're right." Her head dropped to her chest. She couldn't look him in the eyes.

"Of all the betrayals, I think the part that hurt me the most was the fact that you allowed Manning to use your sexual inaccessibility as a lesbian as the ultimate bait to hook me into a relationship with you."

"He suspected that you would be turned on by the challenge of making love to a woman who was not interested in men," she said.

"And Manning was right. And so was Westview. They both played on my weaknesses . . . and they succeeded. Manning played on my weakness for women. Westview played on my weakness for adrenaline. Ironically, the man I was led to believe was the principal villain, Mapplethorpe, turned out to be the one person who from the very beginning suspected Manning's treachery and your involvement. Of course, he needed your confession as proof. But he never got it!"

"So there is no one left with a shred of decency or innocence?" Mary asked plaintively, placing her arms around his neck.

"I don't know the answer to that question."

"The man who has the solution to all problems doesn't know the answer to that simple question. Well . . . well . . . Maybe I could be in love with a human, after all."

"Do you mean that?"

"How can you ever believe me, no matter what I say, since I'm so duplicitous and ruthless?"

"I've taken my chances with more unsavory characters for less of a reason," Desaix said, knowing that he should be more upset with her. But he was responding to his heart.

"That's mighty big of you, sport," she gibed. Now it was her turn to take a white envelope from her satchel. "Desaix, the one thing that has always bothered me was the cavalier way you were willing to take us into a nuclear war with Kulikov."

"I already told you that most crisis systems don't work, be they Russian or American."

"What you're telling me is that never having seen or met Marshal Kulikov, you made a judgment call that he would not go to war. Even after Kulikov's countdown, you were convinced that the Russians would never go to war.

That Kulikov was bluffing." Mary paused for effect. "Please correct me if I'm wrong, but you wanted me to believe that this critical assessment was made from some extraordinary intellectual acumen. Is that right?"

"You could say that I relied on my vast experience in negotiating with the Russians to give me the confidence to call their bluff." He held her close, relieved by the way both of them had handled what could have been a total disaster.

"Bullshit!" she replied.

"All right, I relied on a National Character Study."

"Bullshit!"

"I relied on the Operational Code of Marshal Kulikov."

"Bullshitski!"

"What about the Psychological Profile?" Desaix asked, quizzically.

Mary opened the envelope she was holding. "Let me understand it again."

"What?"

"You have never met or seen Field Marshal Alexander Kulikov before yesterday?"

"That's right," Desaix replied self-righteously.

The envelope contained a letter that Mary read in a loud voice.

"My dearest Desaix! As usual it was good to see you again after such a long time. Please accept my congratulations upon your appointment as Deputy Assistant Secretary of State. Hopefully, someday we can work together once again. Please give my warmest regards to your lovely third, or is it fourth, wife. Yours always, Sasha."

"Where the hell did you get that letter?"

Mary didn't answer. She beamed.

"So, I'm not the only one who goes through people's drawers."

"I think this is the beginning of a fascinating relationship," Mary yelled back to him as she ran toward the water.

"We have so much in common," Desaix said as he caught up to her.

They raised their envelopes high up in the air, and tore them to shreds, letting the small pieces disperse into the winds off the Vineyard.

"You knew all along that Kulikov, or Sasha as you called him, would end up being the new leader of the Commonwealth of Independent States."

"Let's just say I wasn't surprised. Like all good crisis managers, over the years he and I had developed a series of contingency strategies that we gamed out beforehand, just in case our respective countries would be in political turmoil or we would have to confront each other at some later time."

"And that fake nuclear game of chicken you played with Kulikov?"

"It allowed me to get rid of two birds with one stone—Westview and Manning."

"But you didn't get rid of Manning. As Bonner's handpicked Vice President, he's more dangerous than ever."

"At least he's been flushed out into the open, where he will be under continuous public scrutiny."

"You hypocrite, you. Handing me all that bull about how you were manipulated by both Westview and Manning."

"*Plus ça change, moins ça change.* The more things change, the less things change."

"I know. I know. And that other Desaix Axiom: 'Trust is good, but control is better.' Your credo, I presume, Dr. Clark?"

"You've got it, my dear. Control, control, control! The first, second, and third rules of crisis management!" Desaix said tongue in cheek, smiling as he grabbed Mary, forcing her to submerge with him beneath the cool, inviting water.